Praise for
The Effects of Pickled Herring

"A warm and funny coming-of age story, but one that also packs an emotional wallop. *The Effects of Pickled Herring* is a wonderful tale about the gnawing self-doubt and daily humiliations we all suffer at age thirteen. An insightful and provocative read!"

—Derf Backderf, Eisner Award-winning author of *Kent State: Four Dead in Ohio*

"A wonderful story of all the directions we are pulled in our adolescence, and a reminder of the one thing that can ground us—the ones we love."

—Jonathan Hill, author of *Tales of a Seventh-Grade Lizard Boy*

"You'll immediately recognize Micah Gadsky as yourself, your friend, or that slightly awkward Jewish kid in your class. *The Effects of Pickled Herring* is filled with humor and heart and some heartbreak too, but ultimately it's about family and friendship and how these relationships help us navigate change. This is a must-read coming of age graphic novel and I hope not the last we'll see of Micah. The bar mitzvah was one thing, how is he going to make it through high school?"

—Erica Lyons, National Jewish Book Awards Finalist

"*The Effects of Pickled Herring* is a heart-warming hoot that is full of laughs, heart and not the least bit fishy."

—Judd Winick, author of the bestselling Hilo series

"Alex Schumacher has crafted a wonderful coming of age story (like literally: it hinges on a Bar and Bat Mitzvah). It's a poignant tale about the importance of family and faith in a person's life, both young and old. And even though you might need to keep a box of tissues handy for the especially emotional passages, it's also leavened with Alex's trademark sense of humor. A funny, moving story that I highly recommend!"

——Mark Reznicek, drummer of Toadies

The Effects of

PICKLED HERRING

The Effects of

PICKLED HERRING

A Graphic Novel

Alex Schumacher
with color by Allan Ferguson

mango
PUBLISHING GROUP

Coral Gables

Published by Mango Publishing, a division of Mango Publishing Group, Inc.

Cover Design: Elina Diaz
Cover Photo/illustration: Alex Schumacher
Coloring: Allan Ferguson
Layout & Design: Elina Diaz

For permission requests, please contact the publisher at:
Mango Publishing Group
2850 S Douglas Road, 2nd Floor
Coral Gables, FL 33134 USA
info@mango.bz

For special orders, quantity sales, course adoptions and corporate sales, please email the publisher at sales@mango.bz. For trade and wholesale sales, please contact Ingram Publisher Services at customer.service@ingramcontent.com or +1.800.509.4887.

The Effects of Pickled Herring: A Graphic Novel

Library of Congress Cataloging-in-Publication number: 2023945346
ISBN: (pb) 978-1-68481-356-8, (hc) 978-1-68481-357-5, (e) 978-1-68481-358-2
BISAC category code: YAF010070, YOUNG ADULT FICTION / Comics & Graphic Novels / Coming of Age

Printed in the United States of America

FSC
www.fsc.org
MIX
Paper from responsible sources
FSC® C005010

For Grams and Gramps

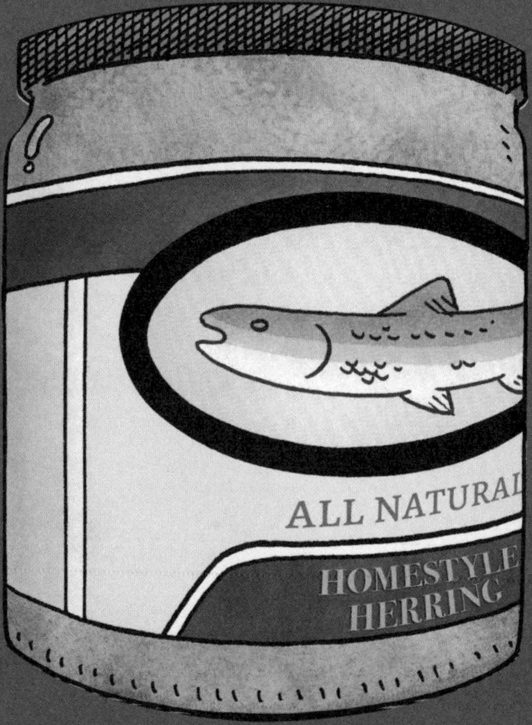
ALL NATURAL
HOMESTYLE
HERRING

PART 1

Winter/
Cold Season

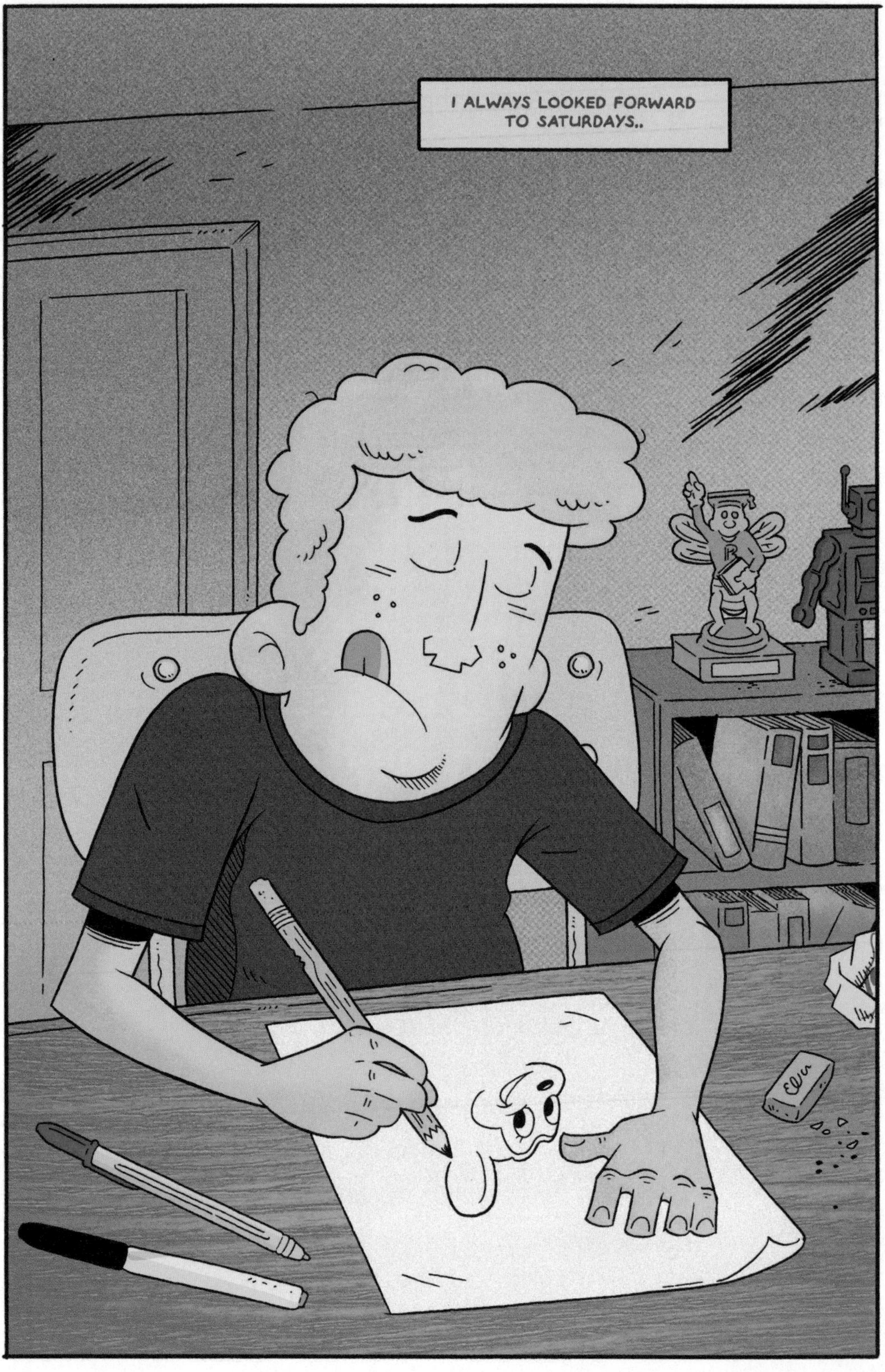
I ALWAYS LOOKED FORWARD TO SATURDAYS..

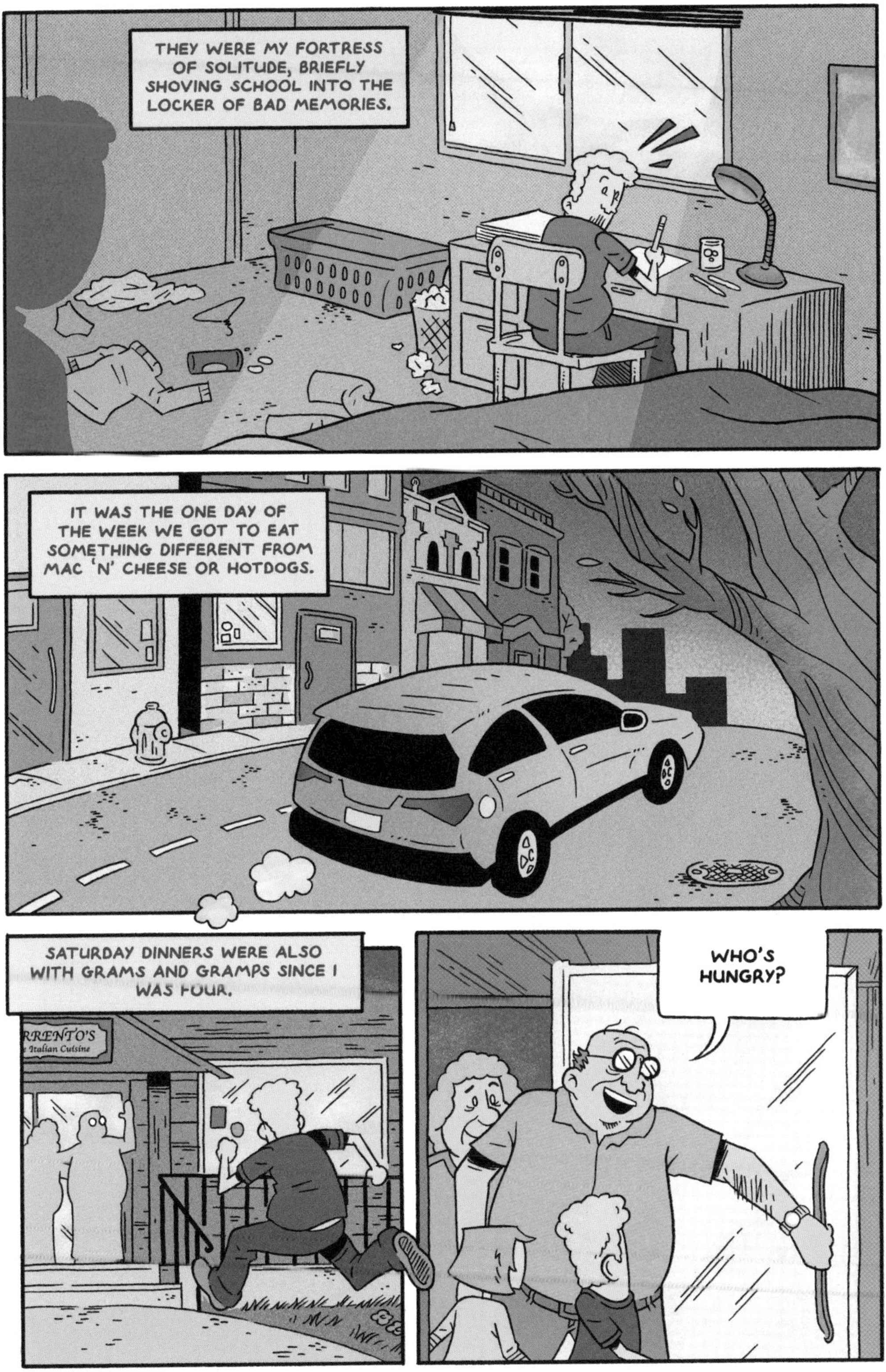
THEY WERE MY FORTRESS OF SOLITUDE, BRIEFLY SHOVING SCHOOL INTO THE LOCKER OF BAD MEMORIES.
IT WAS THE ONE DAY OF THE WEEK WE GOT TO EAT SOMETHING DIFFERENT FROM MAC 'N' CHEESE OR HOTDOGS.
SATURDAY DINNERS WERE ALSO WITH GRAMS AND GRAMPS SINCE I WAS FOUR.
WHO'S HUNGRY?

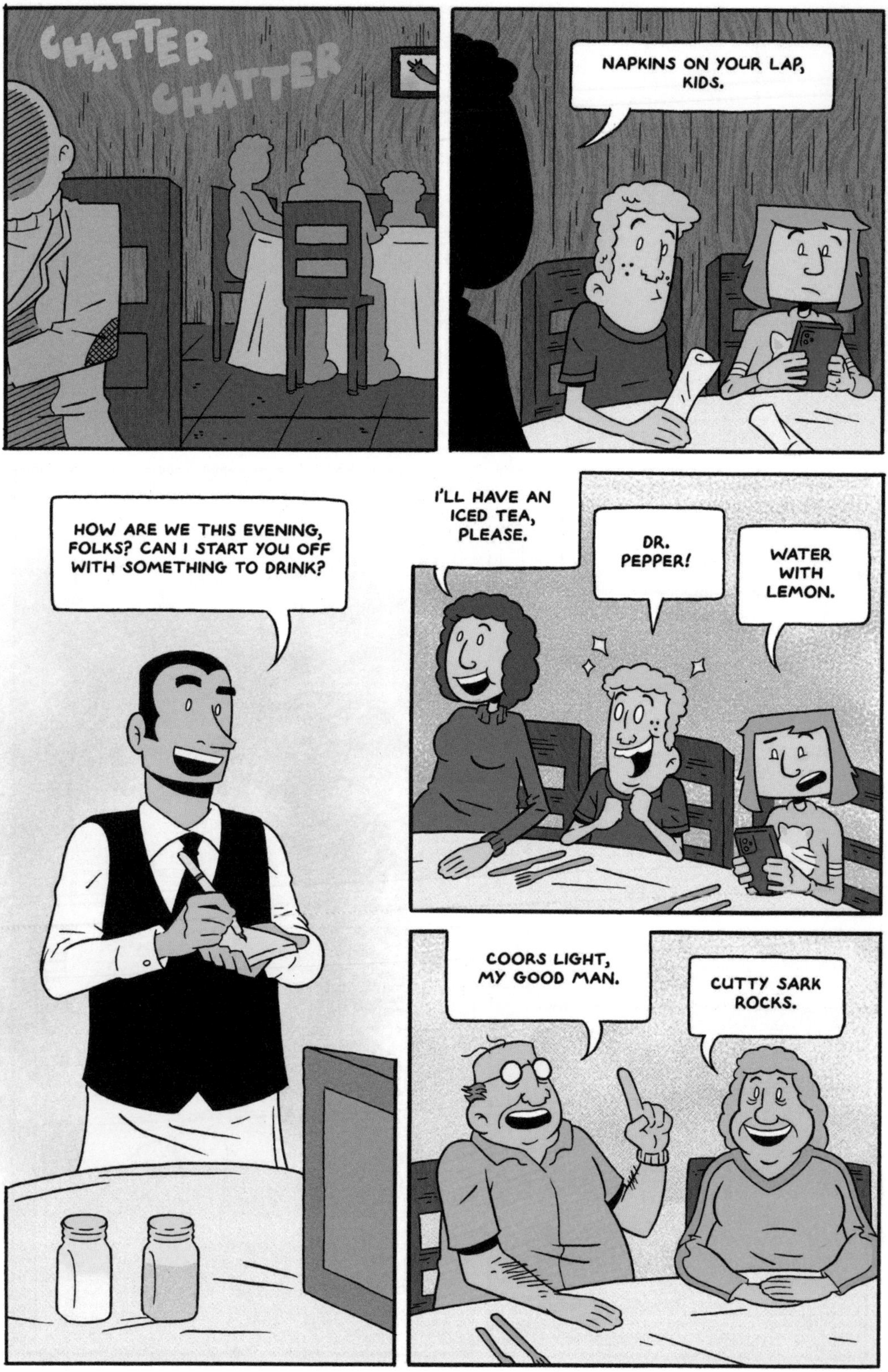
CHATTER
CHATTER
NAPKINS ON YOUR LAP, KIDS.
HOW ARE WE THIS EVENING, FOLKS? CAN I START YOU OFF WITH SOMETHING TO DRINK?
I'LL HAVE AN ICED TEA, PLEASE.
DR. PEPPER!
WATER WITH LEMON.
COORS LIGHT, MY GOOD MAN.
CUTTY SARK ROCKS.

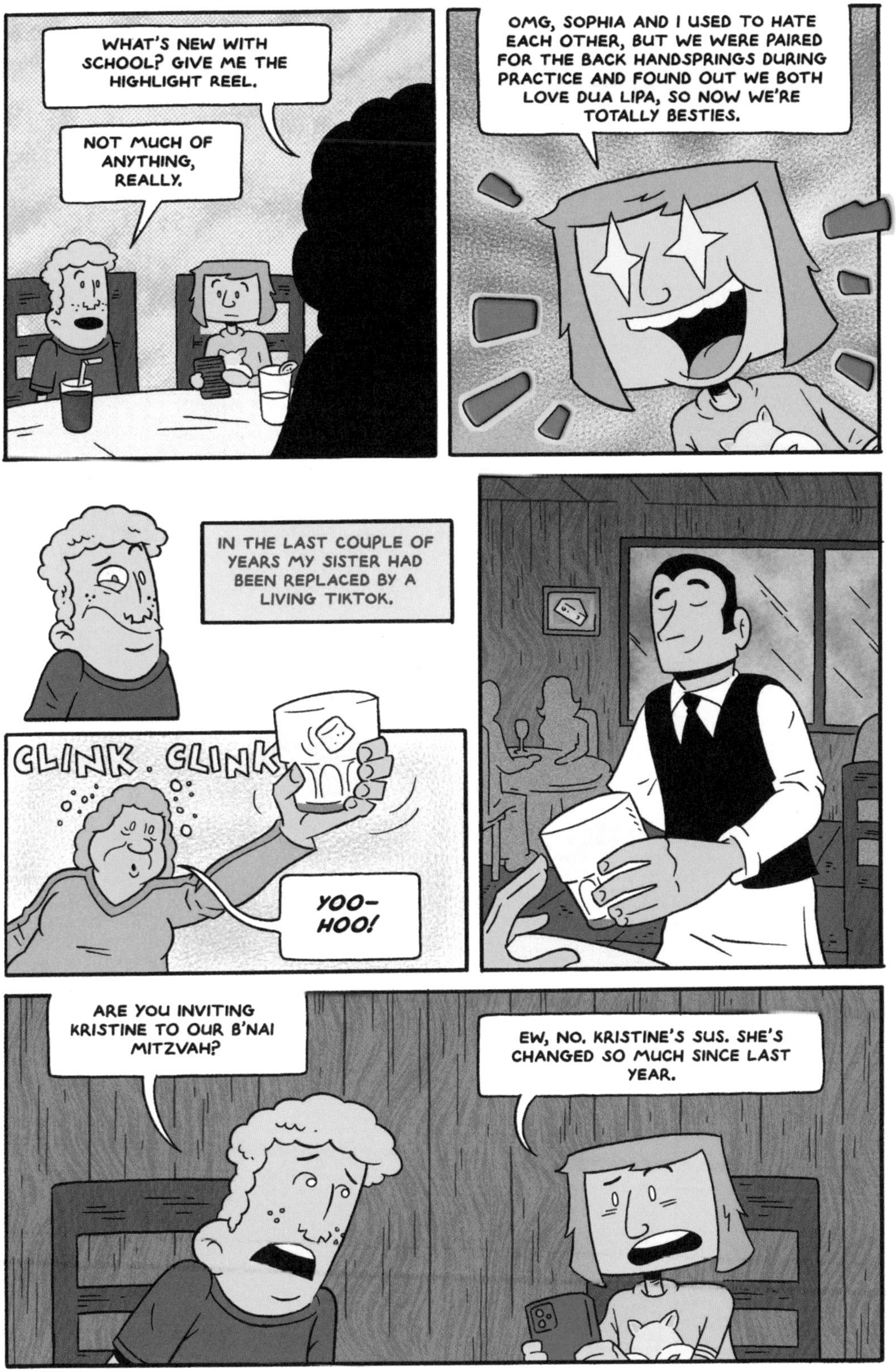

WHAT'S NEW WITH SCHOOL? GIVE ME THE HIGHLIGHT REEL.
NOT MUCH OF ANYTHING, REALLY.
OMG, SOPHIA AND I USED TO HATE EACH OTHER, BUT WE WERE PAIRED FOR THE BACK HANDSPRINGS DURING PRACTICE AND FOUND OUT WE BOTH LOVE DUA LIPA, SO NOW WE'RE TOTALLY BESTIES.
IN THE LAST COUPLE OF YEARS MY SISTER HAD BEEN REPLACED BY A LIVING TIKTOK.
CLINK. CLINK
YOO-HOO!
ARE YOU INVITING KRISTINE TO OUR B'NAI MITZVAH?
EW, NO. KRISTINE'S SUS. SHE'S CHANGED SO MUCH SINCE LAST YEAR.

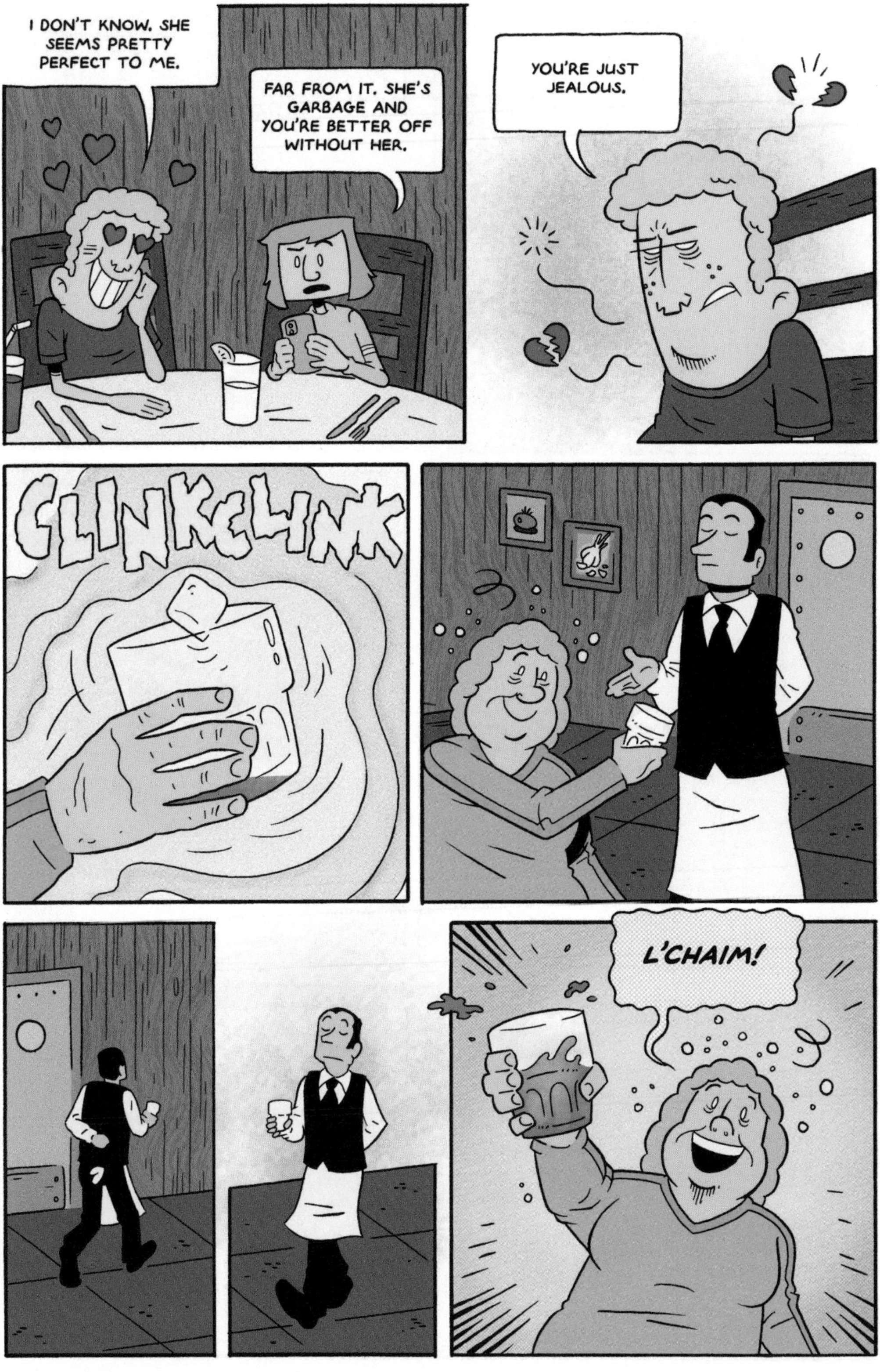
I DON'T KNOW. SHE SEEMS PRETTY PERFECT TO ME.
FAR FROM IT. SHE'S GARBAGE AND YOU'RE BETTER OFF WITHOUT HER.
YOU'RE JUST JEALOUS.
CLINKCLINK
L'CHAIM!

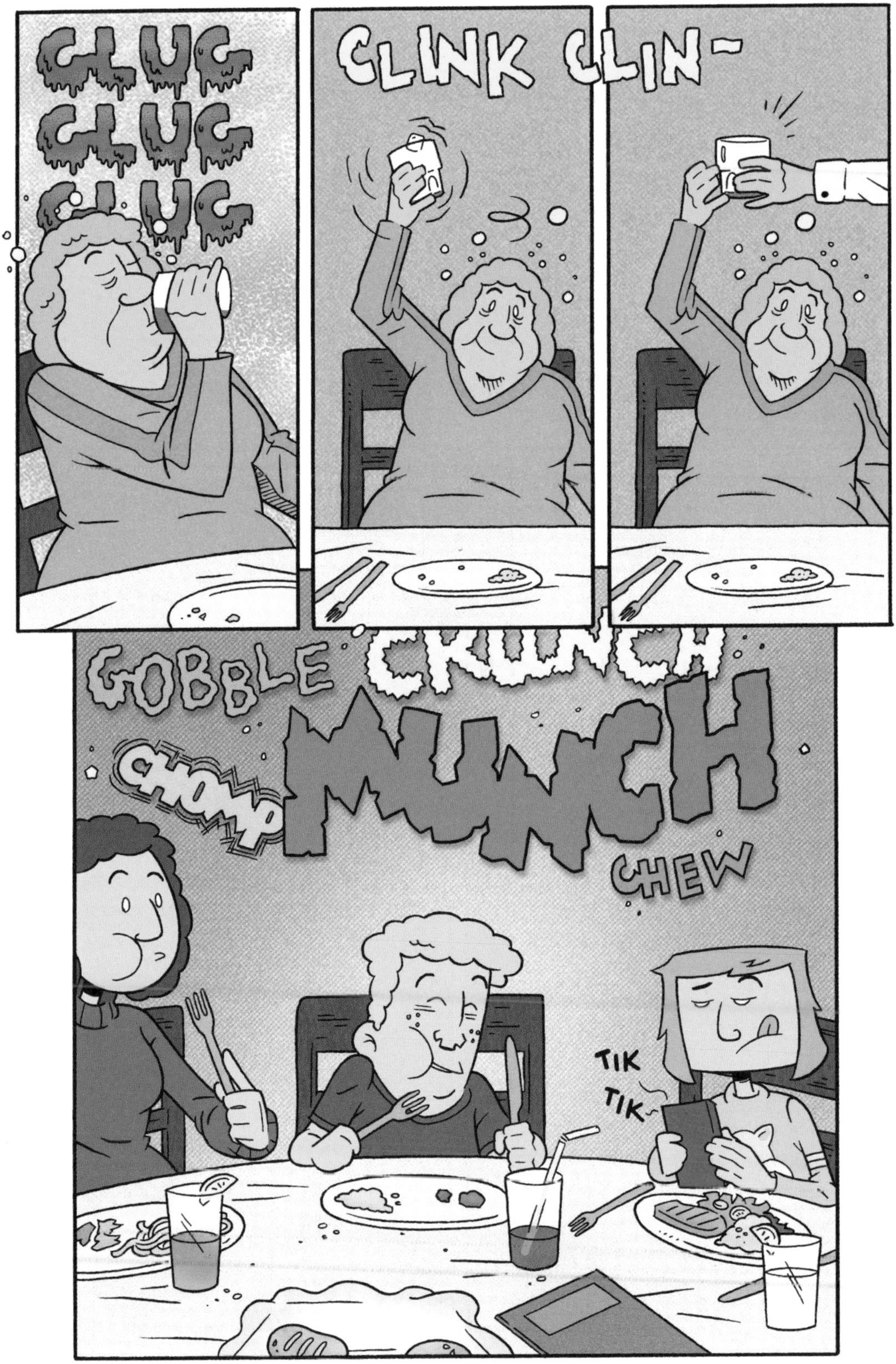
GLUG
GLUG
GLUG
CLINK CLIN-
GOBBLE
CRUNCH
CHOMP
MUNCH
CHEW
TIK
TIK

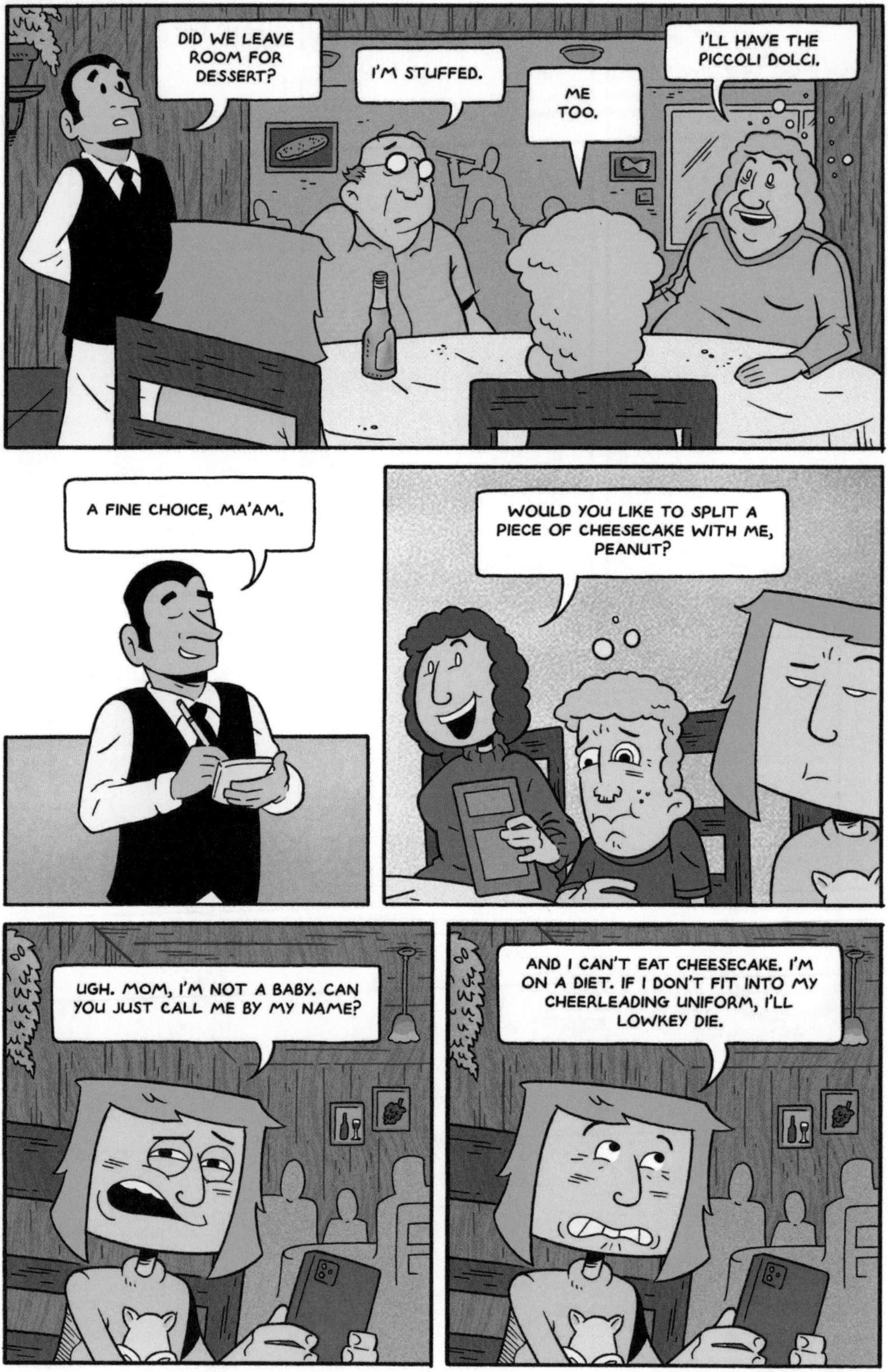
DID WE LEAVE ROOM FOR DESSERT?
I'M STUFFED.
ME TOO.
I'LL HAVE THE PICCOLI DOLCI.
A FINE CHOICE, MA'AM.
WOULD YOU LIKE TO SPLIT A PIECE OF CHEESECAKE WITH ME, PEANUT?
UGH. MOM, I'M NOT A BABY. CAN YOU JUST CALL ME BY MY NAME?
AND I CAN'T EAT CHEESECAKE. I'M ON A DIET. IF I DON'T FIT INTO MY CHEERLEADING UNIFORM, I'LL LOWKEY DIE.

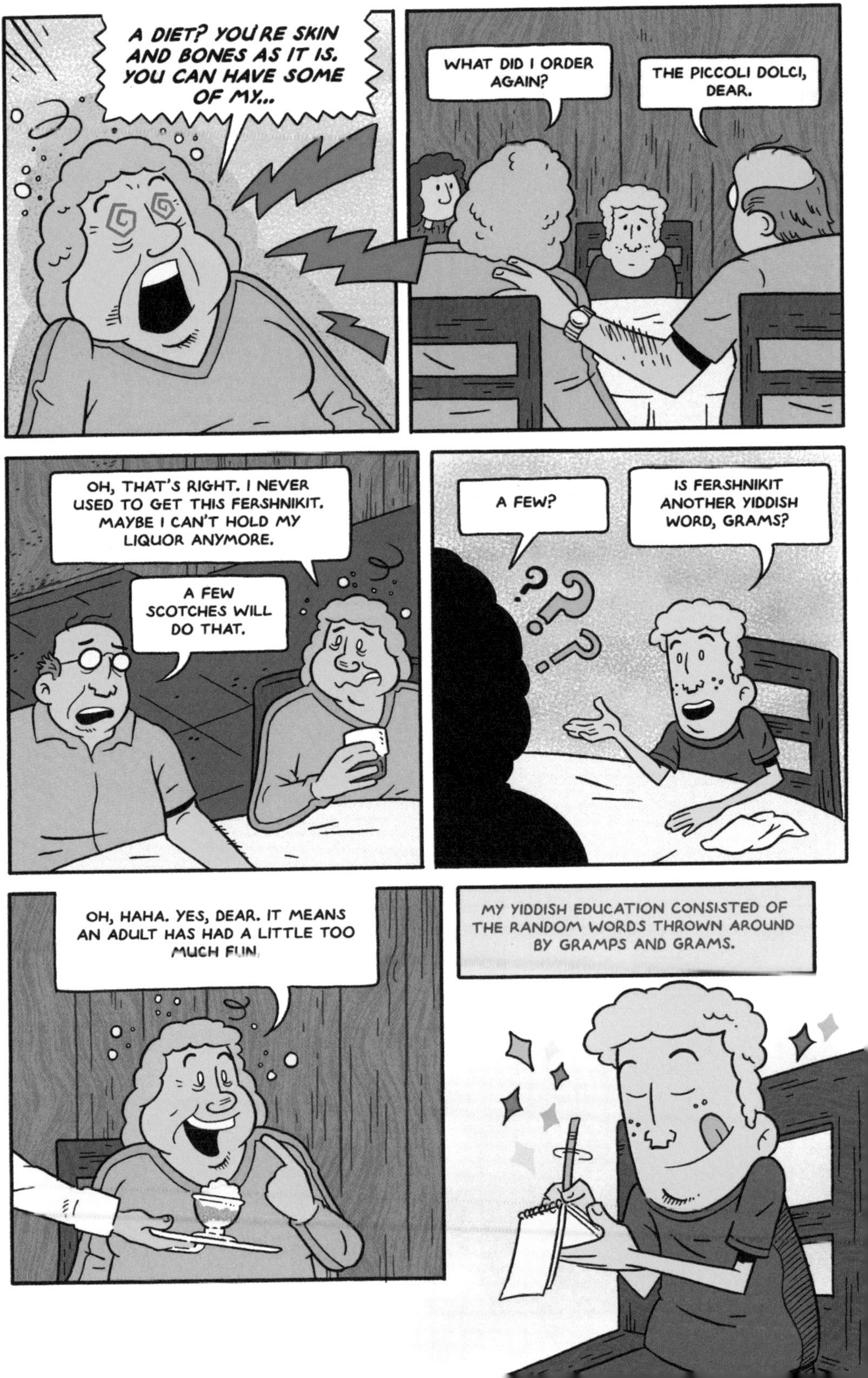
A DIET? YOU'RE SKIN AND BONES AS IT IS. YOU CAN HAVE SOME OF MY...
WHAT DID I ORDER AGAIN?
THE PICCOLI DOLCI, DEAR.
OH, THAT'S RIGHT. I NEVER USED TO GET THIS FERSHNIKIT. MAYBE I CAN'T HOLD MY LIQUOR ANYMORE.
A FEW SCOTCHES WILL DO THAT.
A FEW?
IS FERSHNIKIT ANOTHER YIDDISH WORD, GRAMS?
OH, HAHA. YES, DEAR. IT MEANS AN ADULT HAS HAD A LITTLE TOO MUCH FUN.
MY YIDDISH EDUCATION CONSISTED OF THE RANDOM WORDS THROWN AROUND BY GRAMPS AND GRAMS.

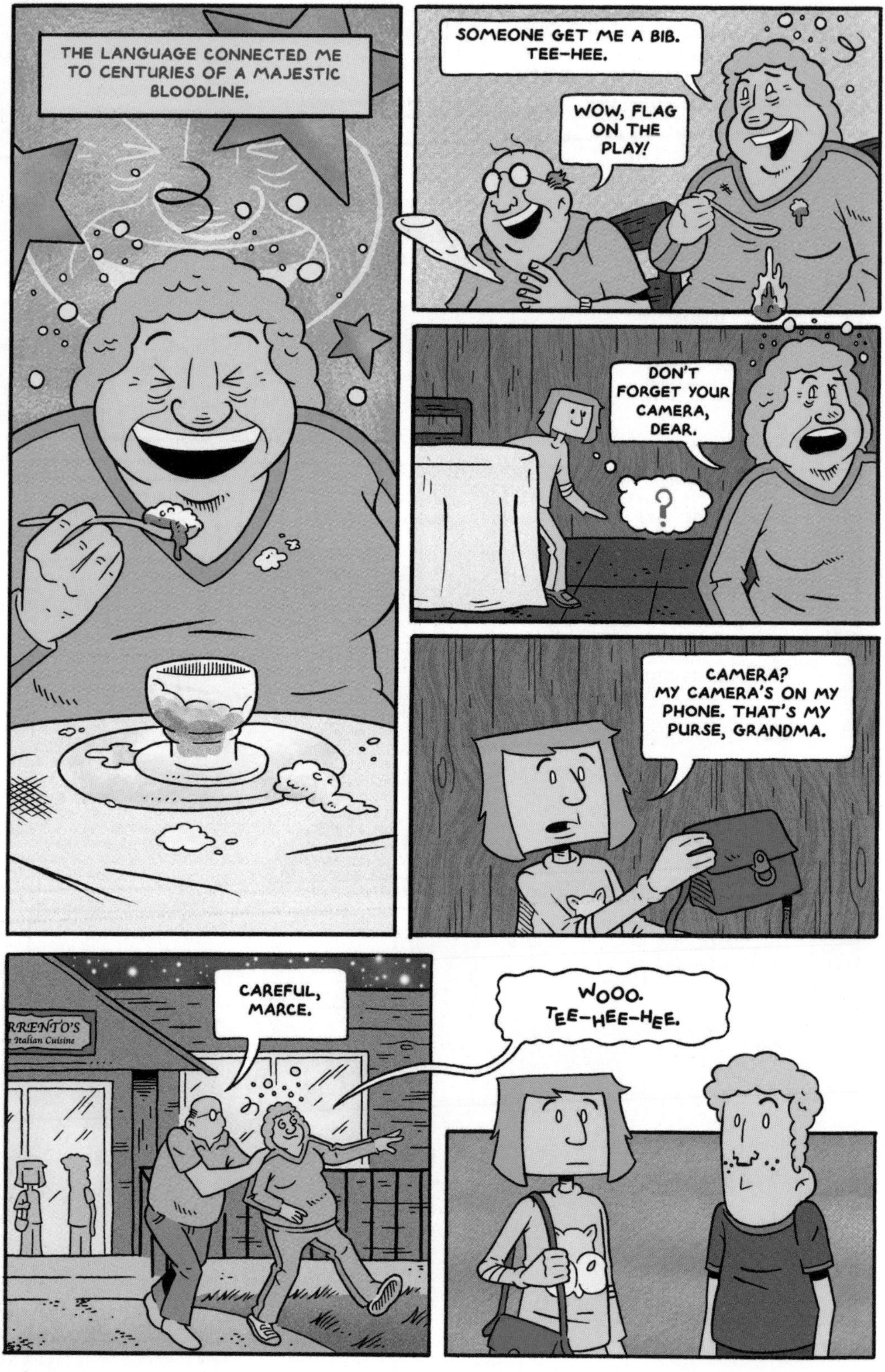
THE LANGUAGE CONNECTED ME TO CENTURIES OF A MAJESTIC BLOODLINE.
SOMEONE GET ME A BIB. TEE-HEE.
WOW, FLAG ON THE PLAY!
DON'T FORGET YOUR CAMERA, DEAR.
?
CAMERA? MY CAMERA'S ON MY PHONE. THAT'S MY PURSE, GRANDMA.
RRENTO'S
Italian Cuisine
CAREFUL, MARCE.
WOOO. TEE-HEE-HEE.

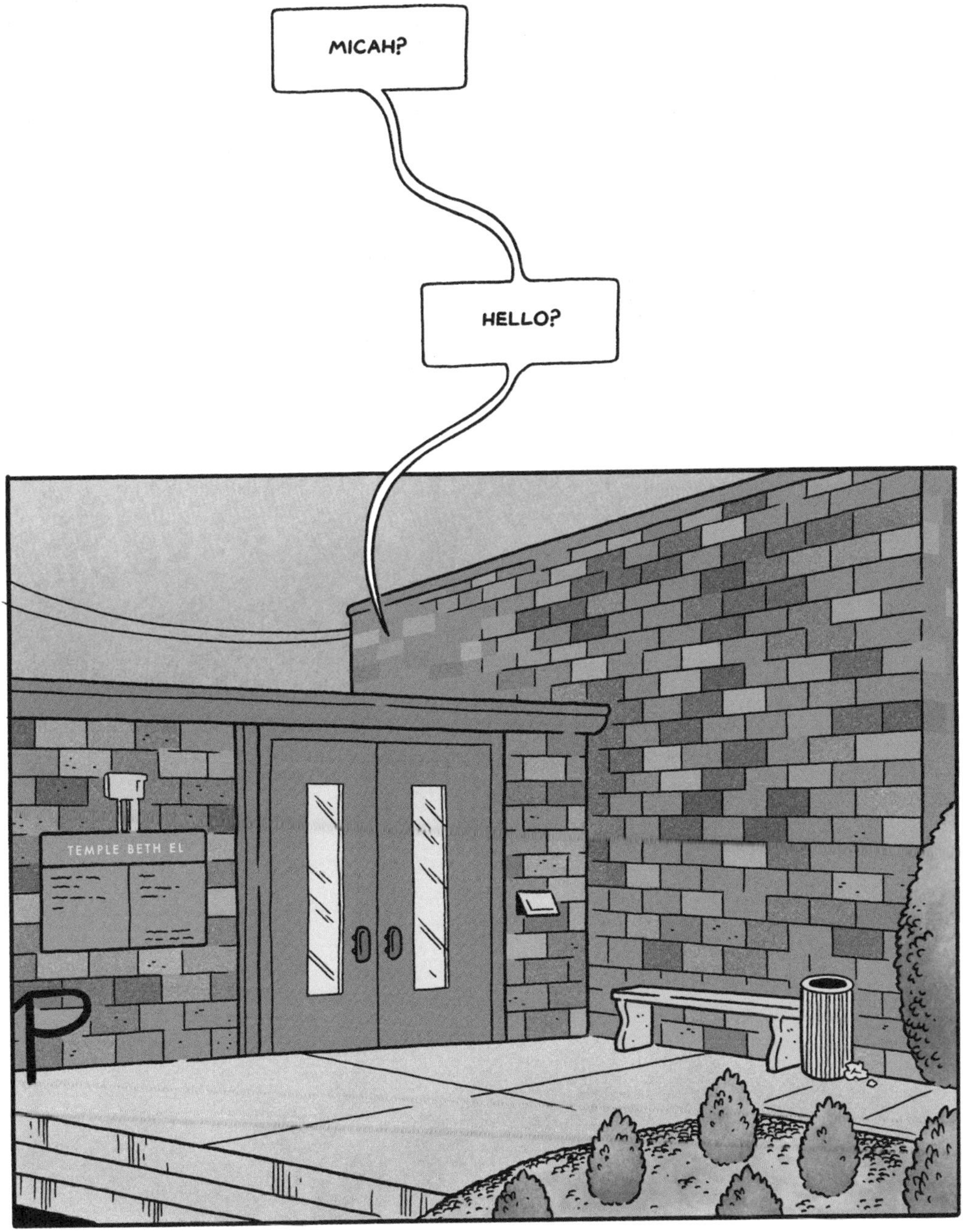
MICAH?
HELLO?
TEMPLE BETH EL

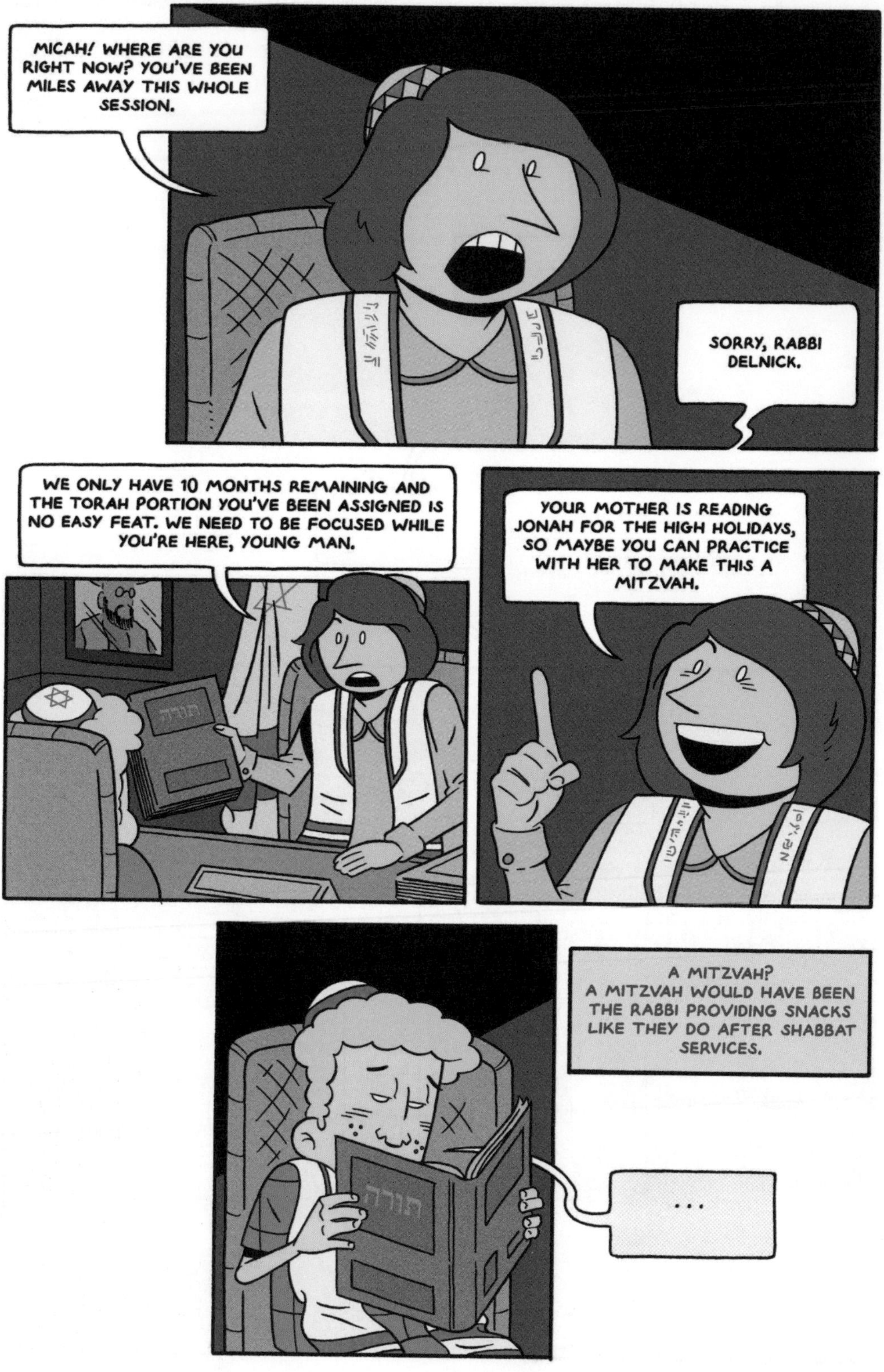
MICAH! WHERE ARE YOU RIGHT NOW? YOU'VE BEEN MILES AWAY THIS WHOLE SESSION.
SORRY, RABBI DELNICK.
WE ONLY HAVE 10 MONTHS REMAINING AND THE TORAH PORTION YOU'VE BEEN ASSIGNED IS NO EASY FEAT. WE NEED TO BE FOCUSED WHILE YOU'RE HERE, YOUNG MAN.
תורה
YOUR MOTHER IS READING JONAH FOR THE HIGH HOLIDAYS, SO MAYBE YOU CAN PRACTICE WITH HER TO MAKE THIS A MITZVAH.
A MITZVAH? A MITZVAH WOULD HAVE BEEN THE RABBI PROVIDING SNACKS LIKE THEY DO AFTER SHABBAT SERVICES.
תורה
...

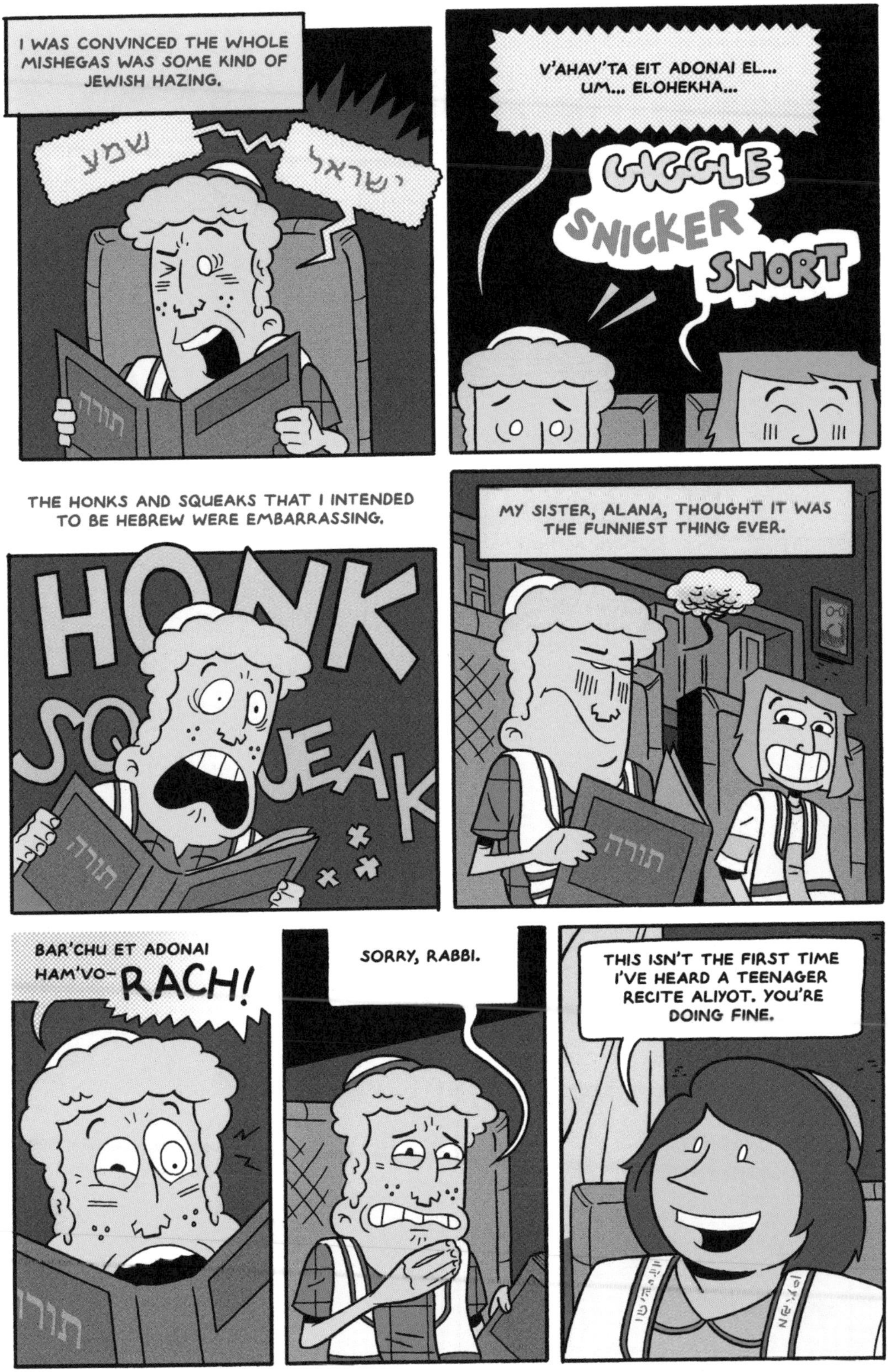
I WAS CONVINCED THE WHOLE MISHEGAS WAS SOME KIND OF JEWISH HAZING.
שמע
ישראל
תורה
V'AHAV'TA EIT ADONAI EL... UM... ELOHEKHA...
GIGGLE
SNICKER
SNORT
THE HONKS AND SQUEAKS THAT I INTENDED TO BE HEBREW WERE EMBARRASSING.
HONK
SQUEAK
תורה
MY SISTER, ALANA, THOUGHT IT WAS THE FUNNIEST THING EVER.
תורה
BAR'CHU ET ADONAI HAM'VO-RACH!
תורה
SORRY, RABBI.
THIS ISN'T THE FIRST TIME I'VE HEARD A TEENAGER RECITE ALIYOT. YOU'RE DOING FINE.

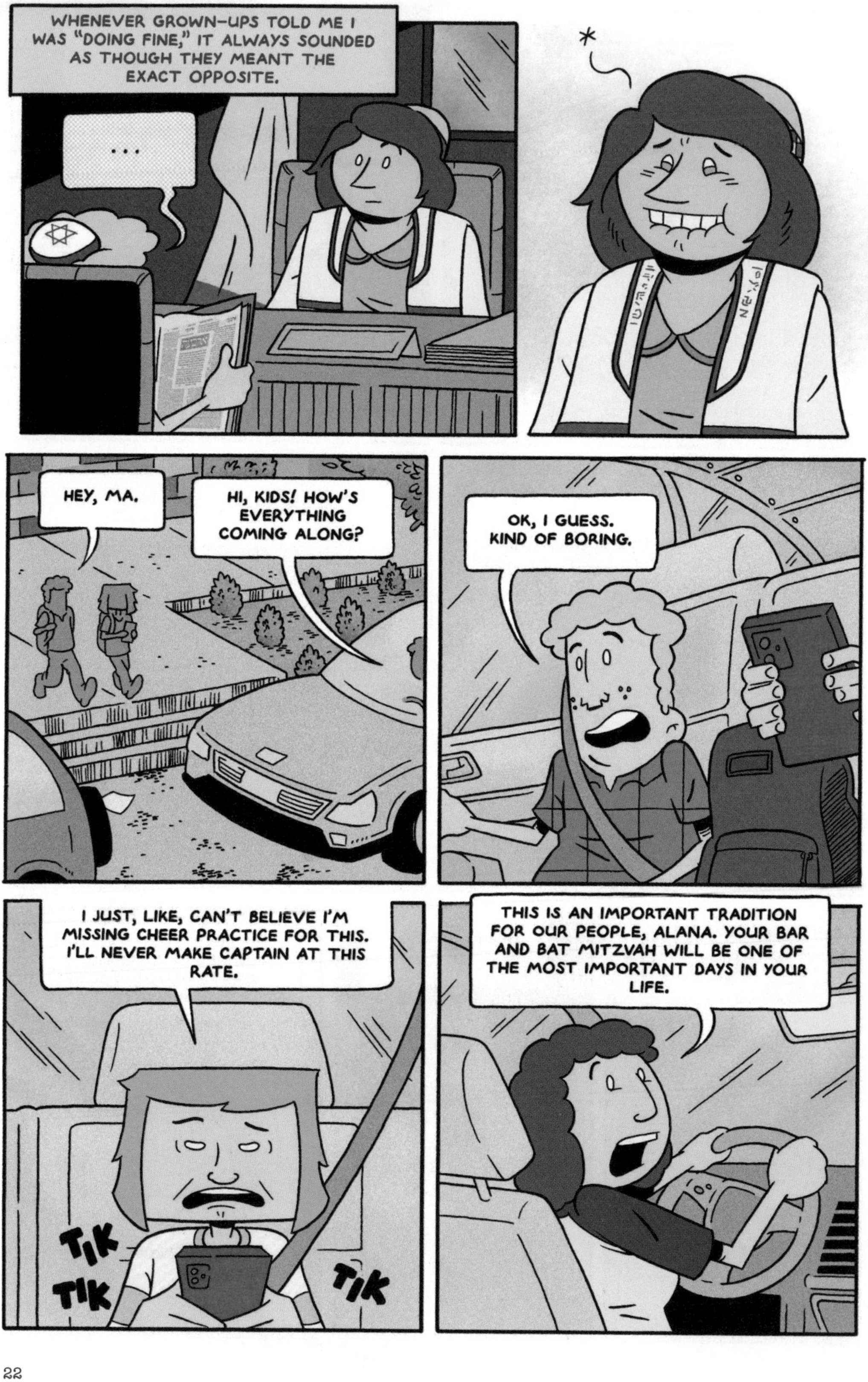
WHENEVER GROWN-UPS TOLD ME I WAS "DOING FINE," IT ALWAYS SOUNDED AS THOUGH THEY MEANT THE EXACT OPPOSITE.
...
*
HEY, MA.
HI, KIDS! HOW'S EVERYTHING COMING ALONG?
OK, I GUESS. KIND OF BORING.
I JUST, LIKE, CAN'T BELIEVE I'M MISSING CHEER PRACTICE FOR THIS. I'LL NEVER MAKE CAPTAIN AT THIS RATE.
TIK
TIK
TIK
THIS IS AN IMPORTANT TRADITION FOR OUR PEOPLE, ALANA. YOUR BAR AND BAT MITZVAH WILL BE ONE OF THE MOST IMPORTANT DAYS IN YOUR LIFE.

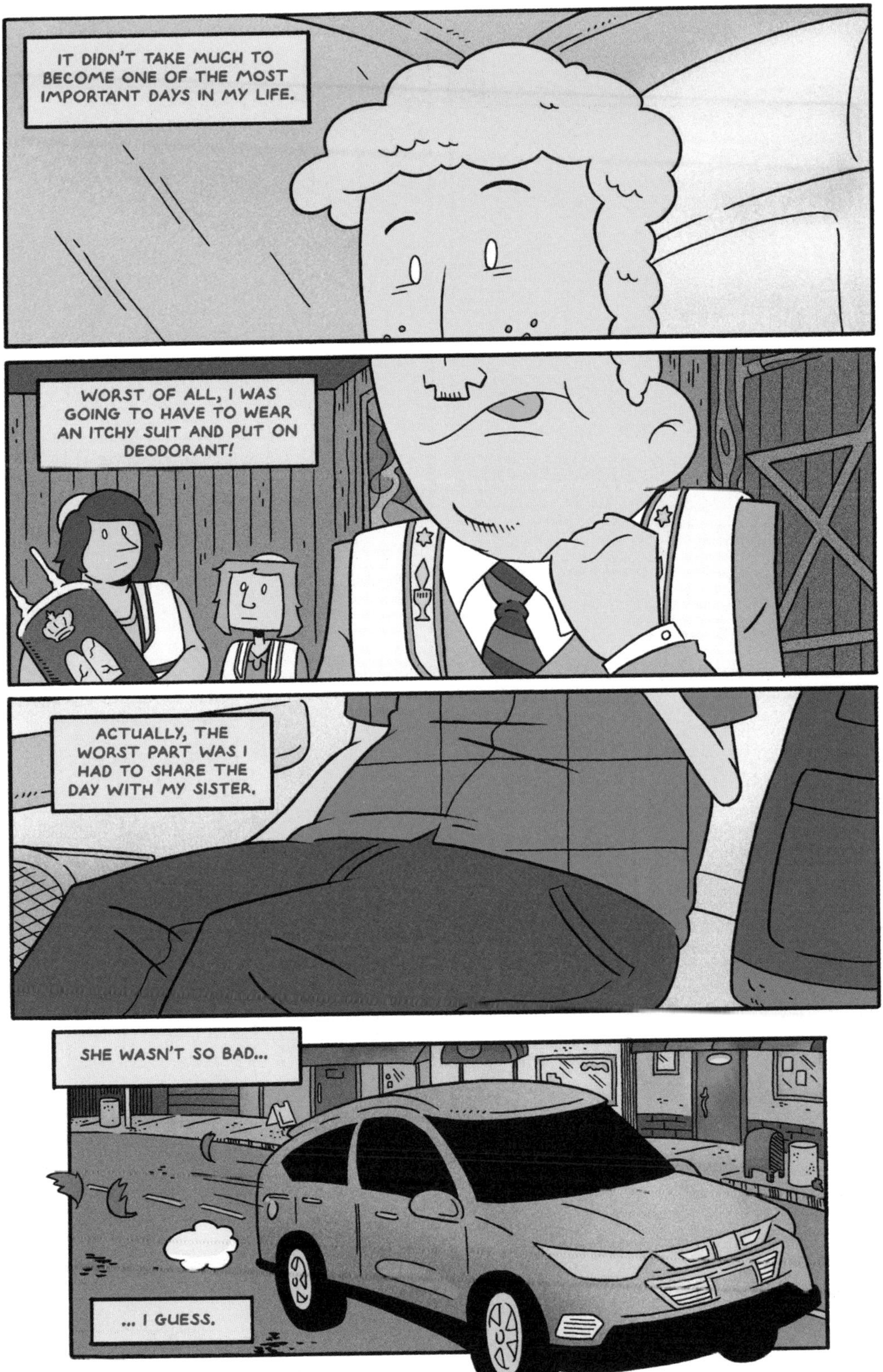
IT DIDN'T TAKE MUCH TO BECOME ONE OF THE MOST IMPORTANT DAYS IN MY LIFE.
WORST OF ALL, I WAS GOING TO HAVE TO WEAR AN ITCHY SUIT AND PUT ON DEODORANT!
ACTUALLY, THE WORST PART WAS I HAD TO SHARE THE DAY WITH MY SISTER.
SHE WASN'T SO BAD...
... I GUESS.

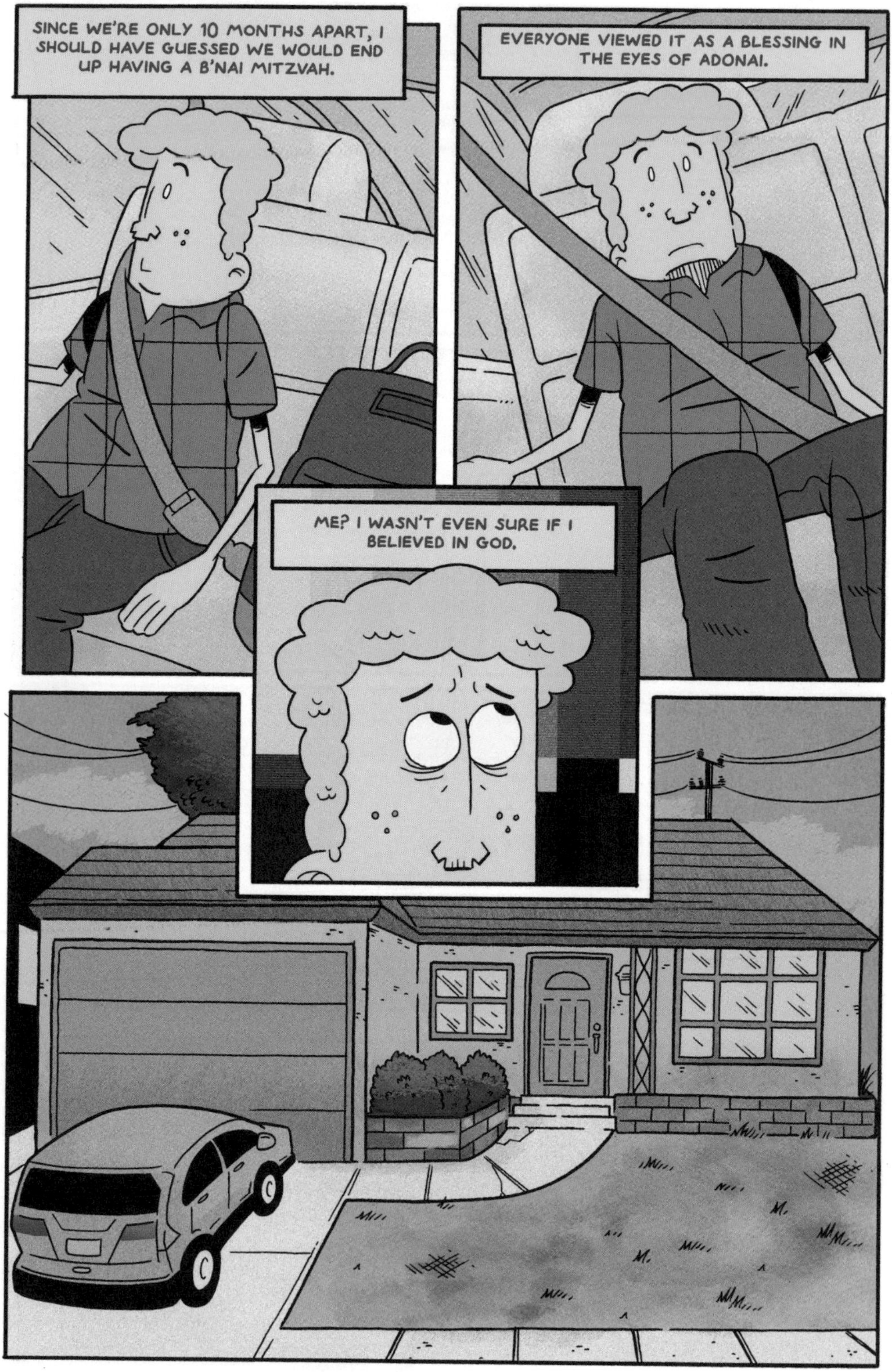
SINCE WE'RE ONLY 10 MONTHS APART, I SHOULD HAVE GUESSED WE WOULD END UP HAVING A B'NAI MITZVAH.
EVERYONE VIEWED IT AS A BLESSING IN THE EYES OF ADONAI.
ME? I WASN'T EVEN SURE IF I BELIEVED IN GOD.

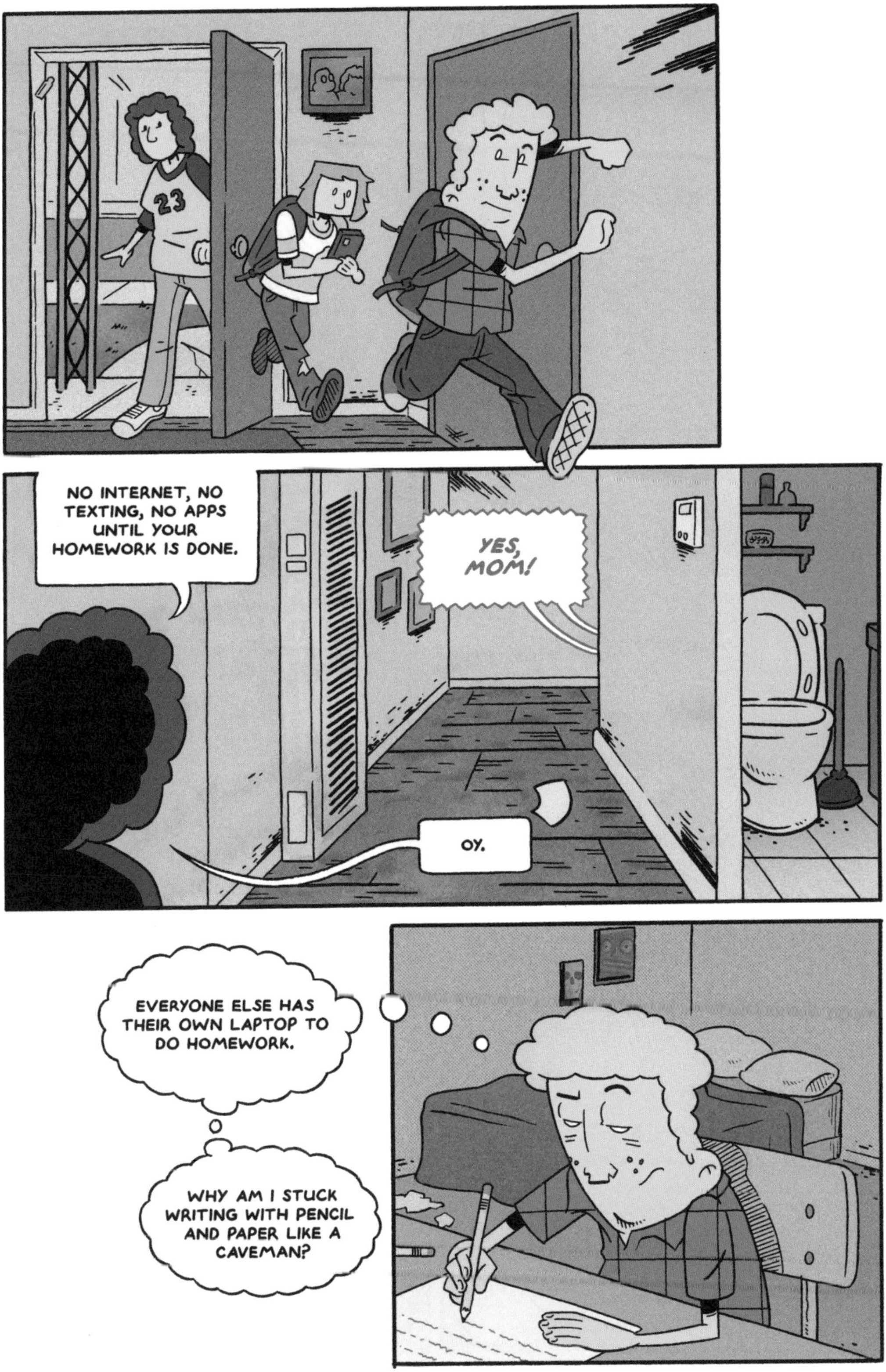
NO INTERNET, NO TEXTING, NO APPS UNTIL YOUR HOMEWORK IS DONE.
YES, MOM!
OY.
EVERYONE ELSE HAS THEIR OWN LAPTOP TO DO HOMEWORK.
WHY AM I STUCK WRITING WITH PENCIL AND PAPER LIKE A CAVEMAN?

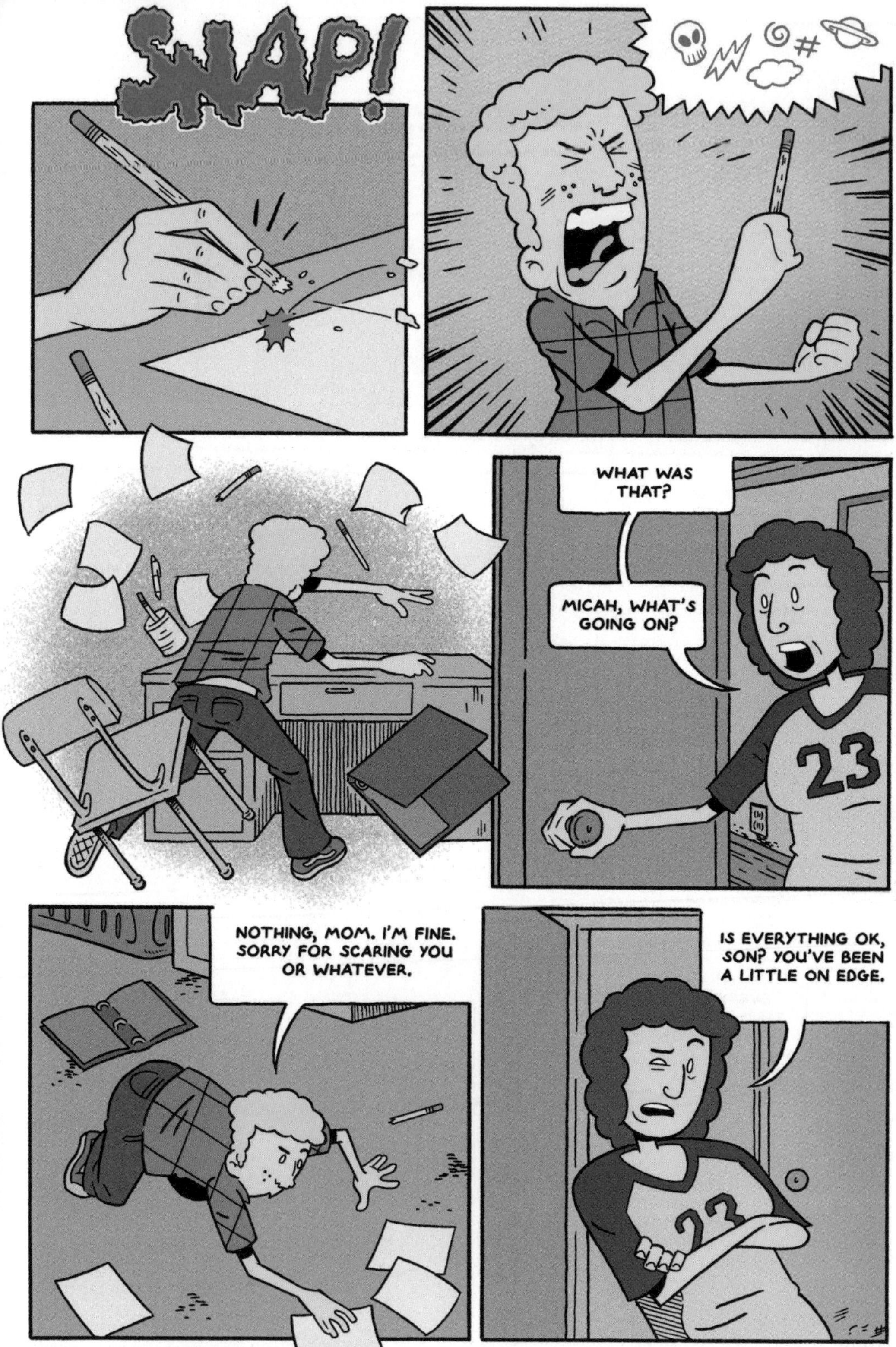
SNAP!
WHAT WAS THAT?
MICAH, WHAT'S GOING ON?
NOTHING, MOM. I'M FINE. SORRY FOR SCARING YOU OR WHATEVER.
IS EVERYTHING OK, SON? YOU'VE BEEN A LITTLE ON EDGE.

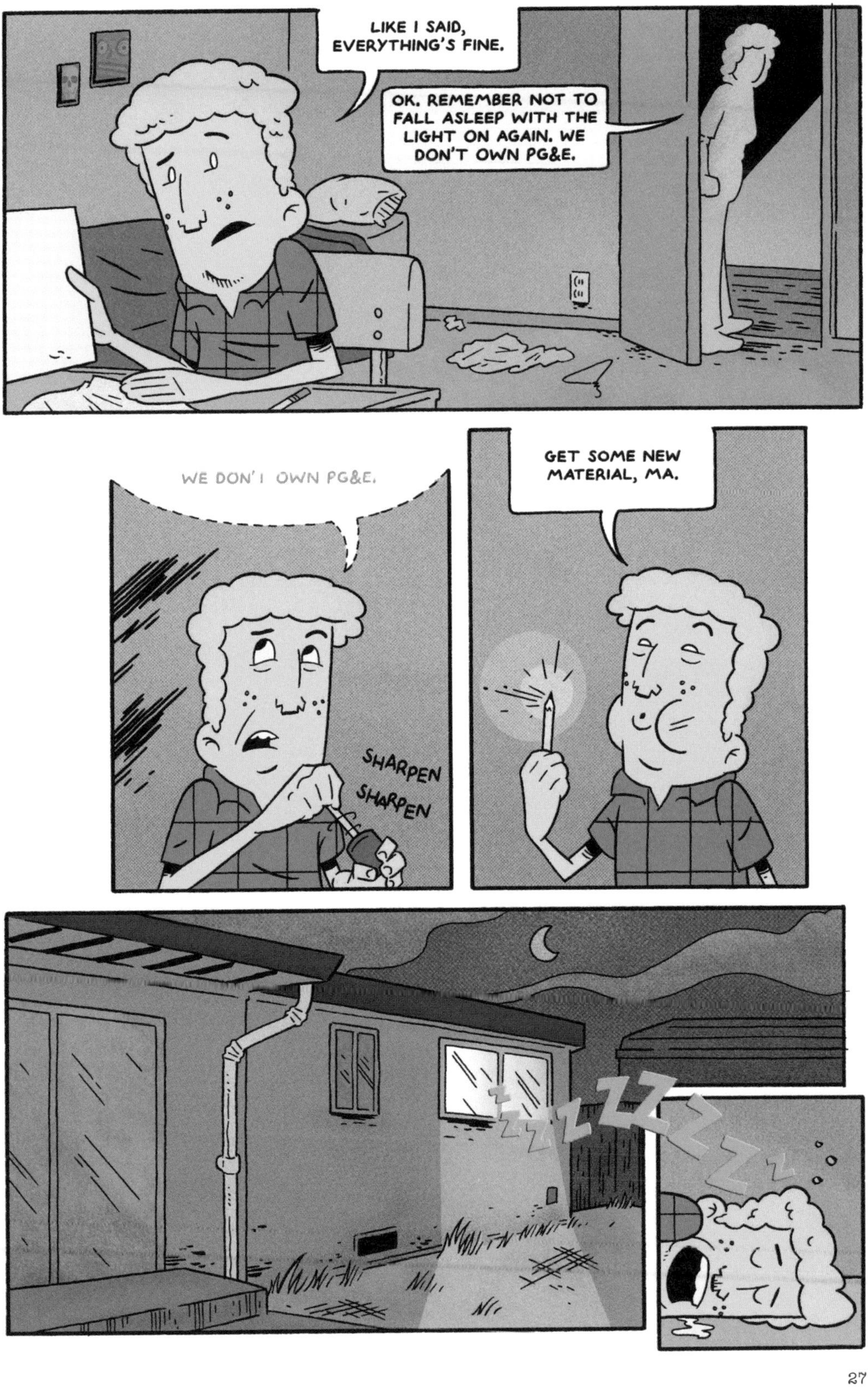
LIKE I SAID, EVERYTHING'S FINE.
OK. REMEMBER NOT TO FALL ASLEEP WITH THE LIGHT ON AGAIN. WE DON'T OWN PG&E.
WE DON'T OWN PG&E.
SHARPEN SHARPEN
GET SOME NEW MATERIAL, MA.

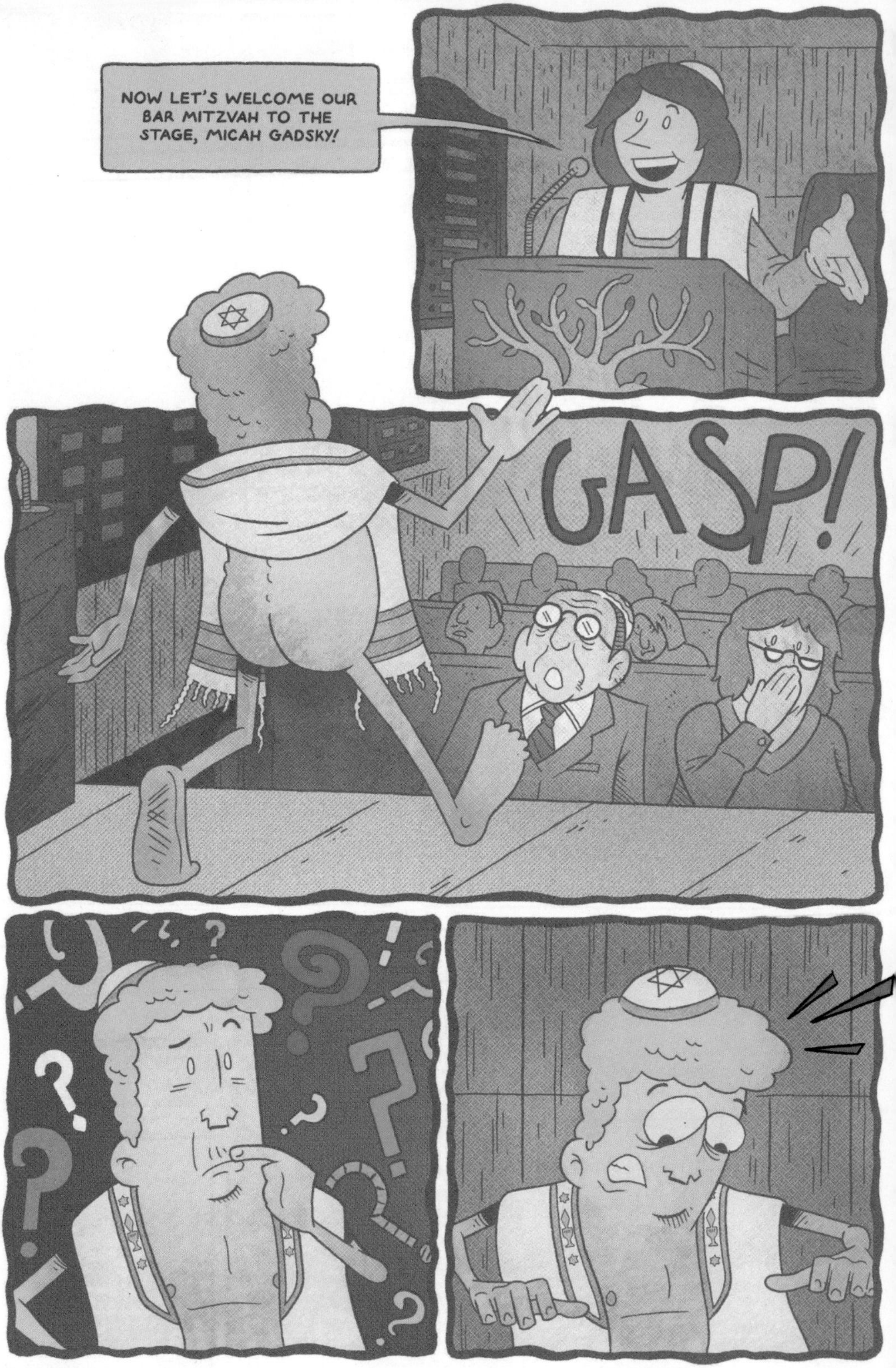
NOW LET'S WELCOME OUR BAR MITZVAH TO THE STAGE, MICAH GADSKY!
GASP!

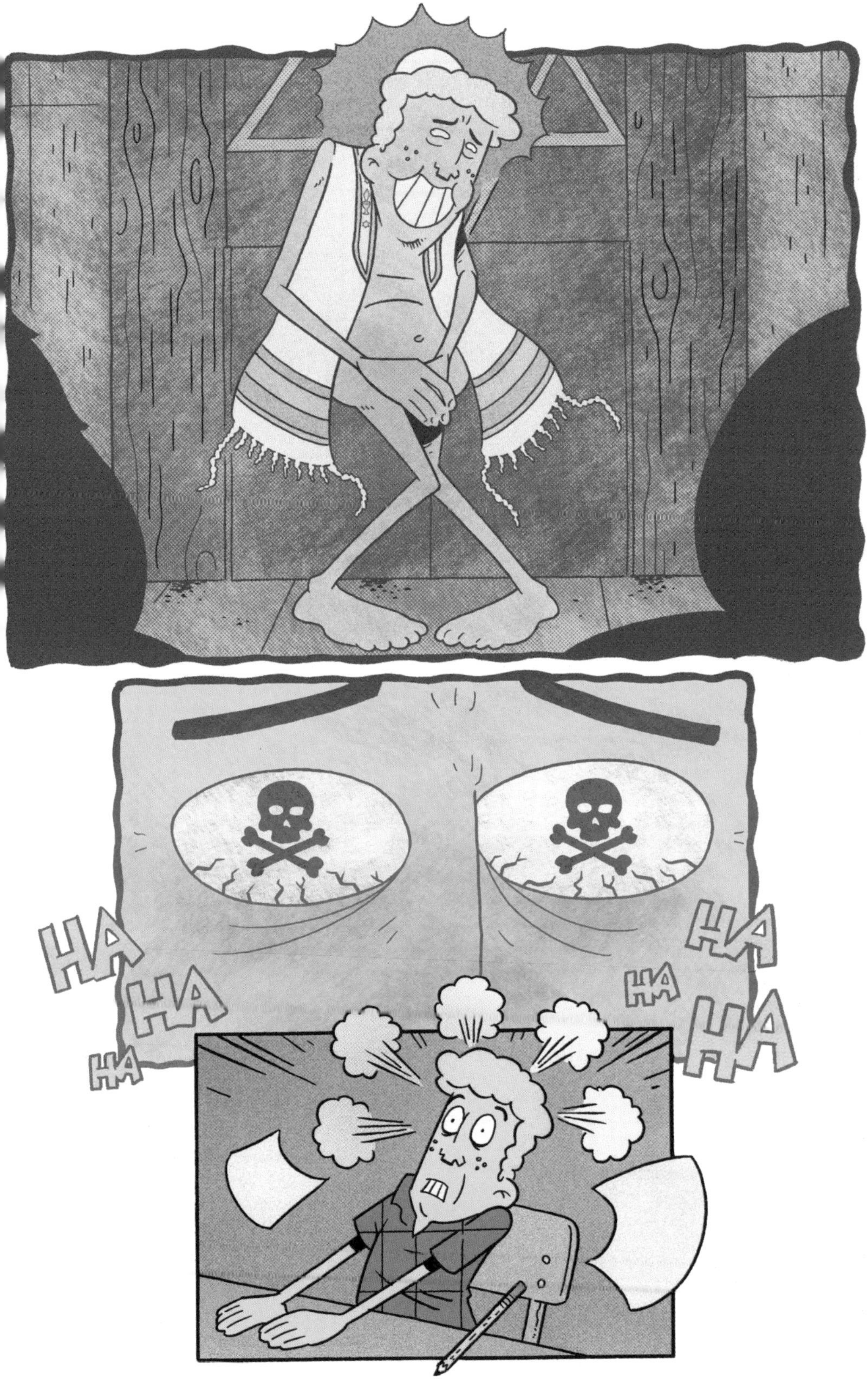
HA
HA
HA
HA
HA
HA

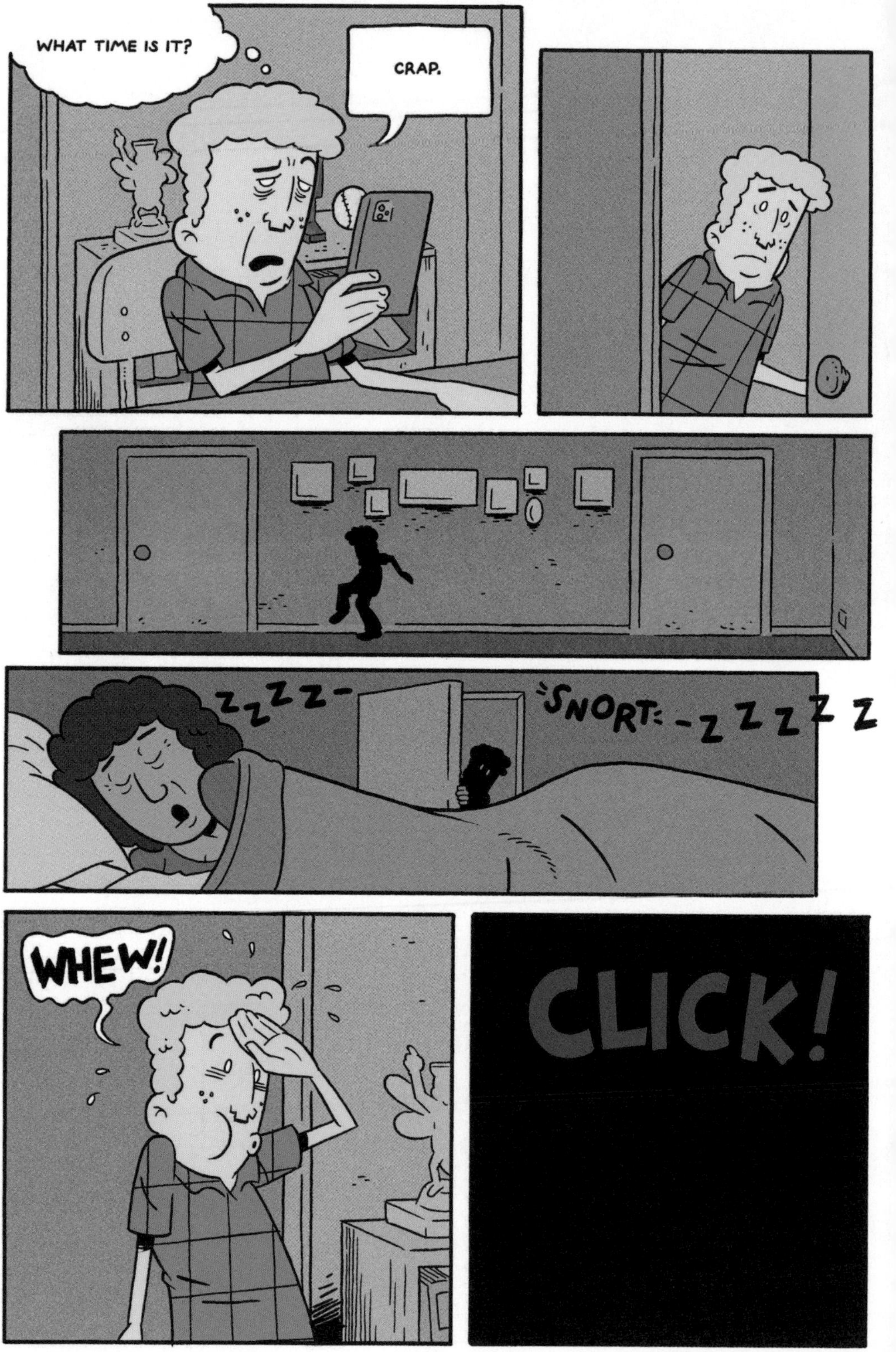

WHAT TIME IS IT?
CRAP.
ZZZZ-
SNORT -ZZZZZ
WHEW!
CLICK!

GROWING UP, MY SISTER AND I SEEMED TO SHARE THE SAME MENTAL LINK AS TWINS.

AS CLOSE AS WE WERE IN AGE, I FIGURED WE JUST MADE THE CUTOFF.

TIK TIK TIK TIK

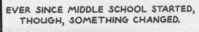

EVER SINCE MIDDLE SCHOOL STARTED, THOUGH, SOMETHING CHANGED.

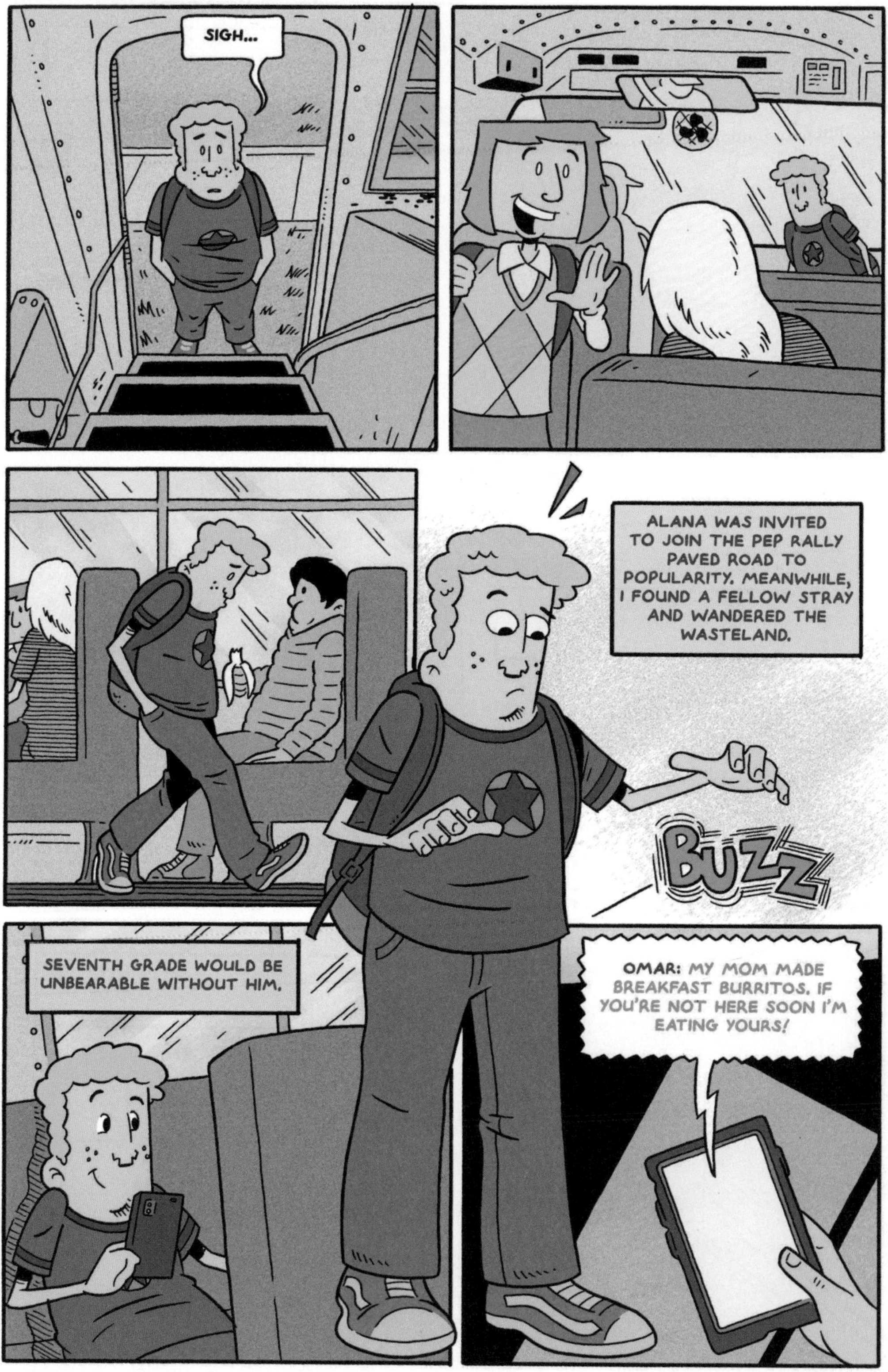
SIGH...
ALANA WAS INVITED TO JOIN THE PEP RALLY PAVED ROAD TO POPULARITY. MEANWHILE, I FOUND A FELLOW STRAY AND WANDERED THE WASTELAND.
BUZZ
SEVENTH GRADE WOULD BE UNBEARABLE WITHOUT HIM.
OMAR: MY MOM MADE BREAKFAST BURRITOS. IF YOU'RE NOT HERE SOON I'M EATING YOURS!

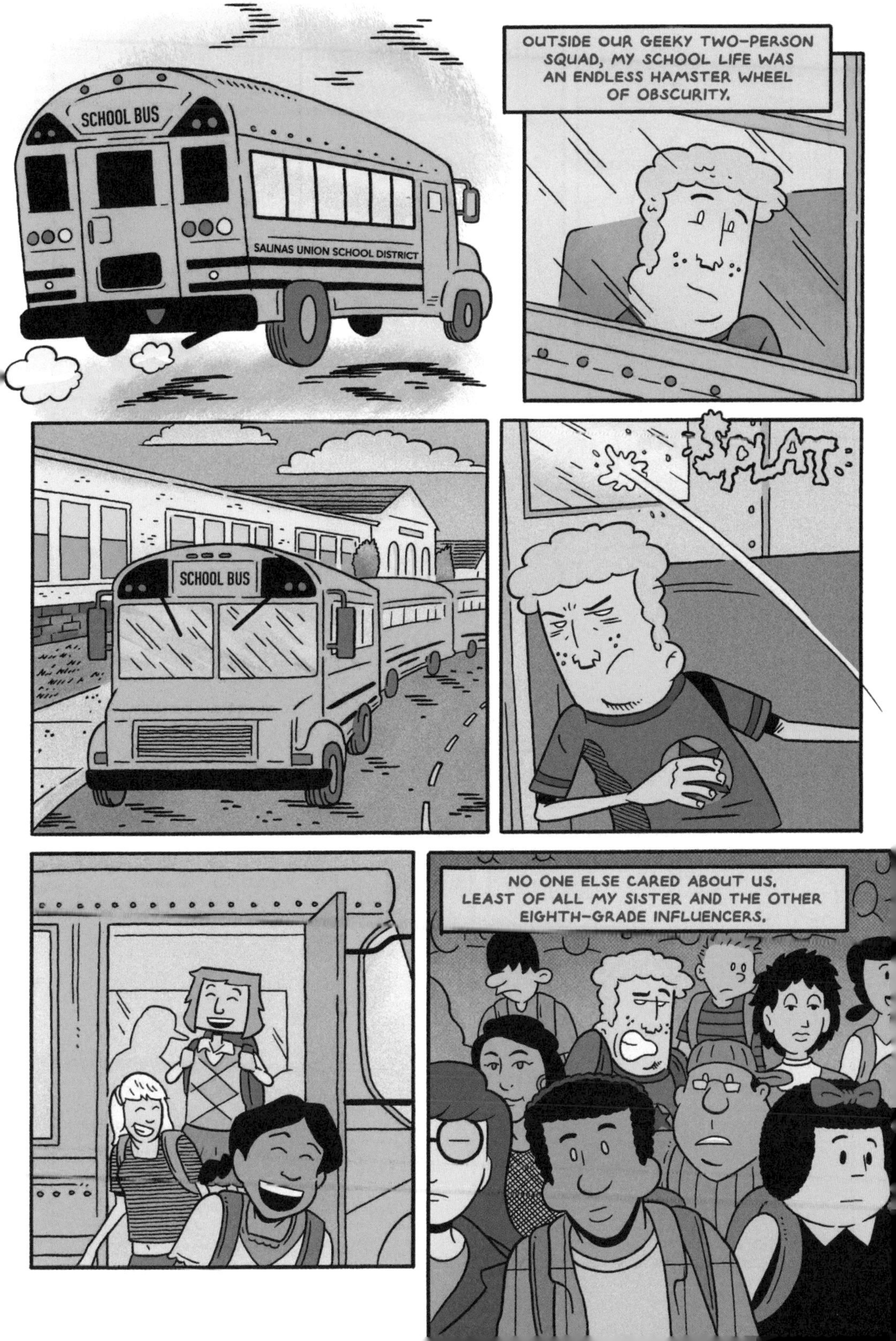
SCHOOL BUS
SALINAS UNION SCHOOL DISTRICT
OUTSIDE OUR GEEKY TWO-PERSON SQUAD, MY SCHOOL LIFE WAS AN ENDLESS HAMSTER WHEEL OF OBSCURITY.
SCHOOL BUS
SPLAT
NO ONE ELSE CARED ABOUT US. LEAST OF ALL MY SISTER AND THE OTHER EIGHTH-GRADE INFLUENCERS.

FIRST BELL WAS THE SCHOOL'S WAY OF ANNOUNCING, "YOU'RE ALL TRAPPED HERE FOR THE NEXT SEVEN HOURS!"

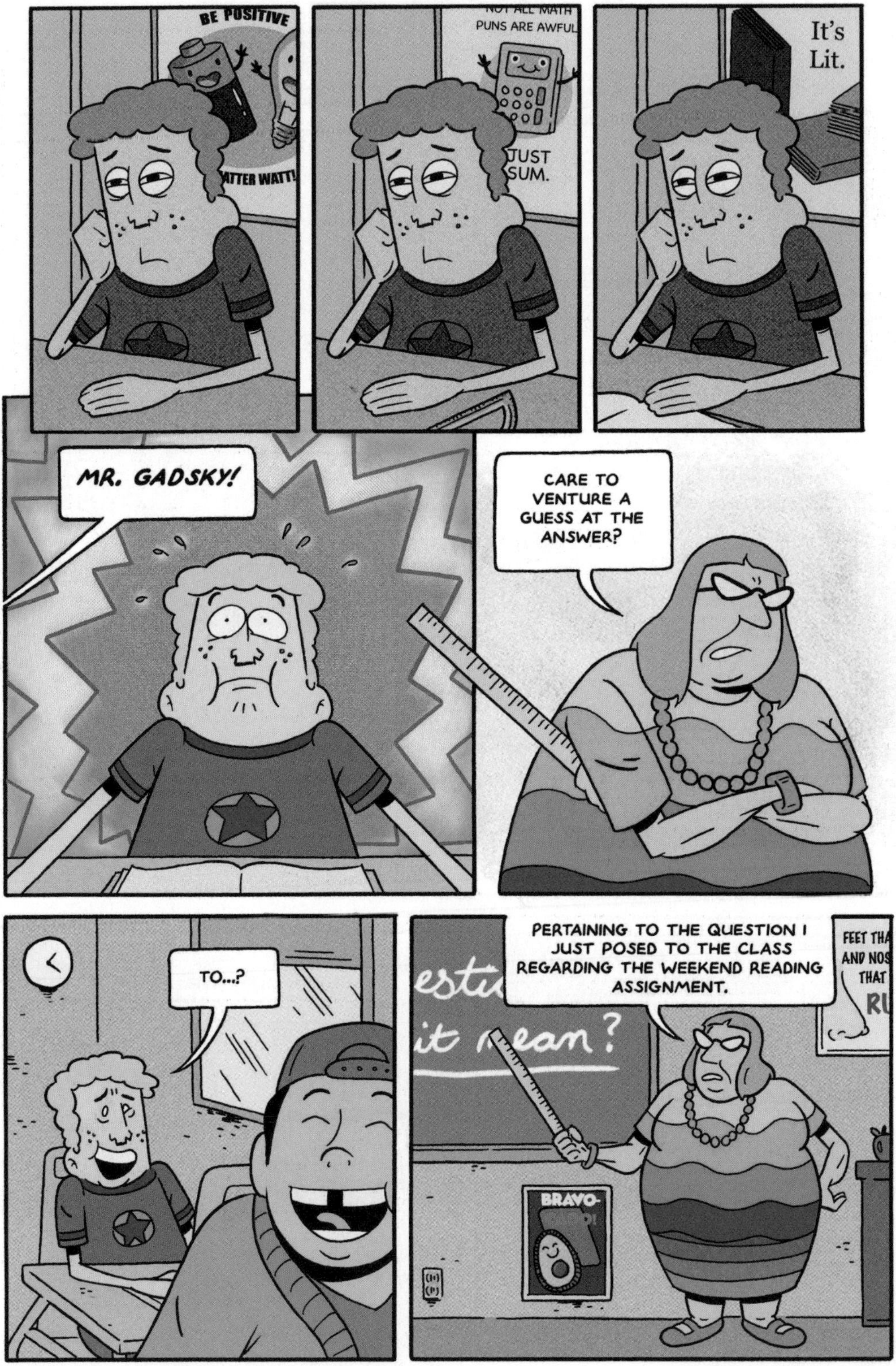

BE POSITIVE
PUNS ARE AWFUL
JUST SUM.
It's Lit.
MR. GADSKY!
CARE TO VENTURE A GUESS AT THE ANSWER?
TO...?
PERTAINING TO THE QUESTION I JUST POSED TO THE CLASS REGARDING THE WEEKEND READING ASSIGNMENT.
BRAVO-

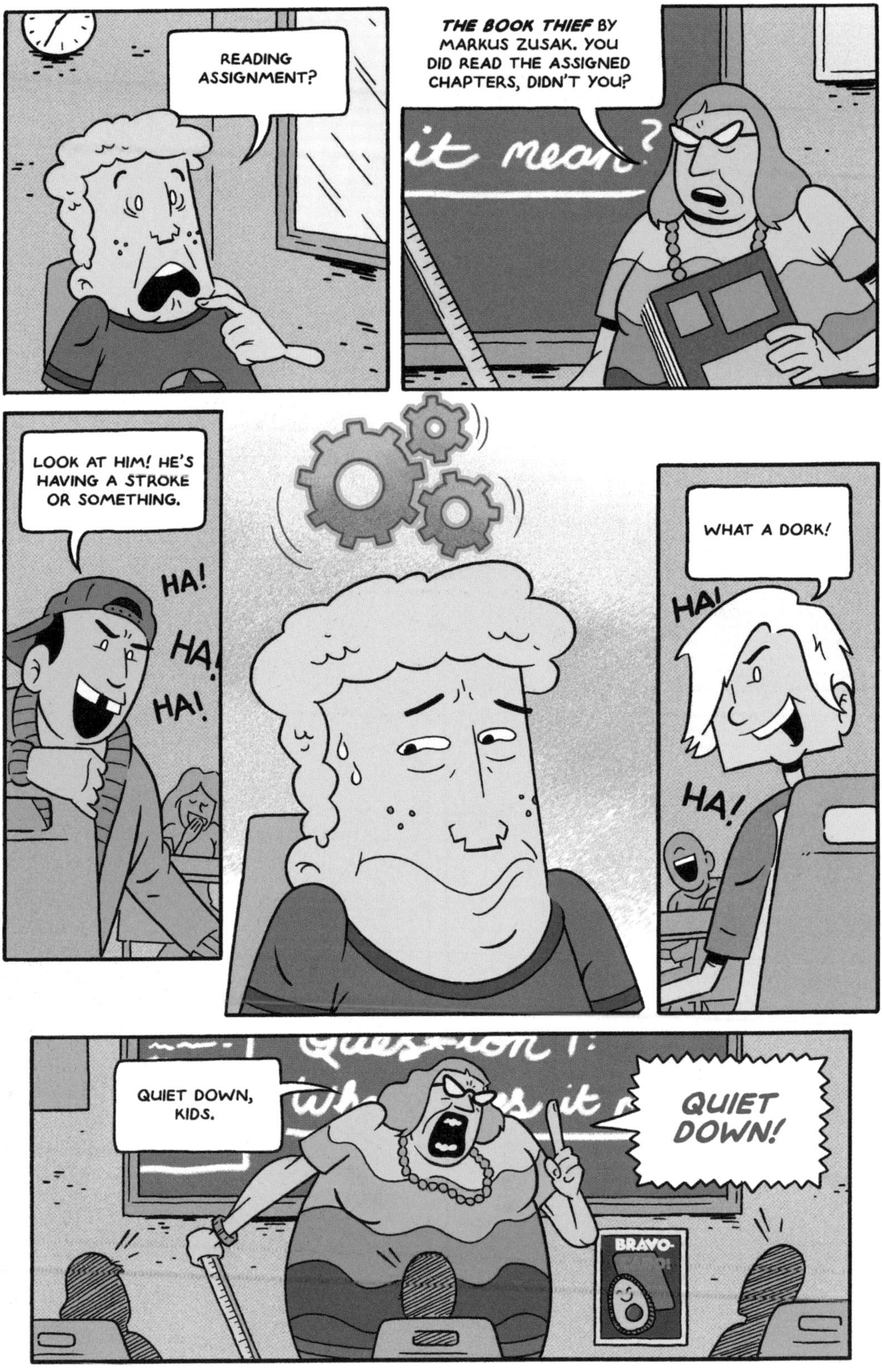
READING ASSIGNMENT?
THE BOOK THIEF BY MARKUS ZUSAK. YOU DID READ THE ASSIGNED CHAPTERS, DIDN'T YOU?
it mean?
LOOK AT HIM! HE'S HAVING A STROKE OR SOMETHING.
HA! HA! HA!
WHAT A DORK!
HA! HA!
QUIET DOWN, KIDS.
QUIET DOWN!
BRAVO-

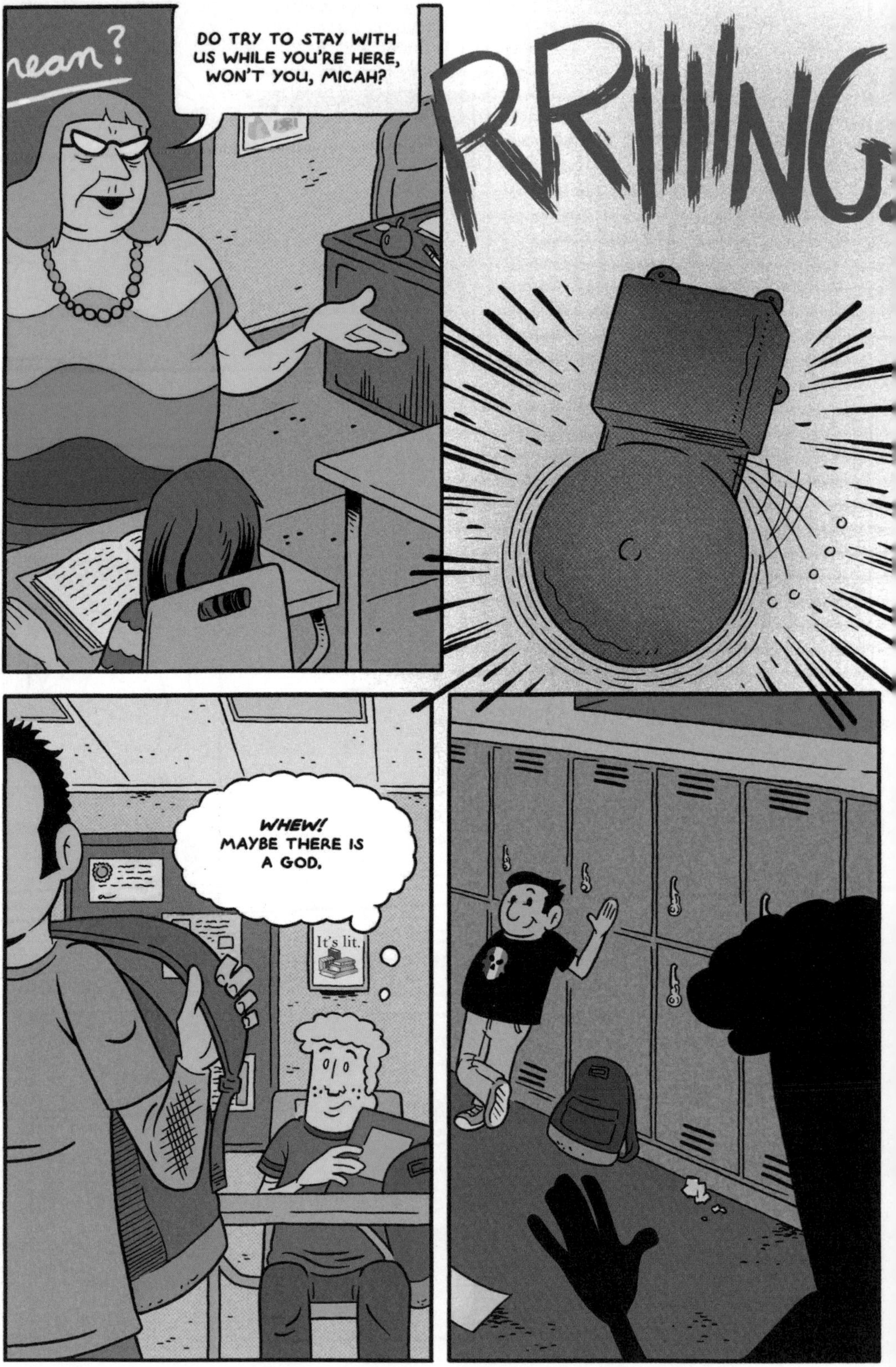
nean?
DO TRY TO STAY WITH US WHILE YOU'RE HERE, WON'T YOU, MICAH?
RRIIING!
WHEW! MAYBE THERE IS A GOD.
It's lit.

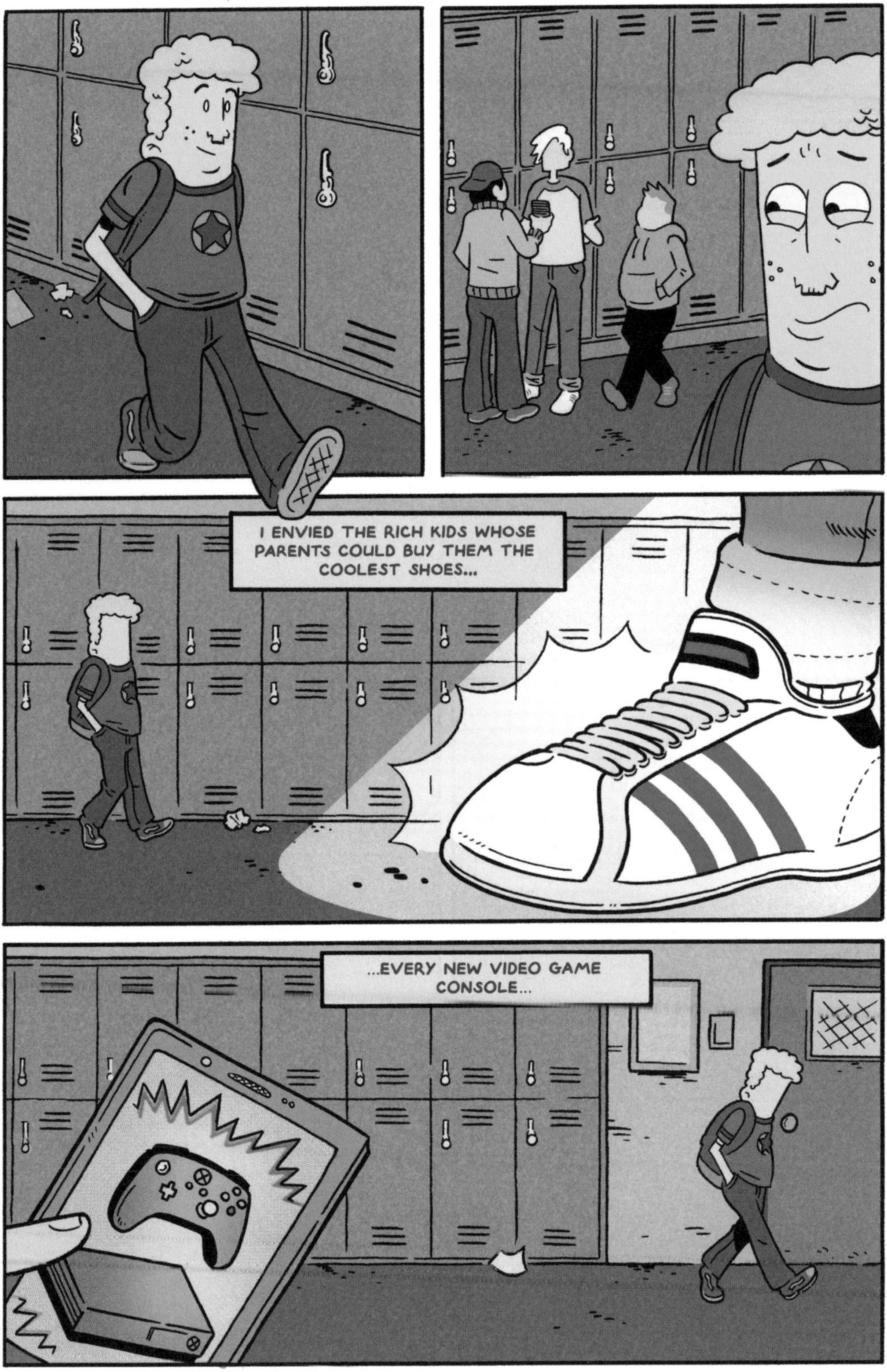
I ENVIED THE RICH KIDS WHOSE PARENTS COULD BUY THEM THE COOLEST SHOES...
...EVERY NEW VIDEO GAME CONSOLE...

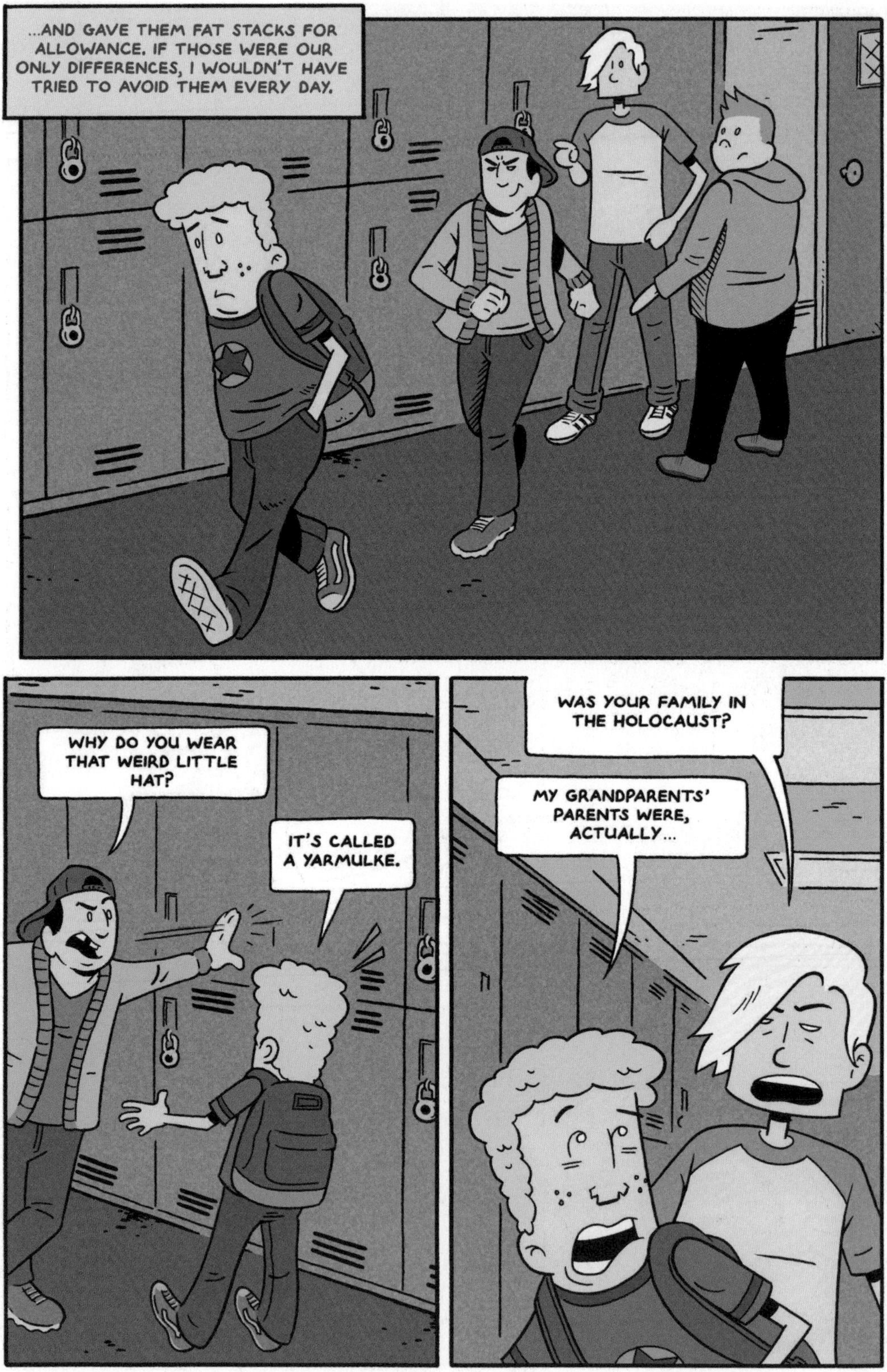
...AND GAVE THEM FAT STACKS FOR ALLOWANCE. IF THOSE WERE OUR ONLY DIFFERENCES, I WOULDN'T HAVE TRIED TO AVOID THEM EVERY DAY.
WHY DO YOU WEAR THAT WEIRD LITTLE HAT?
IT'S CALLED A YARMULKE.
WAS YOUR FAMILY IN THE HOLOCAUST?
MY GRANDPARENTS' PARENTS WERE, ACTUALLY...

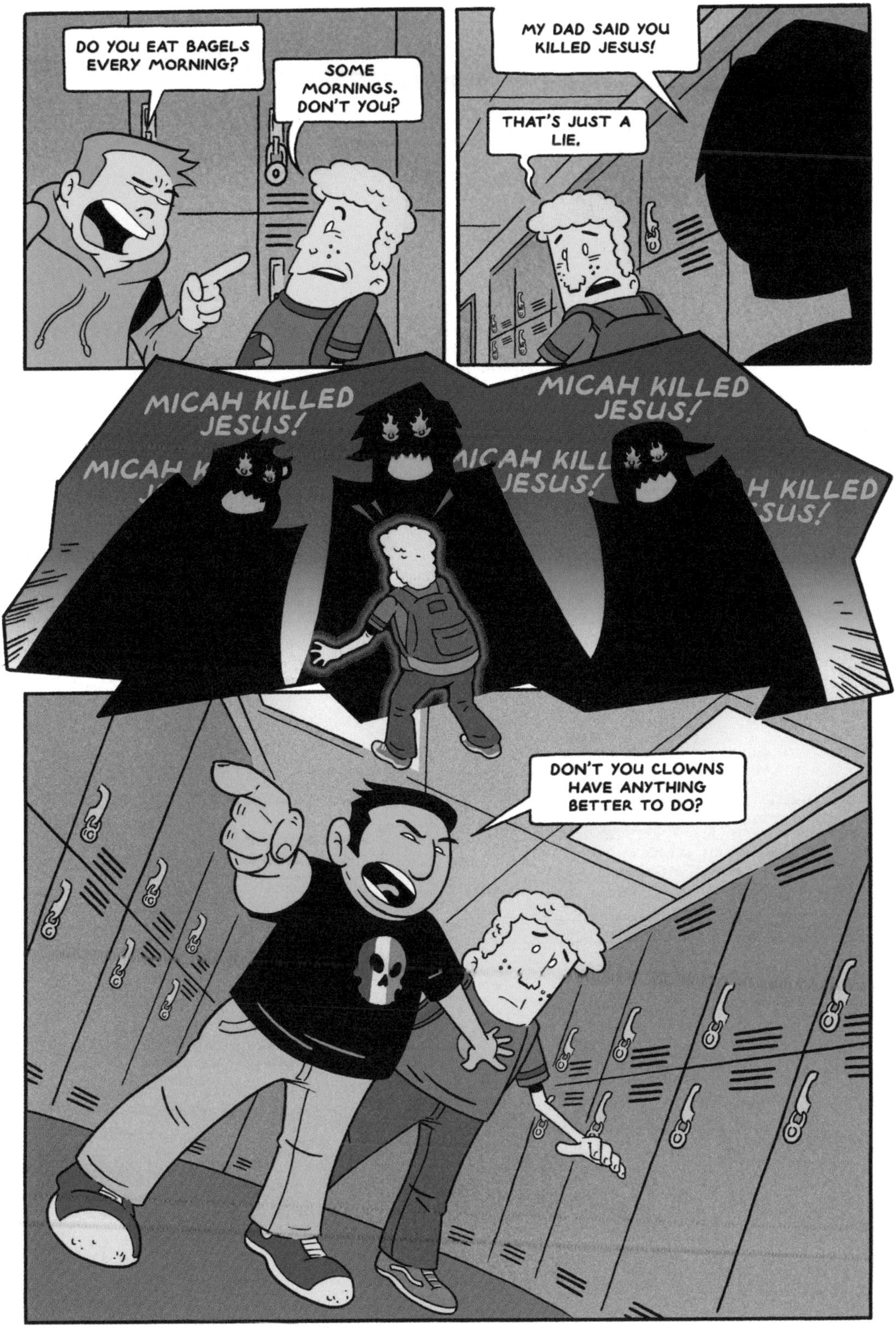

DO YOU EAT BAGELS EVERY MORNING?
SOME MORNINGS. DON'T YOU?
MY DAD SAID YOU KILLED JESUS!
THAT'S JUST A LIE.
MICAH KILLED JESUS!
MICAH KILLED JESUS!
DON'T YOU CLOWNS HAVE ANYTHING BETTER TO DO?

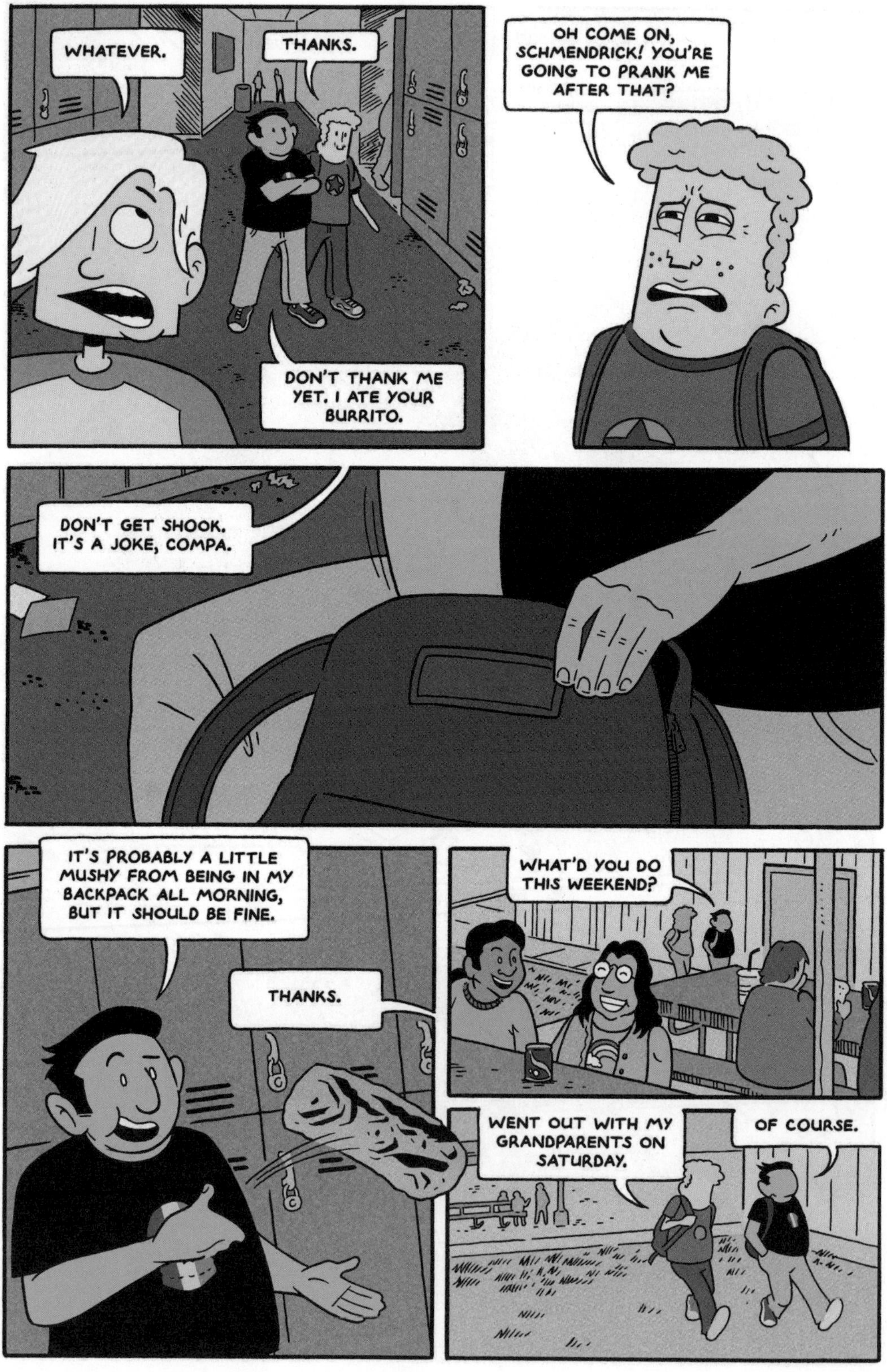
WHATEVER.
THANKS.
DON'T THANK ME YET. I ATE YOUR BURRITO.
OH COME ON, SCHMENDRICK! YOU'RE GOING TO PRANK ME AFTER THAT?
DON'T GET SHOOK. IT'S A JOKE, COMPA.
IT'S PROBABLY A LITTLE MUSHY FROM BEING IN MY BACKPACK ALL MORNING, BUT IT SHOULD BE FINE.
THANKS.
WHAT'D YOU DO THIS WEEKEND?
WENT OUT WITH MY GRANDPARENTS ON SATURDAY.
OF COURSE.

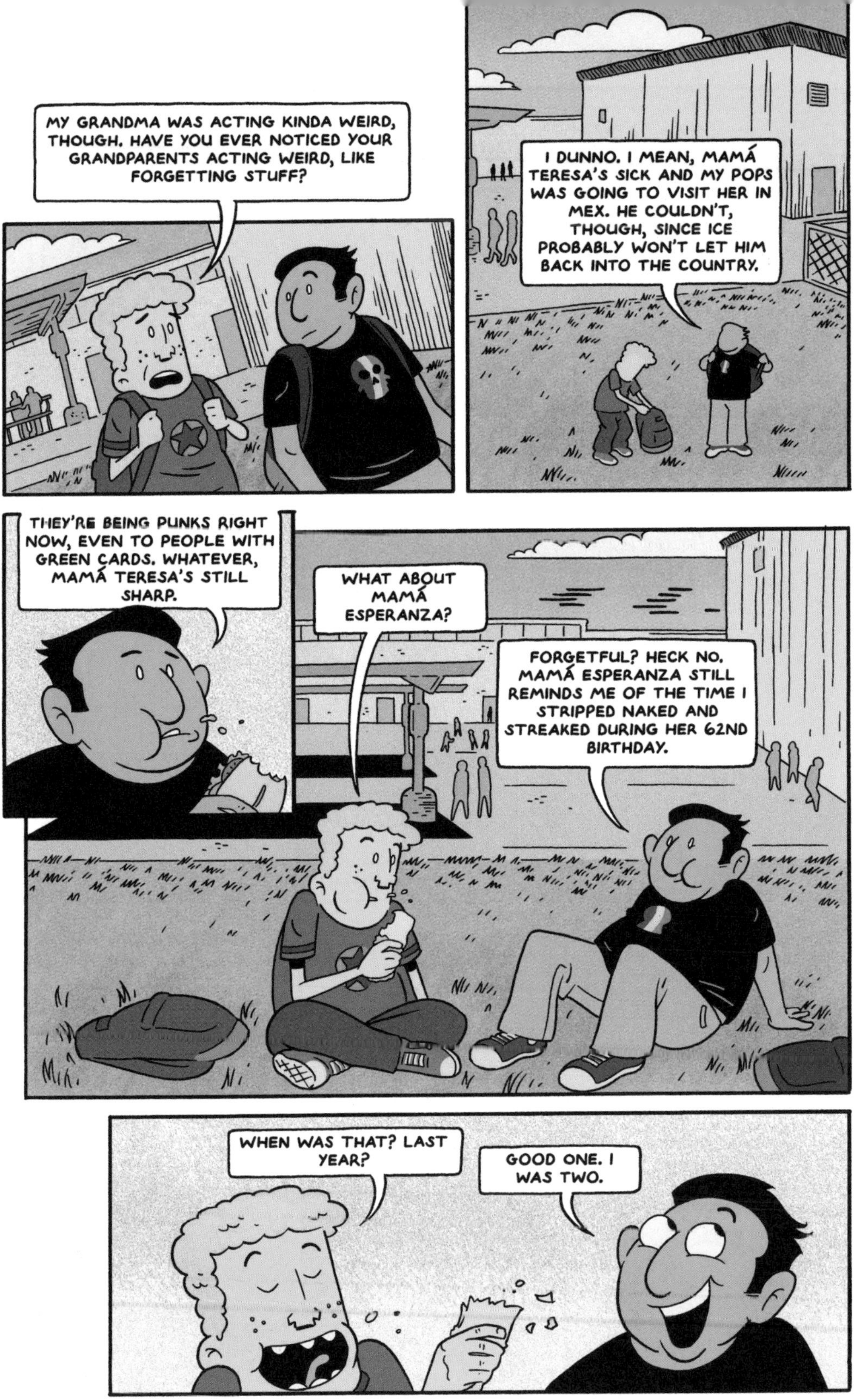
MY GRANDMA WAS ACTING KINDA WEIRD, THOUGH. HAVE YOU EVER NOTICED YOUR GRANDPARENTS ACTING WEIRD, LIKE FORGETTING STUFF?
I DUNNO. I MEAN, MAMÁ TERESA'S SICK AND MY POPS WAS GOING TO VISIT HER IN MEX. HE COULDN'T, THOUGH, SINCE ICE PROBABLY WON'T LET HIM BACK INTO THE COUNTRY.
THEY'RE BEING PUNKS RIGHT NOW, EVEN TO PEOPLE WITH GREEN CARDS. WHATEVER, MAMÁ TERESA'S STILL SHARP.
WHAT ABOUT MAMÁ ESPERANZA?
FORGETFUL? HECK NO. MAMÁ ESPERANZA STILL REMINDS ME OF THE TIME I STRIPPED NAKED AND STREAKED DURING HER 62ND BIRTHDAY.
WHEN WAS THAT? LAST YEAR?
GOOD ONE. I WAS TWO.

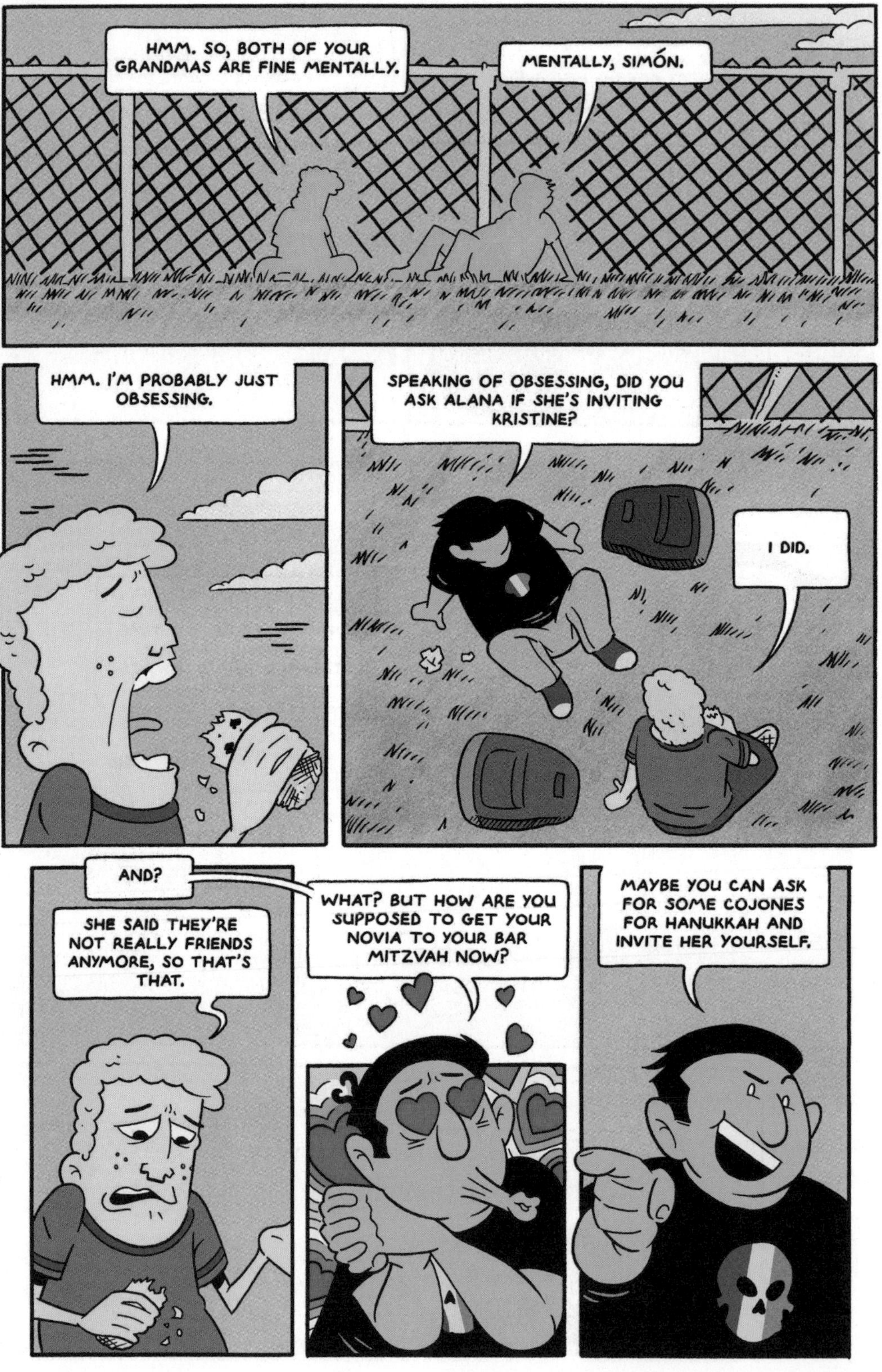
HMM. SO, BOTH OF YOUR GRANDMAS ARE FINE MENTALLY.
MENTALLY, SIMÓN.
HMM. I'M PROBABLY JUST OBSESSING.
SPEAKING OF OBSESSING, DID YOU ASK ALANA IF SHE'S INVITING KRISTINE?
I DID.
AND?
SHE SAID THEY'RE NOT REALLY FRIENDS ANYMORE, SO THAT'S THAT.
WHAT? BUT HOW ARE YOU SUPPOSED TO GET YOUR NOVIA TO YOUR BAR MITZVAH NOW?
MAYBE YOU CAN ASK FOR SOME COJONES FOR HANUKKAH AND INVITE HER YOURSELF.

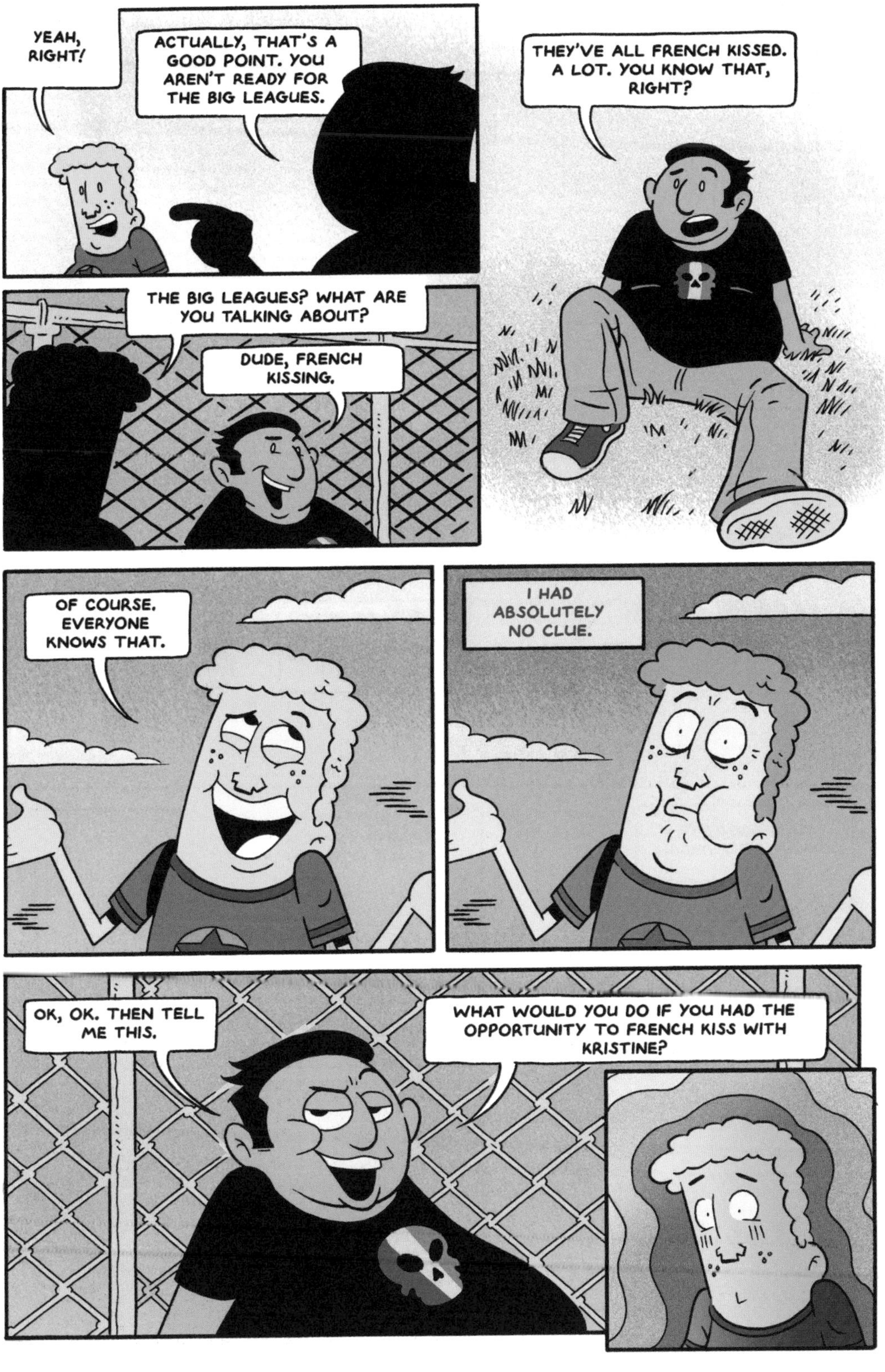
YEAH, RIGHT!
ACTUALLY, THAT'S A GOOD POINT. YOU AREN'T READY FOR THE BIG LEAGUES.
THEY'VE ALL FRENCH KISSED. A LOT. YOU KNOW THAT, RIGHT?
THE BIG LEAGUES? WHAT ARE YOU TALKING ABOUT?
DUDE, FRENCH KISSING.
OF COURSE. EVERYONE KNOWS THAT.
I HAD ABSOLUTELY NO CLUE.
OK, OK. THEN TELL ME THIS.
WHAT WOULD YOU DO IF YOU HAD THE OPPORTUNITY TO FRENCH KISS WITH KRISTINE?

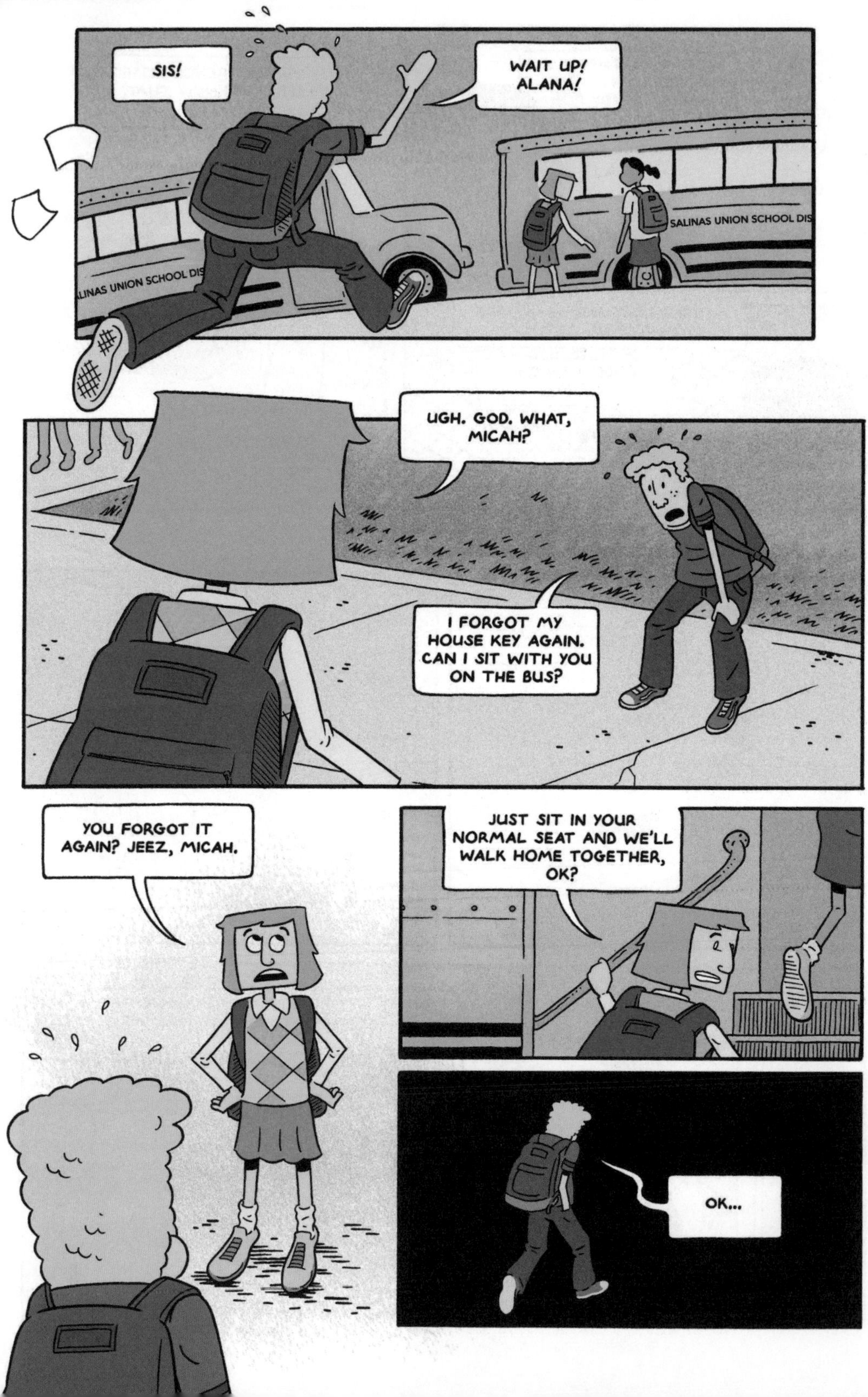
SIS!
WAIT UP! ALANA!
SALINAS UNION SCHOOL DIS
SALINAS UNION SCHOOL DIS
UGH. GOD. WHAT, MICAH?
I FORGOT MY HOUSE KEY AGAIN. CAN I SIT WITH YOU ON THE BUS?
YOU FORGOT IT AGAIN? JEEZ, MICAH.
JUST SIT IN YOUR NORMAL SEAT AND WE'LL WALK HOME TOGETHER, OK?
OK...

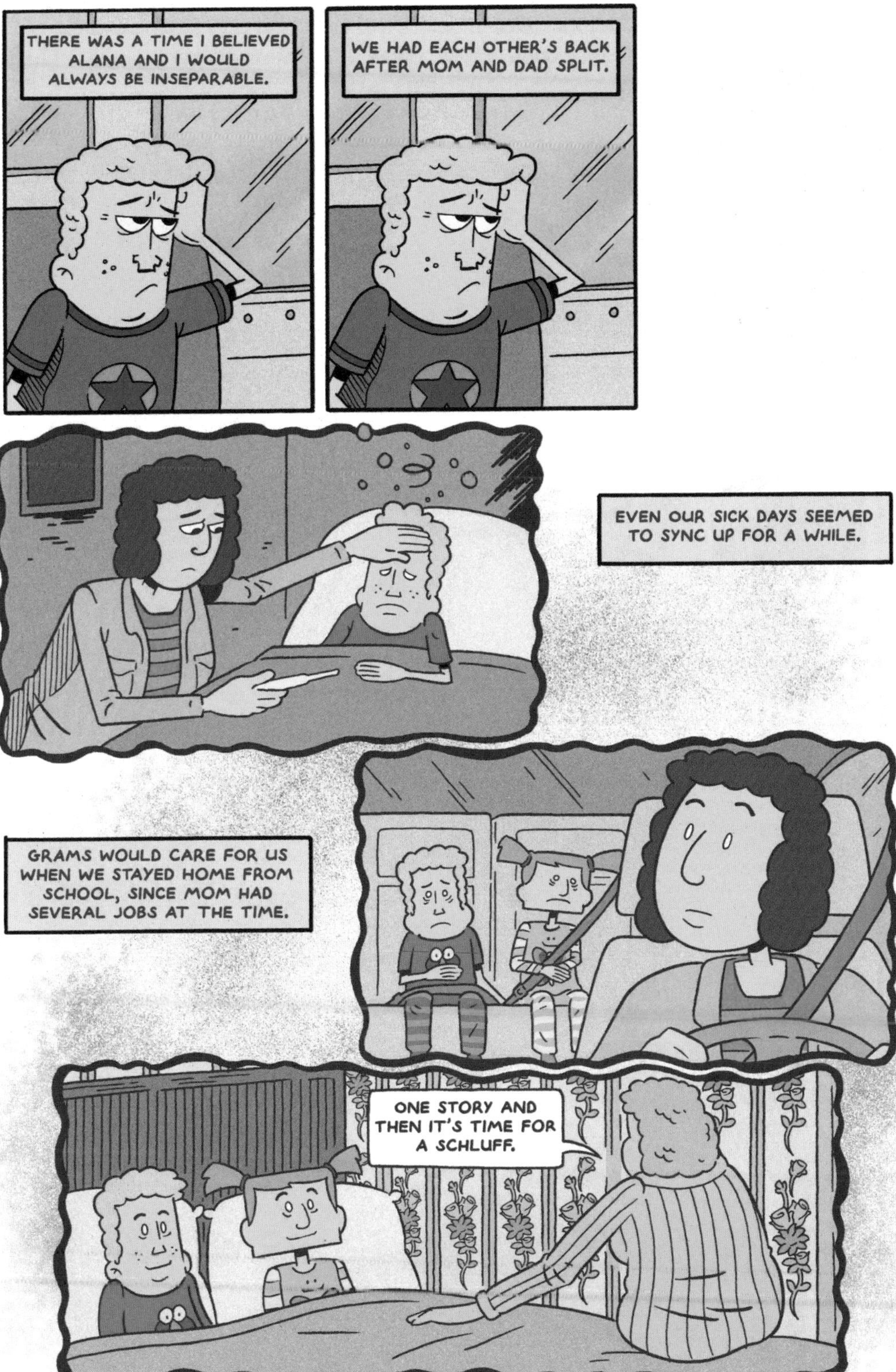
THERE WAS A TIME I BELIEVED ALANA AND I WOULD ALWAYS BE INSEPARABLE.
WE HAD EACH OTHER'S BACK AFTER MOM AND DAD SPLIT.
EVEN OUR SICK DAYS SEEMED TO SYNC UP FOR A WHILE.
GRAMS WOULD CARE FOR US WHEN WE STAYED HOME FROM SCHOOL, SINCE MOM HAD SEVERAL JOBS AT THE TIME.
ONE STORY AND THEN IT'S TIME FOR A SCHLUFF.

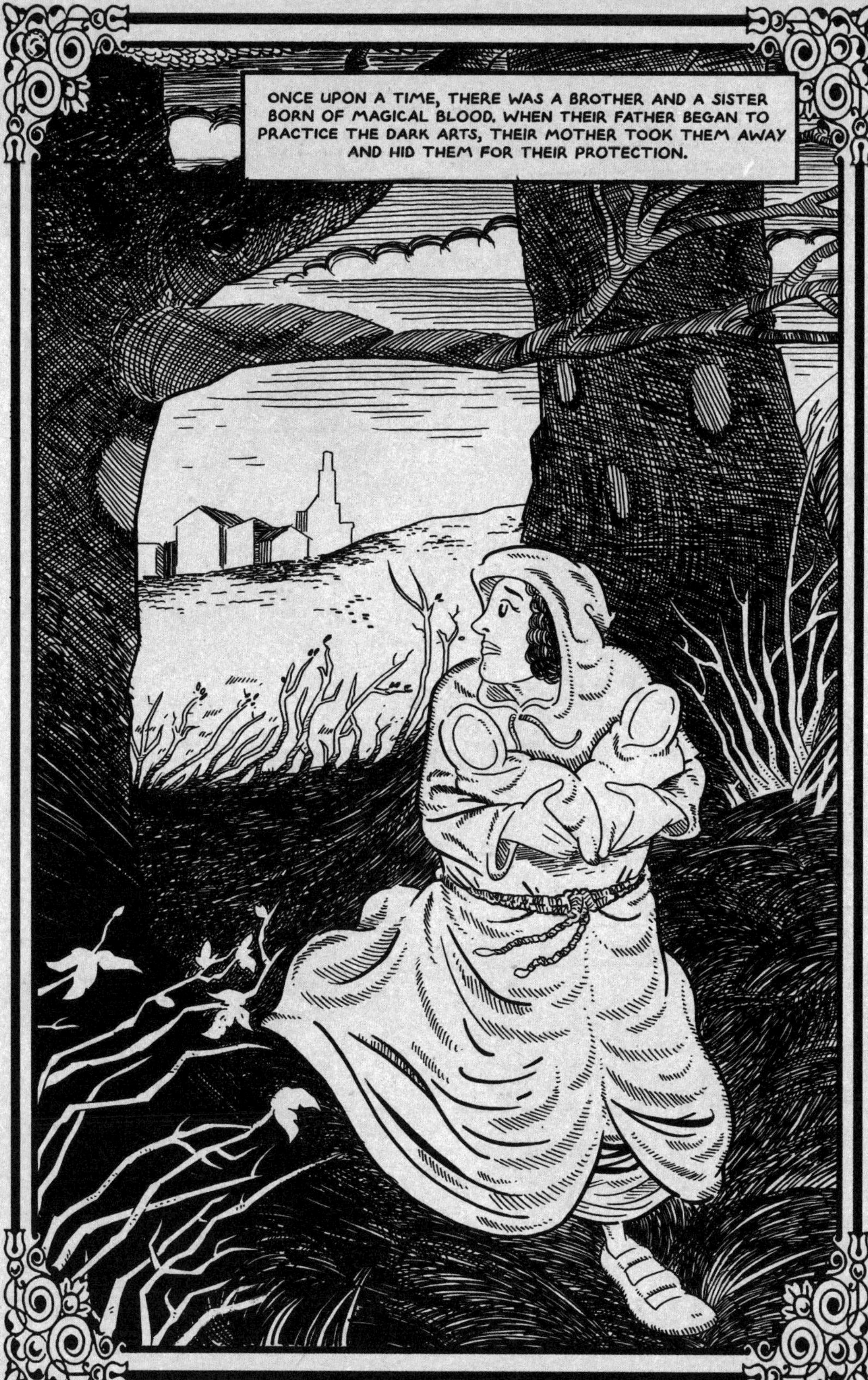
ONCE UPON A TIME, THERE WAS A BROTHER AND A SISTER BORN OF MAGICAL BLOOD. WHEN THEIR FATHER BEGAN TO PRACTICE THE DARK ARTS, THEIR MOTHER TOOK THEM AWAY AND HID THEM FOR THEIR PROTECTION.

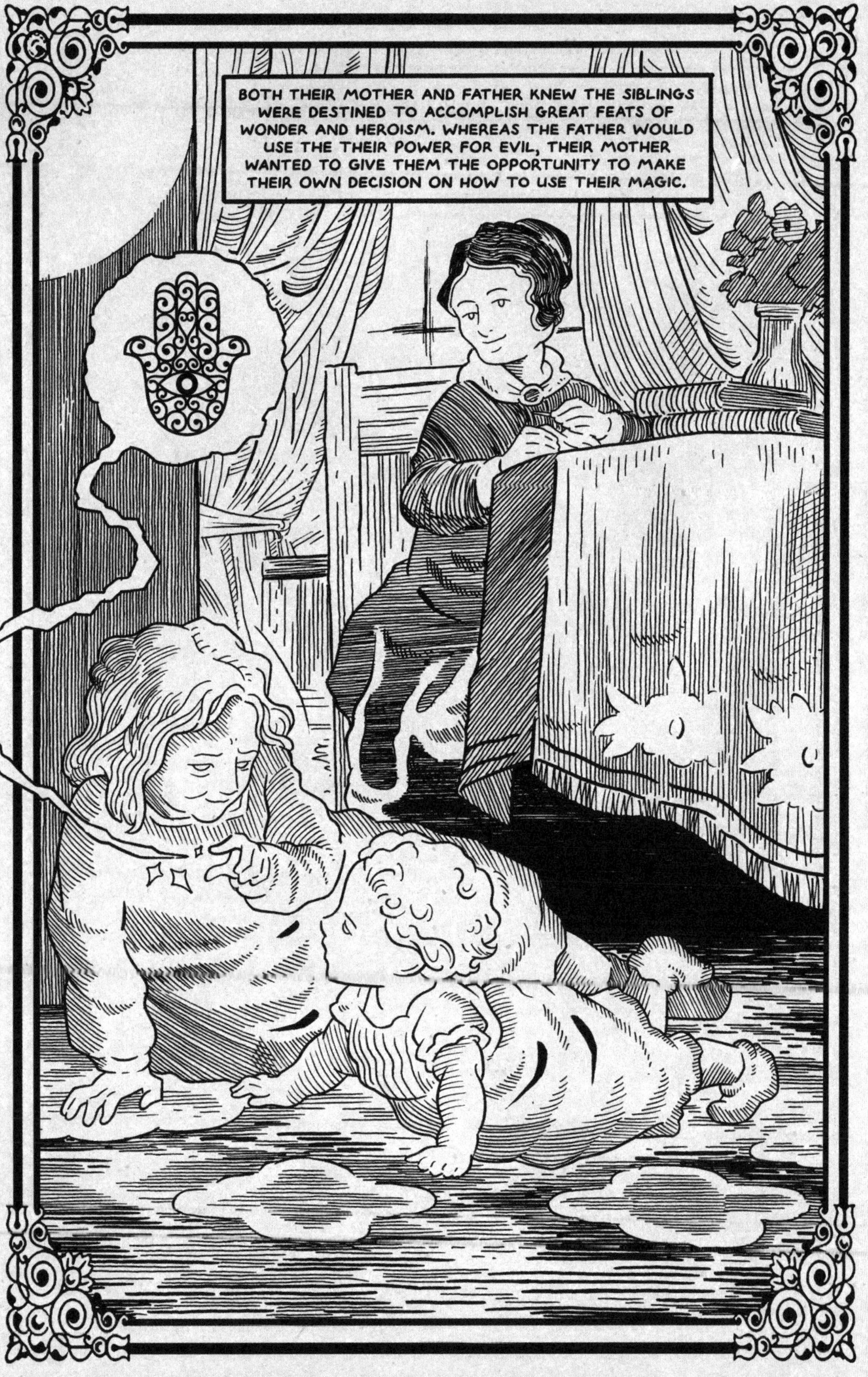
BOTH THEIR MOTHER AND FATHER KNEW THE SIBLINGS WERE DESTINED TO ACCOMPLISH GREAT FEATS OF WONDER AND HEROISM. WHEREAS THE FATHER WOULD USE THE THEIR POWER FOR EVIL, THEIR MOTHER WANTED TO GIVE THEM THE OPPORTUNITY TO MAKE THEIR OWN DECISION ON HOW TO USE THEIR MAGIC.

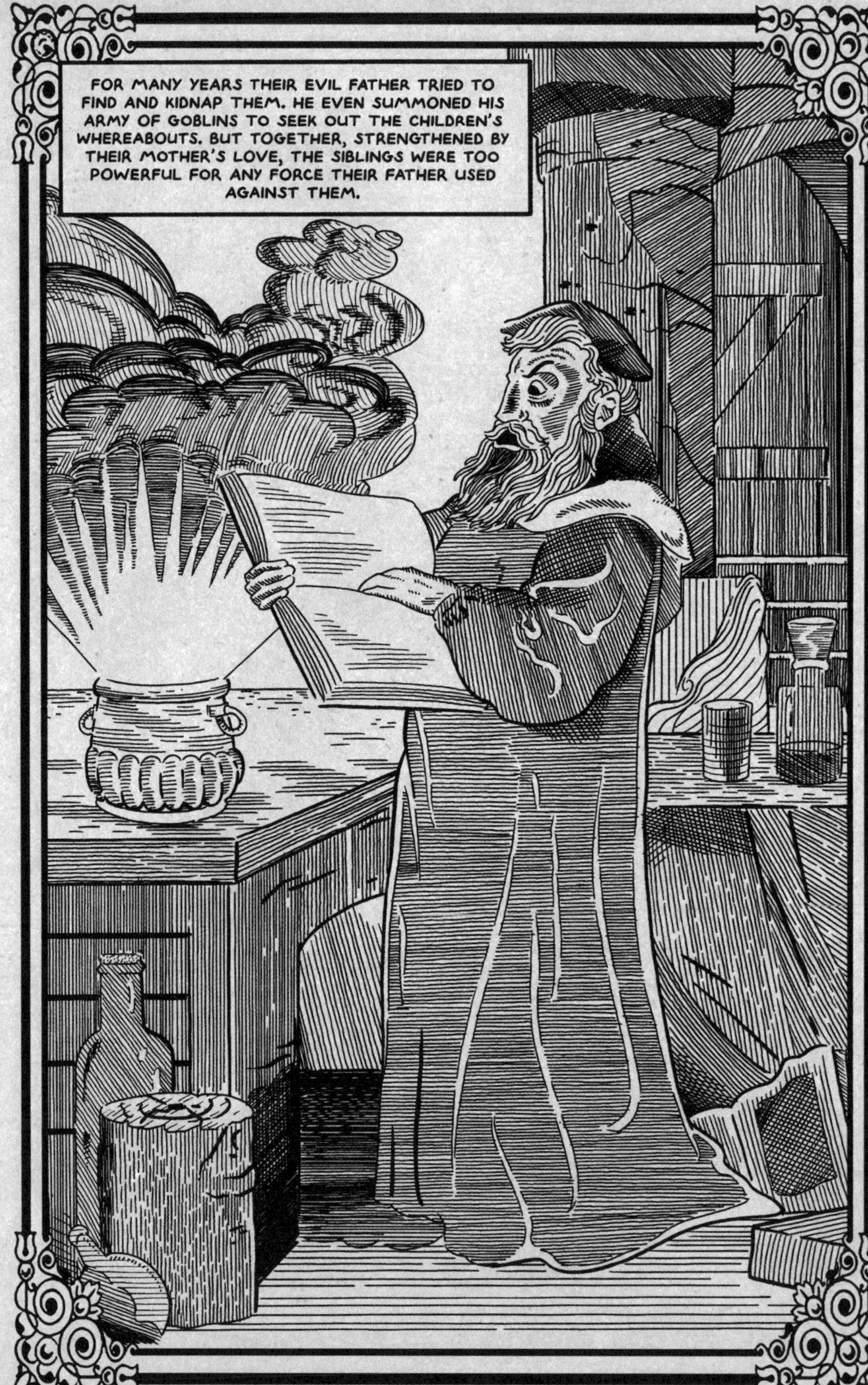
FOR MANY YEARS THEIR EVIL FATHER TRIED TO FIND AND KIDNAP THEM. HE EVEN SUMMONED HIS ARMY OF GOBLINS TO SEEK OUT THE CHILDREN'S WHEREABOUTS. BUT TOGETHER, STRENGTHENED BY THEIR MOTHER'S LOVE, THE SIBLINGS WERE TOO POWERFUL FOR ANY FORCE THEIR FATHER USED AGAINST THEM.

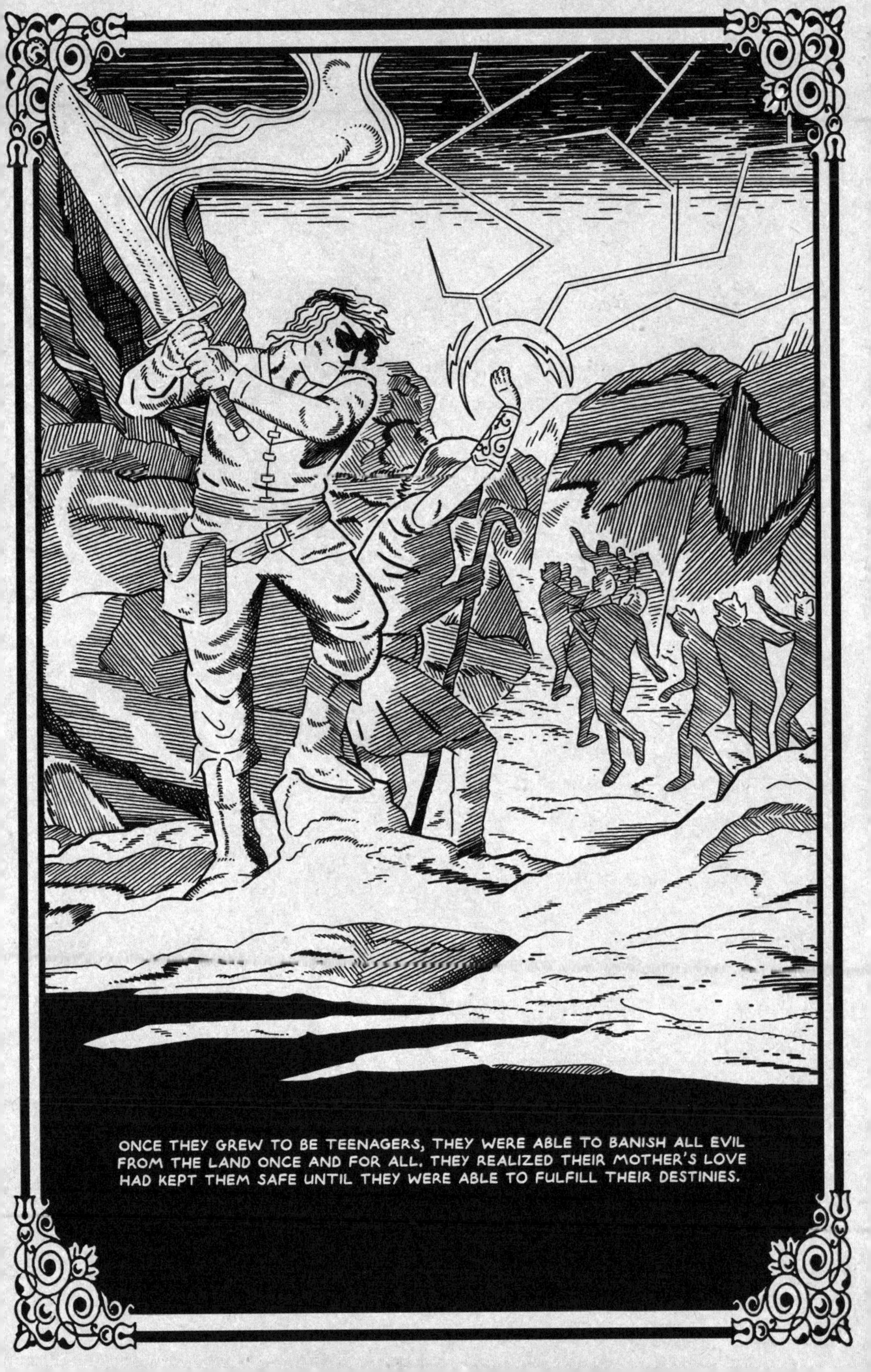
ONCE THEY GREW TO BE TEENAGERS, THEY WERE ABLE TO BANISH ALL EVIL FROM THE LAND ONCE AND FOR ALL. THEY REALIZED THEIR MOTHER'S LOVE HAD KEPT THEM SAFE UNTIL THEY WERE ABLE TO FULFILL THEIR DESTINIES.

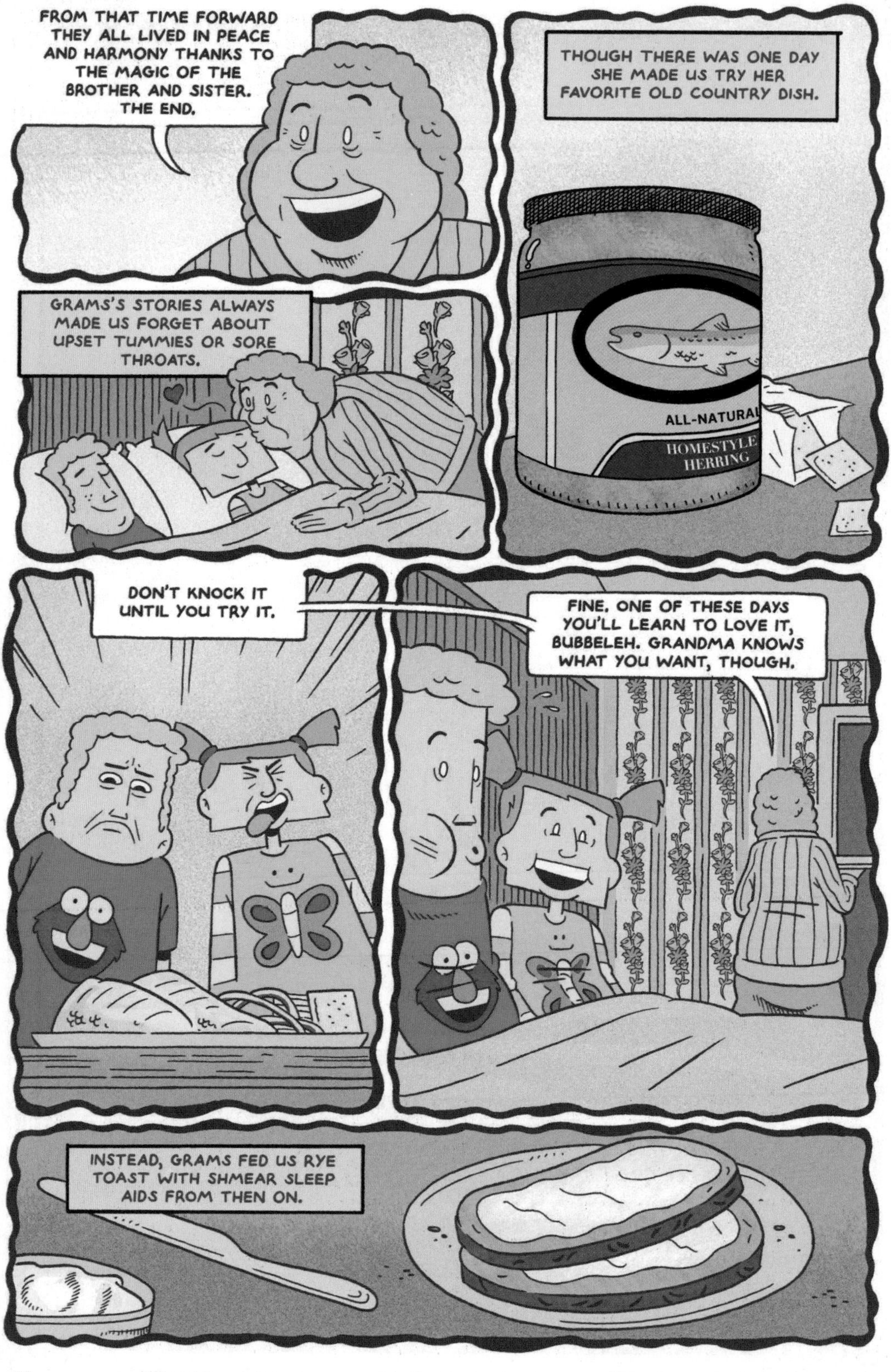

FROM THAT TIME FORWARD THEY ALL LIVED IN PEACE AND HARMONY THANKS TO THE MAGIC OF THE BROTHER AND SISTER. THE END.
THOUGH THERE WAS ONE DAY SHE MADE US TRY HER FAVORITE OLD COUNTRY DISH.
ALL-NATURAL
HOMESTYLE HERRING
GRAMS'S STORIES ALWAYS MADE US FORGET ABOUT UPSET TUMMIES OR SORE THROATS.
DON'T KNOCK IT UNTIL YOU TRY IT.
FINE. ONE OF THESE DAYS YOU'LL LEARN TO LOVE IT, BUBBELEH. GRANDMA KNOWS WHAT YOU WANT, THOUGH.
INSTEAD, GRAMS FED US RYE TOAST WITH SHMEAR SLEEP AIDS FROM THEN ON.

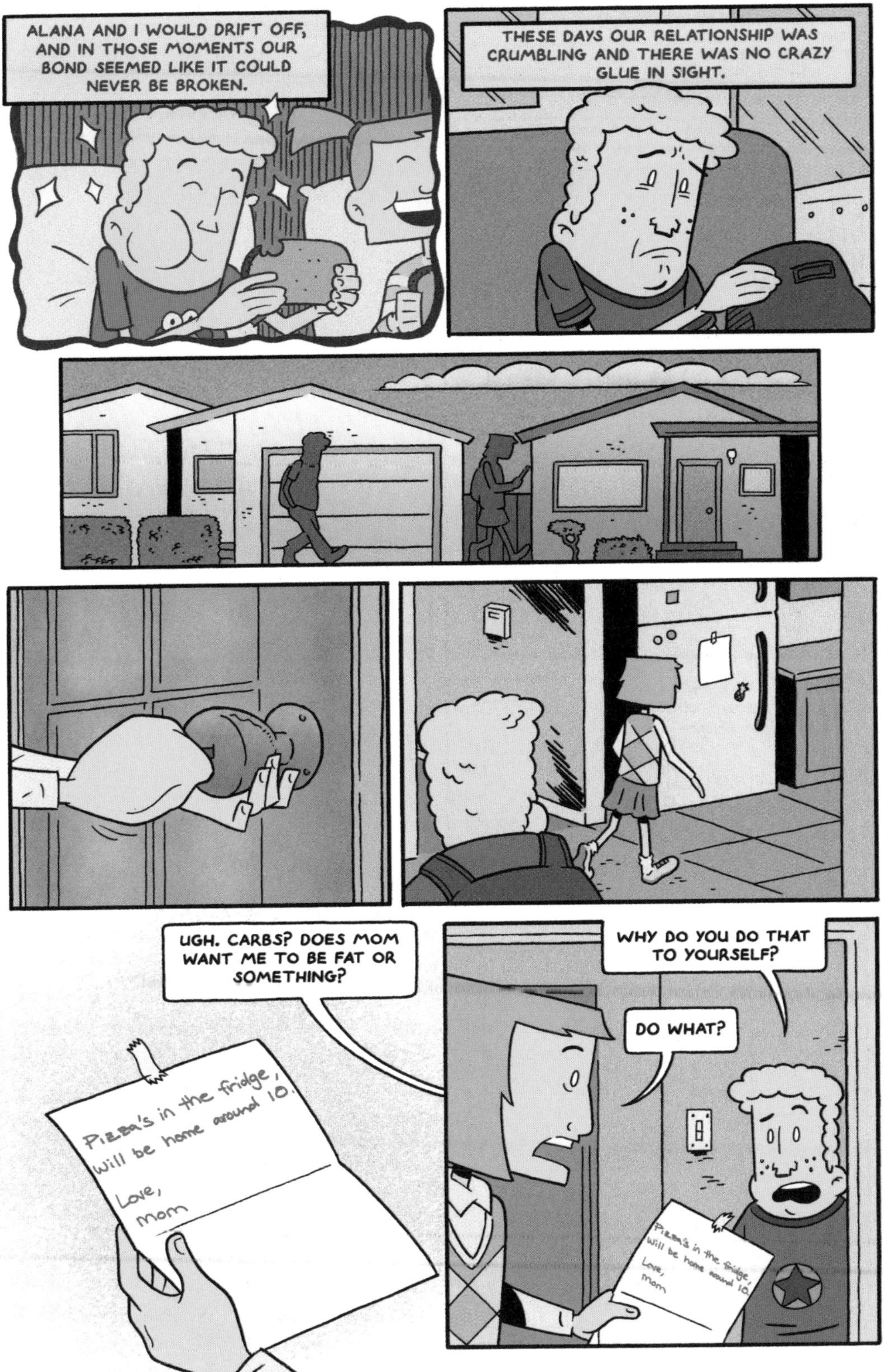
ALANA AND I WOULD DRIFT OFF, AND IN THOSE MOMENTS OUR BOND SEEMED LIKE IT COULD NEVER BE BROKEN.
THESE DAYS OUR RELATIONSHIP WAS CRUMBLING AND THERE WAS NO CRAZY GLUE IN SIGHT.
UGH. CARBS? DOES MOM WANT ME TO BE FAT OR SOMETHING?
Pizza's in the fridge, will be home around 10.
Love, mom
WHY DO YOU DO THAT TO YOURSELF?
DO WHAT?

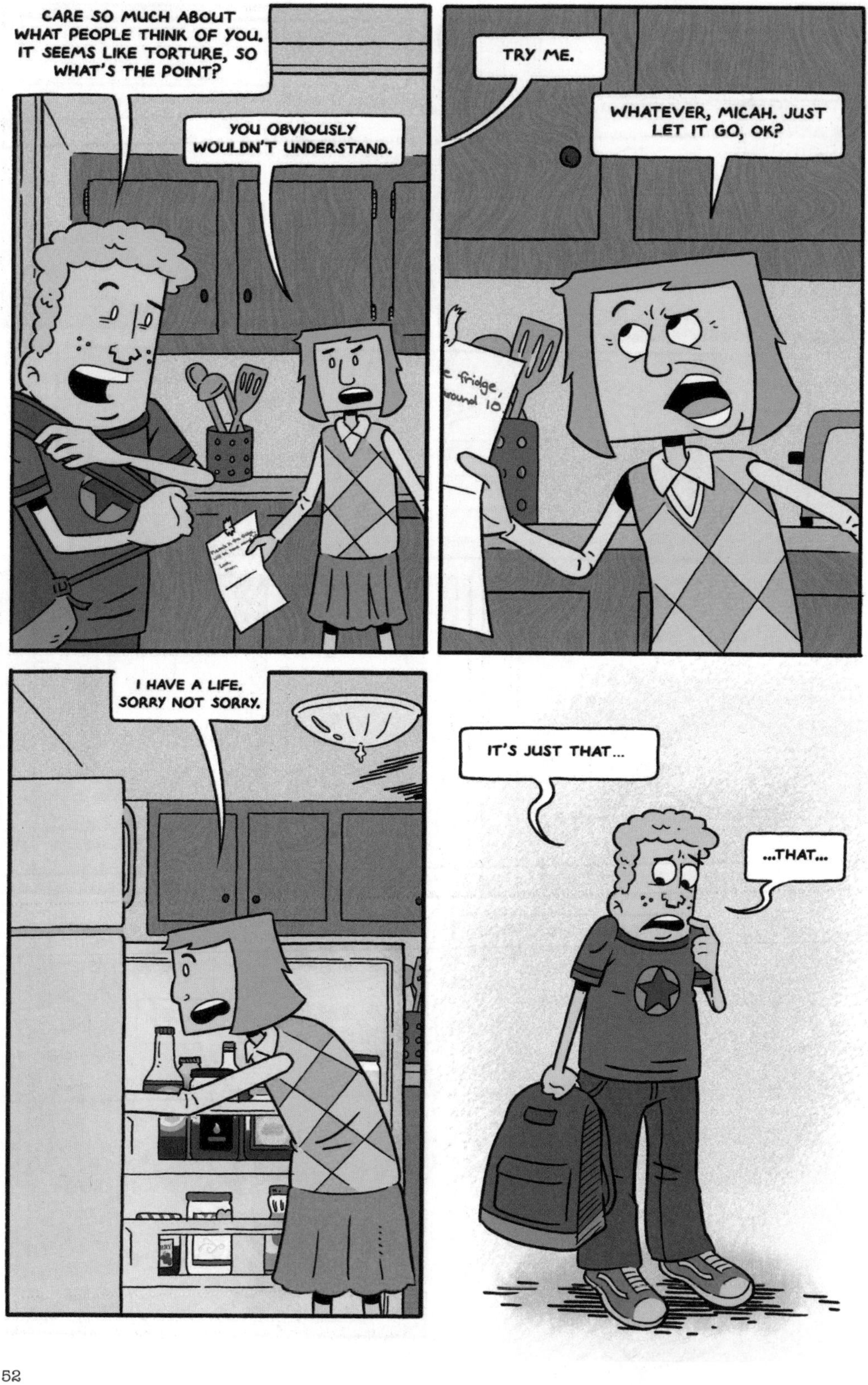
CARE SO MUCH ABOUT WHAT PEOPLE THINK OF YOU. IT SEEMS LIKE TORTURE, SO WHAT'S THE POINT?
YOU OBVIOUSLY WOULDN'T UNDERSTAND.
TRY ME.
WHATEVER, MICAH. JUST LET IT GO, OK?
I HAVE A LIFE. SORRY NOT SORRY.
IT'S JUST THAT...
...THAT...

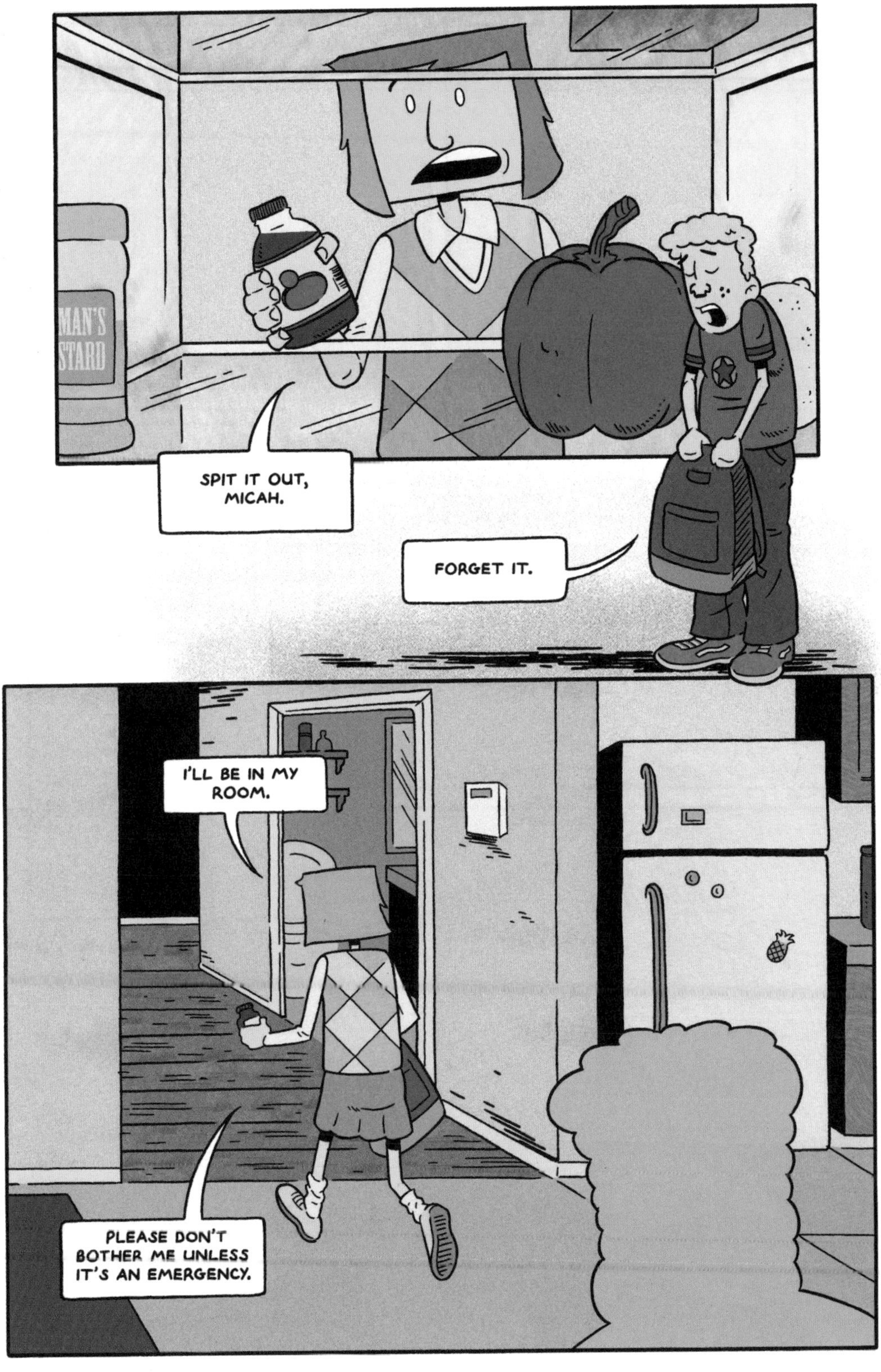
SPIT IT OUT, MICAH.
FORGET IT.
I'LL BE IN MY ROOM.
PLEASE DON'T BOTHER ME UNLESS IT'S AN EMERGENCY.

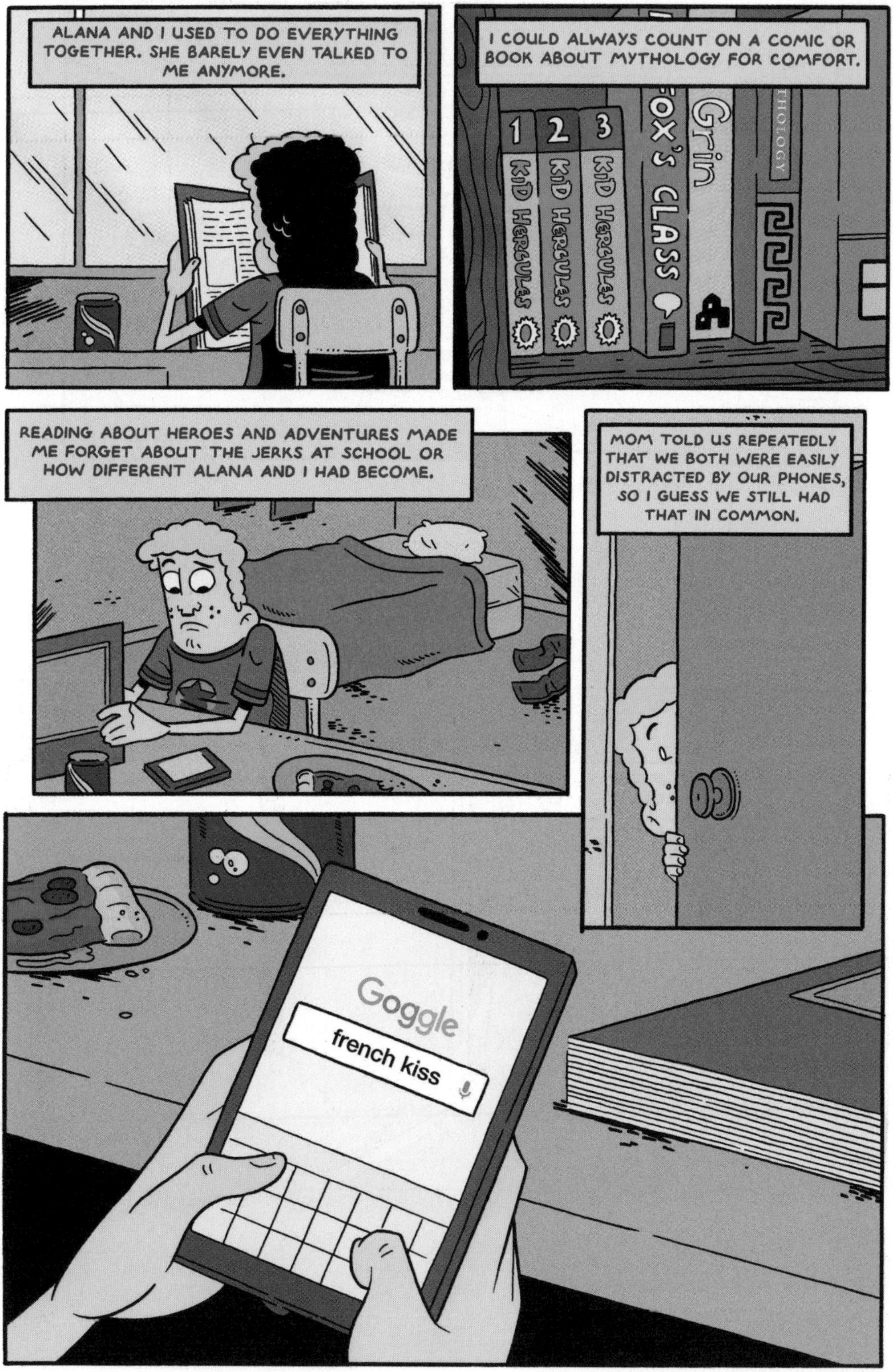
ALANA AND I USED TO DO EVERYTHING TOGETHER. SHE BARELY EVEN TALKED TO ME ANYMORE.
I COULD ALWAYS COUNT ON A COMIC OR BOOK ABOUT MYTHOLOGY FOR COMFORT.
1 KID HERCULES
2 KID HERCULES
3 KID HERCULES
Grin
READING ABOUT HEROES AND ADVENTURES MADE ME FORGET ABOUT THE JERKS AT SCHOOL OR HOW DIFFERENT ALANA AND I HAD BECOME.
MOM TOLD US REPEATEDLY THAT WE BOTH WERE EASILY DISTRACTED BY OUR PHONES, SO I GUESS WE STILL HAD THAT IN COMMON.
Goggle
french kiss

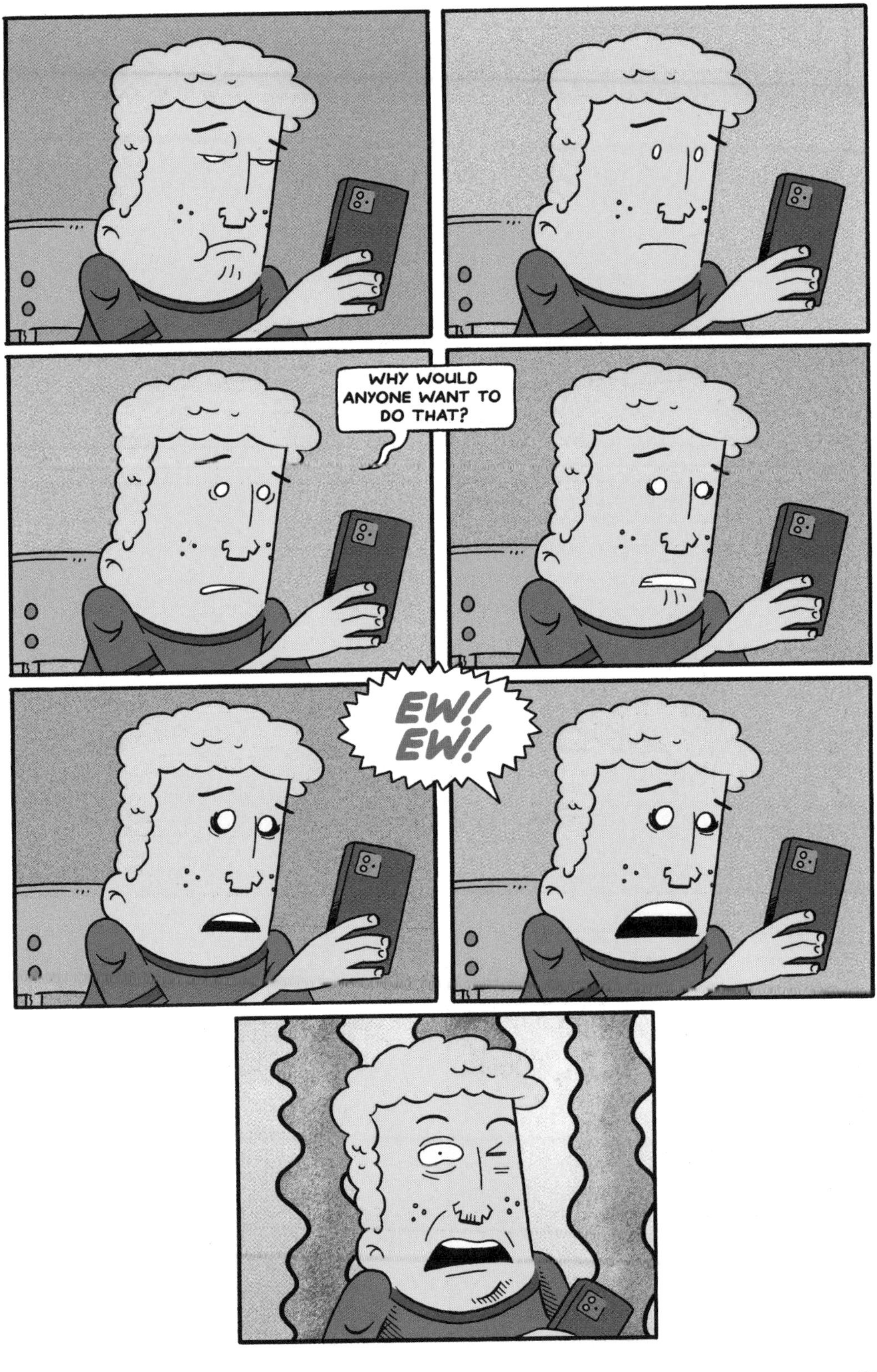
WHY WOULD ANYONE WANT TO DO THAT?
EW! EW!

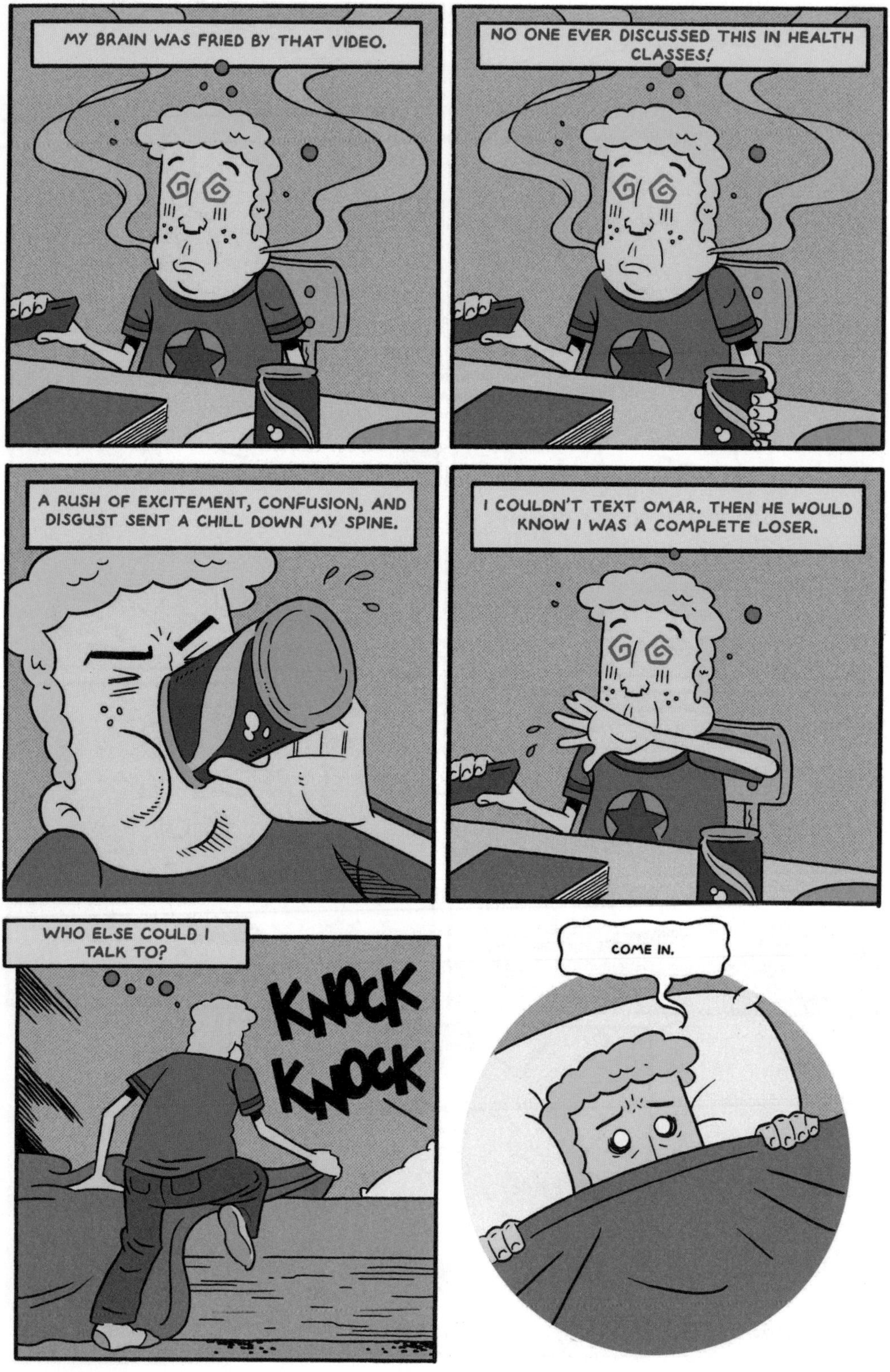
MY BRAIN WAS FRIED BY THAT VIDEO.
NO ONE EVER DISCUSSED THIS IN HEALTH CLASSES!
A RUSH OF EXCITEMENT, CONFUSION, AND DISGUST SENT A CHILL DOWN MY SPINE.
I COULDN'T TEXT OMAR. THEN HE WOULD KNOW I WAS A COMPLETE LOSER.
WHO ELSE COULD I TALK TO?
KNOCK KNOCK
COME IN.

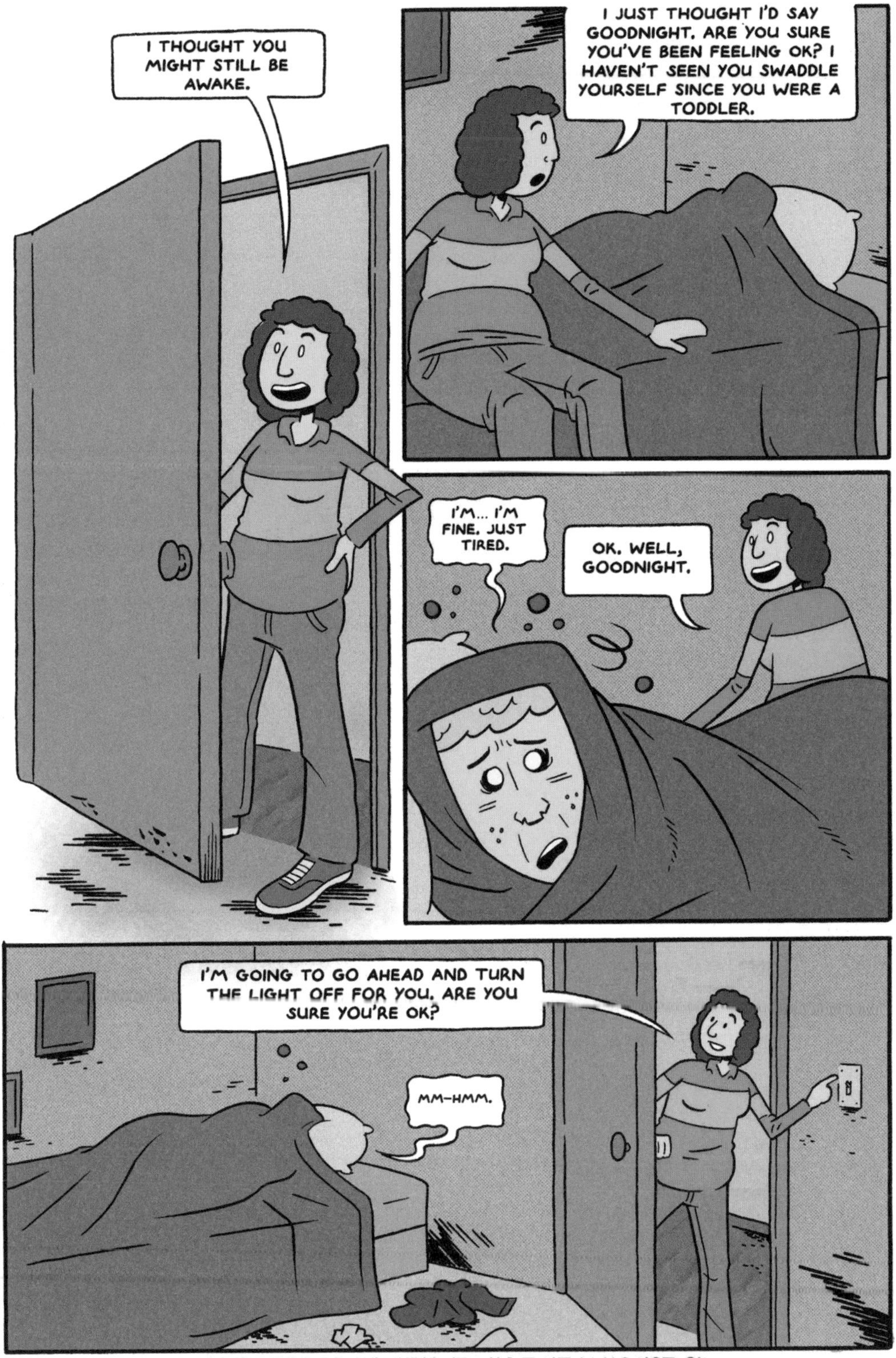
I THOUGHT YOU MIGHT STILL BE AWAKE.
I JUST THOUGHT I'D SAY GOODNIGHT. ARE YOU SURE YOU'VE BEEN FEELING OK? I HAVEN'T SEEN YOU SWADDLE YOURSELF SINCE YOU WERE A TODDLER.
I'M... I'M FINE. JUST TIRED.
OK. WELL, GOODNIGHT.
I'M GOING TO GO AHEAD AND TURN THE LIGHT OFF FOR YOU. ARE YOU SURE YOU'RE OK?
MM-HMM.

IF I WAS SURE OF ANYTHING, IT WAS THAT I WAS NOT OK.

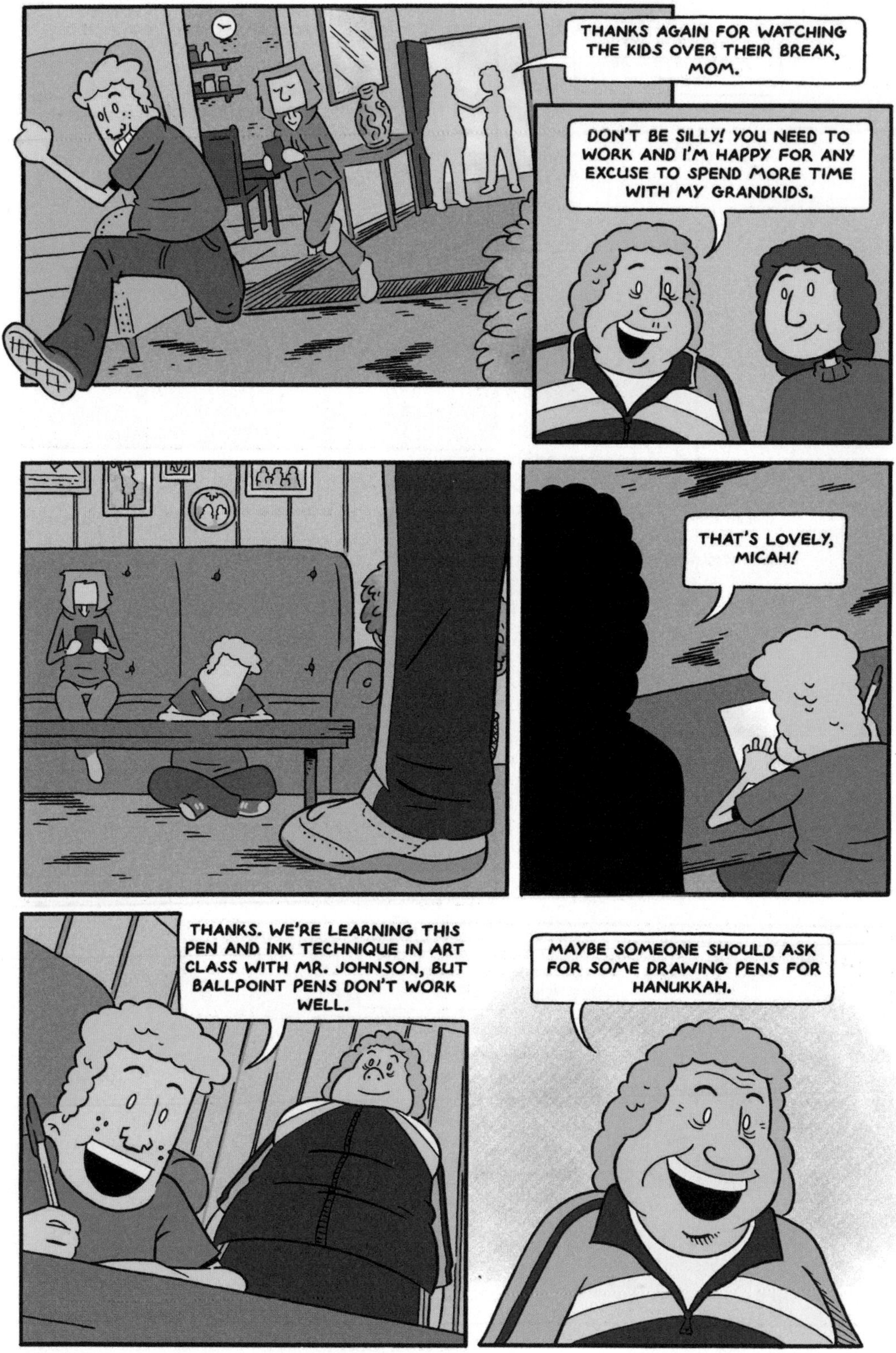
THANKS AGAIN FOR WATCHING THE KIDS OVER THEIR BREAK, MOM.
DON'T BE SILLY! YOU NEED TO WORK AND I'M HAPPY FOR ANY EXCUSE TO SPEND MORE TIME WITH MY GRANDKIDS.
THAT'S LOVELY, MICAH!
THANKS. WE'RE LEARNING THIS PEN AND INK TECHNIQUE IN ART CLASS WITH MR. JOHNSON, BUT BALLPOINT PENS DON'T WORK WELL.
MAYBE SOMEONE SHOULD ASK FOR SOME DRAWING PENS FOR HANUKKAH.

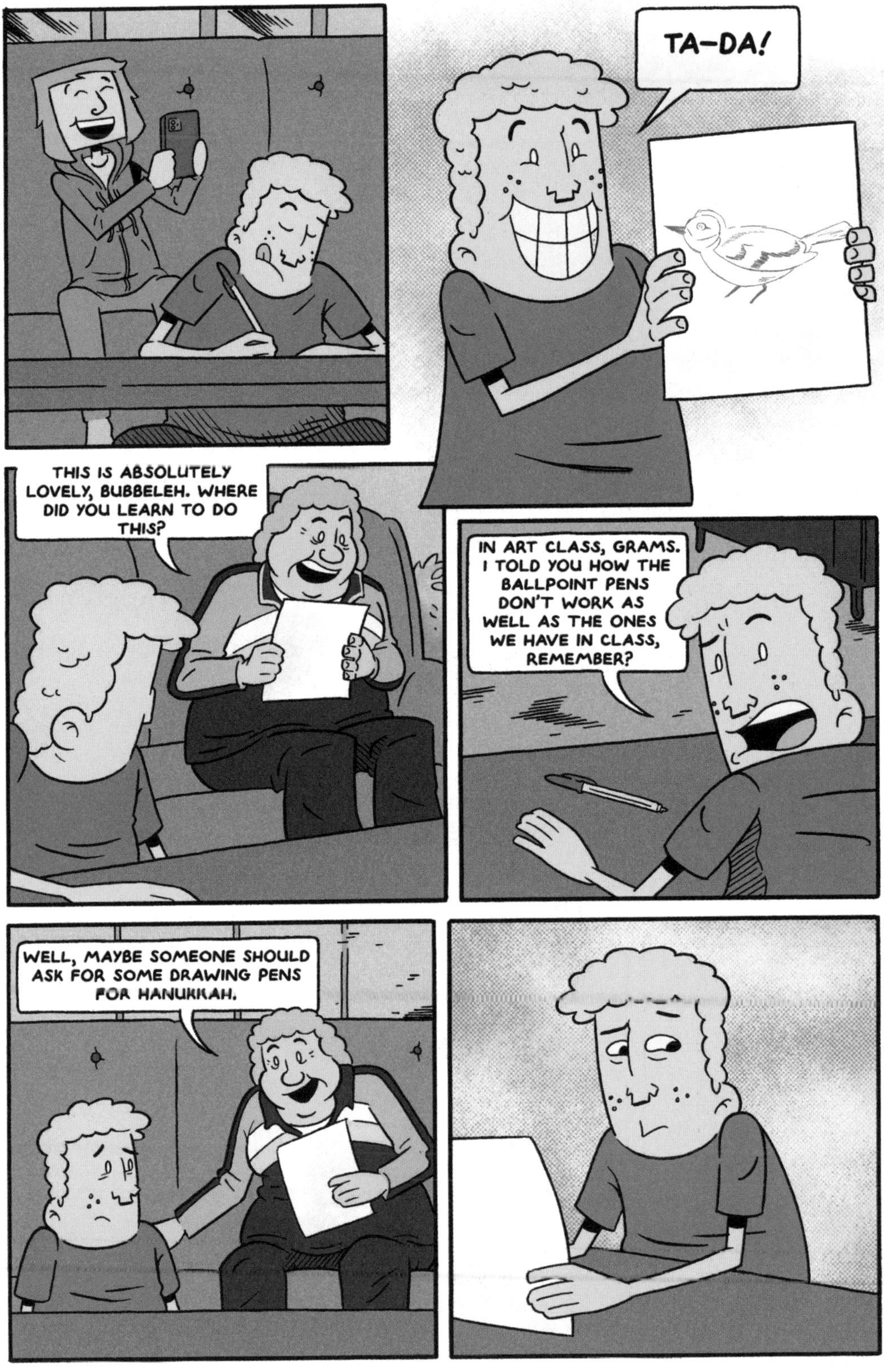
TA-DA!
THIS IS ABSOLUTELY LOVELY, BUBBELEH. WHERE DID YOU LEARN TO DO THIS?
IN ART CLASS, GRAMS. I TOLD YOU HOW THE BALLPOINT PENS DON'T WORK AS WELL AS THE ONES WE HAVE IN CLASS, REMEMBER?
WELL, MAYBE SOMEONE SHOULD ASK FOR SOME DRAWING PENS FOR HANUKKAH.

PART 2
Harvest

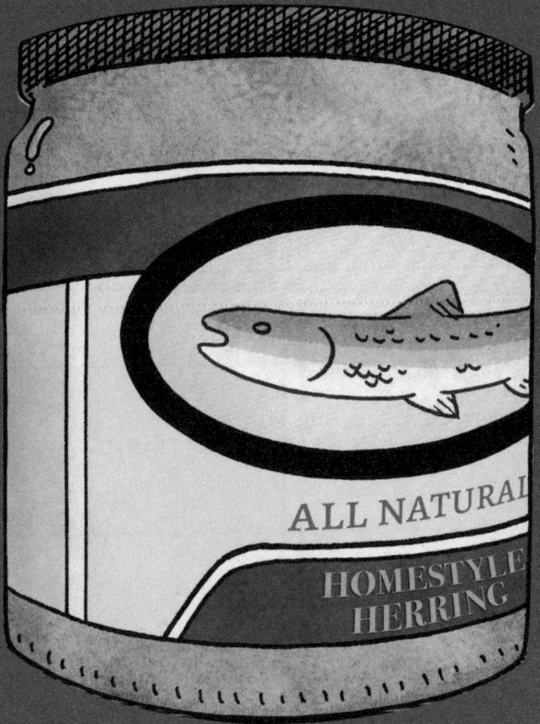
ALL NATURAL
HOMESTYLE
HERRING

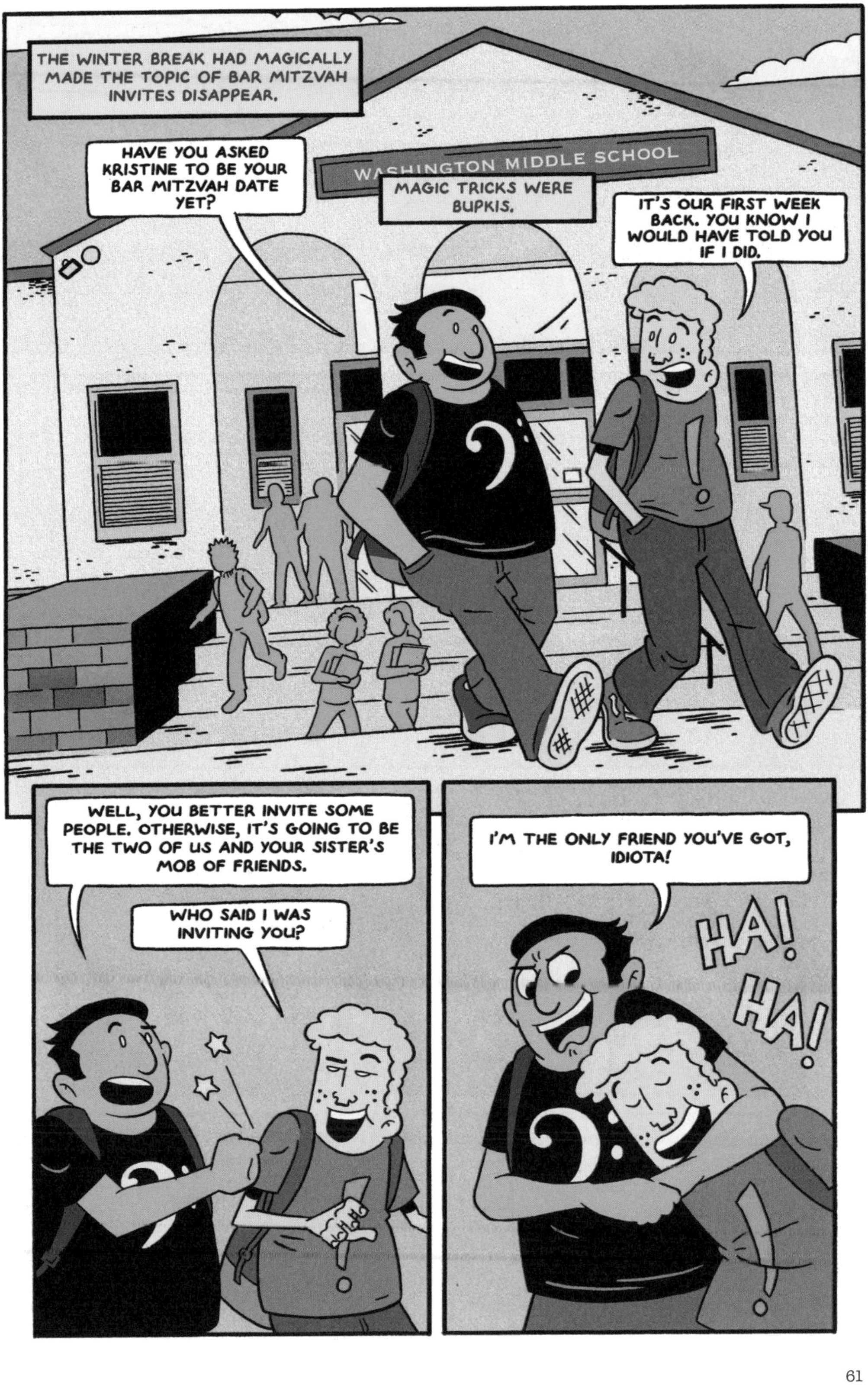
THE WINTER BREAK HAD MAGICALLY MADE THE TOPIC OF BAR MITZVAH INVITES DISAPPEAR.
WASHINGTON MIDDLE SCHOOL
HAVE YOU ASKED KRISTINE TO BE YOUR BAR MITZVAH DATE YET?
MAGIC TRICKS WERE BUPKIS.
IT'S OUR FIRST WEEK BACK. YOU KNOW I WOULD HAVE TOLD YOU IF I DID.
WELL, YOU BETTER INVITE SOME PEOPLE. OTHERWISE, IT'S GOING TO BE THE TWO OF US AND YOUR SISTER'S MOB OF FRIENDS.
WHO SAID I WAS INVITING YOU?
I'M THE ONLY FRIEND YOU'VE GOT, IDIOTA!
HA! HA!

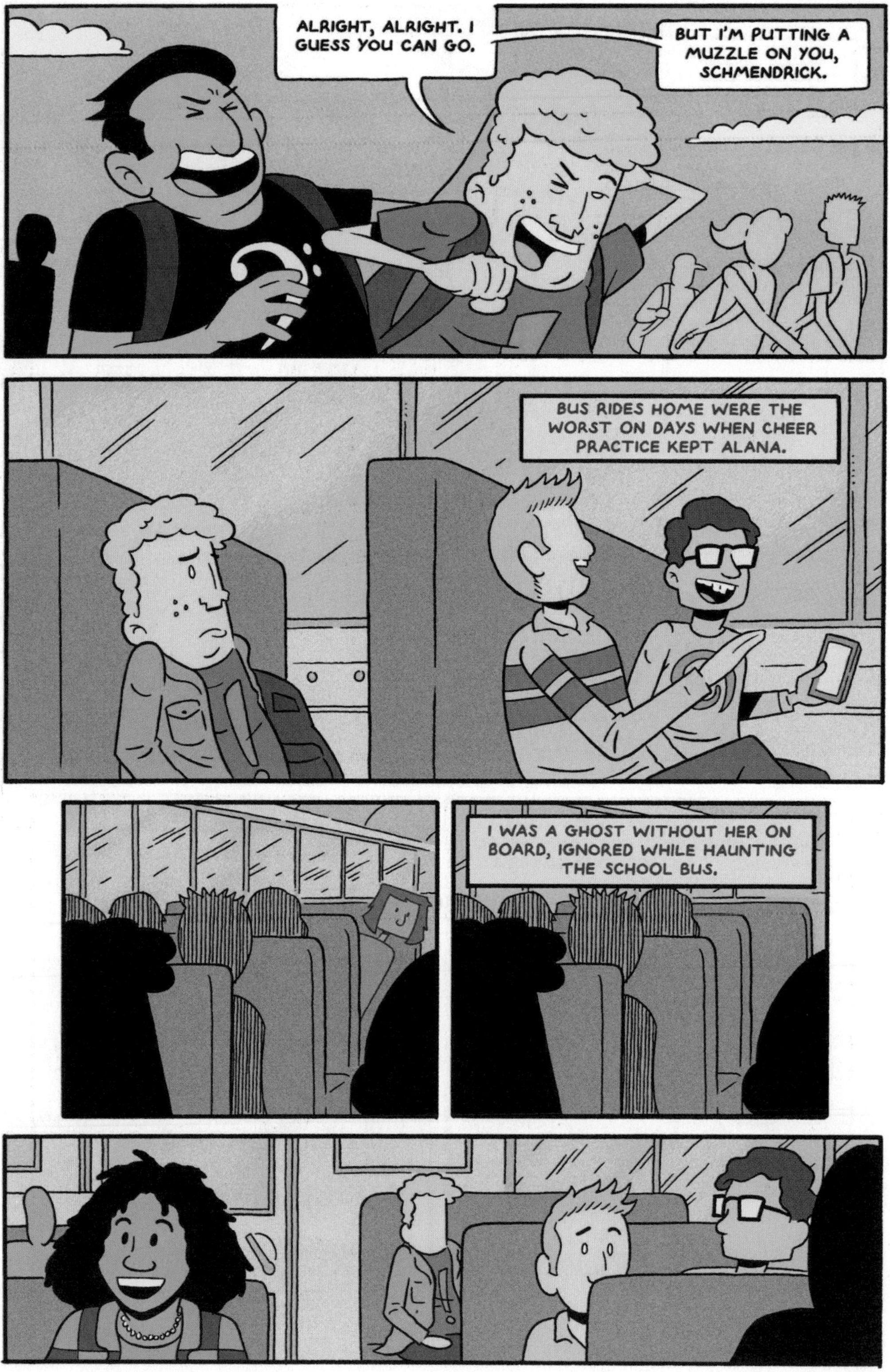
ALRIGHT, ALRIGHT. I GUESS YOU CAN GO.
BUT I'M PUTTING A MUZZLE ON YOU, SCHMENDRICK.
BUS RIDES HOME WERE THE WORST ON DAYS WHEN CHEER PRACTICE KEPT ALANA.
I WAS A GHOST WITHOUT HER ON BOARD, IGNORED WHILE HAUNTING THE SCHOOL BUS.

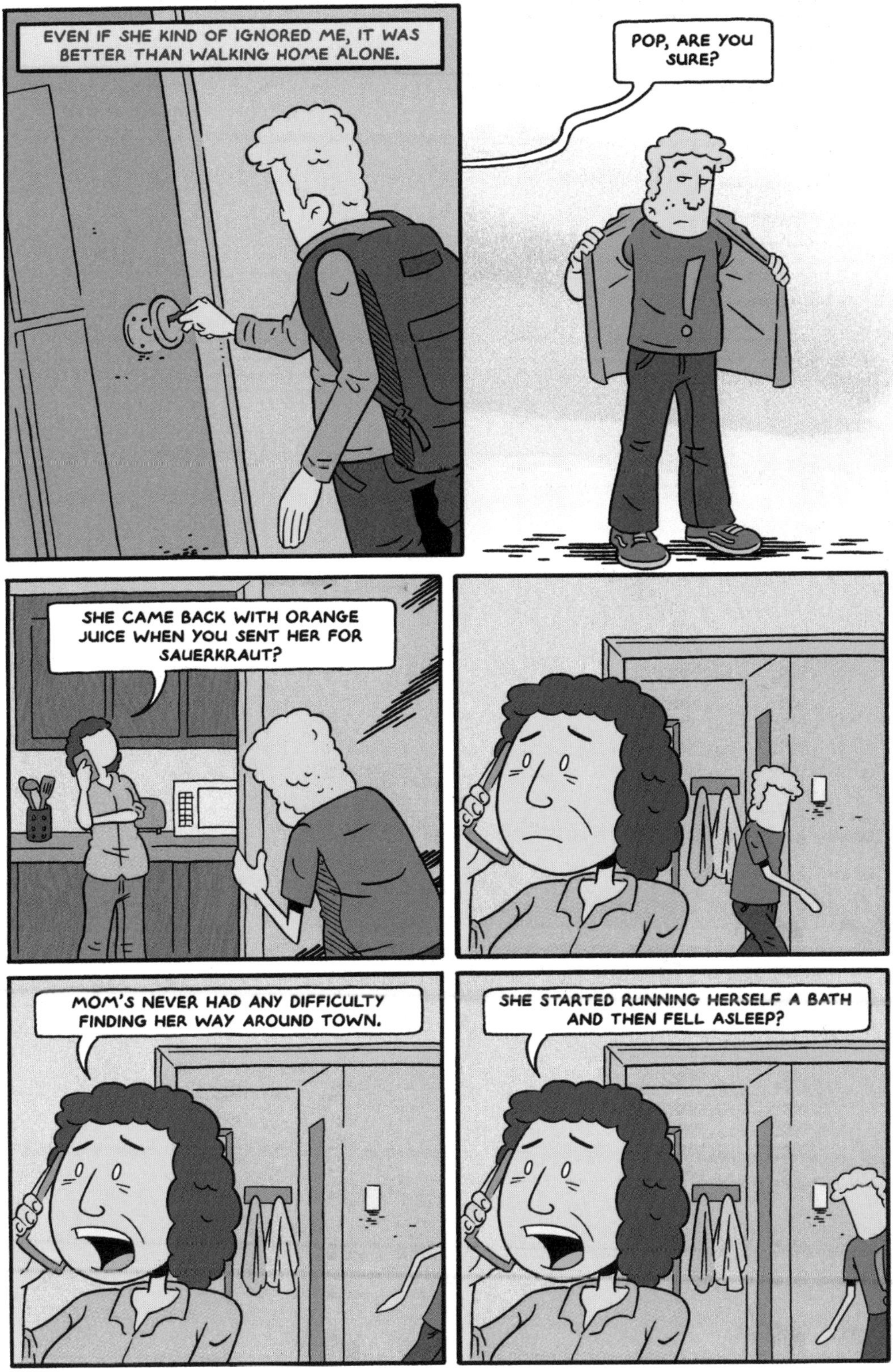
EVEN IF SHE KIND OF IGNORED ME, IT WAS BETTER THAN WALKING HOME ALONE.
POP, ARE YOU SURE?
SHE CAME BACK WITH ORANGE JUICE WHEN YOU SENT HER FOR SAUERKRAUT?
MOM'S NEVER HAD ANY DIFFICULTY FINDING HER WAY AROUND TOWN.
SHE STARTED RUNNING HERSELF A BATH AND THEN FELL ASLEEP?

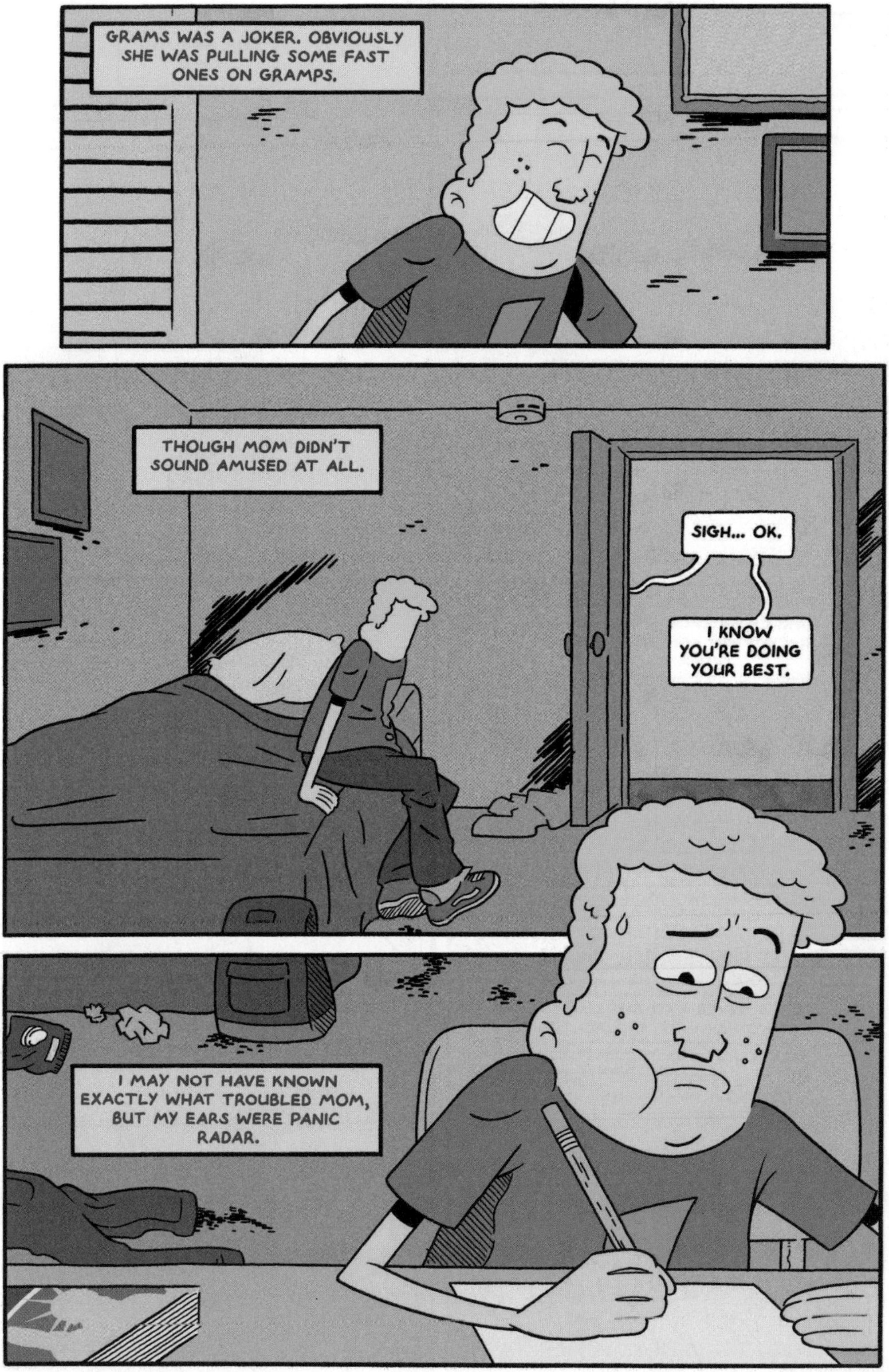
GRAMS WAS A JOKER. OBVIOUSLY SHE WAS PULLING SOME FAST ONES ON GRAMPS.
THOUGH MOM DIDN'T SOUND AMUSED AT ALL.
SIGH... OK.
I KNOW YOU'RE DOING YOUR BEST.
I MAY NOT HAVE KNOWN EXACTLY WHAT TROUBLED MOM, BUT MY EARS WERE PANIC RADAR.

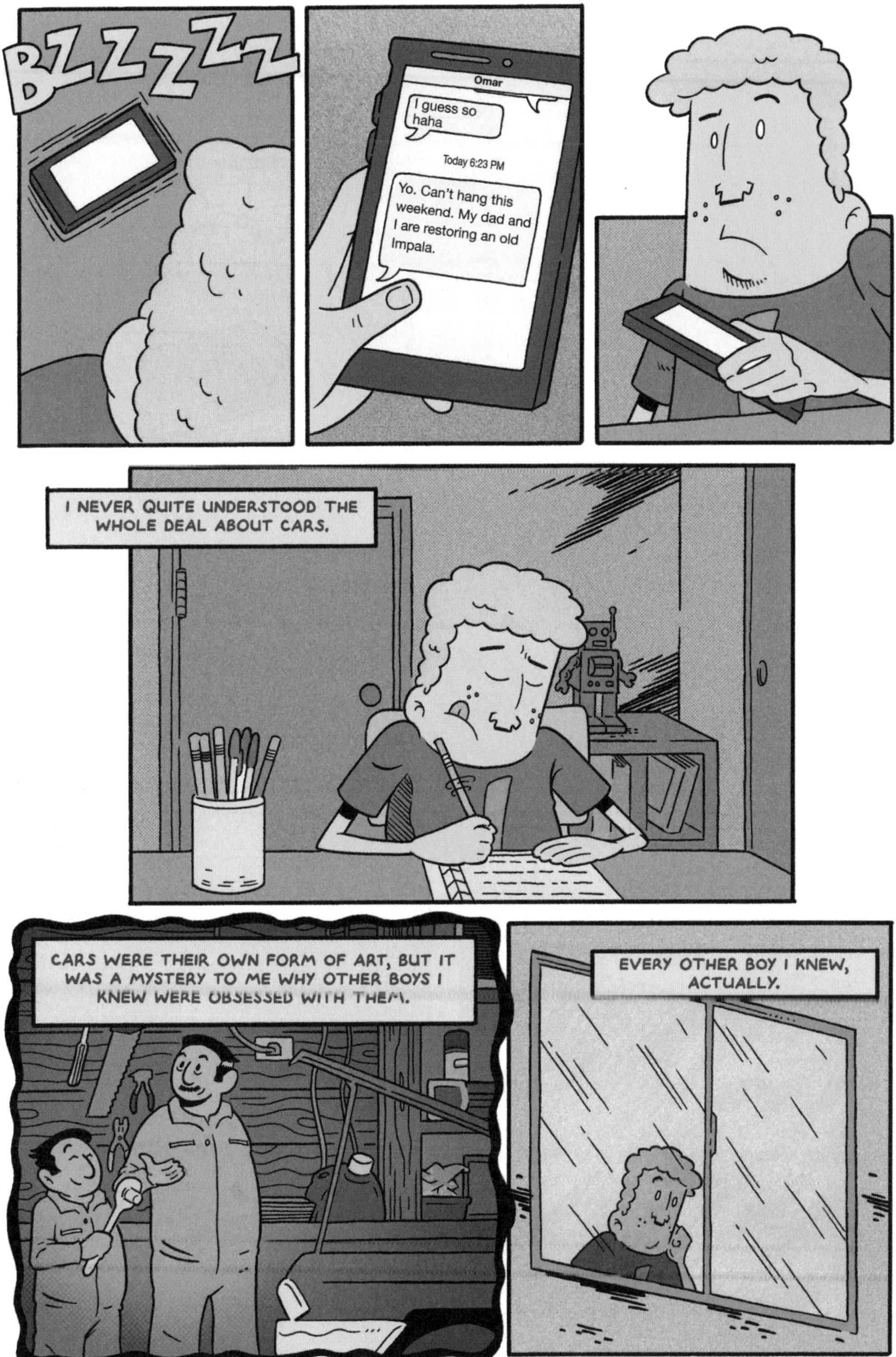

BZZZZZZ
Omar
I guess so haha
Today 6:23 PM
Yo. Can't hang this weekend. My dad and I are restoring an old Impala.
I NEVER QUITE UNDERSTOOD THE WHOLE DEAL ABOUT CARS.
CARS WERE THEIR OWN FORM OF ART, BUT IT WAS A MYSTERY TO ME WHY OTHER BOYS I KNEW WERE OBSESSED WITH THEM.
EVERY OTHER BOY I KNEW, ACTUALLY.

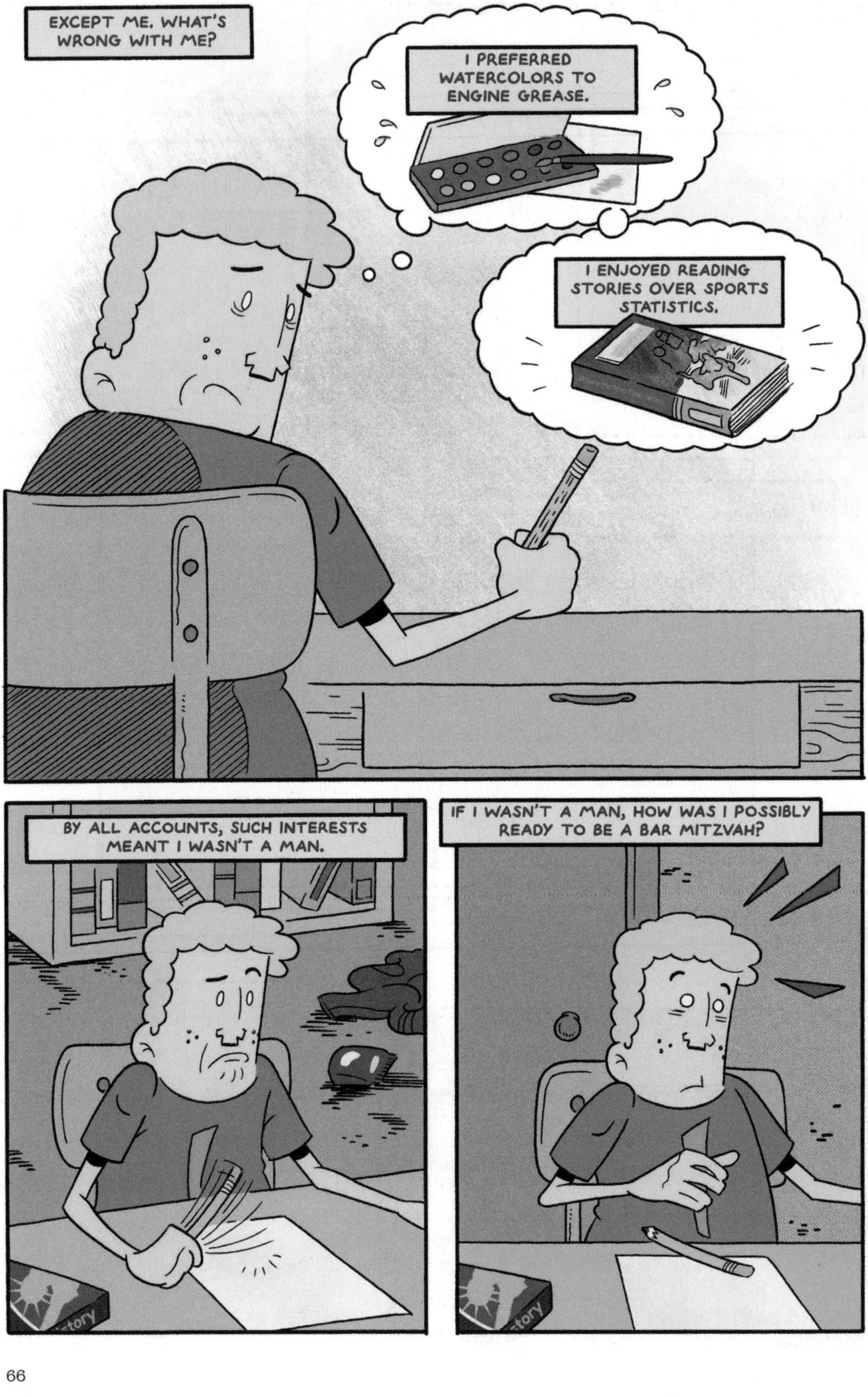
EXCEPT ME. WHAT'S WRONG WITH ME?
I PREFERRED WATERCOLORS TO ENGINE GREASE.
I ENJOYED READING STORIES OVER SPORTS STATISTICS.
BY ALL ACCOUNTS, SUCH INTERESTS MEANT I WASN'T A MAN.
IF I WASN'T A MAN, HOW WAS I POSSIBLY READY TO BE A BAR MITZVAH?

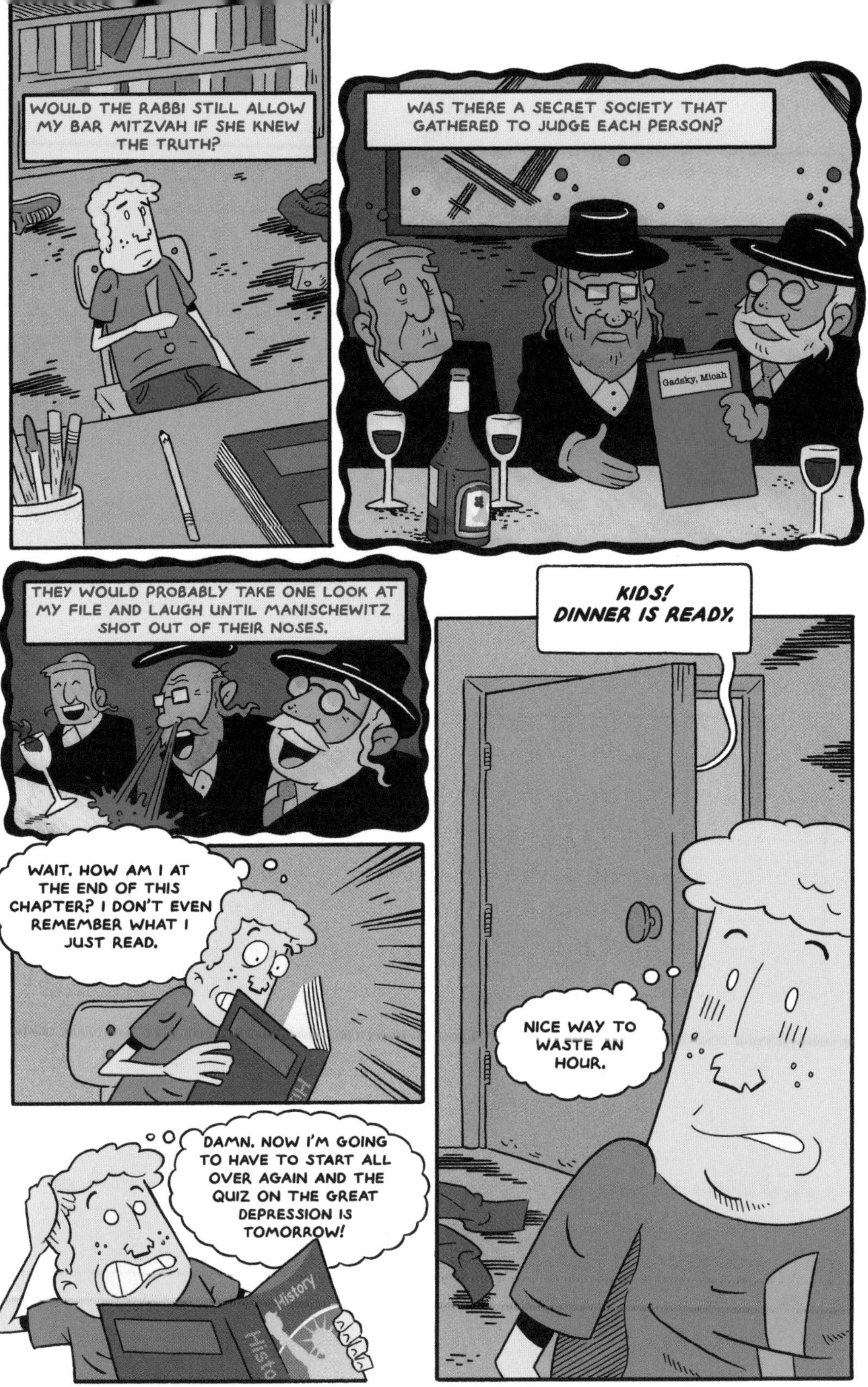
WOULD THE RABBI STILL ALLOW MY BAR MITZVAH IF SHE KNEW THE TRUTH?
WAS THERE A SECRET SOCIETY THAT GATHERED TO JUDGE EACH PERSON?
Gadsky, Micah
THEY WOULD PROBABLY TAKE ONE LOOK AT MY FILE AND LAUGH UNTIL MANISCHEWITZ SHOT OUT OF THEIR NOSES.
KIDS! DINNER IS READY.
WAIT. HOW AM I AT THE END OF THIS CHAPTER? I DON'T EVEN REMEMBER WHAT I JUST READ.
NICE WAY TO WASTE AN HOUR.
DAMN. NOW I'M GOING TO HAVE TO START ALL OVER AGAIN AND THE QUIZ ON THE GREAT DEPRESSION IS TOMORROW!
History

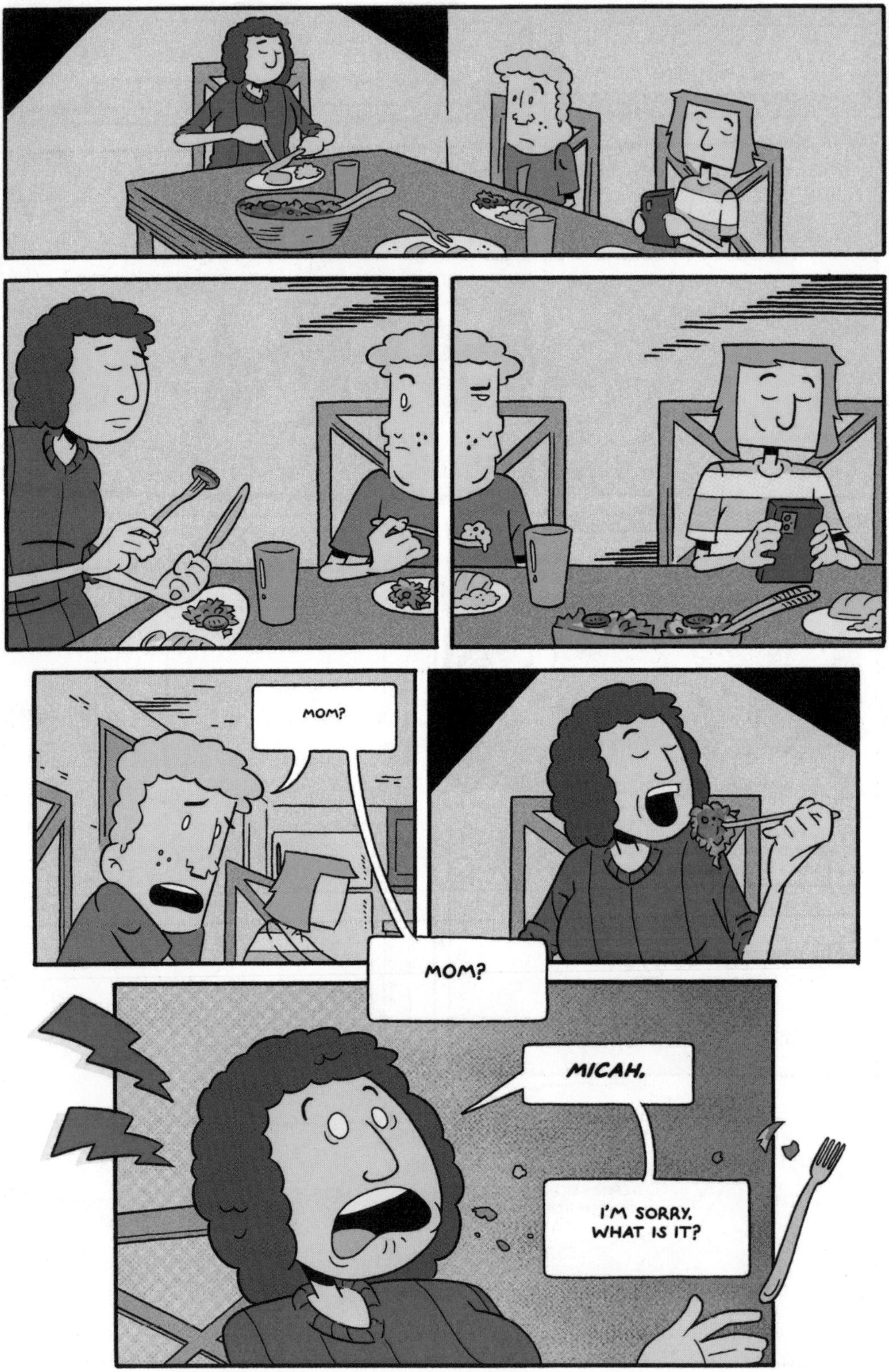
MOM?
MOM?
MICAH.
I'M SORRY. WHAT IS IT?

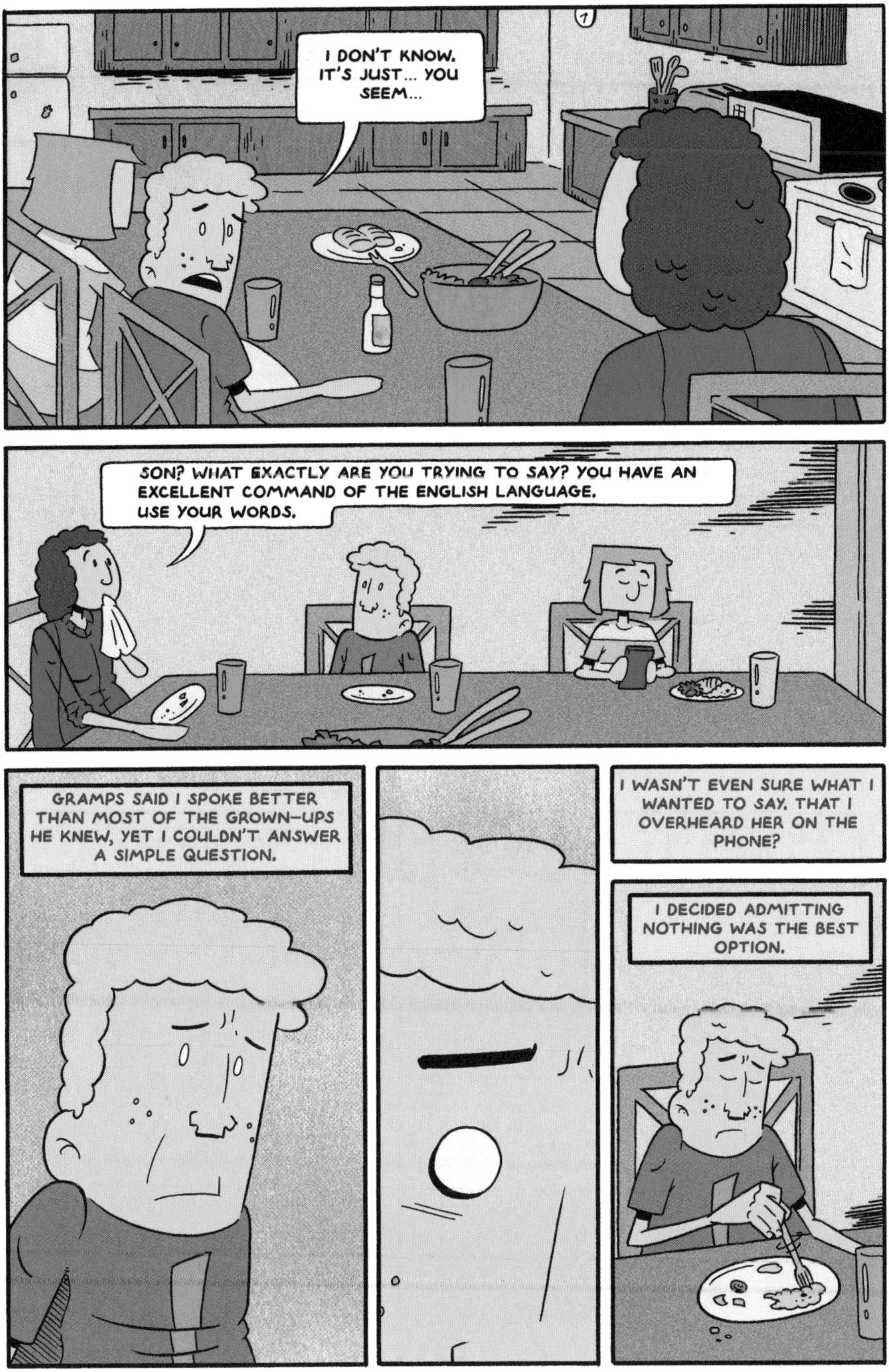
I DON'T KNOW. IT'S JUST... YOU SEEM...
SON? WHAT EXACTLY ARE YOU TRYING TO SAY? YOU HAVE AN EXCELLENT COMMAND OF THE ENGLISH LANGUAGE. USE YOUR WORDS.
GRAMPS SAID I SPOKE BETTER THAN MOST OF THE GROWN-UPS HE KNEW, YET I COULDN'T ANSWER A SIMPLE QUESTION.
I WASN'T EVEN SURE WHAT I WANTED TO SAY. THAT I OVERHEARD HER ON THE PHONE?
I DECIDED ADMITTING NOTHING WAS THE BEST OPTION.

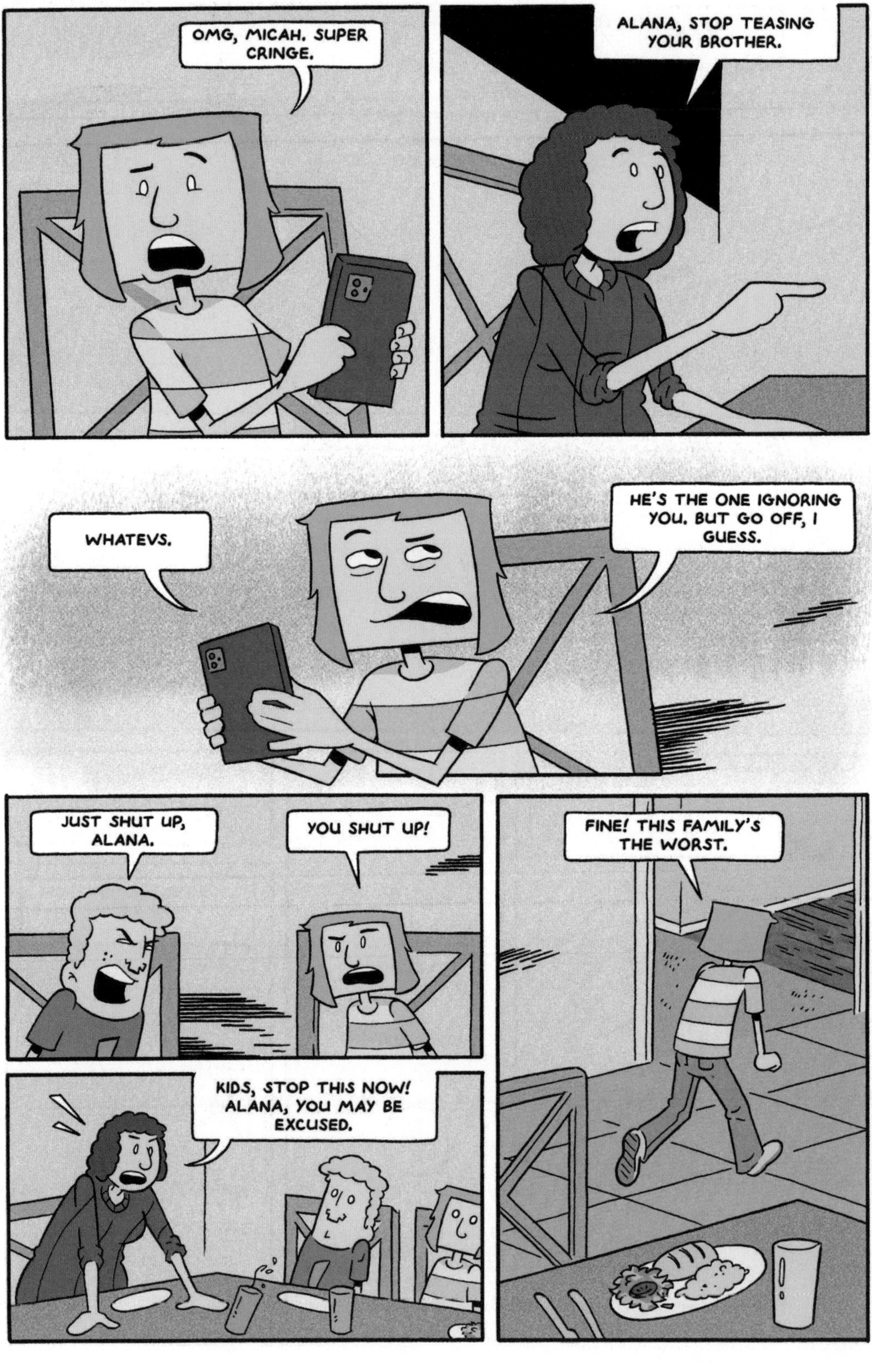
OMG, MICAH. SUPER CRINGE.
ALANA, STOP TEASING YOUR BROTHER.
WHATEVS.
HE'S THE ONE IGNORING YOU. BUT GO OFF, I GUESS.
JUST SHUT UP, ALANA.
YOU SHUT UP!
FINE! THIS FAMILY'S THE WORST.
KIDS, STOP THIS NOW! ALANA, YOU MAY BE EXCUSED.

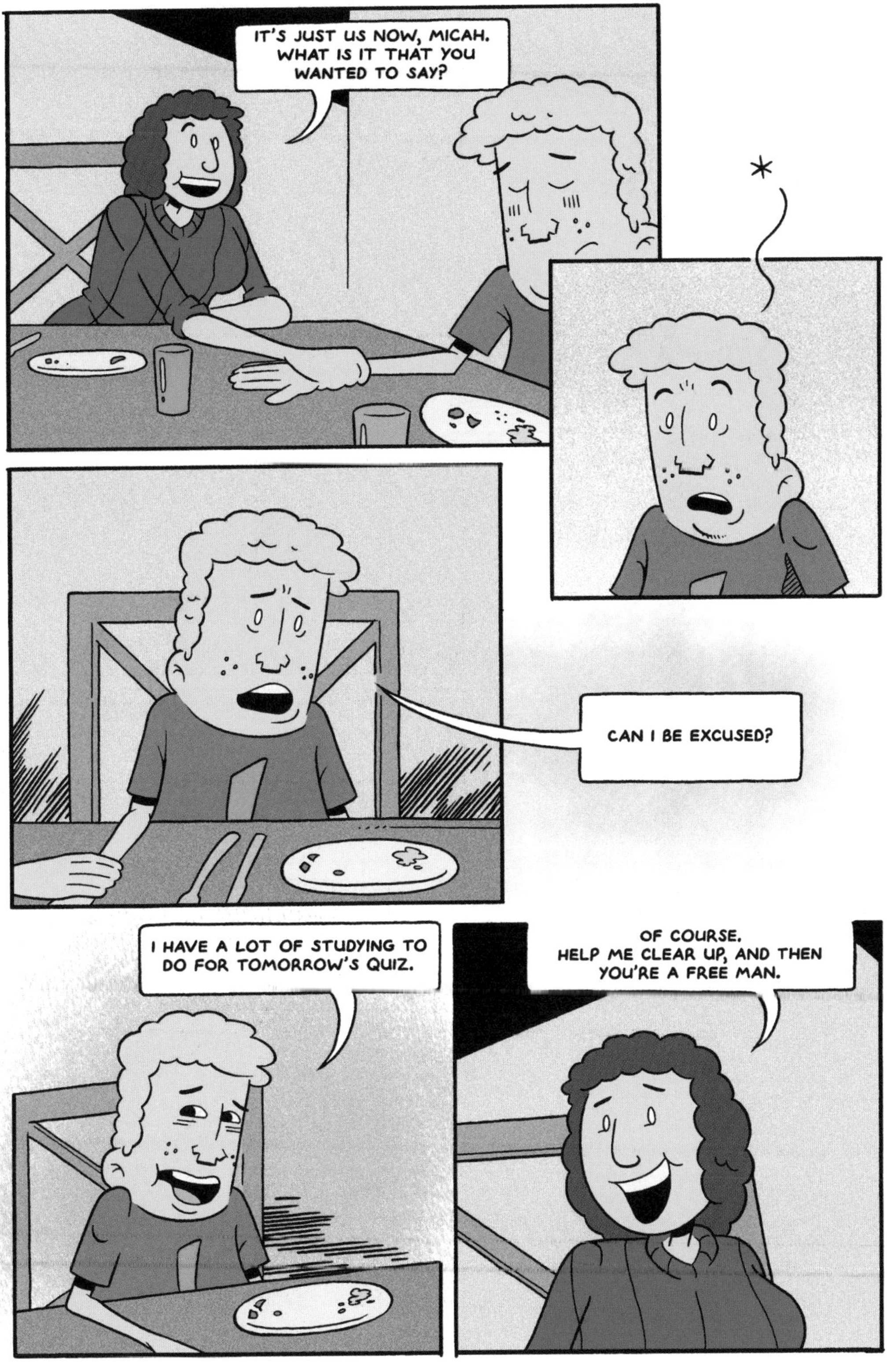
IT'S JUST US NOW, MICAH. WHAT IS IT THAT YOU WANTED TO SAY?
*
CAN I BE EXCUSED?
I HAVE A LOT OF STUDYING TO DO FOR TOMORROW'S QUIZ.
OF COURSE. HELP ME CLEAR UP, AND THEN YOU'RE A FREE MAN.

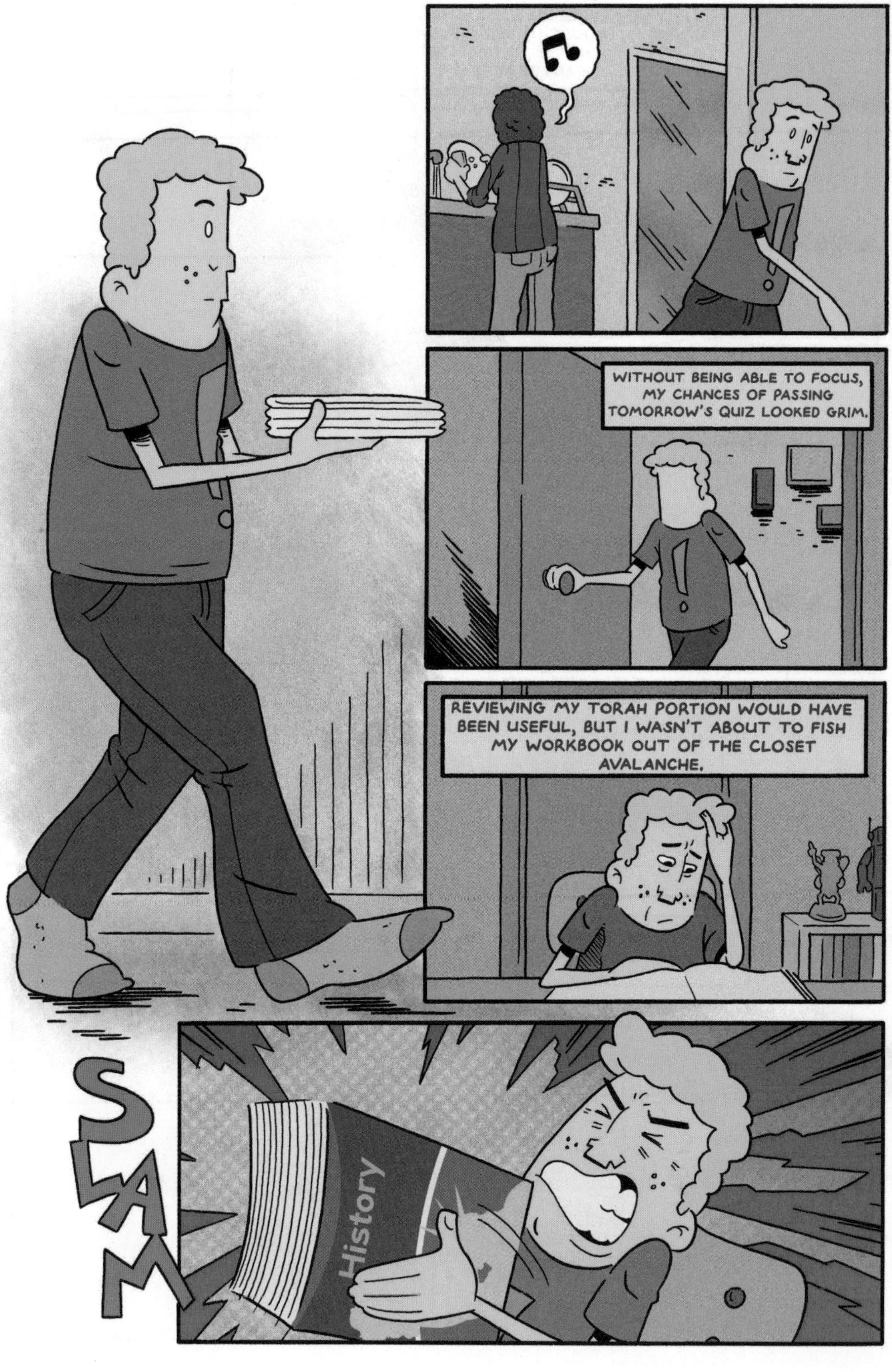
WITHOUT BEING ABLE TO FOCUS, MY CHANCES OF PASSING TOMORROW'S QUIZ LOOKED GRIM.
REVIEWING MY TORAH PORTION WOULD HAVE BEEN USEFUL, BUT I WASN'T ABOUT TO FISH MY WORKBOOK OUT OF THE CLOSET AVALANCHE.
SLAM
History

EVERYTHING WAS JUST PROOF I WAS UNWORTHY OF BEING A BAR MITZVAH.

I HATED TO THINK OF DISAPPOINTING MY FAMILY AND, WORST OF ALL, MY GRANDPARENTS.

THEY TOLD ME SINCE I WAS YOUNG THAT I WAS SPECIAL AND WOULD ACCOMPLISH GREAT THINGS IN LIFE.

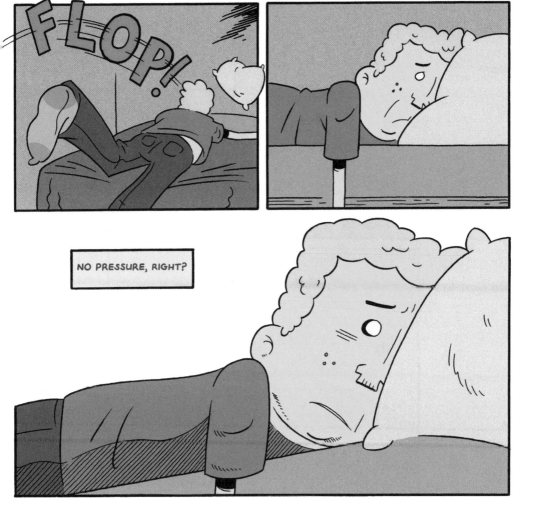

FLOP!

NO PRESSURE, RIGHT?

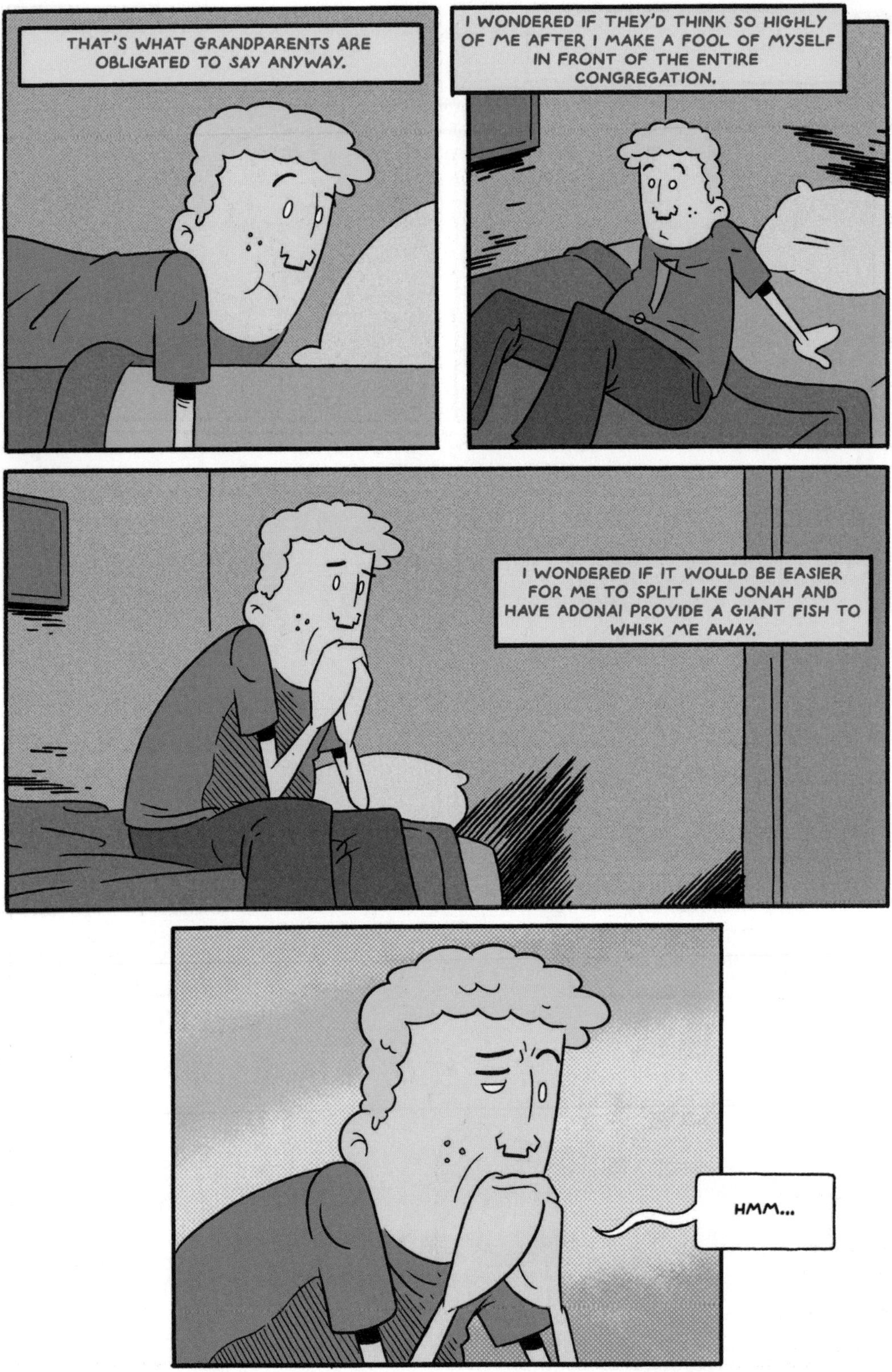
THAT'S WHAT GRANDPARENTS ARE OBLIGATED TO SAY ANYWAY.
I WONDERED IF THEY'D THINK SO HIGHLY OF ME AFTER I MAKE A FOOL OF MYSELF IN FRONT OF THE ENTIRE CONGREGATION.
I WONDERED IF IT WOULD BE EASIER FOR ME TO SPLIT LIKE JONAH AND HAVE ADONAI PROVIDE A GIANT FISH TO WHISK ME AWAY.
HMM...

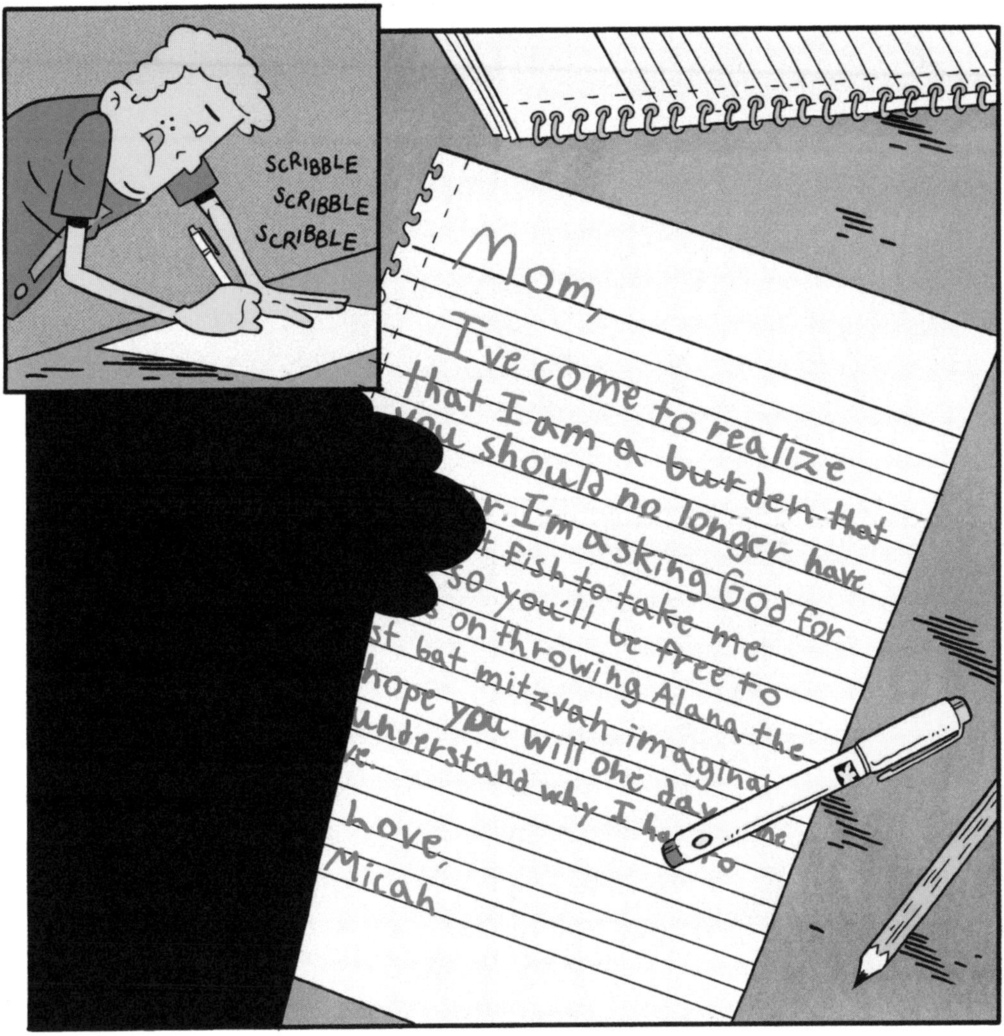
SCRIBBLE
SCRIBBLE
SCRIBBLE
Mom,
I've come to realize
that I am a burden that
should no longer have
I'm asking God for
fish to take me
so you'll be free to
on throwing Alana the
bat mitzvah imagin
hope you will one day
understand why I
Love,
Micah

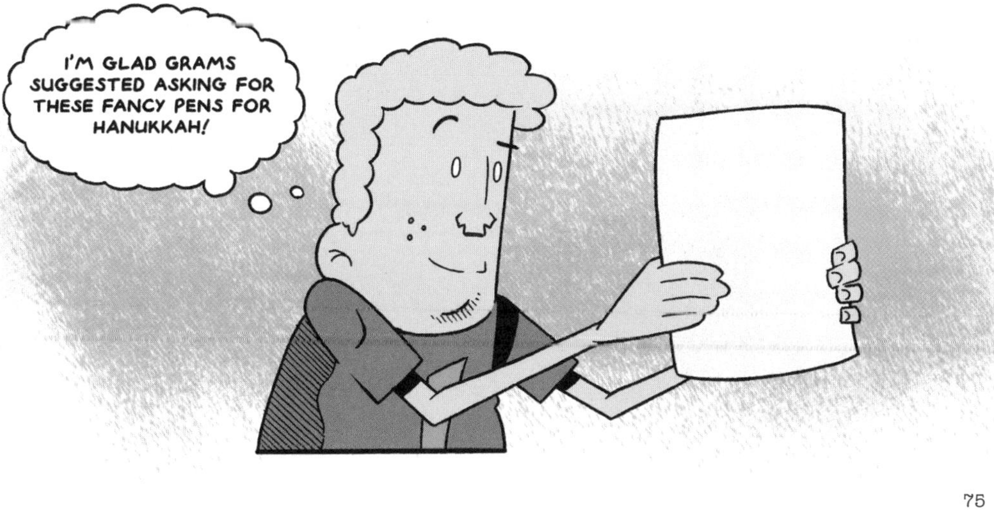
I'M GLAD GRAMS SUGGESTED ASKING FOR THESE FANCY PENS FOR HANUKKAH!

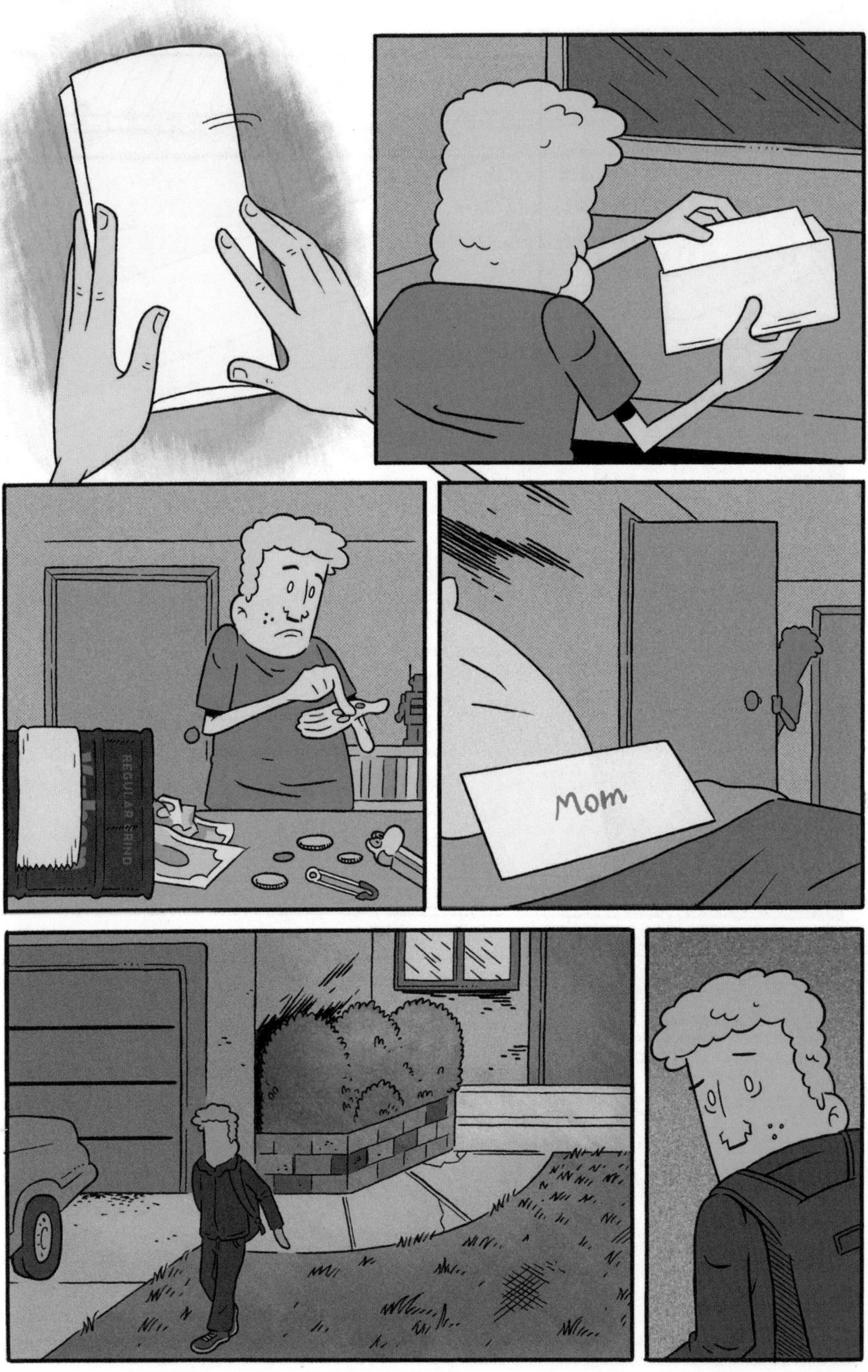
REGULAR GRIND
Mom

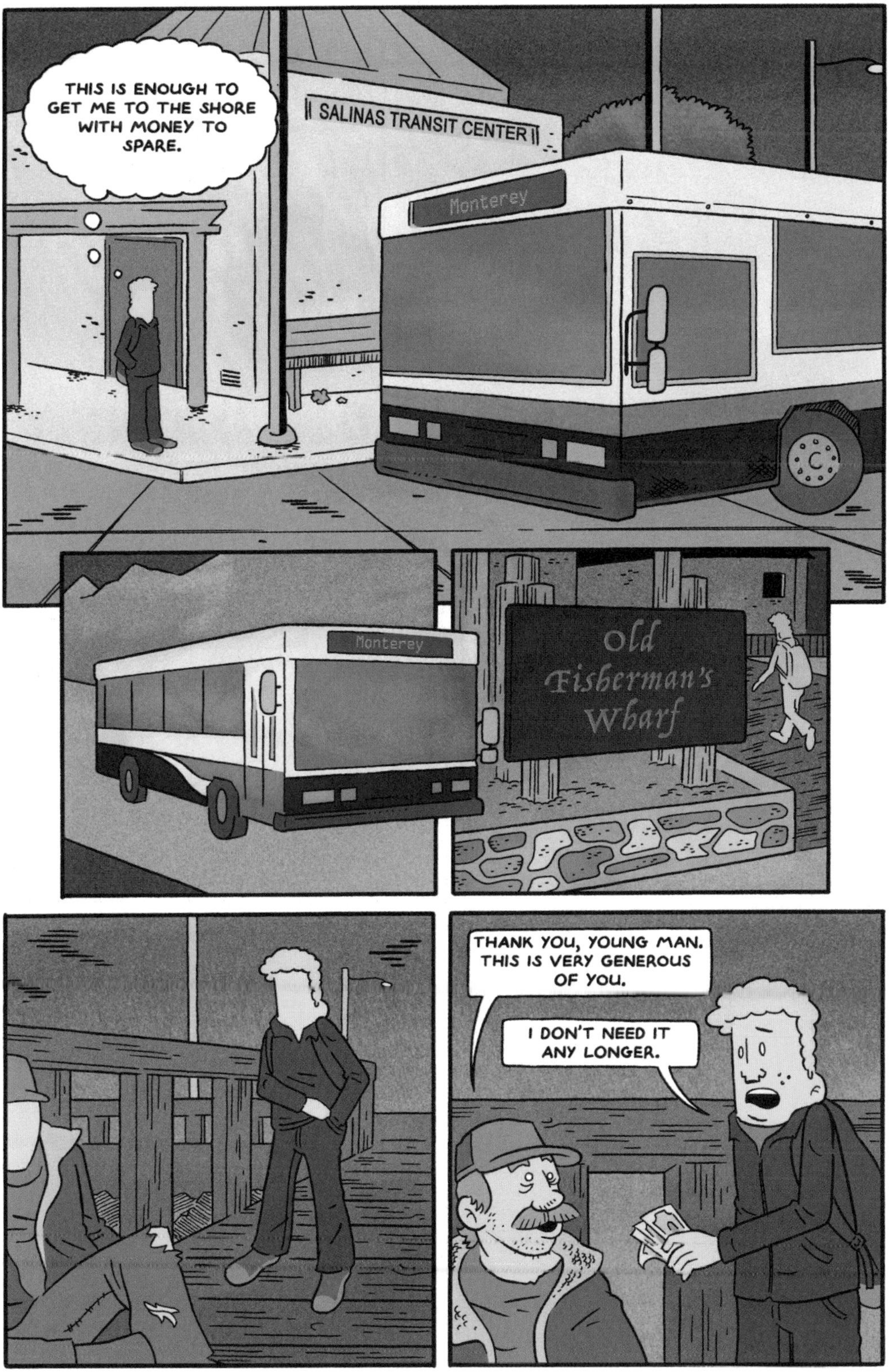
THIS IS ENOUGH TO GET ME TO THE SHORE WITH MONEY TO SPARE.
SALINAS TRANSIT CENTER
Monterey
Monterey
Old Fisherman's Wharf
THANK YOU, YOUNG MAN. THIS IS VERY GENEROUS OF YOU.
I DON'T NEED IT ANY LONGER.

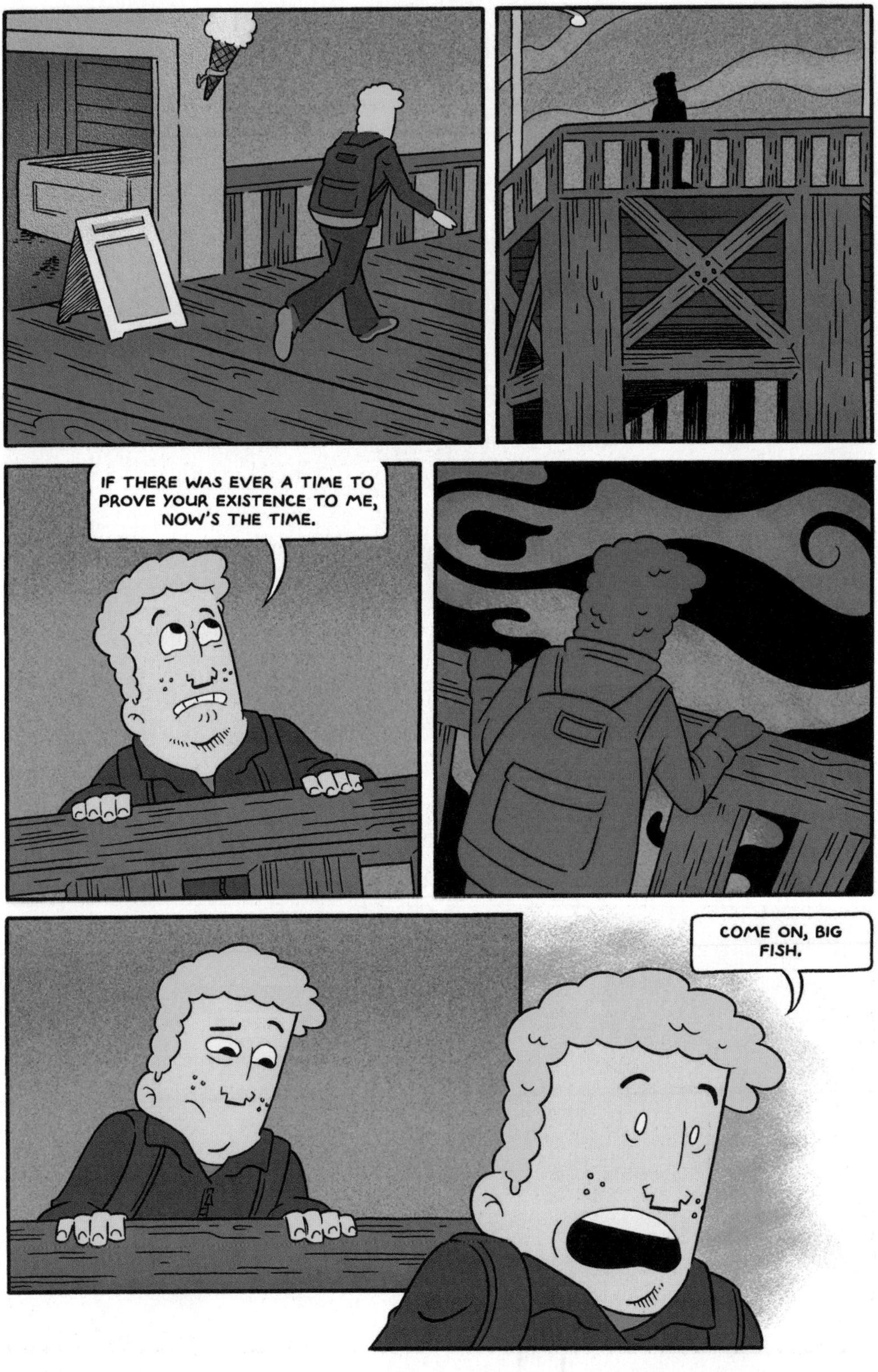
IF THERE WAS EVER A TIME TO PROVE YOUR EXISTENCE TO ME, NOW'S THE TIME.
COME ON, BIG FISH.

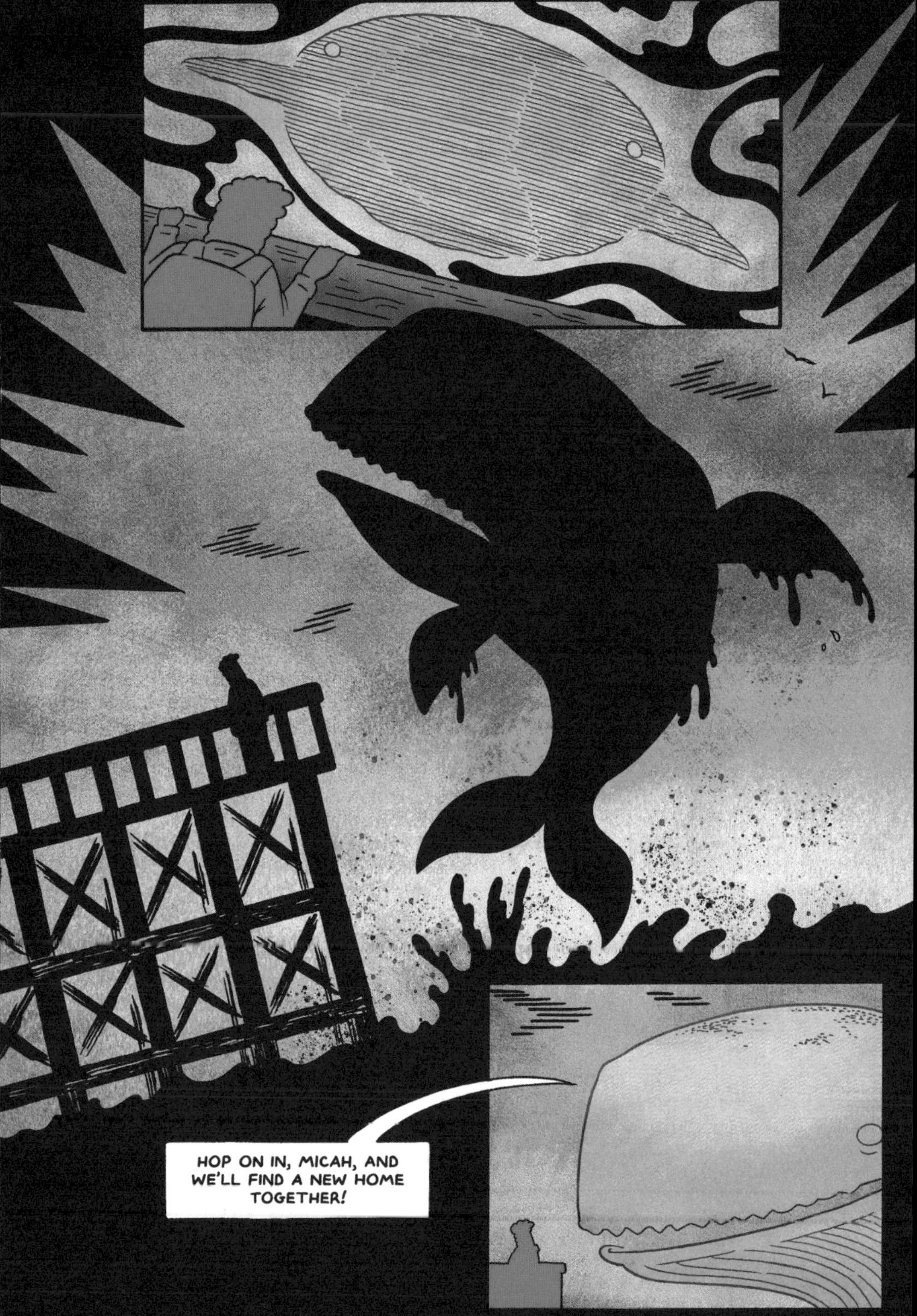
HOP ON IN, MICAH, AND WE'LL FIND A NEW HOME TOGETHER!

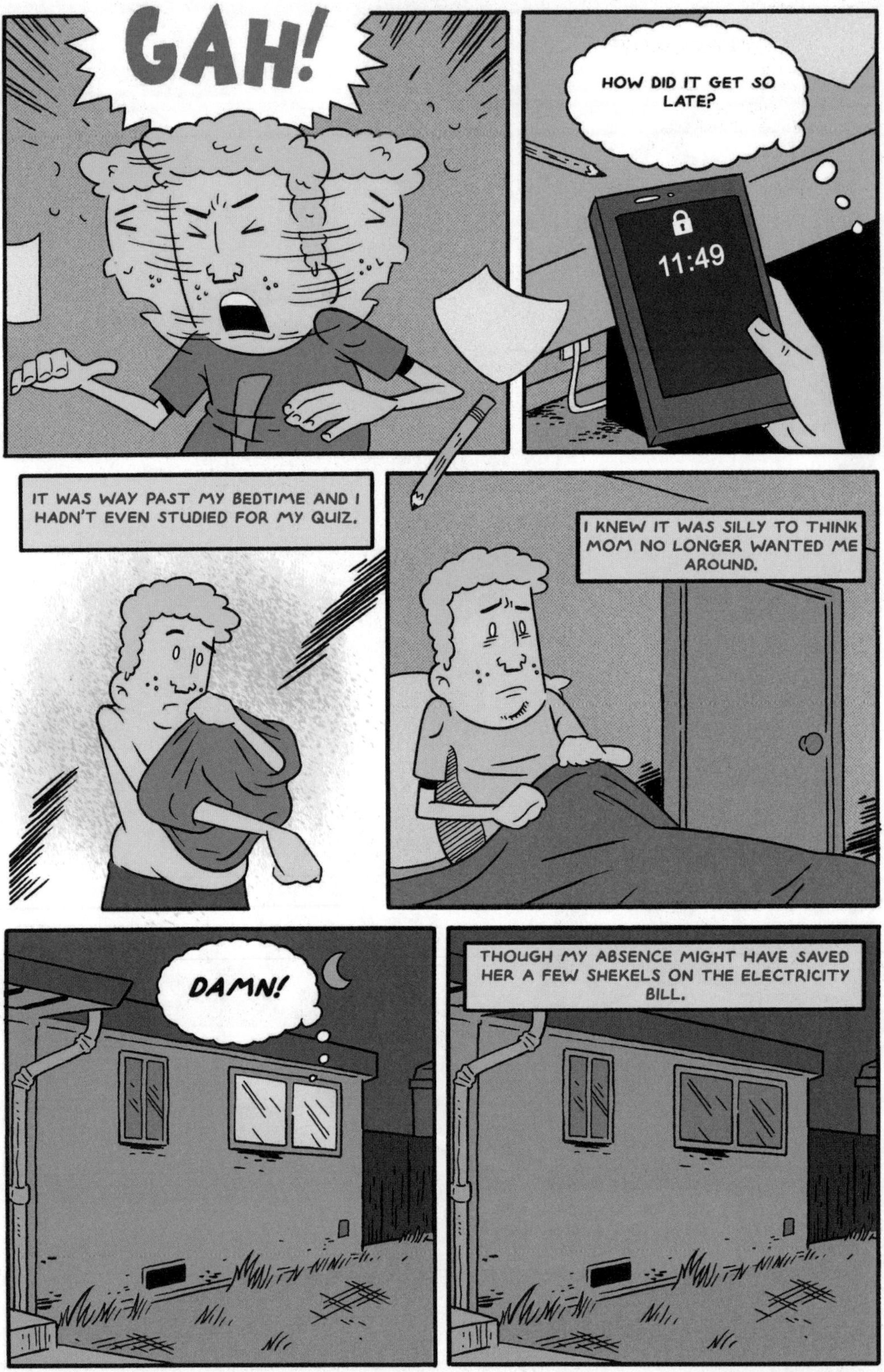
GAH!
HOW DID IT GET SO LATE?
11:49
IT WAS WAY PAST MY BEDTIME AND I HADN'T EVEN STUDIED FOR MY QUIZ.
I KNEW IT WAS SILLY TO THINK MOM NO LONGER WANTED ME AROUND.
DAMN!
THOUGH MY ABSENCE MIGHT HAVE SAVED HER A FEW SHEKELS ON THE ELECTRICITY BILL.

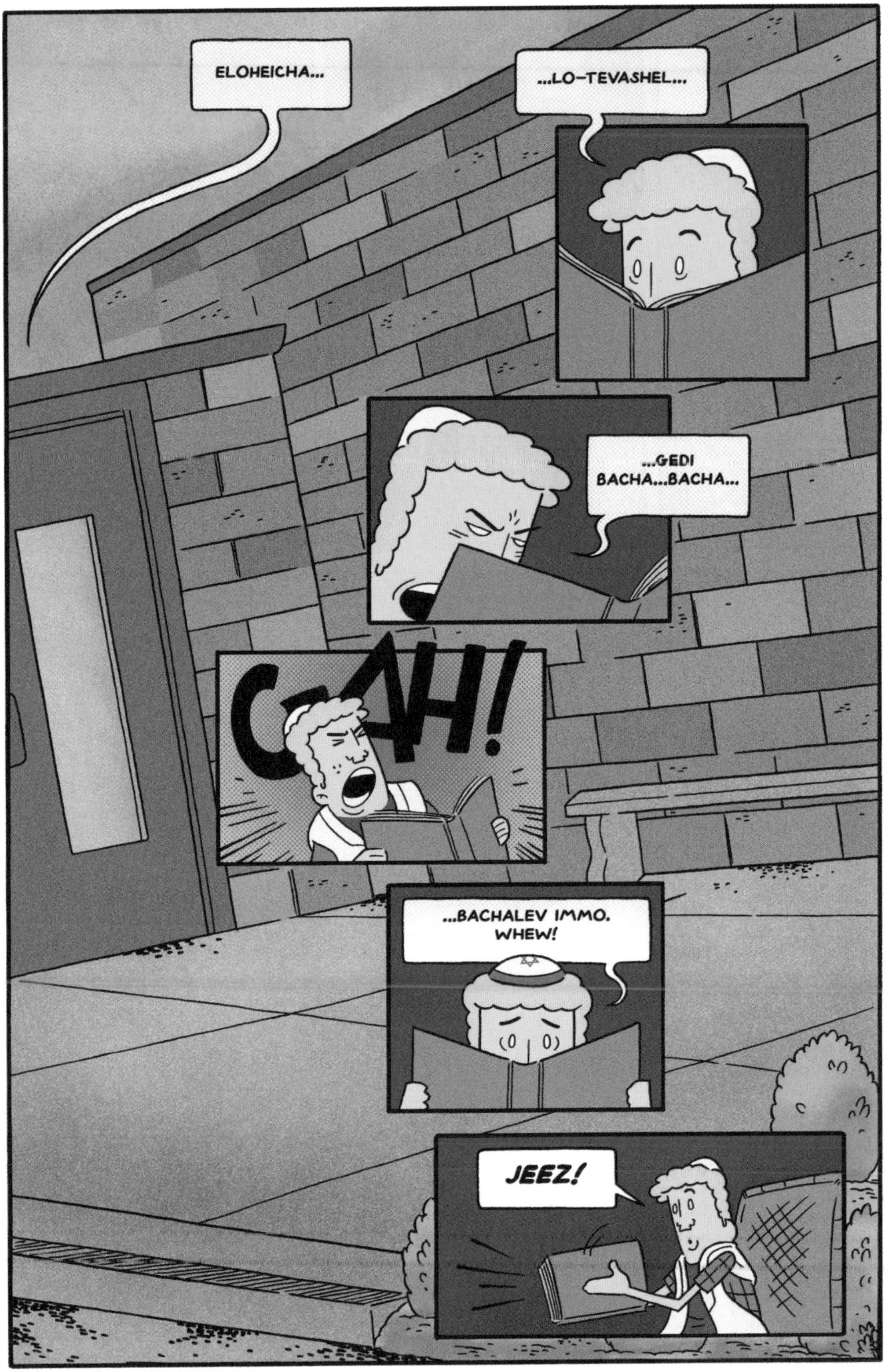
ELOHEICHA...
...LO-TEVASHEL...
...GEDI BACHA...BACHA...
GAH!
...BACHALEV IMMO. WHEW!
JEEZ!

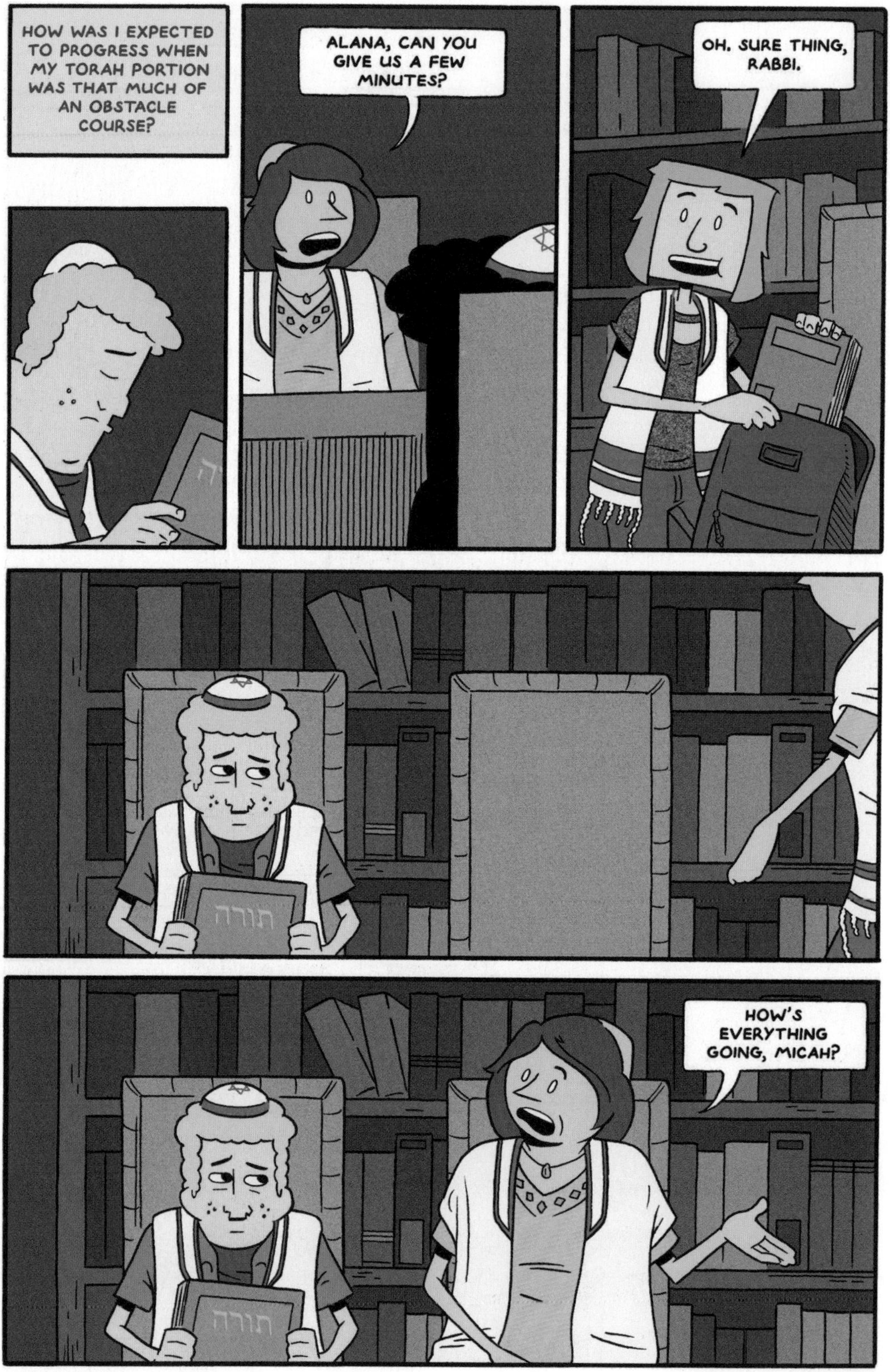
HOW WAS I EXPECTED TO PROGRESS WHEN MY TORAH PORTION WAS THAT MUCH OF AN OBSTACLE COURSE?
ALANA, CAN YOU GIVE US A FEW MINUTES?
OH. SURE THING, RABBI.
תורה
HOW'S EVERYTHING GOING, MICAH?

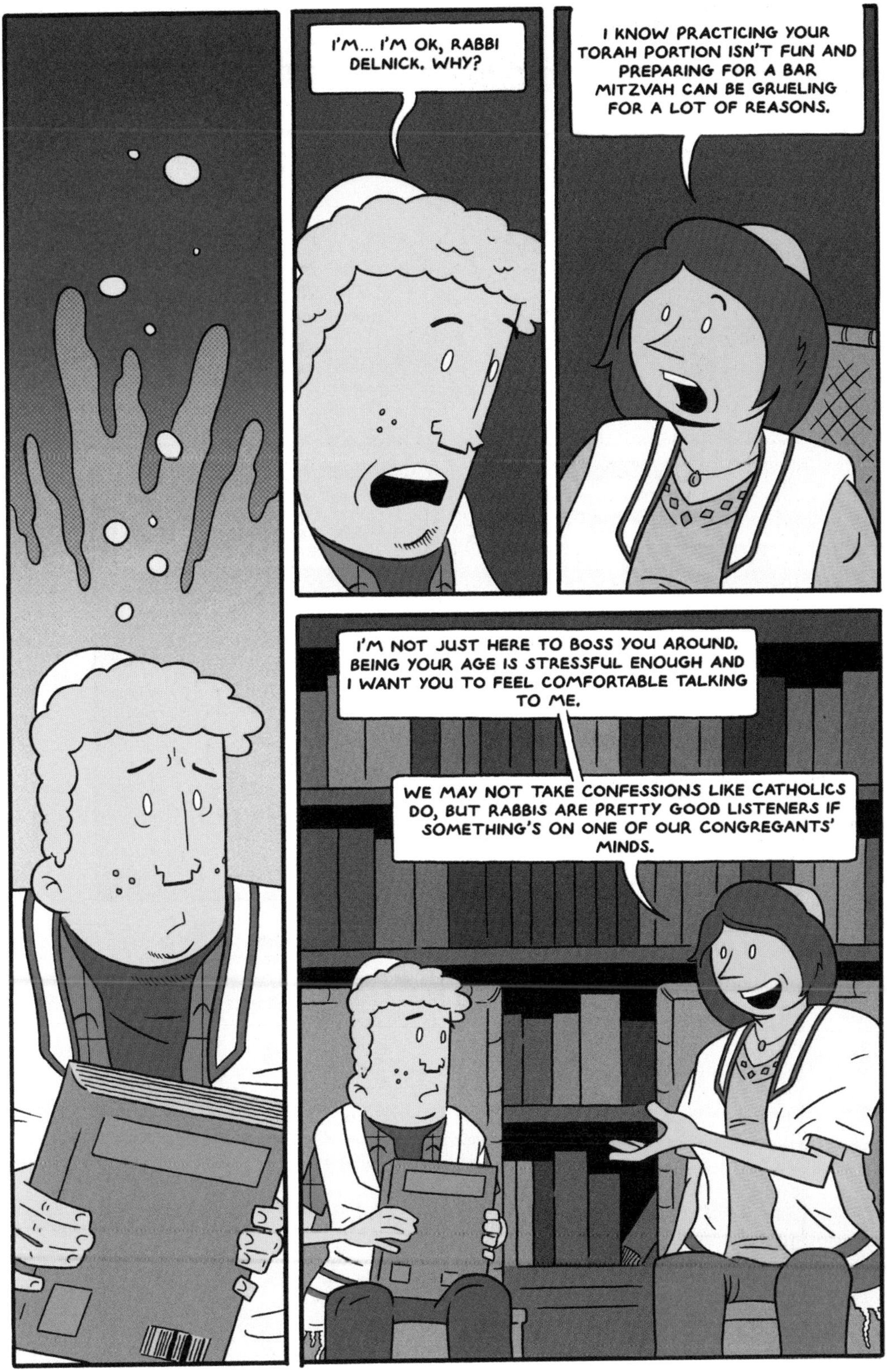
I'M... I'M OK, RABBI DELNICK. WHY?
I KNOW PRACTICING YOUR TORAH PORTION ISN'T FUN AND PREPARING FOR A BAR MITZVAH CAN BE GRUELING FOR A LOT OF REASONS.
I'M NOT JUST HERE TO BOSS YOU AROUND. BEING YOUR AGE IS STRESSFUL ENOUGH AND I WANT YOU TO FEEL COMFORTABLE TALKING TO ME.
WE MAY NOT TAKE CONFESSIONS LIKE CATHOLICS DO, BUT RABBIS ARE PRETTY GOOD LISTENERS IF SOMETHING'S ON ONE OF OUR CONGREGANTS' MINDS.

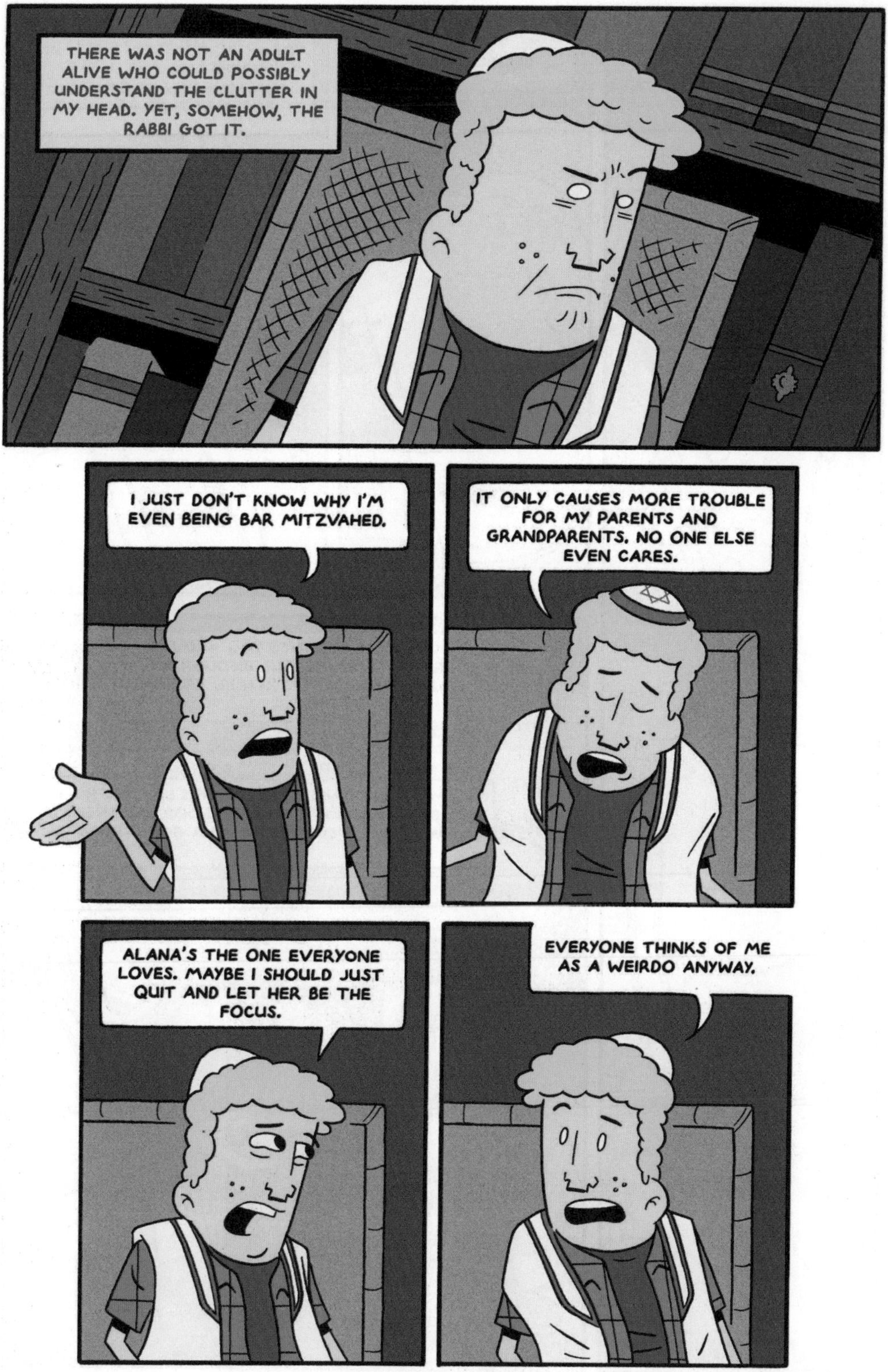
THERE WAS NOT AN ADULT ALIVE WHO COULD POSSIBLY UNDERSTAND THE CLUTTER IN MY HEAD. YET, SOMEHOW, THE RABBI GOT IT.
I JUST DON'T KNOW WHY I'M EVEN BEING BAR MITZVAHED.
IT ONLY CAUSES MORE TROUBLE FOR MY PARENTS AND GRANDPARENTS. NO ONE ELSE EVEN CARES.
ALANA'S THE ONE EVERYONE LOVES. MAYBE I SHOULD JUST QUIT AND LET HER BE THE FOCUS.
EVERYONE THINKS OF ME AS A WEIRDO ANYWAY.

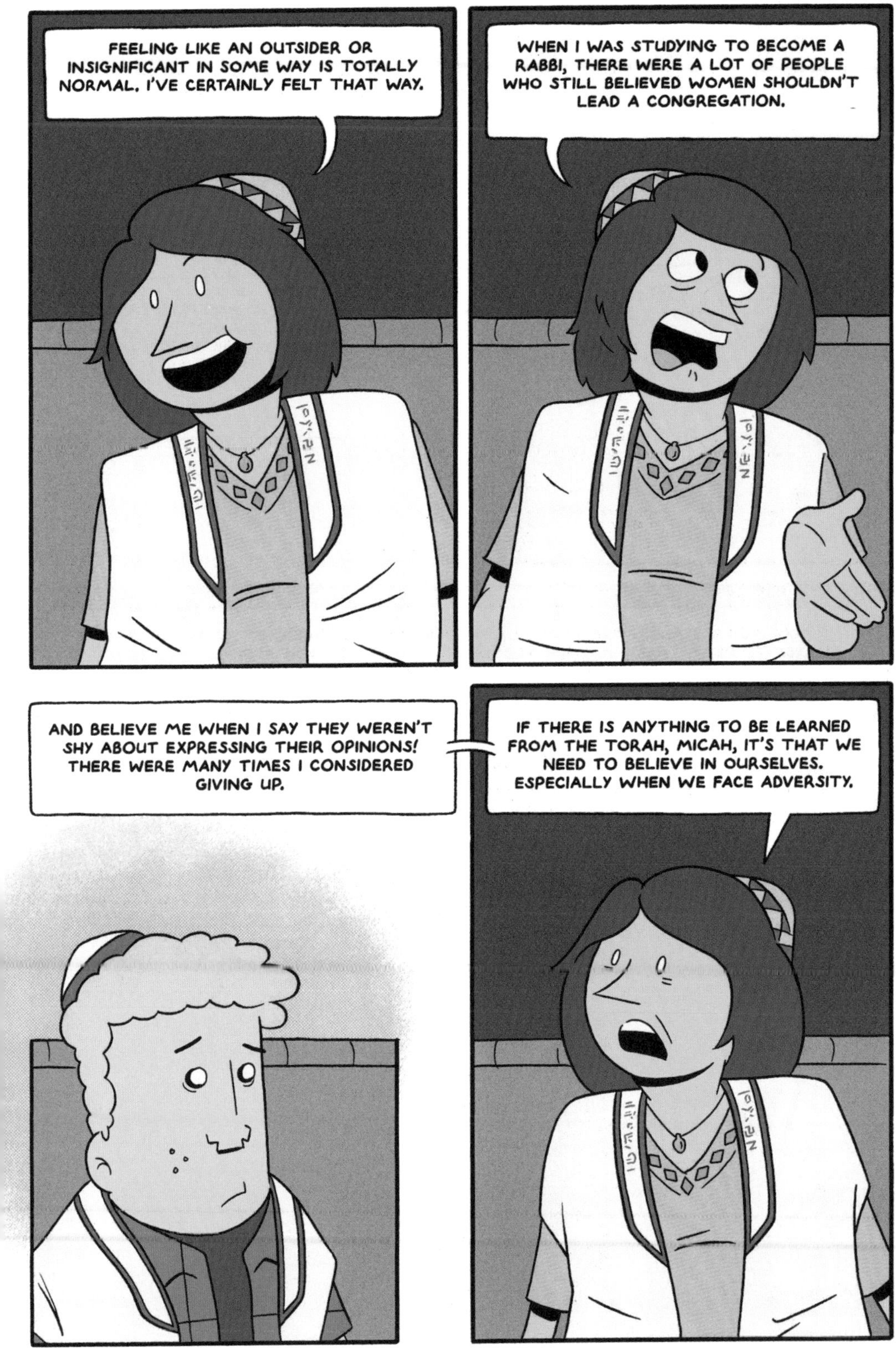
FEELING LIKE AN OUTSIDER OR INSIGNIFICANT IN SOME WAY IS TOTALLY NORMAL. I'VE CERTAINLY FELT THAT WAY.
WHEN I WAS STUDYING TO BECOME A RABBI, THERE WERE A LOT OF PEOPLE WHO STILL BELIEVED WOMEN SHOULDN'T LEAD A CONGREGATION.
AND BELIEVE ME WHEN I SAY THEY WEREN'T SHY ABOUT EXPRESSING THEIR OPINIONS! THERE WERE MANY TIMES I CONSIDERED GIVING UP.
IF THERE IS ANYTHING TO BE LEARNED FROM THE TORAH, MICAH, IT'S THAT WE NEED TO BELIEVE IN OURSELVES. ESPECIALLY WHEN WE FACE ADVERSITY.

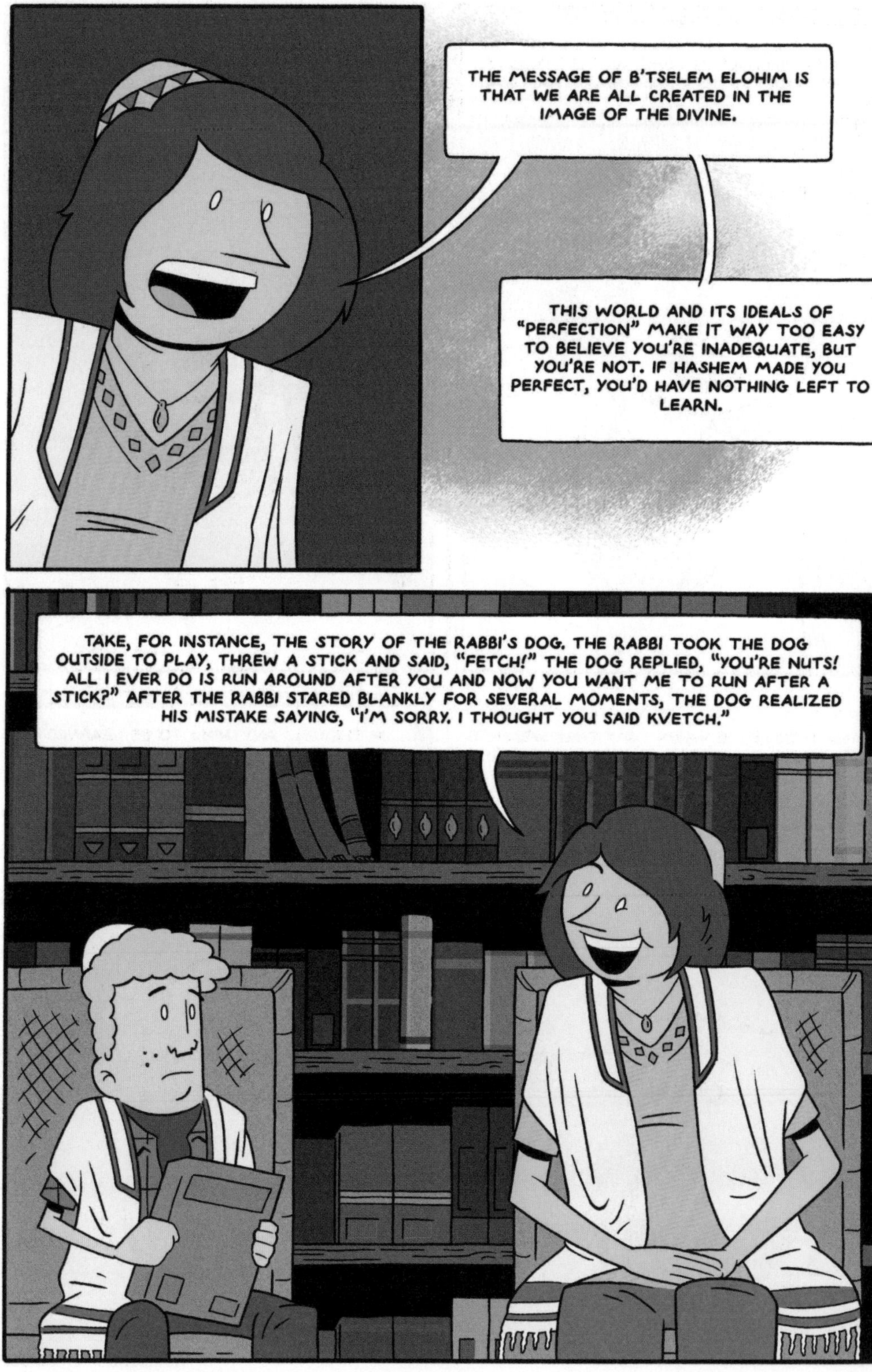
THE MESSAGE OF B'TSELEM ELOHIM IS THAT WE ARE ALL CREATED IN THE IMAGE OF THE DIVINE.
THIS WORLD AND ITS IDEALS OF "PERFECTION" MAKE IT WAY TOO EASY TO BELIEVE YOU'RE INADEQUATE, BUT YOU'RE NOT. IF HASHEM MADE YOU PERFECT, YOU'D HAVE NOTHING LEFT TO LEARN.
TAKE, FOR INSTANCE, THE STORY OF THE RABBI'S DOG. THE RABBI TOOK THE DOG OUTSIDE TO PLAY, THREW A STICK AND SAID, "FETCH!" THE DOG REPLIED, "YOU'RE NUTS! ALL I EVER DO IS RUN AROUND AFTER YOU AND NOW YOU WANT ME TO RUN AFTER A STICK?" AFTER THE RABBI STARED BLANKLY FOR SEVERAL MOMENTS, THE DOG REALIZED HIS MISTAKE SAYING, "I'M SORRY. I THOUGHT YOU SAID KVETCH."

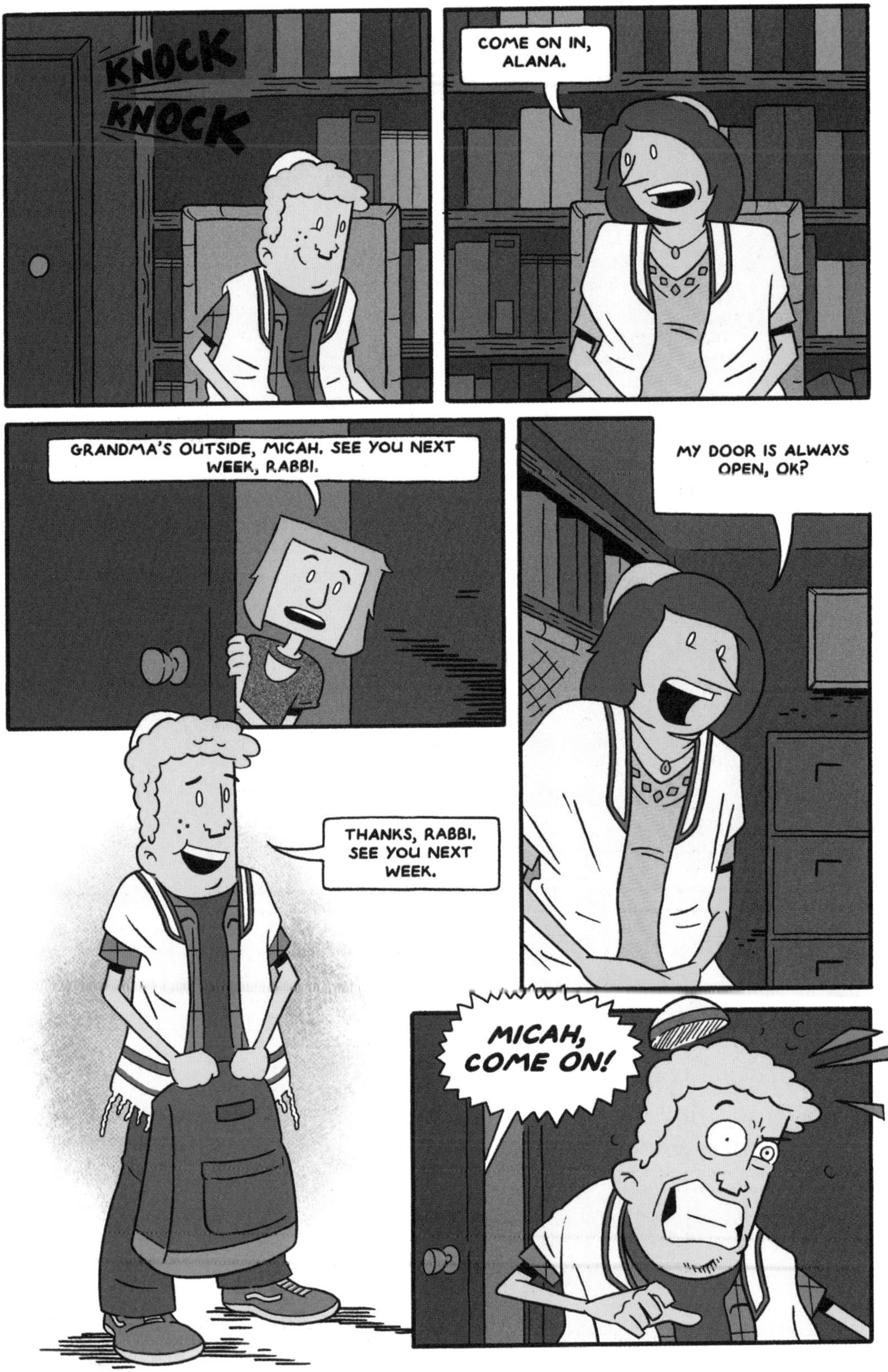
KNOCK KNOCK
COME ON IN, ALANA.
GRANDMA'S OUTSIDE, MICAH. SEE YOU NEXT WEEK, RABBI.
MY DOOR IS ALWAYS OPEN, OK?
THANKS, RABBI. SEE YOU NEXT WEEK.
MICAH, COME ON!

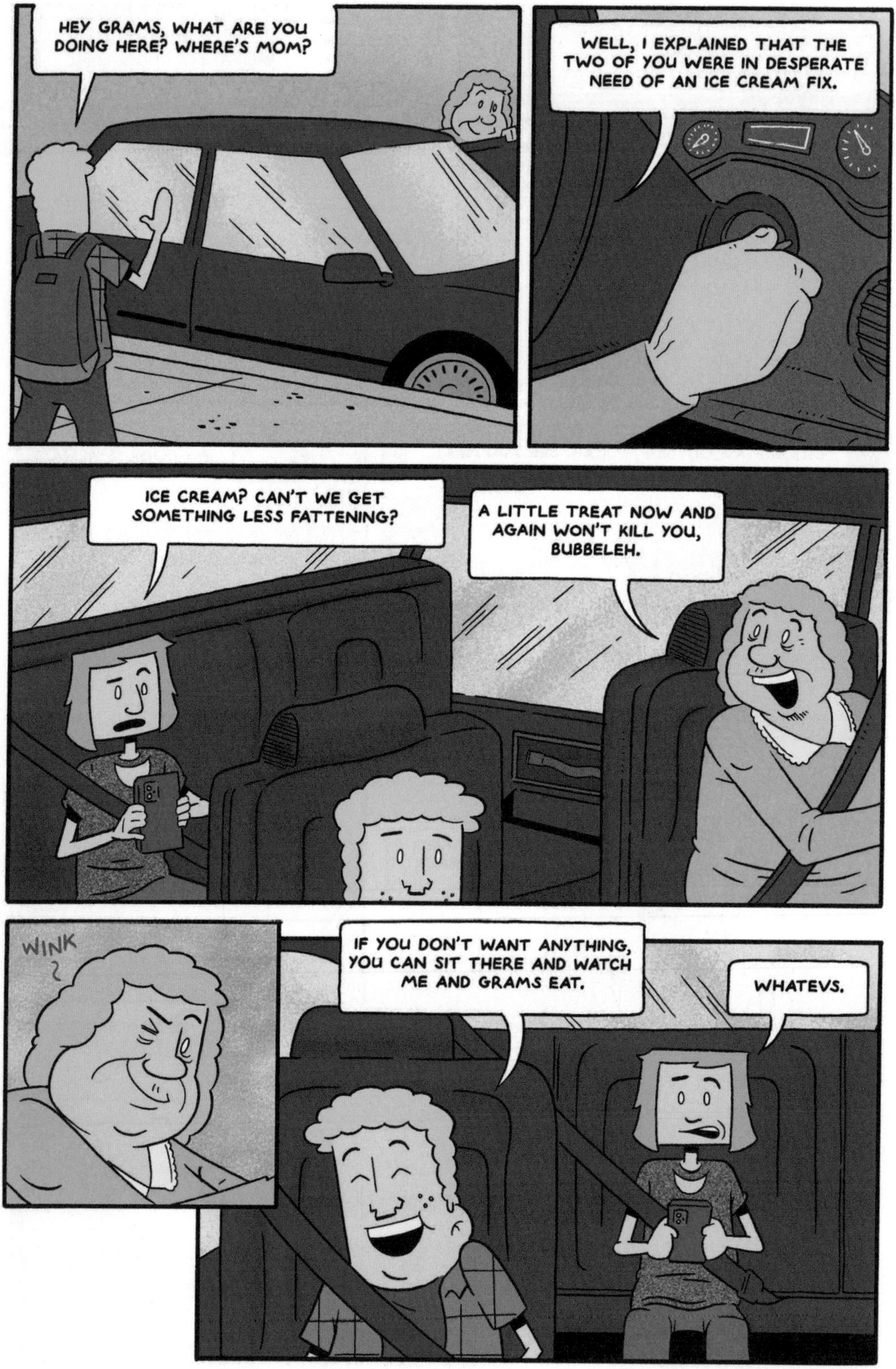
HEY GRAMS, WHAT ARE YOU DOING HERE? WHERE'S MOM?
WELL, I EXPLAINED THAT THE TWO OF YOU WERE IN DESPERATE NEED OF AN ICE CREAM FIX.
ICE CREAM? CAN'T WE GET SOMETHING LESS FATTENING?
A LITTLE TREAT NOW AND AGAIN WON'T KILL YOU, BUBBELEH.
WINK
IF YOU DON'T WANT ANYTHING, YOU CAN SIT THERE AND WATCH ME AND GRAMS EAT.
WHATEVS.

TRIPS TO THE ICE CREAM SHOP WERE GRAMS'S UNDERCOVER WAY OF INDULGING HER OWN SWEET TOOTH.

CENTRAL COAST CREAMERY

IT WAS ALSO A WAY FOR HER TO SPEND WHAT SHE CALLED "ONE-ON-ONE TIME" WITH US.

OH MY... WHAT DO I WANT?

ALANA, WHY DON'T YOU TELL THE NICE MAN WHAT YOU'D LIKE.

CAN I JUST HAVE A CUP FOR WATER? THANKS.

OY GEVALT, MICAH?

BUTTER PECAN
DULCE DE LECHE
MINT CHOCOLATE CHIP
PISTACHIO

CAN I HAVE A SCOOP OF COOKIE DOUGH AND A SCOOP OF BUTTERSCOTCH RIBBON?

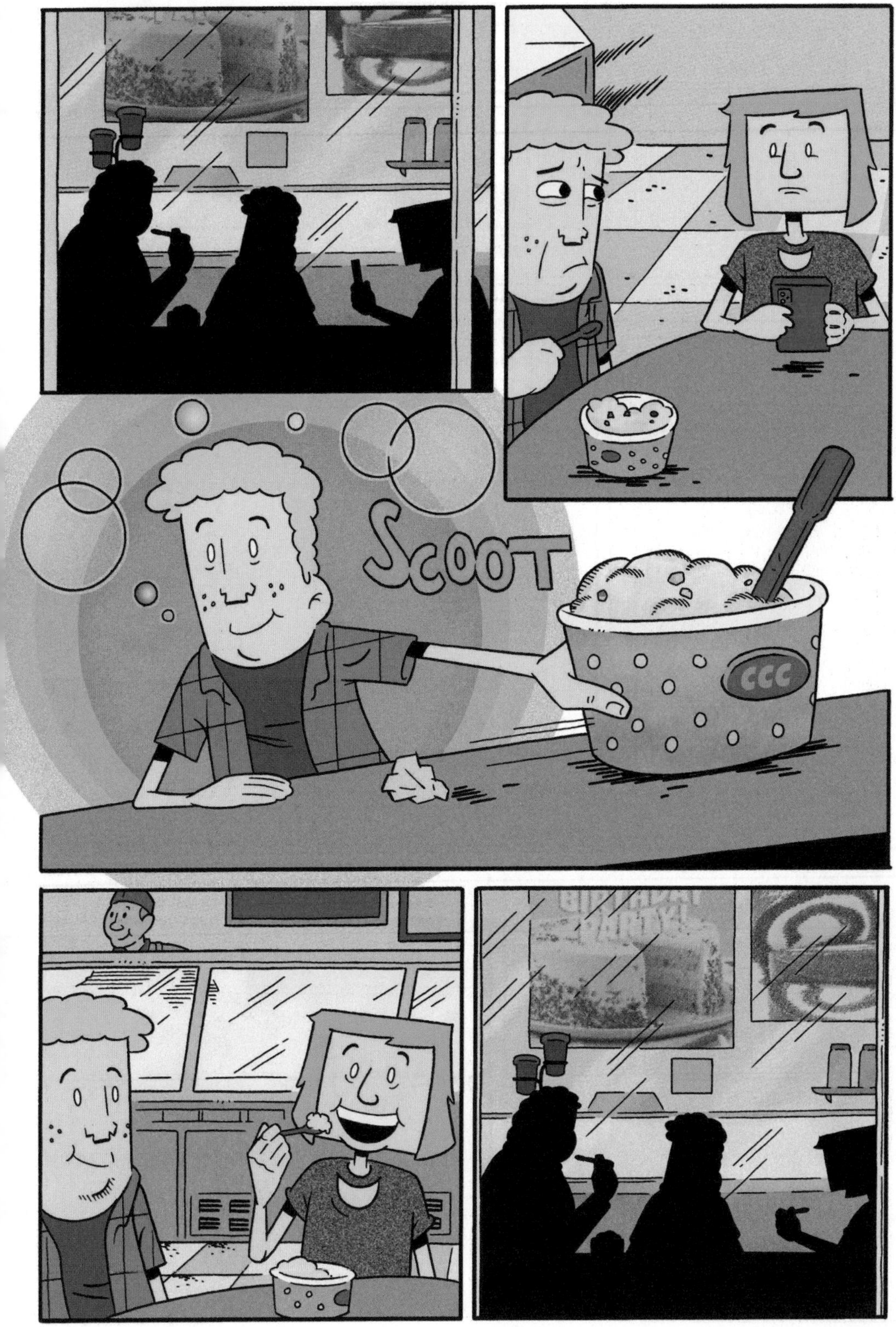
SCOOT
CCC
PARTY!

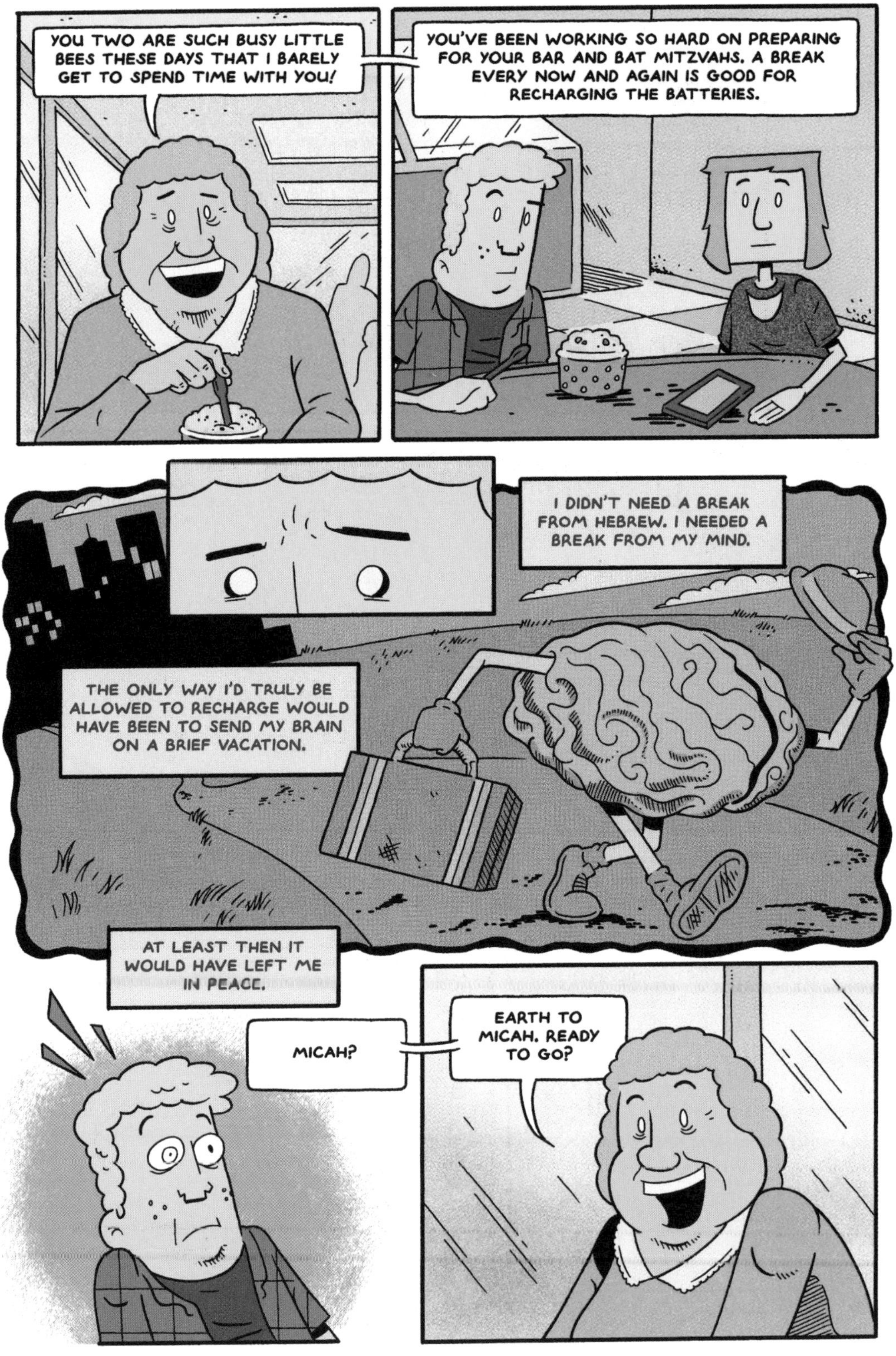
YOU TWO ARE SUCH BUSY LITTLE BEES THESE DAYS THAT I BARELY GET TO SPEND TIME WITH YOU!
YOU'VE BEEN WORKING SO HARD ON PREPARING FOR YOUR BAR AND BAT MITZVAHS. A BREAK EVERY NOW AND AGAIN IS GOOD FOR RECHARGING THE BATTERIES.
I DIDN'T NEED A BREAK FROM HEBREW. I NEEDED A BREAK FROM MY MIND.
THE ONLY WAY I'D TRULY BE ALLOWED TO RECHARGE WOULD HAVE BEEN TO SEND MY BRAIN ON A BRIEF VACATION.
AT LEAST THEN IT WOULD HAVE LEFT ME IN PEACE.
MICAH?
EARTH TO MICAH. READY TO GO?

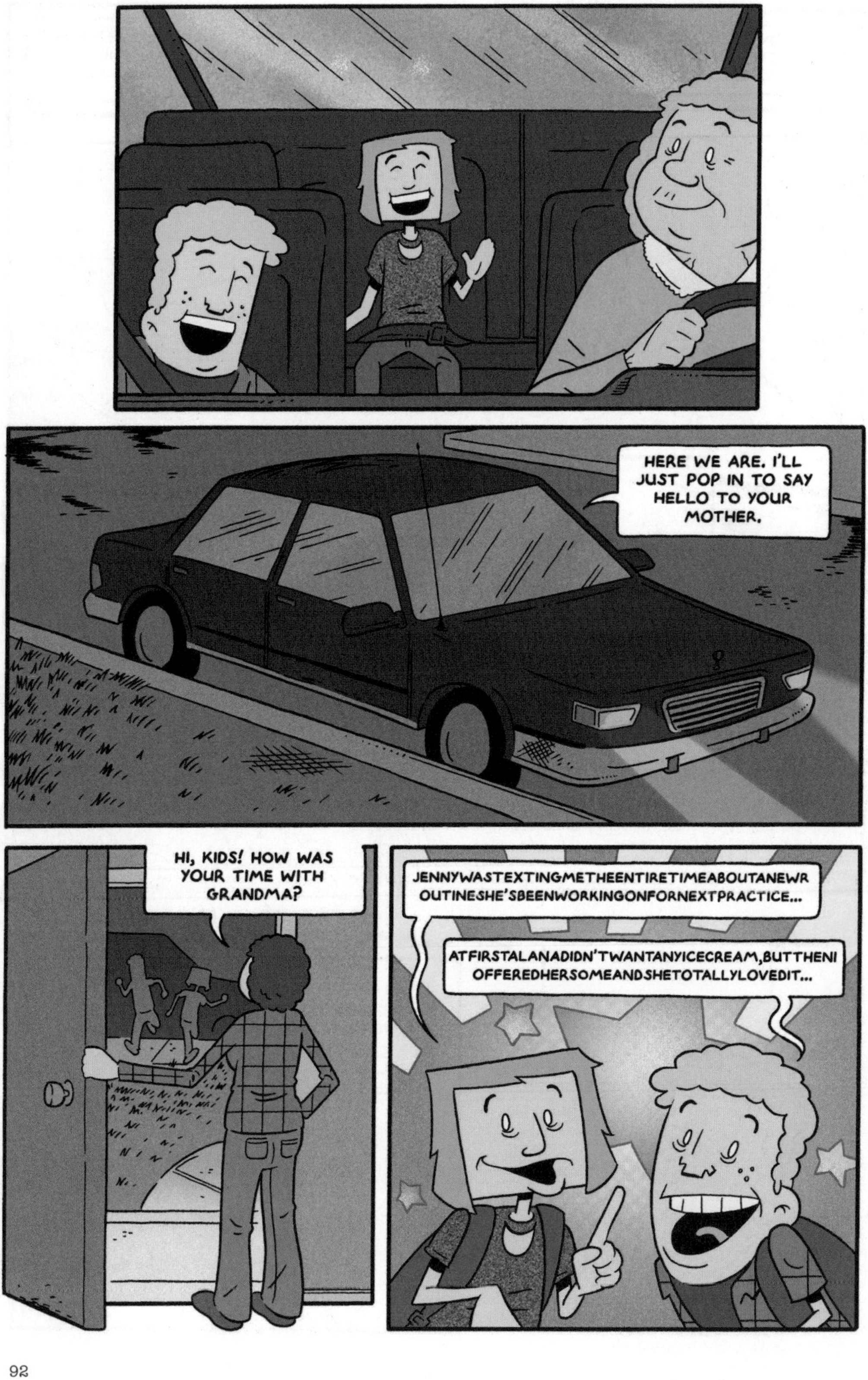
HERE WE ARE. I'LL JUST POP IN TO SAY HELLO TO YOUR MOTHER.
HI, KIDS! HOW WAS YOUR TIME WITH GRANDMA?
JENNYWASTEXTINGMETHEENTIRETIMEABOUTANEWROUTINESHE'SBEENWORKINGONFORNEXTPRACTICE...
ATFIRSTALANADIDN'TWANTANYICECREAM,BUTTHENIOFFEREDHERSOMEANDSHETOTALLYLOVEDIT...

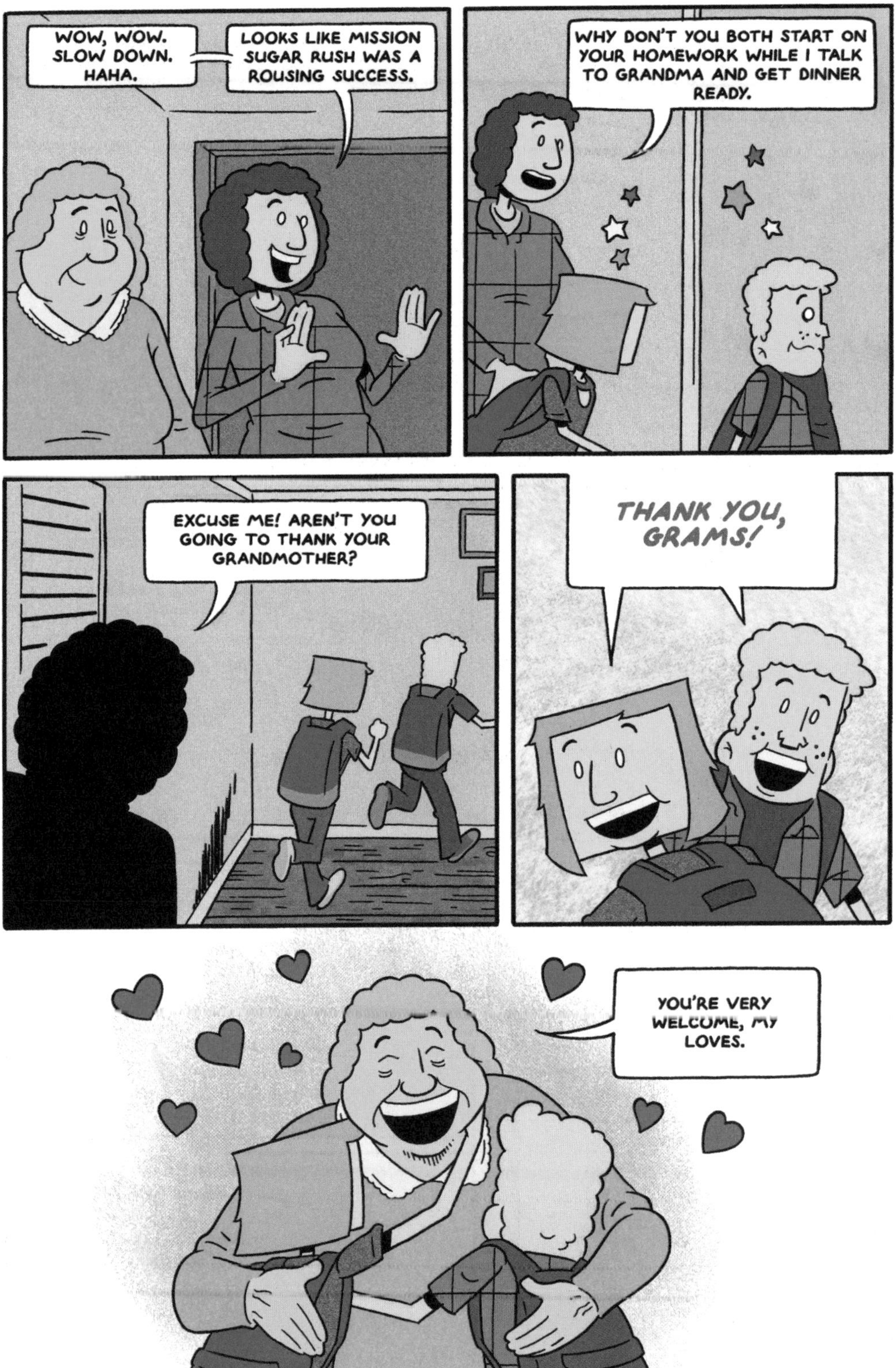
WOW, WOW. SLOW DOWN. HAHA.
LOOKS LIKE MISSION SUGAR RUSH WAS A ROUSING SUCCESS.
WHY DON'T YOU BOTH START ON YOUR HOMEWORK WHILE I TALK TO GRANDMA AND GET DINNER READY.
EXCUSE ME! AREN'T YOU GOING TO THANK YOUR GRANDMOTHER?
THANK YOU, GRAMS!
YOU'RE VERY WELCOME, MY LOVES.

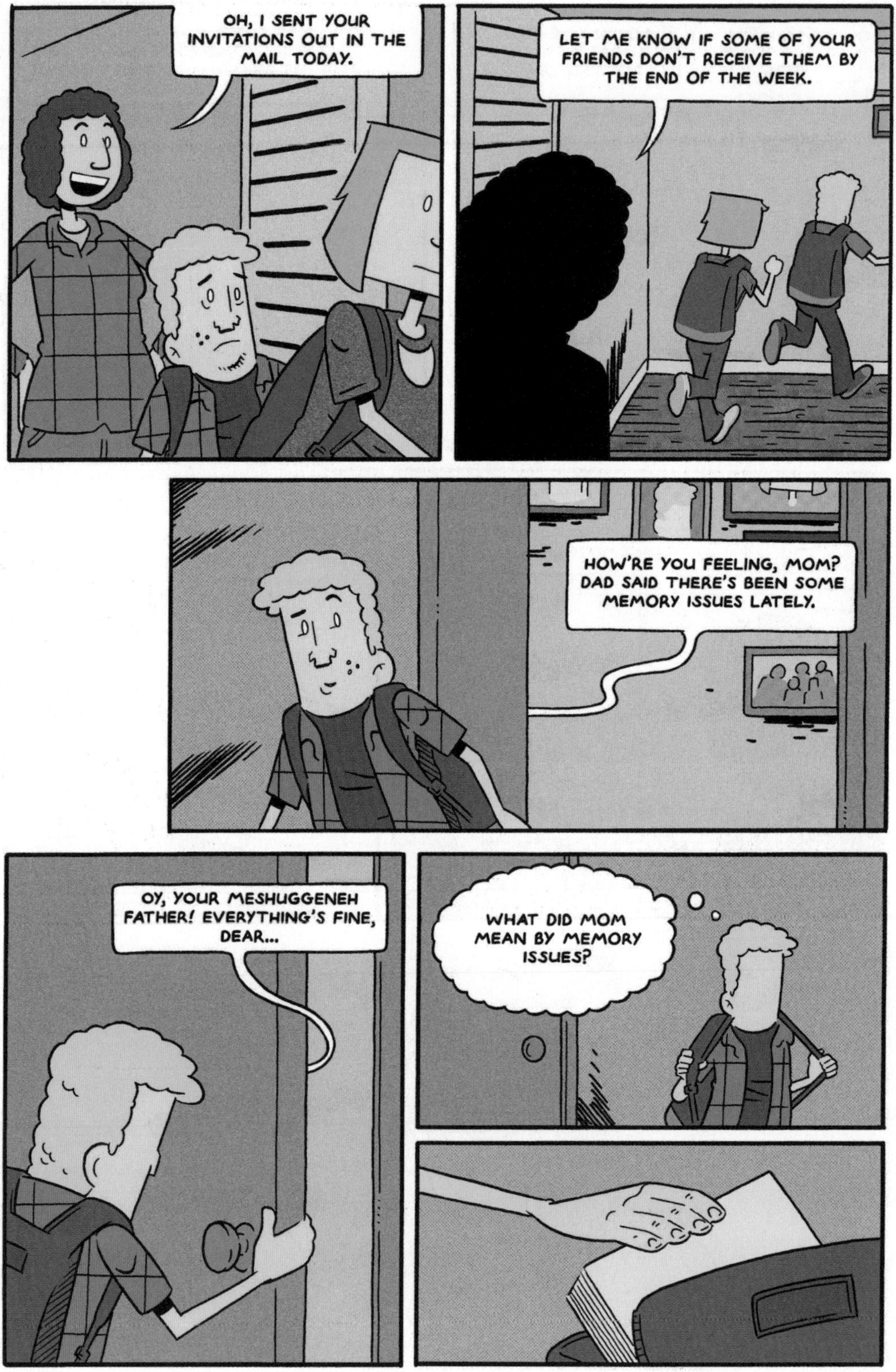

OH, I SENT YOUR INVITATIONS OUT IN THE MAIL TODAY.
LET ME KNOW IF SOME OF YOUR FRIENDS DON'T RECEIVE THEM BY THE END OF THE WEEK.
HOW'RE YOU FEELING, MOM? DAD SAID THERE'S BEEN SOME MEMORY ISSUES LATELY.
OY, YOUR MESHUGGENEH FATHER! EVERYTHING'S FINE, DEAR...
WHAT DID MOM MEAN BY MEMORY ISSUES?

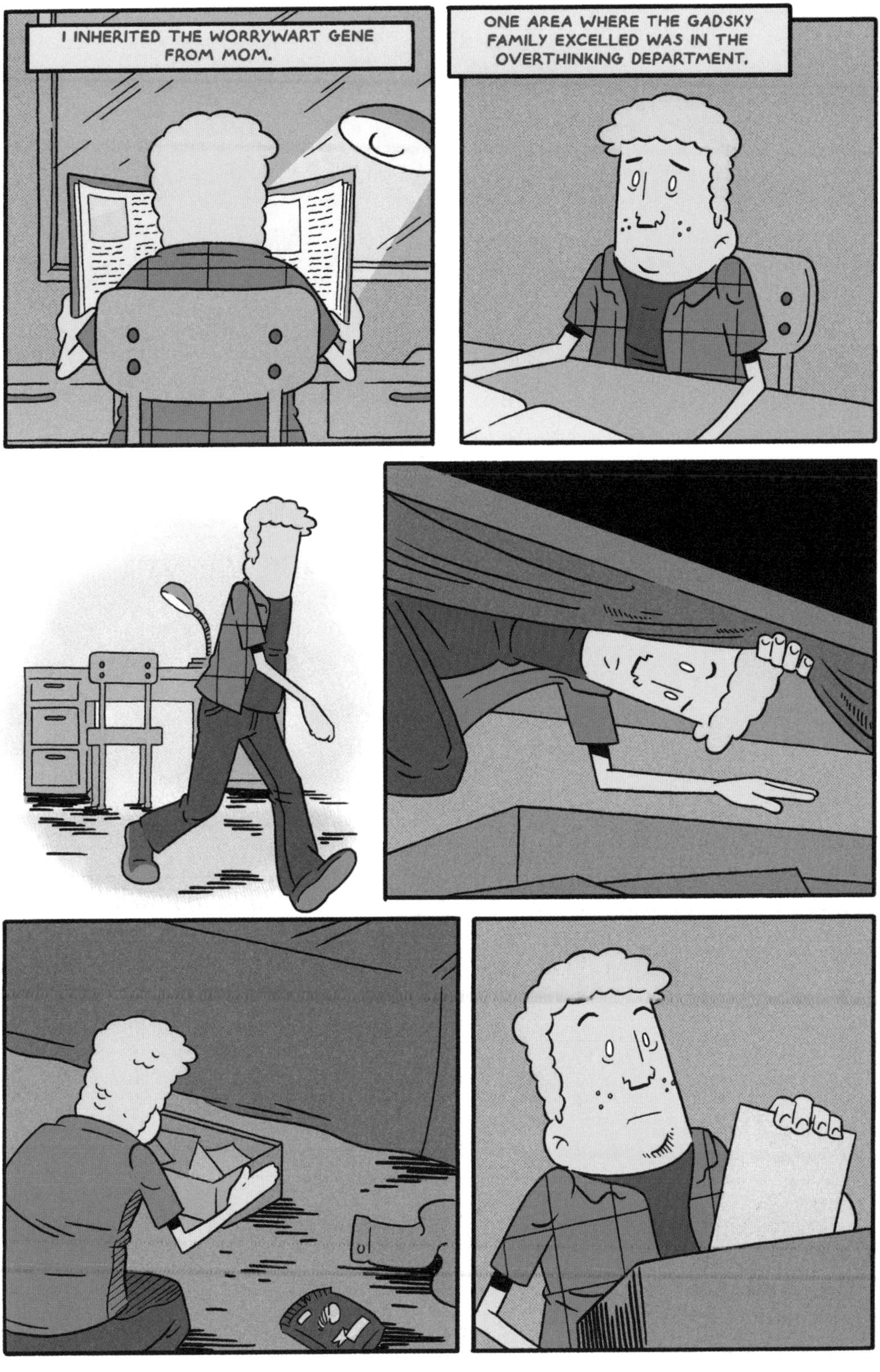
I INHERITED THE WORRYWART GENE FROM MOM.
ONE AREA WHERE THE GADSKY FAMILY EXCELLED WAS IN THE OVERTHINKING DEPARTMENT.

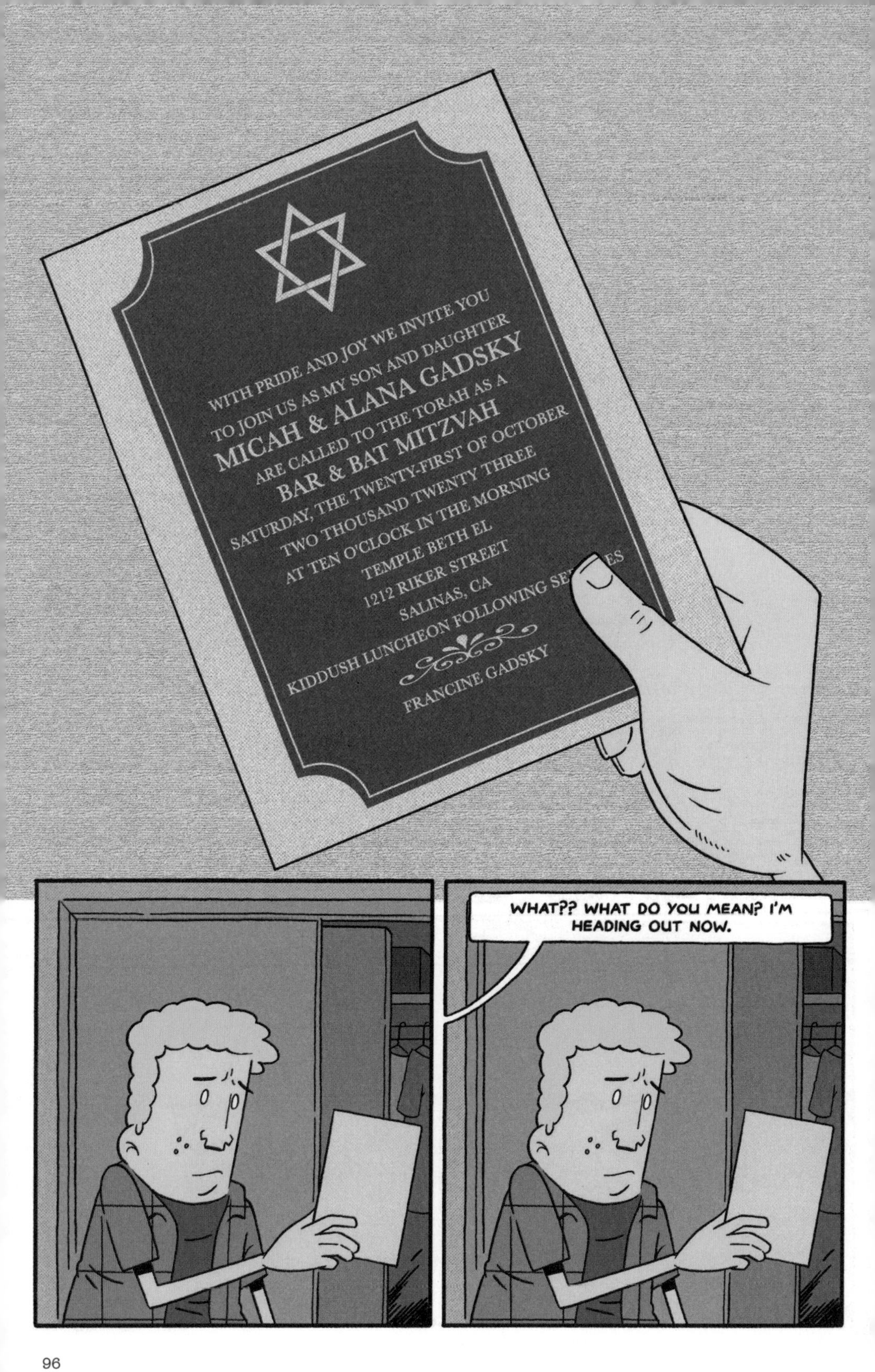
WITH PRIDE AND JOY WE INVITE YOU
TO JOIN US AS MY SON AND DAUGHTER
MICAH & ALANA GADSKY
ARE CALLED TO THE TORAH AS A
BAR & BAT MITZVAH
SATURDAY, THE TWENTY-FIRST OF OCTOBER
TWO THOUSAND TWENTY THREE
AT TEN O'CLOCK IN THE MORNING
TEMPLE BETH EL
1212 RIKER STREET
SALINAS, CA
KIDDUSH LUNCHEON FOLLOWING SE ES
FRANCINE GADSKY
WHAT?? WHAT DO YOU MEAN? I'M HEADING OUT NOW.

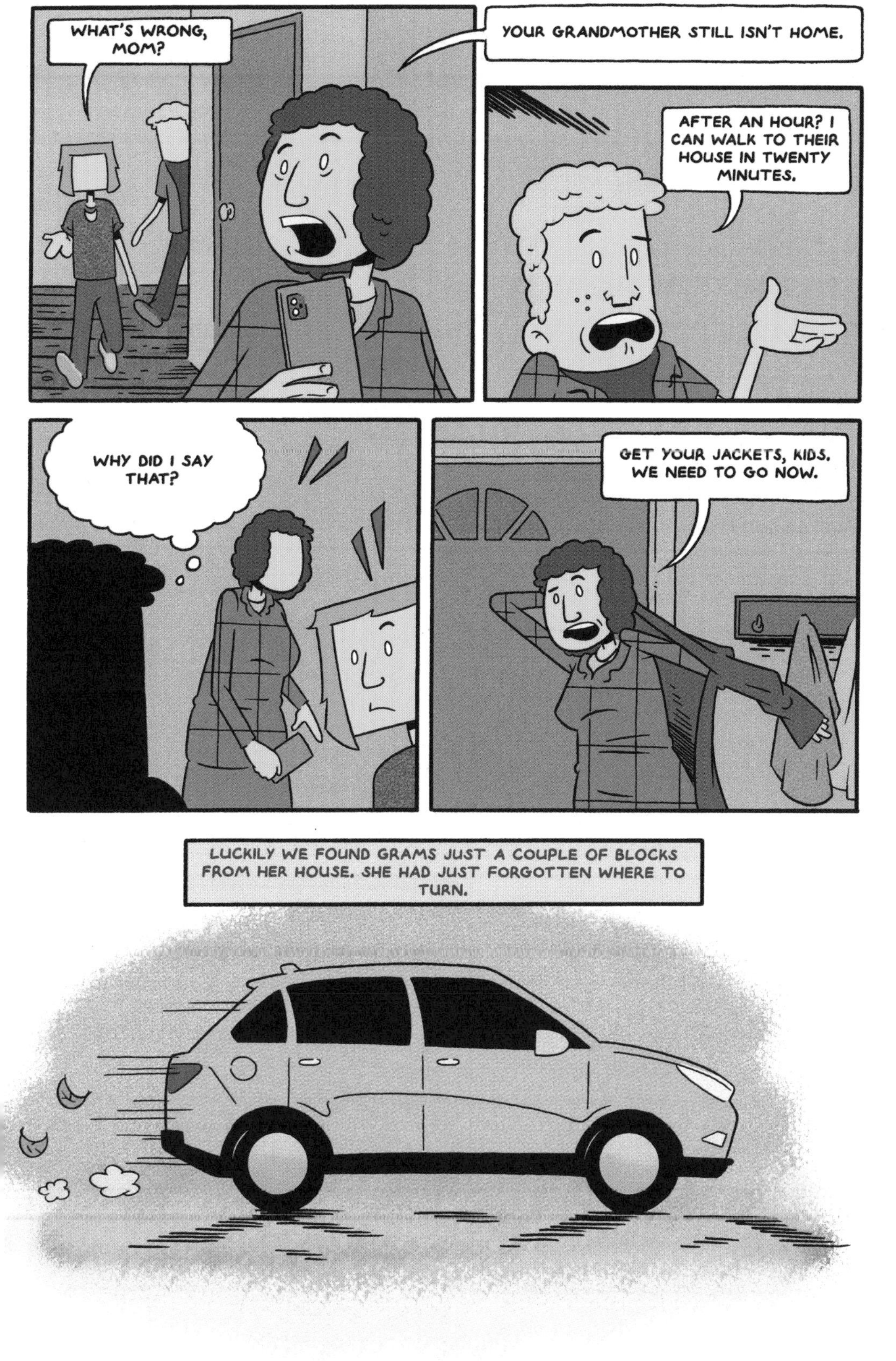
WHAT'S WRONG, MOM?
YOUR GRANDMOTHER STILL ISN'T HOME.
AFTER AN HOUR? I CAN WALK TO THEIR HOUSE IN TWENTY MINUTES.
WHY DID I SAY THAT?
GET YOUR JACKETS, KIDS. WE NEED TO GO NOW.
LUCKILY WE FOUND GRAMS JUST A COUPLE OF BLOCKS FROM HER HOUSE. SHE HAD JUST FORGOTTEN WHERE TO TURN.

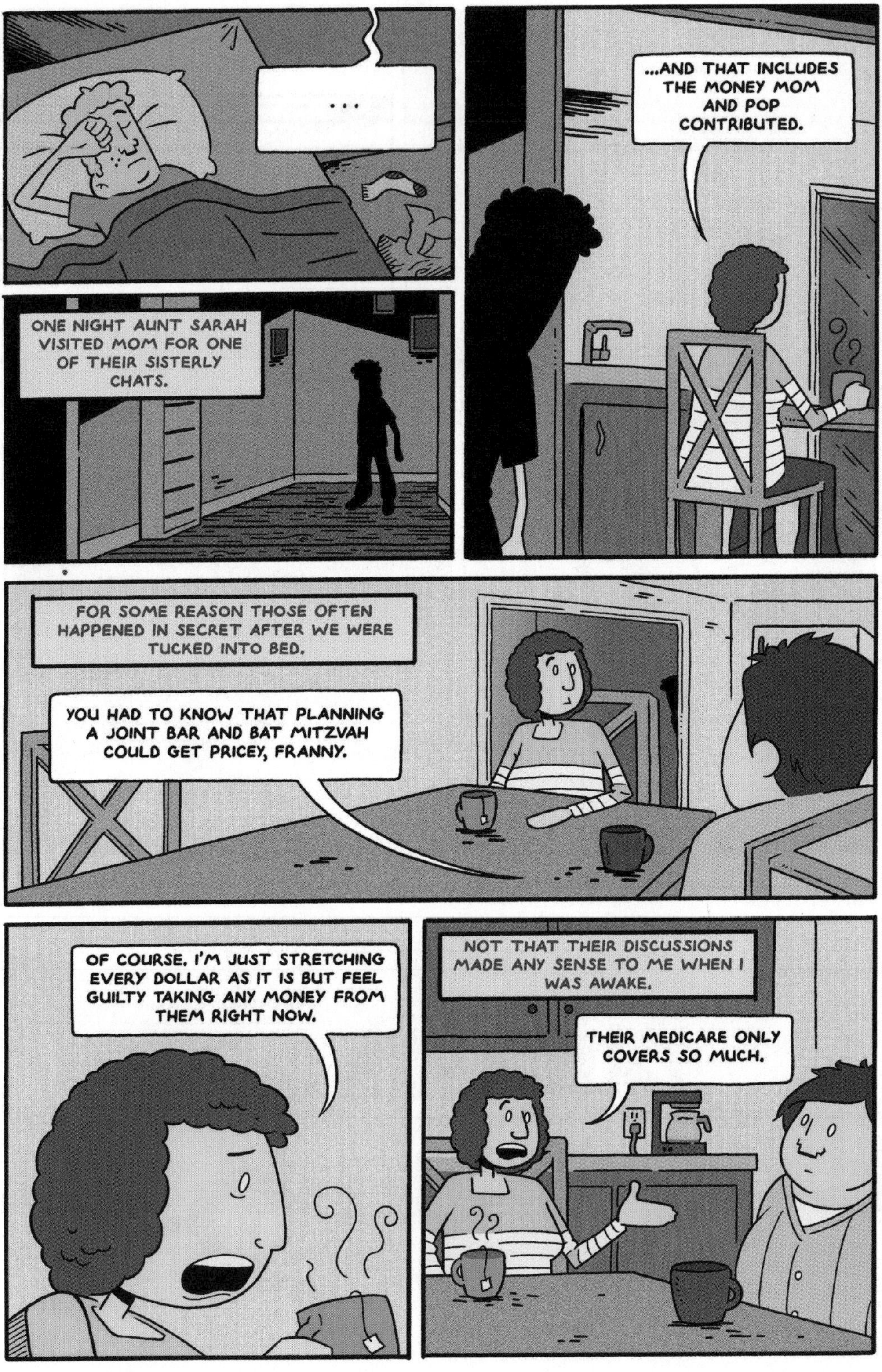
...
ONE NIGHT AUNT SARAH VISITED MOM FOR ONE OF THEIR SISTERLY CHATS.
...AND THAT INCLUDES THE MONEY MOM AND POP CONTRIBUTED.
FOR SOME REASON THOSE OFTEN HAPPENED IN SECRET AFTER WE WERE TUCKED INTO BED.
YOU HAD TO KNOW THAT PLANNING A JOINT BAR AND BAT MITZVAH COULD GET PRICEY, FRANNY.
OF COURSE. I'M JUST STRETCHING EVERY DOLLAR AS IT IS BUT FEEL GUILTY TAKING ANY MONEY FROM THEM RIGHT NOW.
NOT THAT THEIR DISCUSSIONS MADE ANY SENSE TO ME WHEN I WAS AWAKE.
THEIR MEDICARE ONLY COVERS SO MUCH.

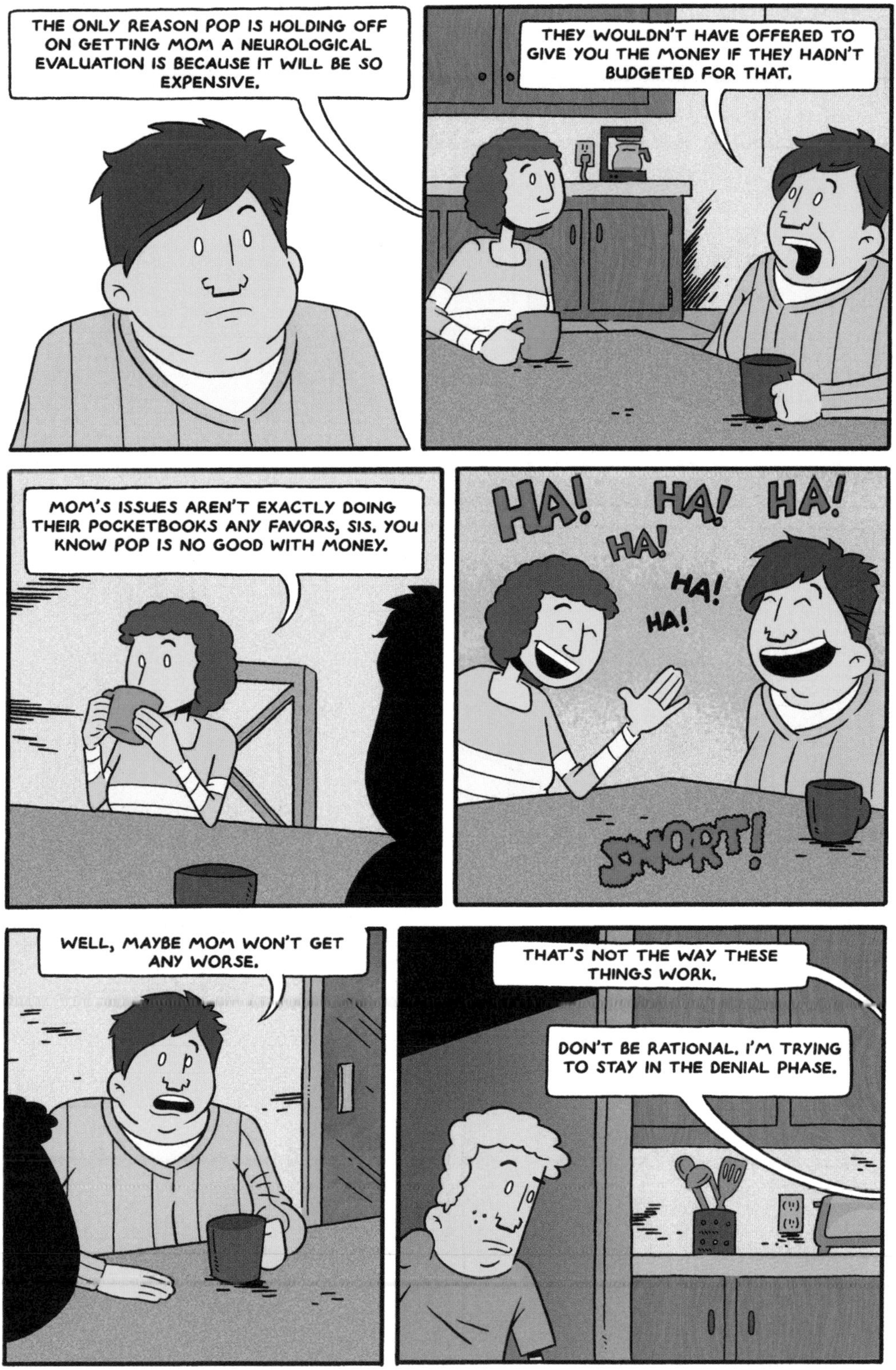
THE ONLY REASON POP IS HOLDING OFF ON GETTING MOM A NEUROLOGICAL EVALUATION IS BECAUSE IT WILL BE SO EXPENSIVE.
THEY WOULDN'T HAVE OFFERED TO GIVE YOU THE MONEY IF THEY HADN'T BUDGETED FOR THAT.
MOM'S ISSUES AREN'T EXACTLY DOING THEIR POCKETBOOKS ANY FAVORS, SIS. YOU KNOW POP IS NO GOOD WITH MONEY.
HA! HA! HA!
HA!
HA!
HA!
SNORT!
WELL, MAYBE MOM WON'T GET ANY WORSE.
THAT'S NOT THE WAY THESE THINGS WORK.
DON'T BE RATIONAL. I'M TRYING TO STAY IN THE DENIAL PHASE.

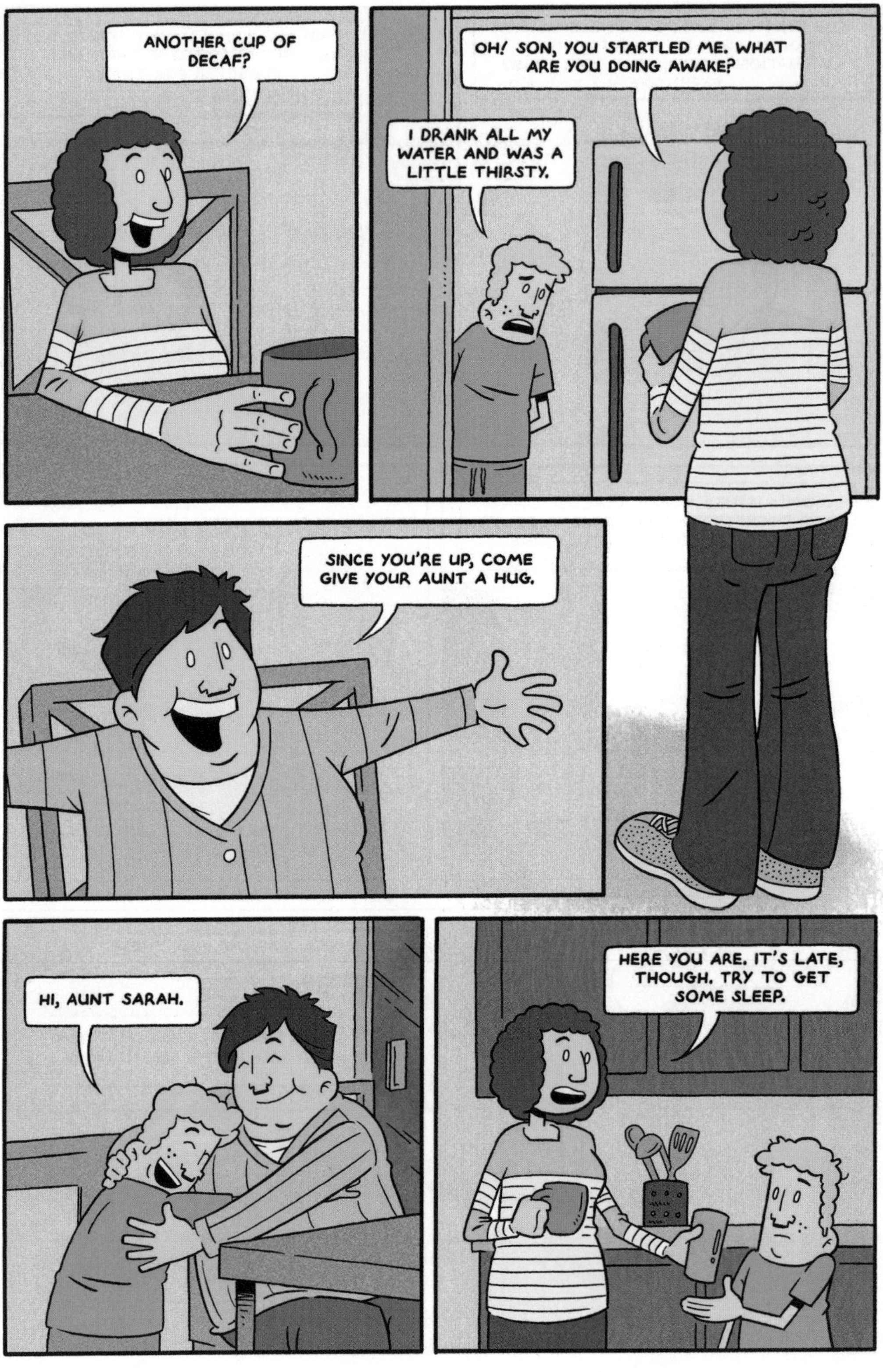
ANOTHER CUP OF DECAF?
OH! SON, YOU STARTLED ME. WHAT ARE YOU DOING AWAKE?
I DRANK ALL MY WATER AND WAS A LITTLE THIRSTY.
SINCE YOU'RE UP, COME GIVE YOUR AUNT A HUG.
HI, AUNT SARAH.
HERE YOU ARE. IT'S LATE, THOUGH. TRY TO GET SOME SLEEP.

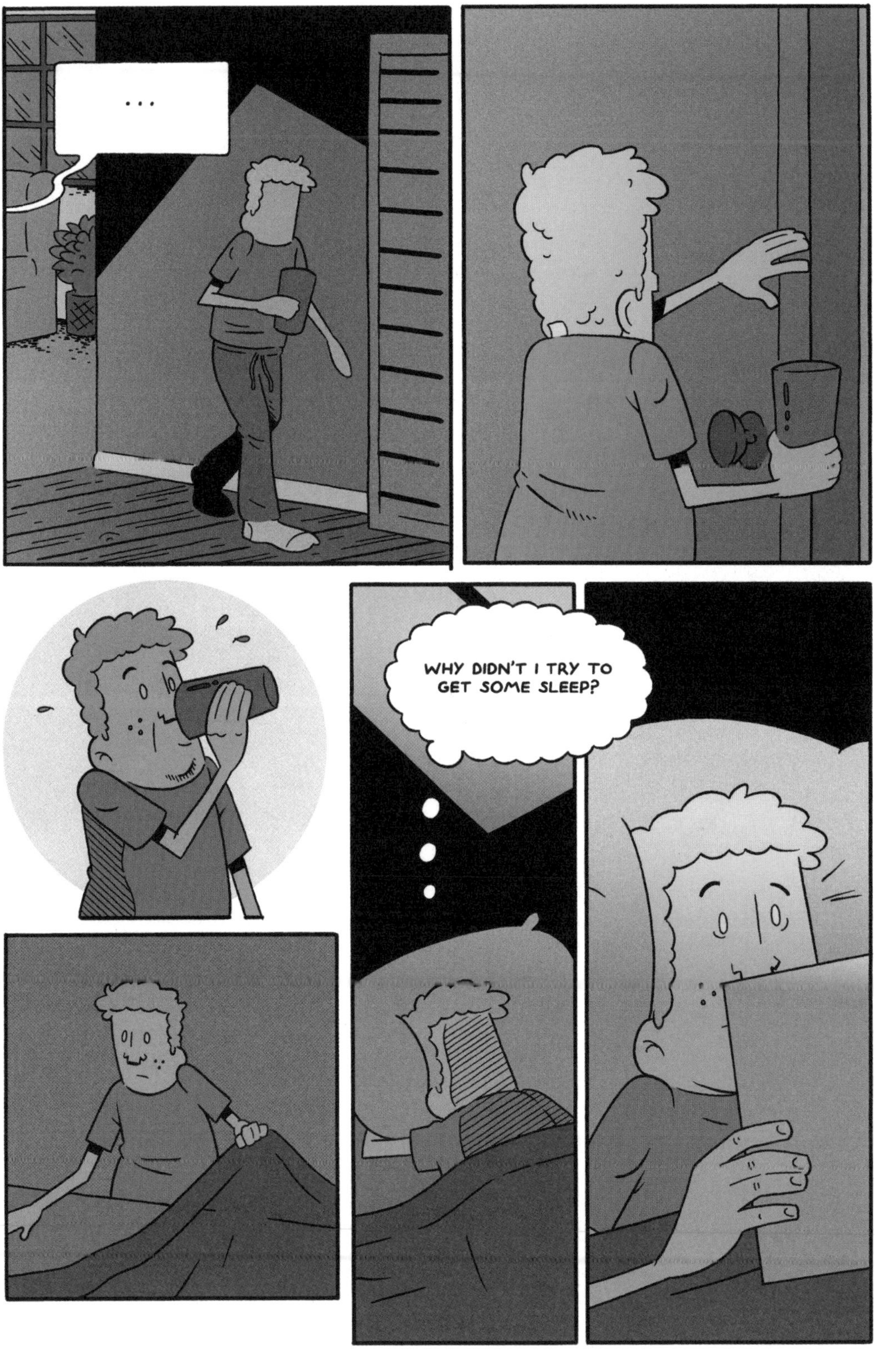
...
WHY DIDN'T I TRY TO GET SOME SLEEP?

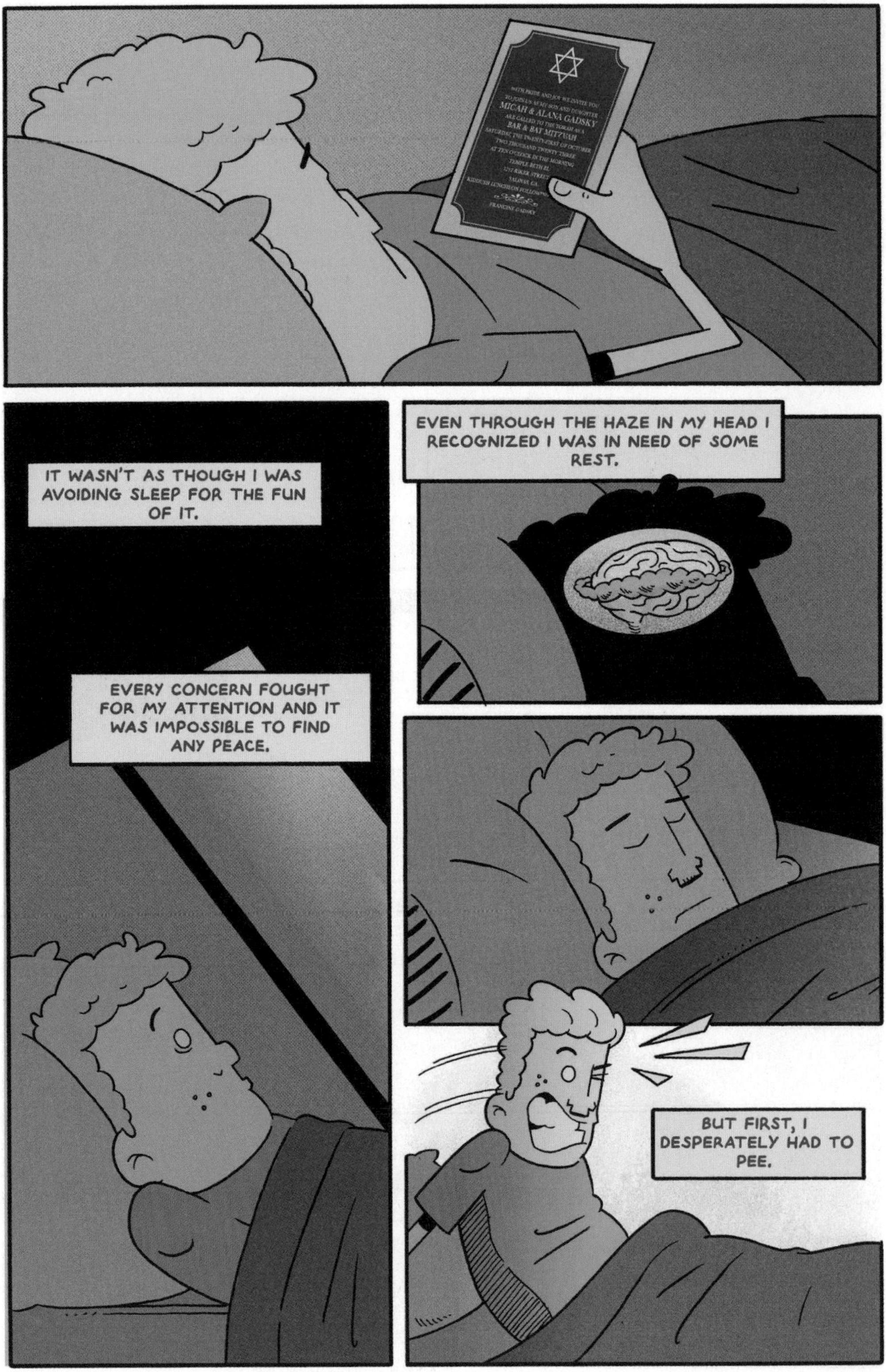
WITH PRIDE AND JOY WE INVITE YOU
TO JOIN US AS MY SON AND DAUGHTER
MICAH & ALANA GADSKY
ARE CALLED TO THE TORAH AS A
BAR & BAT MITZVAH
SATURDAY, THE TWENTY-FIRST OF OCTOBER
TWO THOUSAND TWENTY THREE
AT TEN O'CLOCK IN THE MORNING
TEMPLE BETH EL
SALINAS, CA
FRANCINE GADSKY
IT WASN'T AS THOUGH I WAS AVOIDING SLEEP FOR THE FUN OF IT.
EVERY CONCERN FOUGHT FOR MY ATTENTION AND IT WAS IMPOSSIBLE TO FIND ANY PEACE.
EVEN THROUGH THE HAZE IN MY HEAD I RECOGNIZED I WAS IN NEED OF SOME REST.
BUT FIRST, I DESPERATELY HAD TO PEE.

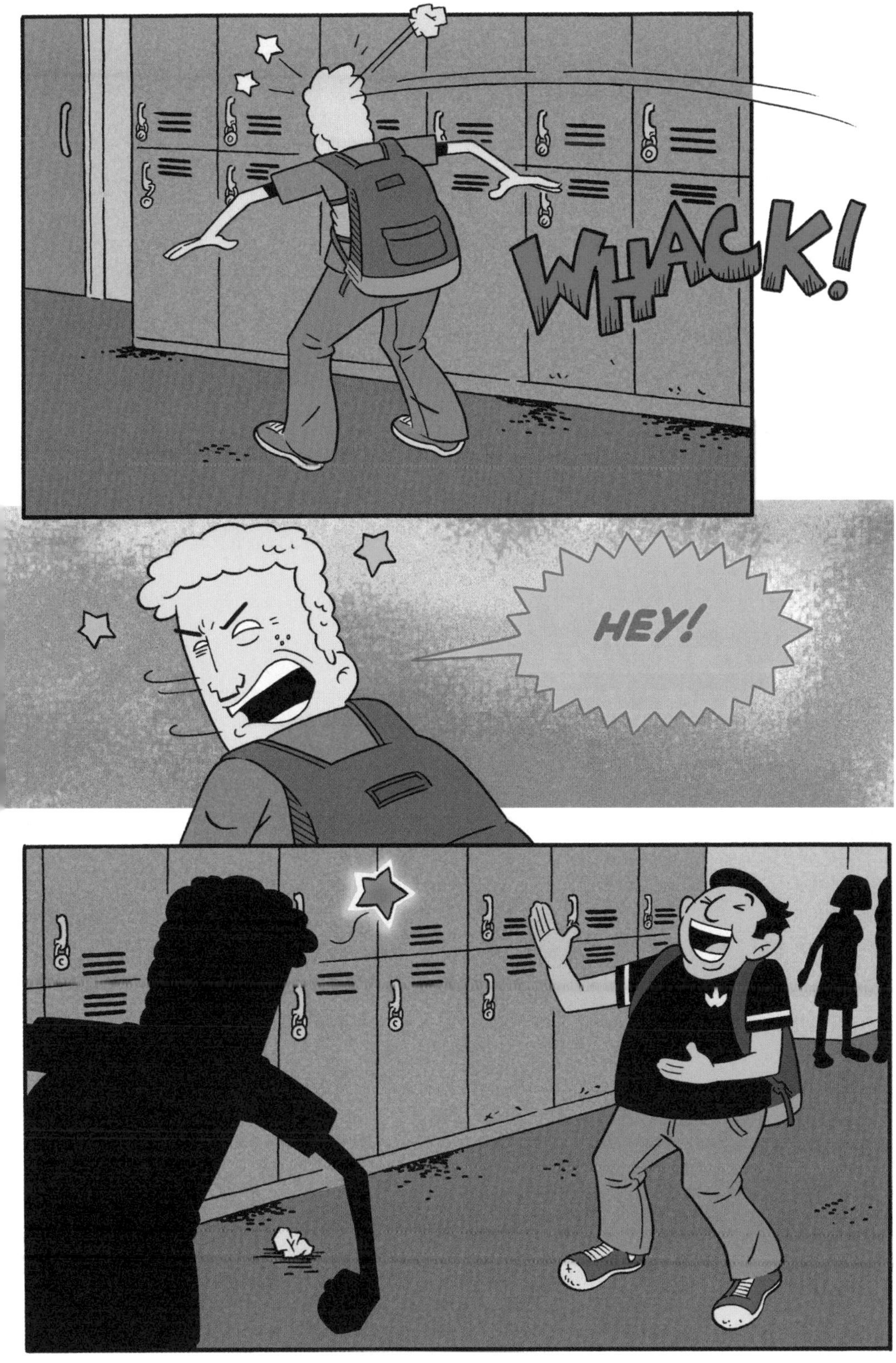
WHACK!
HEY!

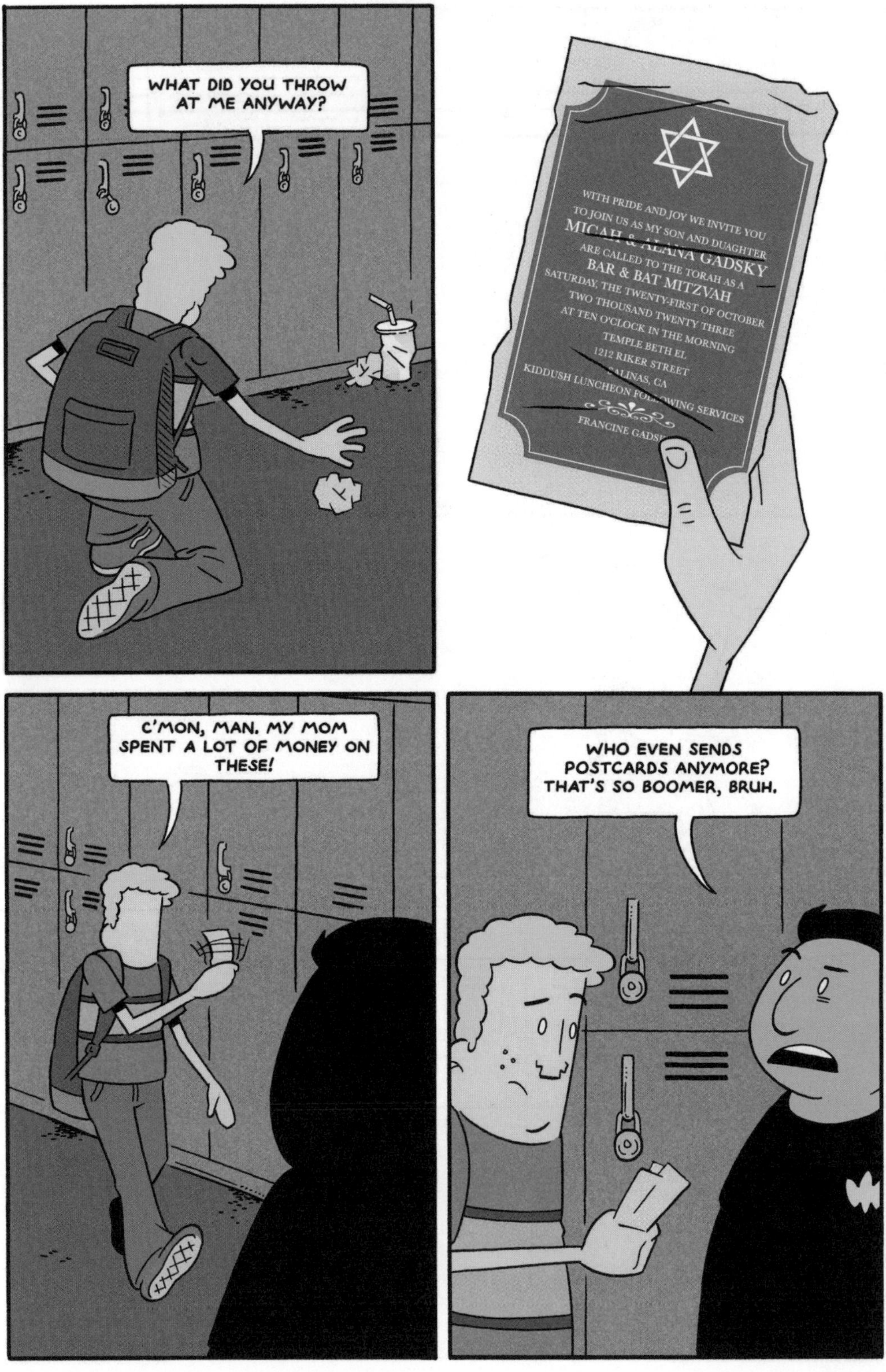
WHAT DID YOU THROW AT ME ANYWAY?
WITH PRIDE AND JOY WE INVITE YOU TO JOIN US AS MY SON AND DUAGHTER
MICAH & ALANA GADSKY
ARE CALLED TO THE TORAH AS A
BAR & BAT MITZVAH
SATURDAY, THE TWENTY-FIRST OF OCTOBER
TWO THOUSAND TWENTY THREE
AT TEN O'CLOCK IN THE MORNING
TEMPLE BETH EL
1212 RIKER STREET
ALINAS, CA
KIDDUSH LUNCHEON FOLLOWING SERVICES
FRANCINE GADS
C'MON, MAN. MY MOM SPENT A LOT OF MONEY ON THESE!
WHO EVEN SENDS POSTCARDS ANYMORE? THAT'S SO BOOMER, BRUH.

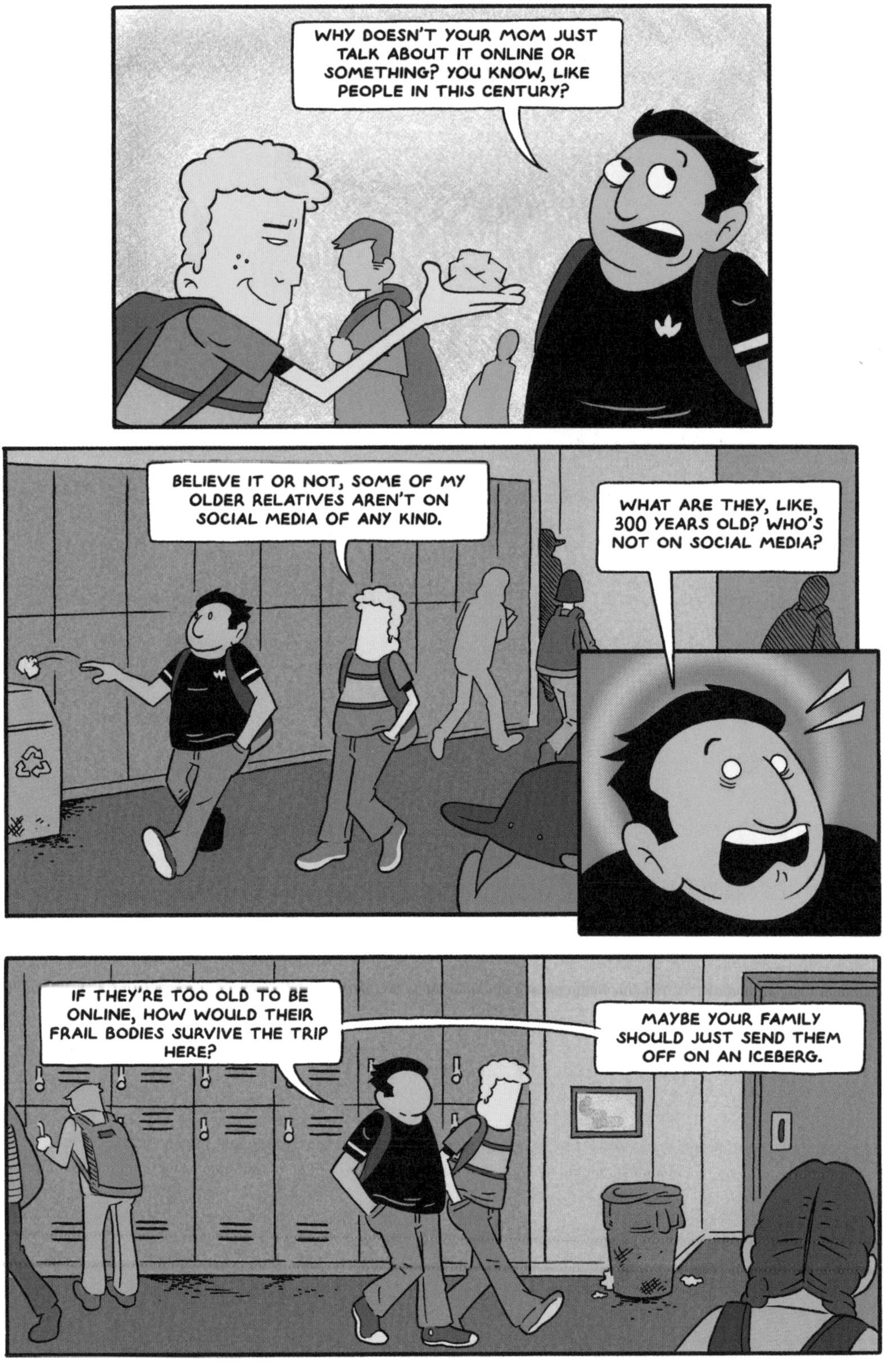
WHY DOESN'T YOUR MOM JUST TALK ABOUT IT ONLINE OR SOMETHING? YOU KNOW, LIKE PEOPLE IN THIS CENTURY?
BELIEVE IT OR NOT, SOME OF MY OLDER RELATIVES AREN'T ON SOCIAL MEDIA OF ANY KIND.
WHAT ARE THEY, LIKE, 300 YEARS OLD? WHO'S NOT ON SOCIAL MEDIA?
IF THEY'RE TOO OLD TO BE ONLINE, HOW WOULD THEIR FRAIL BODIES SURVIVE THE TRIP HERE?
MAYBE YOUR FAMILY SHOULD JUST SEND THEM OFF ON AN ICEBERG.

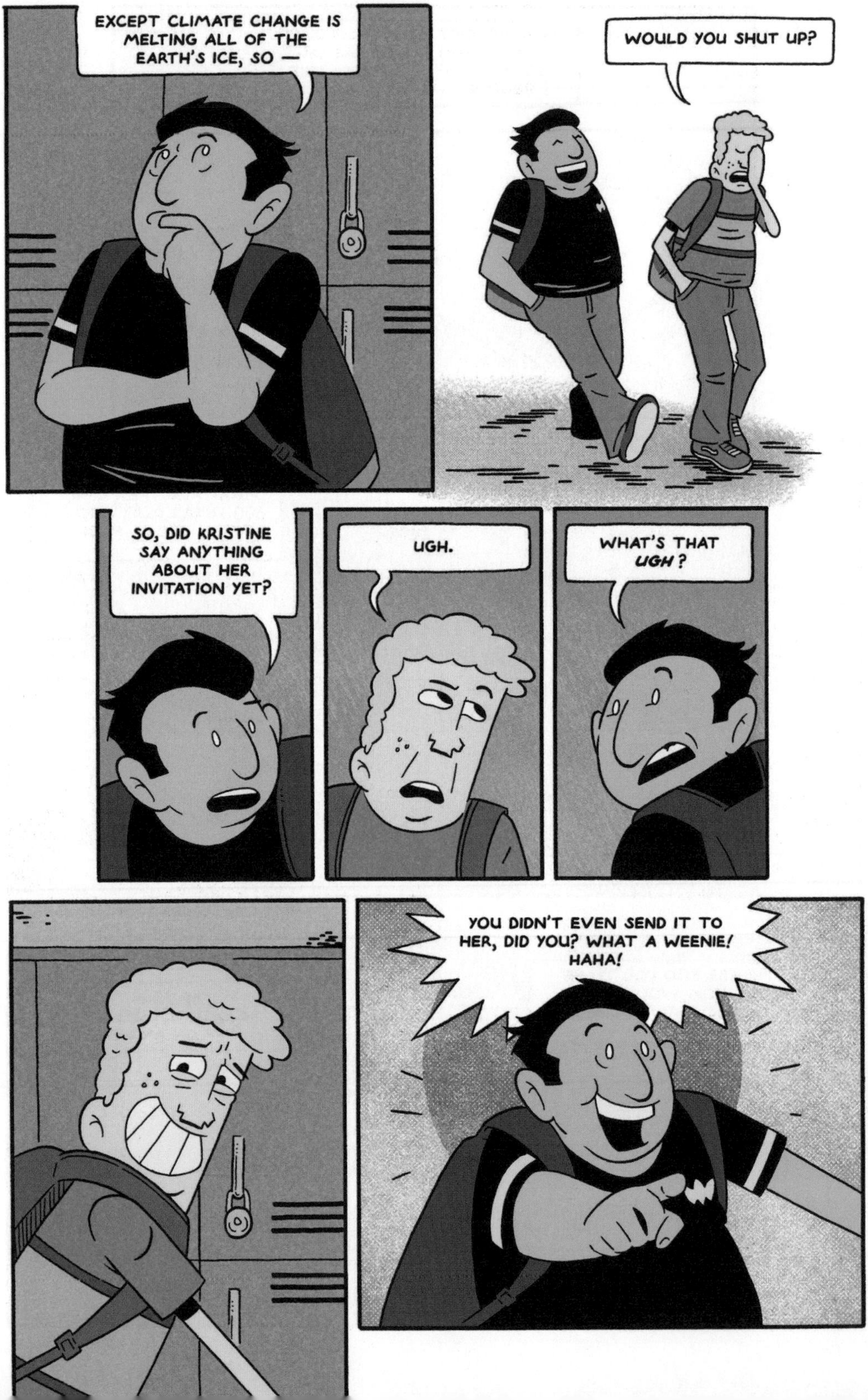
EXCEPT CLIMATE CHANGE IS MELTING ALL OF THE EARTH'S ICE, SO —
WOULD YOU SHUT UP?
SO, DID KRISTINE SAY ANYTHING ABOUT HER INVITATION YET?
UGH.
WHAT'S THAT *UGH*?
YOU DIDN'T EVEN SEND IT TO HER, DID YOU? WHAT A WEENIE! HAHA!

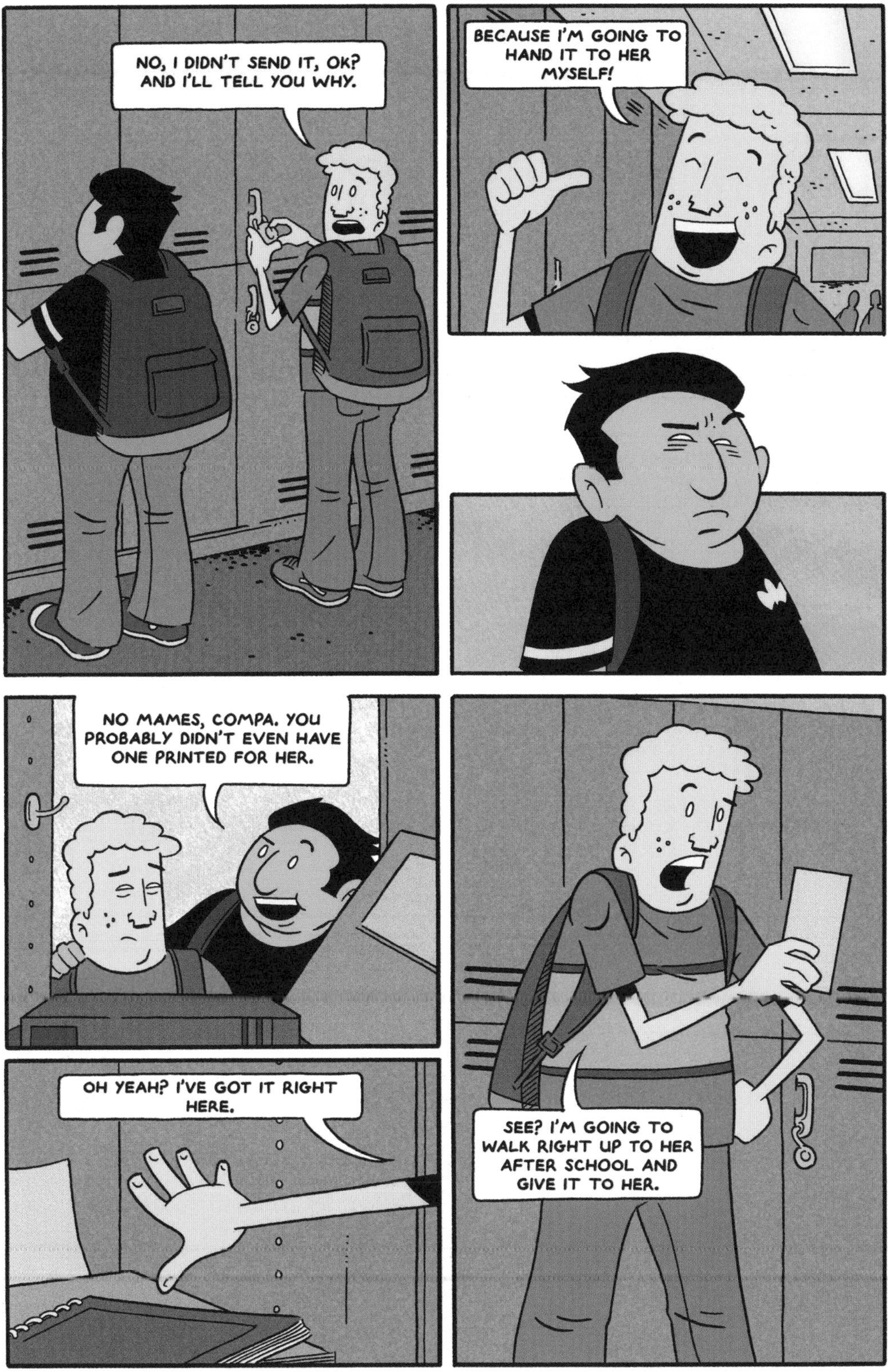

NO, I DIDN'T SEND IT, OK? AND I'LL TELL YOU WHY.
BECAUSE I'M GOING TO HAND IT TO HER MYSELF!
NO MAMES, COMPA. YOU PROBABLY DIDN'T EVEN HAVE ONE PRINTED FOR HER.
OH YEAH? I'VE GOT IT RIGHT HERE.
SEE? I'M GOING TO WALK RIGHT UP TO HER AFTER SCHOOL AND GIVE IT TO HER.

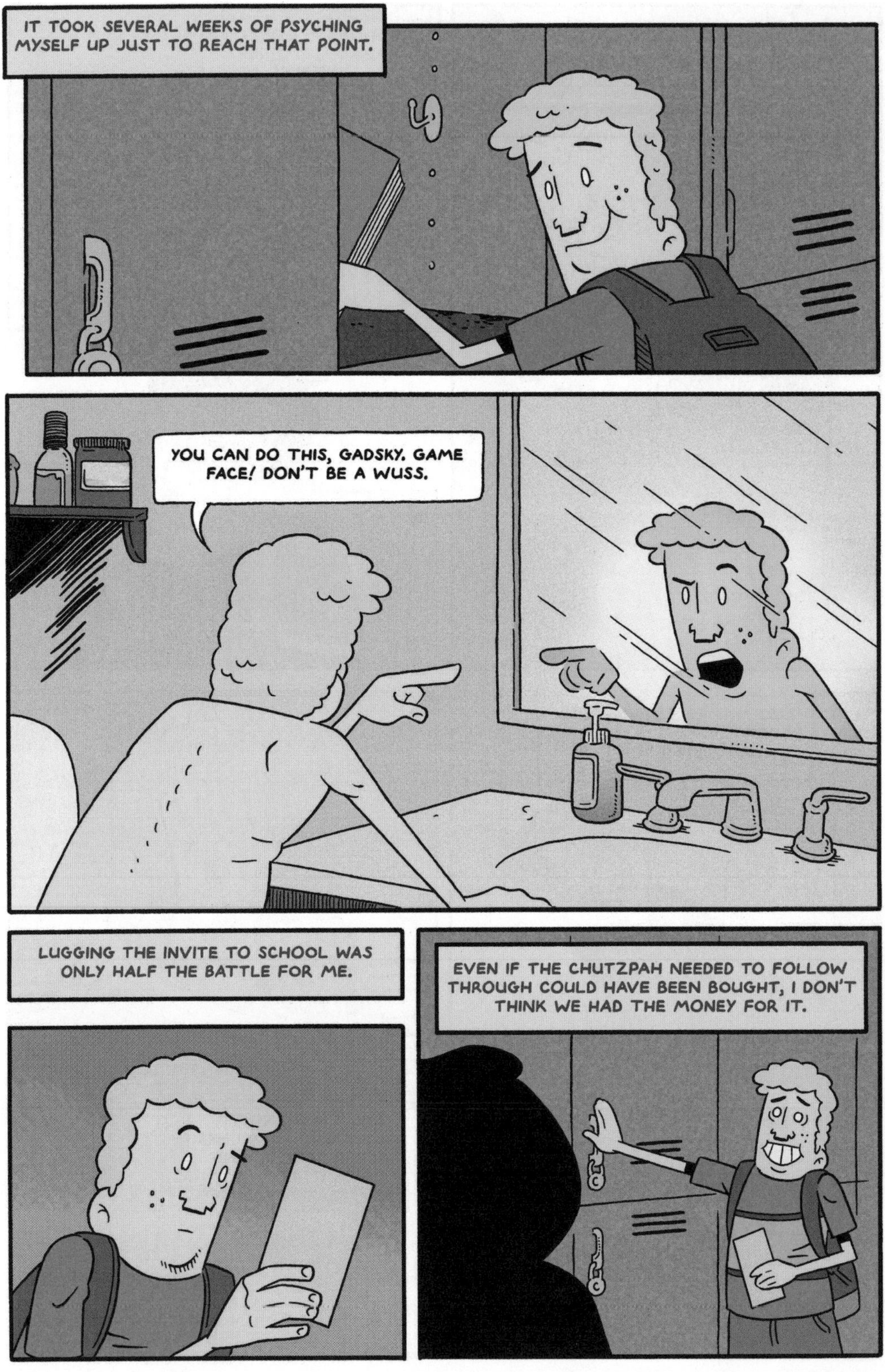
IT TOOK SEVERAL WEEKS OF PSYCHING MYSELF UP JUST TO REACH THAT POINT.
YOU CAN DO THIS, GADSKY. GAME FACE! DON'T BE A WUSS.
LUGGING THE INVITE TO SCHOOL WAS ONLY HALF THE BATTLE FOR ME.
EVEN IF THE CHUTZPAH NEEDED TO FOLLOW THROUGH COULD HAVE BEEN BOUGHT, I DON'T THINK WE HAD THE MONEY FOR IT.

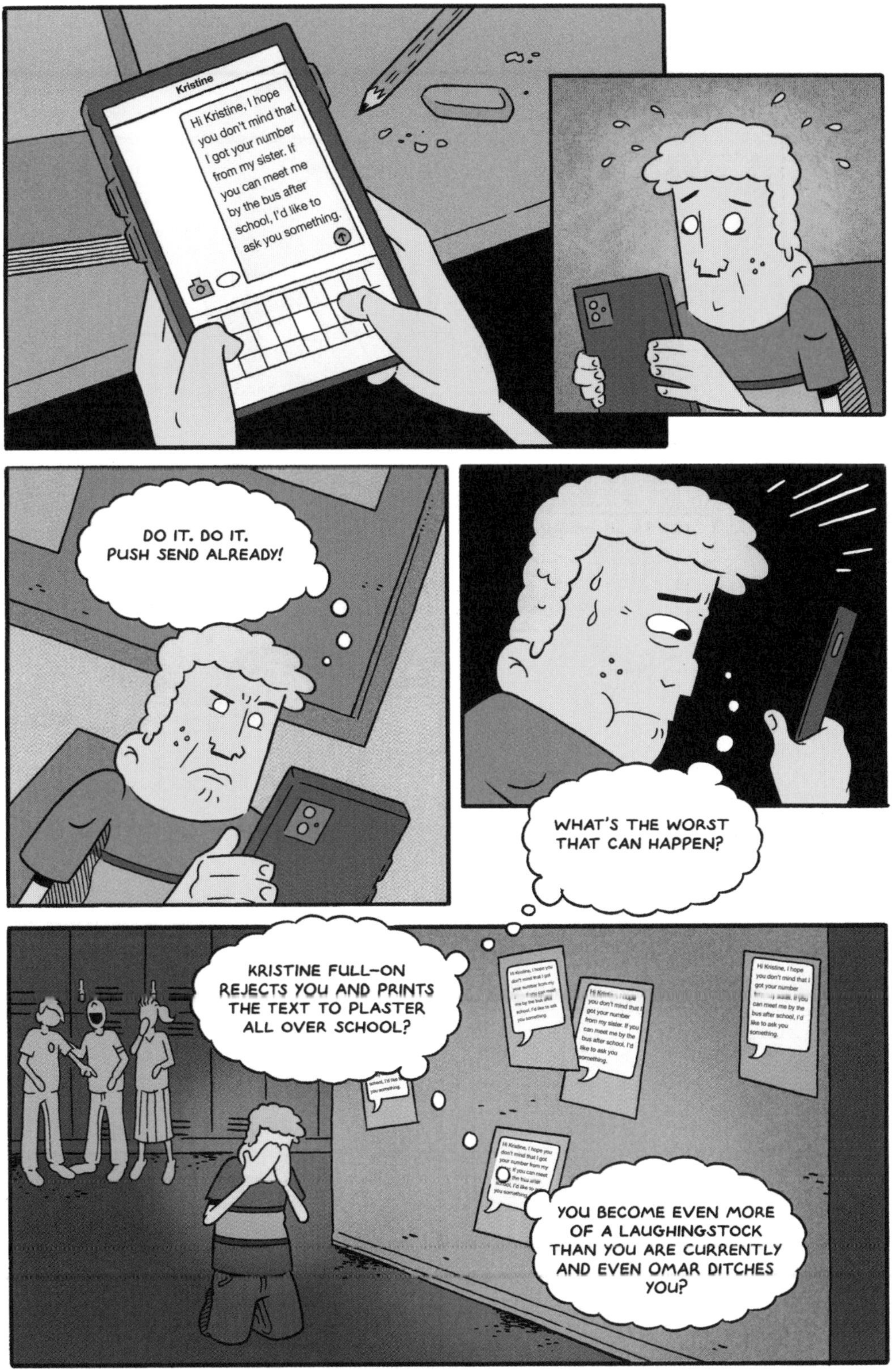
Kristine
Hi Kristine, I hope you don't mind that I got your number from my sister. If you can meet me by the bus after school, I'd like to ask you something.
DO IT. DO IT. PUSH SEND ALREADY!
WHAT'S THE WORST THAT CAN HAPPEN?
KRISTINE FULL-ON REJECTS YOU AND PRINTS THE TEXT TO PLASTER ALL OVER SCHOOL?
YOU BECOME EVEN MORE OF A LAUGHINGSTOCK THAN YOU ARE CURRENTLY AND EVEN OMAR DITCHES YOU?

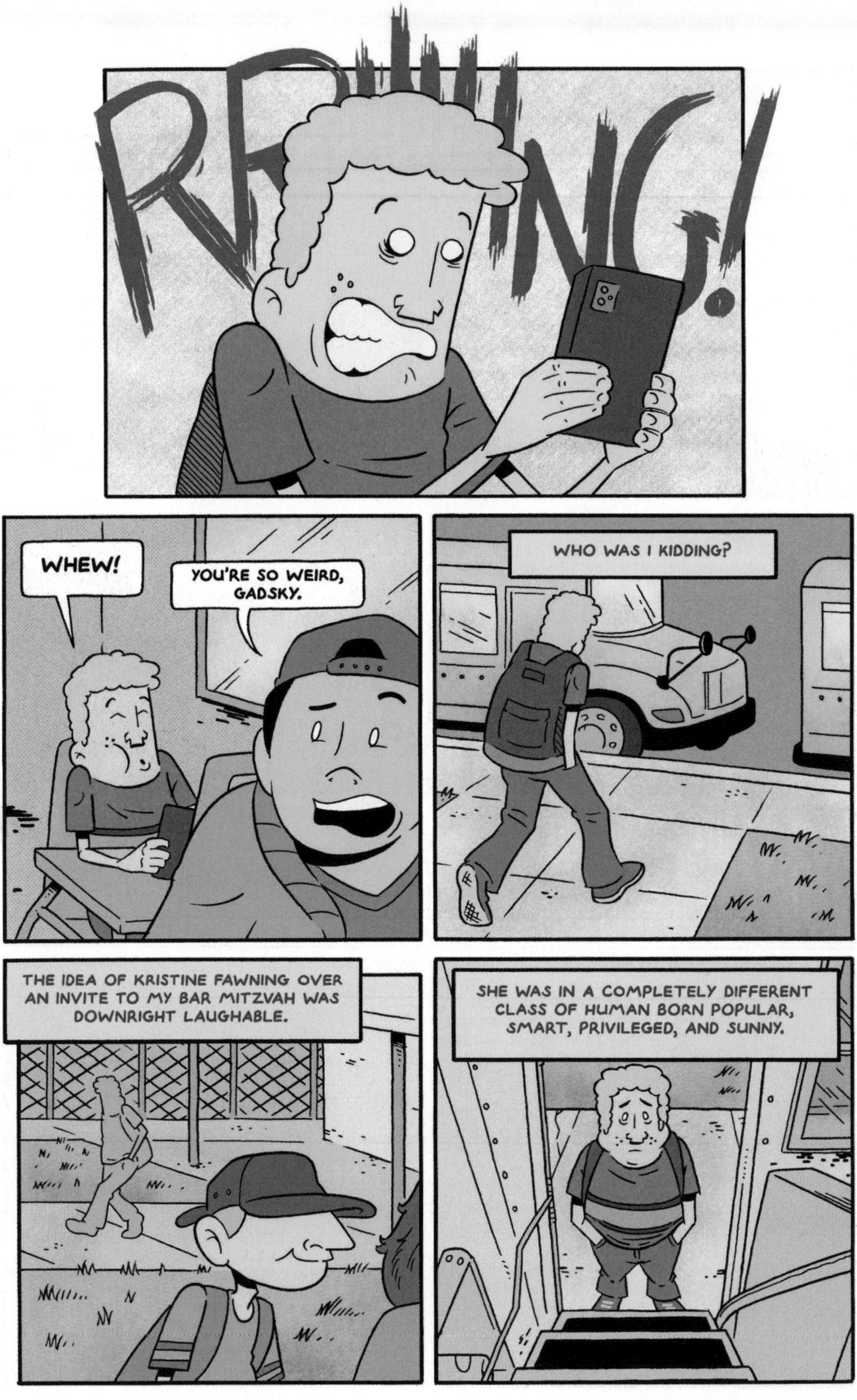
WHEW!
YOU'RE SO WEIRD, GADSKY.
WHO WAS I KIDDING?
THE IDEA OF KRISTINE FAWNING OVER AN INVITE TO MY BAR MITZVAH WAS DOWNRIGHT LAUGHABLE.
SHE WAS IN A COMPLETELY DIFFERENT CLASS OF HUMAN BORN POPULAR, SMART, PRIVILEGED, AND SUNNY.

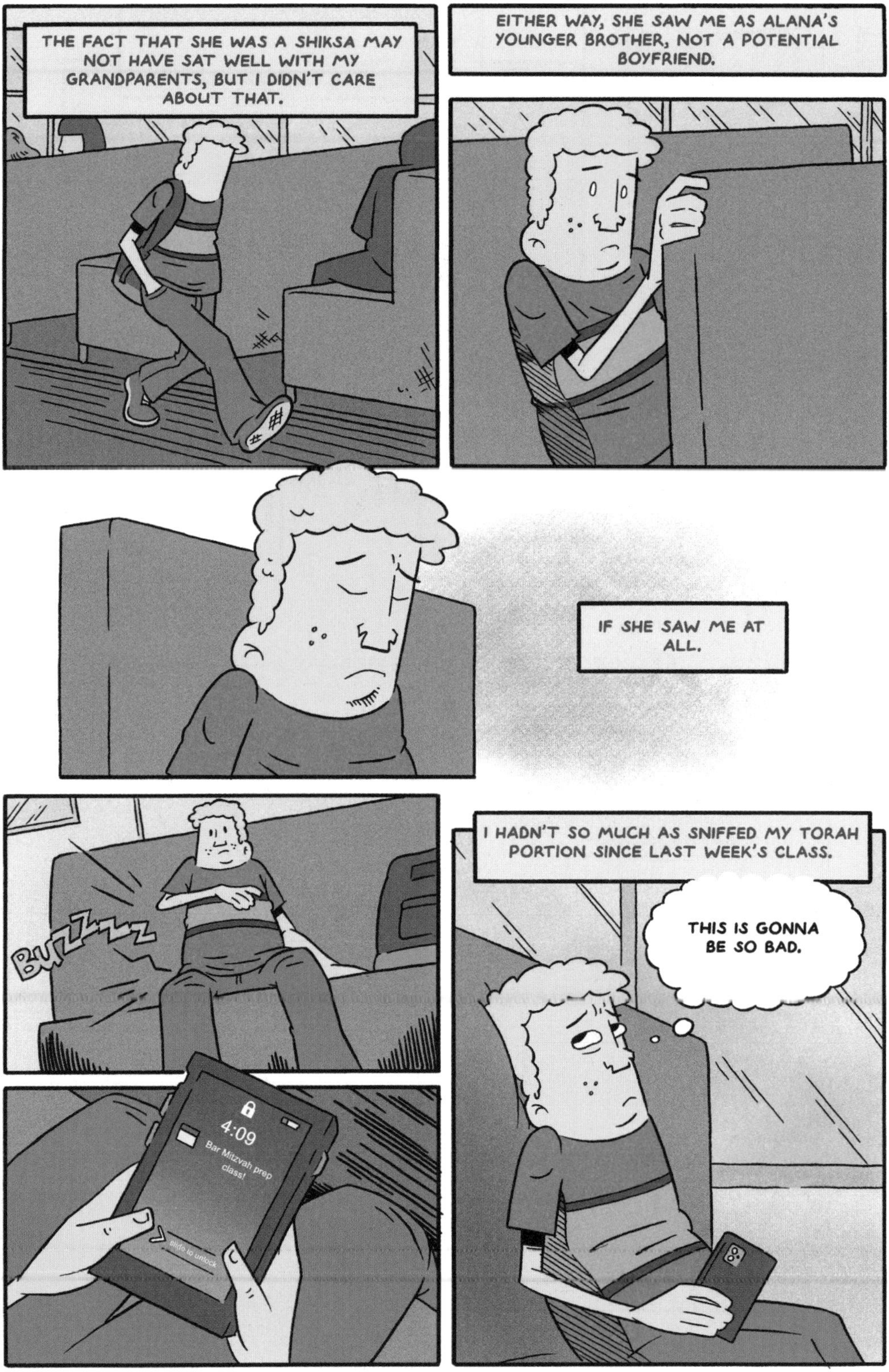

THE FACT THAT SHE WAS A SHIKSA MAY NOT HAVE SAT WELL WITH MY GRANDPARENTS, BUT I DIDN'T CARE ABOUT THAT.
EITHER WAY, SHE SAW ME AS ALANA'S YOUNGER BROTHER, NOT A POTENTIAL BOYFRIEND.
IF SHE SAW ME AT ALL.
BUZZZZZ
4:09
Bar Mitzvah prep class!
slide to unlock
I HADN'T SO MUCH AS SNIFFED MY TORAH PORTION SINCE LAST WEEK'S CLASS.
THIS IS GONNA BE SO BAD.

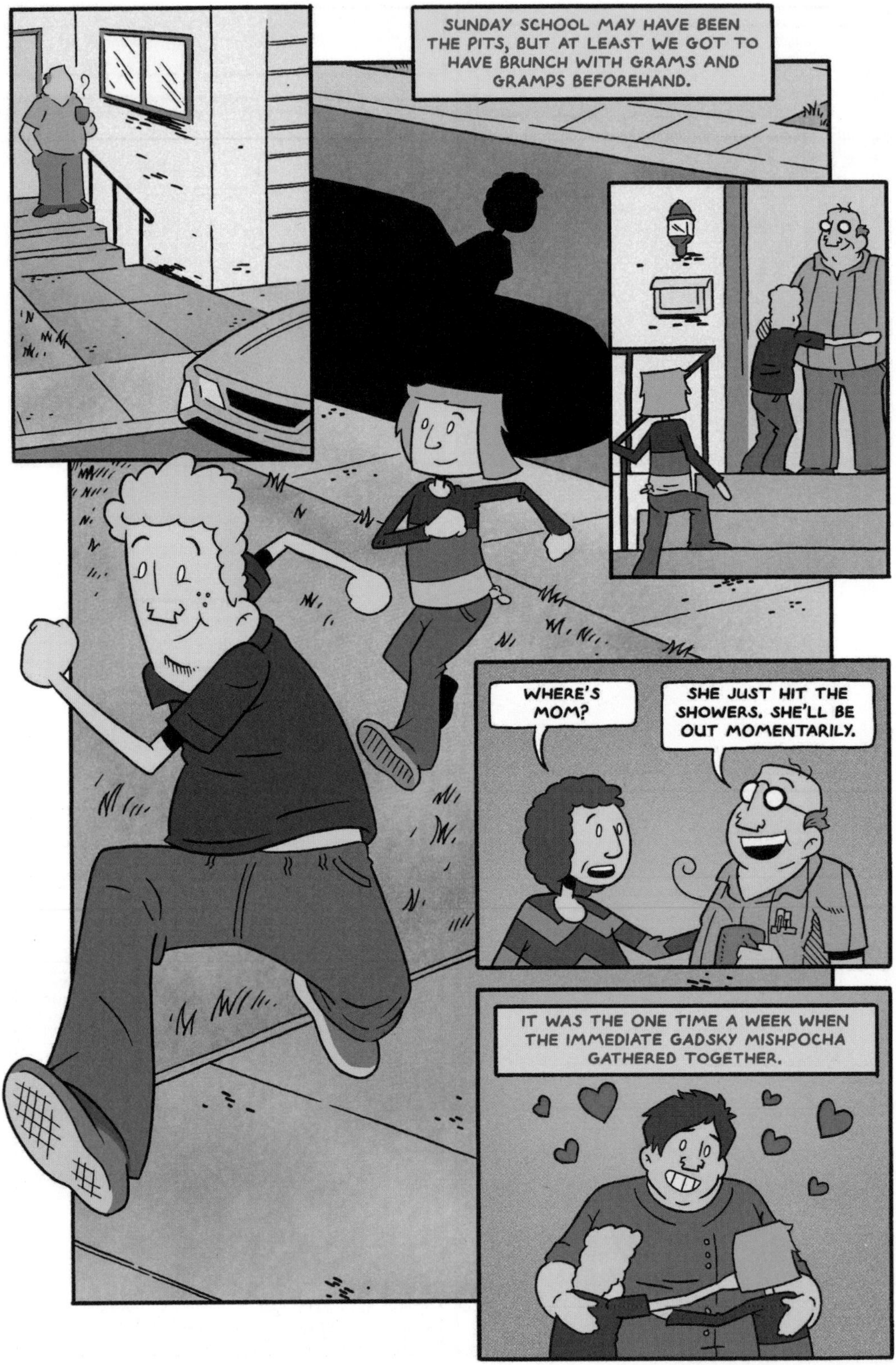
SUNDAY SCHOOL MAY HAVE BEEN THE PITS, BUT AT LEAST WE GOT TO HAVE BRUNCH WITH GRAMS AND GRAMPS BEFOREHAND.
?
WHERE'S MOM?
SHE JUST HIT THE SHOWERS. SHE'LL BE OUT MOMENTARILY.
IT WAS THE ONE TIME A WEEK WHEN THE IMMEDIATE GADSKY MISHPOCHA GATHERED TOGETHER.

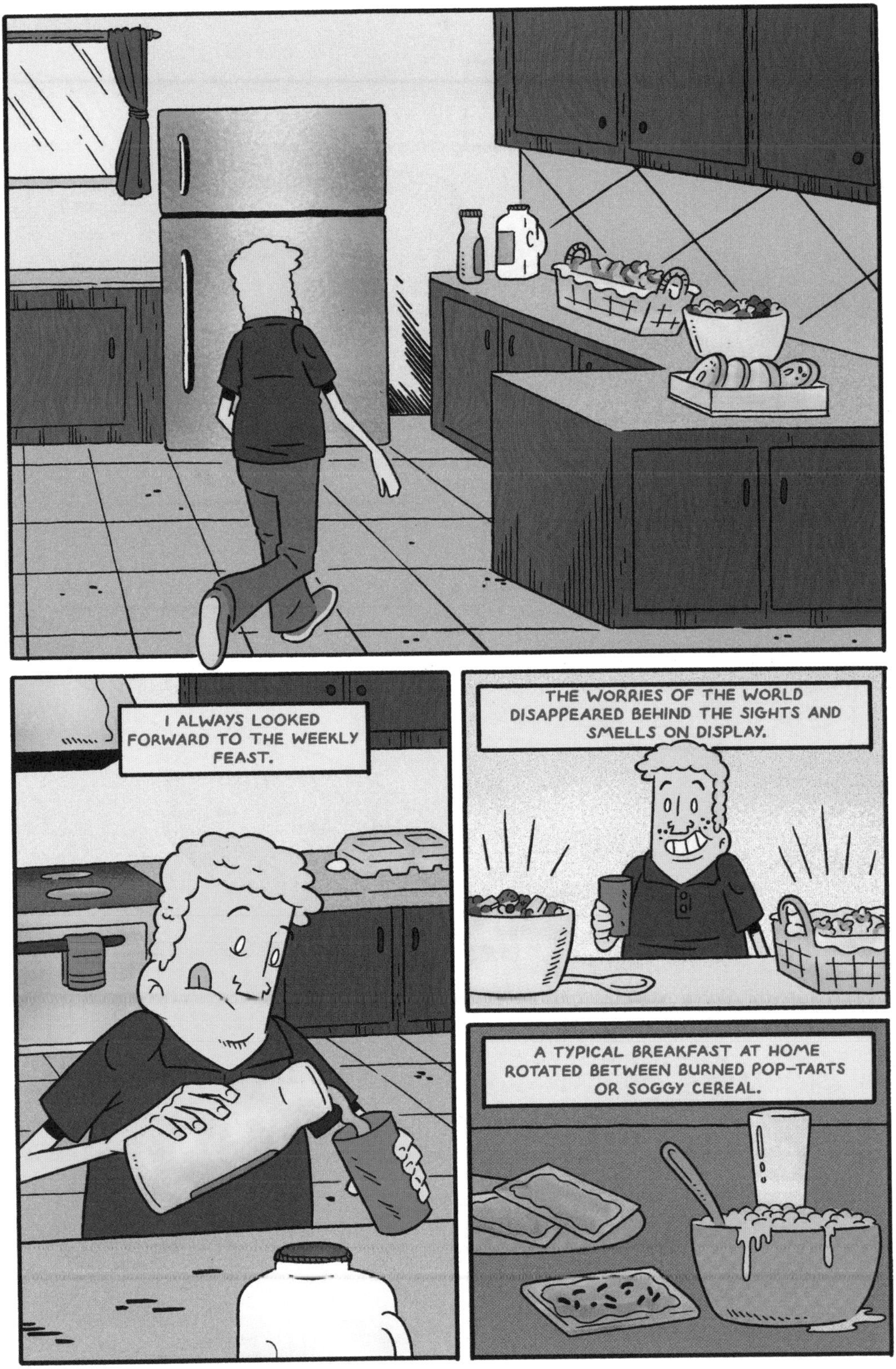
I ALWAYS LOOKED FORWARD TO THE WEEKLY FEAST.
THE WORRIES OF THE WORLD DISAPPEARED BEHIND THE SIGHTS AND SMELLS ON DISPLAY.
A TYPICAL BREAKFAST AT HOME ROTATED BETWEEN BURNED POP-TARTS OR SOGGY CEREAL.

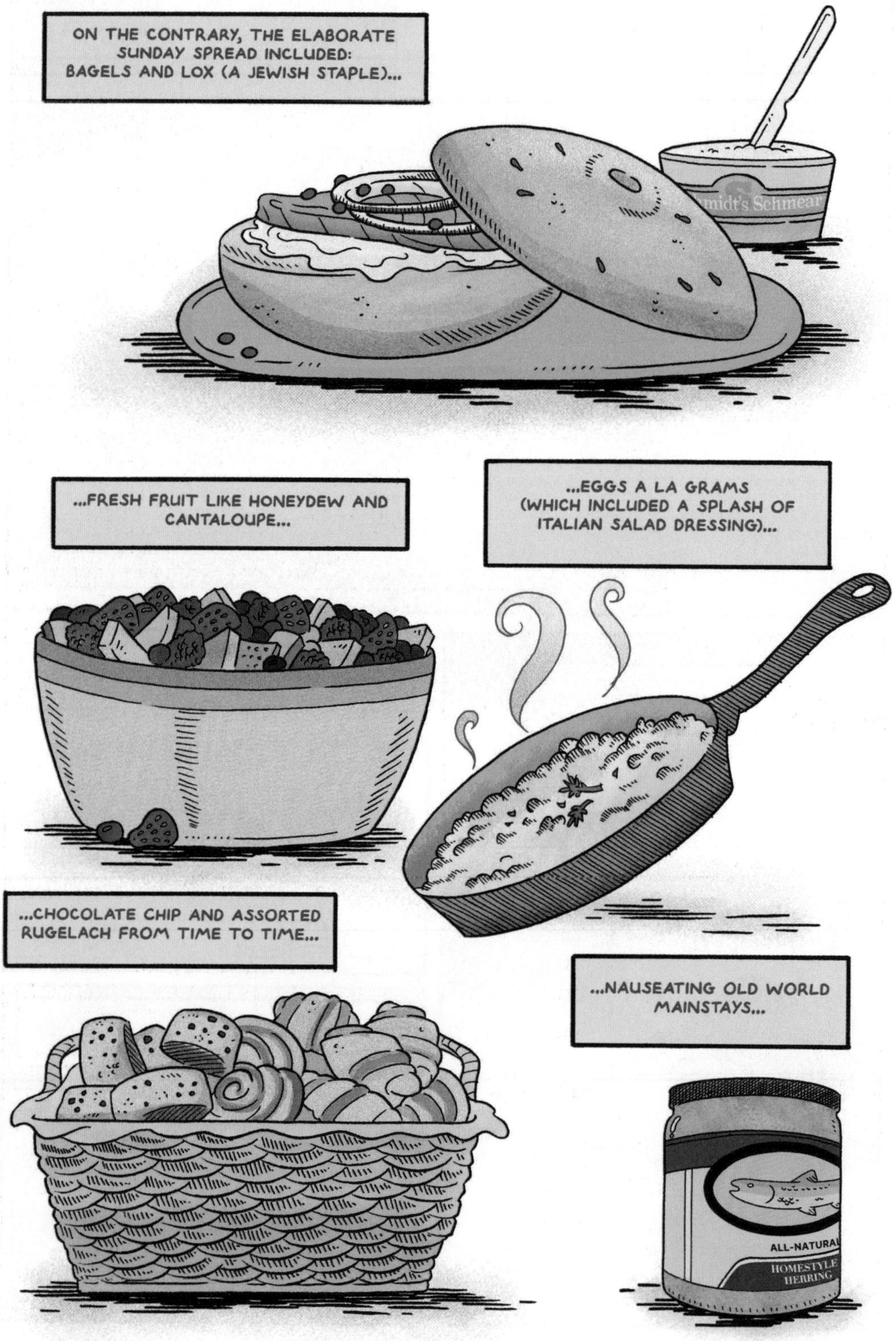
ON THE CONTRARY, THE ELABORATE SUNDAY SPREAD INCLUDED: BAGELS AND LOX (A JEWISH STAPLE)...
...FRESH FRUIT LIKE HONEYDEW AND CANTALOUPE...
...EGGS A LA GRAMS (WHICH INCLUDED A SPLASH OF ITALIAN SALAD DRESSING)...
...CHOCOLATE CHIP AND ASSORTED RUGELACH FROM TIME TO TIME...
...NAUSEATING OLD WORLD MAINSTAYS...
ALL-NATURAL
HOMESTYLE HERRING

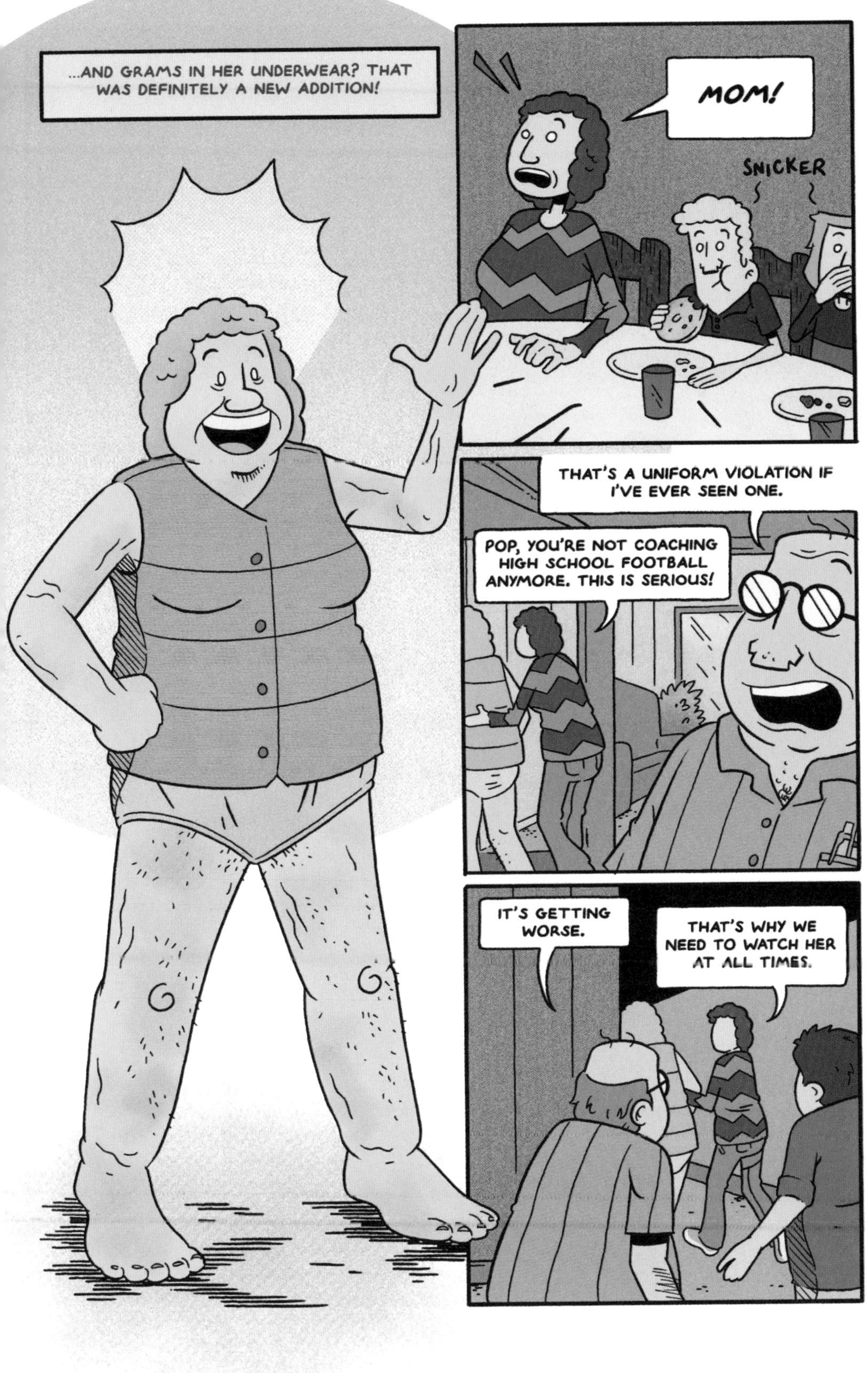
...AND GRAMS IN HER UNDERWEAR? THAT WAS DEFINITELY A NEW ADDITION!
MOM!
SNICKER
THAT'S A UNIFORM VIOLATION IF I'VE EVER SEEN ONE.
POP, YOU'RE NOT COACHING HIGH SCHOOL FOOTBALL ANYMORE. THIS IS SERIOUS!
IT'S GETTING WORSE.
THAT'S WHY WE NEED TO WATCH HER AT ALL TIMES.

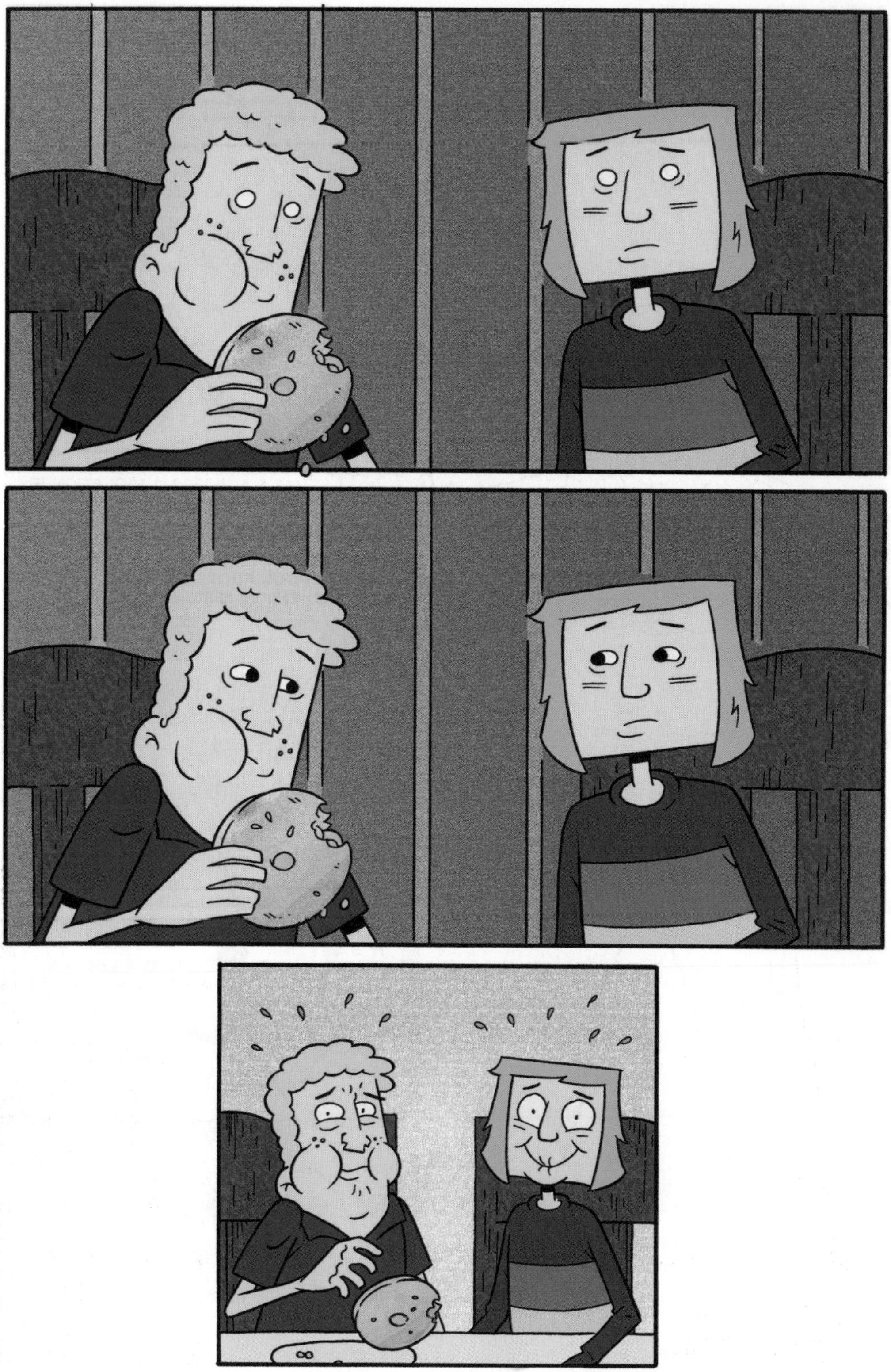

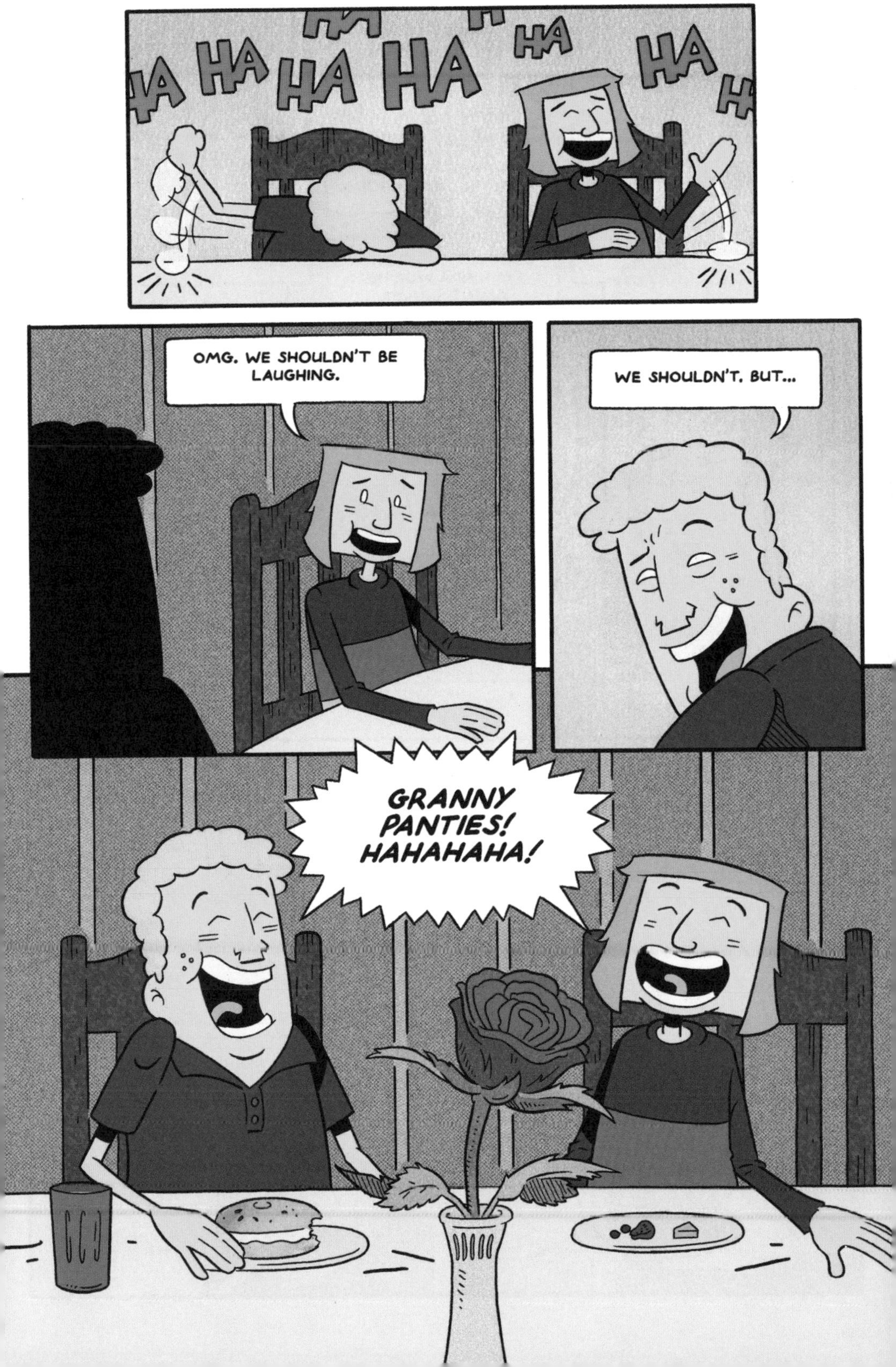
HA HA HA HA HA HA HA HA
OMG. WE SHOULDN'T BE LAUGHING.
WE SHOULDN'T. BUT...
GRANNY PANTIES! HAHAHAHA!

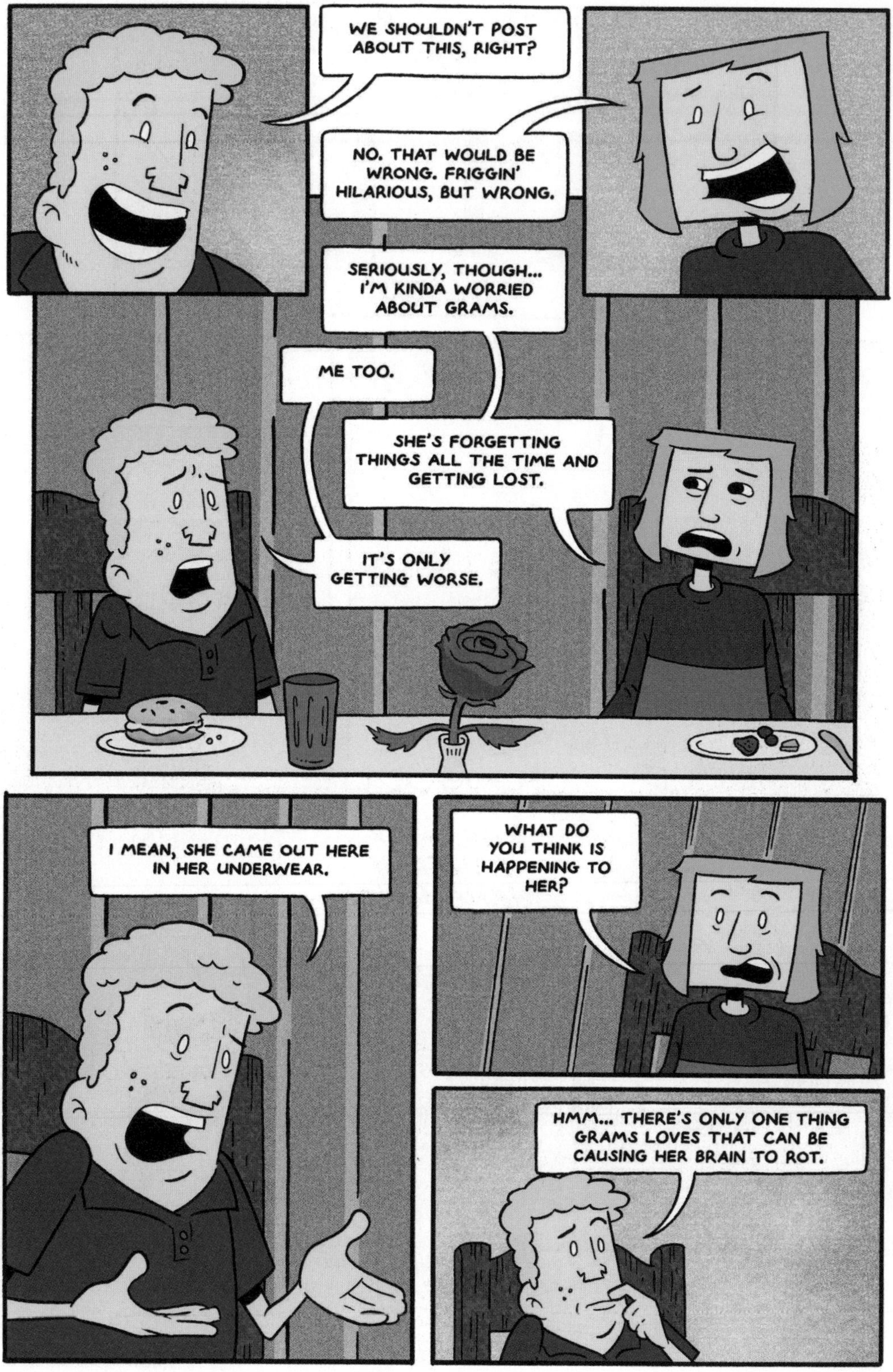
WE SHOULDN'T POST ABOUT THIS, RIGHT?
NO. THAT WOULD BE WRONG. FRIGGIN' HILARIOUS, BUT WRONG.
SERIOUSLY, THOUGH... I'M KINDA WORRIED ABOUT GRAMS.
ME TOO.
SHE'S FORGETTING THINGS ALL THE TIME AND GETTING LOST.
IT'S ONLY GETTING WORSE.
I MEAN, SHE CAME OUT HERE IN HER UNDERWEAR.
WHAT DO YOU THINK IS HAPPENING TO HER?
HMM... THERE'S ONLY ONE THING GRAMS LOVES THAT CAN BE CAUSING HER BRAIN TO ROT.

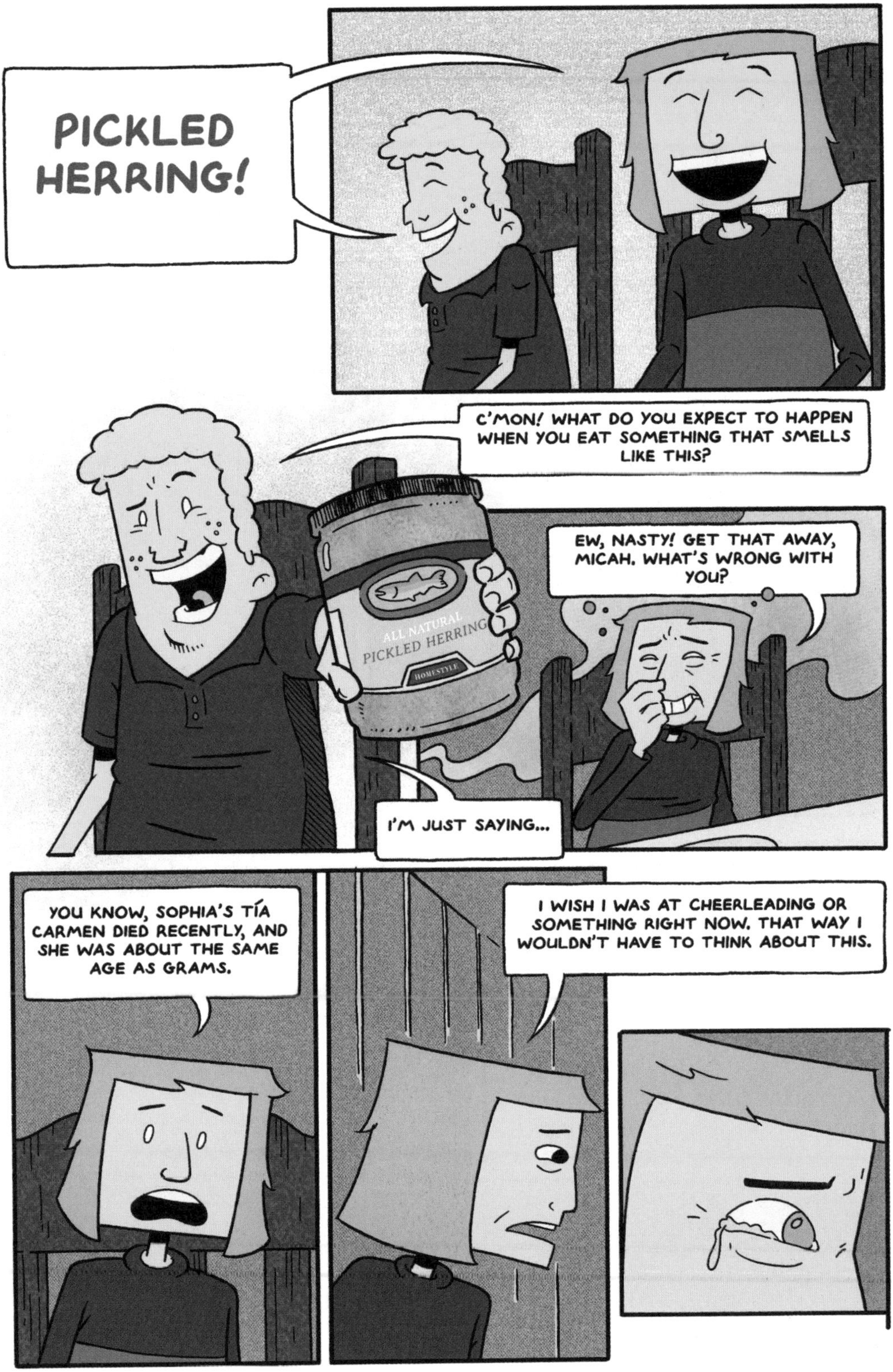

PICKLED HERRING!
C'MON! WHAT DO YOU EXPECT TO HAPPEN WHEN YOU EAT SOMETHING THAT SMELLS LIKE THIS?
ALL NATURAL PICKLED HERRING
HOMESTYLE
EW, NASTY! GET THAT AWAY, MICAH. WHAT'S WRONG WITH YOU?
I'M JUST SAYING...
YOU KNOW, SOPHIA'S TÍA CARMEN DIED RECENTLY, AND SHE WAS ABOUT THE SAME AGE AS GRAMS.
I WISH I WAS AT CHEERLEADING OR SOMETHING RIGHT NOW. THAT WAY I WOULDN'T HAVE TO THINK ABOUT THIS.

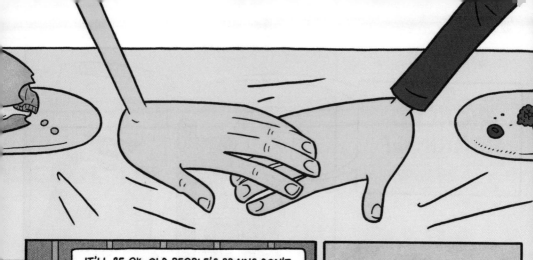

IT'LL BE OK. OLD PEOPLE'S BRAINS DON'T FUNCTION RIGHT SOMETIMES. SHE'S NOT DYING, SIS.

I DON'T KNOW WHY I SAID THAT. GRAMS MIGHT HAVE BEEN DYING FOR ALL I KNEW.

GROSS FOODS AND BRAIN FARTS WERE PART OF BEING OLD, BUT WE WERE IN UNCHARTED TERRITORY.

MISERY MIGHT LOVE COMPANY, BUT NONE OF US INVITED IT TO BRUNCH.

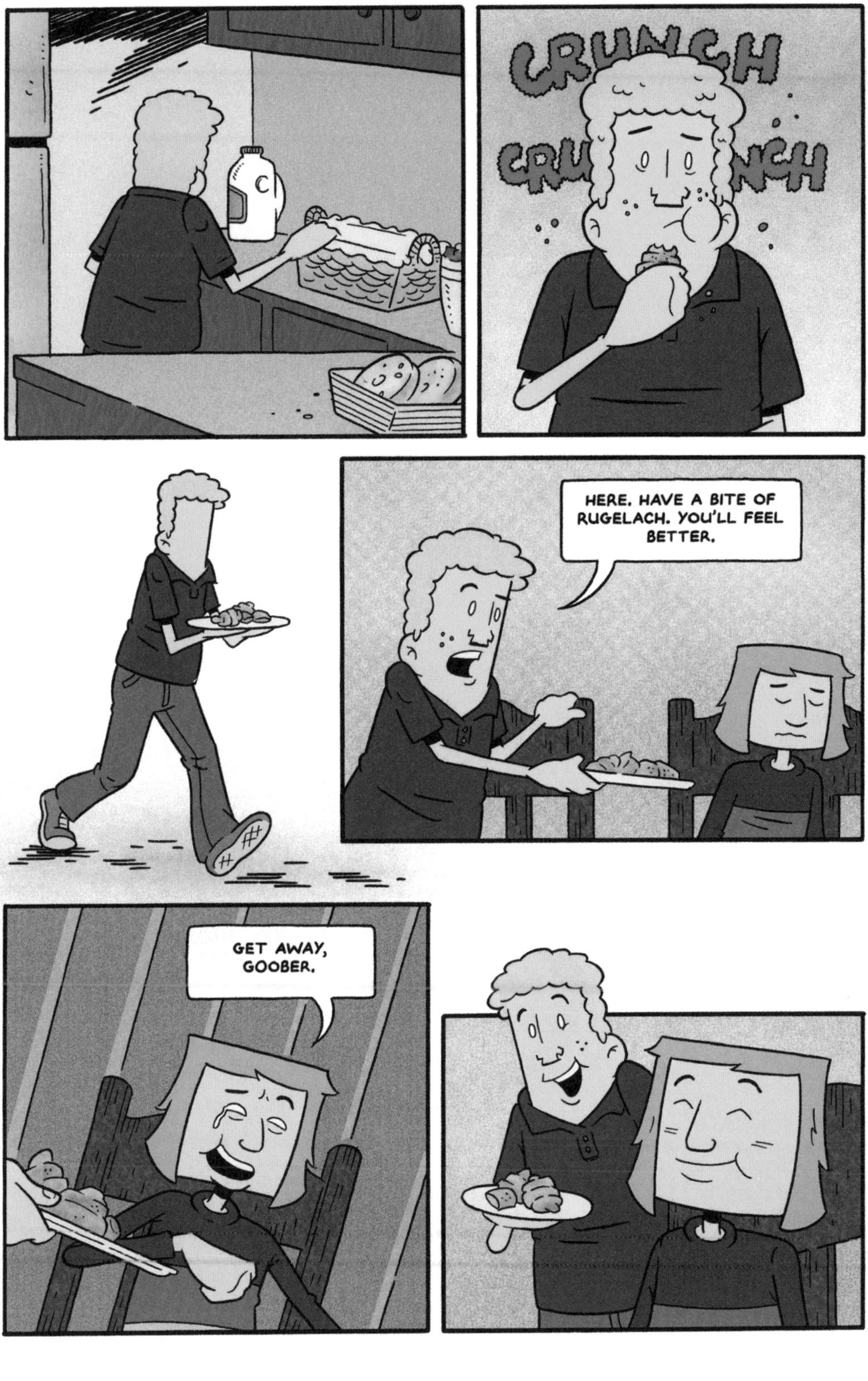
CRUNCH
CRUNCH
HERE. HAVE A BITE OF RUGELACH. YOU'LL FEEL BETTER.
GET AWAY, GOOBER.

PART 3

Hot Season

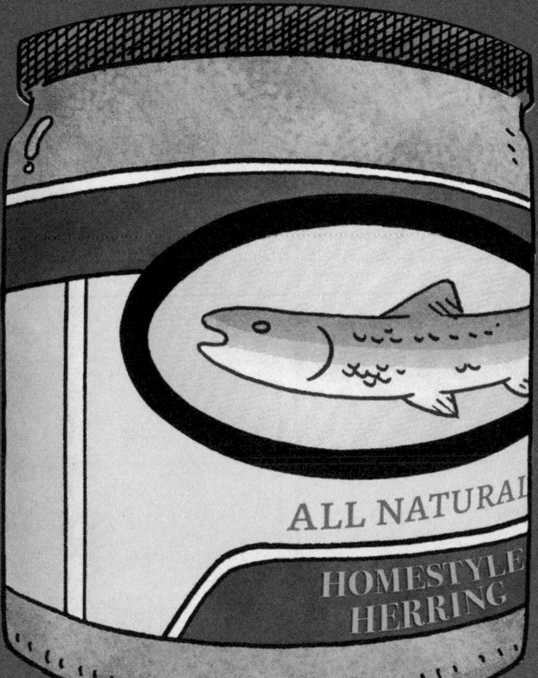
ALL NATURAL
HOMESTYLE
HERRING

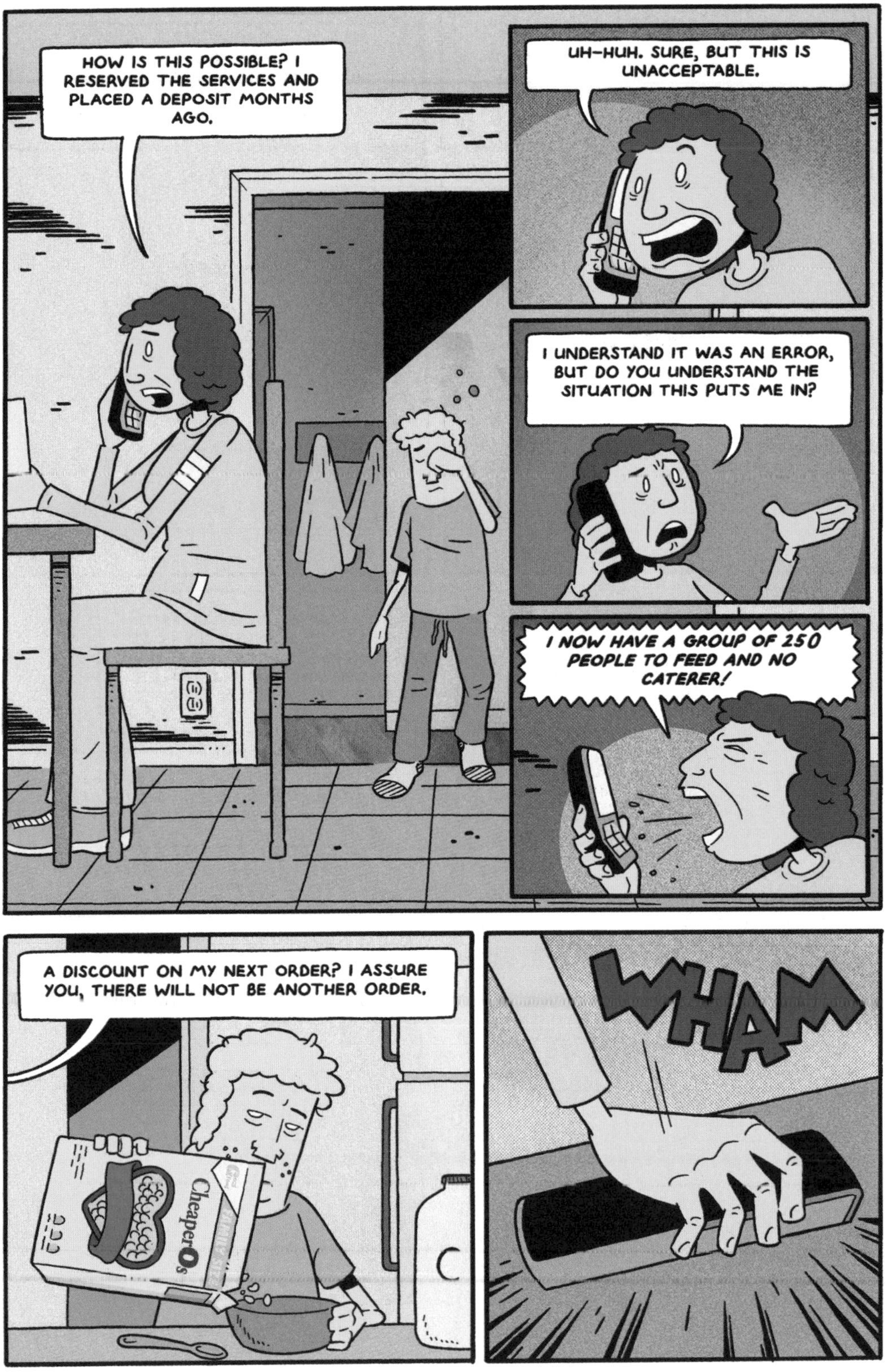
HOW IS THIS POSSIBLE? I RESERVED THE SERVICES AND PLACED A DEPOSIT MONTHS AGO.
UH-HUH. SURE, BUT THIS IS UNACCEPTABLE.
I UNDERSTAND IT WAS AN ERROR, BUT DO YOU UNDERSTAND THE SITUATION THIS PUTS ME IN?
I NOW HAVE A GROUP OF 250 PEOPLE TO FEED AND NO CATERER!
A DISCOUNT ON MY NEXT ORDER? I ASSURE YOU, THERE WILL NOT BE ANOTHER ORDER.
CheaperOs
WHAM

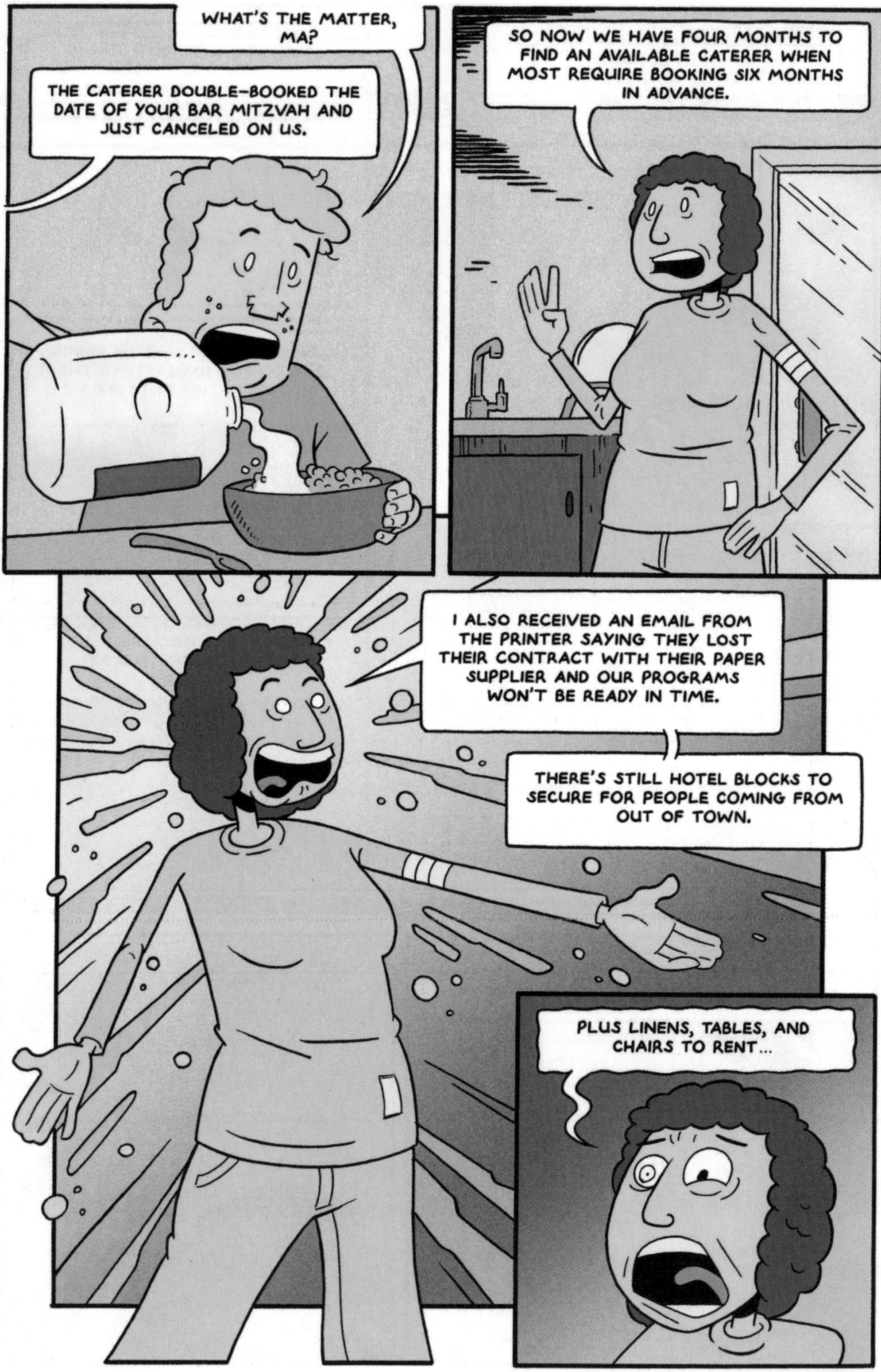
WHAT'S THE MATTER, MA?
THE CATERER DOUBLE-BOOKED THE DATE OF YOUR BAR MITZVAH AND JUST CANCELED ON US.
SO NOW WE HAVE FOUR MONTHS TO FIND AN AVAILABLE CATERER WHEN MOST REQUIRE BOOKING SIX MONTHS IN ADVANCE.
I ALSO RECEIVED AN EMAIL FROM THE PRINTER SAYING THEY LOST THEIR CONTRACT WITH THEIR PAPER SUPPLIER AND OUR PROGRAMS WON'T BE READY IN TIME.
THERE'S STILL HOTEL BLOCKS TO SECURE FOR PEOPLE COMING FROM OUT OF TOWN.
PLUS LINENS, TABLES, AND CHAIRS TO RENT...

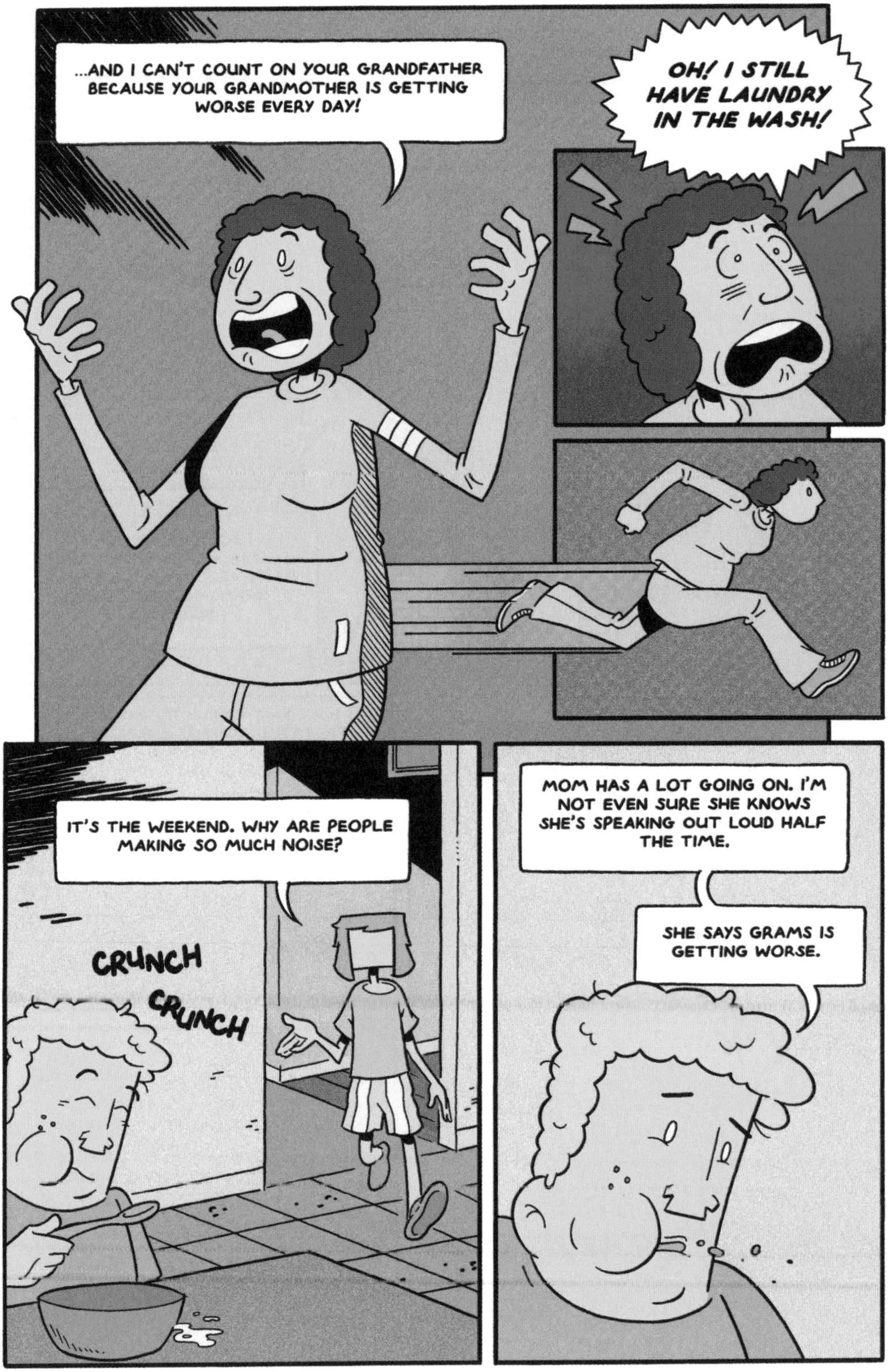
...AND I CAN'T COUNT ON YOUR GRANDFATHER BECAUSE YOUR GRANDMOTHER IS GETTING WORSE EVERY DAY!
OH! I STILL HAVE LAUNDRY IN THE WASH!
IT'S THE WEEKEND. WHY ARE PEOPLE MAKING SO MUCH NOISE?
CRUNCH
CRUNCH
MOM HAS A LOT GOING ON. I'M NOT EVEN SURE SHE KNOWS SHE'S SPEAKING OUT LOUD HALF THE TIME.
SHE SAYS GRAMS IS GETTING WORSE.

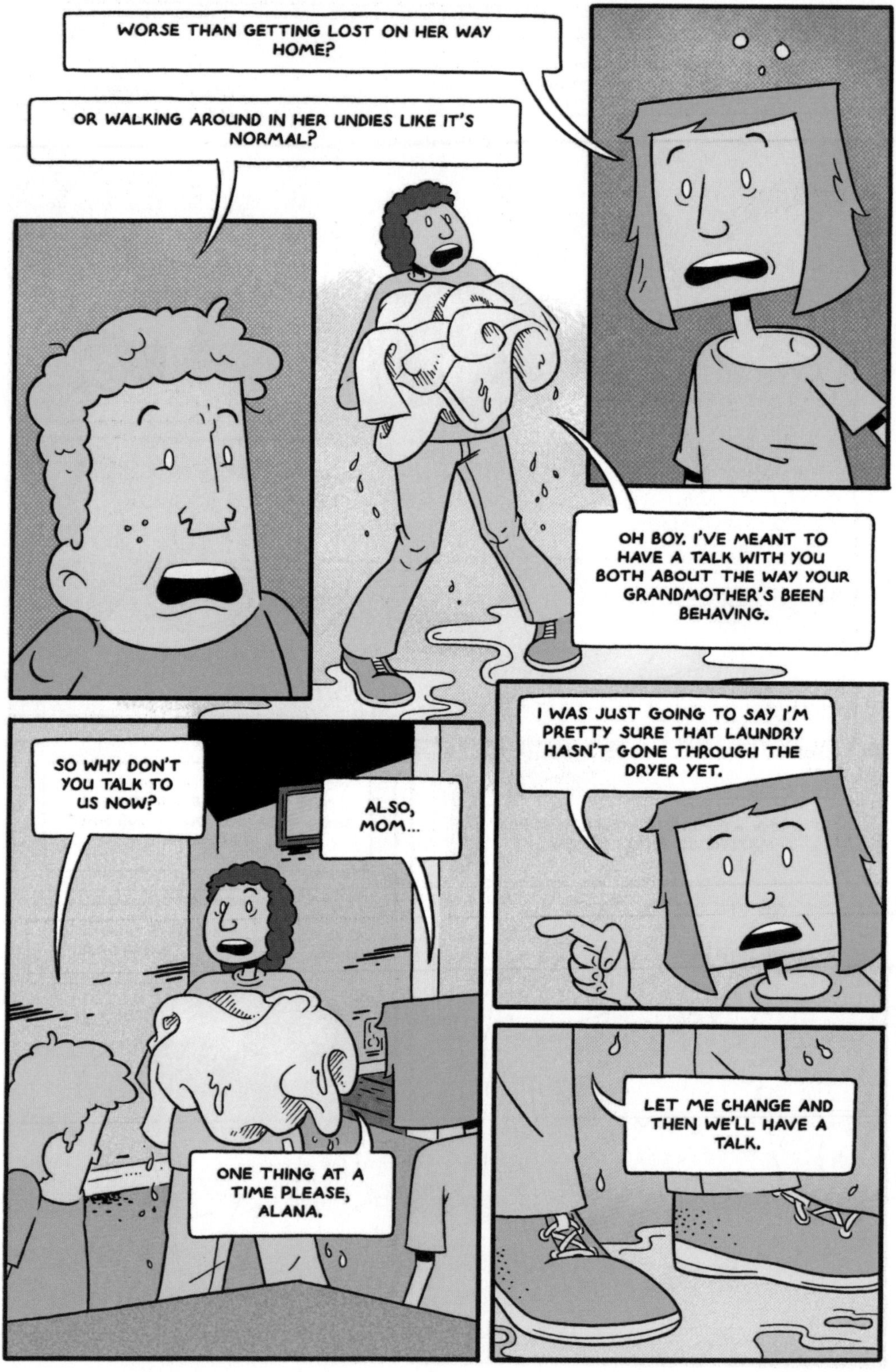
WORSE THAN GETTING LOST ON HER WAY HOME?
OR WALKING AROUND IN HER UNDIES LIKE IT'S NORMAL?
OH BOY. I'VE MEANT TO HAVE A TALK WITH YOU BOTH ABOUT THE WAY YOUR GRANDMOTHER'S BEEN BEHAVING.
SO WHY DON'T YOU TALK TO US NOW?
ALSO, MOM...
ONE THING AT A TIME PLEASE, ALANA.
I WAS JUST GOING TO SAY I'M PRETTY SURE THAT LAUNDRY HASN'T GONE THROUGH THE DRYER YET.
LET ME CHANGE AND THEN WE'LL HAVE A TALK.

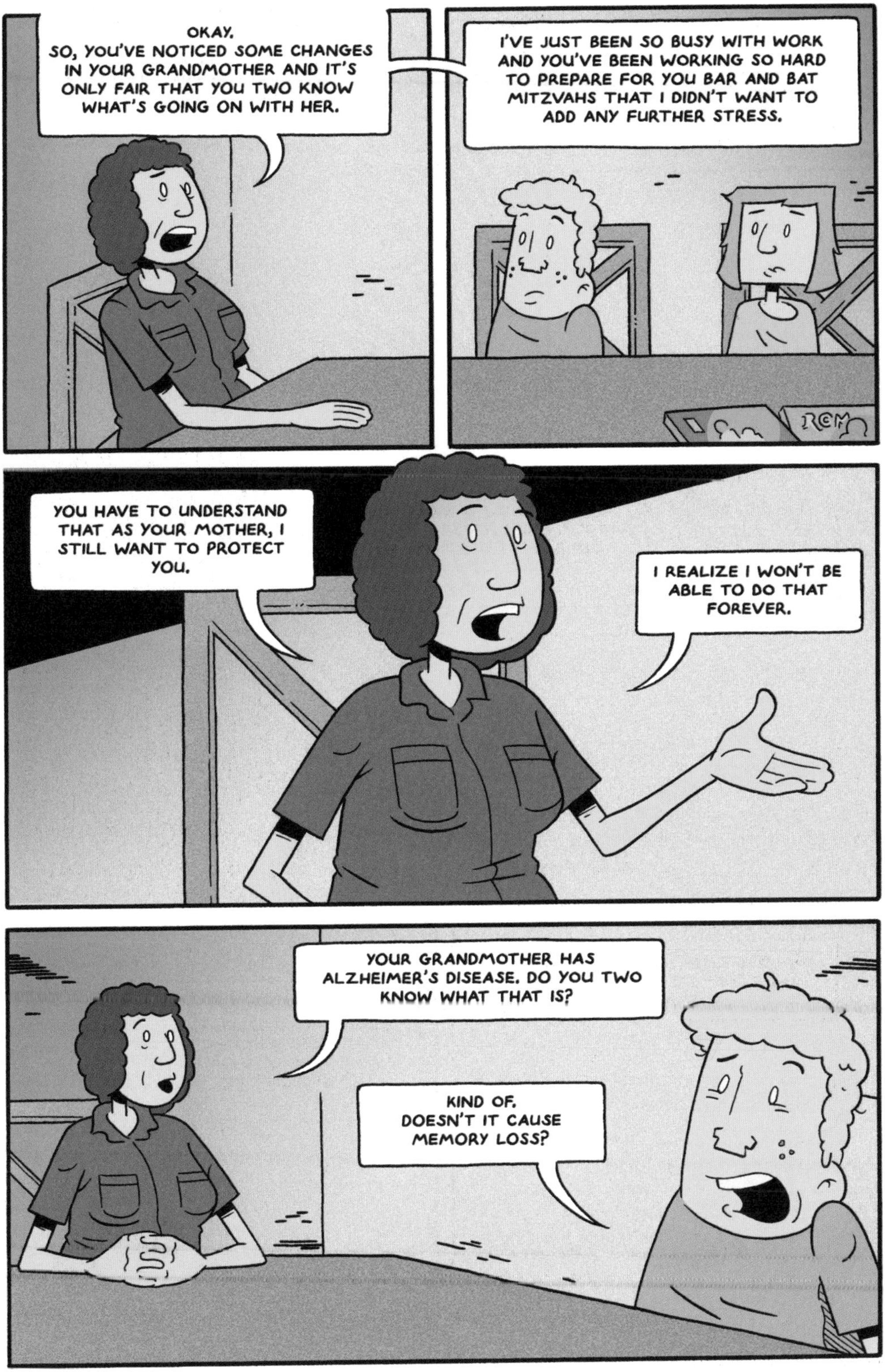
OKAY. SO, YOU'VE NOTICED SOME CHANGES IN YOUR GRANDMOTHER AND IT'S ONLY FAIR THAT YOU TWO KNOW WHAT'S GOING ON WITH HER.
I'VE JUST BEEN SO BUSY WITH WORK AND YOU'VE BEEN WORKING SO HARD TO PREPARE FOR YOU BAR AND BAT MITZVAHS THAT I DIDN'T WANT TO ADD ANY FURTHER STRESS.
YOU HAVE TO UNDERSTAND THAT AS YOUR MOTHER, I STILL WANT TO PROTECT YOU.
I REALIZE I WON'T BE ABLE TO DO THAT FOREVER.
YOUR GRANDMOTHER HAS ALZHEIMER'S DISEASE. DO YOU TWO KNOW WHAT THAT IS?
KIND OF. DOESN'T IT CAUSE MEMORY LOSS?

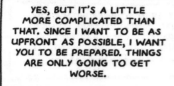

YES, BUT IT'S A LITTLE MORE COMPLICATED THAN THAT. SINCE I WANT TO BE AS UPFRONT AS POSSIBLE, I WANT YOU TO BE PREPARED. THINGS ARE ONLY GOING TO GET WORSE.

THE DOCTORS CAN'T GIVE US AN EXACT TIMEFRAME, BUT OVER THE NEXT FEW MONTHS TO A YEAR GRANDMA IS GOING TO BE VERY DIFFERENT.

I DON'T KNOW EVERYTHING ABOUT THE DISEASE, BUT ARE THERE ANY QUESTIONS YOU TWO WANT TO ASK RIGHT NOW?

WHAT CAUSED THIS TO HAPPEN? WAS IT SOMETHING GRAMS ATE?

NO ONE'S REALLY SURE WHAT CAUSES IT, BUT IT'S CERTAINLY NOT SOMETHING GRANDMA DID OR DIDN'T DO.

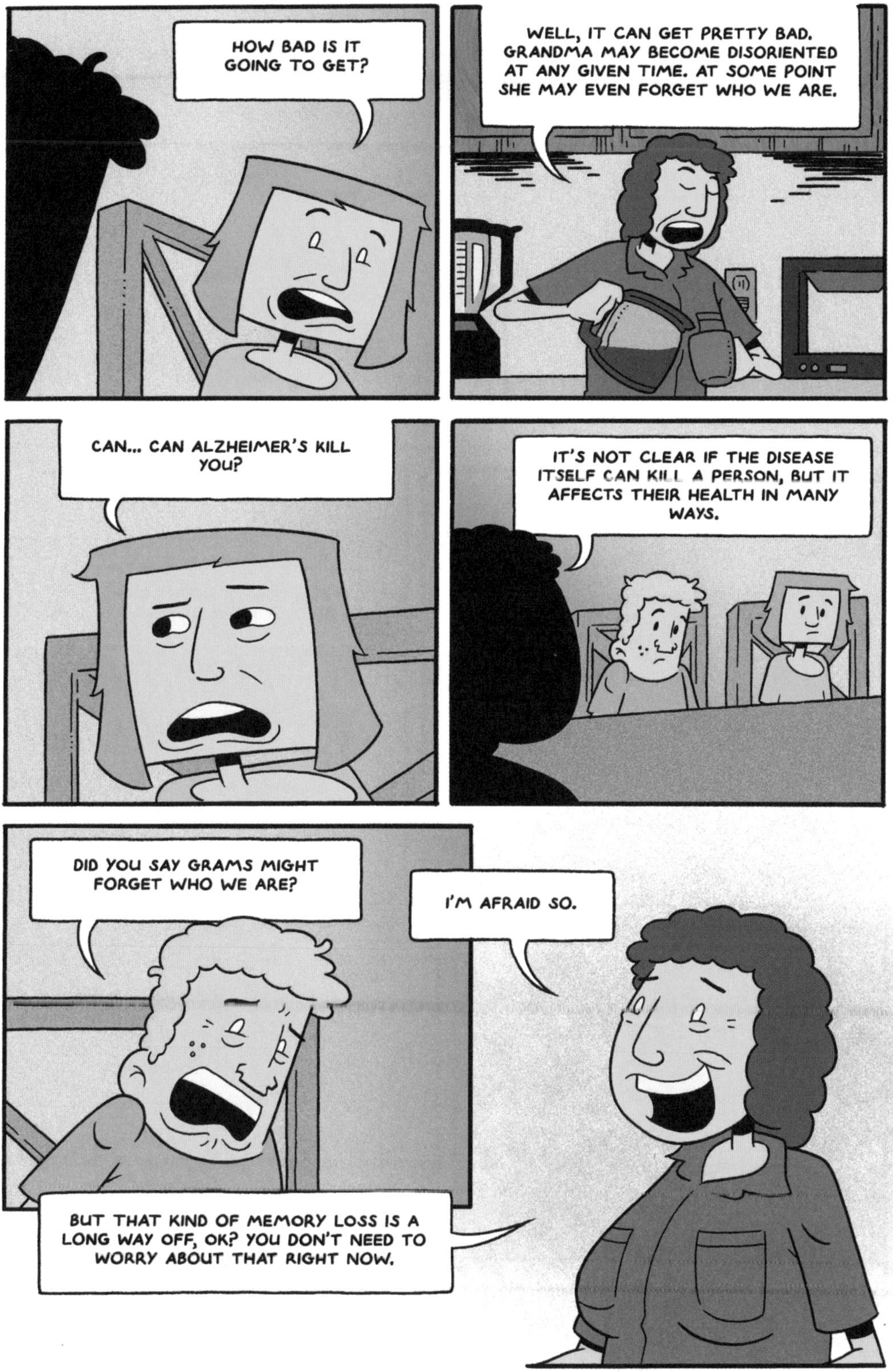
HOW BAD IS IT GOING TO GET?
WELL, IT CAN GET PRETTY BAD. GRANDMA MAY BECOME DISORIENTED AT ANY GIVEN TIME. AT SOME POINT SHE MAY EVEN FORGET WHO WE ARE.
CAN... CAN ALZHEIMER'S KILL YOU?
IT'S NOT CLEAR IF THE DISEASE ITSELF CAN KILL A PERSON, BUT IT AFFECTS THEIR HEALTH IN MANY WAYS.
DID YOU SAY GRAMS MIGHT FORGET WHO WE ARE?
I'M AFRAID SO.
BUT THAT KIND OF MEMORY LOSS IS A LONG WAY OFF, OK? YOU DON'T NEED TO WORRY ABOUT THAT RIGHT NOW.

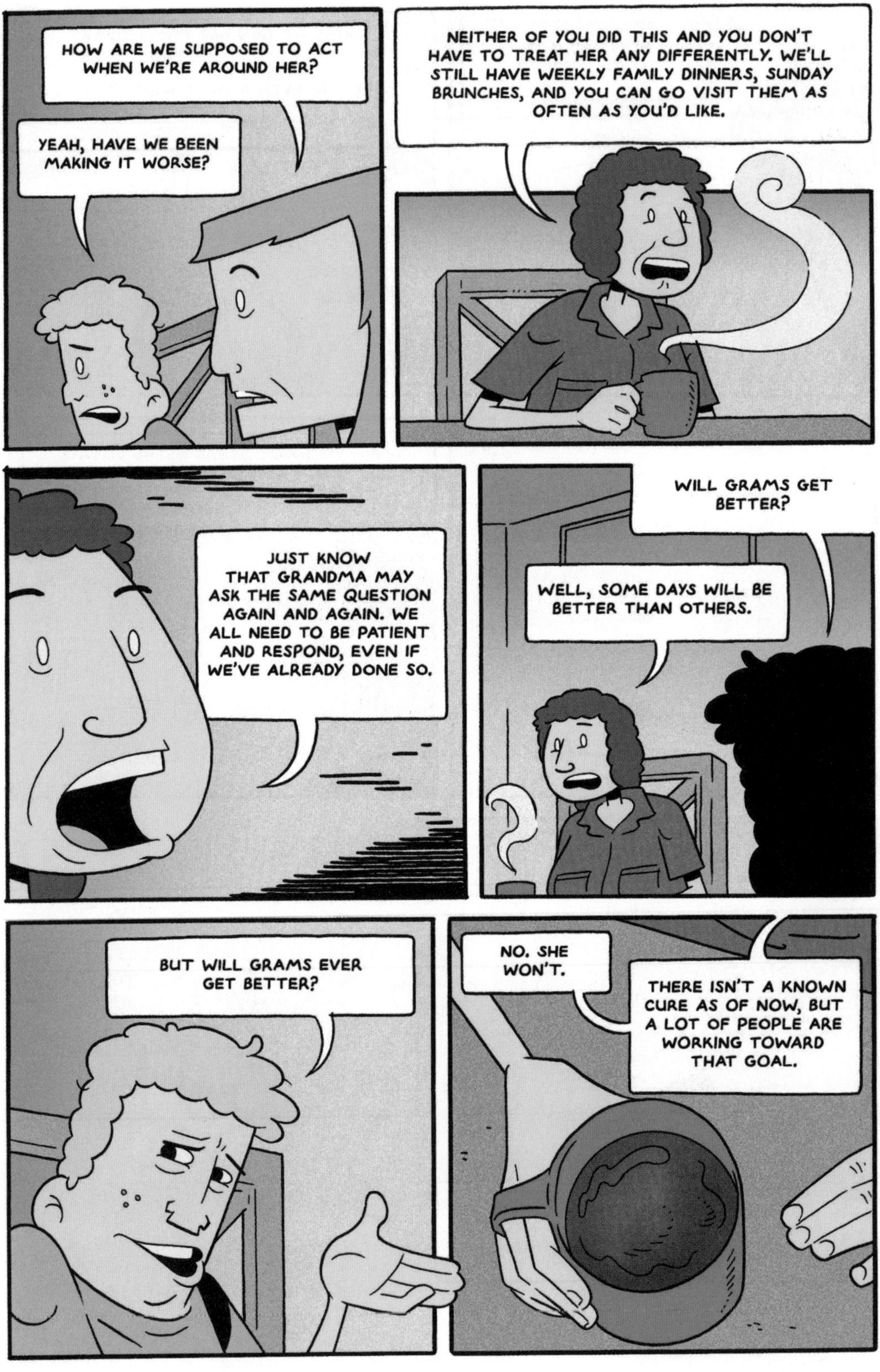
HOW ARE WE SUPPOSED TO ACT WHEN WE'RE AROUND HER?
YEAH, HAVE WE BEEN MAKING IT WORSE?
NEITHER OF YOU DID THIS AND YOU DON'T HAVE TO TREAT HER ANY DIFFERENTLY. WE'LL STILL HAVE WEEKLY FAMILY DINNERS, SUNDAY BRUNCHES, AND YOU CAN GO VISIT THEM AS OFTEN AS YOU'D LIKE.
JUST KNOW THAT GRANDMA MAY ASK THE SAME QUESTION AGAIN AND AGAIN. WE ALL NEED TO BE PATIENT AND RESPOND, EVEN IF WE'VE ALREADY DONE SO.
WILL GRAMS GET BETTER?
WELL, SOME DAYS WILL BE BETTER THAN OTHERS.
BUT WILL GRAMS EVER GET BETTER?
NO. SHE WON'T.
THERE ISN'T A KNOWN CURE AS OF NOW, BUT A LOT OF PEOPLE ARE WORKING TOWARD THAT GOAL.

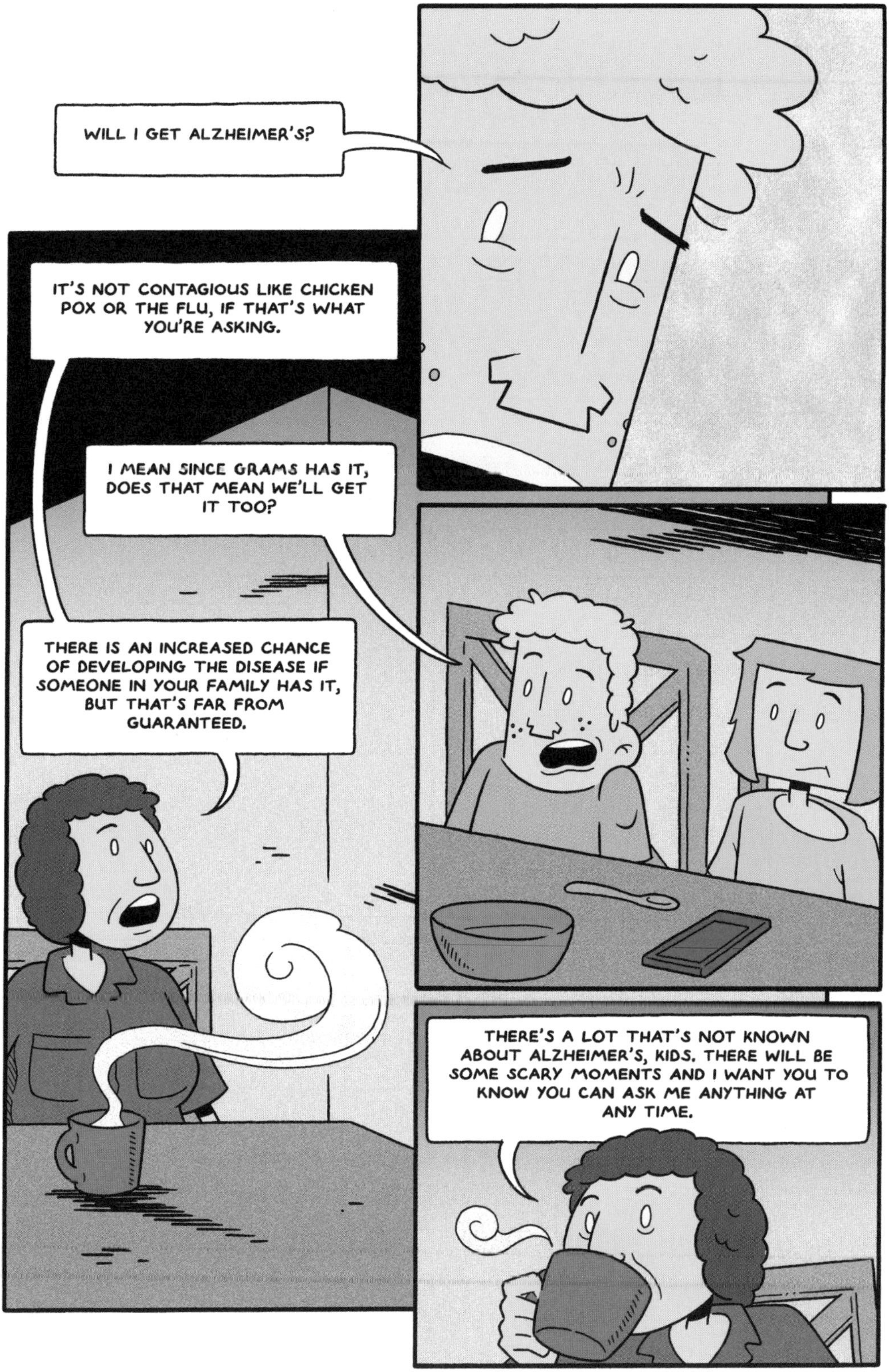
WILL I GET ALZHEIMER'S?
IT'S NOT CONTAGIOUS LIKE CHICKEN POX OR THE FLU, IF THAT'S WHAT YOU'RE ASKING.
I MEAN SINCE GRAMS HAS IT, DOES THAT MEAN WE'LL GET IT TOO?
THERE IS AN INCREASED CHANCE OF DEVELOPING THE DISEASE IF SOMEONE IN YOUR FAMILY HAS IT, BUT THAT'S FAR FROM GUARANTEED.
THERE'S A LOT THAT'S NOT KNOWN ABOUT ALZHEIMER'S, KIDS. THERE WILL BE SOME SCARY MOMENTS AND I WANT YOU TO KNOW YOU CAN ASK ME ANYTHING AT ANY TIME.

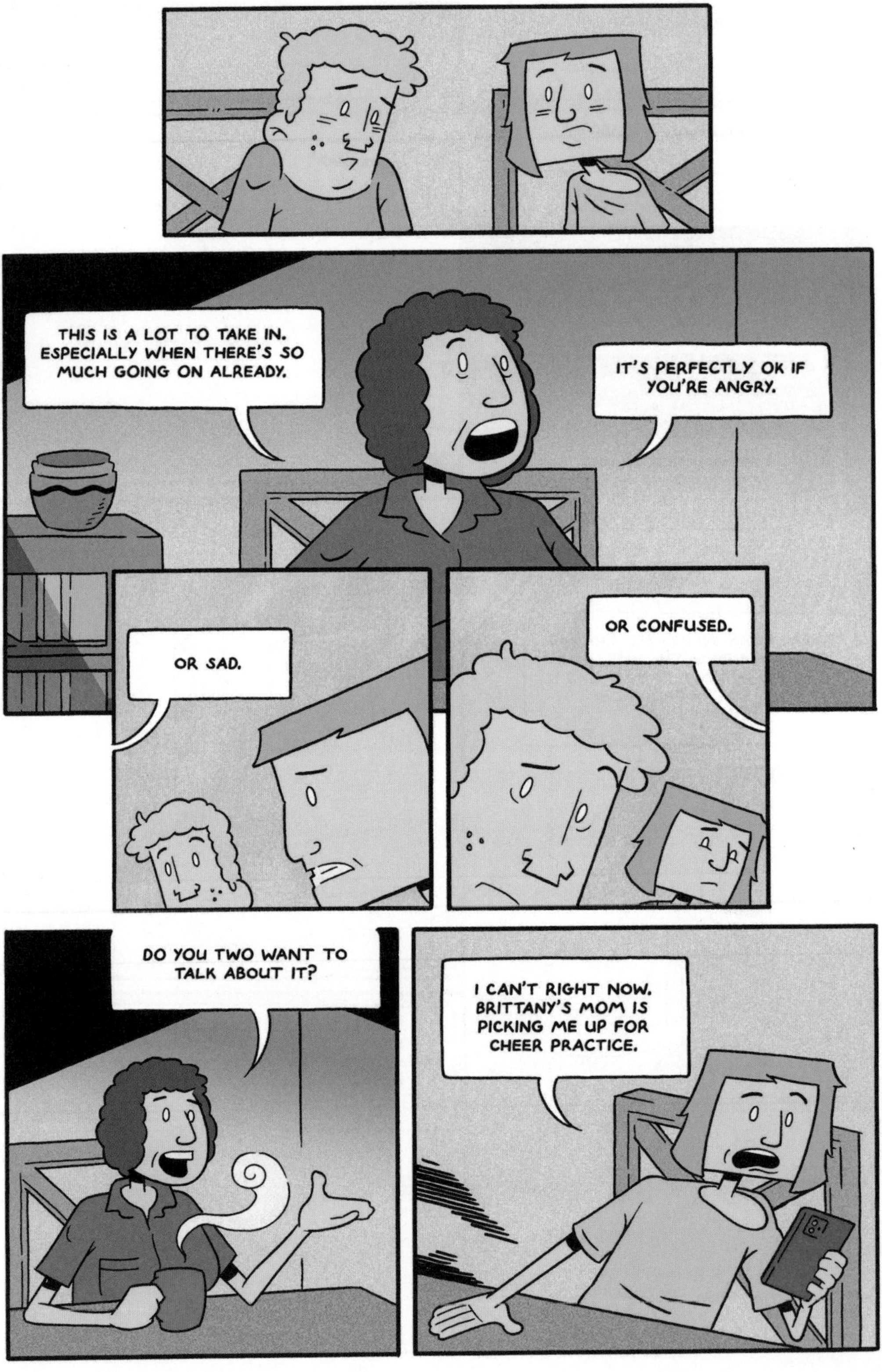
THIS IS A LOT TO TAKE IN. ESPECIALLY WHEN THERE'S SO MUCH GOING ON ALREADY.
IT'S PERFECTLY OK IF YOU'RE ANGRY.
OR SAD.
OR CONFUSED.
DO YOU TWO WANT TO TALK ABOUT IT?
I CAN'T RIGHT NOW. BRITTANY'S MOM IS PICKING ME UP FOR CHEER PRACTICE.

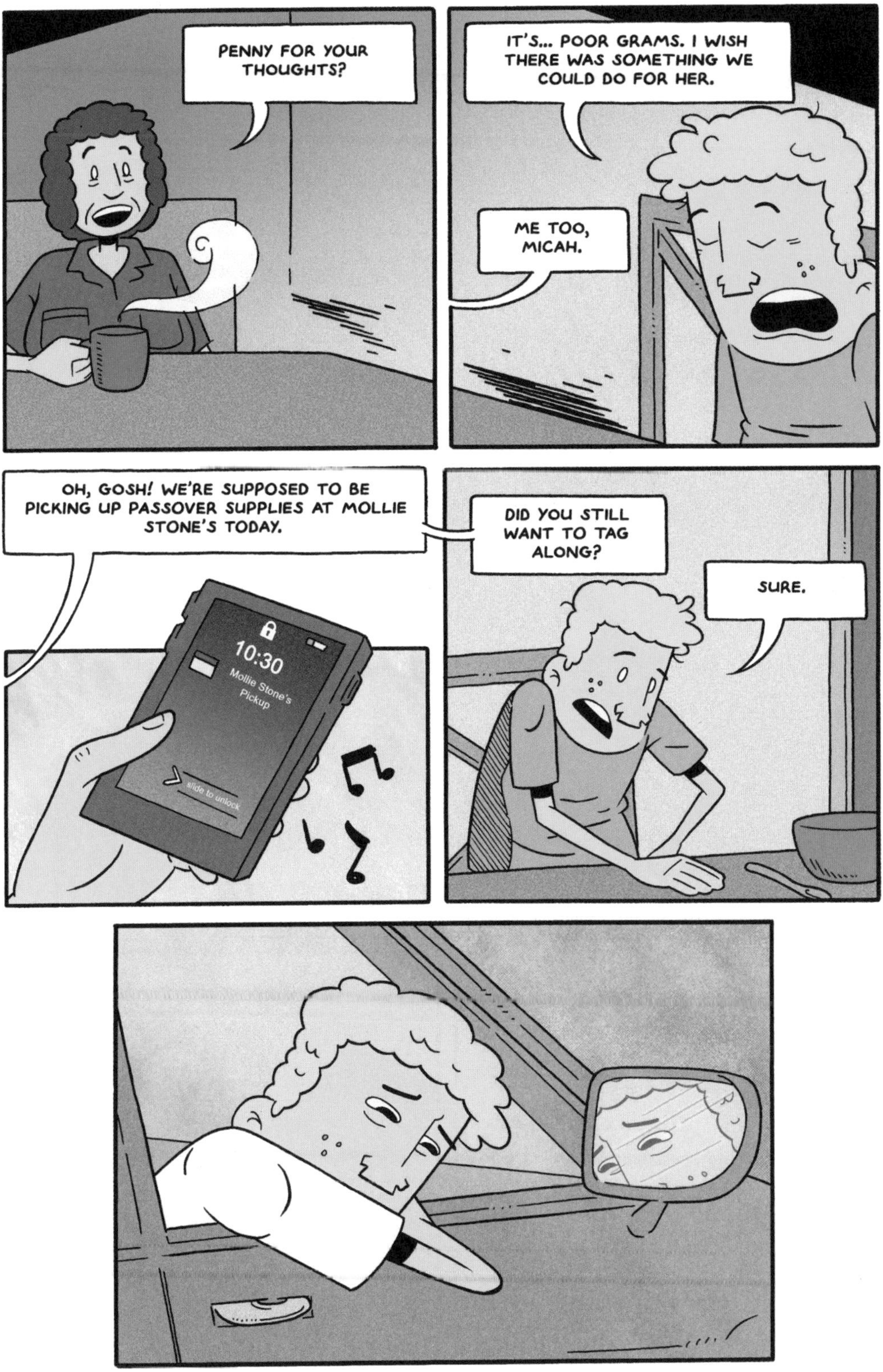
PENNY FOR YOUR THOUGHTS?
IT'S... POOR GRAMS. I WISH THERE WAS SOMETHING WE COULD DO FOR HER.
ME TOO, MICAH.
OH, GOSH! WE'RE SUPPOSED TO BE PICKING UP PASSOVER SUPPLIES AT MOLLIE STONE'S TODAY.
10:30
Mollie Stone's Pickup
slide to unlock
DID YOU STILL WANT TO TAG ALONG?
SURE.

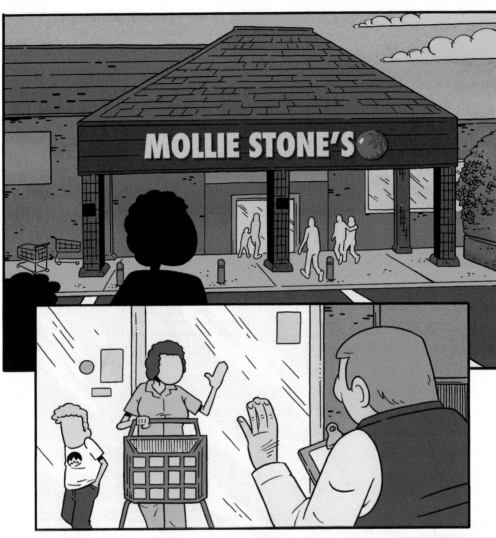

I CONSTANTLY LEFT MY LIGHTS ON ALL NIGHT ACCIDENTALLY.

I ALSO REPEATEDLY LOST MY HOUSE KEYS.

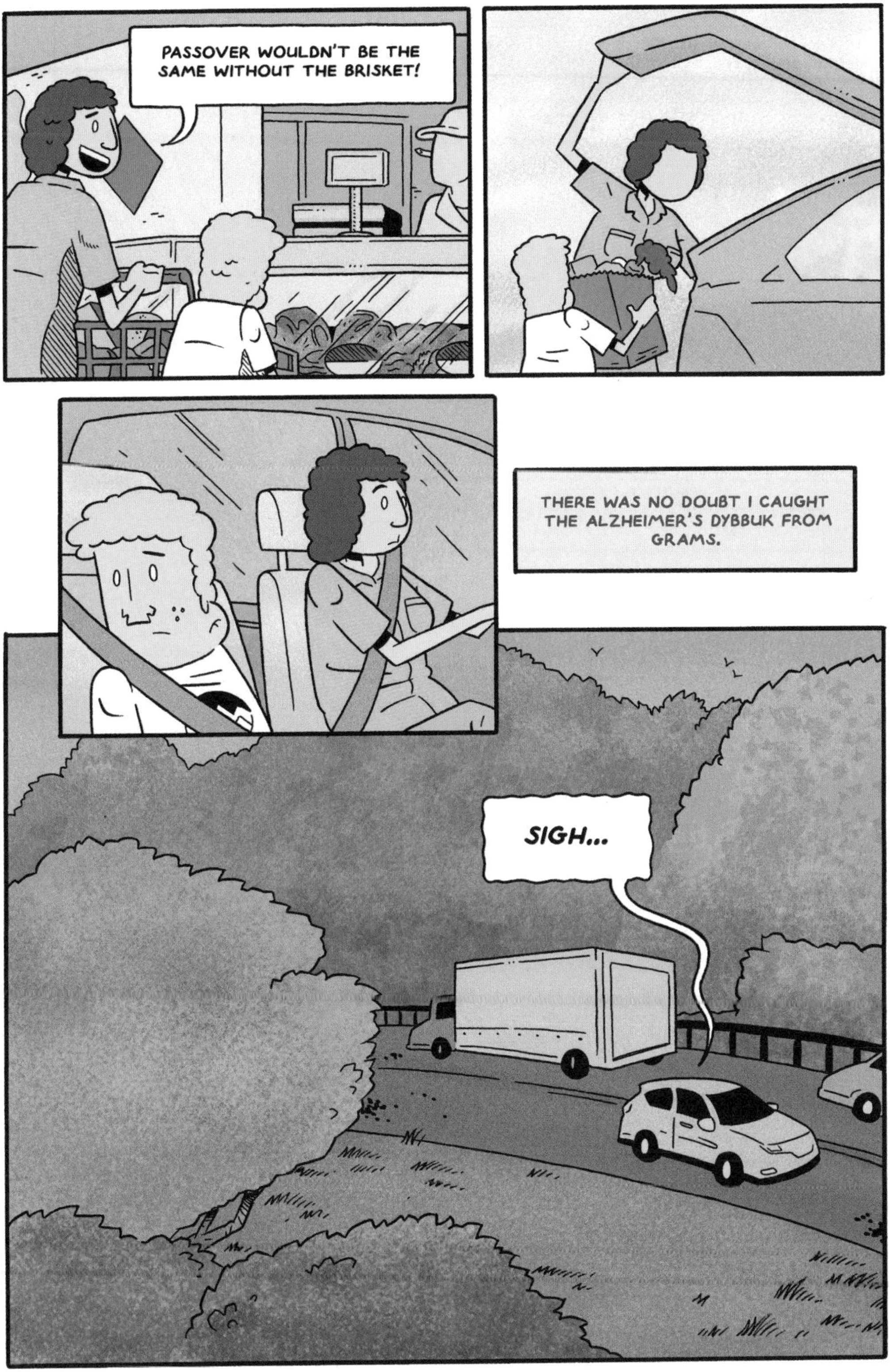
PASSOVER WOULDN'T BE THE SAME WITHOUT THE BRISKET!
THERE WAS NO DOUBT I CAUGHT THE ALZHEIMER'S DYBBUK FROM GRAMS.
SIGH...

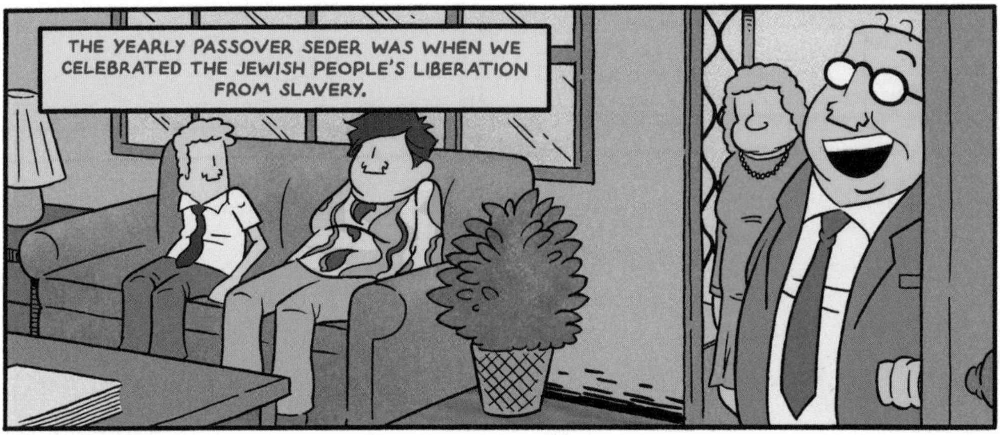
THE YEARLY PASSOVER SEDER WAS WHEN WE CELEBRATED THE JEWISH PEOPLE'S LIBERATION FROM SLAVERY.

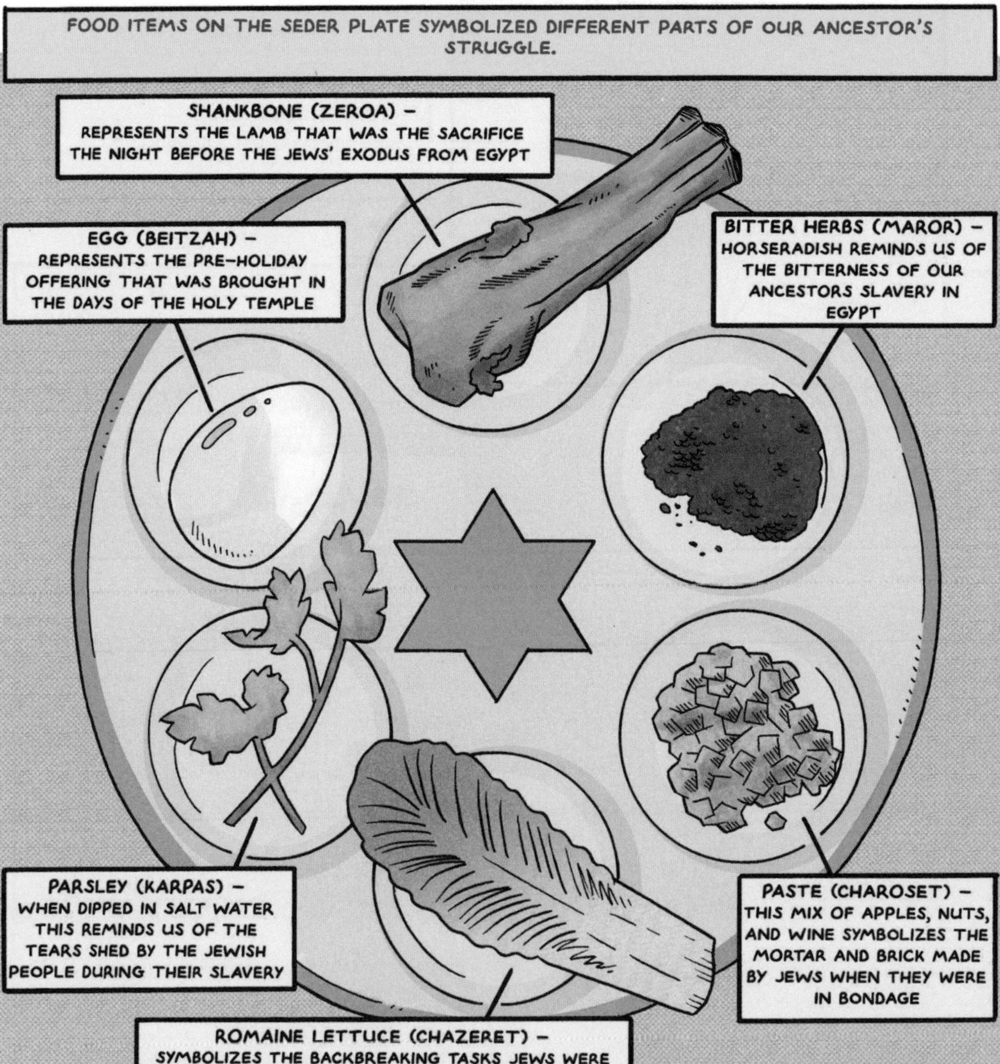
FOOD ITEMS ON THE SEDER PLATE SYMBOLIZED DIFFERENT PARTS OF OUR ANCESTOR'S STRUGGLE.
SHANKBONE (ZEROA) – REPRESENTS THE LAMB THAT WAS THE SACRIFICE THE NIGHT BEFORE THE JEWS' EXODUS FROM EGYPT
EGG (BEITZAH) – REPRESENTS THE PRE-HOLIDAY OFFERING THAT WAS BROUGHT IN THE DAYS OF THE HOLY TEMPLE
BITTER HERBS (MAROR) – HORSERADISH REMINDS US OF THE BITTERNESS OF OUR ANCESTORS SLAVERY IN EGYPT
PARSLEY (KARPAS) – WHEN DIPPED IN SALT WATER THIS REMINDS US OF THE TEARS SHED BY THE JEWISH PEOPLE DURING THEIR SLAVERY
PASTE (CHAROSET) – THIS MIX OF APPLES, NUTS, AND WINE SYMBOLIZES THE MORTAR AND BRICK MADE BY JEWS WHEN THEY WERE IN BONDAGE
ROMAINE LETTUCE (CHAZERET) – SYMBOLIZES THE BACKBREAKING TASKS JEWS WERE FORCED TO PERFORM AS SLAVES

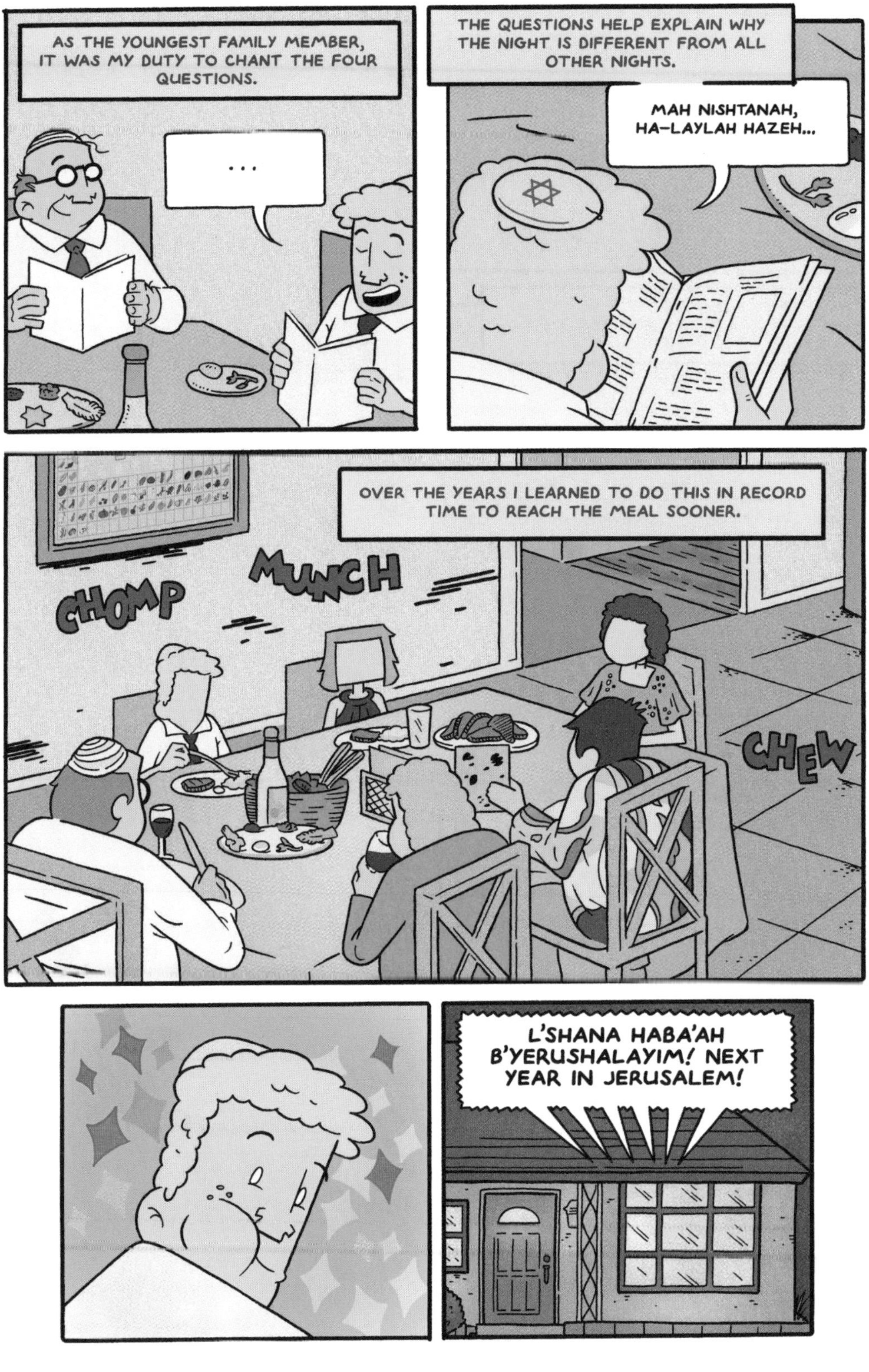

AS THE YOUNGEST FAMILY MEMBER, IT WAS MY DUTY TO CHANT THE FOUR QUESTIONS.
...
THE QUESTIONS HELP EXPLAIN WHY THE NIGHT IS DIFFERENT FROM ALL OTHER NIGHTS.
MAH NISHTANAH, HA-LAYLAH HAZEH...
OVER THE YEARS I LEARNED TO DO THIS IN RECORD TIME TO REACH THE MEAL SOONER.
CHOMP
MUNCH
CHEW
L'SHANA HABA'AH B'YERUSHALAYIM! NEXT YEAR IN JERUSALEM!

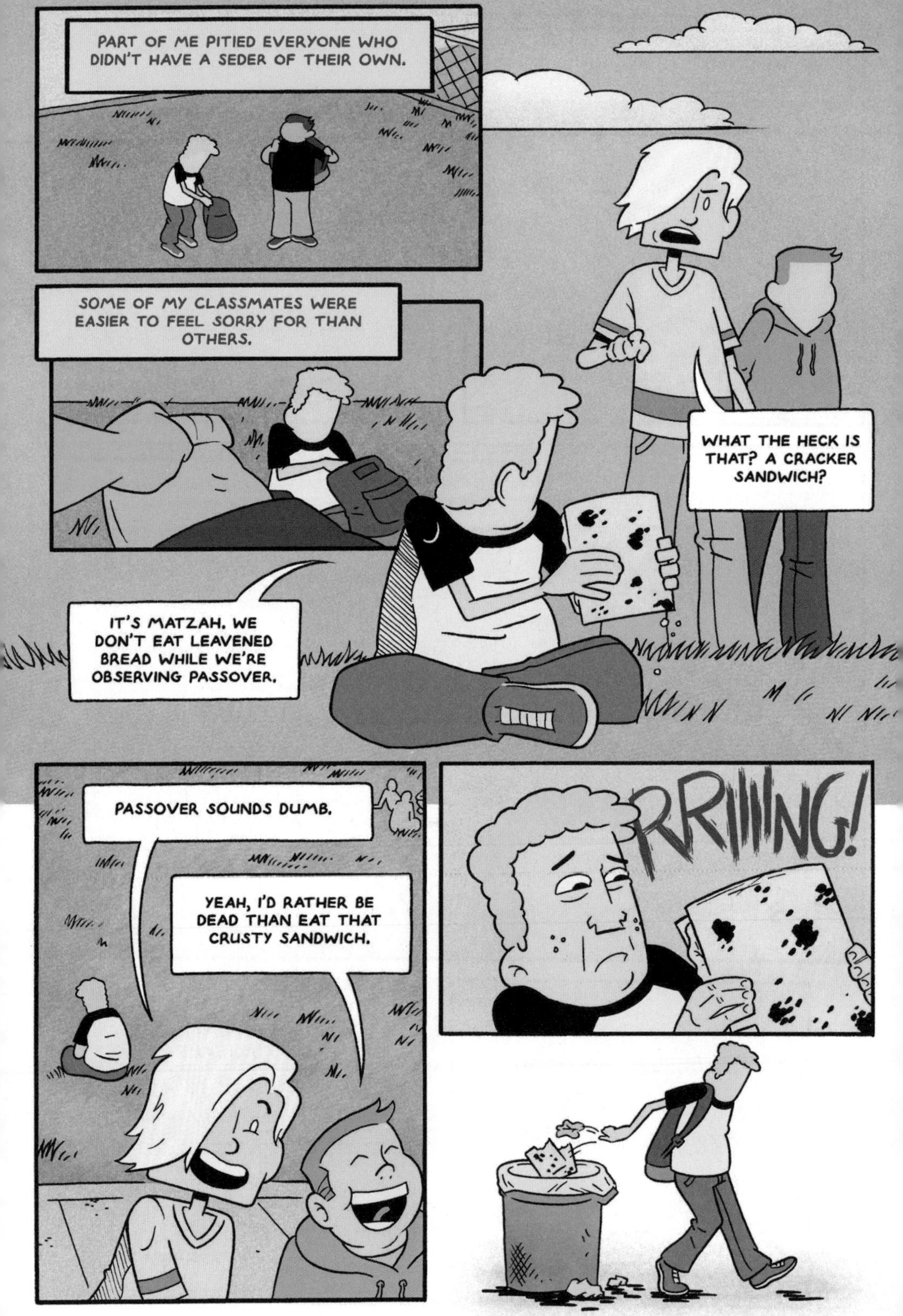
PART OF ME PITIED EVERYONE WHO DIDN'T HAVE A SEDER OF THEIR OWN.
SOME OF MY CLASSMATES WERE EASIER TO FEEL SORRY FOR THAN OTHERS.
WHAT THE HECK IS THAT? A CRACKER SANDWICH?
IT'S MATZAH. WE DON'T EAT LEAVENED BREAD WHILE WE'RE OBSERVING PASSOVER.
PASSOVER SOUNDS DUMB.
YEAH, I'D RATHER BE DEAD THAN EAT THAT CRUSTY SANDWICH.
RRIIIING!

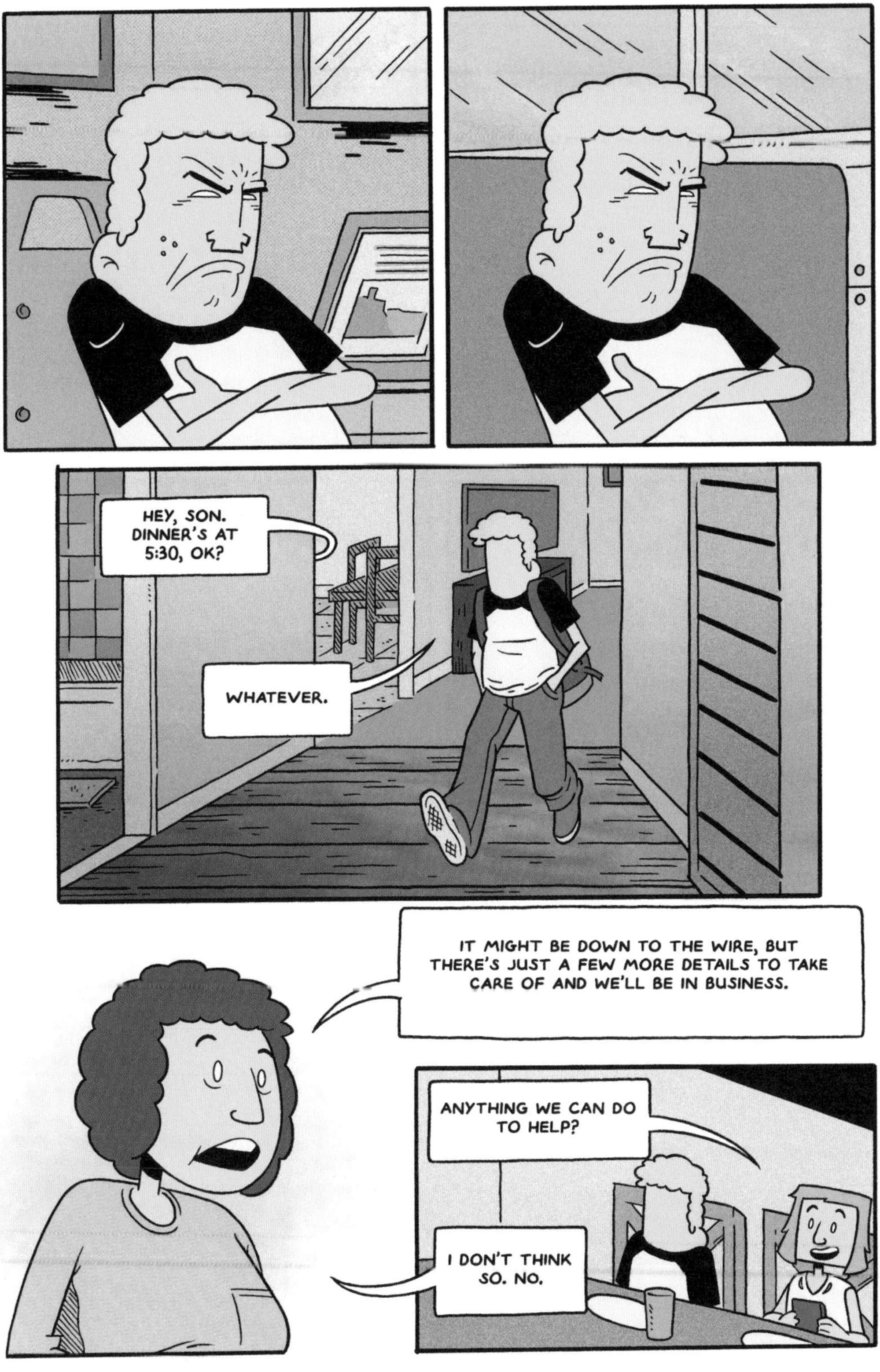
HEY, SON. DINNER'S AT 5:30, OK?
WHATEVER.
IT MIGHT BE DOWN TO THE WIRE, BUT THERE'S JUST A FEW MORE DETAILS TO TAKE CARE OF AND WE'LL BE IN BUSINESS.
ANYTHING WE CAN DO TO HELP?
I DON'T THINK SO. NO.

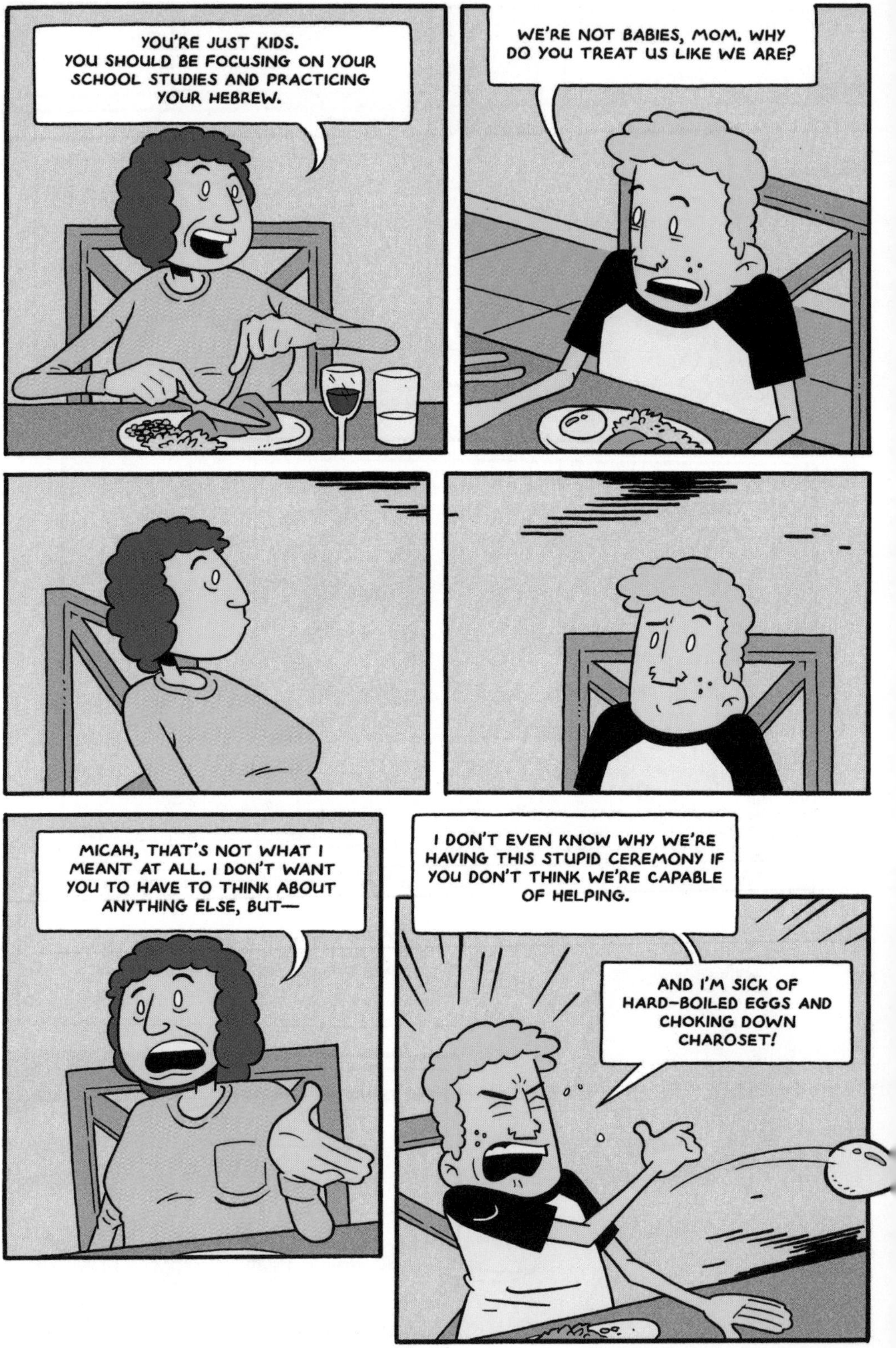
YOU'RE JUST KIDS. YOU SHOULD BE FOCUSING ON YOUR SCHOOL STUDIES AND PRACTICING YOUR HEBREW.
WE'RE NOT BABIES, MOM. WHY DO YOU TREAT US LIKE WE ARE?
MICAH, THAT'S NOT WHAT I MEANT AT ALL. I DON'T WANT YOU TO HAVE TO THINK ABOUT ANYTHING ELSE, BUT—
I DON'T EVEN KNOW WHY WE'RE HAVING THIS STUPID CEREMONY IF YOU DON'T THINK WE'RE CAPABLE OF HELPING.
AND I'M SICK OF HARD-BOILED EGGS AND CHOKING DOWN CHAROSET!

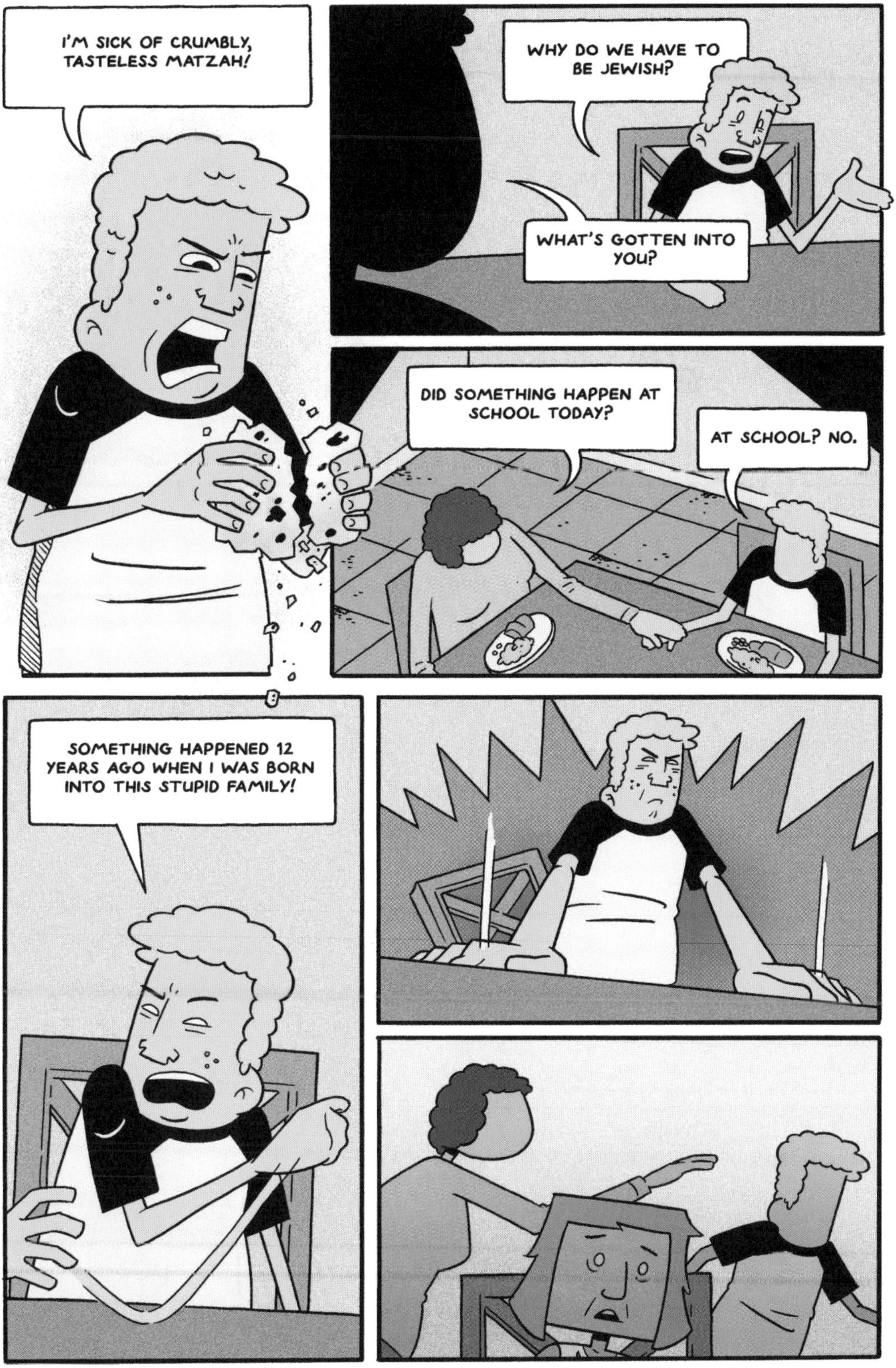

I'M SICK OF CRUMBLY, TASTELESS MATZAH!
WHY DO WE HAVE TO BE JEWISH?
WHAT'S GOTTEN INTO YOU?
DID SOMETHING HAPPEN AT SCHOOL TODAY?
AT SCHOOL? NO.
SOMETHING HAPPENED 12 YEARS AGO WHEN I WAS BORN INTO THIS STUPID FAMILY!

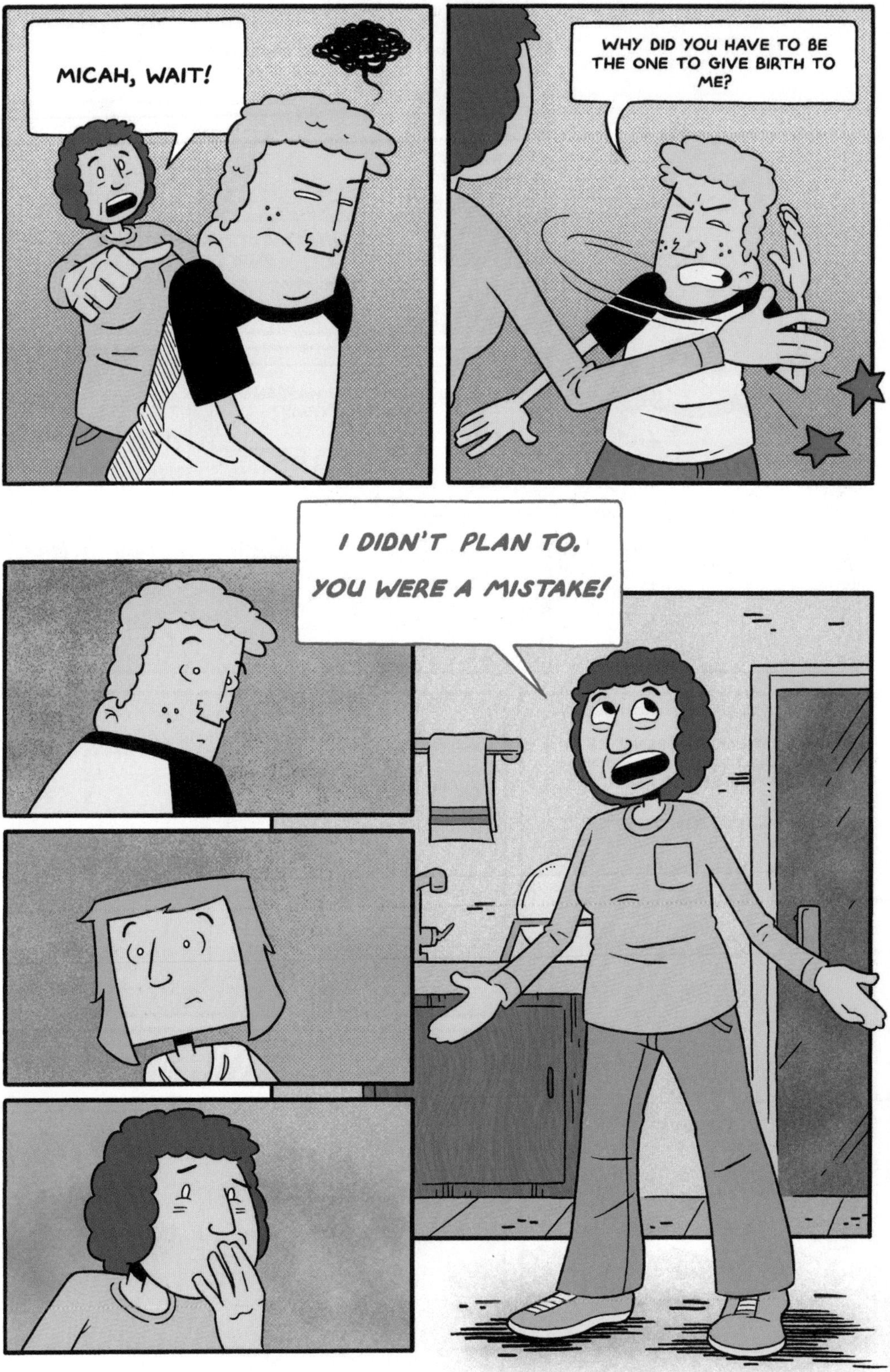
MICAH, WAIT!
WHY DID YOU HAVE TO BE THE ONE TO GIVE BIRTH TO ME?
I DIDN'T PLAN TO. YOU WERE A MISTAKE!

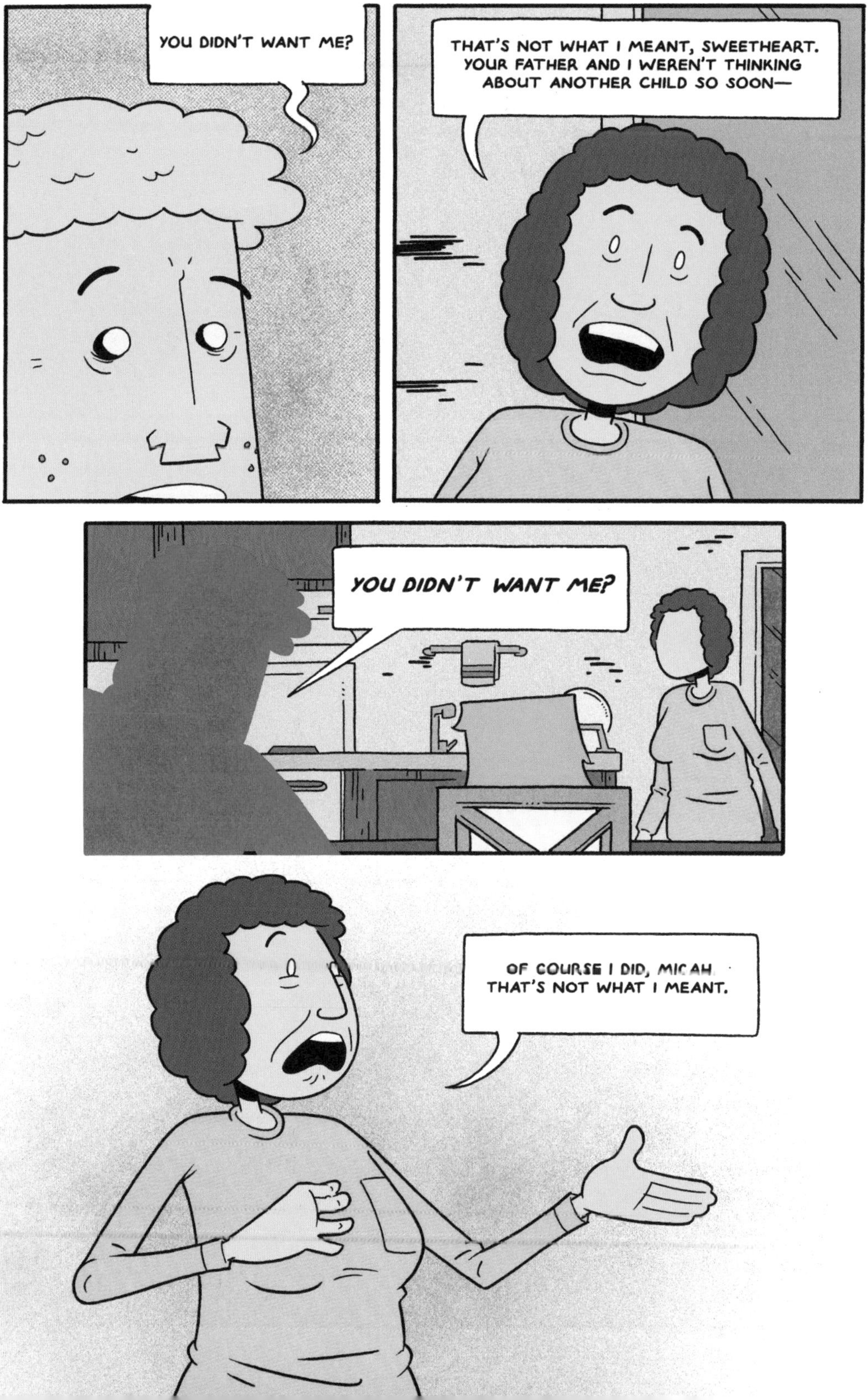
YOU DIDN'T WANT ME?
THAT'S NOT WHAT I MEANT, SWEETHEART. YOUR FATHER AND I WEREN'T THINKING ABOUT ANOTHER CHILD SO SOON—
YOU DIDN'T WANT ME?
OF COURSE I DID, MICAH. THAT'S NOT WHAT I MEANT.

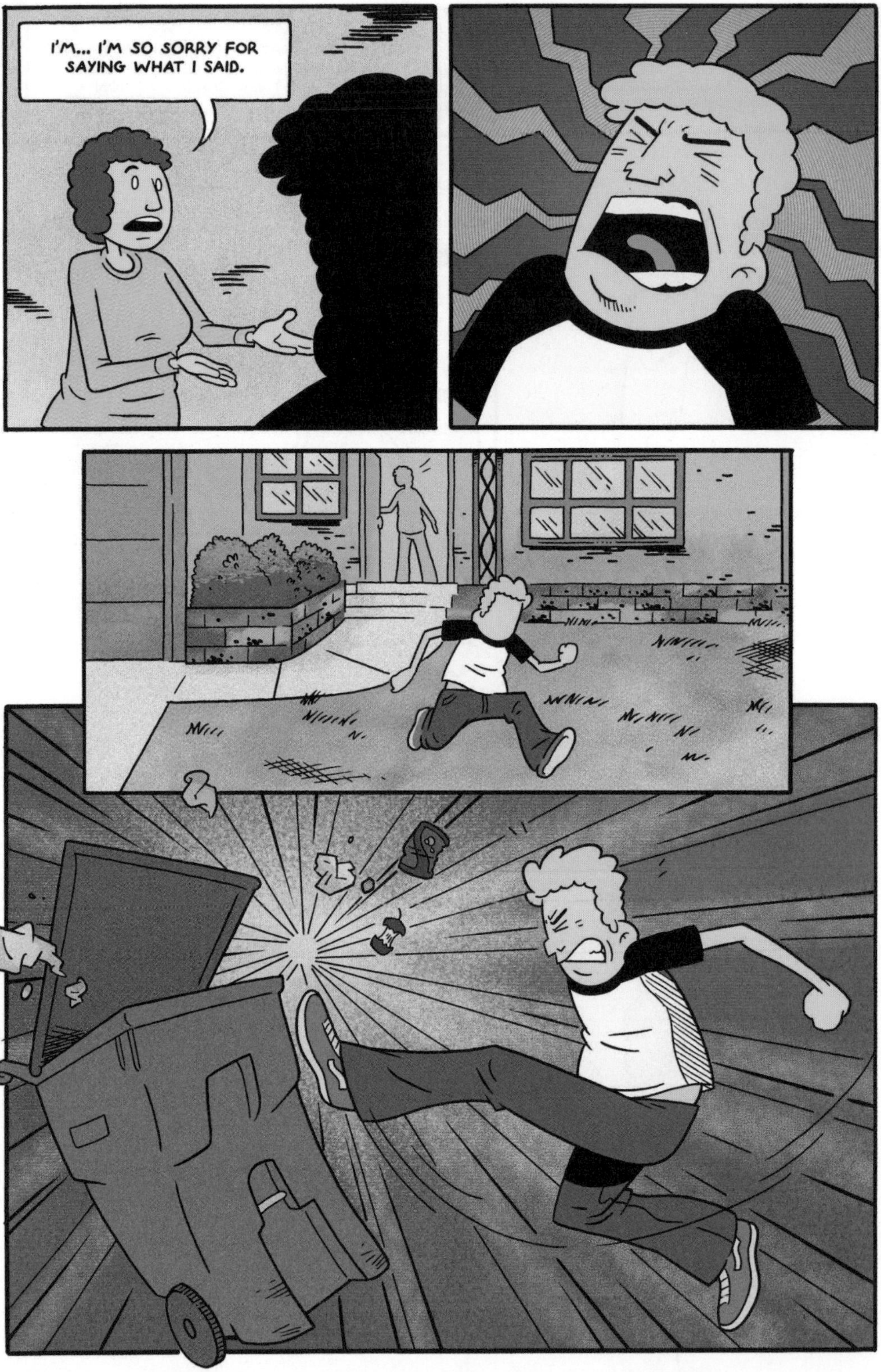
I'M... I'M SO SORRY FOR SAYING WHAT I SAID.

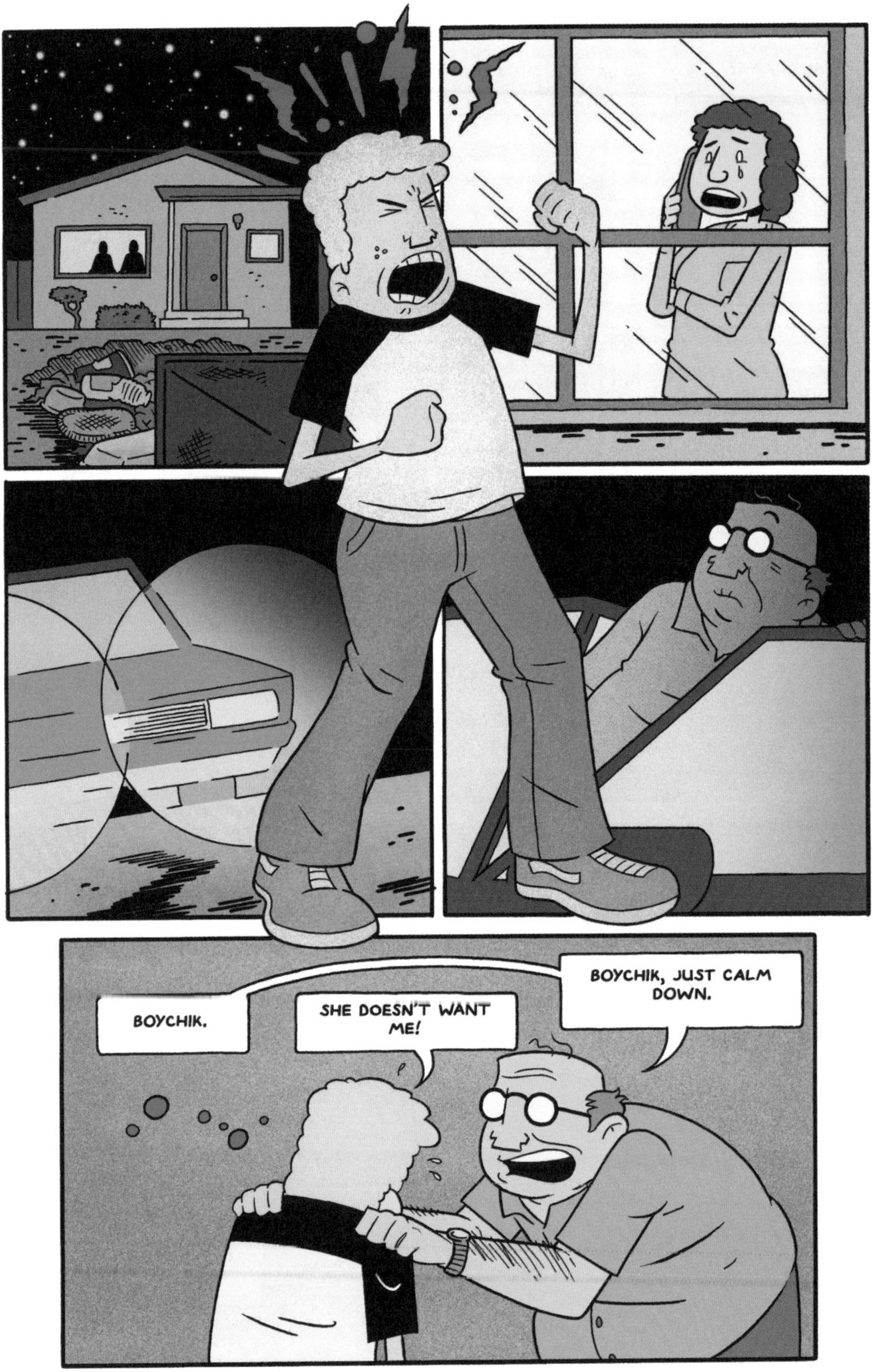
BOYCHIK.
SHE DOESN'T WANT ME!
BOYCHIK, JUST CALM DOWN.

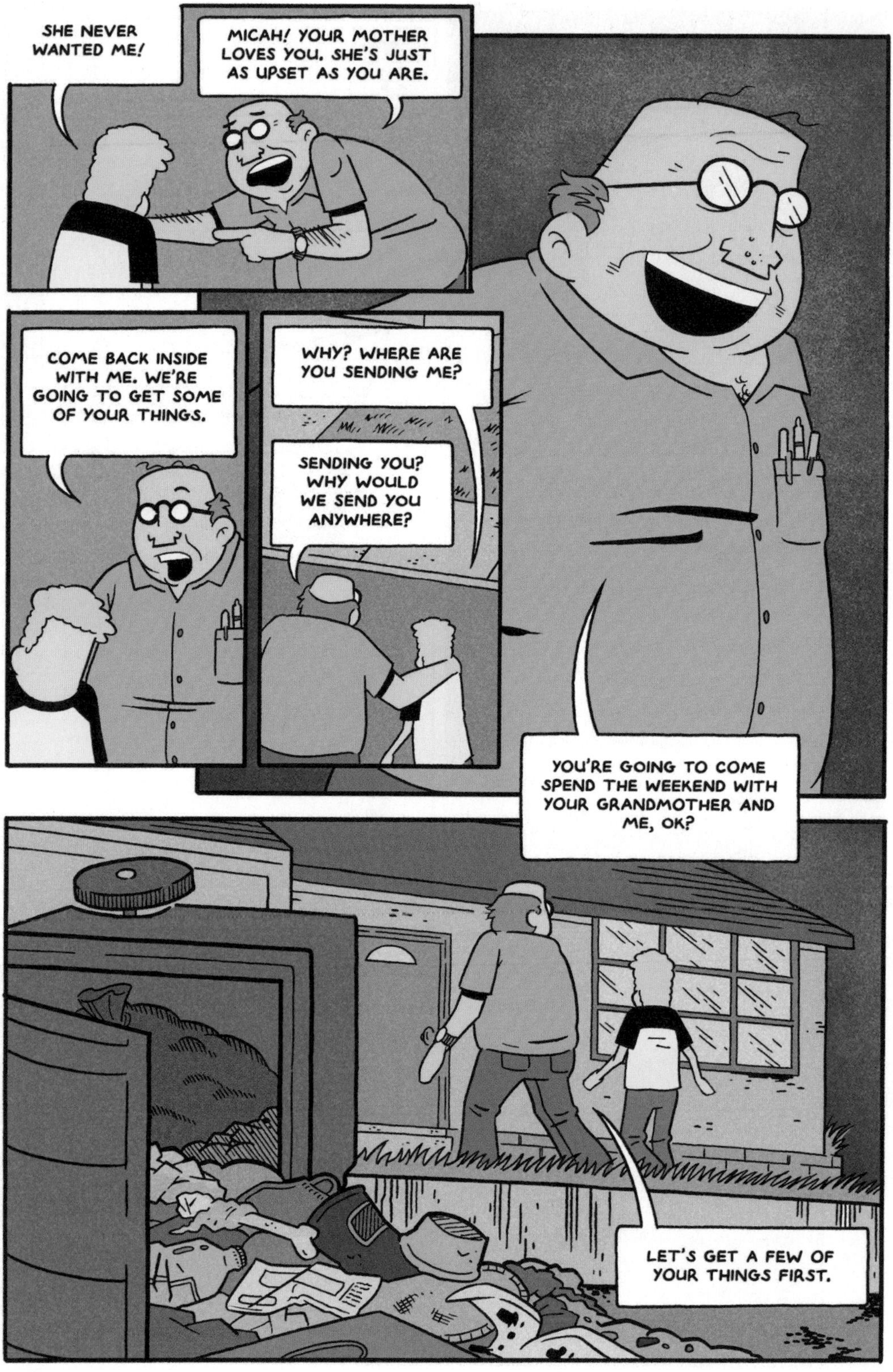
SHE NEVER WANTED ME!
MICAH! YOUR MOTHER LOVES YOU. SHE'S JUST AS UPSET AS YOU ARE.
COME BACK INSIDE WITH ME. WE'RE GOING TO GET SOME OF YOUR THINGS.
WHY? WHERE ARE YOU SENDING ME?
SENDING YOU? WHY WOULD WE SEND YOU ANYWHERE?
YOU'RE GOING TO COME SPEND THE WEEKEND WITH YOUR GRANDMOTHER AND ME, OK?
LET'S GET A FEW OF YOUR THINGS FIRST.

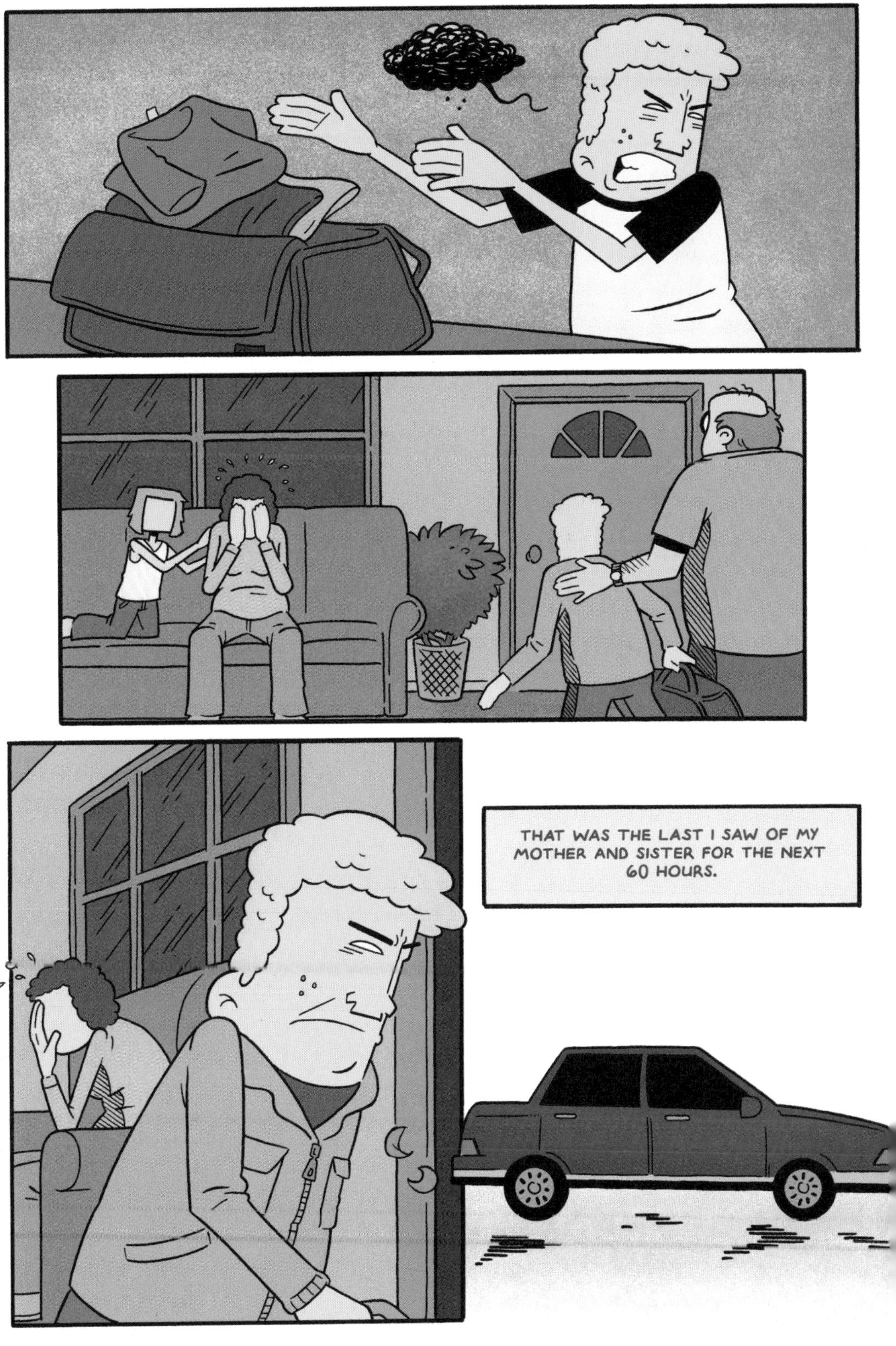
THAT WAS THE LAST I SAW OF MY MOTHER AND SISTER FOR THE NEXT 60 HOURS.

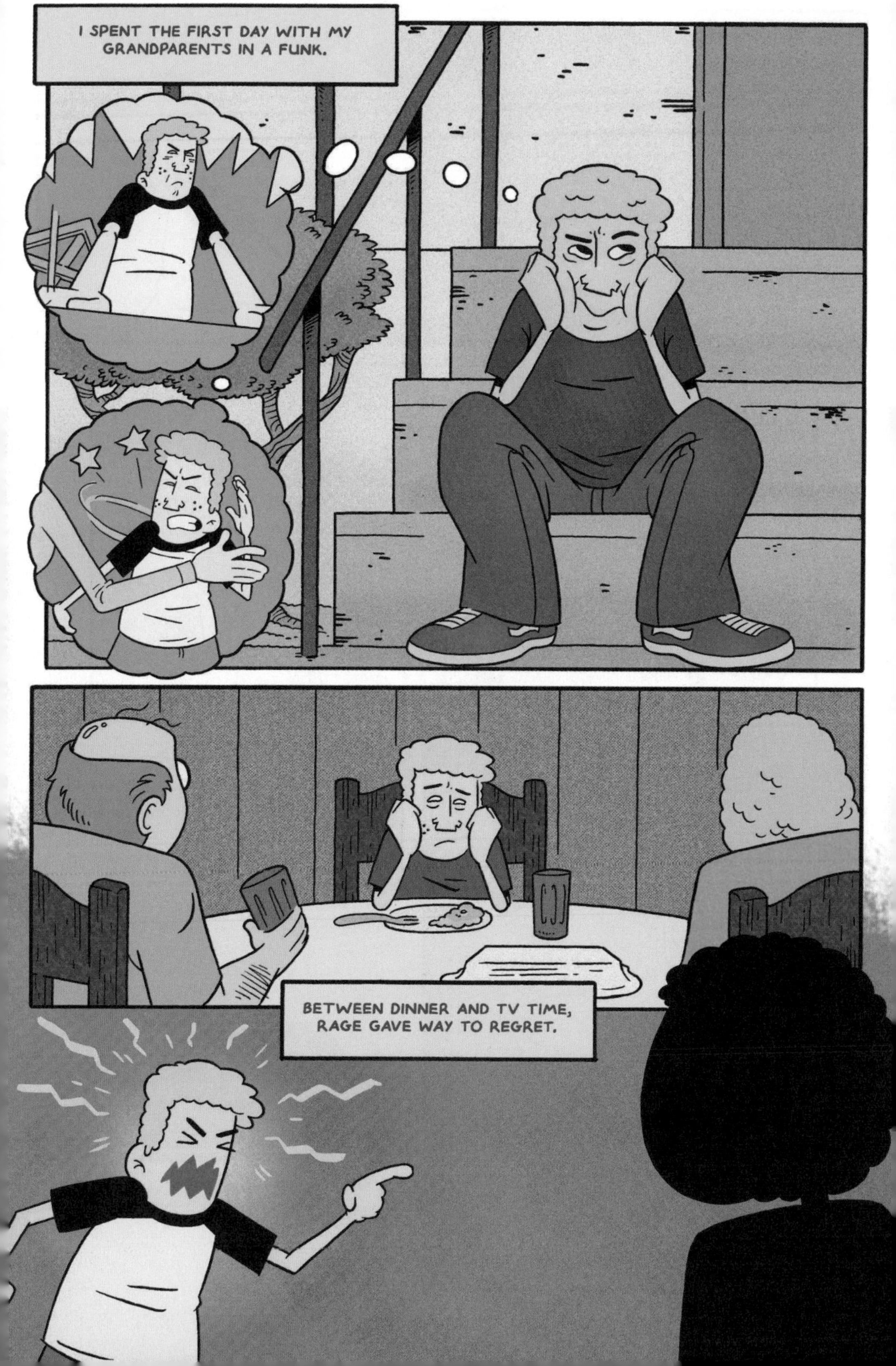
I SPENT THE FIRST DAY WITH MY GRANDPARENTS IN A FUNK.
BETWEEN DINNER AND TV TIME, RAGE GAVE WAY TO REGRET.

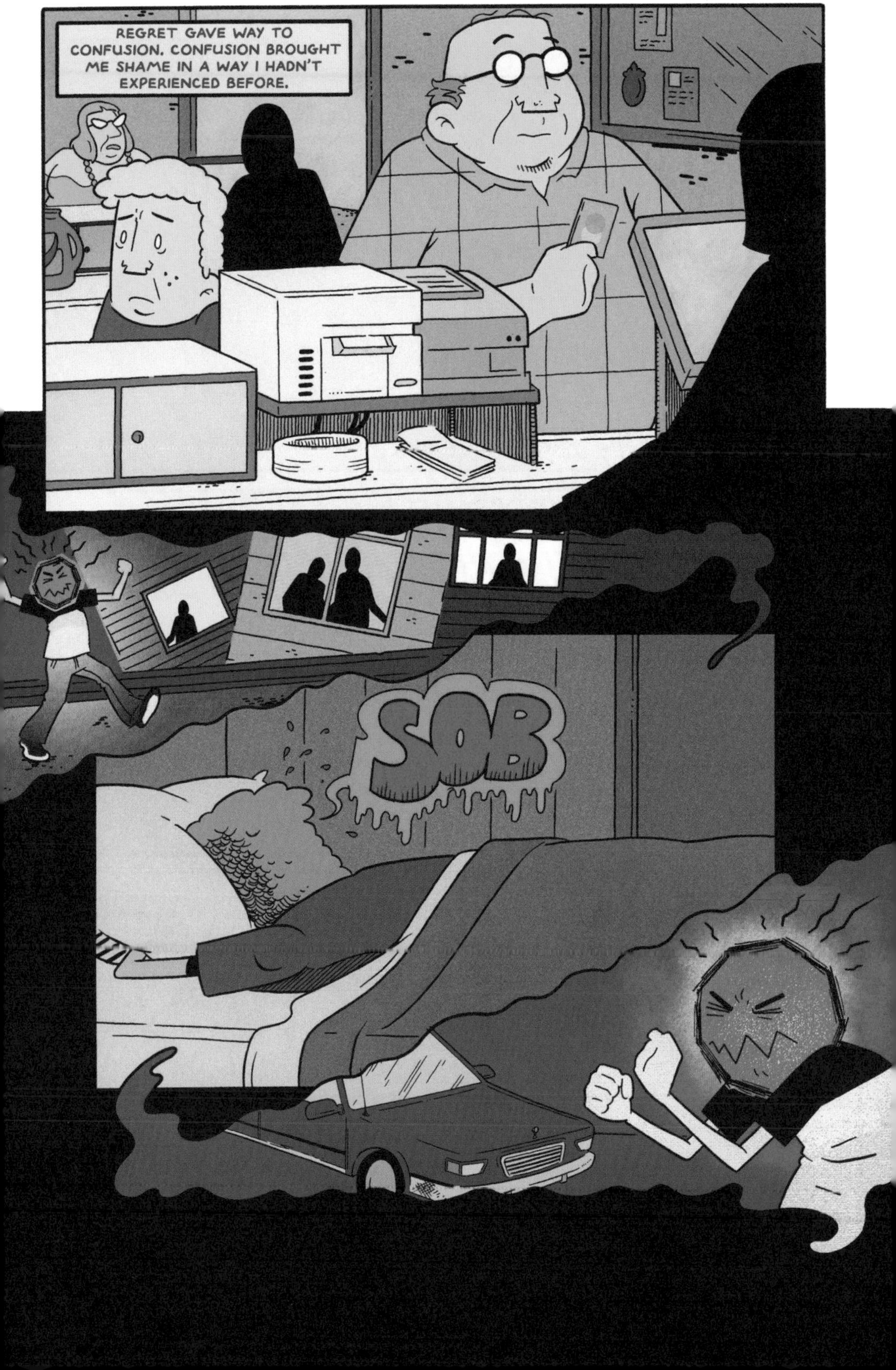
REGRET GAVE WAY TO CONFUSION. CONFUSION BROUGHT ME SHAME IN A WAY I HADN'T EXPERIENCED BEFORE.
SOB

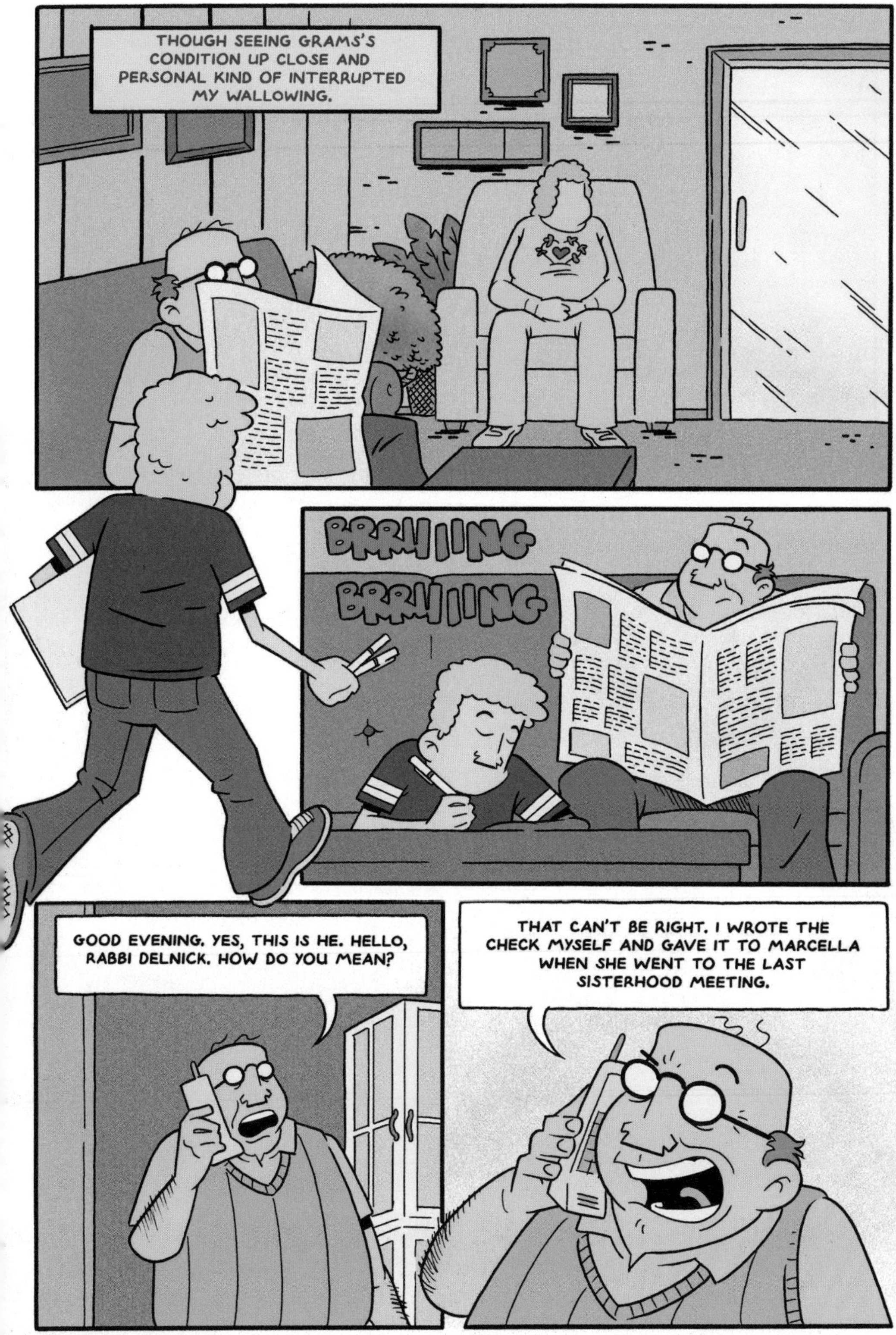
THOUGH SEEING GRAMS'S CONDITION UP CLOSE AND PERSONAL KIND OF INTERRUPTED MY WALLOWING.
BRRIIIING
BRRIIIING
GOOD EVENING. YES, THIS IS HE. HELLO, RABBI DELNICK. HOW DO YOU MEAN?
THAT CAN'T BE RIGHT. I WROTE THE CHECK MYSELF AND GAVE IT TO MARCELLA WHEN SHE WENT TO THE LAST SISTERHOOD MEETING.

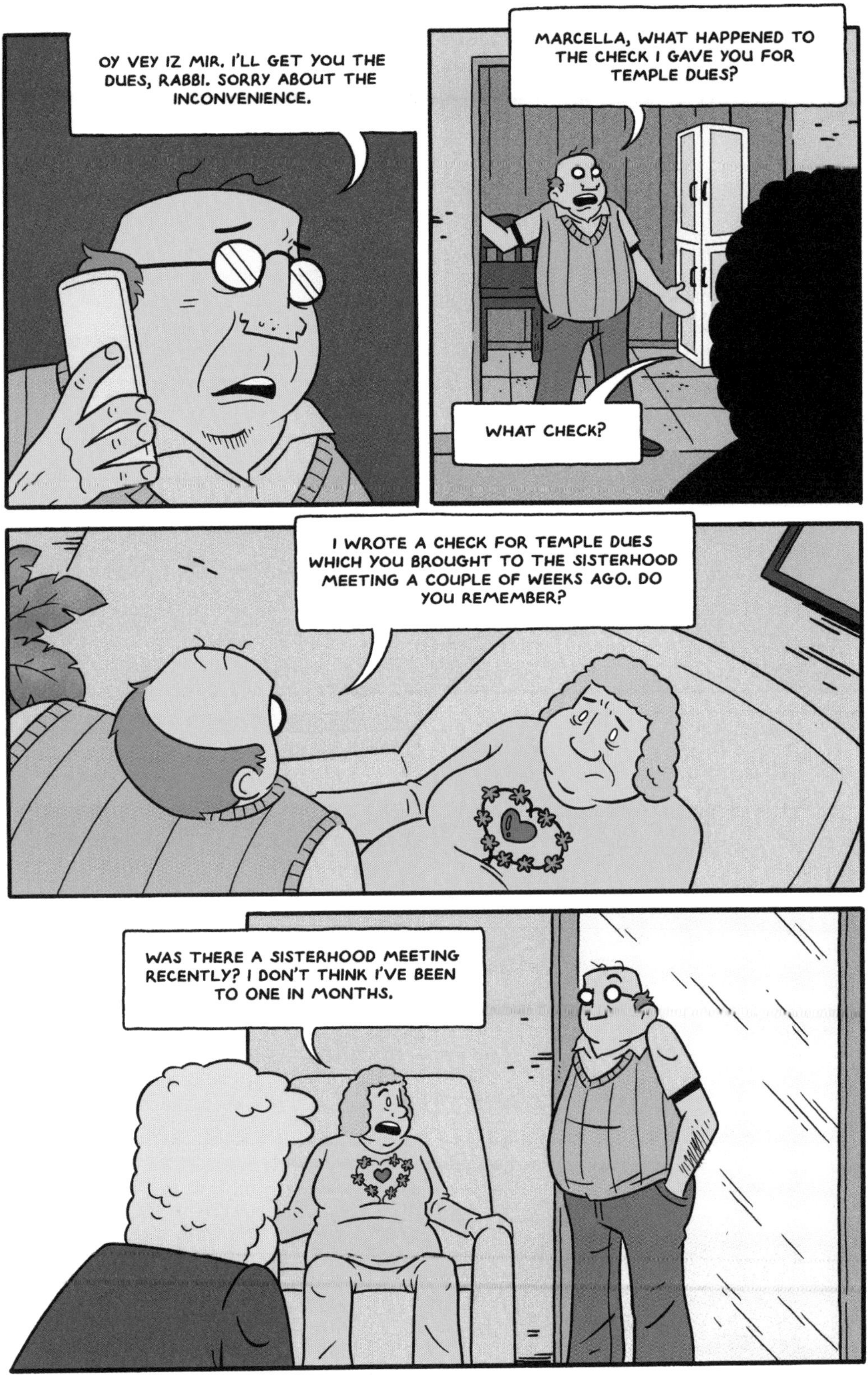
OY VEY IZ MIR. I'LL GET YOU THE DUES, RABBI. SORRY ABOUT THE INCONVENIENCE.
MARCELLA, WHAT HAPPENED TO THE CHECK I GAVE YOU FOR TEMPLE DUES?
WHAT CHECK?
I WROTE A CHECK FOR TEMPLE DUES WHICH YOU BROUGHT TO THE SISTERHOOD MEETING A COUPLE OF WEEKS AGO. DO YOU REMEMBER?
WAS THERE A SISTERHOOD MEETING RECENTLY? I DON'T THINK I'VE BEEN TO ONE IN MONTHS.

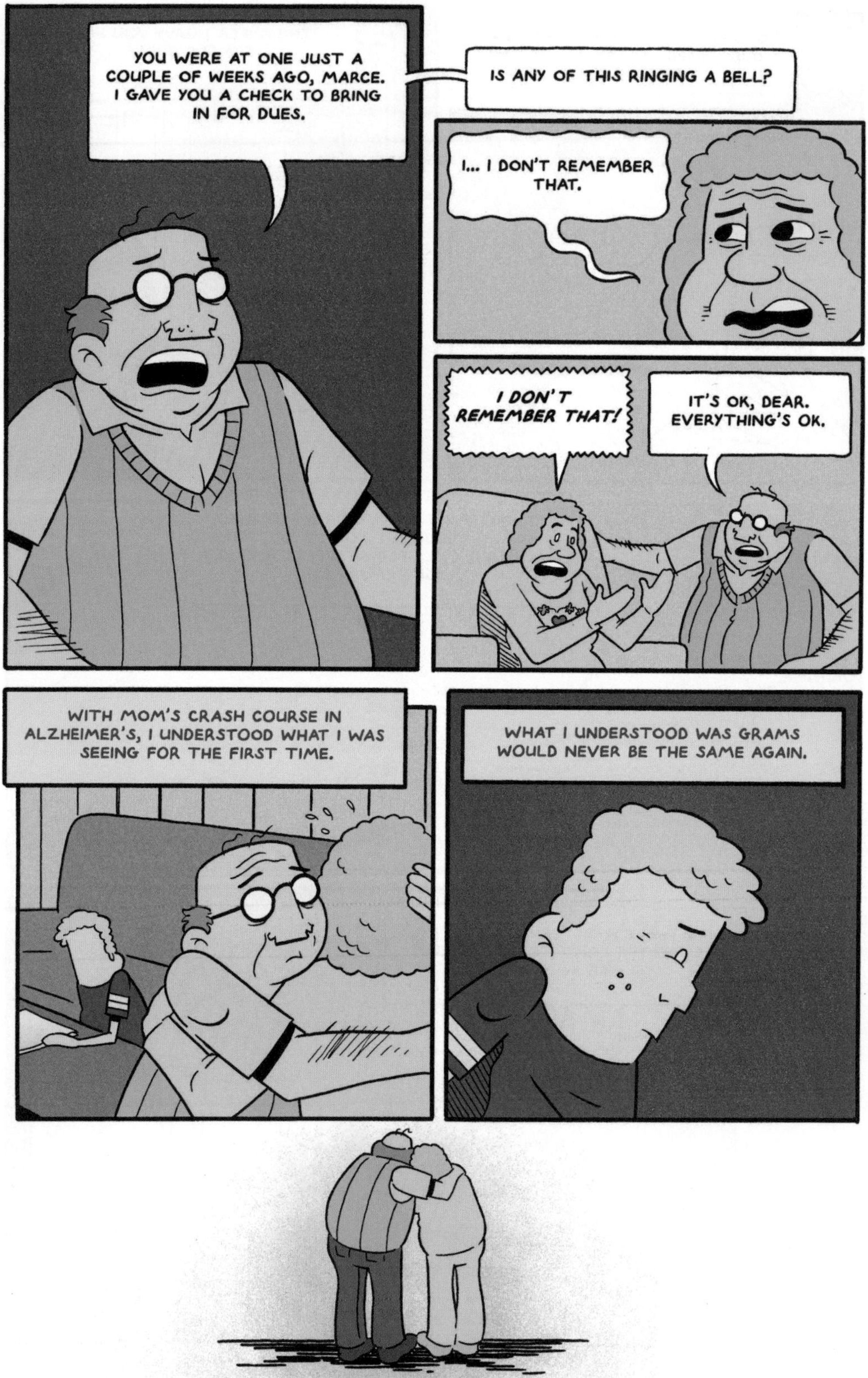

YOU WERE AT ONE JUST A COUPLE OF WEEKS AGO, MARCE. I GAVE YOU A CHECK TO BRING IN FOR DUES.
IS ANY OF THIS RINGING A BELL?
I... I DON'T REMEMBER THAT.
I DON'T REMEMBER THAT!
IT'S OK, DEAR. EVERYTHING'S OK.
WITH MOM'S CRASH COURSE IN ALZHEIMER'S, I UNDERSTOOD WHAT I WAS SEEING FOR THE FIRST TIME.
WHAT I UNDERSTOOD WAS GRAMS WOULD NEVER BE THE SAME AGAIN.

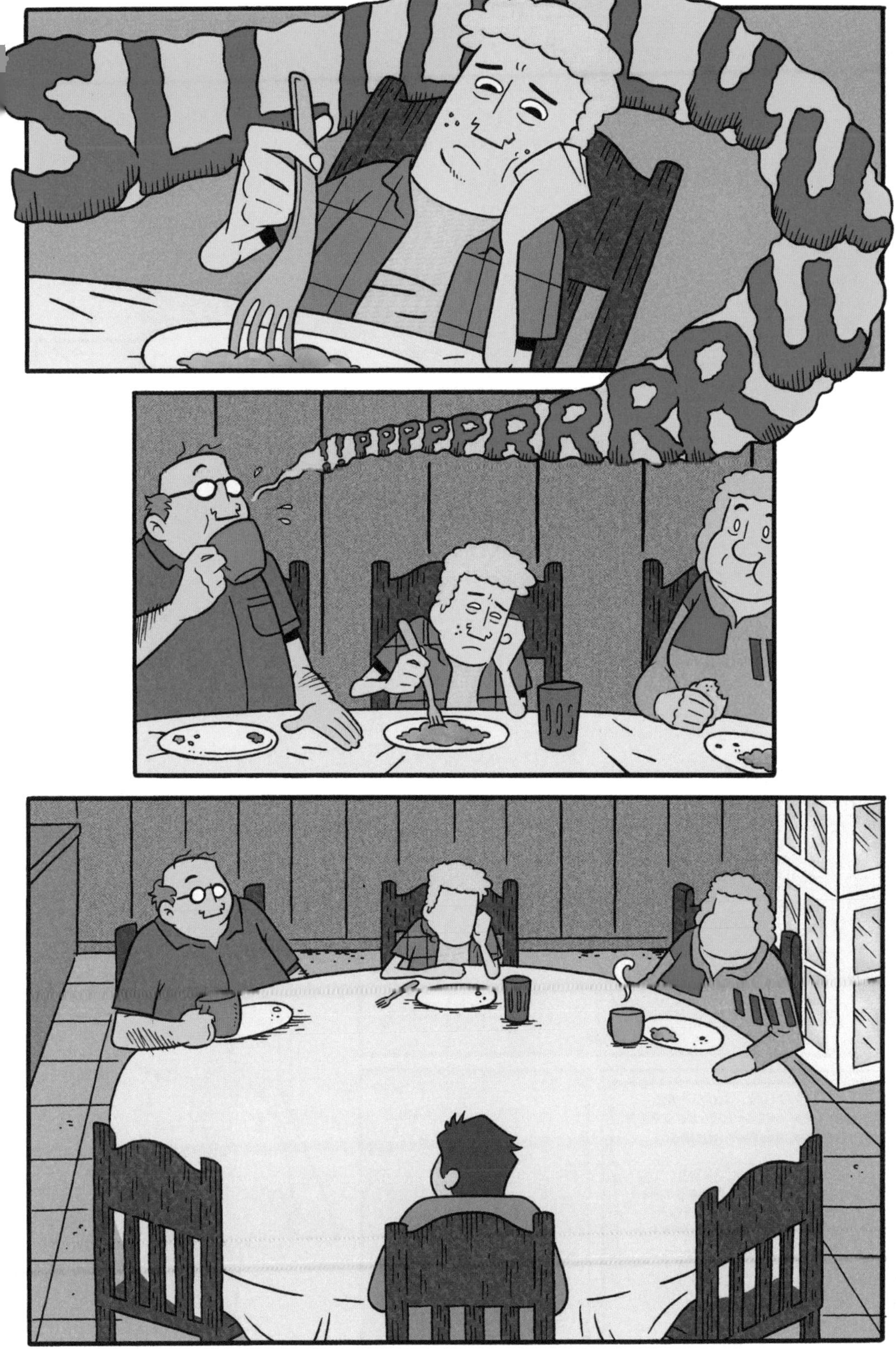
SLLLLLLUUURRRRPPPPPP!!

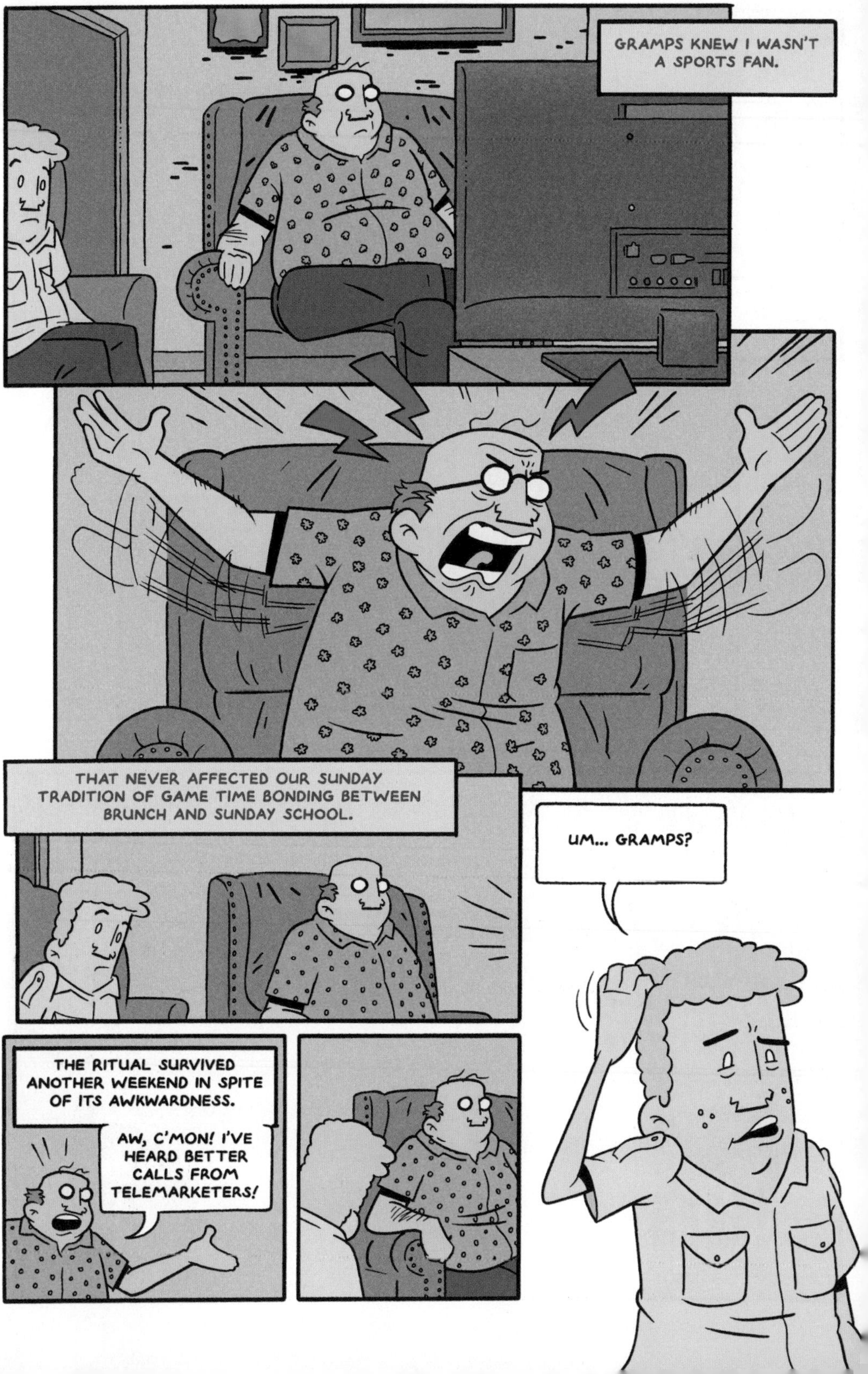
GRAMPS KNEW I WASN'T A SPORTS FAN.
THAT NEVER AFFECTED OUR SUNDAY TRADITION OF GAME TIME BONDING BETWEEN BRUNCH AND SUNDAY SCHOOL.
UM... GRAMPS?
THE RITUAL SURVIVED ANOTHER WEEKEND IN SPITE OF ITS AWKWARDNESS.
AW, C'MON! I'VE HEARD BETTER CALLS FROM TELEMARKETERS!

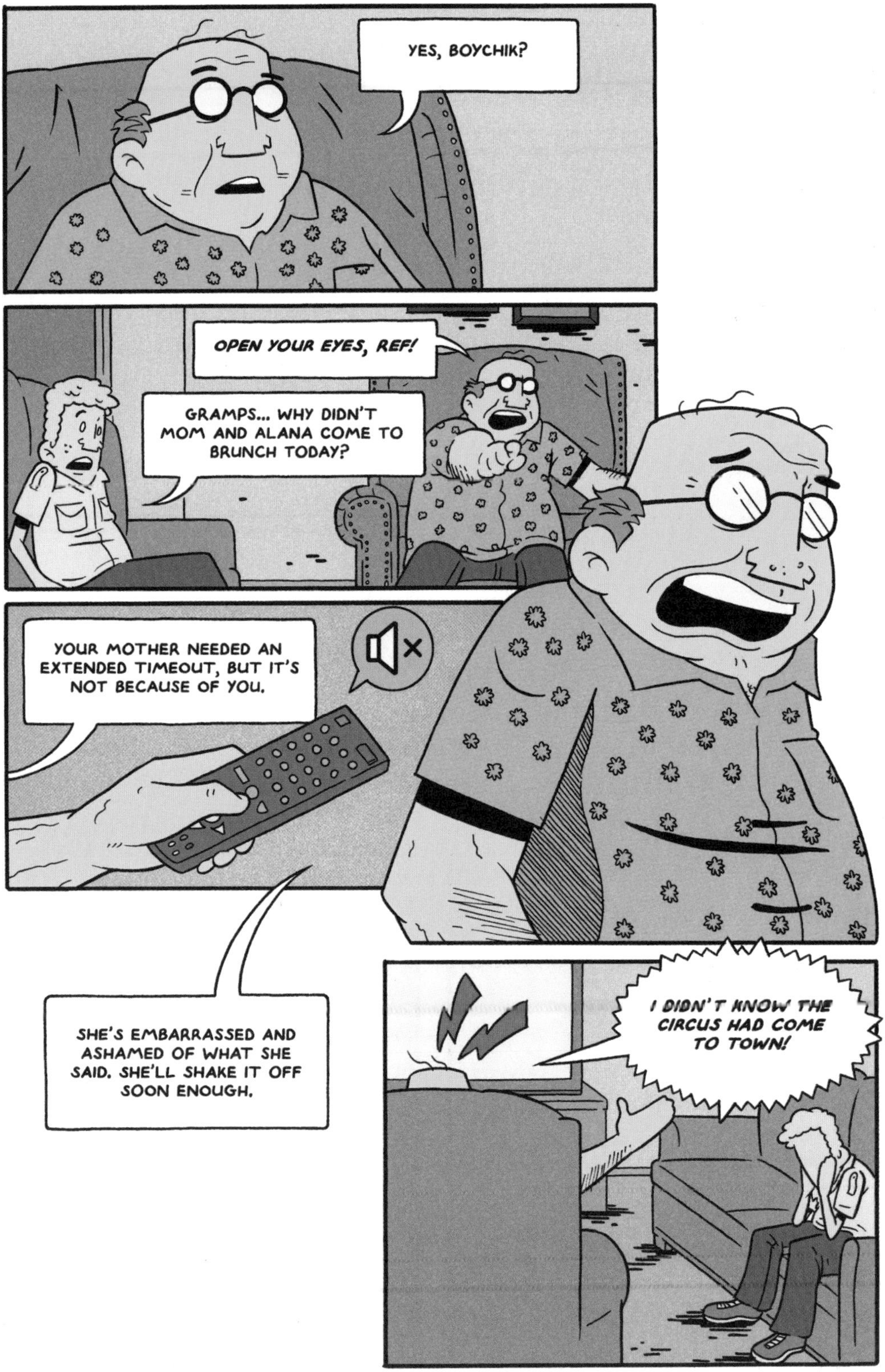
YES, BOYCHIK?
OPEN YOUR EYES, REF!
GRAMPS... WHY DIDN'T MOM AND ALANA COME TO BRUNCH TODAY?
YOUR MOTHER NEEDED AN EXTENDED TIMEOUT, BUT IT'S NOT BECAUSE OF YOU.
SHE'S EMBARRASSED AND ASHAMED OF WHAT SHE SAID. SHE'LL SHAKE IT OFF SOON ENOUGH.
I DIDN'T KNOW THE CIRCUS HAD COME TO TOWN!

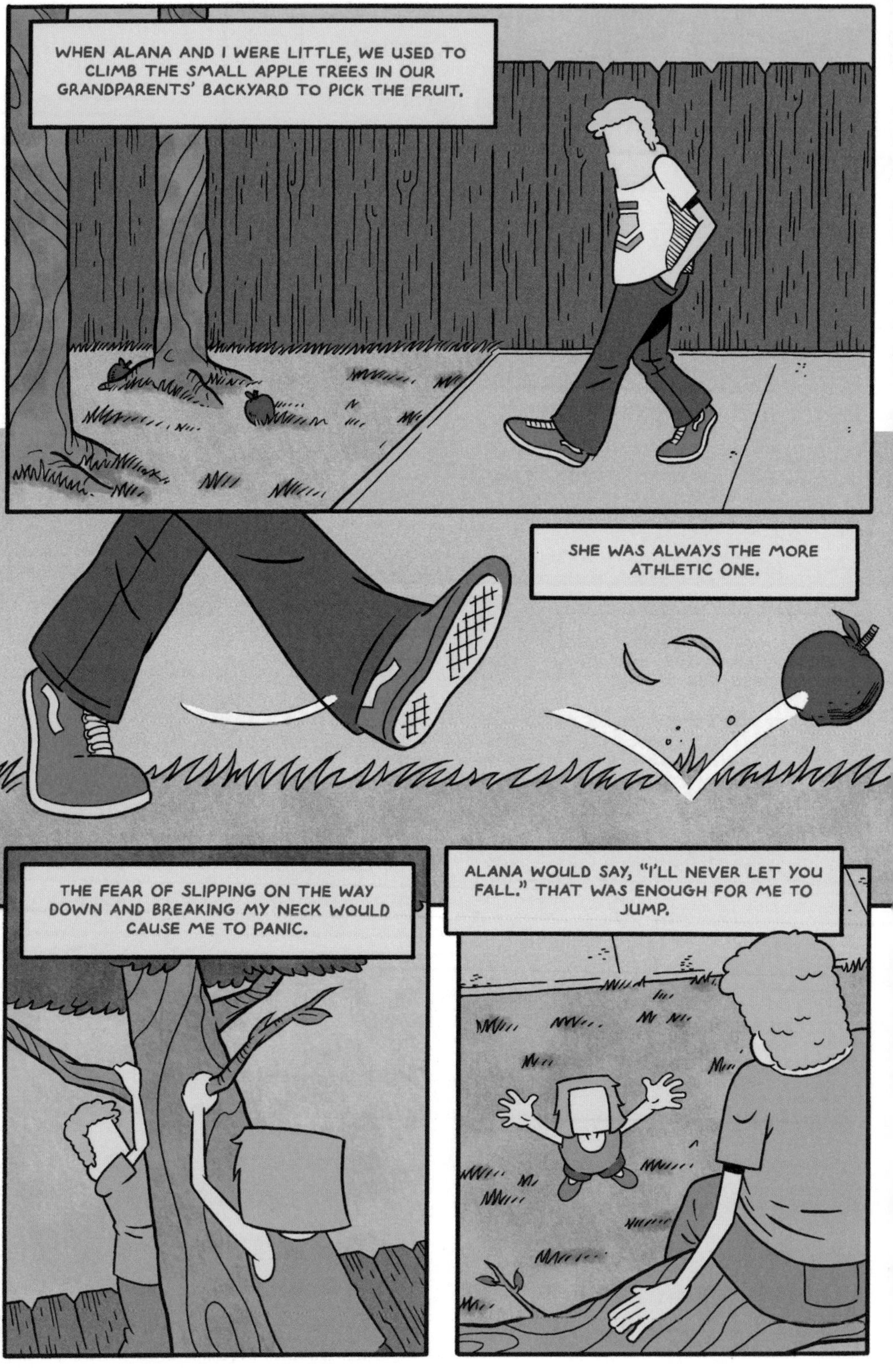
WHEN ALANA AND I WERE LITTLE, WE USED TO CLIMB THE SMALL APPLE TREES IN OUR GRANDPARENTS' BACKYARD TO PICK THE FRUIT.
SHE WAS ALWAYS THE MORE ATHLETIC ONE.
THE FEAR OF SLIPPING ON THE WAY DOWN AND BREAKING MY NECK WOULD CAUSE ME TO PANIC.
ALANA WOULD SAY, "I'LL NEVER LET YOU FALL." THAT WAS ENOUGH FOR ME TO JUMP.

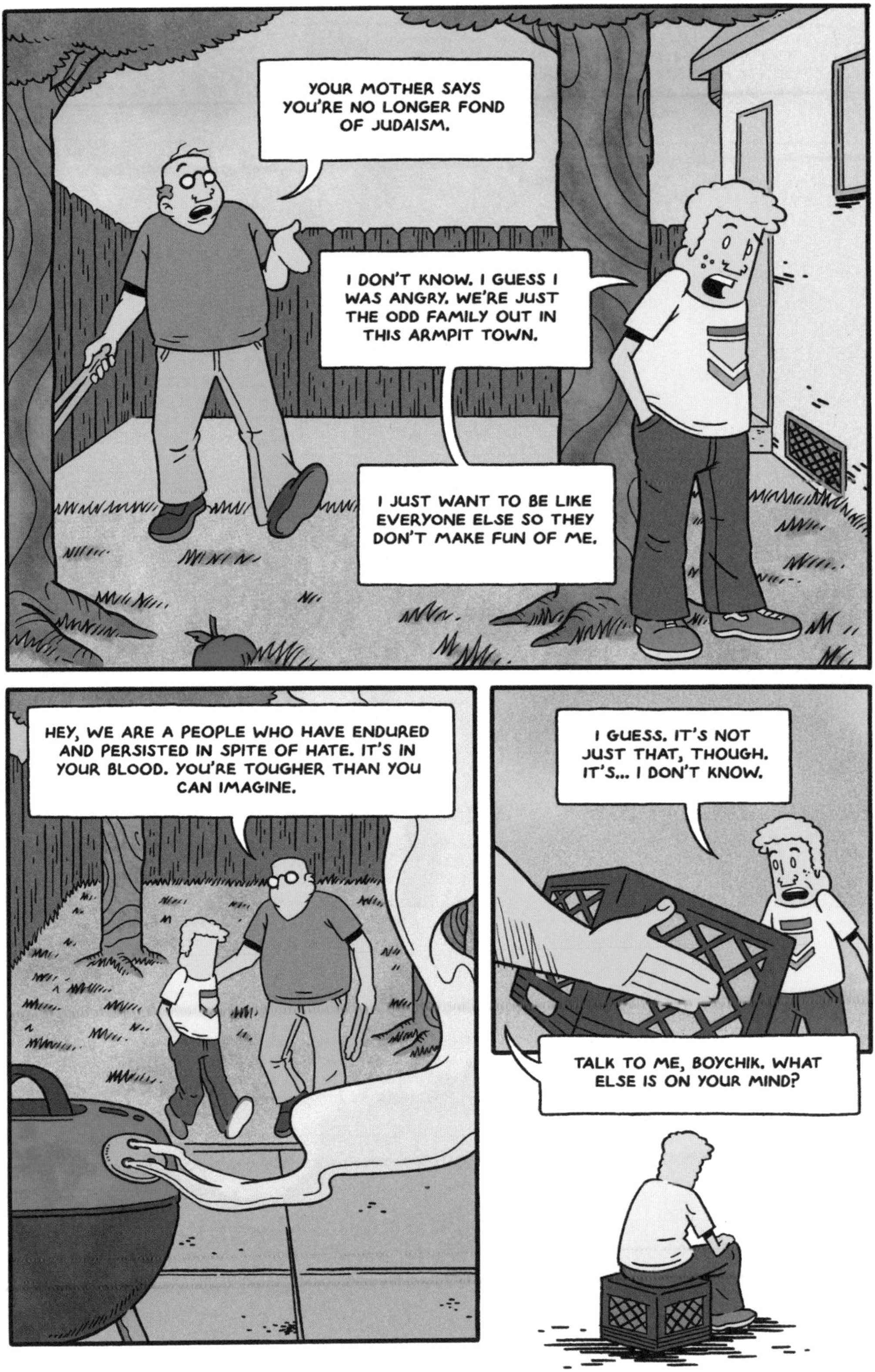
YOUR MOTHER SAYS YOU'RE NO LONGER FOND OF JUDAISM.
I DON'T KNOW. I GUESS I WAS ANGRY. WE'RE JUST THE ODD FAMILY OUT IN THIS ARMPIT TOWN.
I JUST WANT TO BE LIKE EVERYONE ELSE SO THEY DON'T MAKE FUN OF ME.
HEY, WE ARE A PEOPLE WHO HAVE ENDURED AND PERSISTED IN SPITE OF HATE. IT'S IN YOUR BLOOD. YOU'RE TOUGHER THAN YOU CAN IMAGINE.
I GUESS. IT'S NOT JUST THAT, THOUGH. IT'S... I DON'T KNOW.
TALK TO ME, BOYCHIK. WHAT ELSE IS ON YOUR MIND?

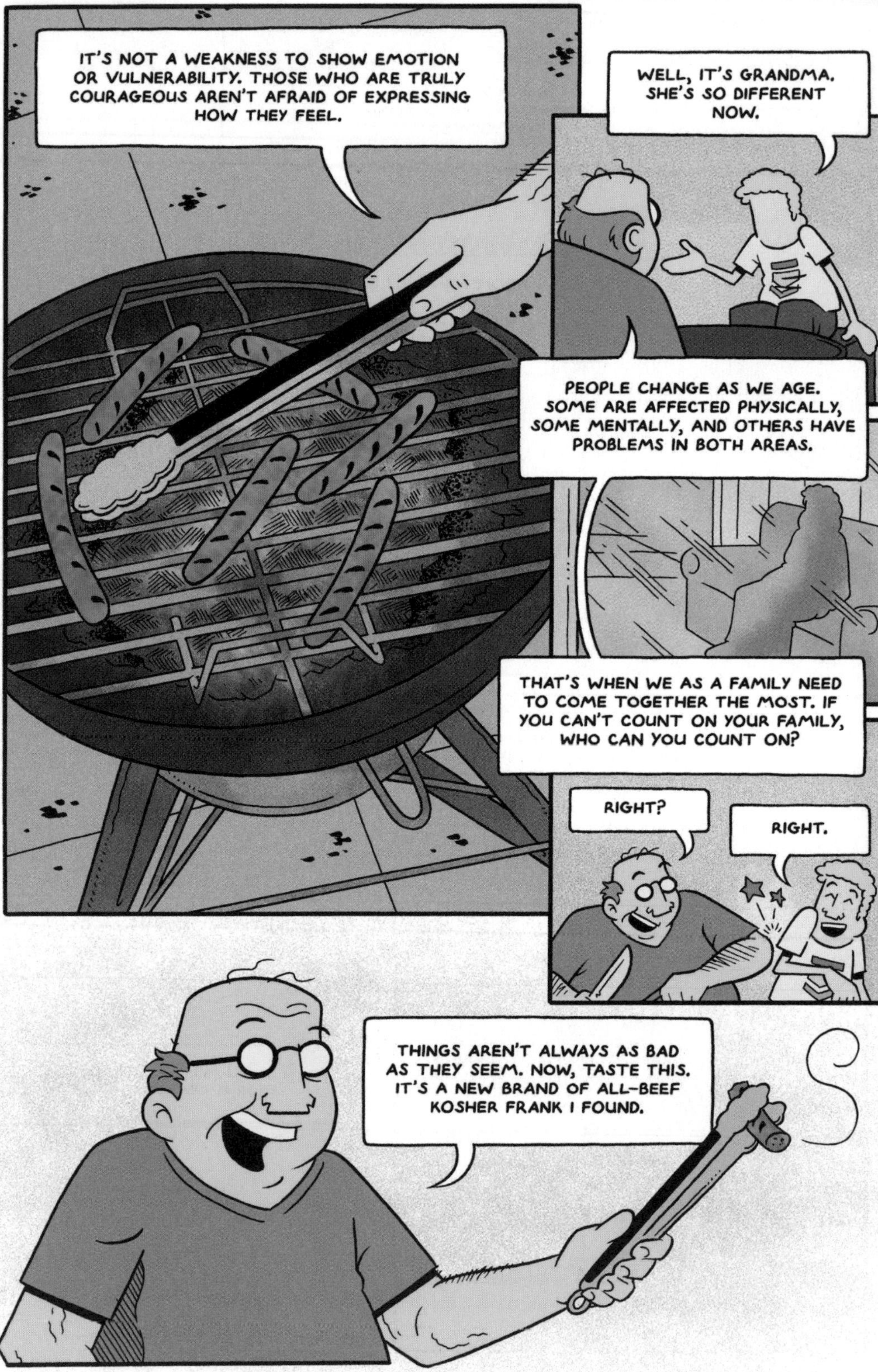
IT'S NOT A WEAKNESS TO SHOW EMOTION OR VULNERABILITY. THOSE WHO ARE TRULY COURAGEOUS AREN'T AFRAID OF EXPRESSING HOW THEY FEEL.
WELL, IT'S GRANDMA. SHE'S SO DIFFERENT NOW.
PEOPLE CHANGE AS WE AGE. SOME ARE AFFECTED PHYSICALLY, SOME MENTALLY, AND OTHERS HAVE PROBLEMS IN BOTH AREAS.
THAT'S WHEN WE AS A FAMILY NEED TO COME TOGETHER THE MOST. IF YOU CAN'T COUNT ON YOUR FAMILY, WHO CAN YOU COUNT ON?
RIGHT?
RIGHT.
THINGS AREN'T ALWAYS AS BAD AS THEY SEEM. NOW, TASTE THIS. IT'S A NEW BRAND OF ALL-BEEF KOSHER FRANK I FOUND.

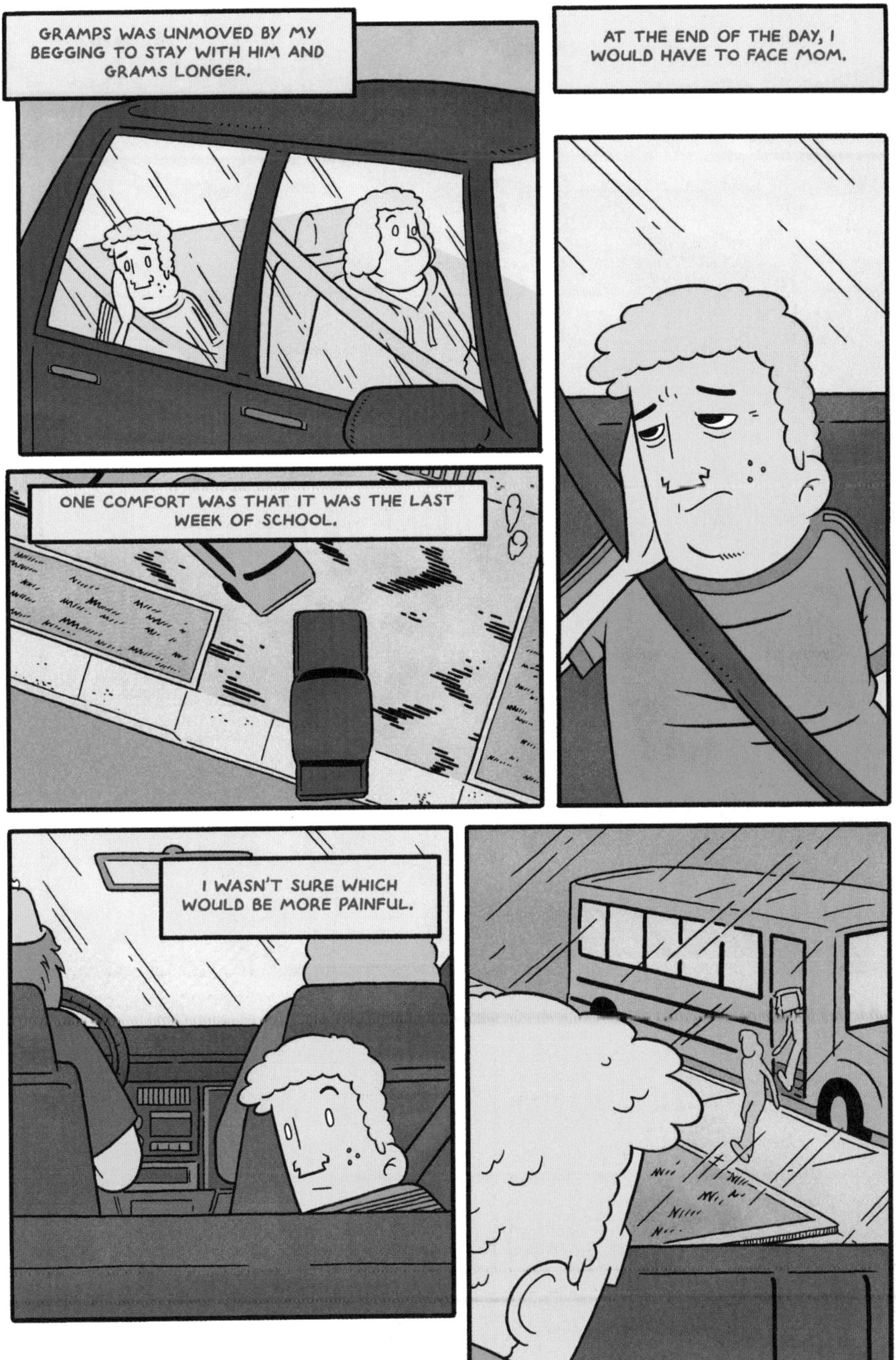
GRAMPS WAS UNMOVED BY MY BEGGING TO STAY WITH HIM AND GRAMS LONGER.
AT THE END OF THE DAY, I WOULD HAVE TO FACE MOM.
ONE COMFORT WAS THAT IT WAS THE LAST WEEK OF SCHOOL.
I WASN'T SURE WHICH WOULD BE MORE PAINFUL.

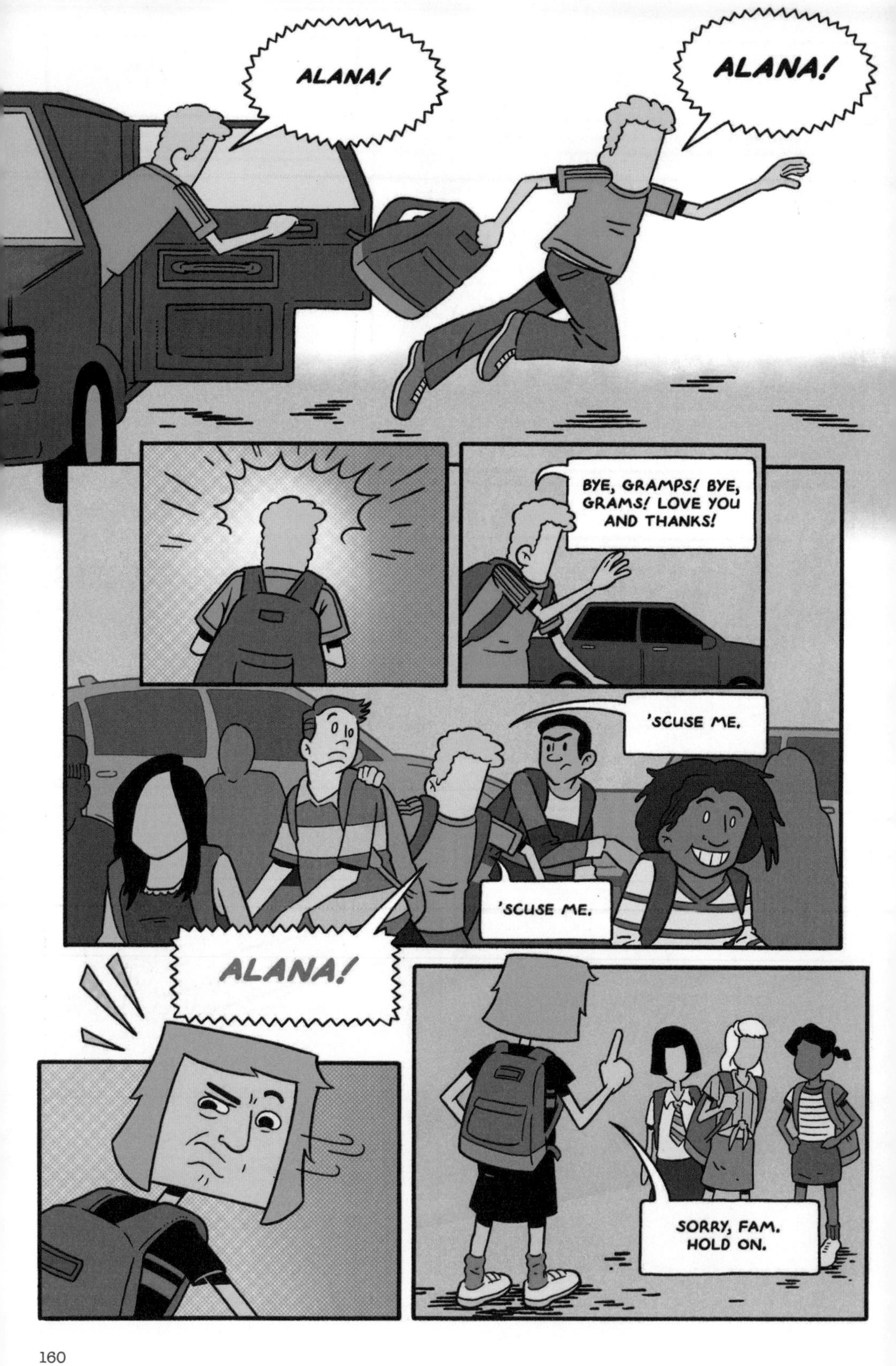
ALANA!
ALANA!
BYE, GRAMPS! BYE, GRAMS! LOVE YOU AND THANKS!
'SCUSE ME.
'SCUSE ME.
ALANA!
SORRY, FAM. HOLD ON.

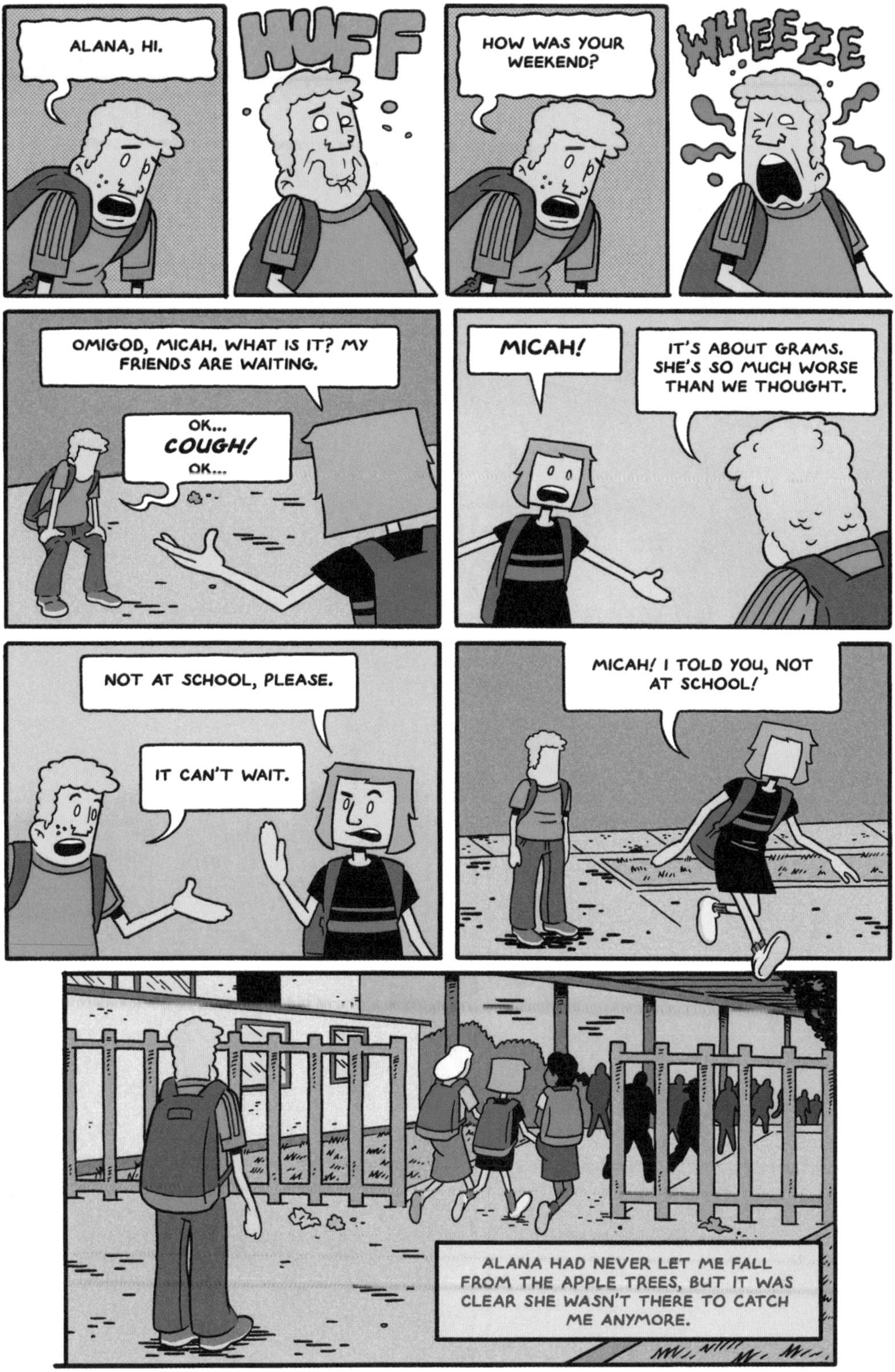

ALANA, HI.
HUFF
HOW WAS YOUR WEEKEND?
WHEEZE
OMIGOD, MICAH. WHAT IS IT? MY FRIENDS ARE WAITING.
OK... COUGH! OK...
MICAH!
IT'S ABOUT GRAMS. SHE'S SO MUCH WORSE THAN WE THOUGHT.
NOT AT SCHOOL, PLEASE.
IT CAN'T WAIT.
MICAH! I TOLD YOU, NOT AT SCHOOL!
ALANA HAD NEVER LET ME FALL FROM THE APPLE TREES, BUT IT WAS CLEAR SHE WASN'T THERE TO CATCH ME ANYMORE.

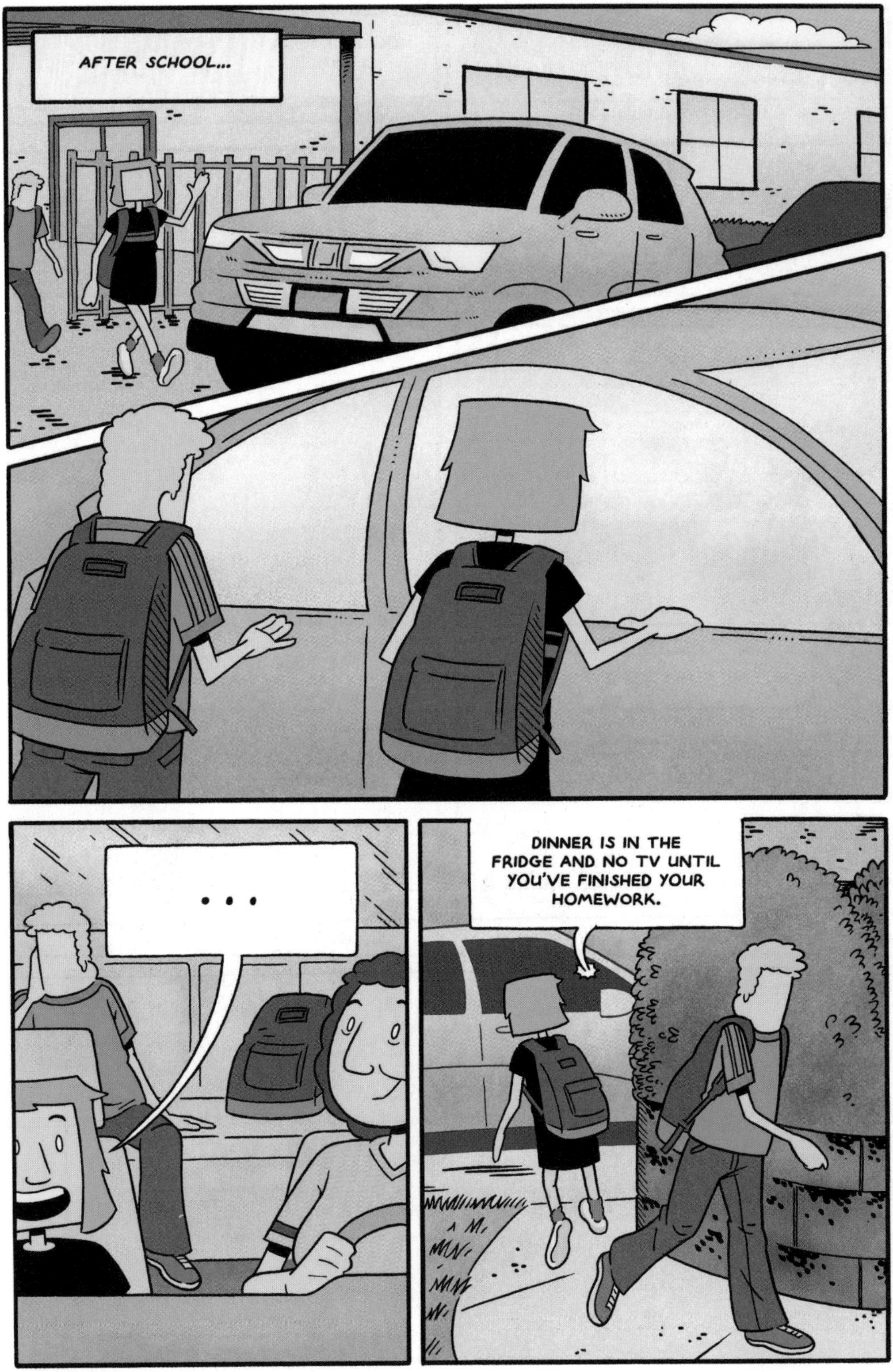
AFTER SCHOOL...
. . .
DINNER IS IN THE FRIDGE AND NO TV UNTIL YOU'VE FINISHED YOUR HOMEWORK.

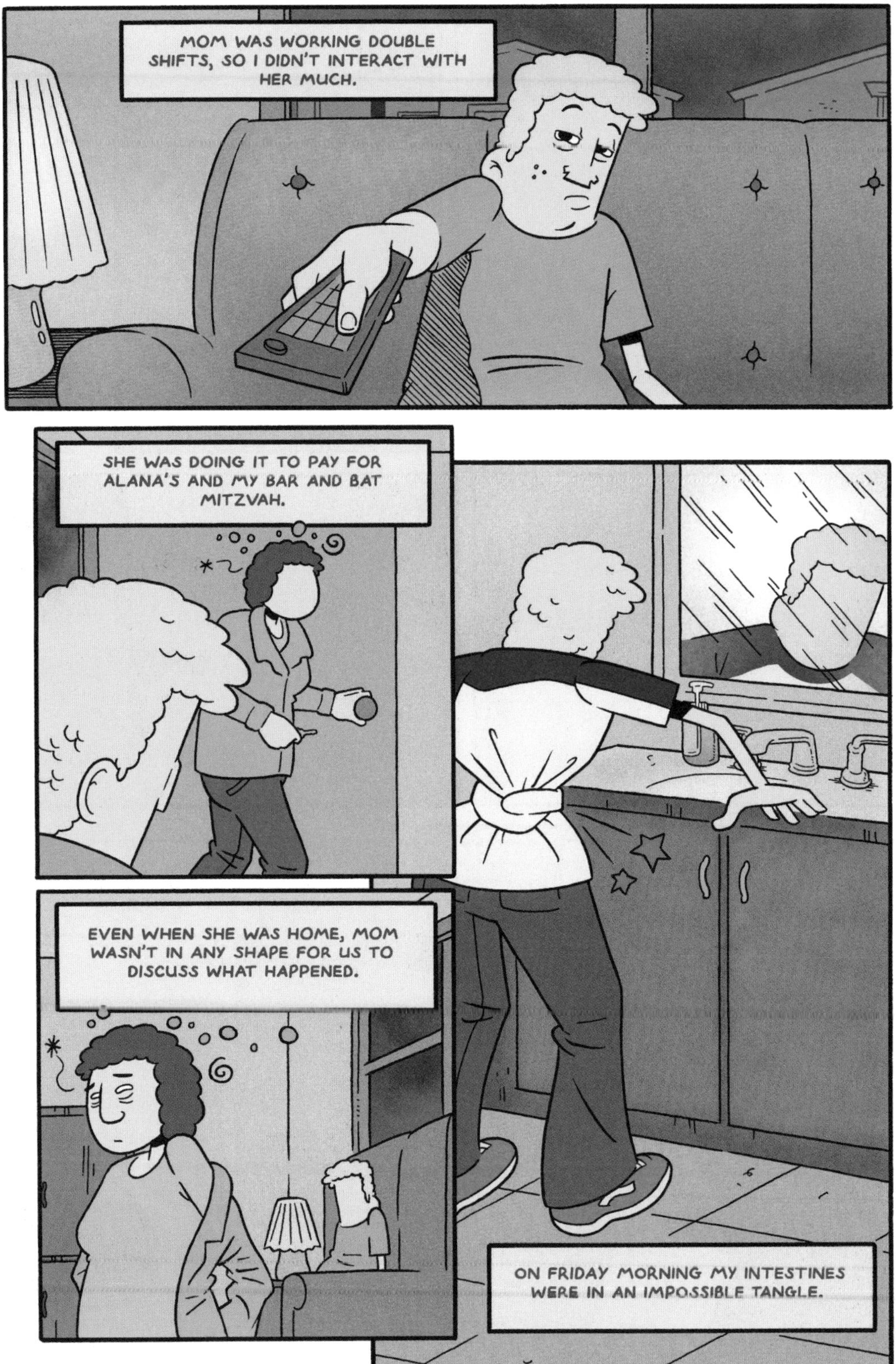
MOM WAS WORKING DOUBLE SHIFTS, SO I DIDN'T INTERACT WITH HER MUCH.
SHE WAS DOING IT TO PAY FOR ALANA'S AND MY BAR AND BAT MITZVAH.
EVEN WHEN SHE WAS HOME, MOM WASN'T IN ANY SHAPE FOR US TO DISCUSS WHAT HAPPENED.
ON FRIDAY MORNING MY INTESTINES WERE IN AN IMPOSSIBLE TANGLE.

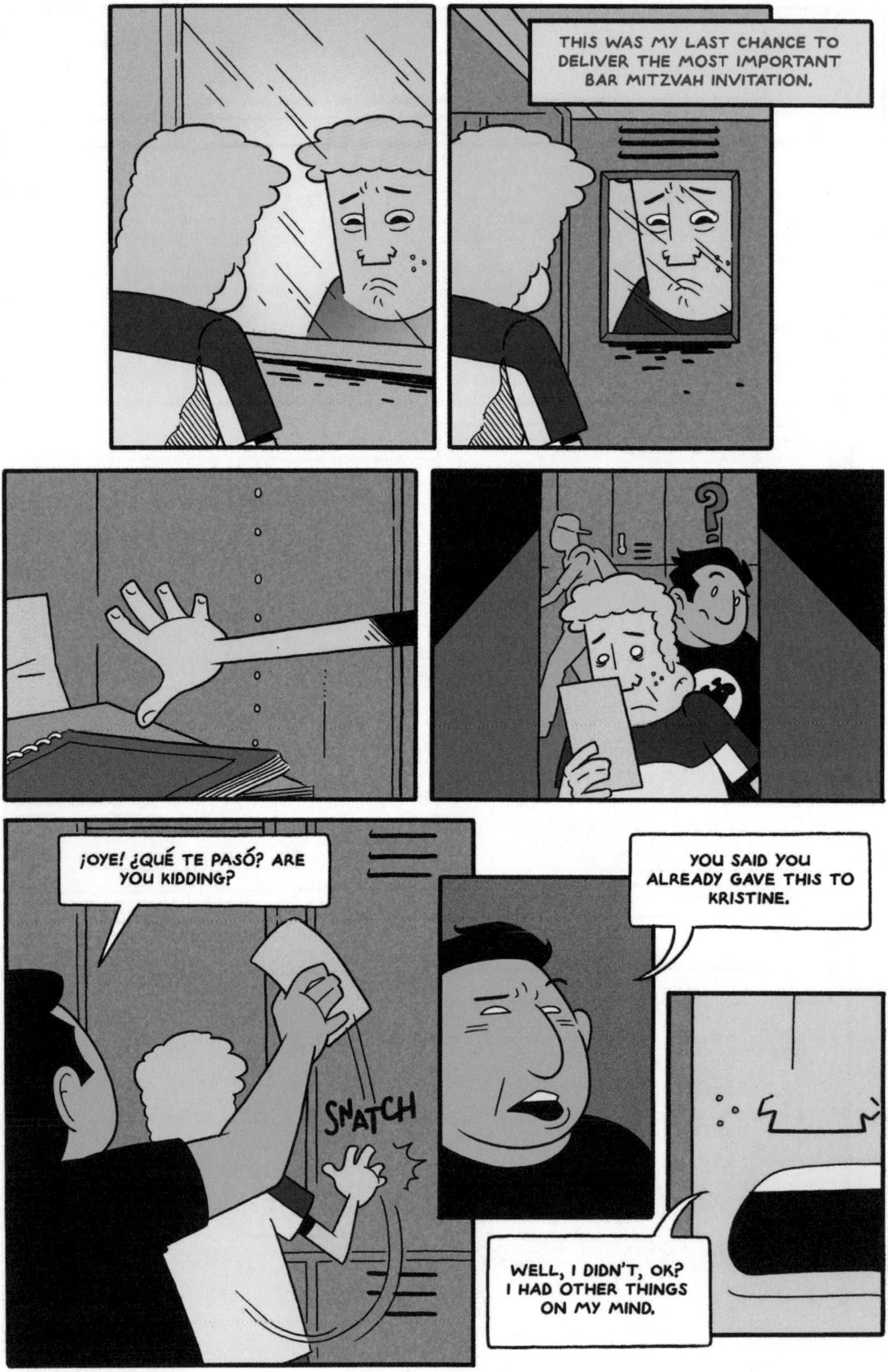
THIS WAS MY LAST CHANCE TO DELIVER THE MOST IMPORTANT BAR MITZVAH INVITATION.
?
¡OYE! ¿QUÉ TE PASÓ? ARE YOU KIDDING?
SNATCH
YOU SAID YOU ALREADY GAVE THIS TO KRISTINE.
WELL, I DIDN'T, OK? I HAD OTHER THINGS ON MY MIND.

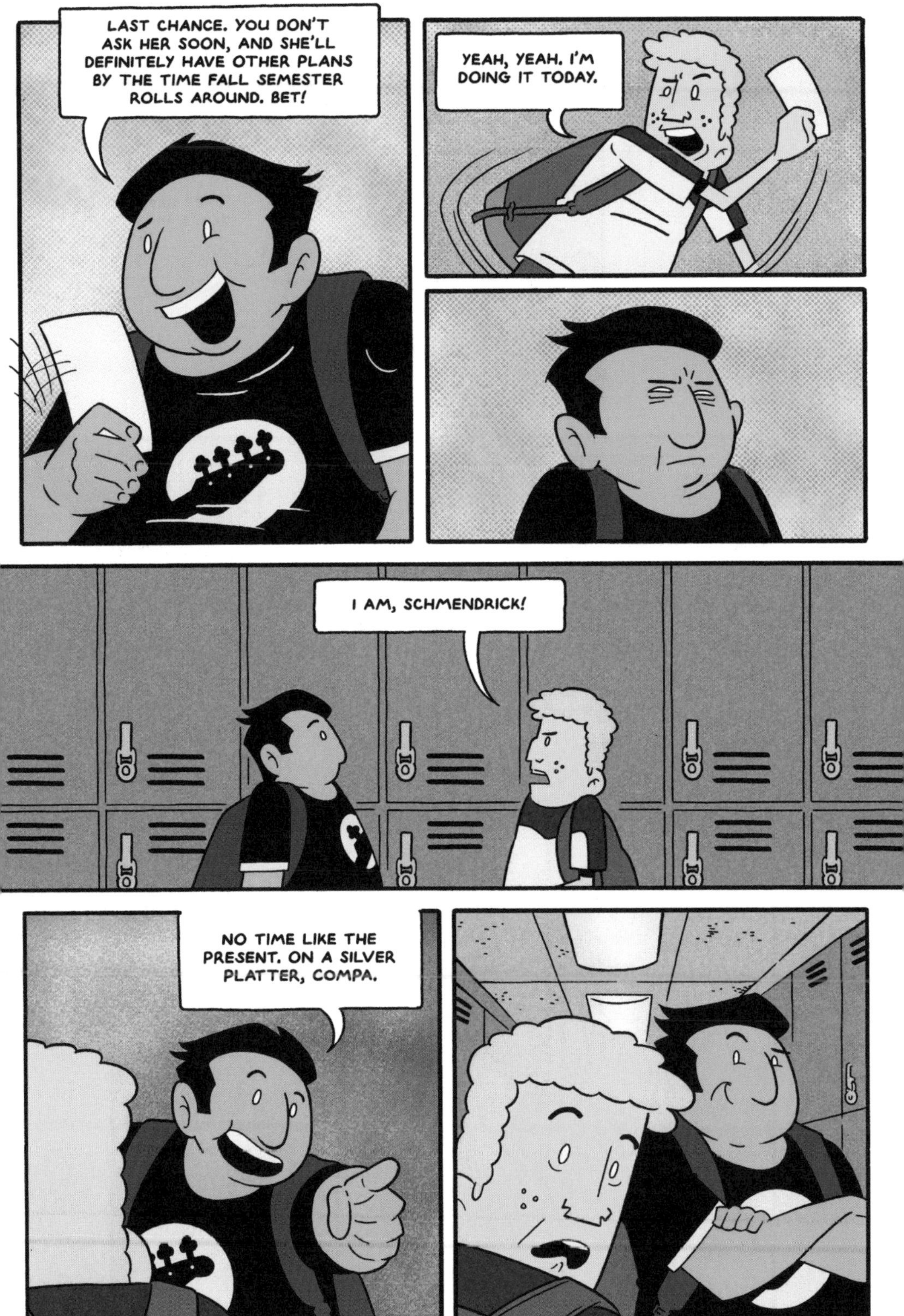
LAST CHANCE. YOU DON'T ASK HER SOON, AND SHE'LL DEFINITELY HAVE OTHER PLANS BY THE TIME FALL SEMESTER ROLLS AROUND. BET!
YEAH, YEAH. I'M DOING IT TODAY.
I AM, SCHMENDRICK!
NO TIME LIKE THE PRESENT. ON A SILVER PLATTER, COMPA.

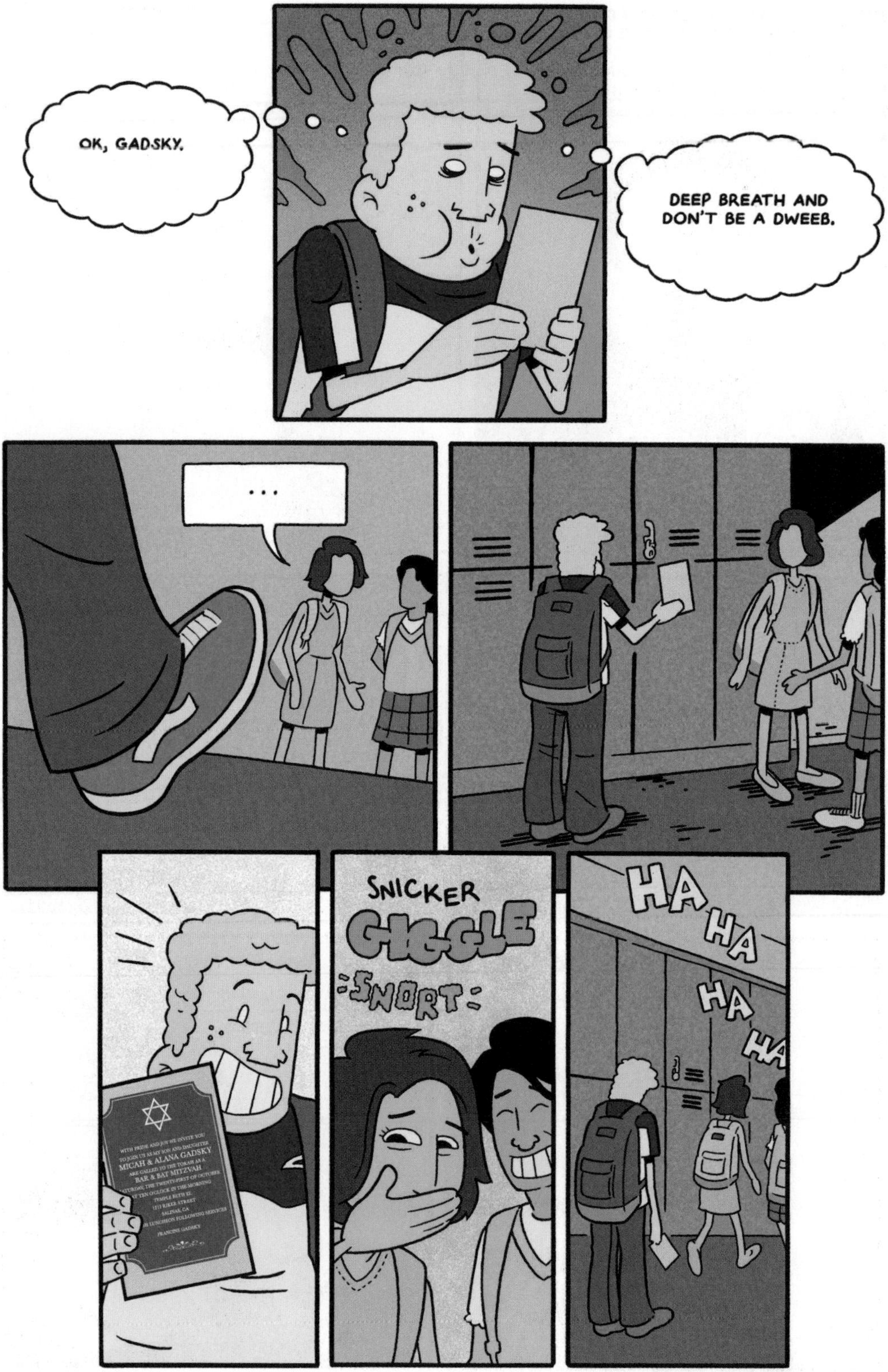
OK, GADSKY.
DEEP BREATH AND DON'T BE A DWEEB.
. . .
WITH PRIDE AND JOY WE INVITE YOU
TO JOIN US AS MY SON AND DAUGHTER
MICAH & ALANA GADSKY
ARE CALLED TO THE TORAH AS A
BAR & BAT MITZVAH
THE TWENTY-FIRST OF OCTOBER
O'CLOCK IN THE MORNING
TEMPLE BETH EL
1212 RIKER STREET
SALINAS, CA
LUNCHEON FOLLOWING SERVICES
FRANCINE GADSKY
SNICKER
GIGGLE
SNORT
HA HA HA HA

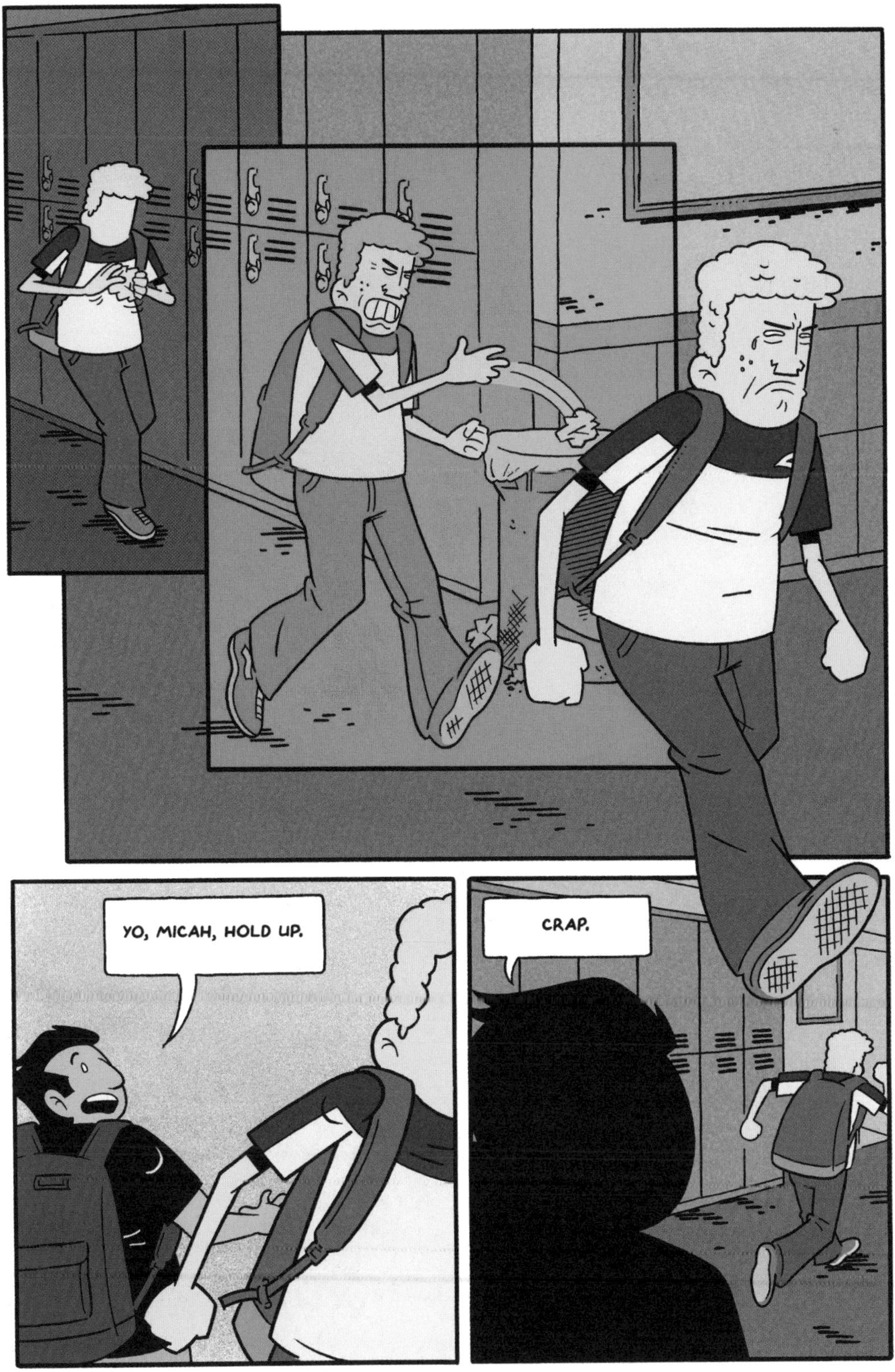
YO, MICAH, HOLD UP.
CRAP.

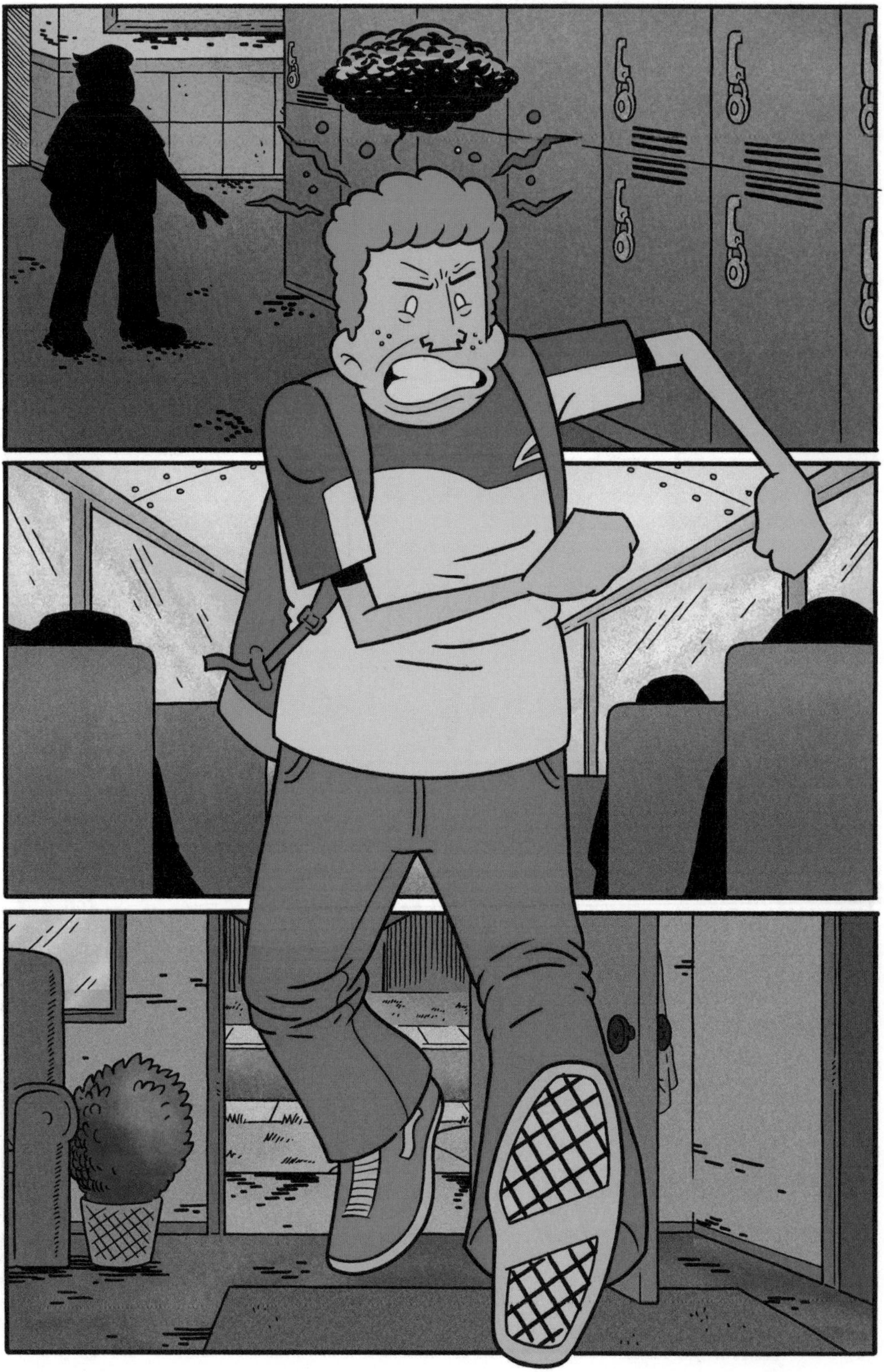

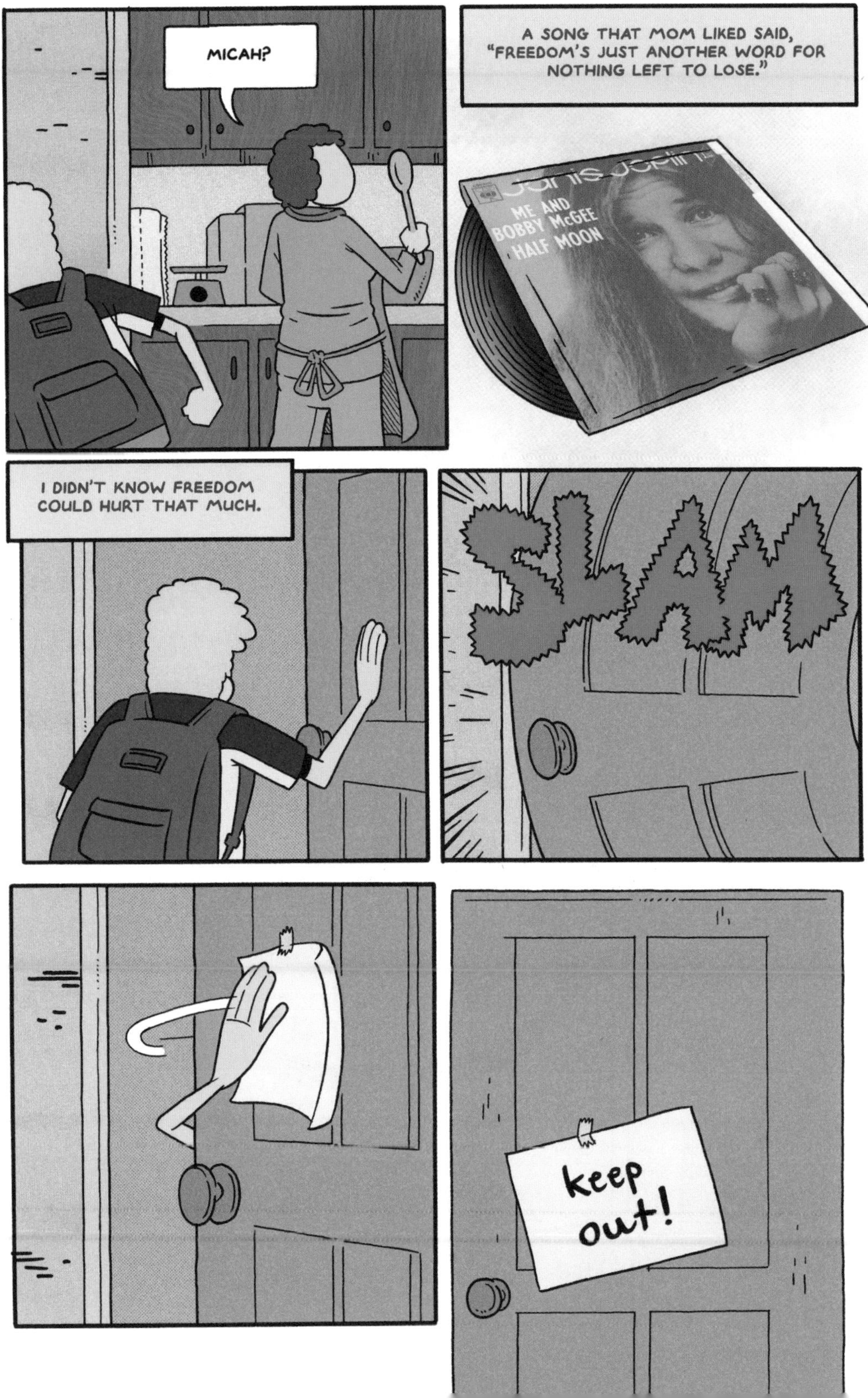

MICAH?
A SONG THAT MOM LIKED SAID, "FREEDOM'S JUST ANOTHER WORD FOR NOTHING LEFT TO LOSE."
ME AND
BOBBY McGEE
HALF MOON
I DIDN'T KNOW FREEDOM COULD HURT THAT MUCH.
SLAM
keep out!

PART 4

Seed Time

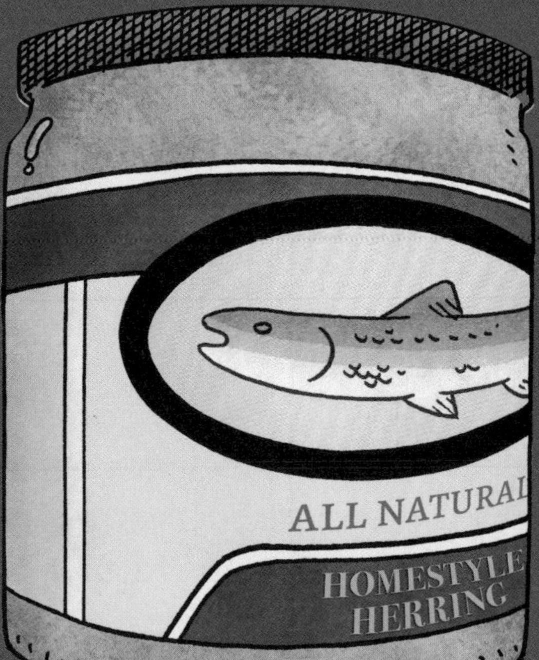
ALL NATURAL
HOMESTYLE
HERRING

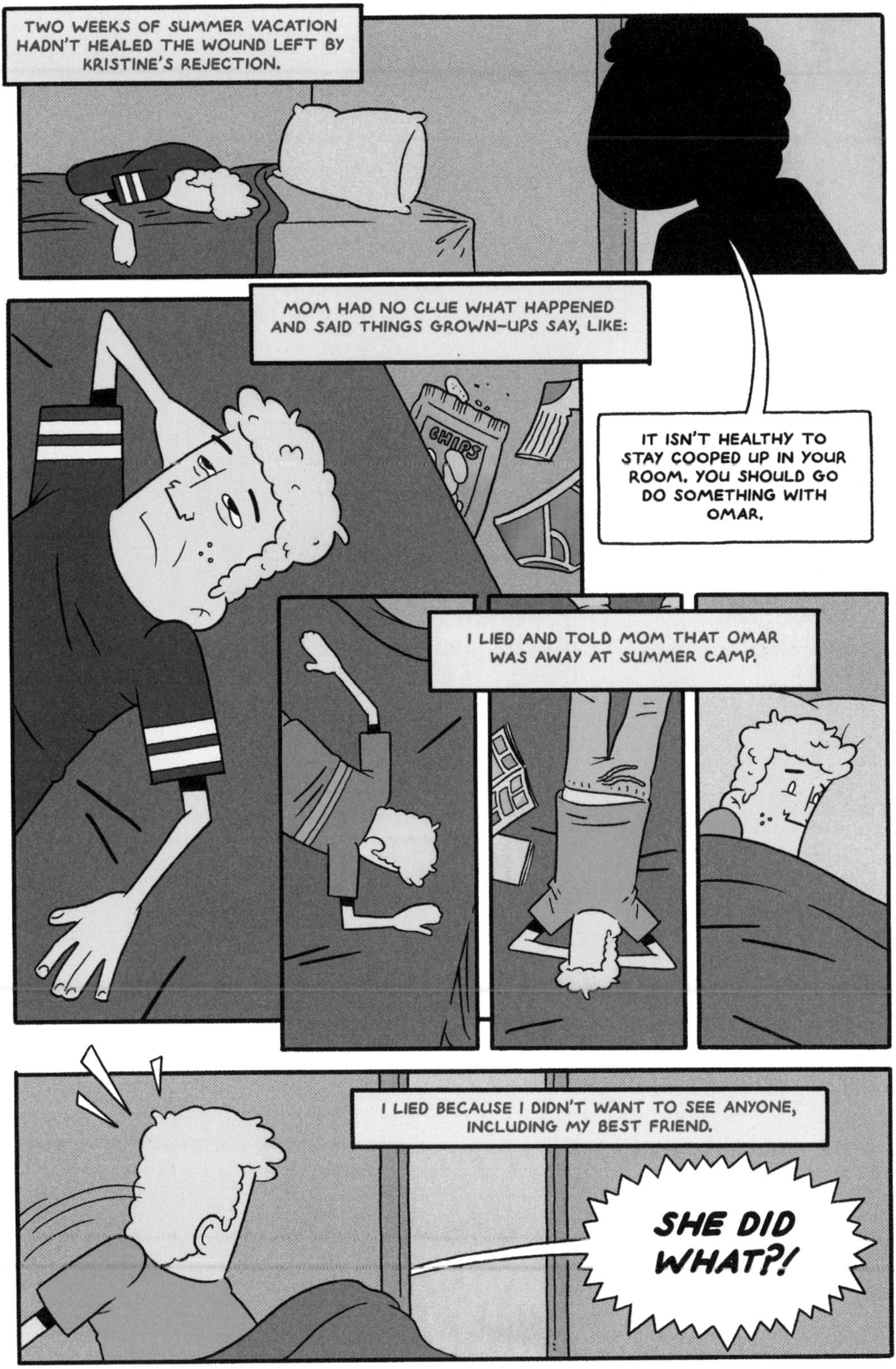
TWO WEEKS OF SUMMER VACATION HADN'T HEALED THE WOUND LEFT BY KRISTINE'S REJECTION.
MOM HAD NO CLUE WHAT HAPPENED AND SAID THINGS GROWN-UPS SAY, LIKE:
IT ISN'T HEALTHY TO STAY COOPED UP IN YOUR ROOM. YOU SHOULD GO DO SOMETHING WITH OMAR.
CHIPS
I LIED AND TOLD MOM THAT OMAR WAS AWAY AT SUMMER CAMP.
I LIED BECAUSE I DIDN'T WANT TO SEE ANYONE, INCLUDING MY BEST FRIEND.
SHE DID WHAT?!

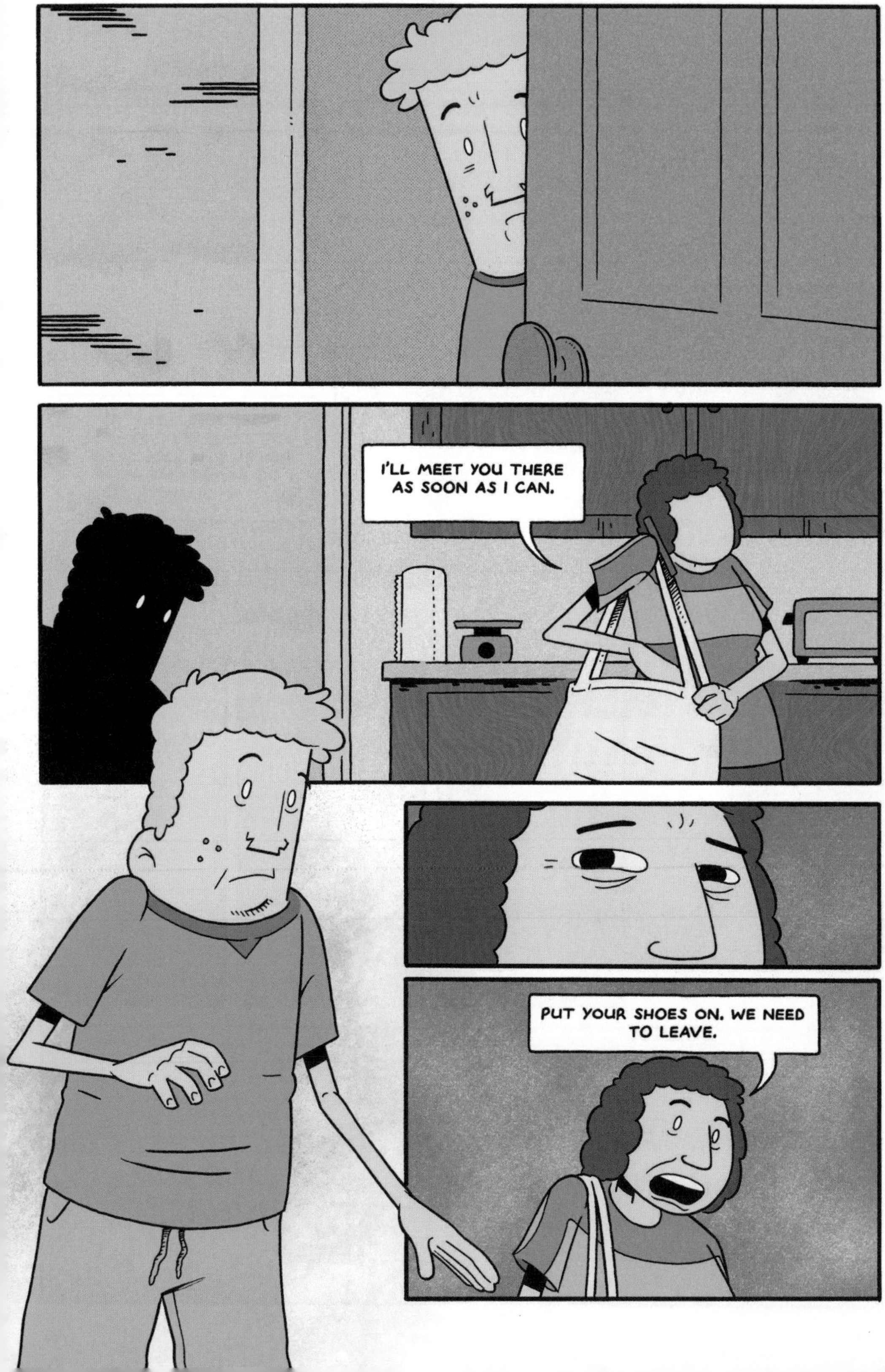

I'LL MEET YOU THERE AS SOON AS I CAN.
PUT YOUR SHOES ON. WE NEED TO LEAVE.

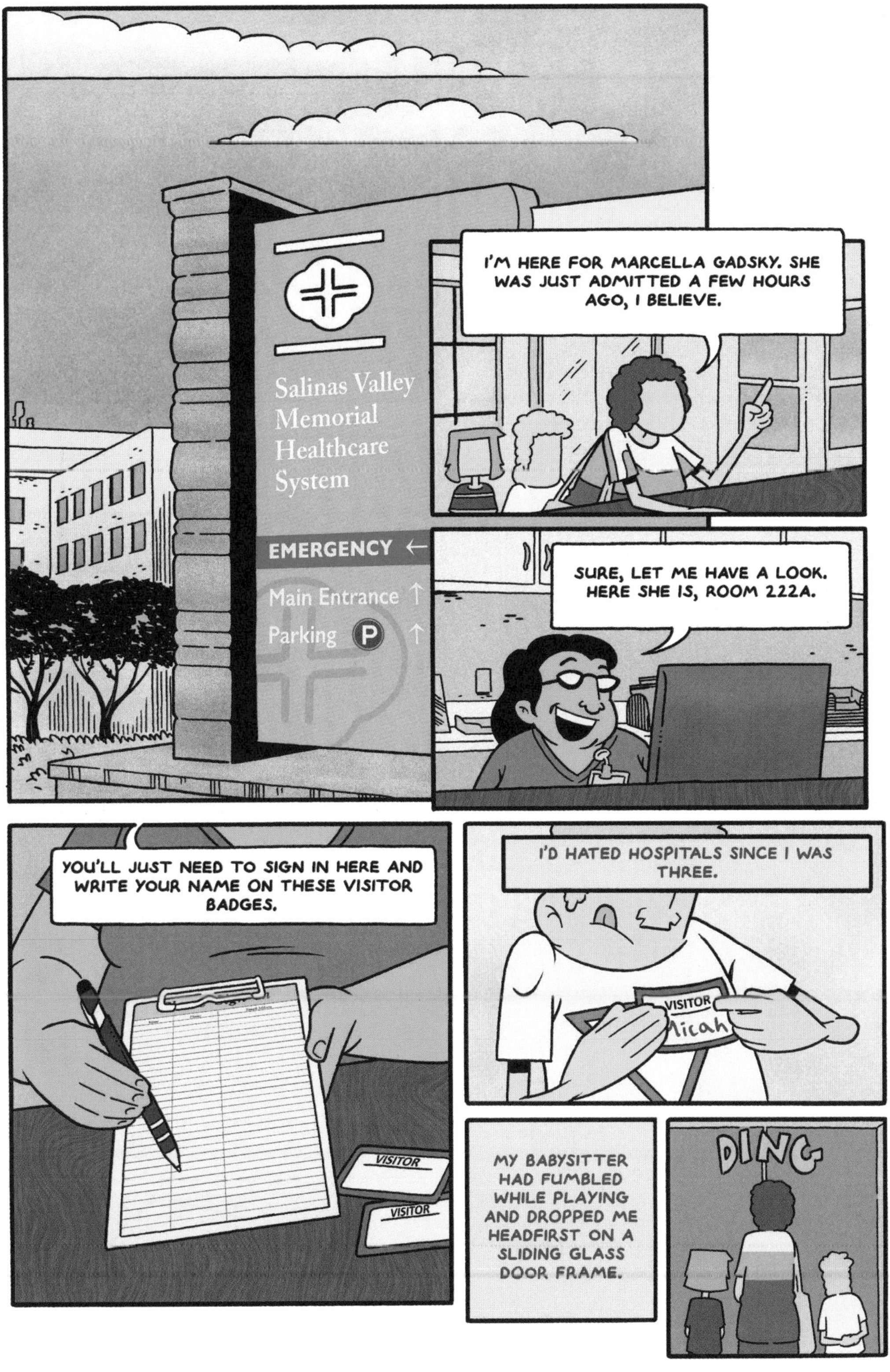
Salinas Valley Memorial Healthcare System
EMERGENCY
Main Entrance
Parking
P
I'M HERE FOR MARCELLA GADSKY. SHE WAS JUST ADMITTED A FEW HOURS AGO, I BELIEVE.
SURE, LET ME HAVE A LOOK. HERE SHE IS, ROOM 222A.
YOU'LL JUST NEED TO SIGN IN HERE AND WRITE YOUR NAME ON THESE VISITOR BADGES.
VISITOR
VISITOR
I'D HATED HOSPITALS SINCE I WAS THREE.
VISITOR
Micah
MY BABYSITTER HAD FUMBLED WHILE PLAYING AND DROPPED ME HEADFIRST ON A SLIDING GLASS DOOR FRAME.
DING

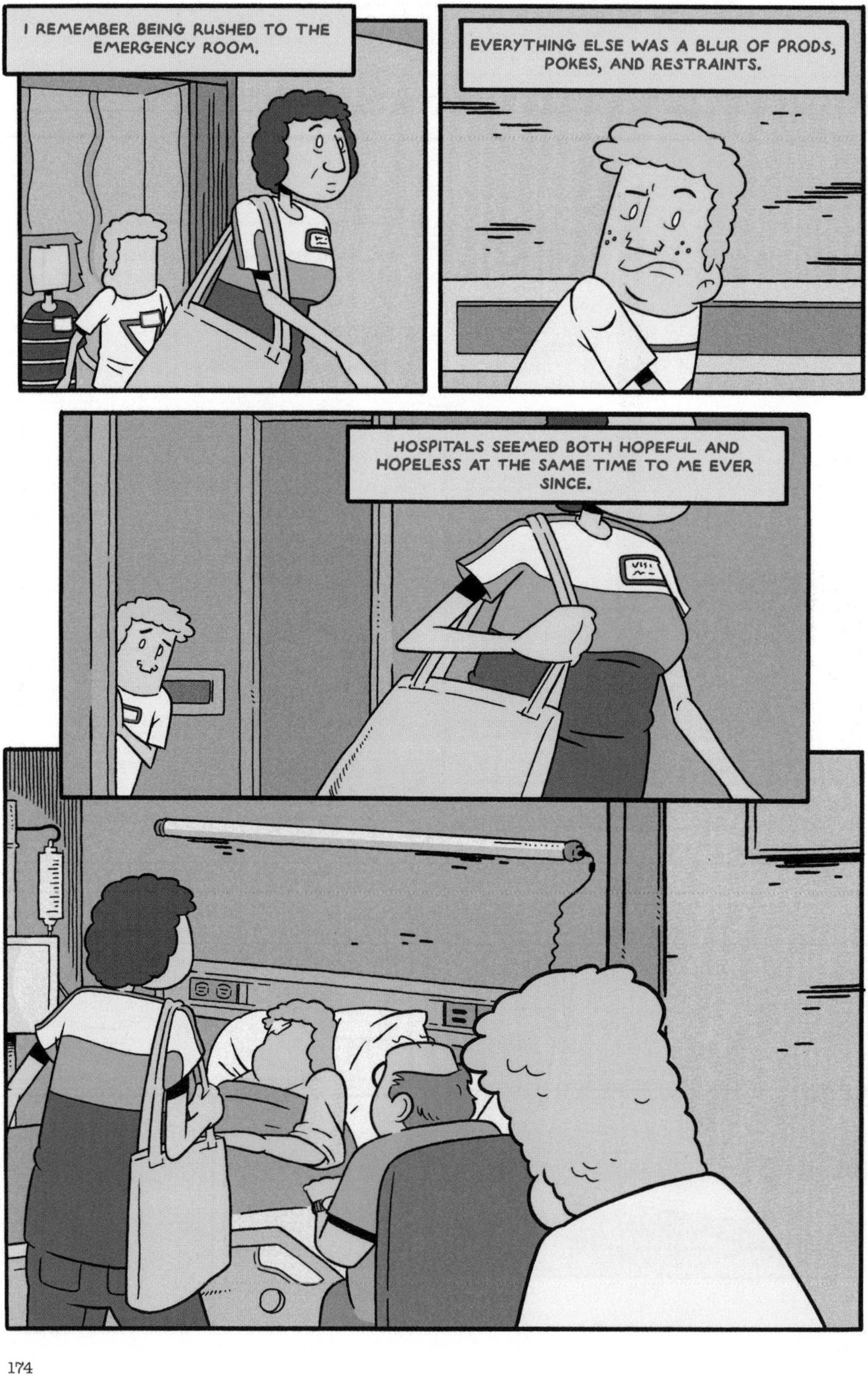
I REMEMBER BEING RUSHED TO THE EMERGENCY ROOM.
EVERYTHING ELSE WAS A BLUR OF PRODS, POKES, AND RESTRAINTS.
HOSPITALS SEEMED BOTH HOPEFUL AND HOPELESS AT THE SAME TIME TO ME EVER SINCE.

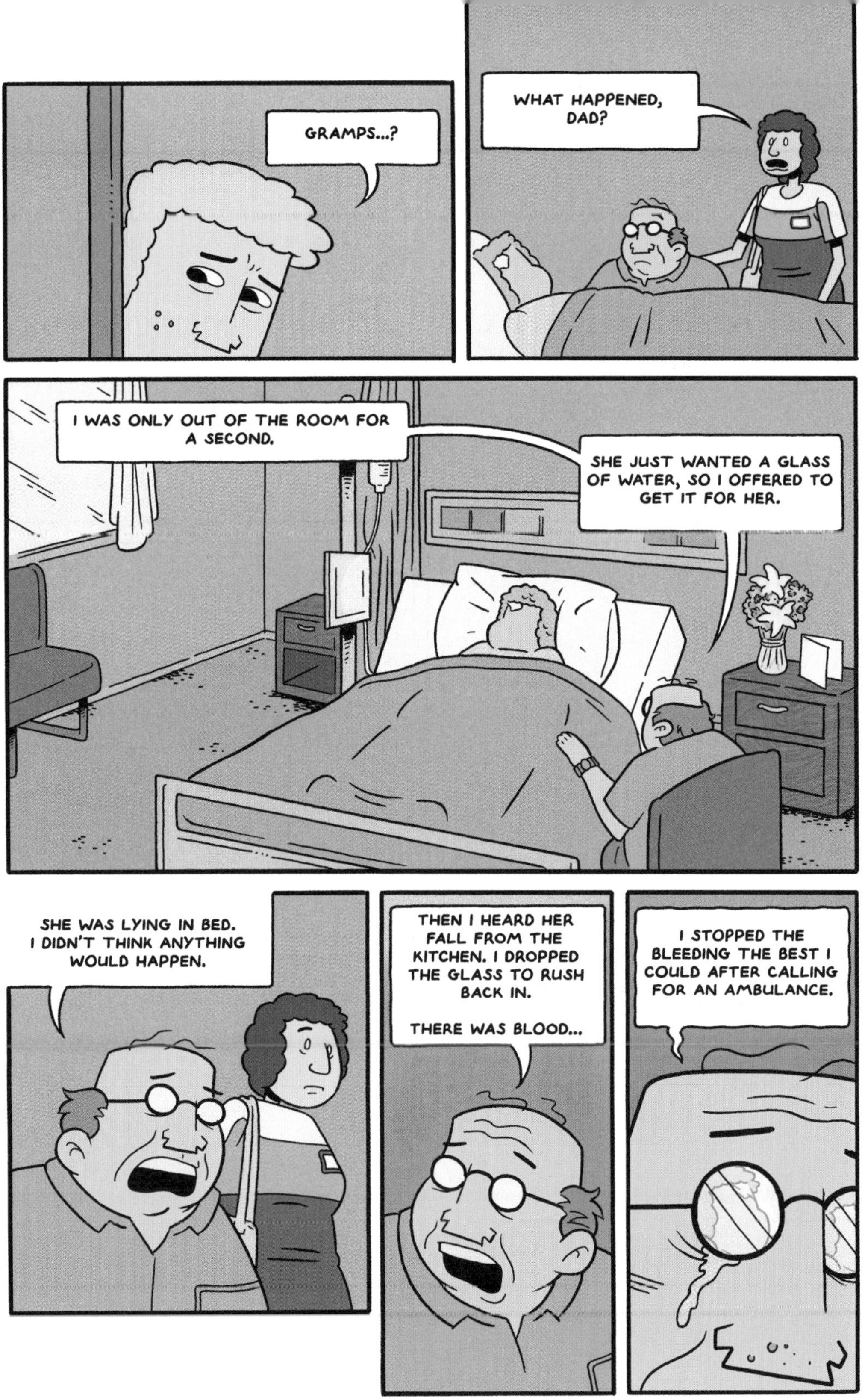
GRAMPS...?
WHAT HAPPENED, DAD?
I WAS ONLY OUT OF THE ROOM FOR A SECOND.
SHE JUST WANTED A GLASS OF WATER, SO I OFFERED TO GET IT FOR HER.
SHE WAS LYING IN BED. I DIDN'T THINK ANYTHING WOULD HAPPEN.
THEN I HEARD HER FALL FROM THE KITCHEN. I DROPPED THE GLASS TO RUSH BACK IN.
THERE WAS BLOOD...
I STOPPED THE BLEEDING THE BEST I COULD AFTER CALLING FOR AN AMBULANCE.

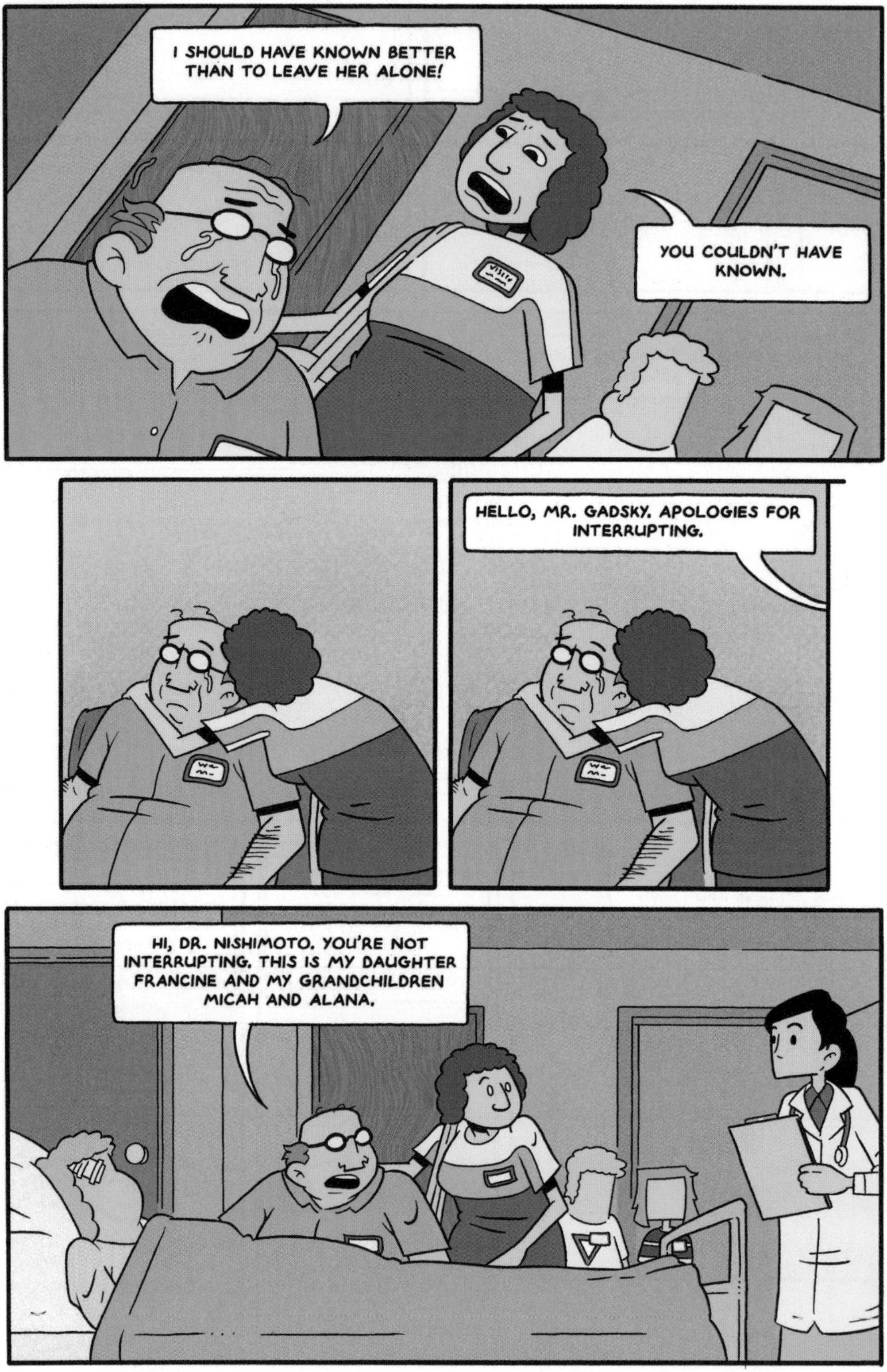
I SHOULD HAVE KNOWN BETTER THAN TO LEAVE HER ALONE!
YOU COULDN'T HAVE KNOWN.
HELLO, MR. GADSKY. APOLOGIES FOR INTERRUPTING.
HI, DR. NISHIMOTO. YOU'RE NOT INTERRUPTING. THIS IS MY DAUGHTER FRANCINE AND MY GRANDCHILDREN MICAH AND ALANA.

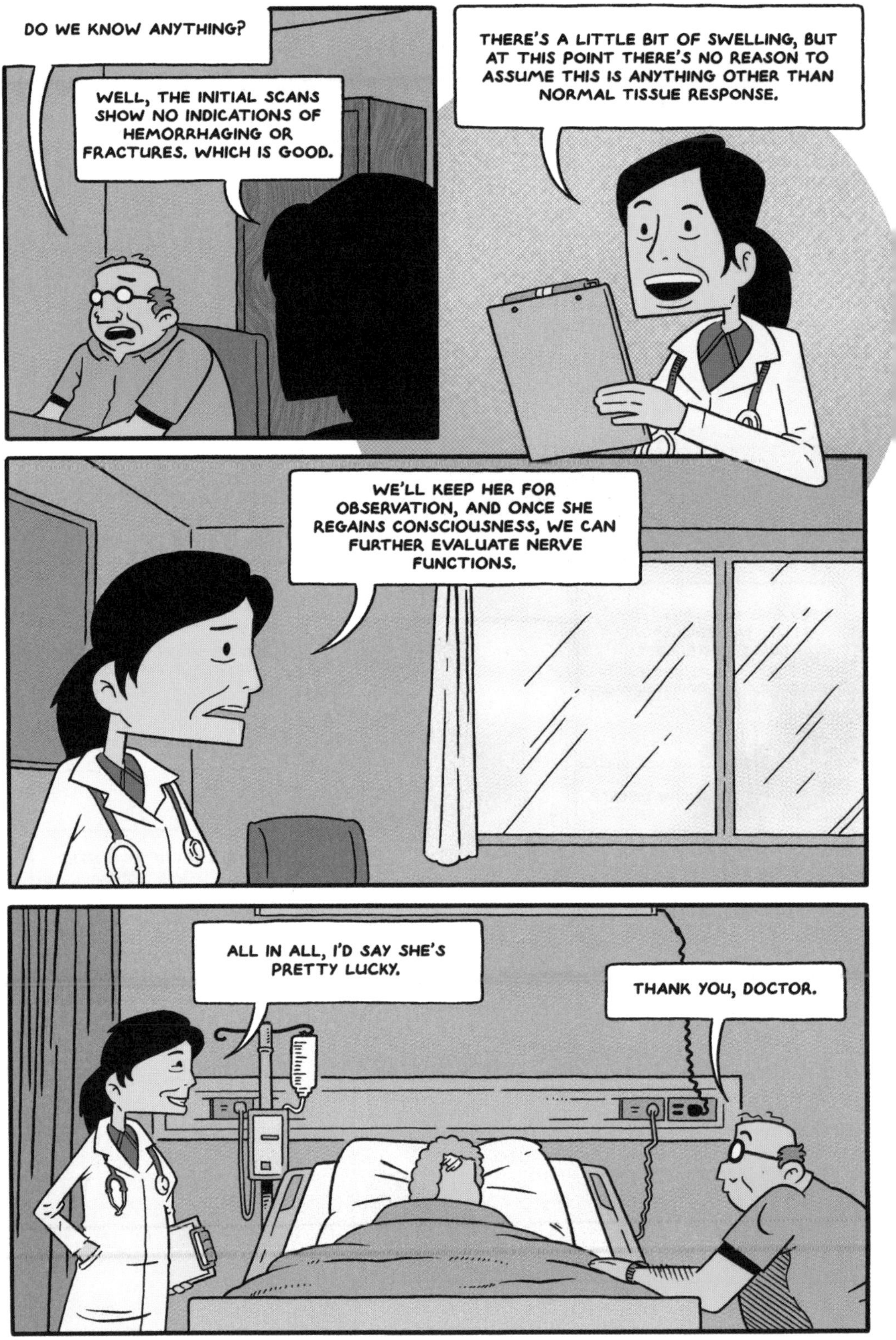
DO WE KNOW ANYTHING?
WELL, THE INITIAL SCANS SHOW NO INDICATIONS OF HEMORRHAGING OR FRACTURES. WHICH IS GOOD.
THERE'S A LITTLE BIT OF SWELLING, BUT AT THIS POINT THERE'S NO REASON TO ASSUME THIS IS ANYTHING OTHER THAN NORMAL TISSUE RESPONSE.
WE'LL KEEP HER FOR OBSERVATION, AND ONCE SHE REGAINS CONSCIOUSNESS, WE CAN FURTHER EVALUATE NERVE FUNCTIONS.
ALL IN ALL, I'D SAY SHE'S PRETTY LUCKY.
THANK YOU, DOCTOR.

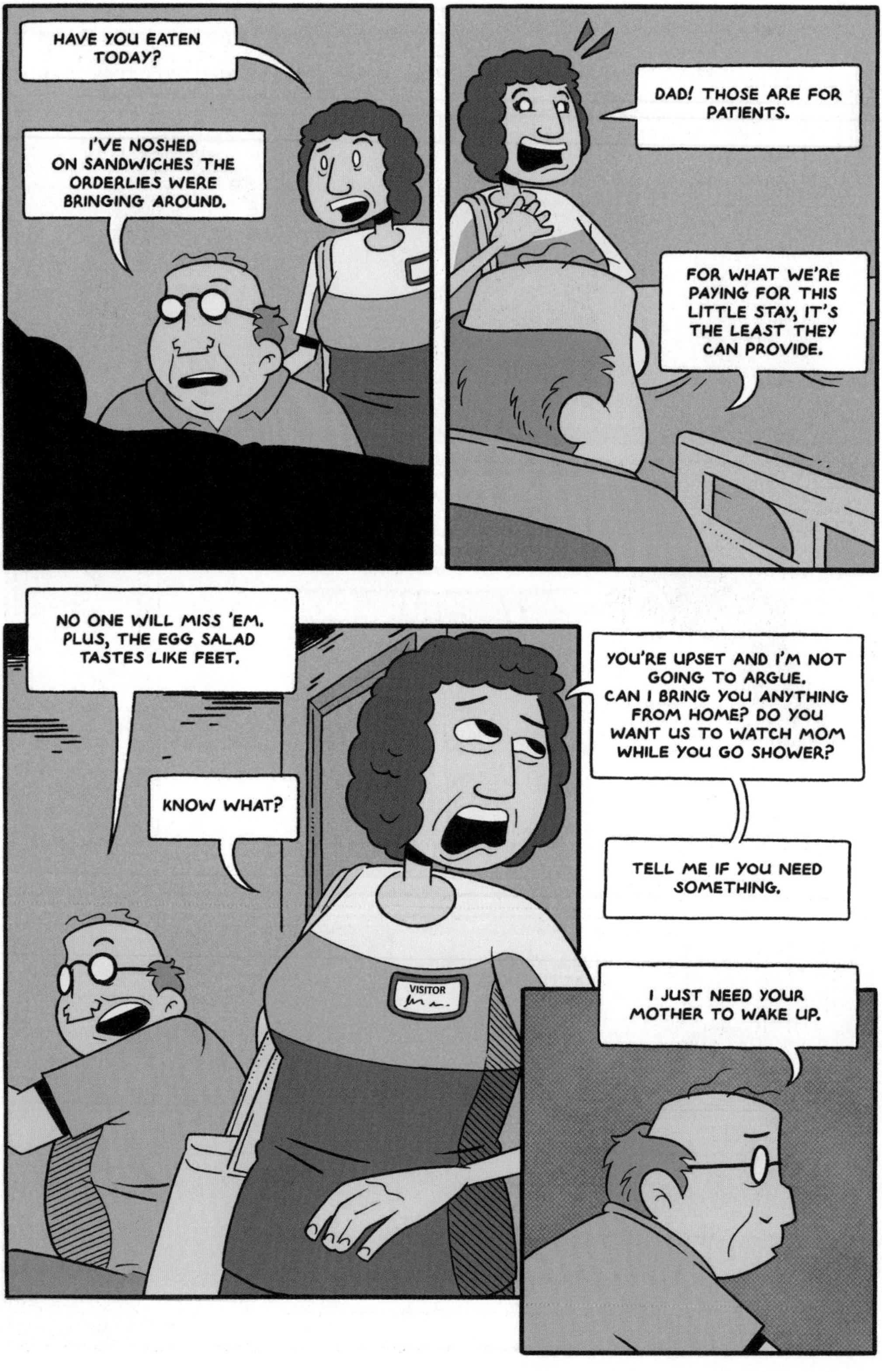
HAVE YOU EATEN TODAY?
I'VE NOSHED ON SANDWICHES THE ORDERLIES WERE BRINGING AROUND.
DAD! THOSE ARE FOR PATIENTS.
FOR WHAT WE'RE PAYING FOR THIS LITTLE STAY, IT'S THE LEAST THEY CAN PROVIDE.
NO ONE WILL MISS 'EM. PLUS, THE EGG SALAD TASTES LIKE FEET.
KNOW WHAT?
YOU'RE UPSET AND I'M NOT GOING TO ARGUE. CAN I BRING YOU ANYTHING FROM HOME? DO YOU WANT US TO WATCH MOM WHILE YOU GO SHOWER?
TELL ME IF YOU NEED SOMETHING.
VISITOR
I JUST NEED YOUR MOTHER TO WAKE UP.

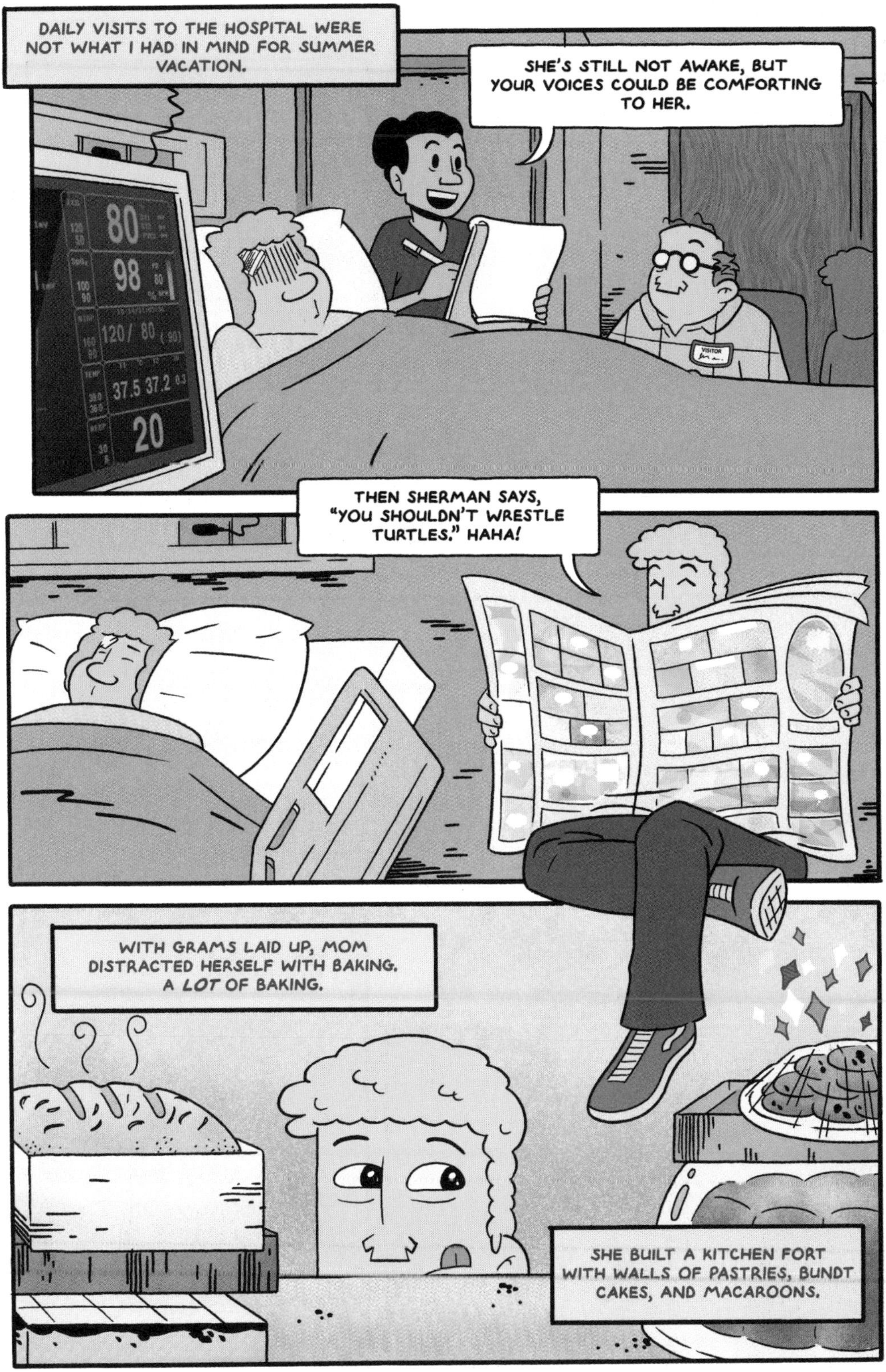
DAILY VISITS TO THE HOSPITAL WERE NOT WHAT I HAD IN MIND FOR SUMMER VACATION.
SHE'S STILL NOT AWAKE, BUT YOUR VOICES COULD BE COMFORTING TO HER.
VISITOR
THEN SHERMAN SAYS, "YOU SHOULDN'T WRESTLE TURTLES." HAHA!
WITH GRAMS LAID UP, MOM DISTRACTED HERSELF WITH BAKING. A *LOT* OF BAKING.
SHE BUILT A KITCHEN FORT WITH WALLS OF PASTRIES, BUNDT CAKES, AND MACAROONS.

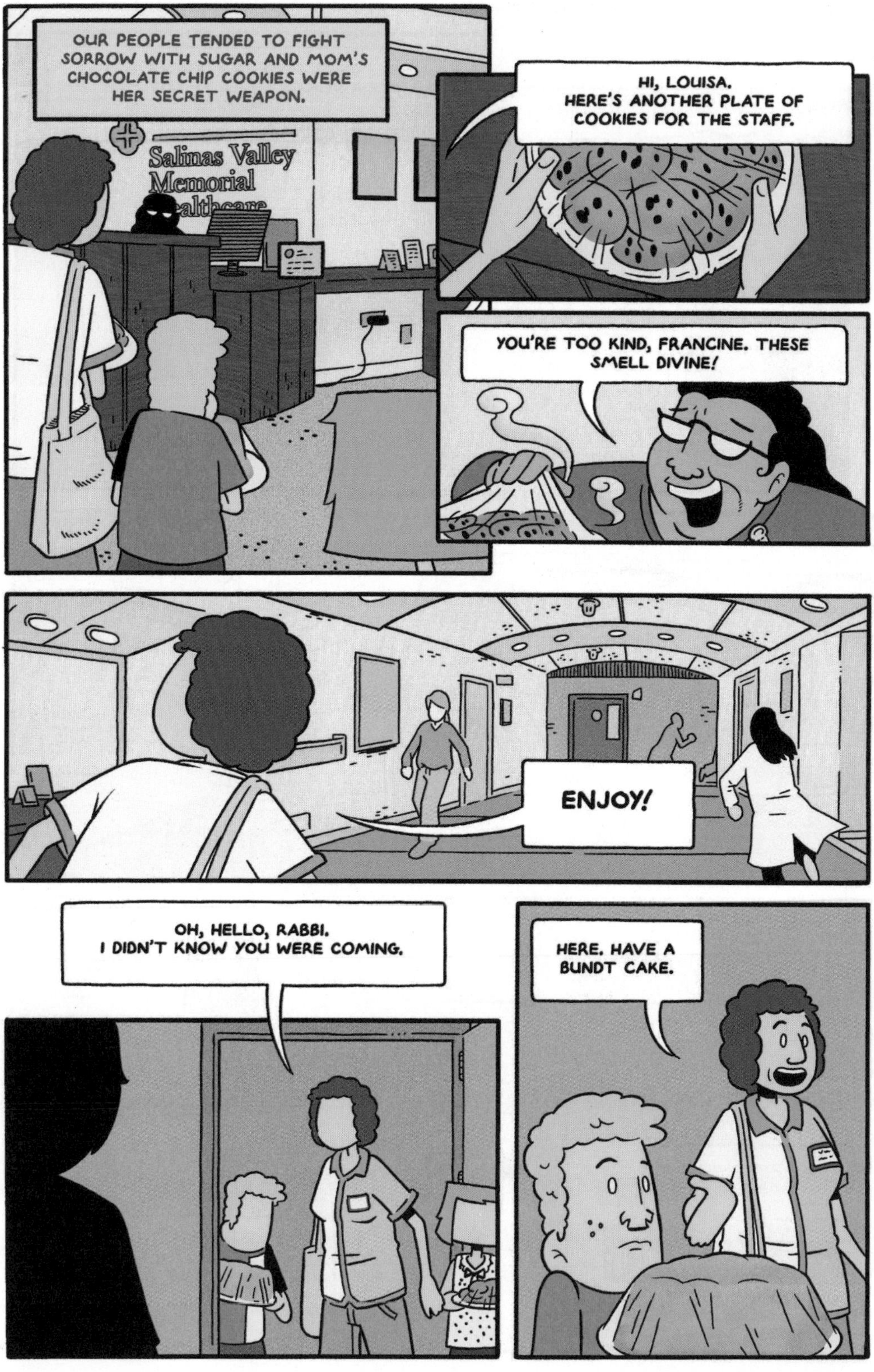
OUR PEOPLE TENDED TO FIGHT SORROW WITH SUGAR AND MOM'S CHOCOLATE CHIP COOKIES WERE HER SECRET WEAPON.
Salinas Valley
Memorial
HI, LOUISA. HERE'S ANOTHER PLATE OF COOKIES FOR THE STAFF.
YOU'RE TOO KIND, FRANCINE. THESE SMELL DIVINE!
ENJOY!
OH, HELLO, RABBI. I DIDN'T KNOW YOU WERE COMING.
HERE. HAVE A BUNDT CAKE.

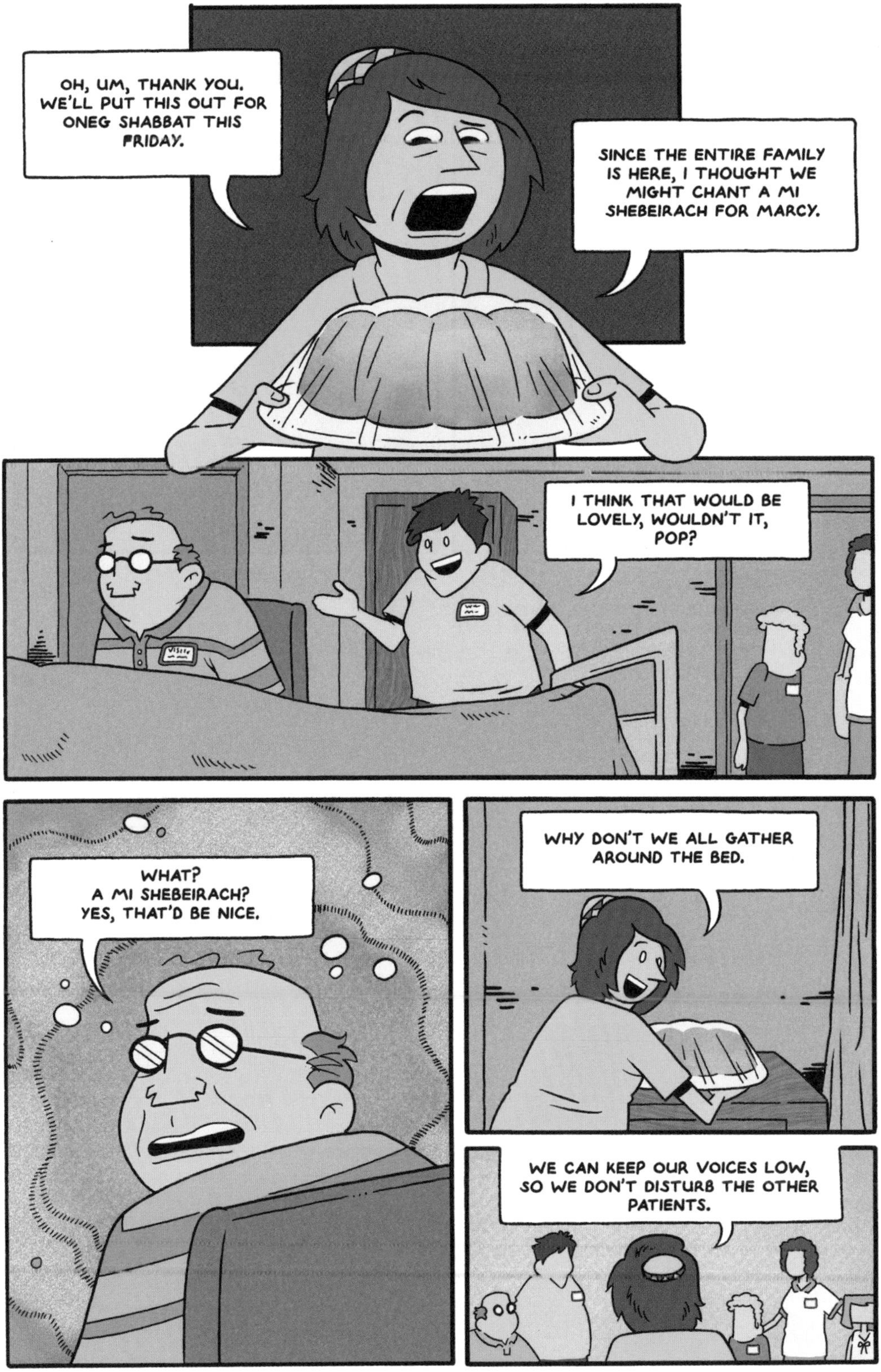
OH, UM, THANK YOU. WE'LL PUT THIS OUT FOR ONEG SHABBAT THIS FRIDAY.
SINCE THE ENTIRE FAMILY IS HERE, I THOUGHT WE MIGHT CHANT A MI SHEBEIRACH FOR MARCY.
I THINK THAT WOULD BE LOVELY, WOULDN'T IT, POP?
WHAT? A MI SHEBEIRACH? YES, THAT'D BE NICE.
WHY DON'T WE ALL GATHER AROUND THE BED.
WE CAN KEEP OUR VOICES LOW, SO WE DON'T DISTURB THE OTHER PATIENTS.

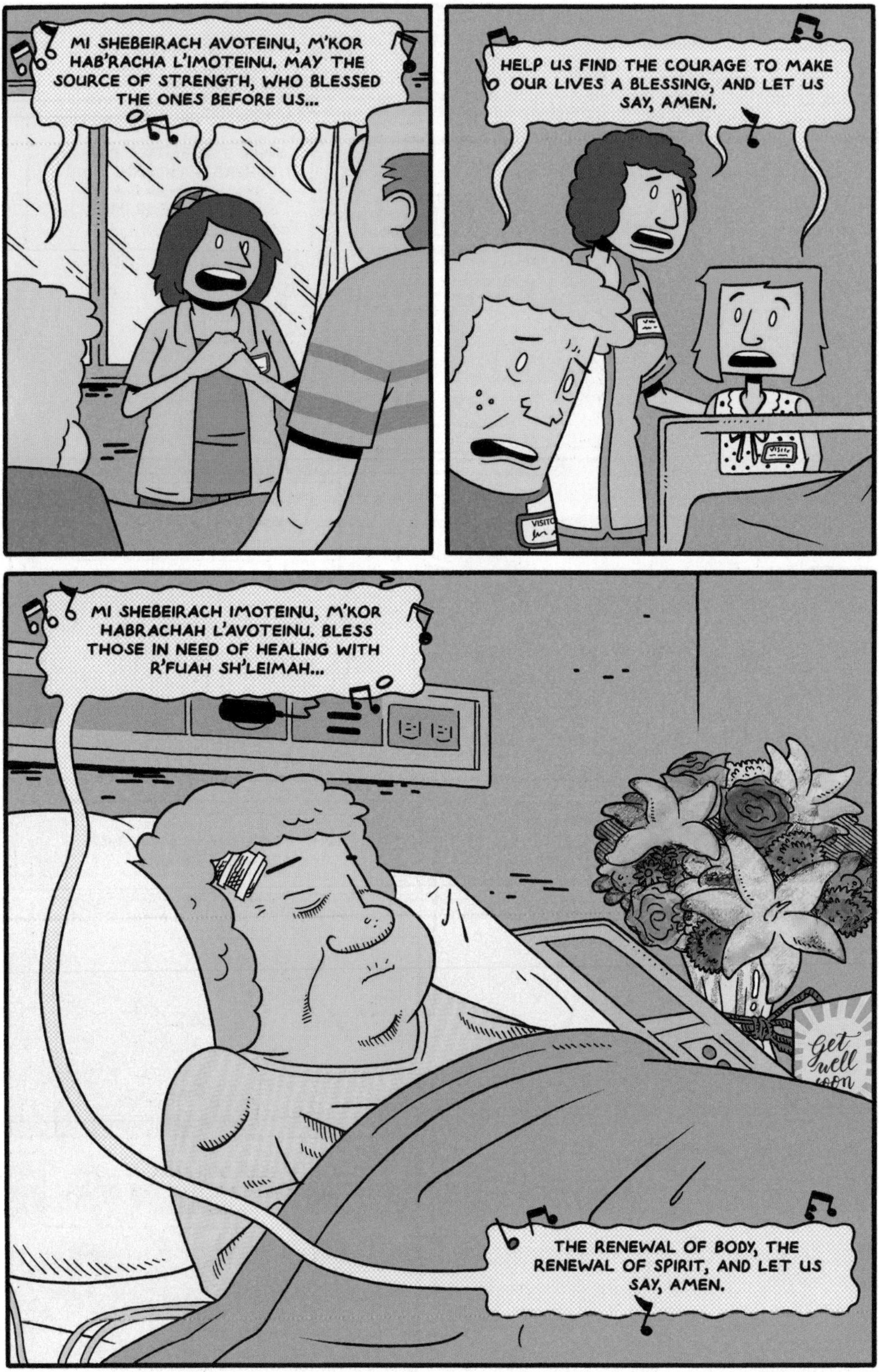
MI SHEBEIRACH AVOTEINU, M'KOR HAB'RACHA L'IMOTEINU. MAY THE SOURCE OF STRENGTH, WHO BLESSED THE ONES BEFORE US...
HELP US FIND THE COURAGE TO MAKE OUR LIVES A BLESSING, AND LET US SAY, AMEN.
MI SHEBEIRACH IMOTEINU, M'KOR HABRACHAH L'AVOTEINU. BLESS THOSE IN NEED OF HEALING WITH R'FUAH SH'LEIMAH...
Get well
THE RENEWAL OF BODY, THE RENEWAL OF SPIRIT, AND LET US SAY, AMEN.

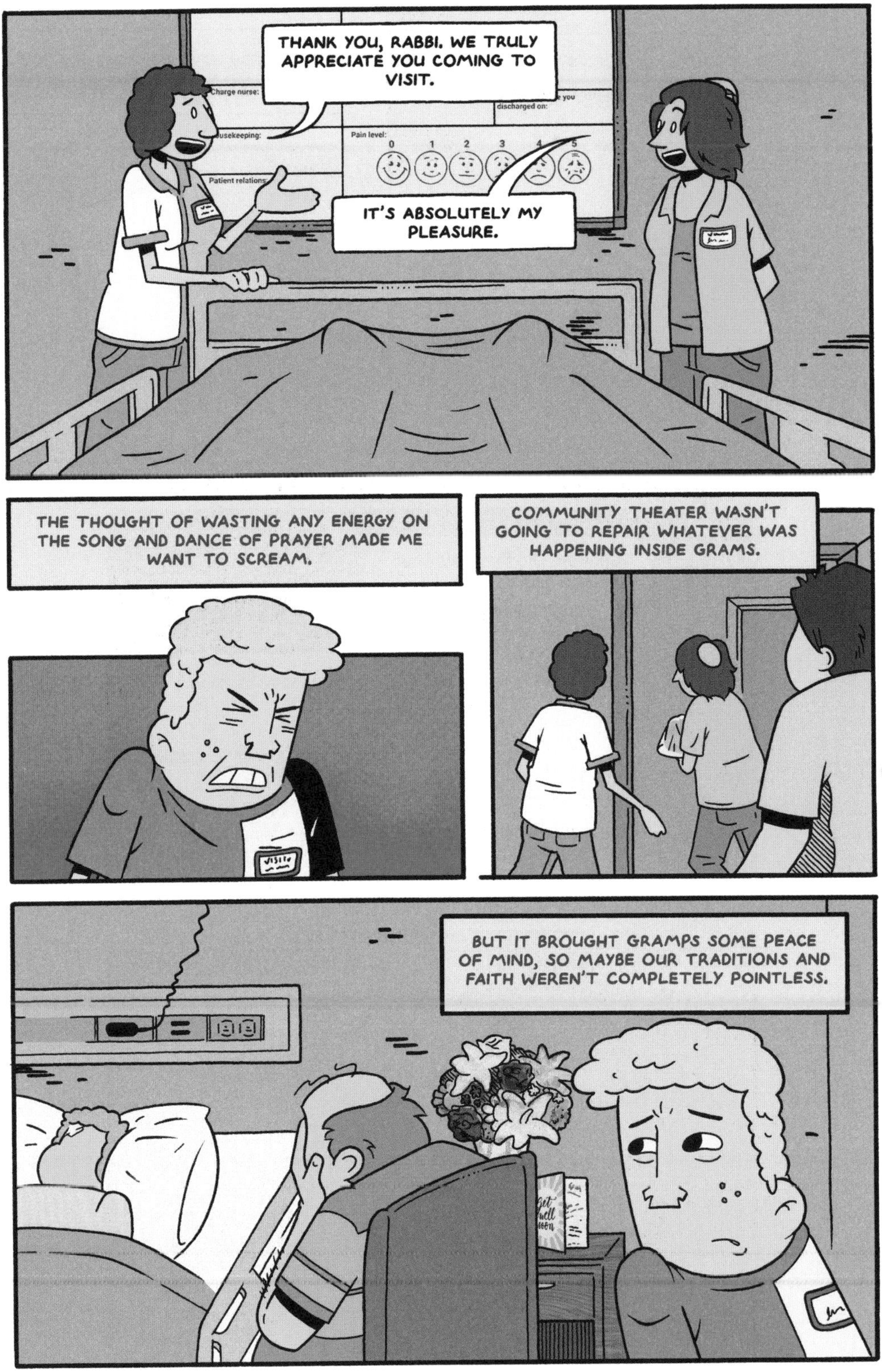
THANK YOU, RABBI. WE TRULY APPRECIATE YOU COMING TO VISIT.
Charge nurse:
discharged on:
Pain level:
Patient relations
IT'S ABSOLUTELY MY PLEASURE.
THE THOUGHT OF WASTING ANY ENERGY ON THE SONG AND DANCE OF PRAYER MADE ME WANT TO SCREAM.
COMMUNITY THEATER WASN'T GOING TO REPAIR WHATEVER WAS HAPPENING INSIDE GRAMS.
BUT IT BROUGHT GRAMPS SOME PEACE OF MIND, SO MAYBE OUR TRADITIONS AND FAITH WEREN'T COMPLETELY POINTLESS.

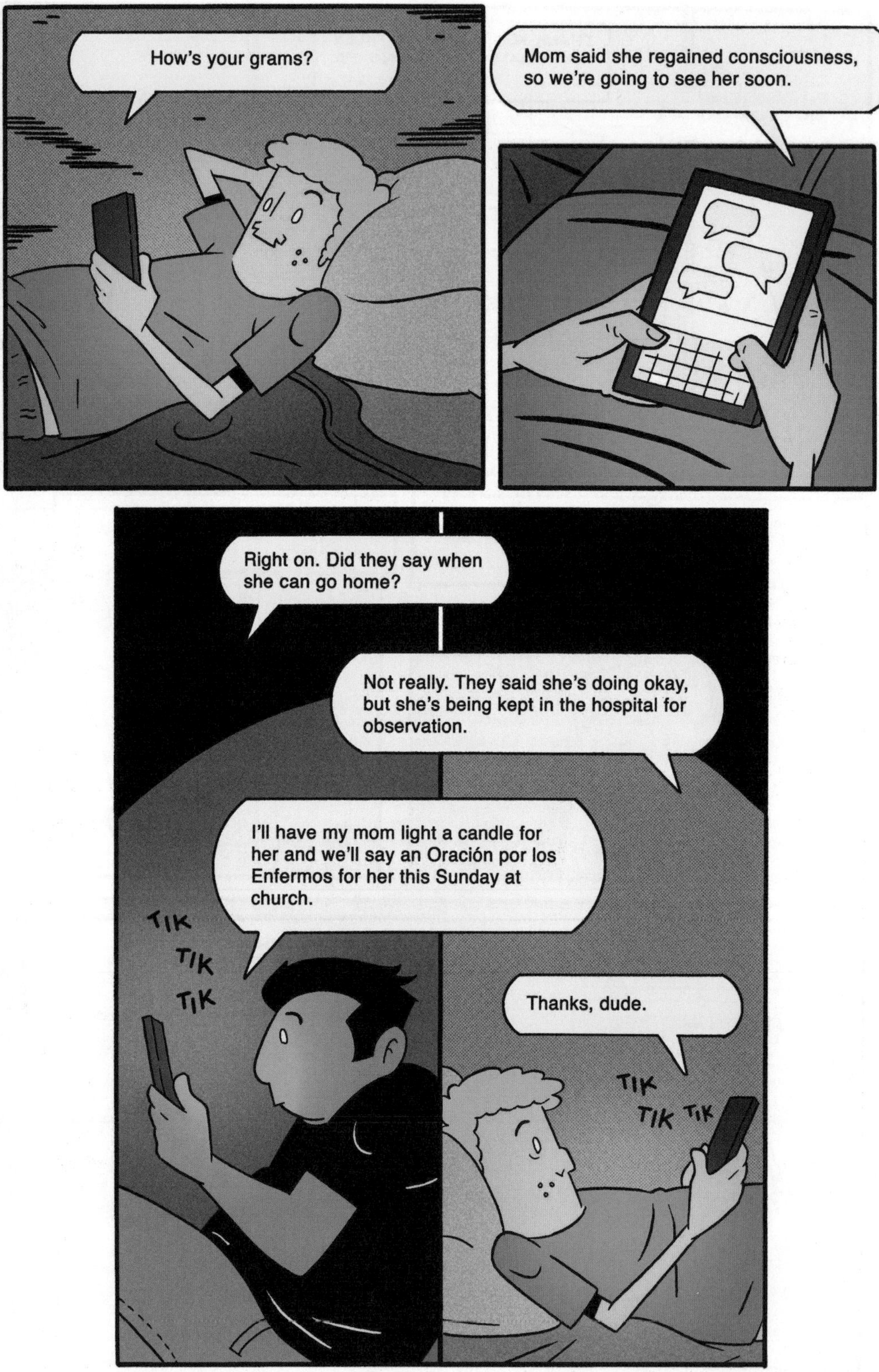
How's your grams?
Mom said she regained consciousness, so we're going to see her soon.
Right on. Did they say when she can go home?
Not really. They said she's doing okay, but she's being kept in the hospital for observation.
I'll have my mom light a candle for her and we'll say an Oración por los Enfermos for her this Sunday at church.
TIK TIK TIK
Thanks, dude.
TIK TIK TIK

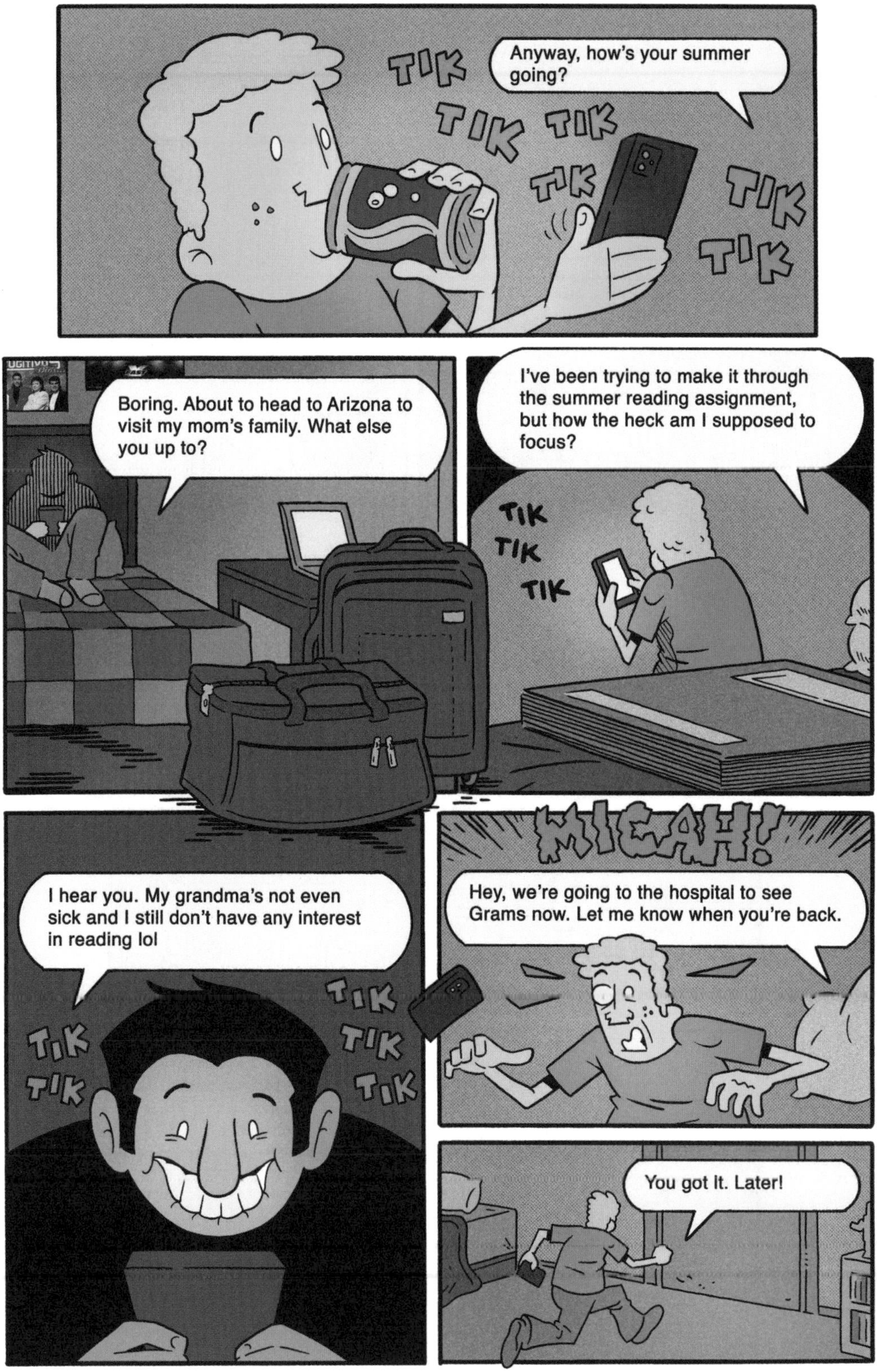
TIK
Anyway, how's your summer going?
TIK TIK
TIK
TIK
TIK
Boring. About to head to Arizona to visit my mom's family. What else you up to?
I've been trying to make it through the summer reading assignment, but how the heck am I supposed to focus?
TIK
TIK
TIK
I hear you. My grandma's not even sick and I still don't have any interest in reading lol
TIK
TIK
TIK
TIK
TIK
MICAH!
Hey, we're going to the hospital to see Grams now. Let me know when you're back.
You got it. Later!

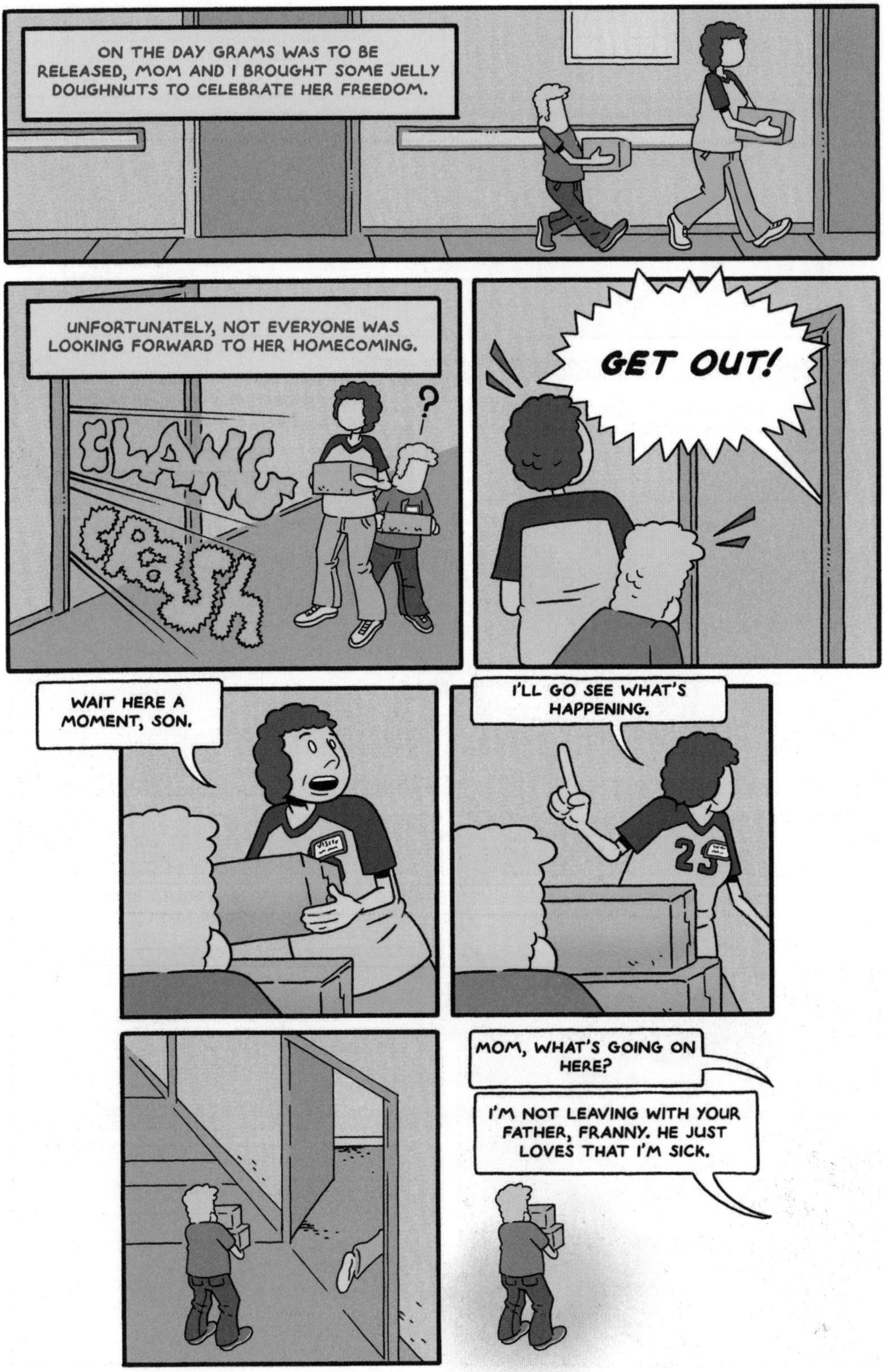
ON THE DAY GRAMS WAS TO BE RELEASED, MOM AND I BROUGHT SOME JELLY DOUGHNUTS TO CELEBRATE HER FREEDOM.
UNFORTUNATELY, NOT EVERYONE WAS LOOKING FORWARD TO HER HOMECOMING.
CLANG
CRASH
?
GET OUT!
WAIT HERE A MOMENT, SON.
I'LL GO SEE WHAT'S HAPPENING.
MOM, WHAT'S GOING ON HERE?
I'M NOT LEAVING WITH YOUR FATHER, FRANNY. HE JUST LOVES THAT I'M SICK.

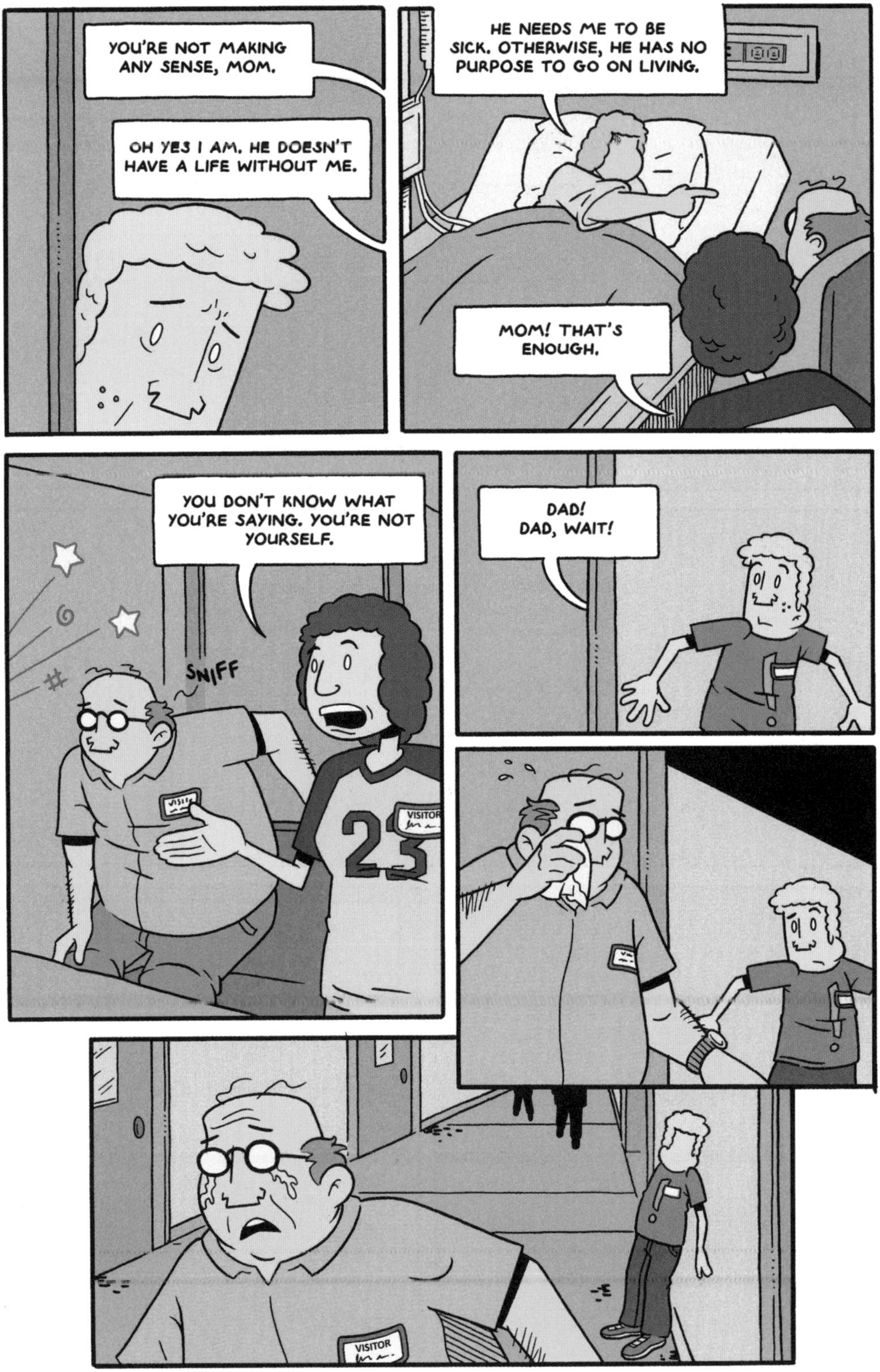
YOU'RE NOT MAKING ANY SENSE, MOM.
OH YES I AM. HE DOESN'T HAVE A LIFE WITHOUT ME.
HE NEEDS ME TO BE SICK. OTHERWISE, HE HAS NO PURPOSE TO GO ON LIVING.
MOM! THAT'S ENOUGH.
YOU DON'T KNOW WHAT YOU'RE SAYING. YOU'RE NOT YOURSELF.
SNIFF
VISITOR
DAD! DAD, WAIT!
VISITOR

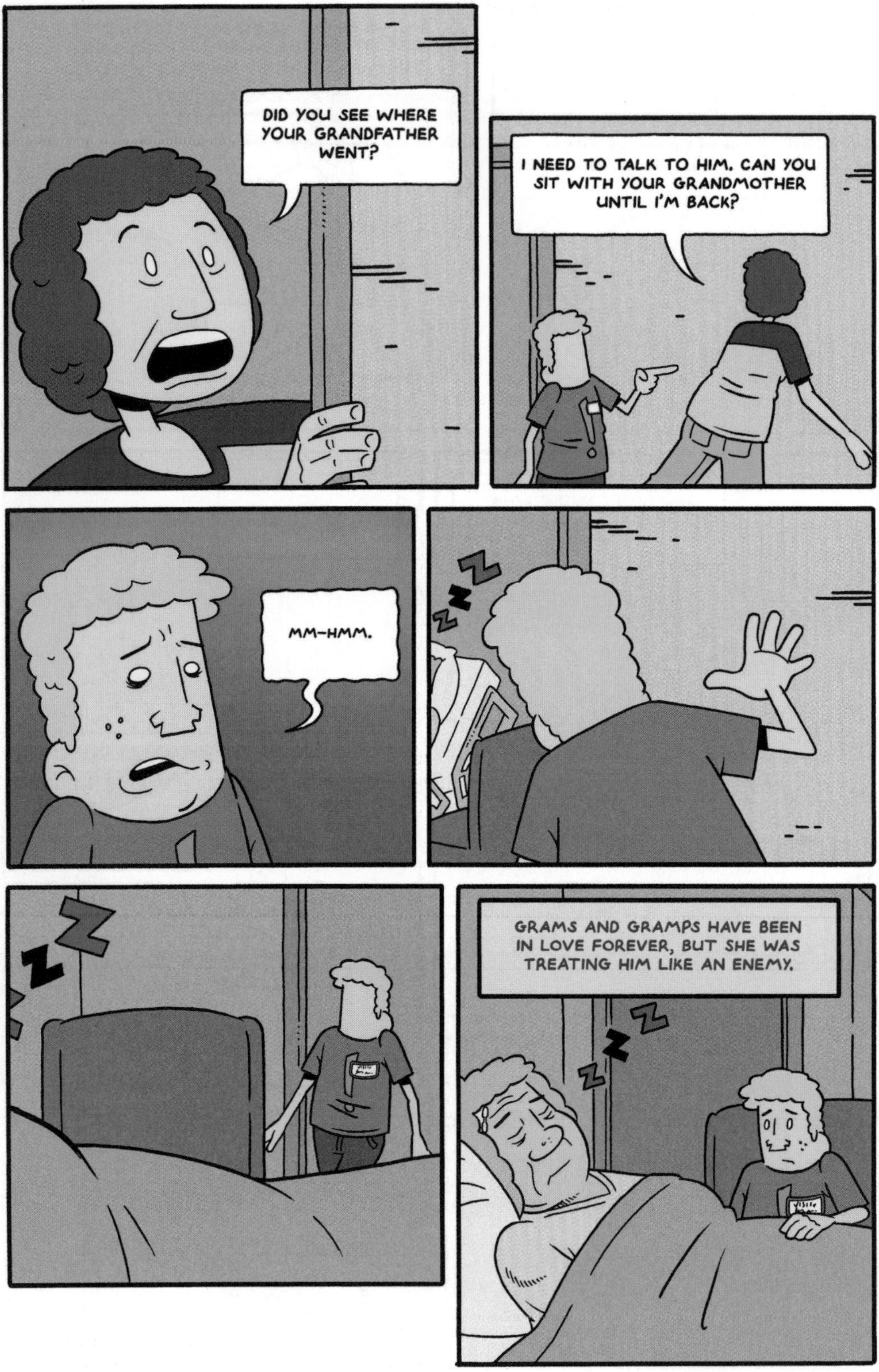
DID YOU SEE WHERE YOUR GRANDFATHER WENT?
I NEED TO TALK TO HIM. CAN YOU SIT WITH YOUR GRANDMOTHER UNTIL I'M BACK?
MM-HMM.
GRAMS AND GRAMPS HAVE BEEN IN LOVE FOREVER, BUT SHE WAS TREATING HIM LIKE AN ENEMY.

THERE WAS NO WAY TO GAUGE JUST HOW FAR THE VENOM HAD SPREAD IN HER SYSTEM.

MICAH?

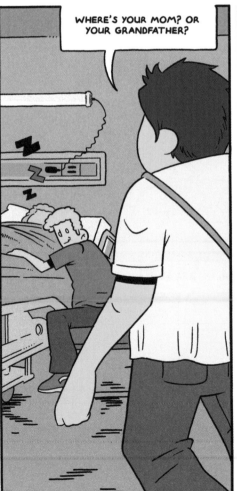

WHERE'S YOUR MOM? OR YOUR GRANDFATHER?

GRANDMA YELLED AT GRANDPA AND MOM WENT TO TALK TO HIM. I DON'T KNOW WHERE THEY WENT.

AGAIN? OY. I'M SORRY YOU HEARD THAT, MICAH.

WHAT DO YOU MEAN, AGAIN?

OH, UM, NEVER MIND. WHY DON'T WE SIT HERE AND WAIT FOR THEM TO GET BACK?

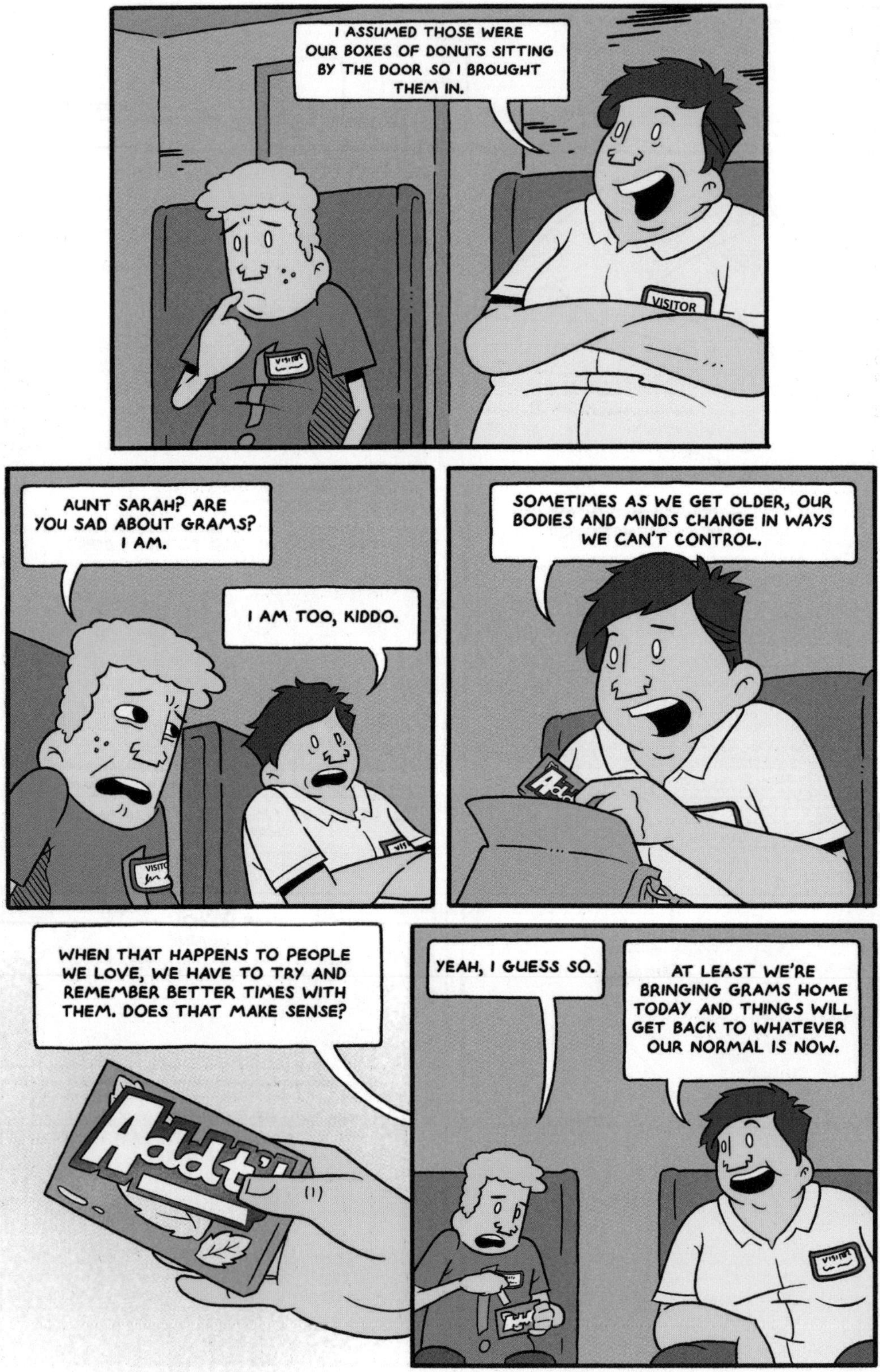
I ASSUMED THOSE WERE OUR BOXES OF DONUTS SITTING BY THE DOOR SO I BROUGHT THEM IN.
VISITOR
AUNT SARAH? ARE YOU SAD ABOUT GRAMS? I AM.
I AM TOO, KIDDO.
SOMETIMES AS WE GET OLDER, OUR BODIES AND MINDS CHANGE IN WAYS WE CAN'T CONTROL.
WHEN THAT HAPPENS TO PEOPLE WE LOVE, WE HAVE TO TRY AND REMEMBER BETTER TIMES WITH THEM. DOES THAT MAKE SENSE?
YEAH, I GUESS SO.
AT LEAST WE'RE BRINGING GRAMS HOME TODAY AND THINGS WILL GET BACK TO WHATEVER OUR NORMAL IS NOW.

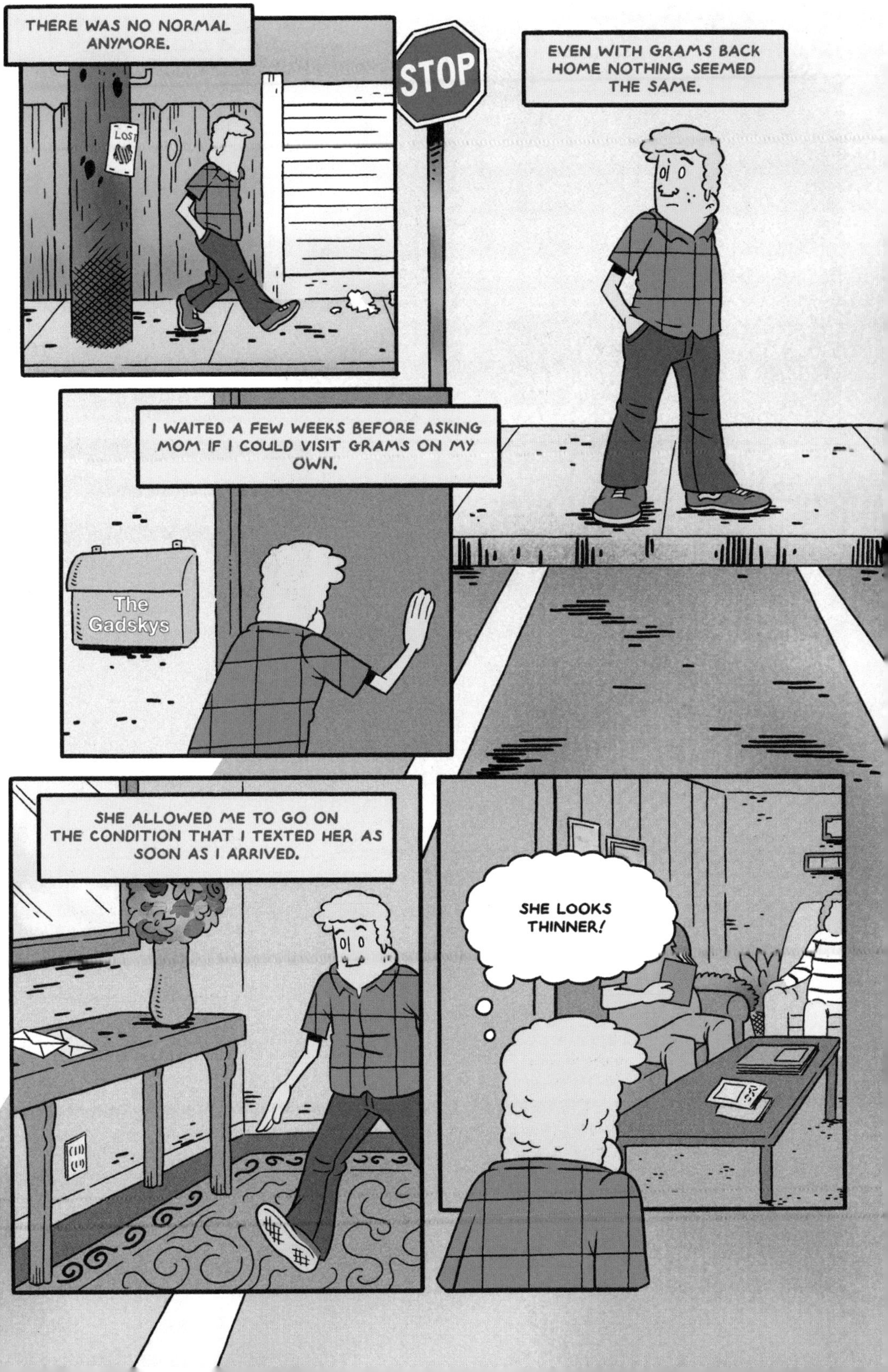
THERE WAS NO NORMAL ANYMORE.
LOST
STOP
EVEN WITH GRAMS BACK HOME NOTHING SEEMED THE SAME.
I WAITED A FEW WEEKS BEFORE ASKING MOM IF I COULD VISIT GRAMS ON MY OWN.
The Gadskys
SHE ALLOWED ME TO GO ON THE CONDITION THAT I TEXTED HER AS SOON AS I ARRIVED.
SHE LOOKS THINNER!

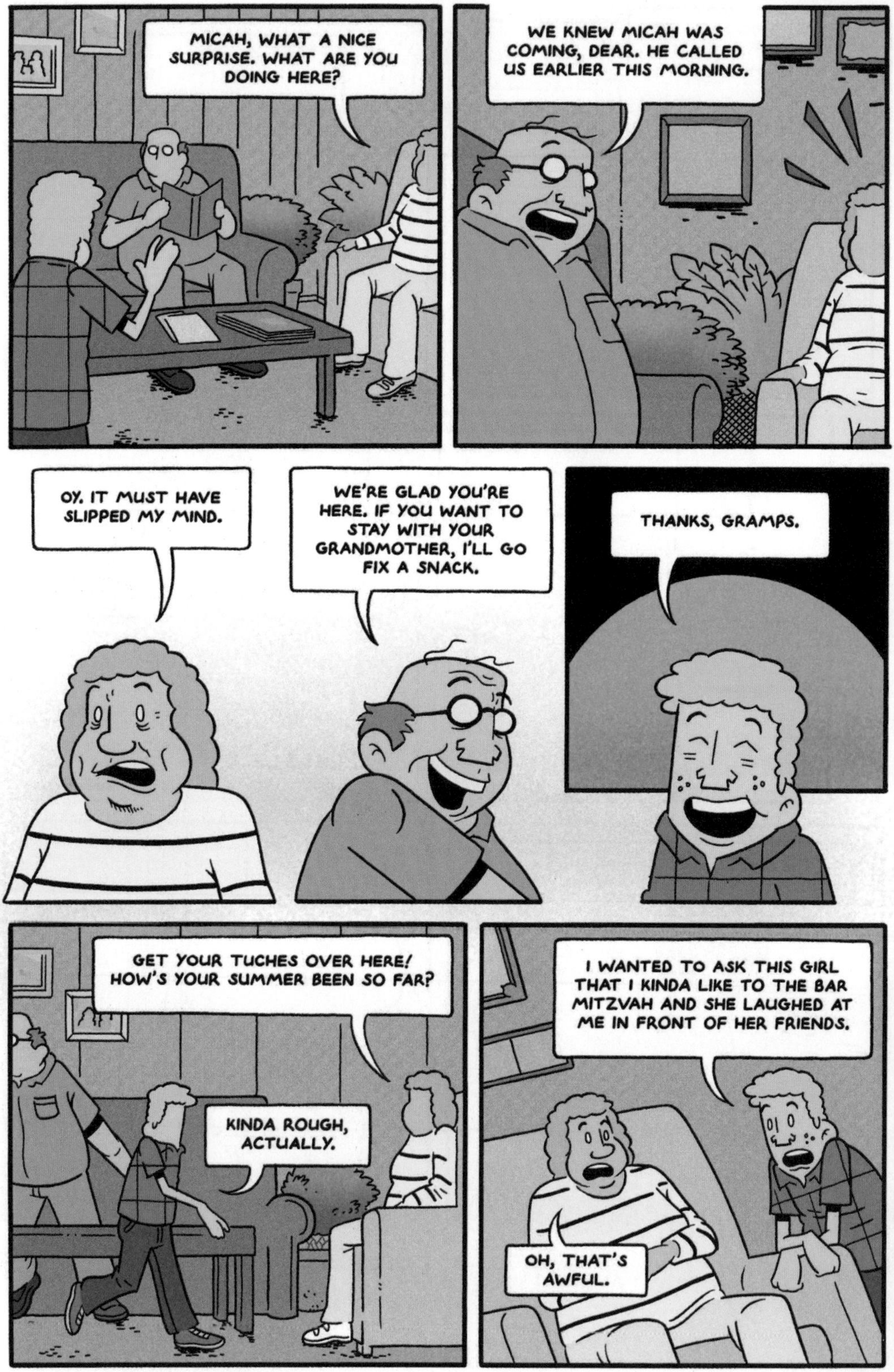
MICAH, WHAT A NICE SURPRISE. WHAT ARE YOU DOING HERE?
WE KNEW MICAH WAS COMING, DEAR. HE CALLED US EARLIER THIS MORNING.
OY. IT MUST HAVE SLIPPED MY MIND.
WE'RE GLAD YOU'RE HERE. IF YOU WANT TO STAY WITH YOUR GRANDMOTHER, I'LL GO FIX A SNACK.
THANKS, GRAMPS.
GET YOUR TUCHES OVER HERE! HOW'S YOUR SUMMER BEEN SO FAR?
KINDA ROUGH, ACTUALLY.
I WANTED TO ASK THIS GIRL THAT I KINDA LIKE TO THE BAR MITZVAH AND SHE LAUGHED AT ME IN FRONT OF HER FRIENDS.
OH, THAT'S AWFUL.

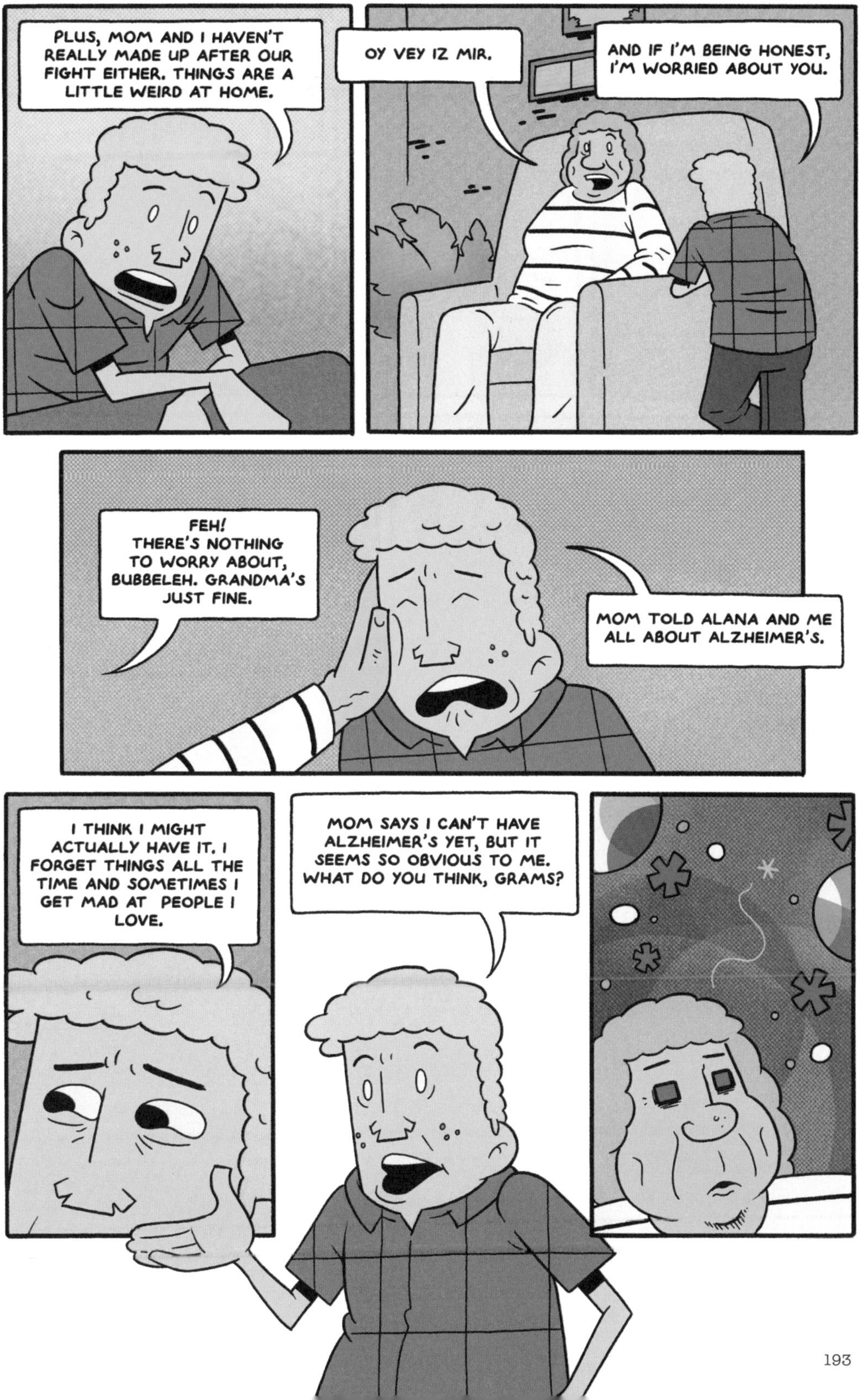
PLUS, MOM AND I HAVEN'T REALLY MADE UP AFTER OUR FIGHT EITHER. THINGS ARE A LITTLE WEIRD AT HOME.
OY VEY IZ MIR.
AND IF I'M BEING HONEST, I'M WORRIED ABOUT YOU.
FEH! THERE'S NOTHING TO WORRY ABOUT, BUBBELEH. GRANDMA'S JUST FINE.
MOM TOLD ALANA AND ME ALL ABOUT ALZHEIMER'S.
I THINK I MIGHT ACTUALLY HAVE IT. I FORGET THINGS ALL THE TIME AND SOMETIMES I GET MAD AT PEOPLE I LOVE.
MOM SAYS I CAN'T HAVE ALZHEIMER'S YET, BUT IT SEEMS SO OBVIOUS TO ME. WHAT DO YOU THINK, GRAMS?

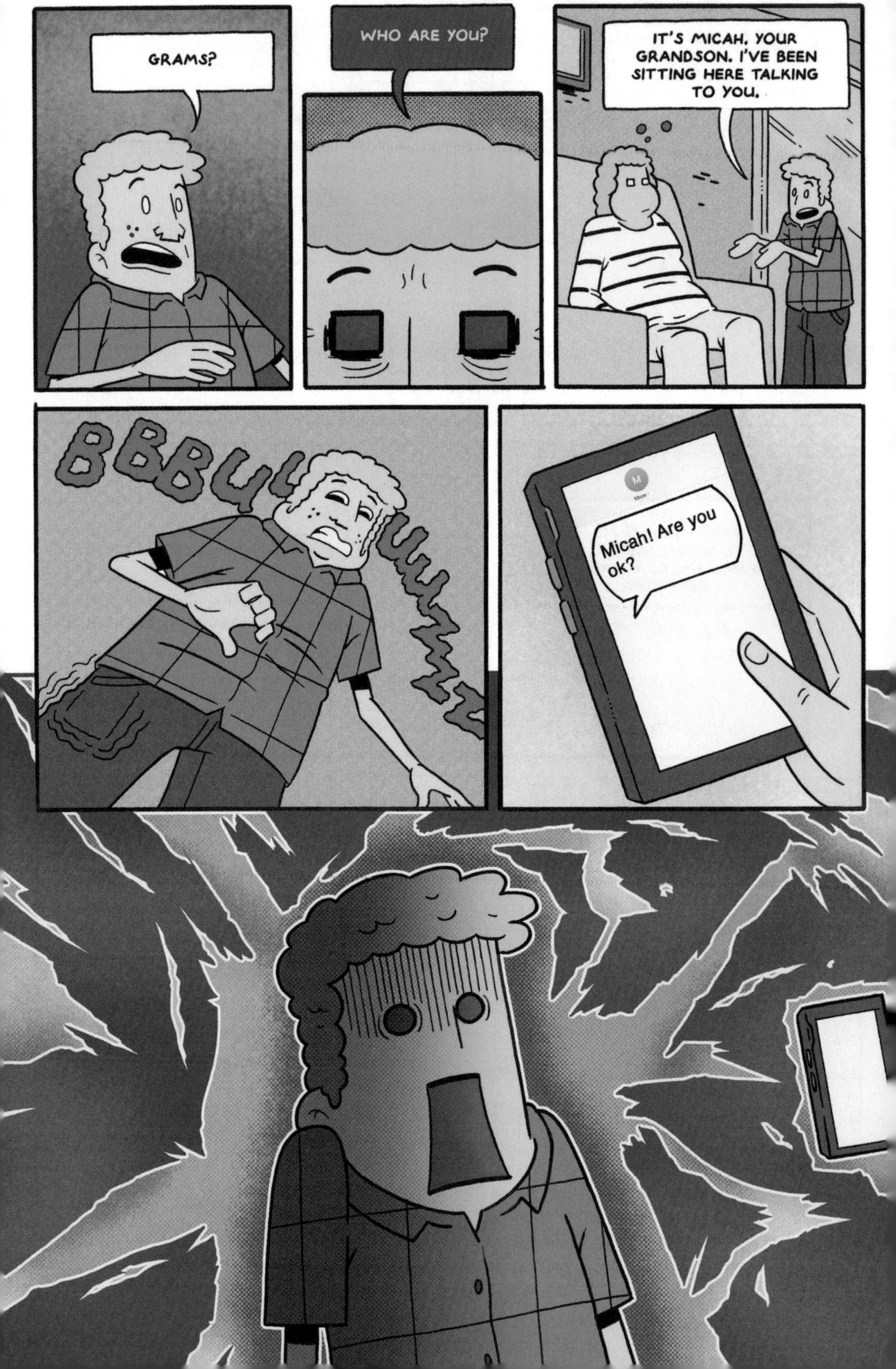
GRAMS?
WHO ARE YOU?
IT'S MICAH. YOUR GRANDSON. I'VE BEEN SITTING HERE TALKING TO YOU.
BBBUUUUUUZZZ
Micah! Are you ok?

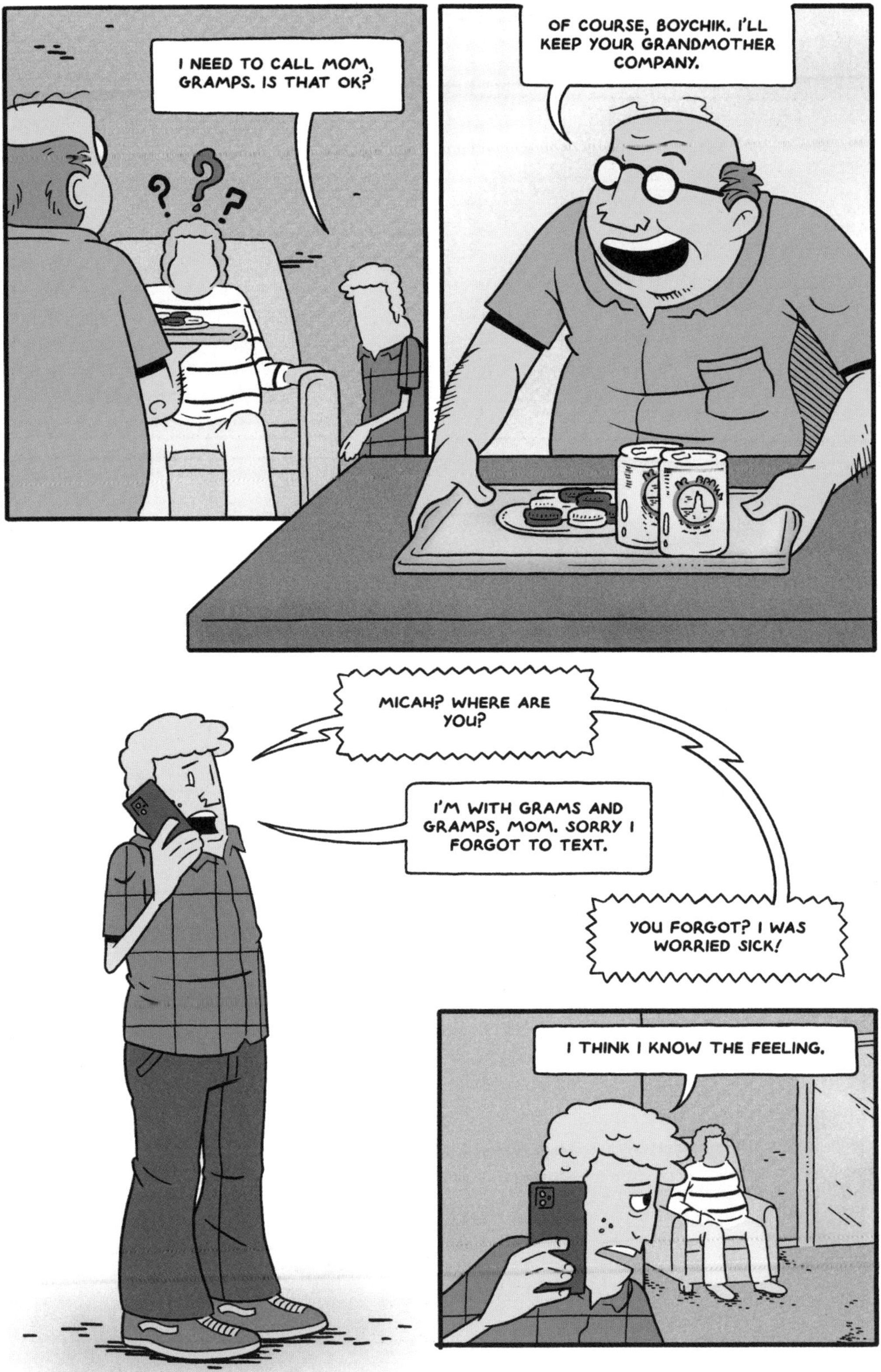
I NEED TO CALL MOM, GRAMPS. IS THAT OK?
OF COURSE, BOYCHIK. I'LL KEEP YOUR GRANDMOTHER COMPANY.
MICAH? WHERE ARE YOU?
I'M WITH GRAMS AND GRAMPS, MOM. SORRY I FORGOT TO TEXT.
YOU FORGOT? I WAS WORRIED SICK!
I THINK I KNOW THE FEELING.

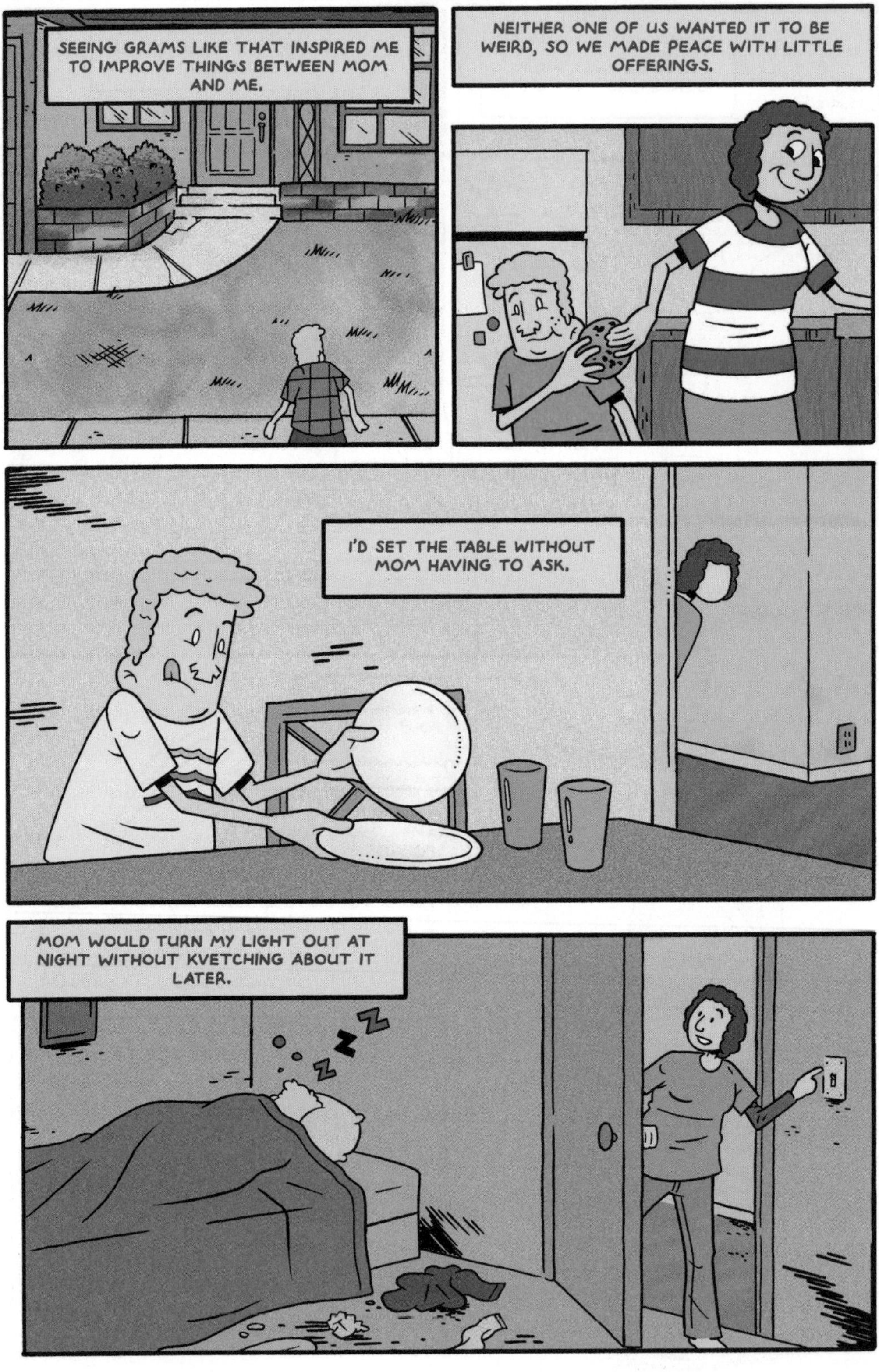
SEEING GRAMS LIKE THAT INSPIRED ME TO IMPROVE THINGS BETWEEN MOM AND ME.
NEITHER ONE OF US WANTED IT TO BE WEIRD, SO WE MADE PEACE WITH LITTLE OFFERINGS.
I'D SET THE TABLE WITHOUT MOM HAVING TO ASK.
MOM WOULD TURN MY LIGHT OUT AT NIGHT WITHOUT KVETCHING ABOUT IT LATER.
ZZZ

I MADE SURE TO PICK UP MY TRAIL OF STUFF THROUGH THE FRONT ROOM.

SHE RATIONED PIECES OF BUNDT CAKE WHILE I STUDIED.

SURE, WE HAD A SURPLUS TO GET RID OF, BUT IT WAS THE THOUGHT THAT COUNTED.

HEY, MOM?

YES, SON?

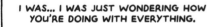

I WAS... I WAS JUST WONDERING HOW YOU'RE DOING WITH EVERYTHING.

HEH. AREN'T YOU SWEET TO ASK.

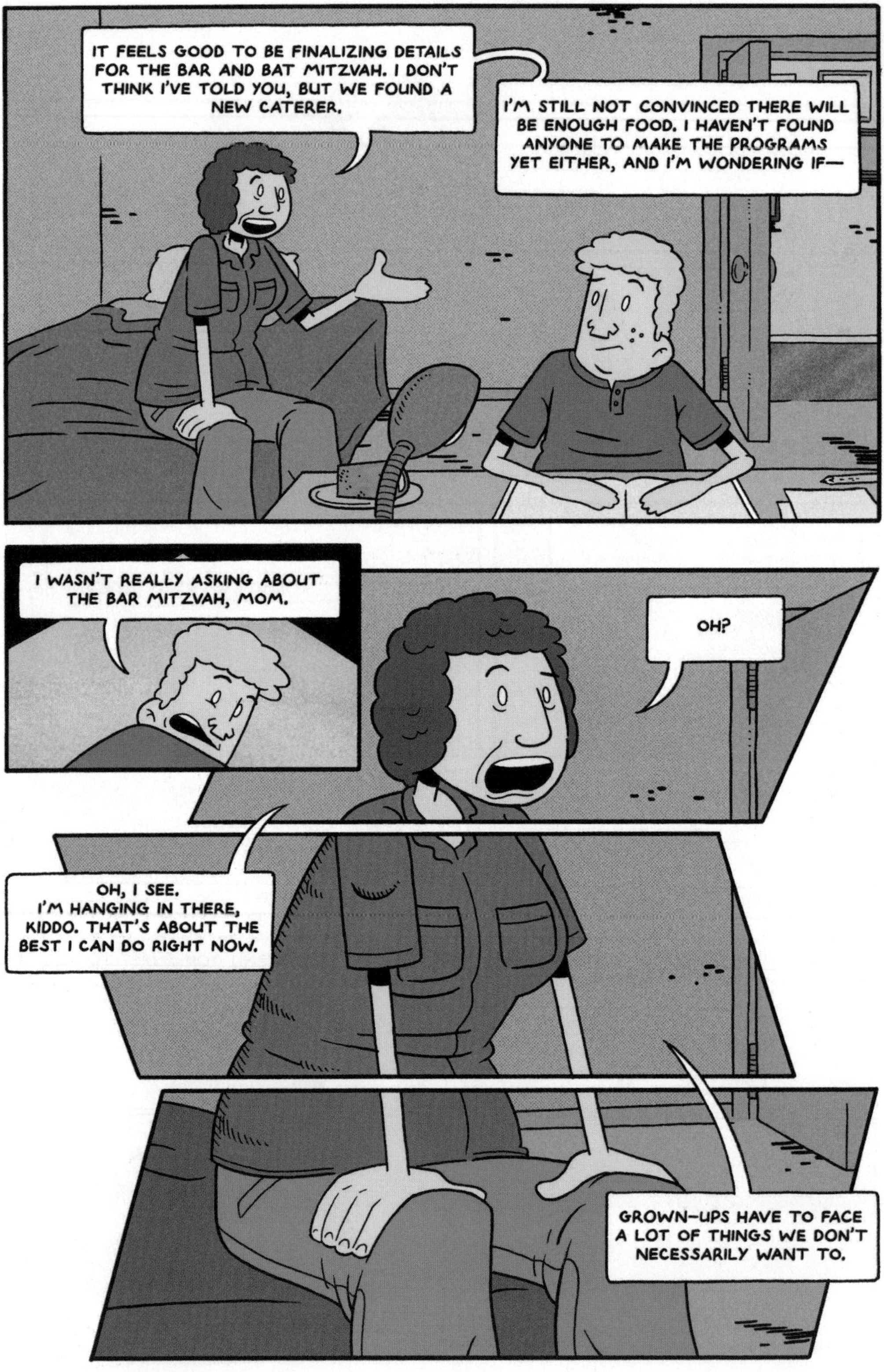
IT FEELS GOOD TO BE FINALIZING DETAILS FOR THE BAR AND BAT MITZVAH. I DON'T THINK I'VE TOLD YOU, BUT WE FOUND A NEW CATERER.
I'M STILL NOT CONVINCED THERE WILL BE ENOUGH FOOD. I HAVEN'T FOUND ANYONE TO MAKE THE PROGRAMS YET EITHER, AND I'M WONDERING IF—
I WASN'T REALLY ASKING ABOUT THE BAR MITZVAH, MOM.
OH?
OH, I SEE. I'M HANGING IN THERE, KIDDO. THAT'S ABOUT THE BEST I CAN DO RIGHT NOW.
GROWN-UPS HAVE TO FACE A LOT OF THINGS WE DON'T NECESSARILY WANT TO.

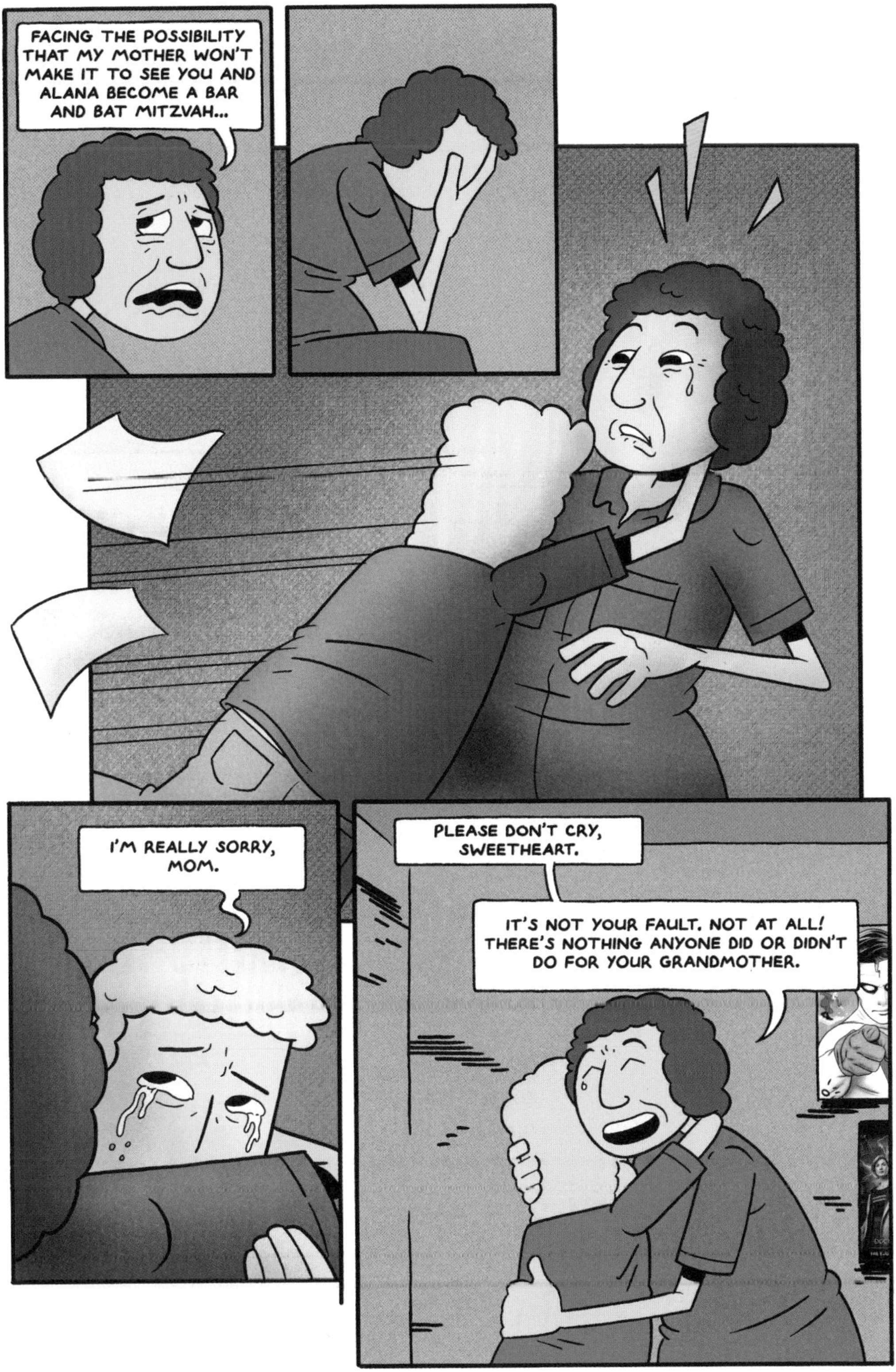
FACING THE POSSIBILITY THAT MY MOTHER WON'T MAKE IT TO SEE YOU AND ALANA BECOME A BAR AND BAT MITZVAH...
I'M REALLY SORRY, MOM.
PLEASE DON'T CRY, SWEETHEART.
IT'S NOT YOUR FAULT. NOT AT ALL! THERE'S NOTHING ANYONE DID OR DIDN'T DO FOR YOUR GRANDMOTHER.

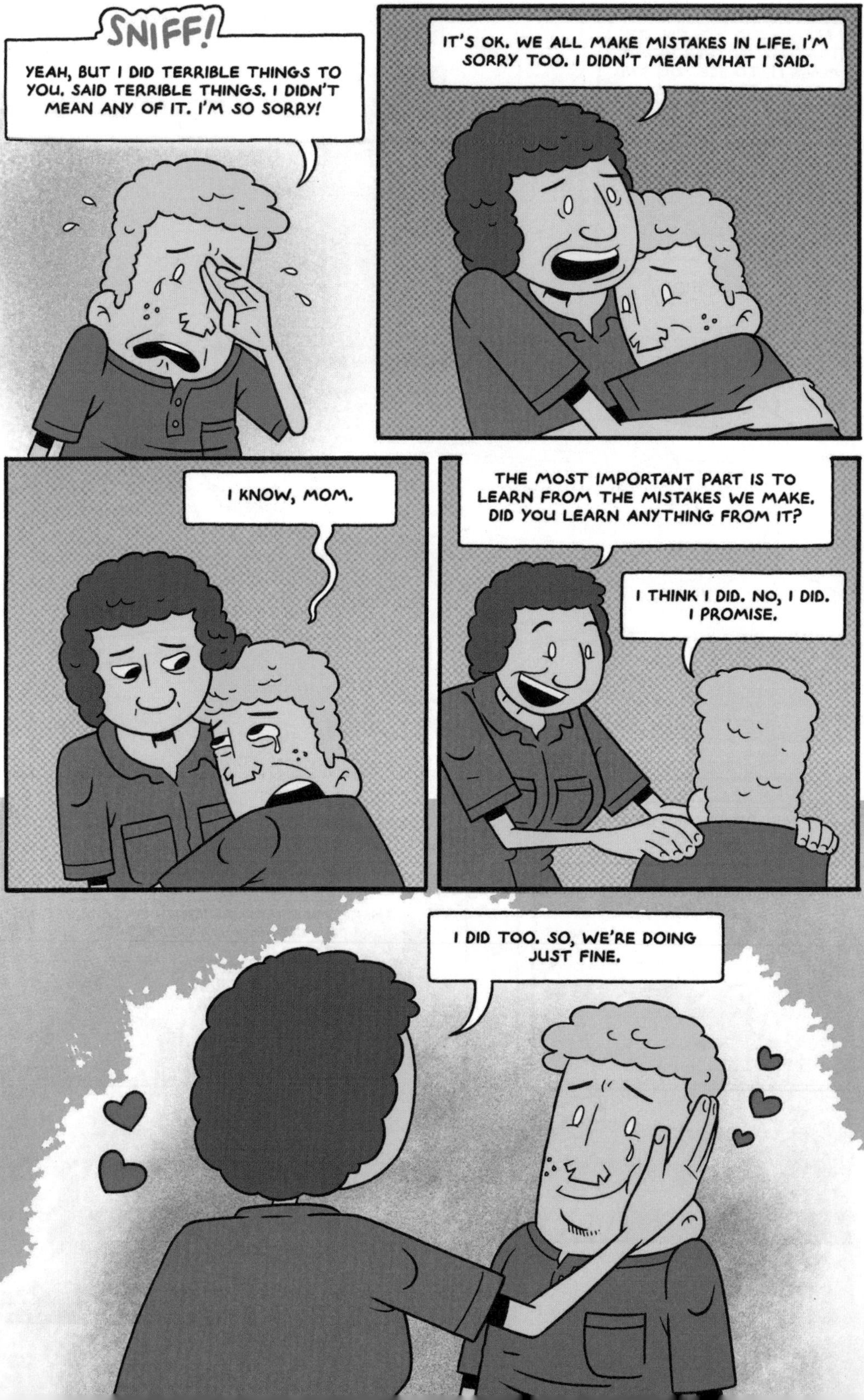
SNIFF!
YEAH, BUT I DID TERRIBLE THINGS TO YOU. SAID TERRIBLE THINGS. I DIDN'T MEAN ANY OF IT. I'M SO SORRY!
IT'S OK. WE ALL MAKE MISTAKES IN LIFE. I'M SORRY TOO. I DIDN'T MEAN WHAT I SAID.
I KNOW, MOM.
THE MOST IMPORTANT PART IS TO LEARN FROM THE MISTAKES WE MAKE. DID YOU LEARN ANYTHING FROM IT?
I THINK I DID. NO, I DID. I PROMISE.
I DID TOO. SO, WE'RE DOING JUST FINE.

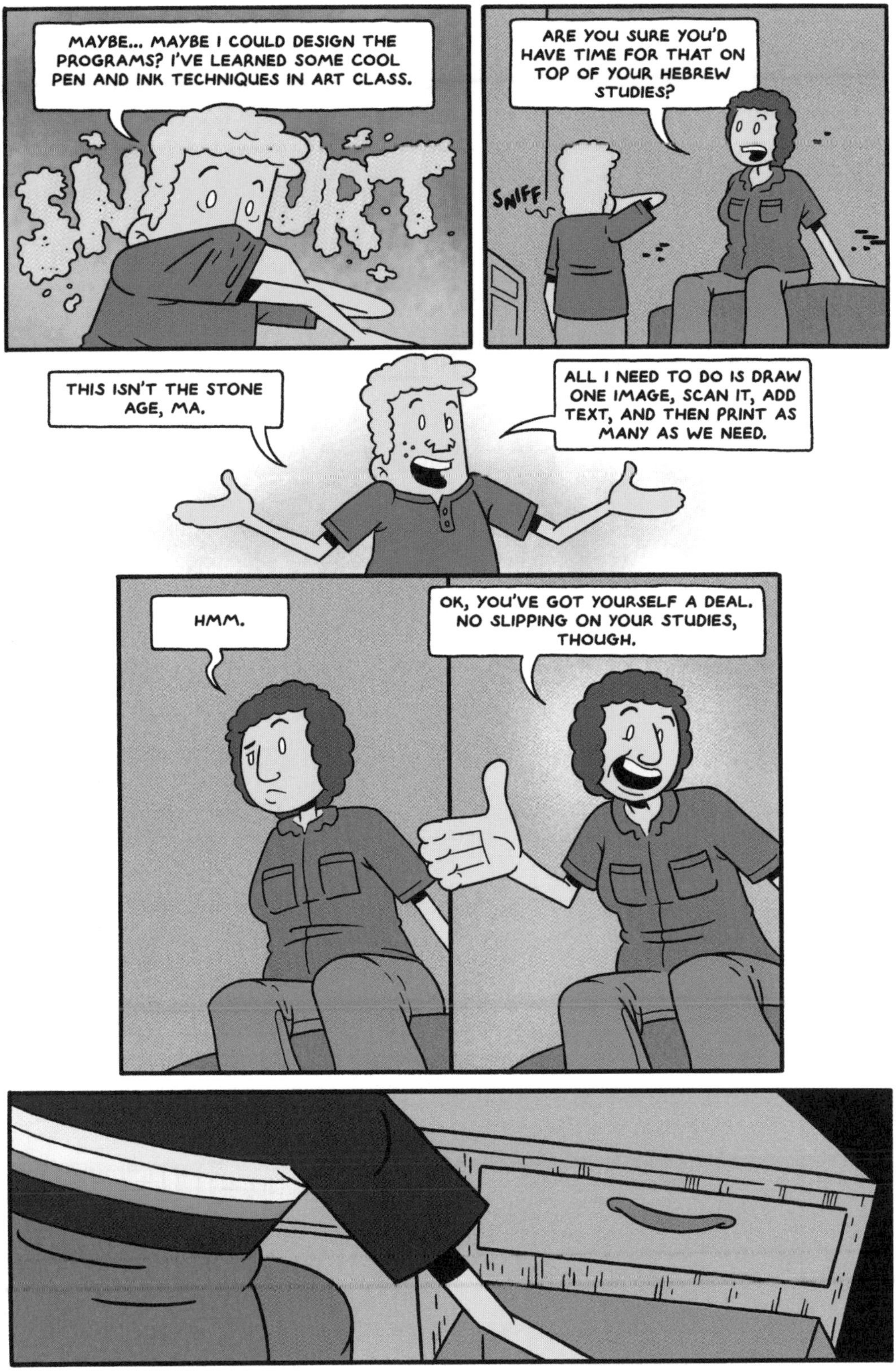
MAYBE... MAYBE I COULD DESIGN THE PROGRAMS? I'VE LEARNED SOME COOL PEN AND INK TECHNIQUES IN ART CLASS.
SNORT
ARE YOU SURE YOU'D HAVE TIME FOR THAT ON TOP OF YOUR HEBREW STUDIES?
SNIFF
THIS ISN'T THE STONE AGE, MA.
ALL I NEED TO DO IS DRAW ONE IMAGE, SCAN IT, ADD TEXT, AND THEN PRINT AS MANY AS WE NEED.
HMM.
OK, YOU'VE GOT YOURSELF A DEAL. NO SLIPPING ON YOUR STUDIES, THOUGH.

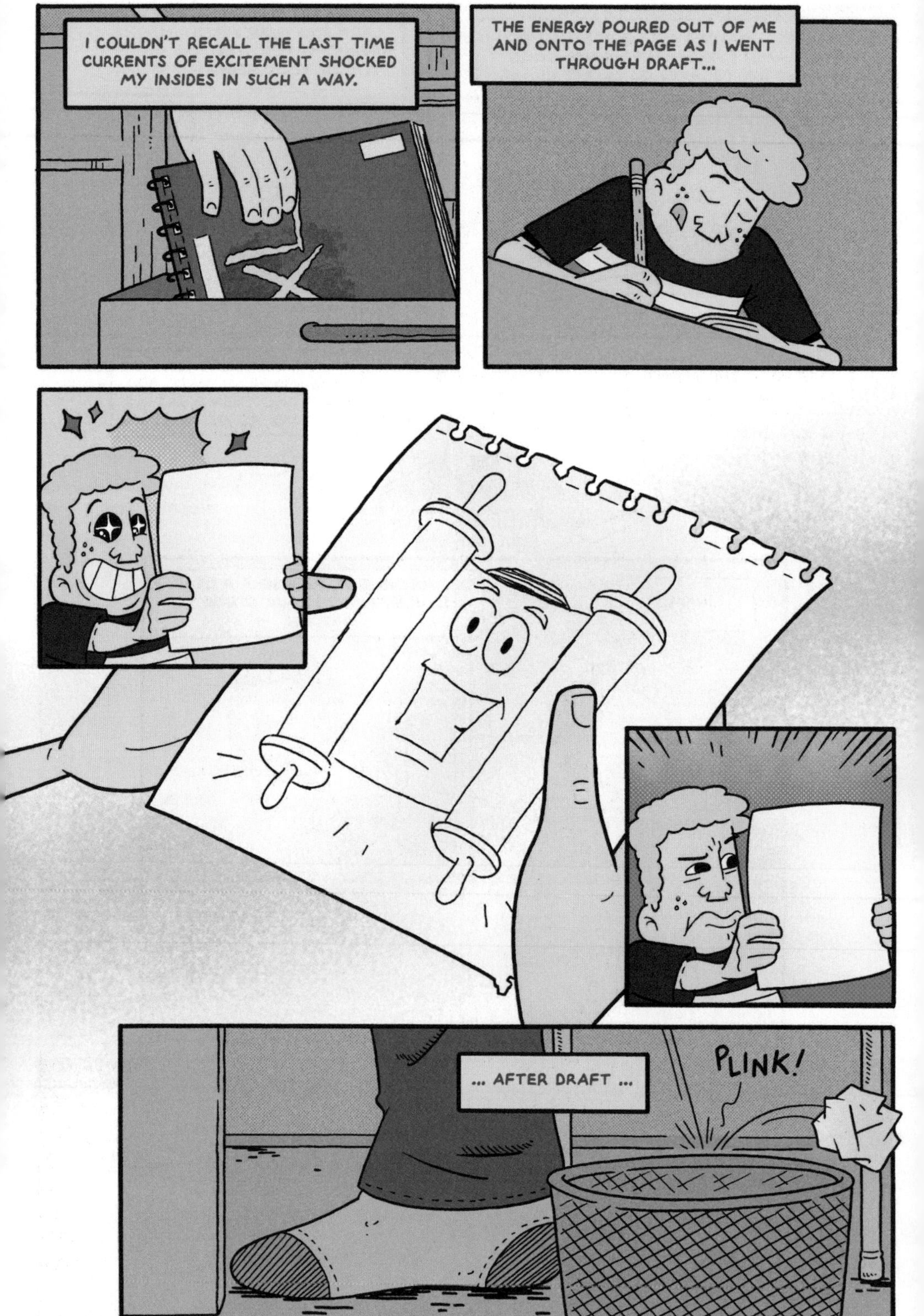

I COULDN'T RECALL THE LAST TIME CURRENTS OF EXCITEMENT SHOCKED MY INSIDES IN SUCH A WAY.
THE ENERGY POURED OUT OF ME AND ONTO THE PAGE AS I WENT THROUGH DRAFT...
... AFTER DRAFT ...
PLINK!

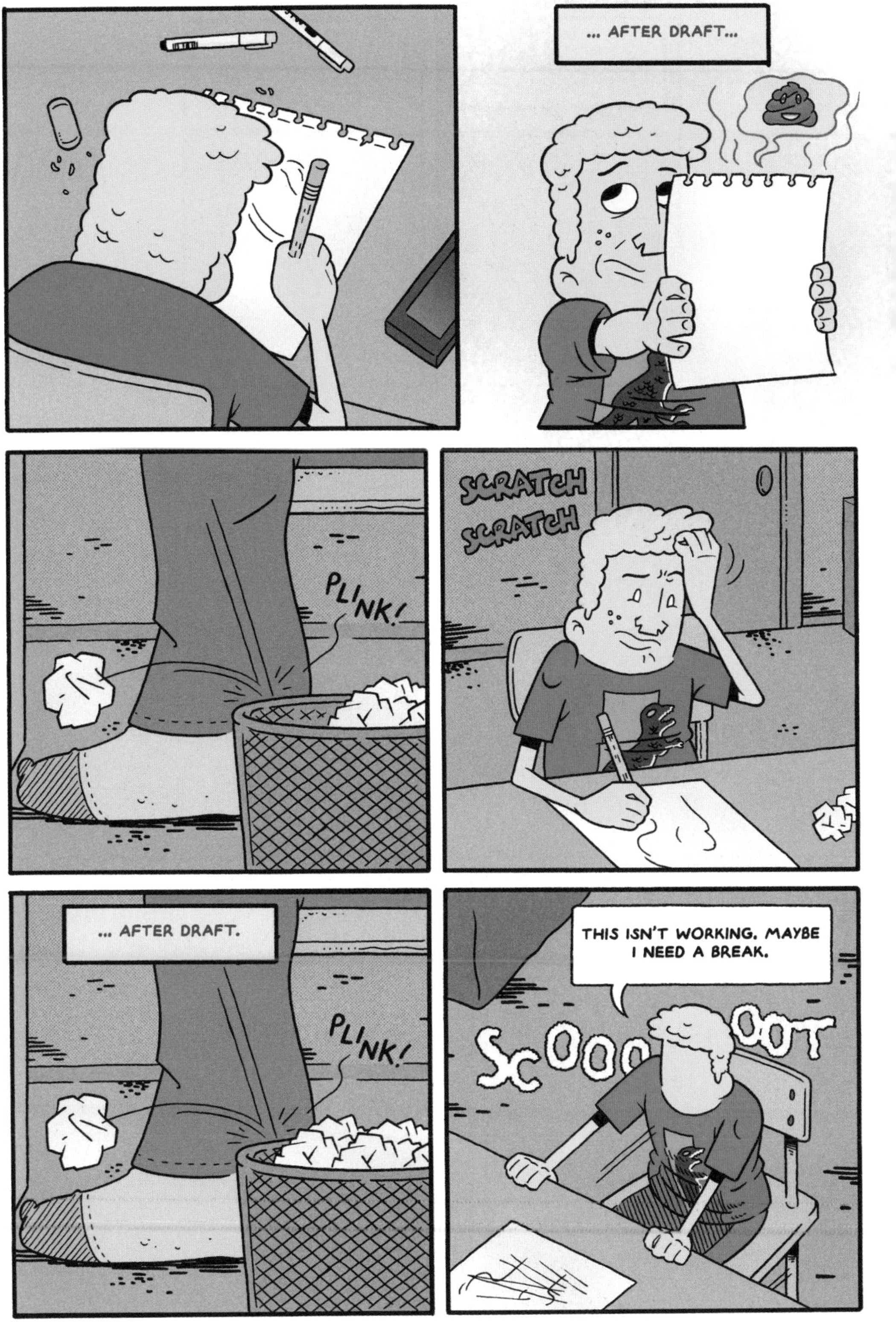
... AFTER DRAFT...
PLINK!
SCRATCH
SCRATCH
... AFTER DRAFT.
PLINK!
THIS ISN'T WORKING. MAYBE I NEED A BREAK.
SCOOO OOT

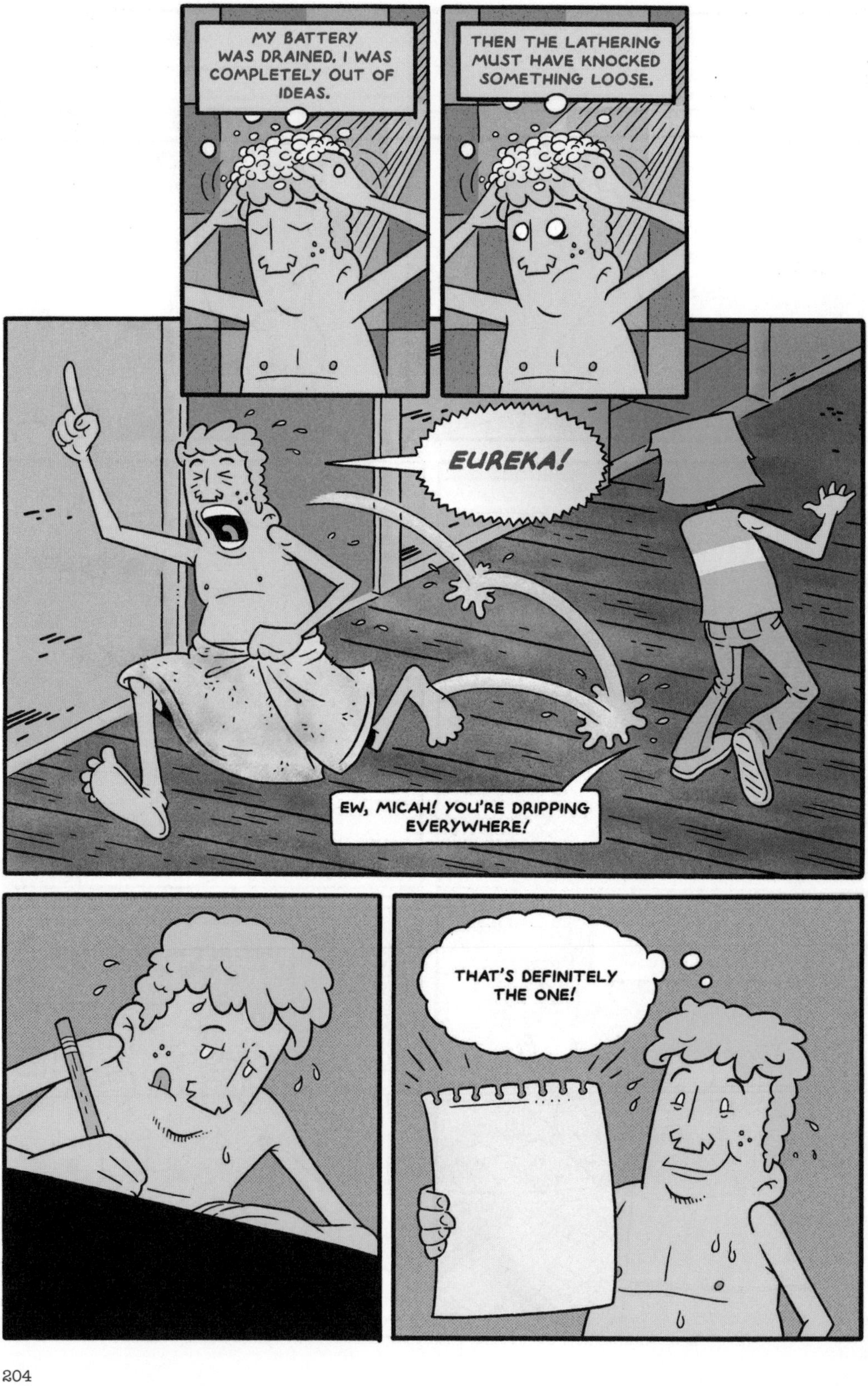
MY BATTERY WAS DRAINED. I WAS COMPLETELY OUT OF IDEAS.
THEN THE LATHERING MUST HAVE KNOCKED SOMETHING LOOSE.
EUREKA!
EW, MICAH! YOU'RE DRIPPING EVERYWHERE!
THAT'S DEFINITELY THE ONE!

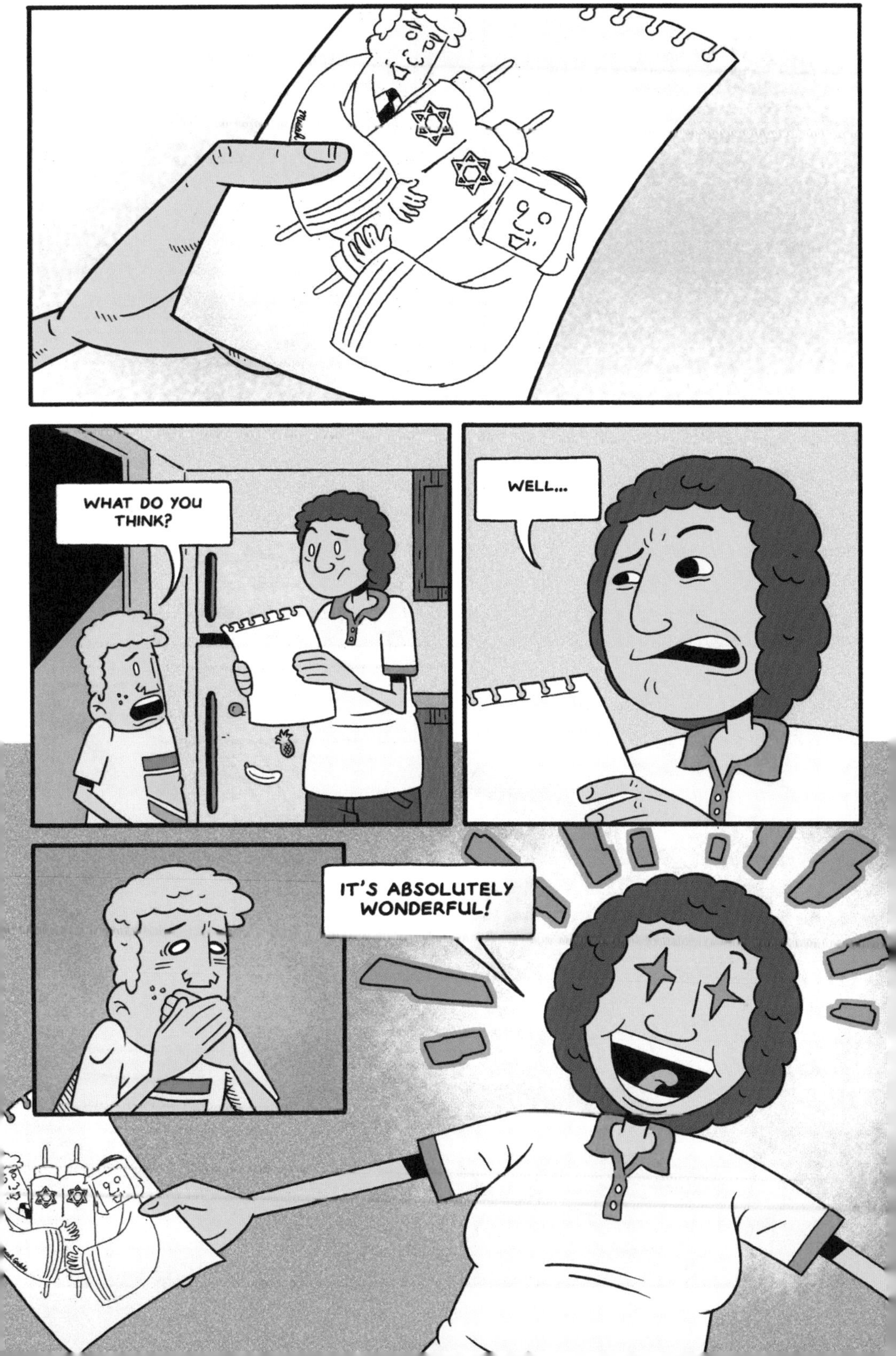
WHAT DO YOU THINK?
WELL...
IT'S ABSOLUTELY WONDERFUL!

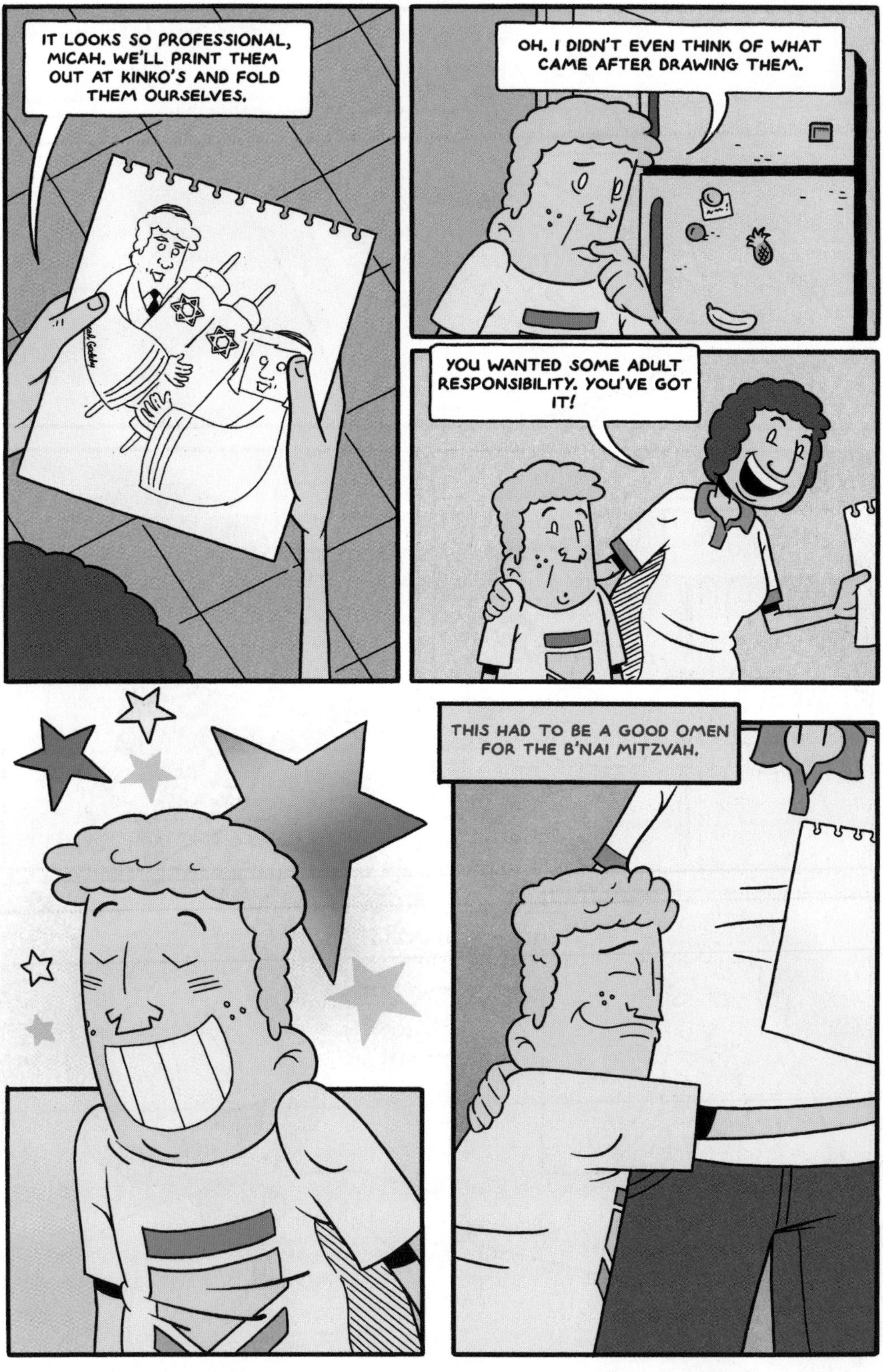
IT LOOKS SO PROFESSIONAL, MICAH. WE'LL PRINT THEM OUT AT KINKO'S AND FOLD THEM OURSELVES.
OH. I DIDN'T EVEN THINK OF WHAT CAME AFTER DRAWING THEM.
YOU WANTED SOME ADULT RESPONSIBILITY. YOU'VE GOT IT!
THIS HAD TO BE A GOOD OMEN FOR THE B'NAI MITZVAH.

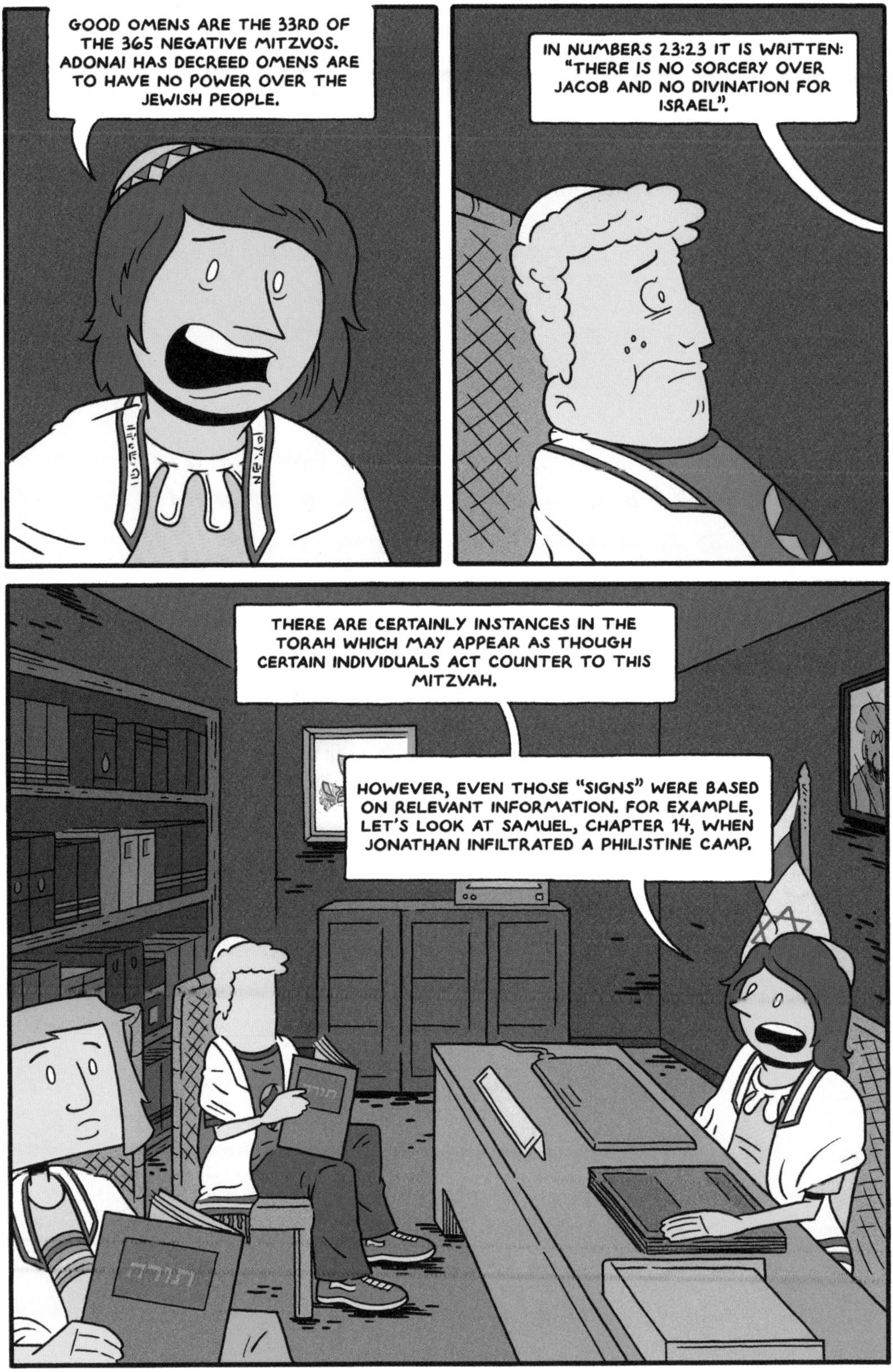
GOOD OMENS ARE THE 33RD OF THE 365 NEGATIVE MITZVOS. ADONAI HAS DECREED OMENS ARE TO HAVE NO POWER OVER THE JEWISH PEOPLE.
IN NUMBERS 23:23 IT IS WRITTEN: "THERE IS NO SORCERY OVER JACOB AND NO DIVINATION FOR ISRAEL".
THERE ARE CERTAINLY INSTANCES IN THE TORAH WHICH MAY APPEAR AS THOUGH CERTAIN INDIVIDUALS ACT COUNTER TO THIS MITZVAH.
HOWEVER, EVEN THOSE "SIGNS" WERE BASED ON RELEVANT INFORMATION. FOR EXAMPLE, LET'S LOOK AT SAMUEL, CHAPTER 14, WHEN JONATHAN INFILTRATED A PHILISTINE CAMP.

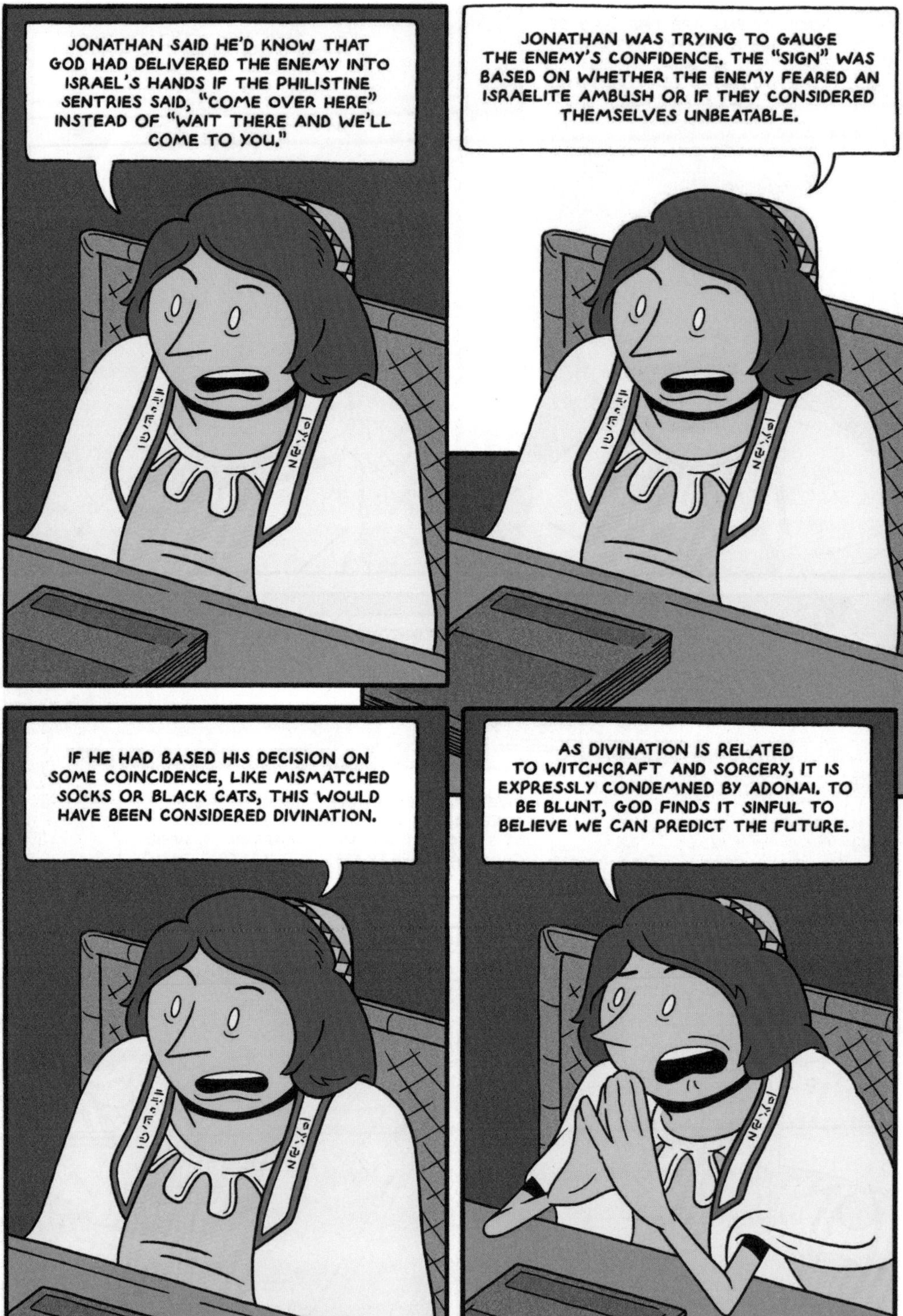
JONATHAN SAID HE'D KNOW THAT GOD HAD DELIVERED THE ENEMY INTO ISRAEL'S HANDS IF THE PHILISTINE SENTRIES SAID, "COME OVER HERE" INSTEAD OF "WAIT THERE AND WE'LL COME TO YOU."
JONATHAN WAS TRYING TO GAUGE THE ENEMY'S CONFIDENCE. THE "SIGN" WAS BASED ON WHETHER THE ENEMY FEARED AN ISRAELITE AMBUSH OR IF THEY CONSIDERED THEMSELVES UNBEATABLE.
IF HE HAD BASED HIS DECISION ON SOME COINCIDENCE, LIKE MISMATCHED SOCKS OR BLACK CATS, THIS WOULD HAVE BEEN CONSIDERED DIVINATION.
AS DIVINATION IS RELATED TO WITCHCRAFT AND SORCERY, IT IS EXPRESSLY CONDEMNED BY ADONAI. TO BE BLUNT, GOD FINDS IT SINFUL TO BELIEVE WE CAN PREDICT THE FUTURE.

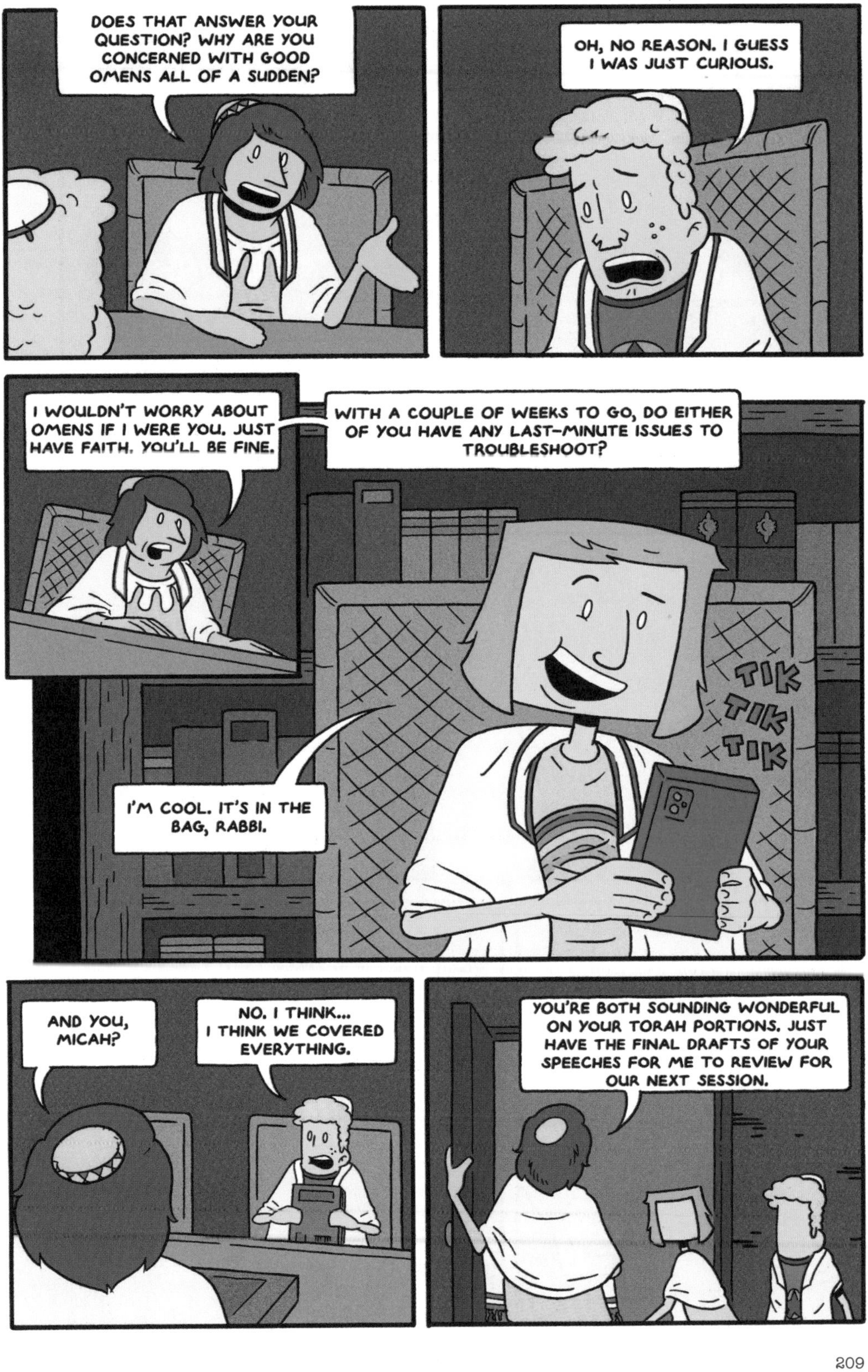
DOES THAT ANSWER YOUR QUESTION? WHY ARE YOU CONCERNED WITH GOOD OMENS ALL OF A SUDDEN?
OH, NO REASON. I GUESS I WAS JUST CURIOUS.
I WOULDN'T WORRY ABOUT OMENS IF I WERE YOU. JUST HAVE FAITH. YOU'LL BE FINE.
WITH A COUPLE OF WEEKS TO GO, DO EITHER OF YOU HAVE ANY LAST-MINUTE ISSUES TO TROUBLESHOOT?
TIK
TIK
TIK
I'M COOL. IT'S IN THE BAG, RABBI.
AND YOU, MICAH?
NO. I THINK... I THINK WE COVERED EVERYTHING.
YOU'RE BOTH SOUNDING WONDERFUL ON YOUR TORAH PORTIONS. JUST HAVE THE FINAL DRAFTS OF YOUR SPEECHES FOR ME TO REVIEW FOR OUR NEXT SESSION.

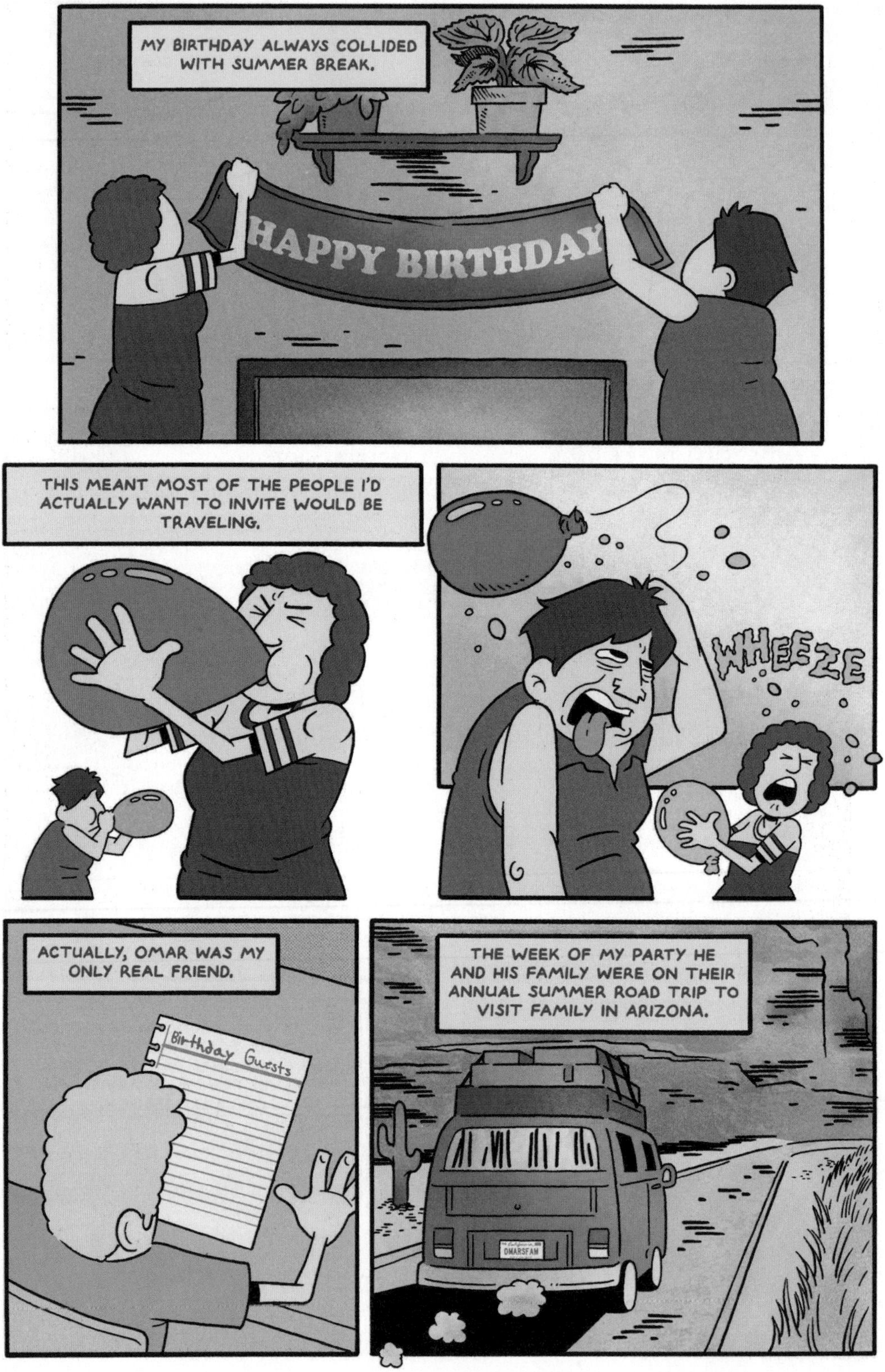
MY BIRTHDAY ALWAYS COLLIDED WITH SUMMER BREAK.
HAPPY BIRTHDAY
THIS MEANT MOST OF THE PEOPLE I'D ACTUALLY WANT TO INVITE WOULD BE TRAVELING.
WHEEZE
ACTUALLY, OMAR WAS MY ONLY REAL FRIEND.
Birthday Guests
THE WEEK OF MY PARTY HE AND HIS FAMILY WERE ON THEIR ANNUAL SUMMER ROAD TRIP TO VISIT FAMILY IN ARIZONA.
OMARSFAM

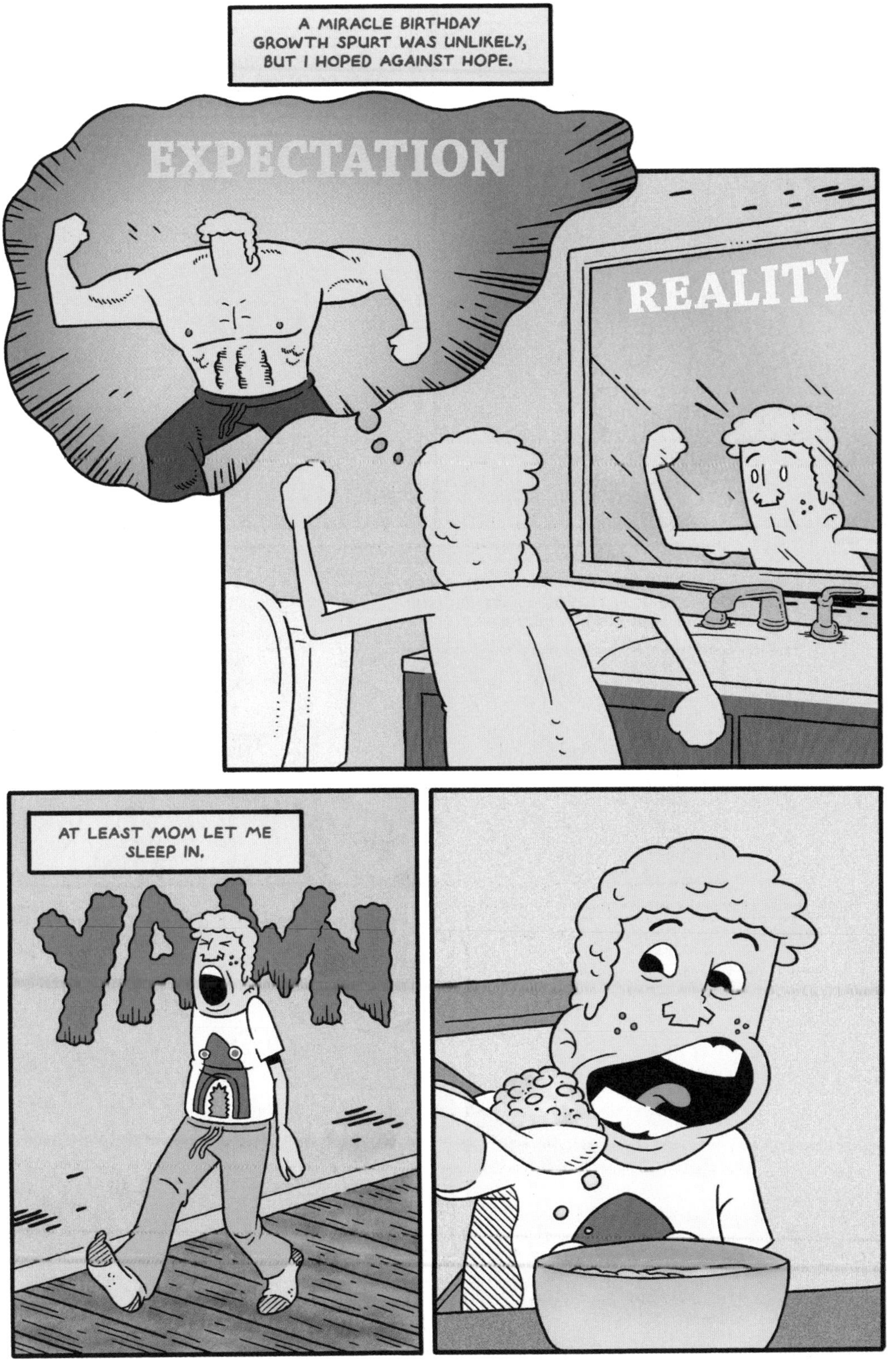
A MIRACLE BIRTHDAY GROWTH SPURT WAS UNLIKELY, BUT I HOPED AGAINST HOPE.
EXPECTATION
REALITY
AT LEAST MOM LET ME SLEEP IN.
YAWN

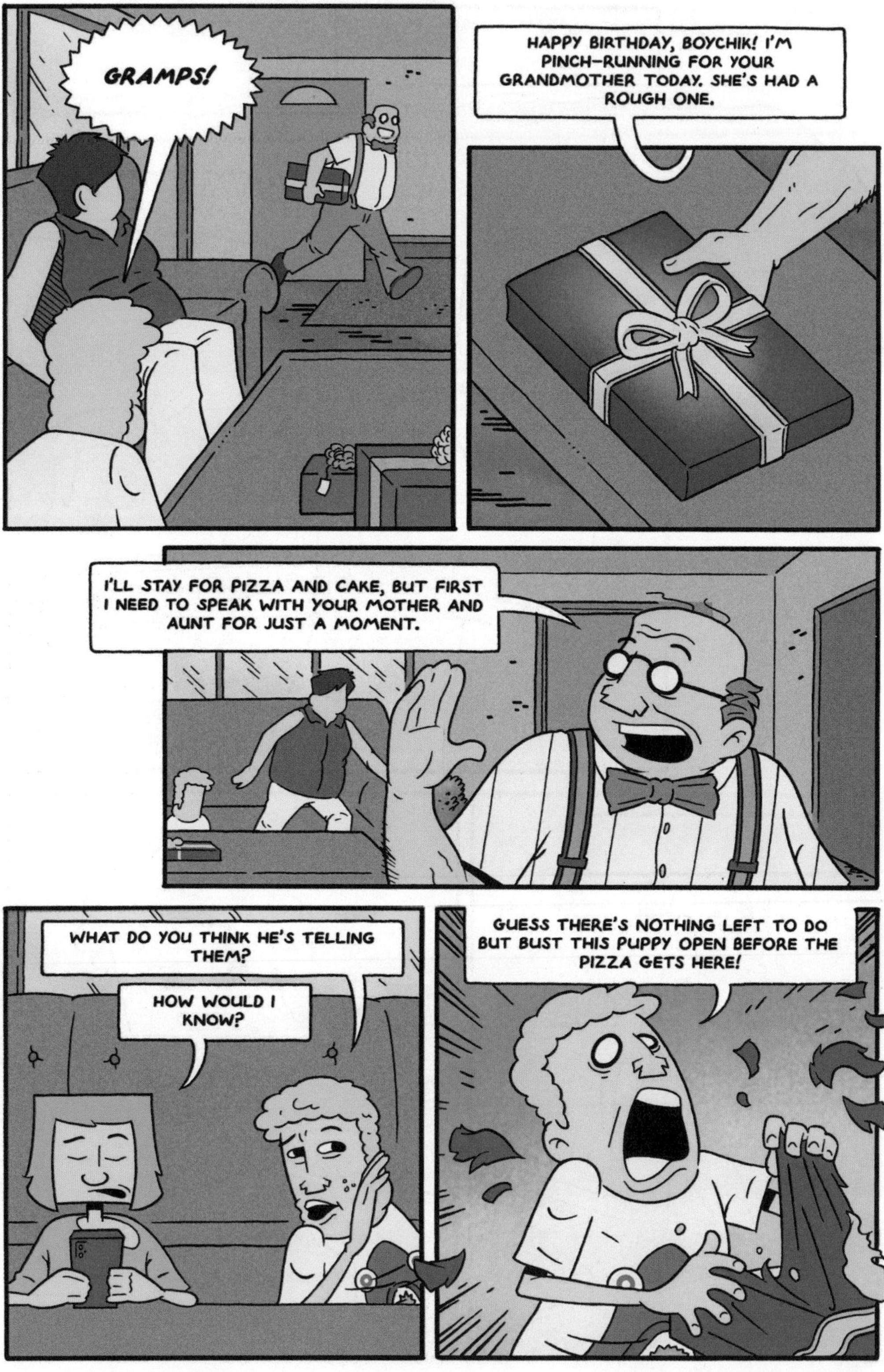
GRAMPS!
HAPPY BIRTHDAY, BOYCHIK! I'M PINCH-RUNNING FOR YOUR GRANDMOTHER TODAY. SHE'S HAD A ROUGH ONE.
I'LL STAY FOR PIZZA AND CAKE, BUT FIRST I NEED TO SPEAK WITH YOUR MOTHER AND AUNT FOR JUST A MOMENT.
WHAT DO YOU THINK HE'S TELLING THEM?
HOW WOULD I KNOW?
GUESS THERE'S NOTHING LEFT TO DO BUT BUST THIS PUPPY OPEN BEFORE THE PIZZA GETS HERE!

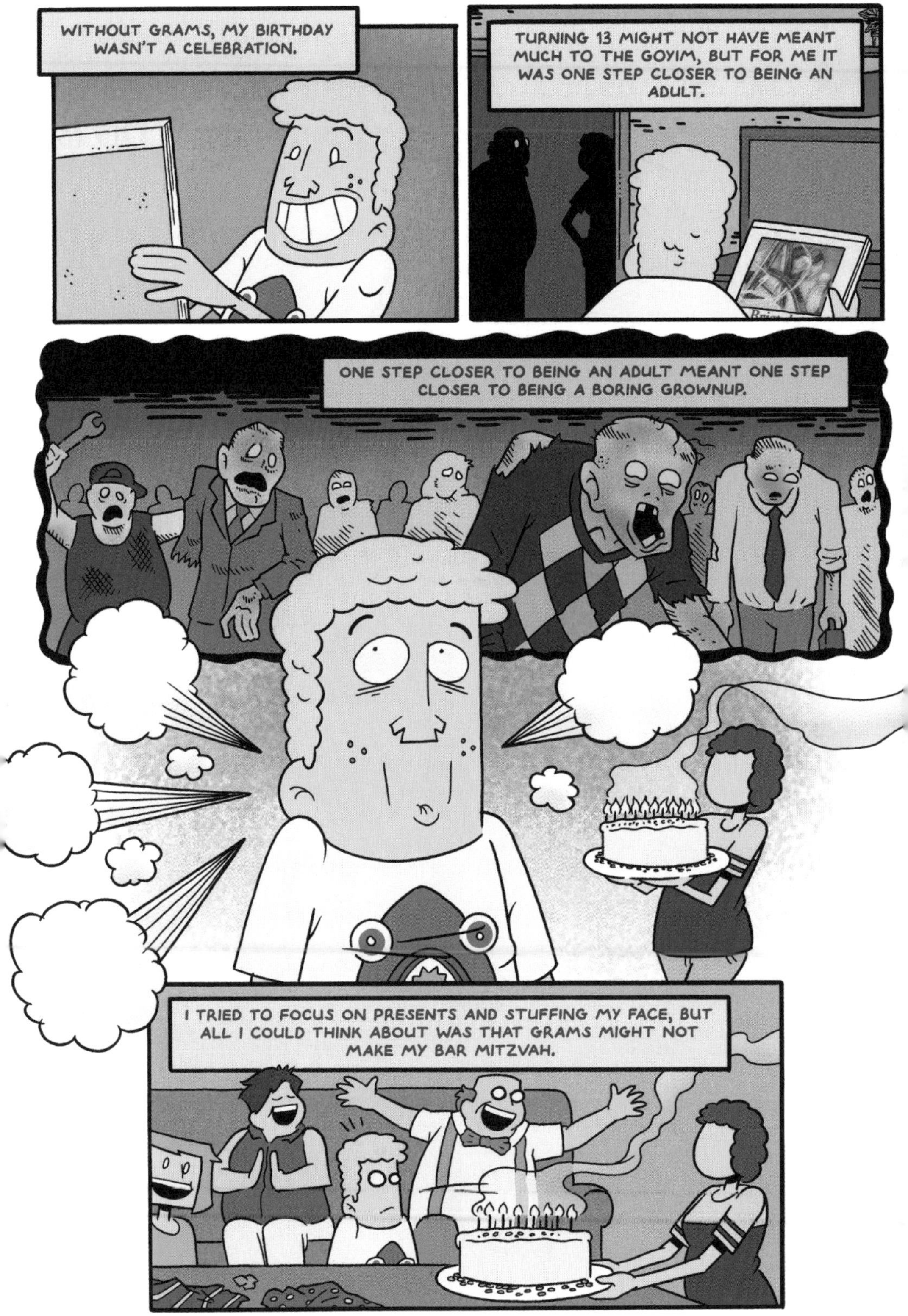
WITHOUT GRAMS, MY BIRTHDAY WASN'T A CELEBRATION.
TURNING 13 MIGHT NOT HAVE MEANT MUCH TO THE GOYIM, BUT FOR ME IT WAS ONE STEP CLOSER TO BEING AN ADULT.
ONE STEP CLOSER TO BEING AN ADULT MEANT ONE STEP CLOSER TO BEING A BORING GROWNUP.
I TRIED TO FOCUS ON PRESENTS AND STUFFING MY FACE, BUT ALL I COULD THINK ABOUT WAS THAT GRAMS MIGHT NOT MAKE MY BAR MITZVAH.

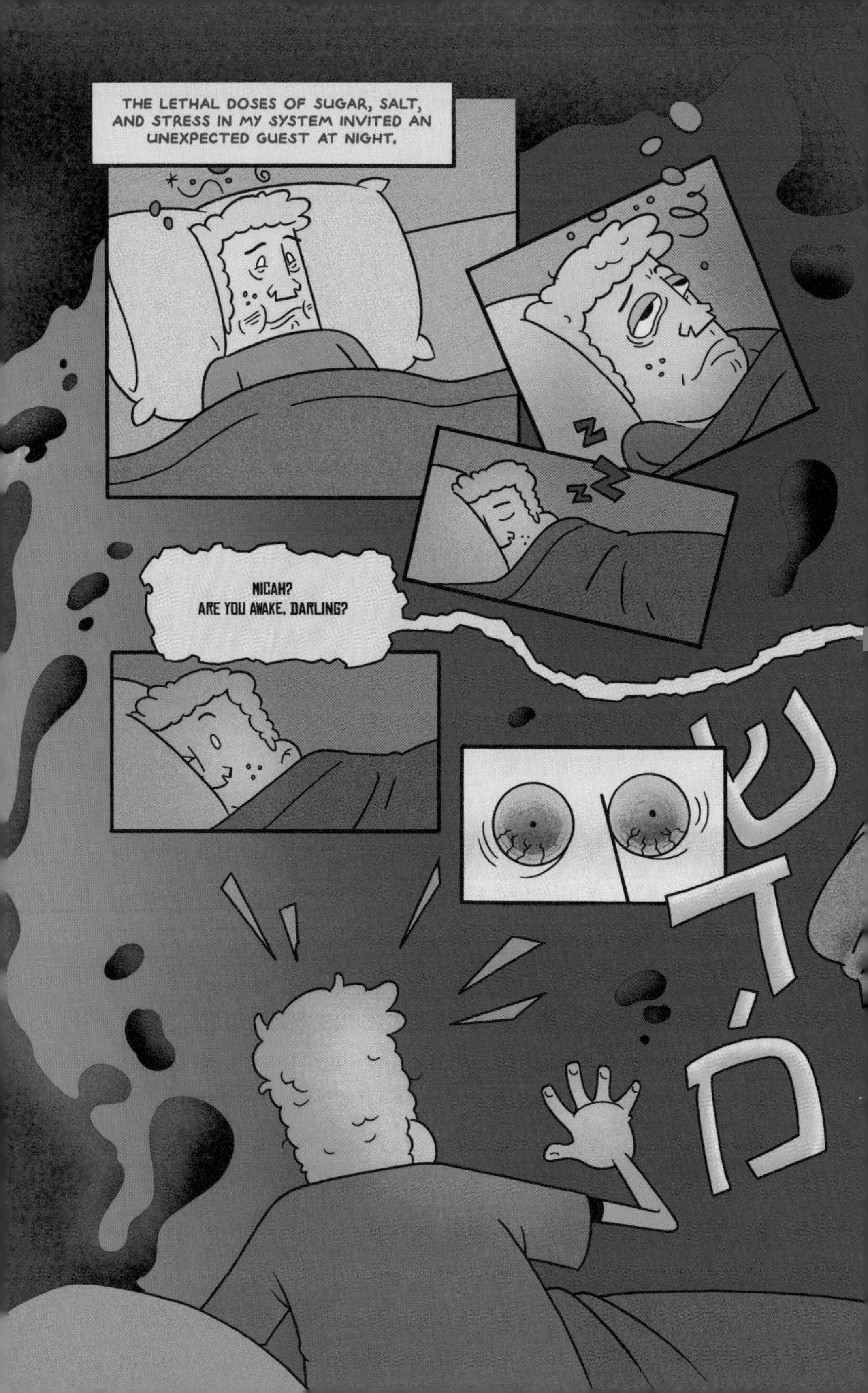
THE LETHAL DOSES OF SUGAR, SALT, AND STRESS IN MY SYSTEM INVITED AN UNEXPECTED GUEST AT NIGHT.
MICAH? ARE YOU AWAKE, DARLING?

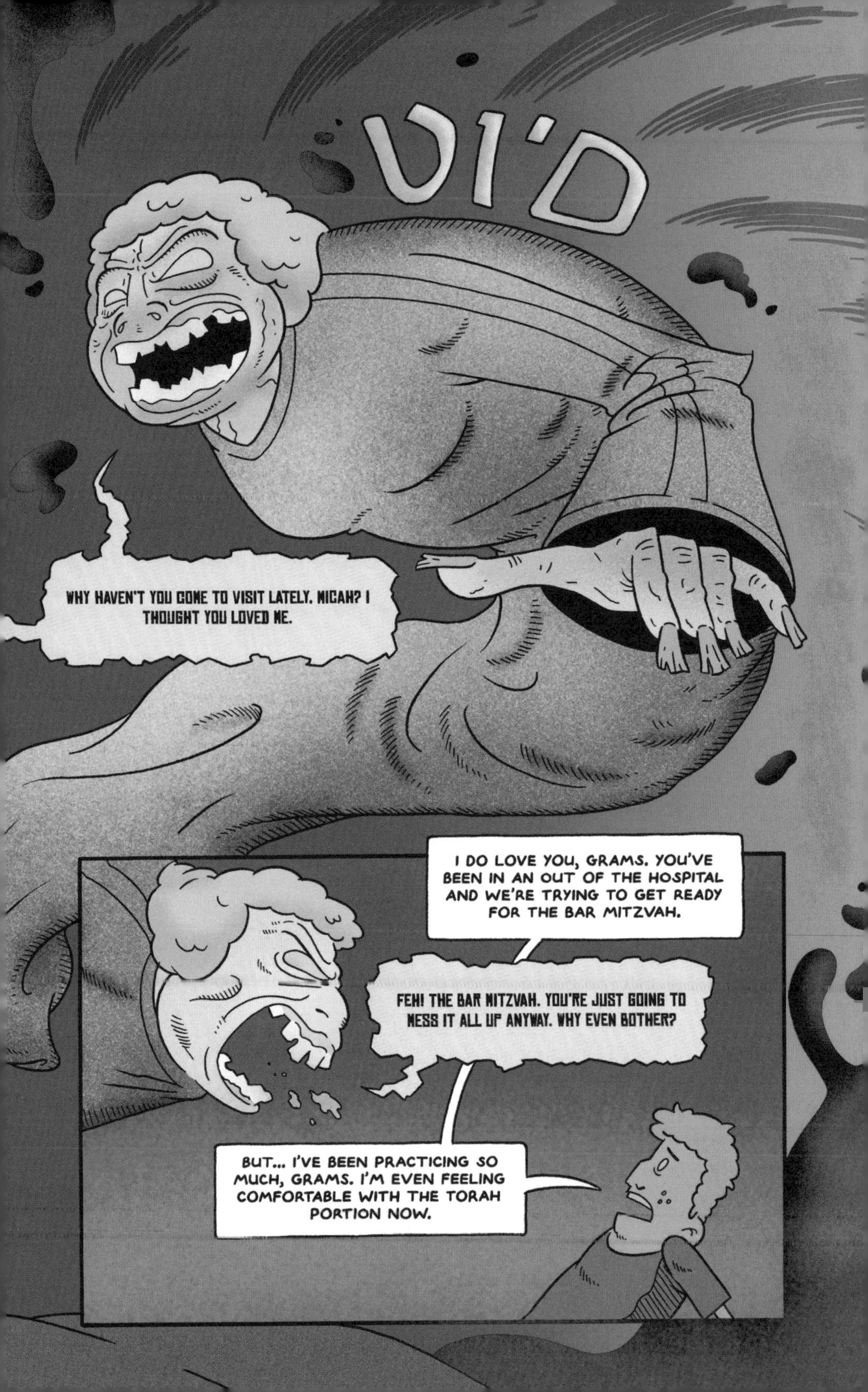
VI'D
WHY HAVEN'T YOU COME TO VISIT LATELY, MICAH? I THOUGHT YOU LOVED ME.
I DO LOVE YOU, GRAMS. YOU'VE BEEN IN AN OUT OF THE HOSPITAL AND WE'RE TRYING TO GET READY FOR THE BAR MITZVAH.
FEH! THE BAR MITZVAH. YOU'RE JUST GOING TO MESS IT ALL UP ANYWAY. WHY EVEN BOTHER?
BUT... I'VE BEEN PRACTICING SO MUCH, GRAMS. I'M EVEN FEELING COMFORTABLE WITH THE TORAH PORTION NOW.

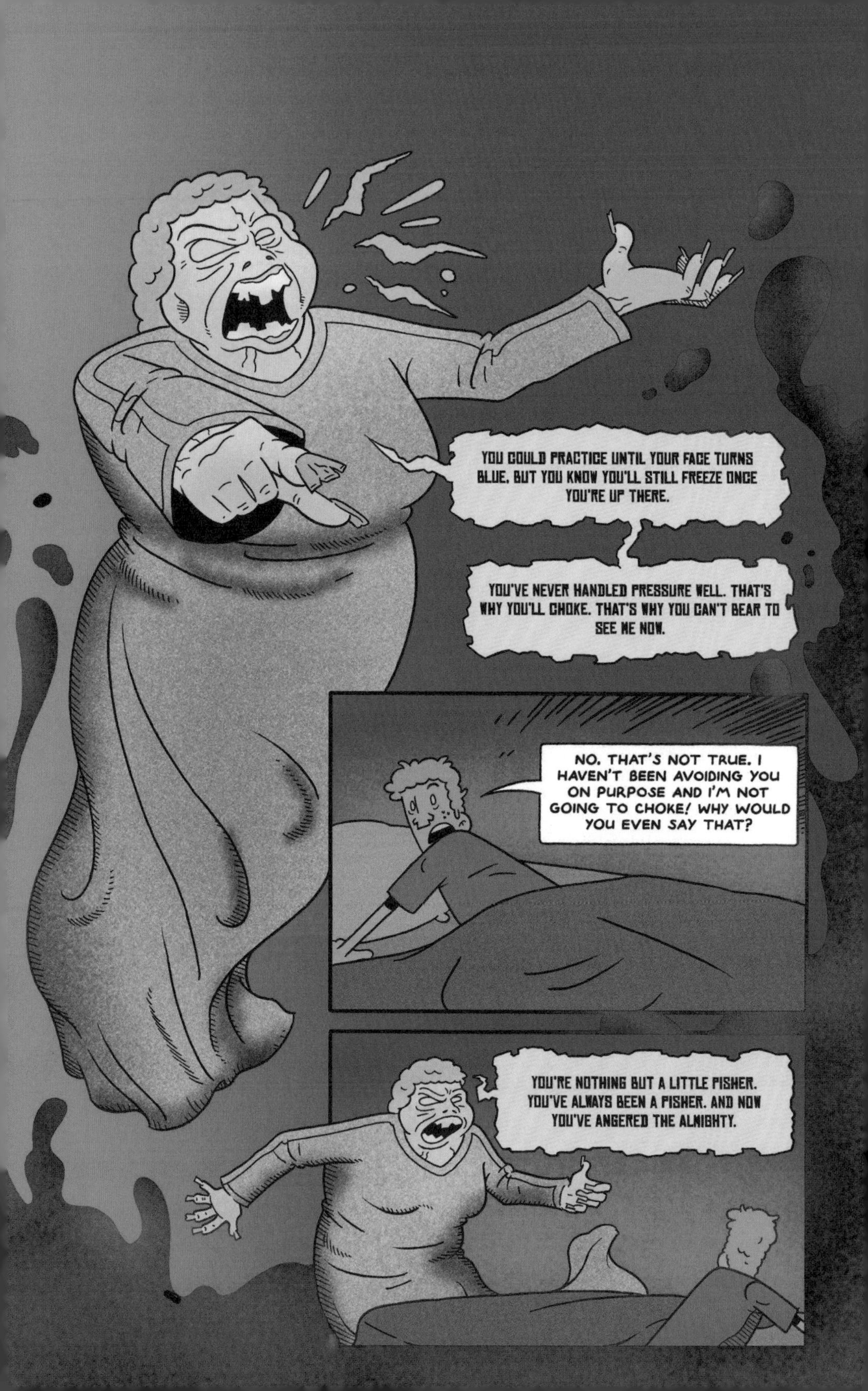
YOU COULD PRACTICE UNTIL YOUR FACE TURNS BLUE, BUT YOU KNOW YOU'LL STILL FREEZE ONCE YOU'RE UP THERE.
YOU'VE NEVER HANDLED PRESSURE WELL. THAT'S WHY YOU'LL CHOKE. THAT'S WHY YOU CAN'T BEAR TO SEE ME NOW.
NO. THAT'S NOT TRUE. I HAVEN'T BEEN AVOIDING YOU ON PURPOSE AND I'M NOT GOING TO CHOKE! WHY WOULD YOU EVEN SAY THAT?
YOU'RE NOTHING BUT A LITTLE PISHER. YOU'VE ALWAYS BEEN A PISHER. AND NOW YOU'VE ANGERED THE ALMIGHTY.

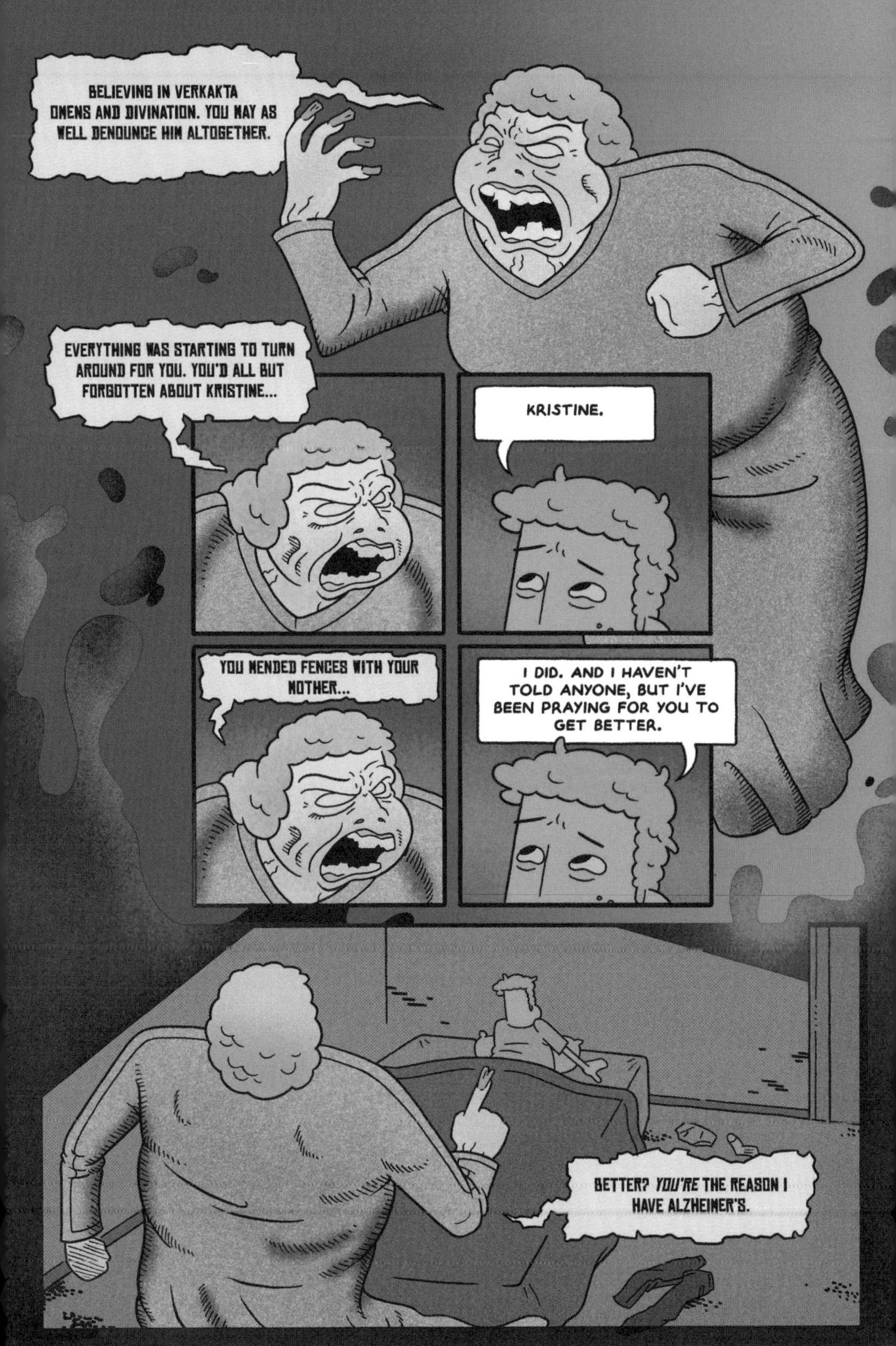
BELIEVING IN VERKAKTA OMENS AND DIVINATION. YOU MAY AS WELL DENOUNCE HIM ALTOGETHER.
EVERYTHING WAS STARTING TO TURN AROUND FOR YOU. YOU'D ALL BUT FORGOTTEN ABOUT KRISTINE...
KRISTINE.
YOU MENDED FENCES WITH YOUR MOTHER...
I DID. AND I HAVEN'T TOLD ANYONE, BUT I'VE BEEN PRAYING FOR YOU TO GET BETTER.
BETTER? *YOU'RE* THE REASON I HAVE ALZHEIMER'S.

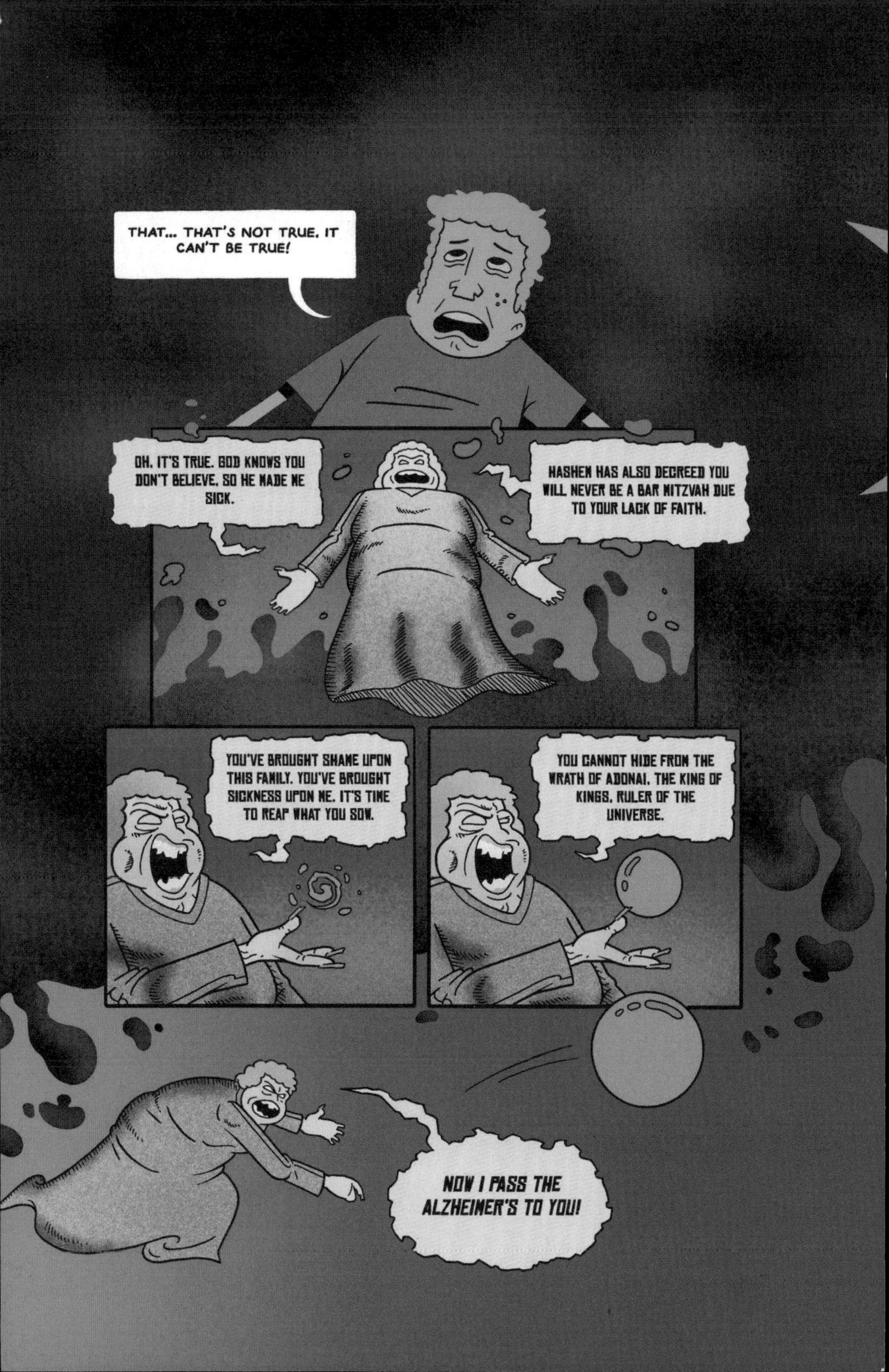
THAT... THAT'S NOT TRUE. IT CAN'T BE TRUE!
OH, IT'S TRUE. GOD KNOWS YOU DON'T BELIEVE, SO HE MADE ME SICK.
HASHEM HAS ALSO DECREED YOU WILL NEVER BE A BAR MITZVAH DUE TO YOUR LACK OF FAITH.
YOU'VE BROUGHT SHAME UPON THIS FAMILY. YOU'VE BROUGHT SICKNESS UPON ME. IT'S TIME TO REAP WHAT YOU SOW.
YOU CANNOT HIDE FROM THE WRATH OF ADONAI, THE KING OF KINGS, RULER OF THE UNIVERSE.
NOW I PASS THE ALZHEIMER'S TO YOU!

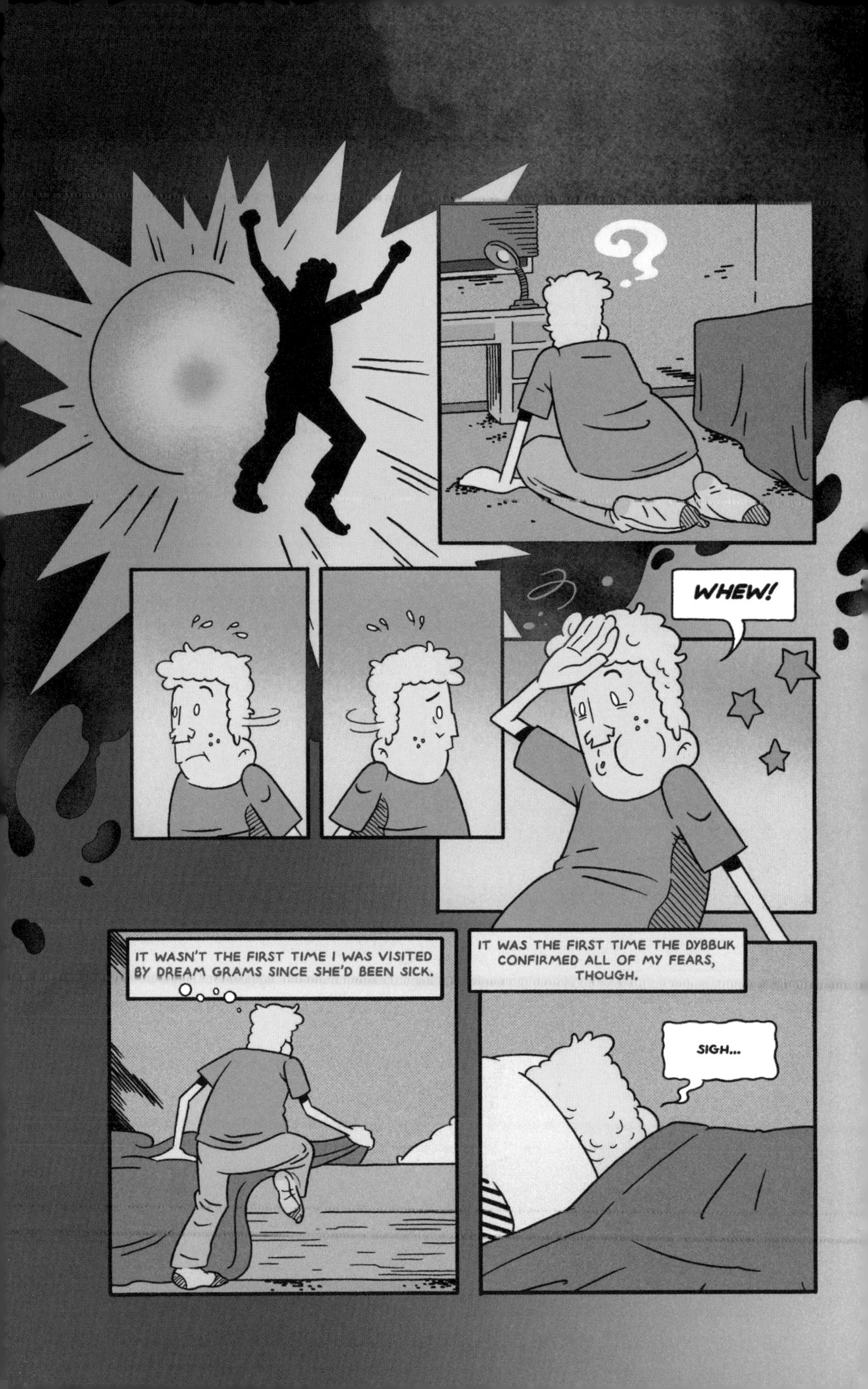
WHEW!
IT WASN'T THE FIRST TIME I WAS VISITED BY DREAM GRAMS SINCE SHE'D BEEN SICK.
IT WAS THE FIRST TIME THE DYBBUK CONFIRMED ALL OF MY FEARS, THOUGH.
SIGH...

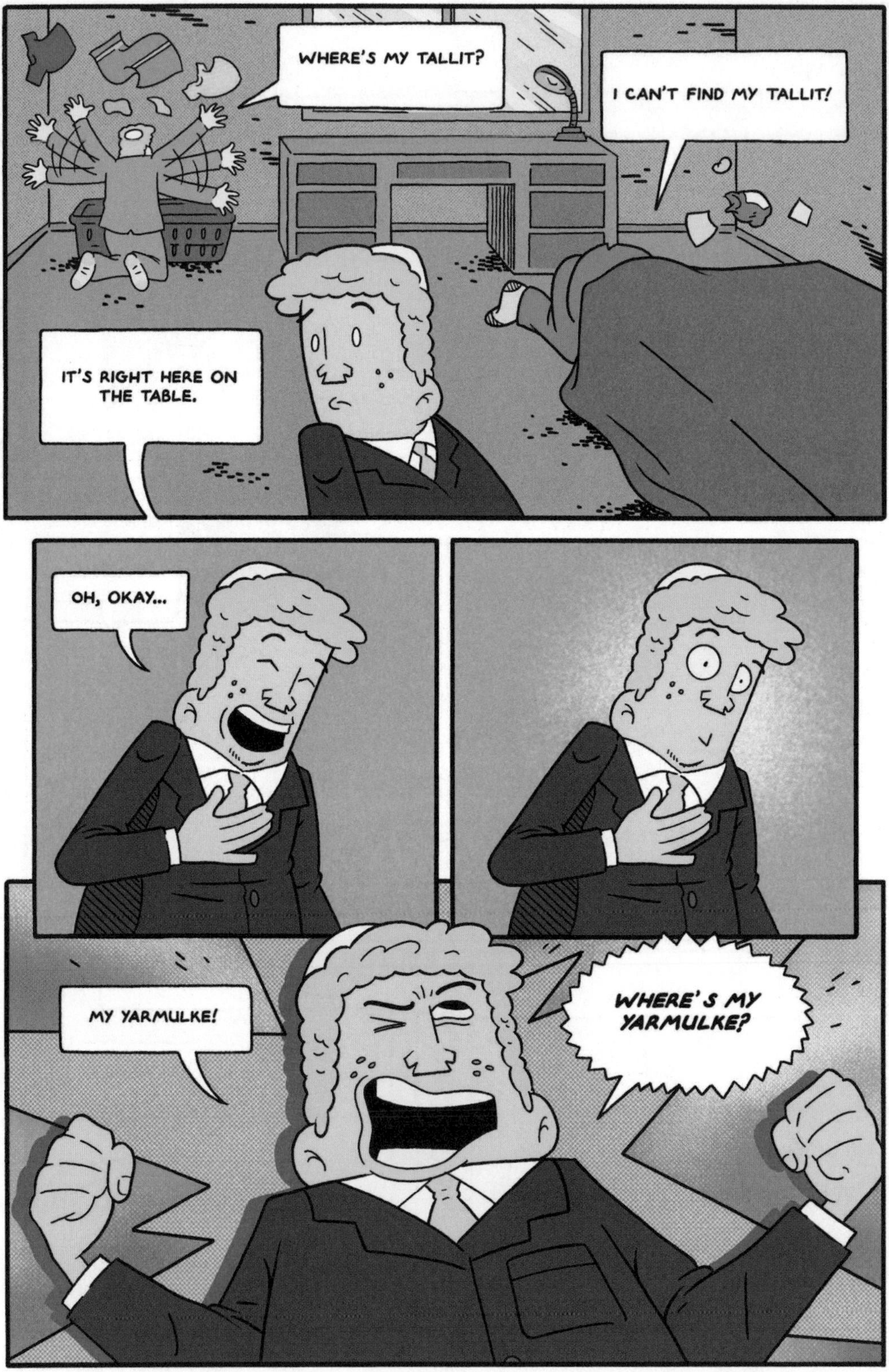
WHERE'S MY TALLIT?
I CAN'T FIND MY TALLIT!
IT'S RIGHT HERE ON THE TABLE.
OH, OKAY...
MY YARMULKE!
WHERE'S MY YARMULKE?

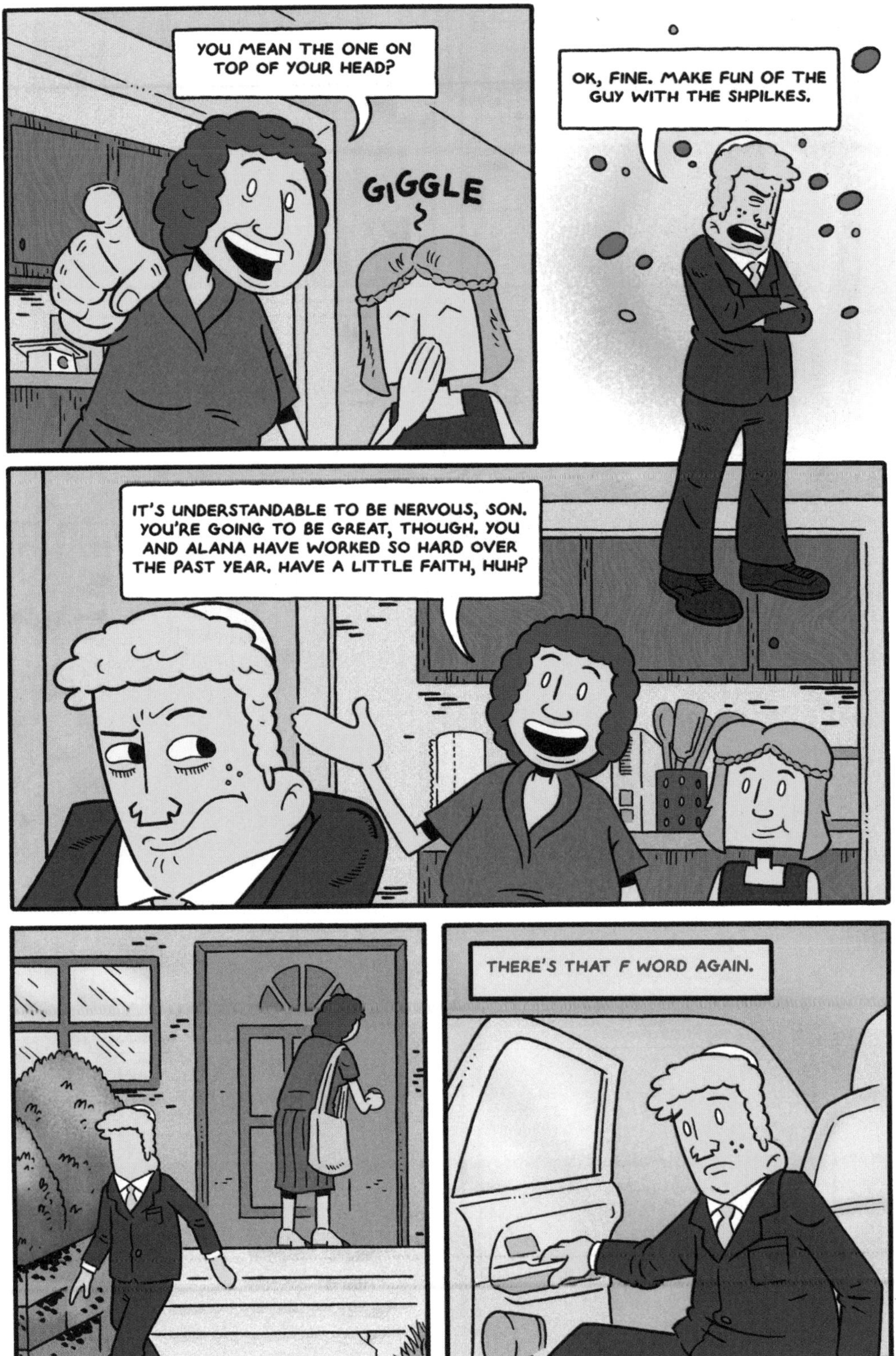
YOU MEAN THE ONE ON TOP OF YOUR HEAD?
GIGGLE
OK, FINE. MAKE FUN OF THE GUY WITH THE SHPILKES.
IT'S UNDERSTANDABLE TO BE NERVOUS, SON. YOU'RE GOING TO BE GREAT, THOUGH. YOU AND ALANA HAVE WORKED SO HARD OVER THE PAST YEAR. HAVE A LITTLE FAITH, HUH?
THERE'S THAT *F* WORD AGAIN.

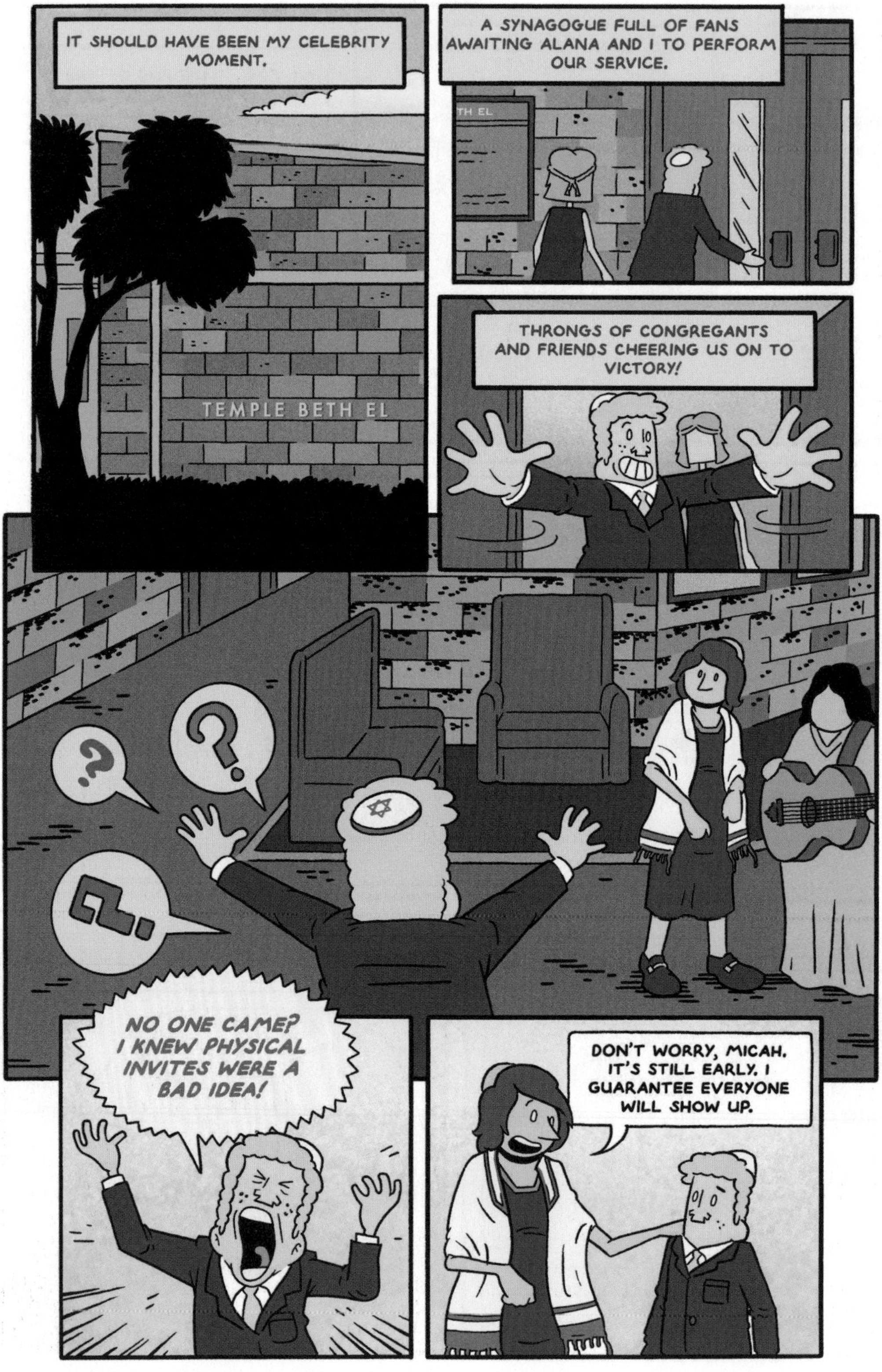
IT SHOULD HAVE BEEN MY CELEBRITY MOMENT.
TEMPLE BETH EL
A SYNAGOGUE FULL OF FANS AWAITING ALANA AND I TO PERFORM OUR SERVICE.
THRONGS OF CONGREGANTS AND FRIENDS CHEERING US ON TO VICTORY!
?
?
?
NO ONE CAME? I KNEW PHYSICAL INVITES WERE A BAD IDEA!
DON'T WORRY, MICAH. IT'S STILL EARLY. I GUARANTEE EVERYONE WILL SHOW UP.

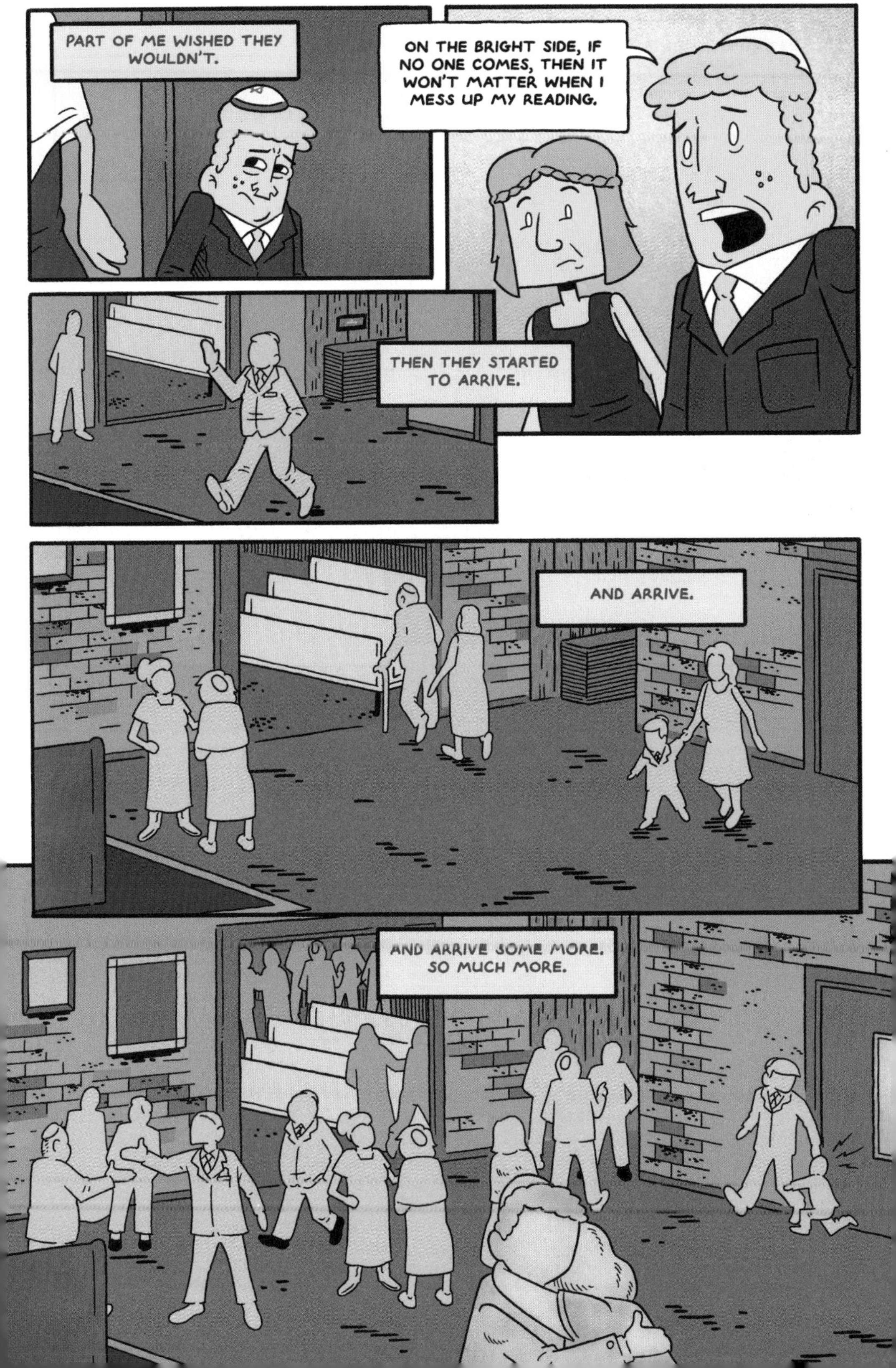
PART OF ME WISHED THEY WOULDN'T.
ON THE BRIGHT SIDE, IF NO ONE COMES, THEN IT WON'T MATTER WHEN I MESS UP MY READING.
THEN THEY STARTED TO ARRIVE.
AND ARRIVE.
AND ARRIVE SOME MORE. SO MUCH MORE.

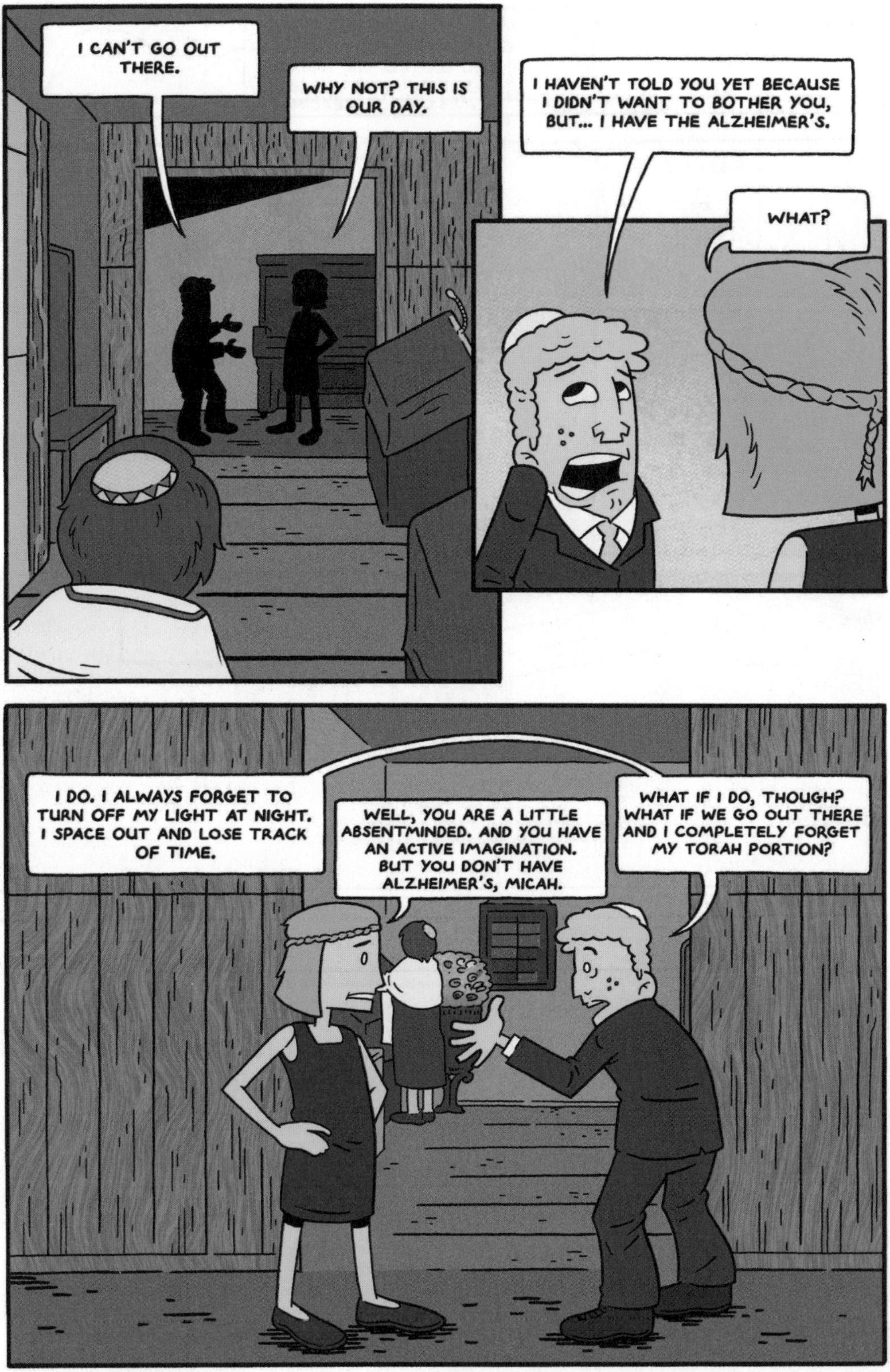
I CAN'T GO OUT THERE.
WHY NOT? THIS IS OUR DAY.
I HAVEN'T TOLD YOU YET BECAUSE I DIDN'T WANT TO BOTHER YOU, BUT... I HAVE THE ALZHEIMER'S.
WHAT?
I DO. I ALWAYS FORGET TO TURN OFF MY LIGHT AT NIGHT. I SPACE OUT AND LOSE TRACK OF TIME.
WELL, YOU ARE A LITTLE ABSENTMINDED. AND YOU HAVE AN ACTIVE IMAGINATION. BUT YOU DON'T HAVE ALZHEIMER'S, MICAH.
WHAT IF I DO, THOUGH? WHAT IF WE GO OUT THERE AND I COMPLETELY FORGET MY TORAH PORTION?

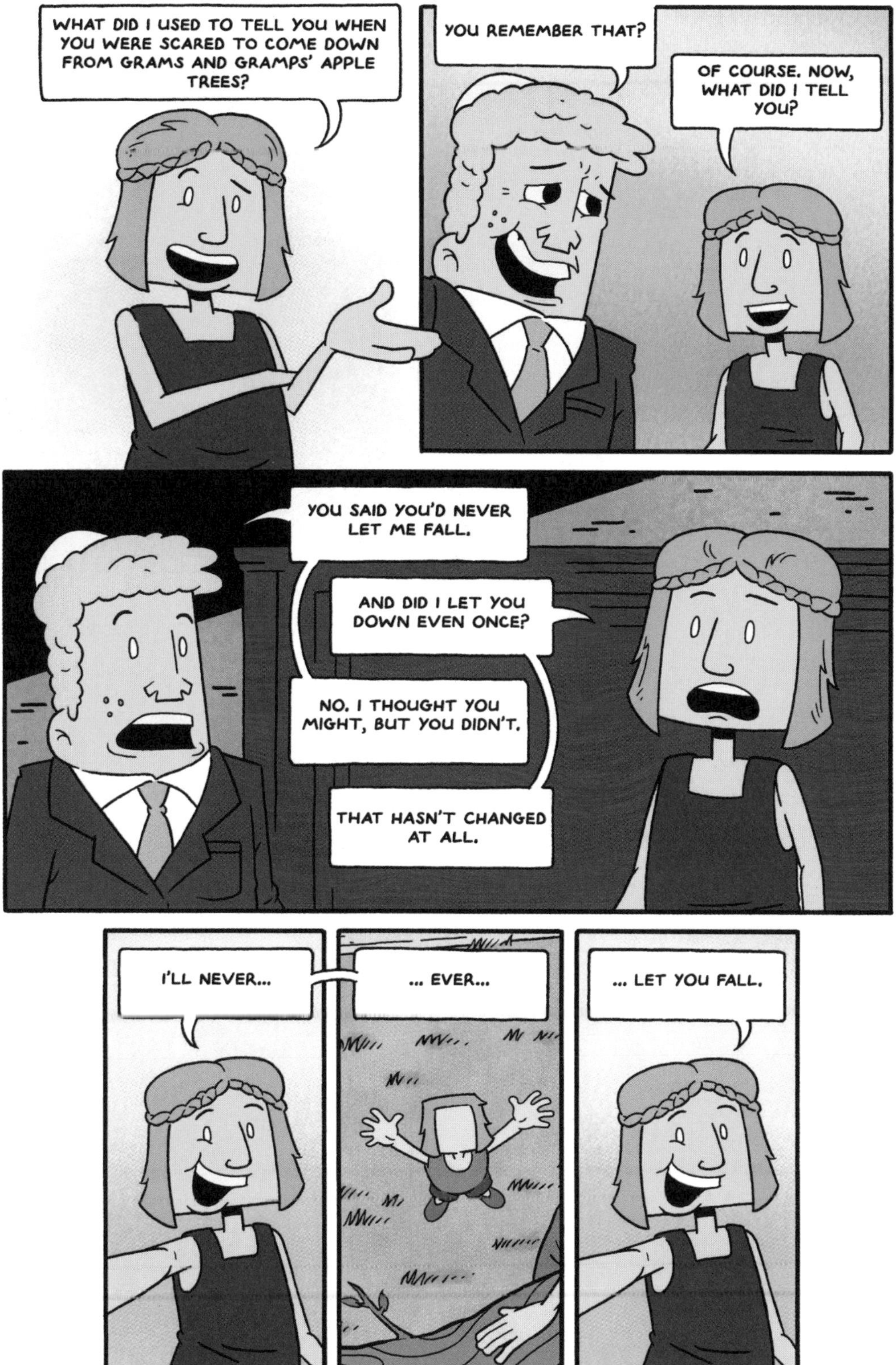
WHAT DID I USED TO TELL YOU WHEN YOU WERE SCARED TO COME DOWN FROM GRAMS AND GRAMPS' APPLE TREES?
YOU REMEMBER THAT?
OF COURSE. NOW, WHAT DID I TELL YOU?
YOU SAID YOU'D NEVER LET ME FALL.
AND DID I LET YOU DOWN EVEN ONCE?
NO. I THOUGHT YOU MIGHT, BUT YOU DIDN'T.
THAT HASN'T CHANGED AT ALL.
I'LL NEVER...
... EVER...
... LET YOU FALL.

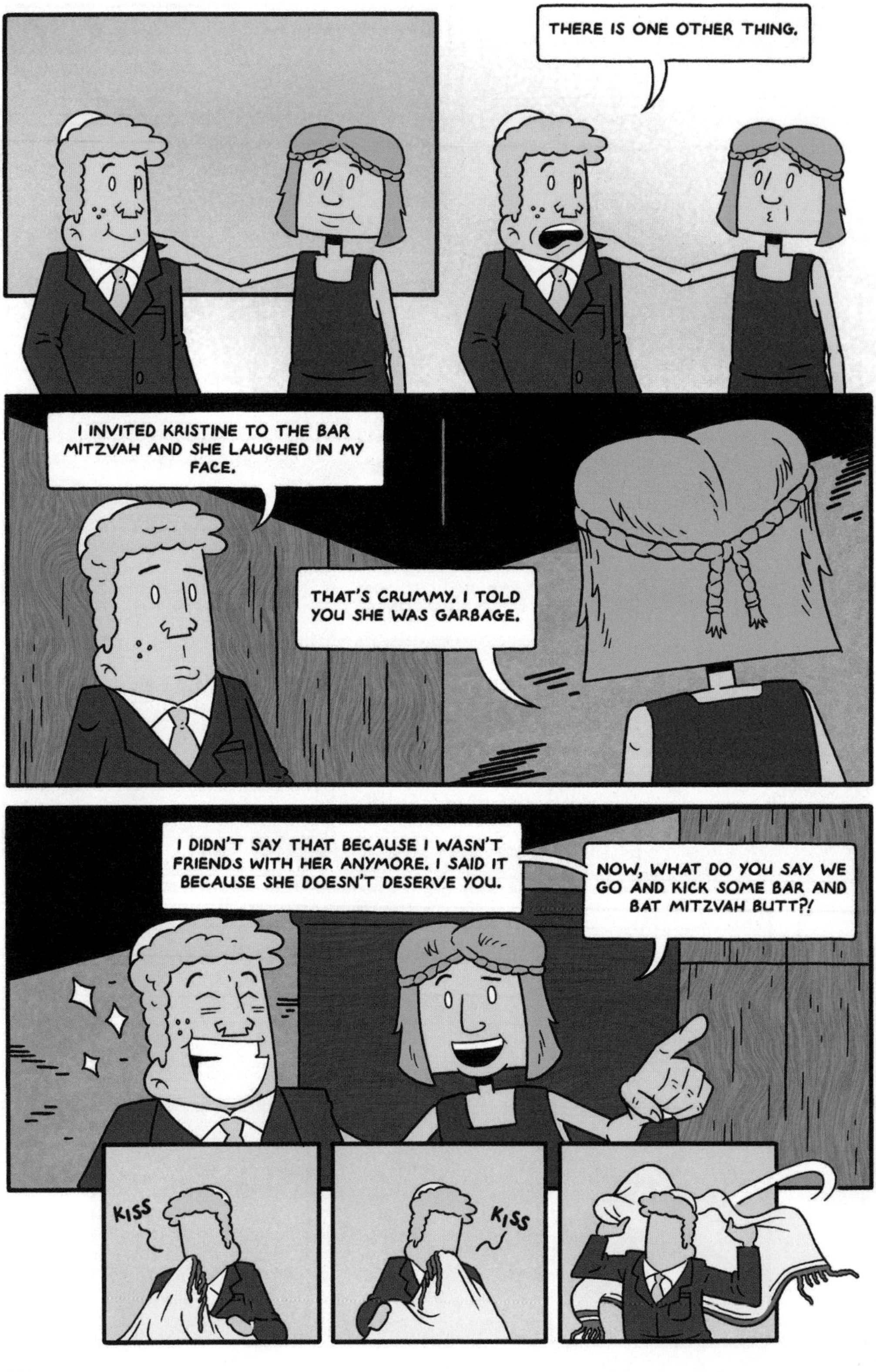
THERE IS ONE OTHER THING.
I INVITED KRISTINE TO THE BAR MITZVAH AND SHE LAUGHED IN MY FACE.
THAT'S CRUMMY. I TOLD YOU SHE WAS GARBAGE.
I DIDN'T SAY THAT BECAUSE I WASN'T FRIENDS WITH HER ANYMORE. I SAID IT BECAUSE SHE DOESN'T DESERVE YOU.
NOW, WHAT DO YOU SAY WE GO AND KICK SOME BAR AND BAT MITZVAH BUTT?!
KISS
KISS

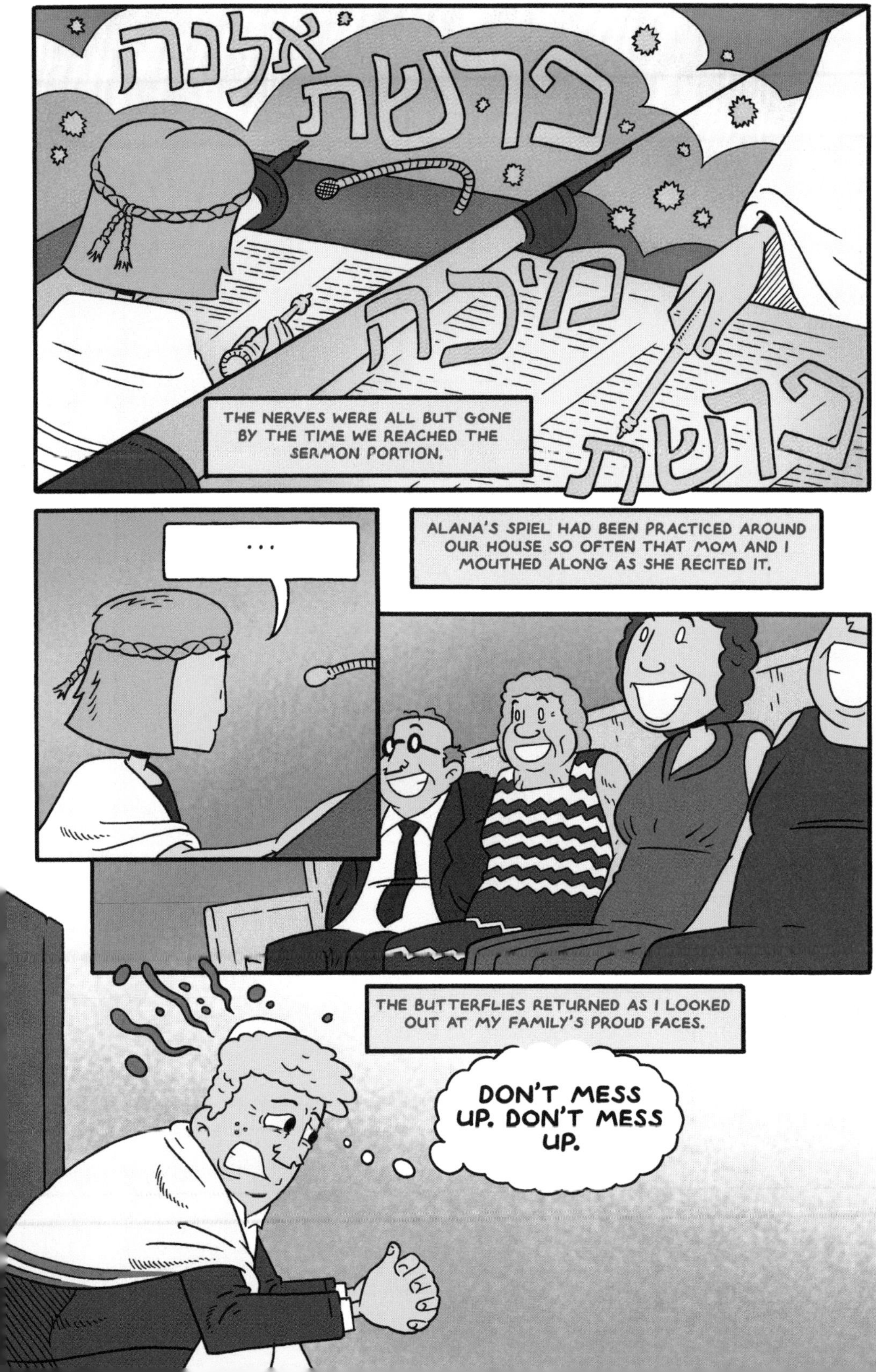
אלנה
פרשת
מיכה
פרשת
THE NERVES WERE ALL BUT GONE BY THE TIME WE REACHED THE SERMON PORTION.
...
ALANA'S SPIEL HAD BEEN PRACTICED AROUND OUR HOUSE SO OFTEN THAT MOM AND I MOUTHED ALONG AS SHE RECITED IT.
THE BUTTERFLIES RETURNED AS I LOOKED OUT AT MY FAMILY'S PROUD FACES.
DON'T MESS UP. DON'T MESS UP.

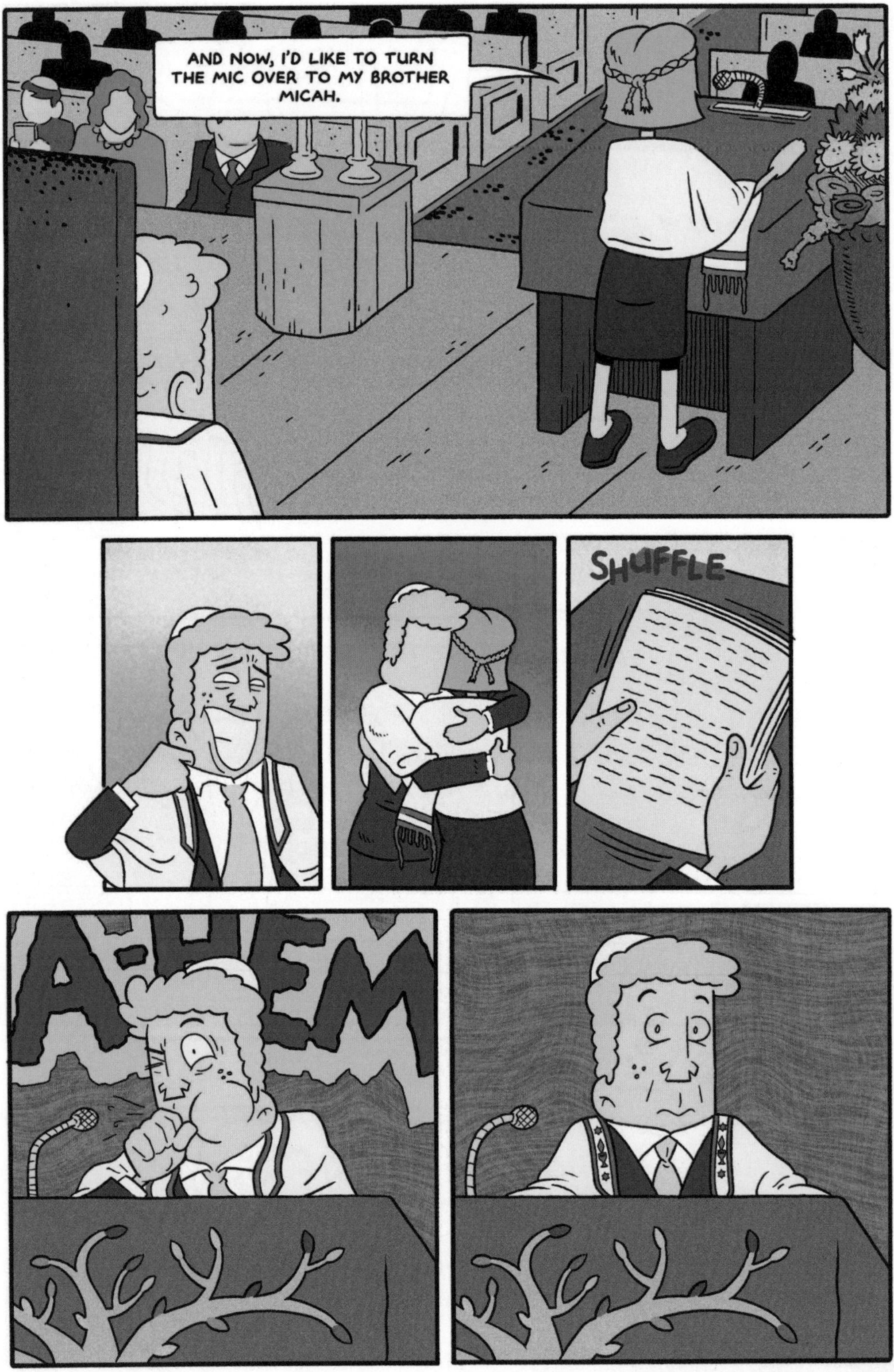
AND NOW, I'D LIKE TO TURN THE MIC OVER TO MY BROTHER MICAH.
SHUFFLE
A-HEM

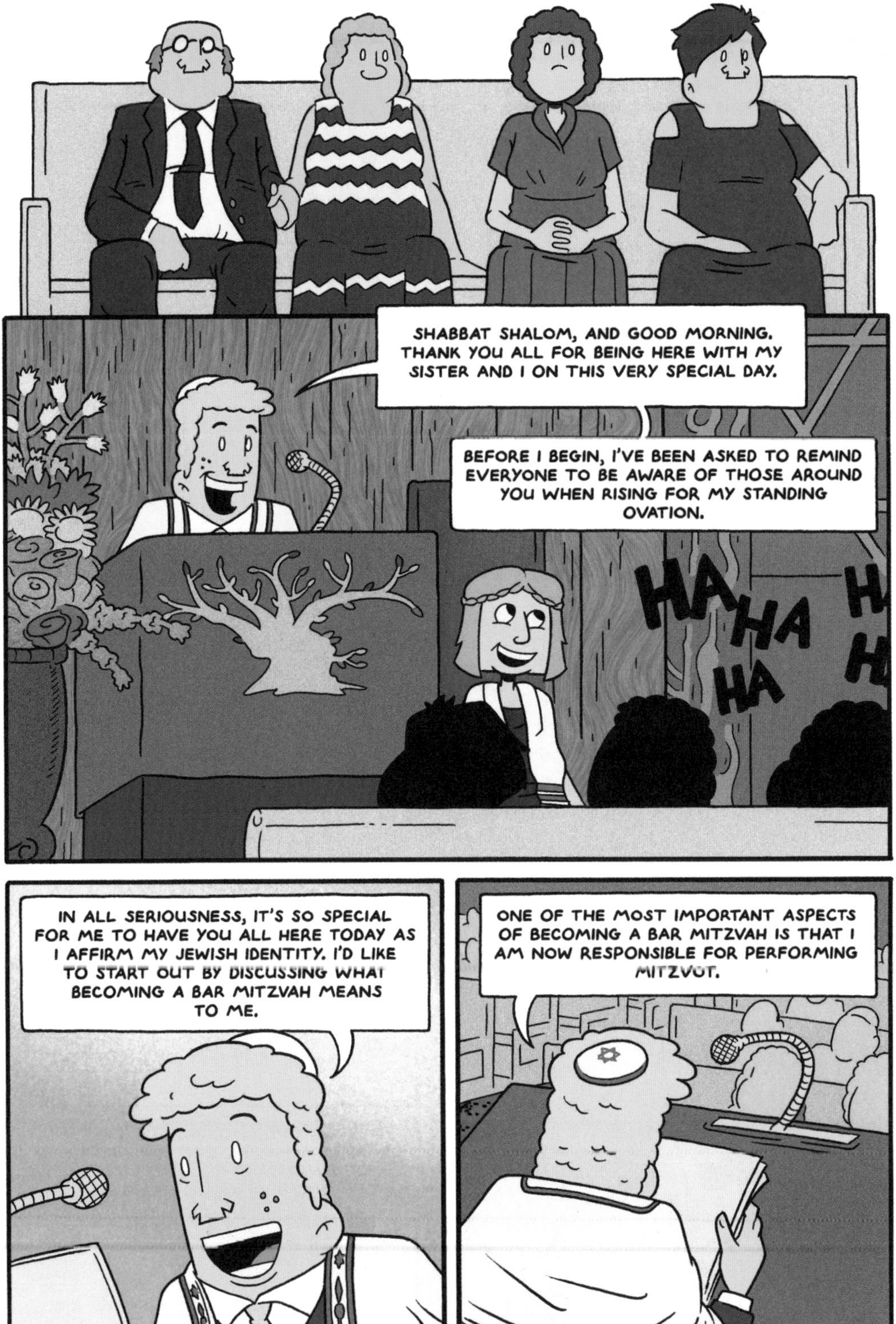
SHABBAT SHALOM, AND GOOD MORNING. THANK YOU ALL FOR BEING HERE WITH MY SISTER AND I ON THIS VERY SPECIAL DAY.
BEFORE I BEGIN, I'VE BEEN ASKED TO REMIND EVERYONE TO BE AWARE OF THOSE AROUND YOU WHEN RISING FOR MY STANDING OVATION.
HAHAHA
HA
IN ALL SERIOUSNESS, IT'S SO SPECIAL FOR ME TO HAVE YOU ALL HERE TODAY AS I AFFIRM MY JEWISH IDENTITY. I'D LIKE TO START OUT BY DISCUSSING WHAT BECOMING A BAR MITZVAH MEANS TO ME.
ONE OF THE MOST IMPORTANT ASPECTS OF BECOMING A BAR MITZVAH IS THAT I AM NOW RESPONSIBLE FOR PERFORMING MITZVOT.

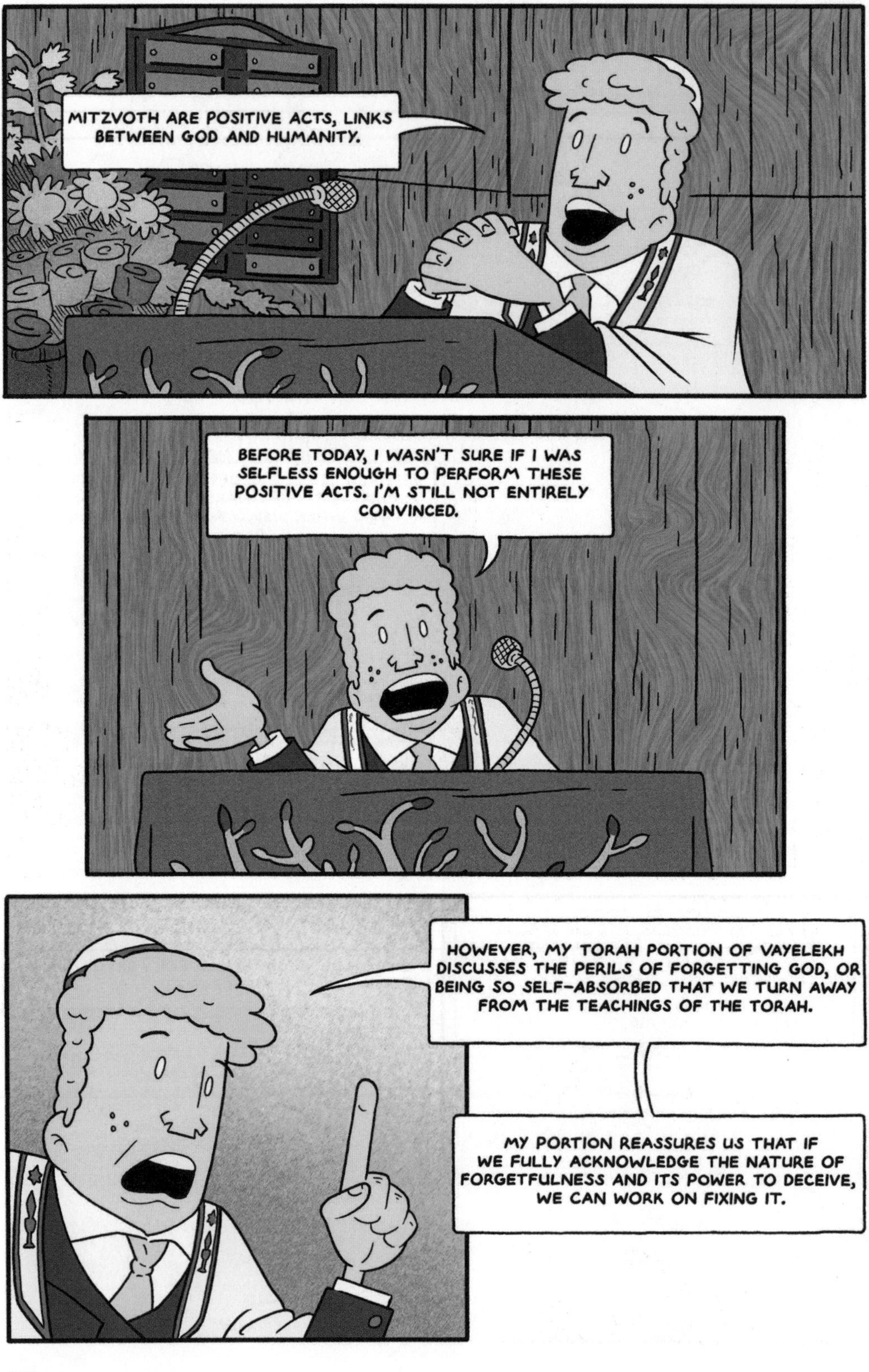
MITZVOTH ARE POSITIVE ACTS, LINKS BETWEEN GOD AND HUMANITY.
BEFORE TODAY, I WASN'T SURE IF I WAS SELFLESS ENOUGH TO PERFORM THESE POSITIVE ACTS. I'M STILL NOT ENTIRELY CONVINCED.
HOWEVER, MY TORAH PORTION OF VAYELEKH DISCUSSES THE PERILS OF FORGETTING GOD, OR BEING SO SELF-ABSORBED THAT WE TURN AWAY FROM THE TEACHINGS OF THE TORAH.
MY PORTION REASSURES US THAT IF WE FULLY ACKNOWLEDGE THE NATURE OF FORGETFULNESS AND ITS POWER TO DECEIVE, WE CAN WORK ON FIXING IT.

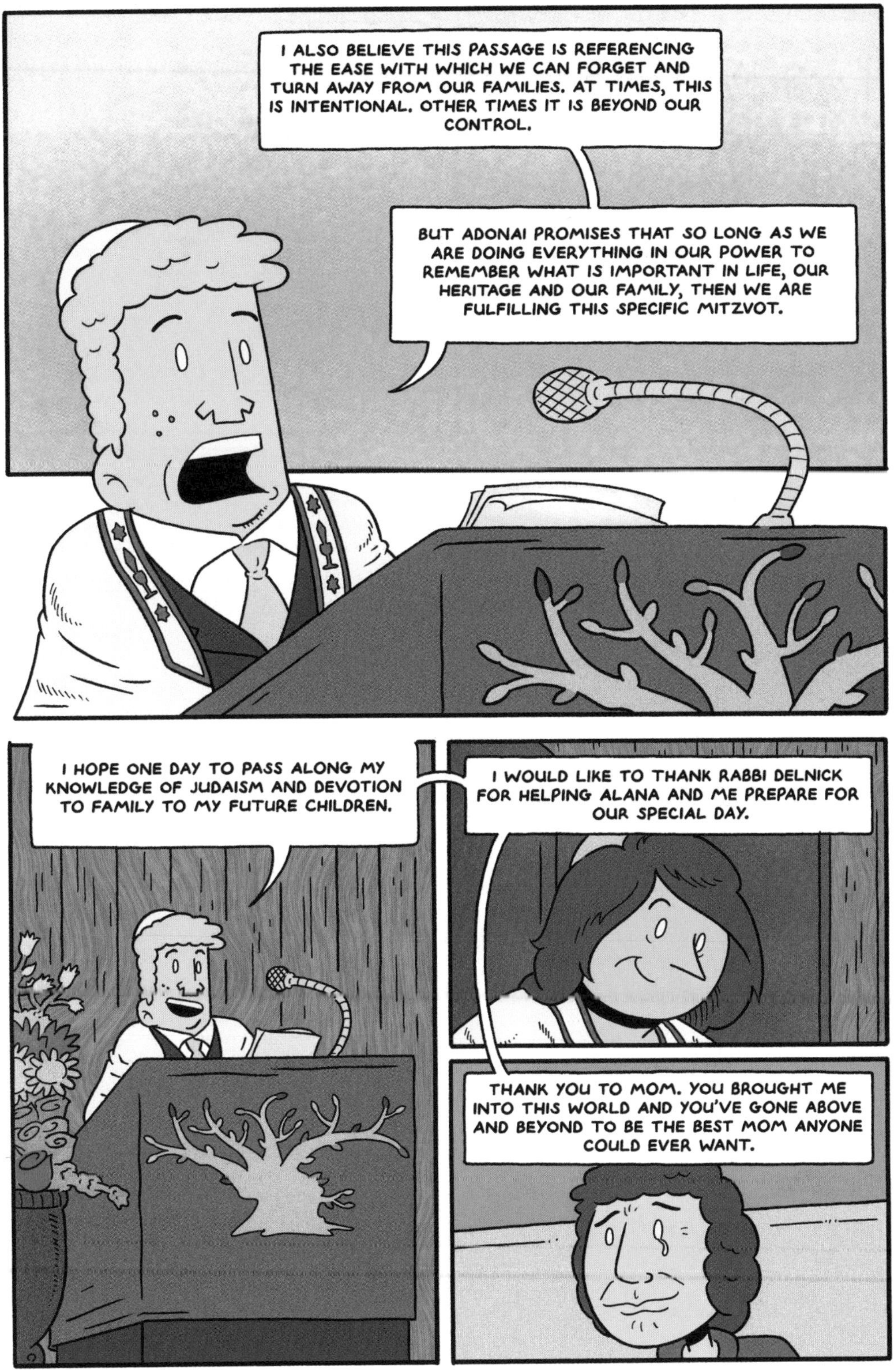
I ALSO BELIEVE THIS PASSAGE IS REFERENCING THE EASE WITH WHICH WE CAN FORGET AND TURN AWAY FROM OUR FAMILIES. AT TIMES, THIS IS INTENTIONAL. OTHER TIMES IT IS BEYOND OUR CONTROL.
BUT ADONAI PROMISES THAT SO LONG AS WE ARE DOING EVERYTHING IN OUR POWER TO REMEMBER WHAT IS IMPORTANT IN LIFE, OUR HERITAGE AND OUR FAMILY, THEN WE ARE FULFILLING THIS SPECIFIC MITZVOT.
I HOPE ONE DAY TO PASS ALONG MY KNOWLEDGE OF JUDAISM AND DEVOTION TO FAMILY TO MY FUTURE CHILDREN.
I WOULD LIKE TO THANK RABBI DELNICK FOR HELPING ALANA AND ME PREPARE FOR OUR SPECIAL DAY.
THANK YOU TO MOM. YOU BROUGHT ME INTO THIS WORLD AND YOU'VE GONE ABOVE AND BEYOND TO BE THE BEST MOM ANYONE COULD EVER WANT.

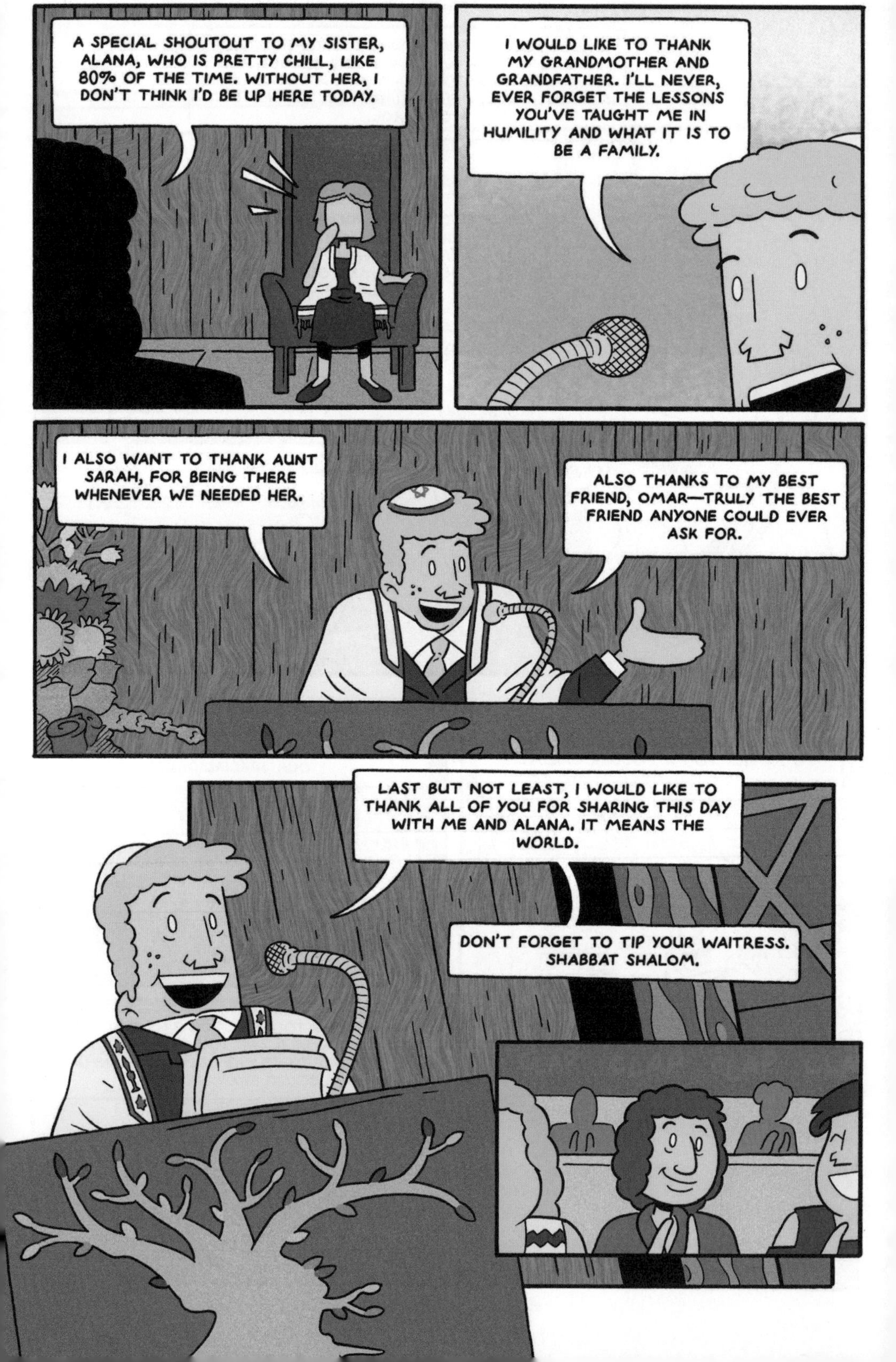
A SPECIAL SHOUTOUT TO MY SISTER, ALANA, WHO IS PRETTY CHILL, LIKE 80% OF THE TIME. WITHOUT HER, I DON'T THINK I'D BE UP HERE TODAY.
I WOULD LIKE TO THANK MY GRANDMOTHER AND GRANDFATHER. I'LL NEVER, EVER FORGET THE LESSONS YOU'VE TAUGHT ME IN HUMILITY AND WHAT IT IS TO BE A FAMILY.
I ALSO WANT TO THANK AUNT SARAH, FOR BEING THERE WHENEVER WE NEEDED HER.
ALSO THANKS TO MY BEST FRIEND, OMAR—TRULY THE BEST FRIEND ANYONE COULD EVER ASK FOR.
LAST BUT NOT LEAST, I WOULD LIKE TO THANK ALL OF YOU FOR SHARING THIS DAY WITH ME AND ALANA. IT MEANS THE WORLD.
DON'T FORGET TO TIP YOUR WAITRESS. SHABBAT SHALOM.

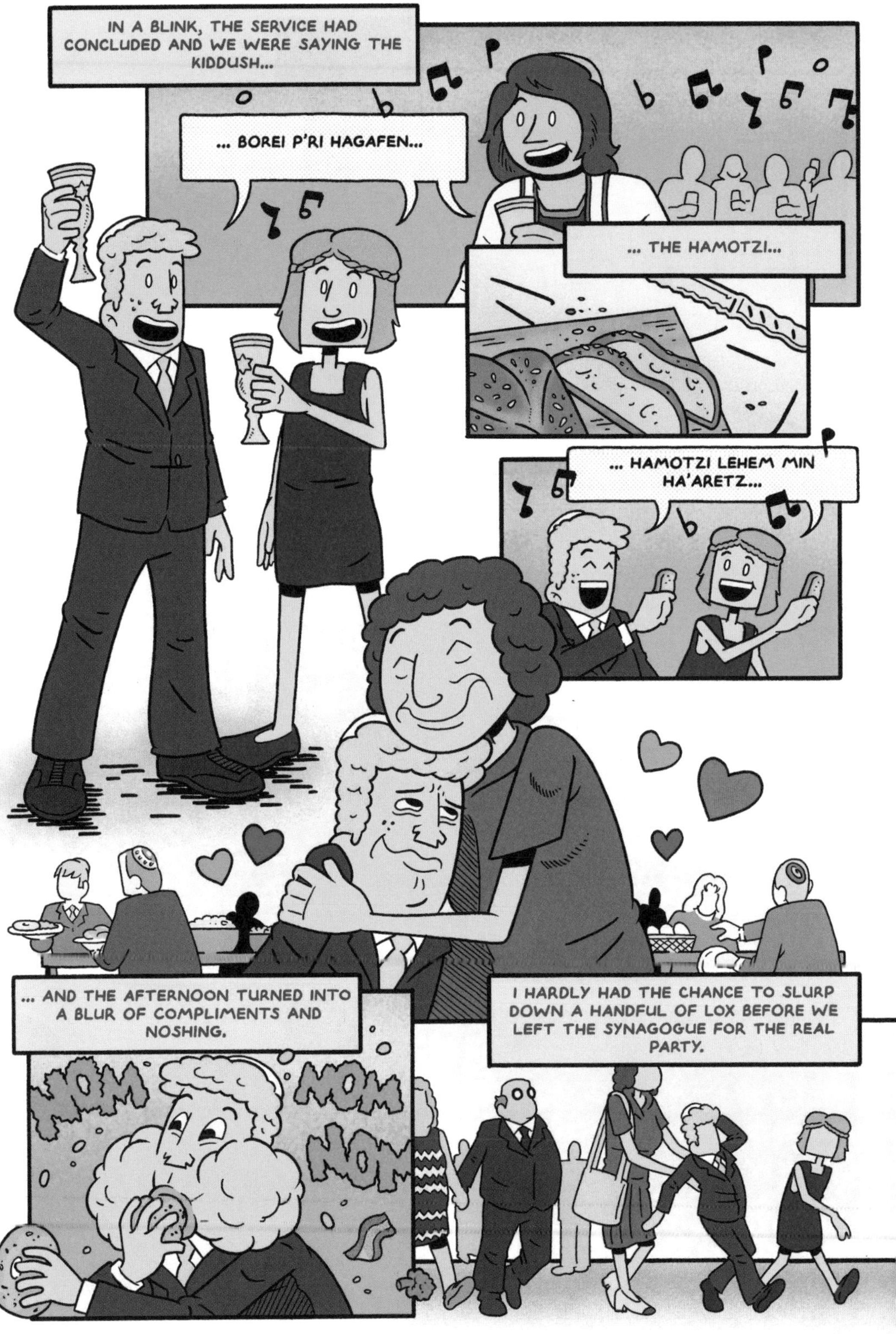

IN A BLINK, THE SERVICE HAD CONCLUDED AND WE WERE SAYING THE KIDDUSH...
... BOREI P'RI HAGAFEN...
... THE HAMOTZI...
... HAMOTZI LEHEM MIN HA'ARETZ...
... AND THE AFTERNOON TURNED INTO A BLUR OF COMPLIMENTS AND NOSHING.
NOM NOM NOM
I HARDLY HAD THE CHANCE TO SLURP DOWN A HANDFUL OF LOX BEFORE WE LEFT THE SYNAGOGUE FOR THE REAL PARTY.

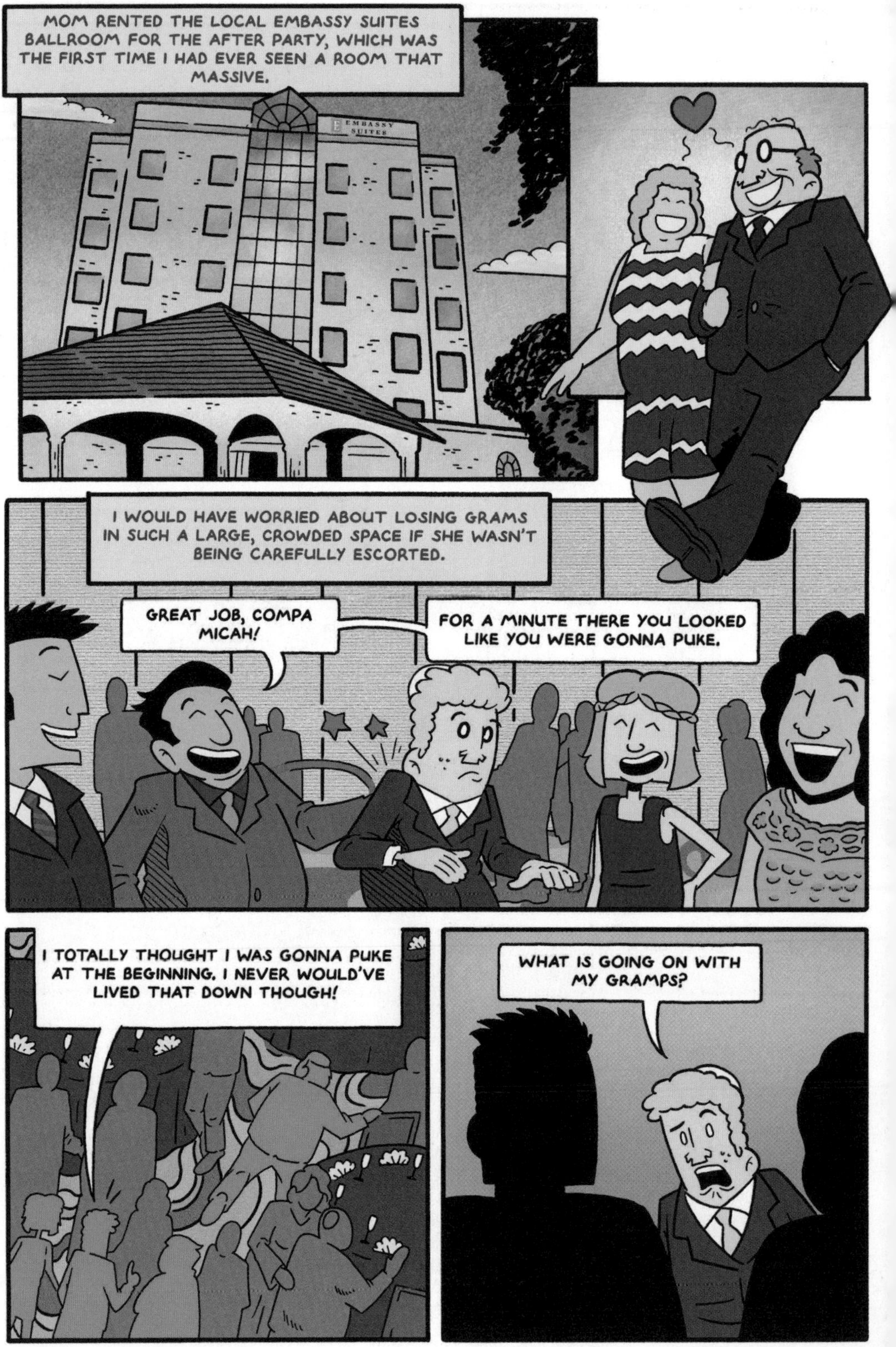
MOM RENTED THE LOCAL EMBASSY SUITES BALLROOM FOR THE AFTER PARTY, WHICH WAS THE FIRST TIME I HAD EVER SEEN A ROOM THAT MASSIVE.
EMBASSY SUITES
I WOULD HAVE WORRIED ABOUT LOSING GRAMS IN SUCH A LARGE, CROWDED SPACE IF SHE WASN'T BEING CAREFULLY ESCORTED.
GREAT JOB, COMPA MICAH!
FOR A MINUTE THERE YOU LOOKED LIKE YOU WERE GONNA PUKE.
I TOTALLY THOUGHT I WAS GONNA PUKE AT THE BEGINNING. I NEVER WOULD'VE LIVED THAT DOWN THOUGH!
WHAT IS GOING ON WITH MY GRAMPS?

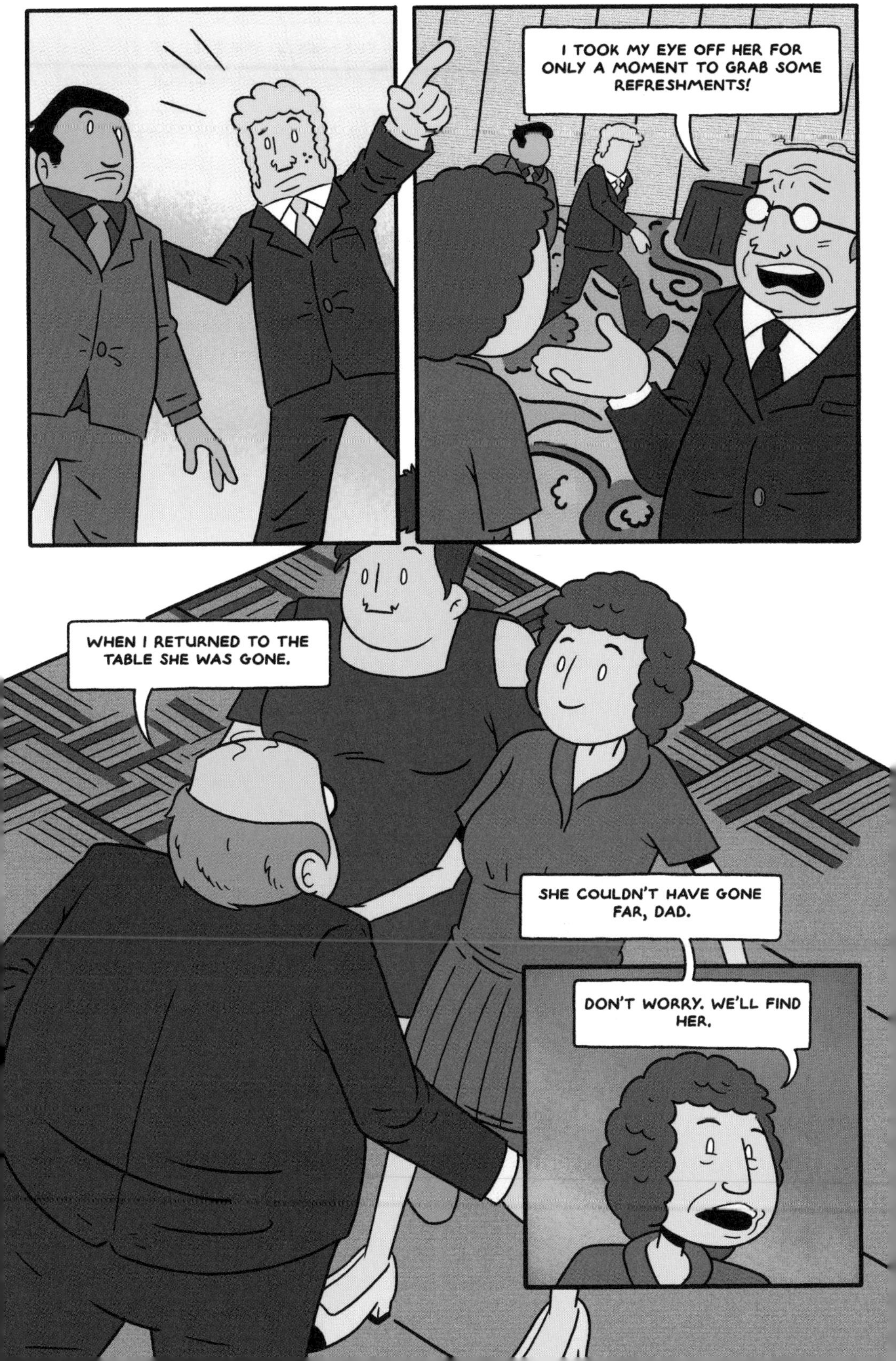
I TOOK MY EYE OFF HER FOR ONLY A MOMENT TO GRAB SOME REFRESHMENTS!
WHEN I RETURNED TO THE TABLE SHE WAS GONE.
SHE COULDN'T HAVE GONE FAR, DAD.
DON'T WORRY. WE'LL FIND HER.

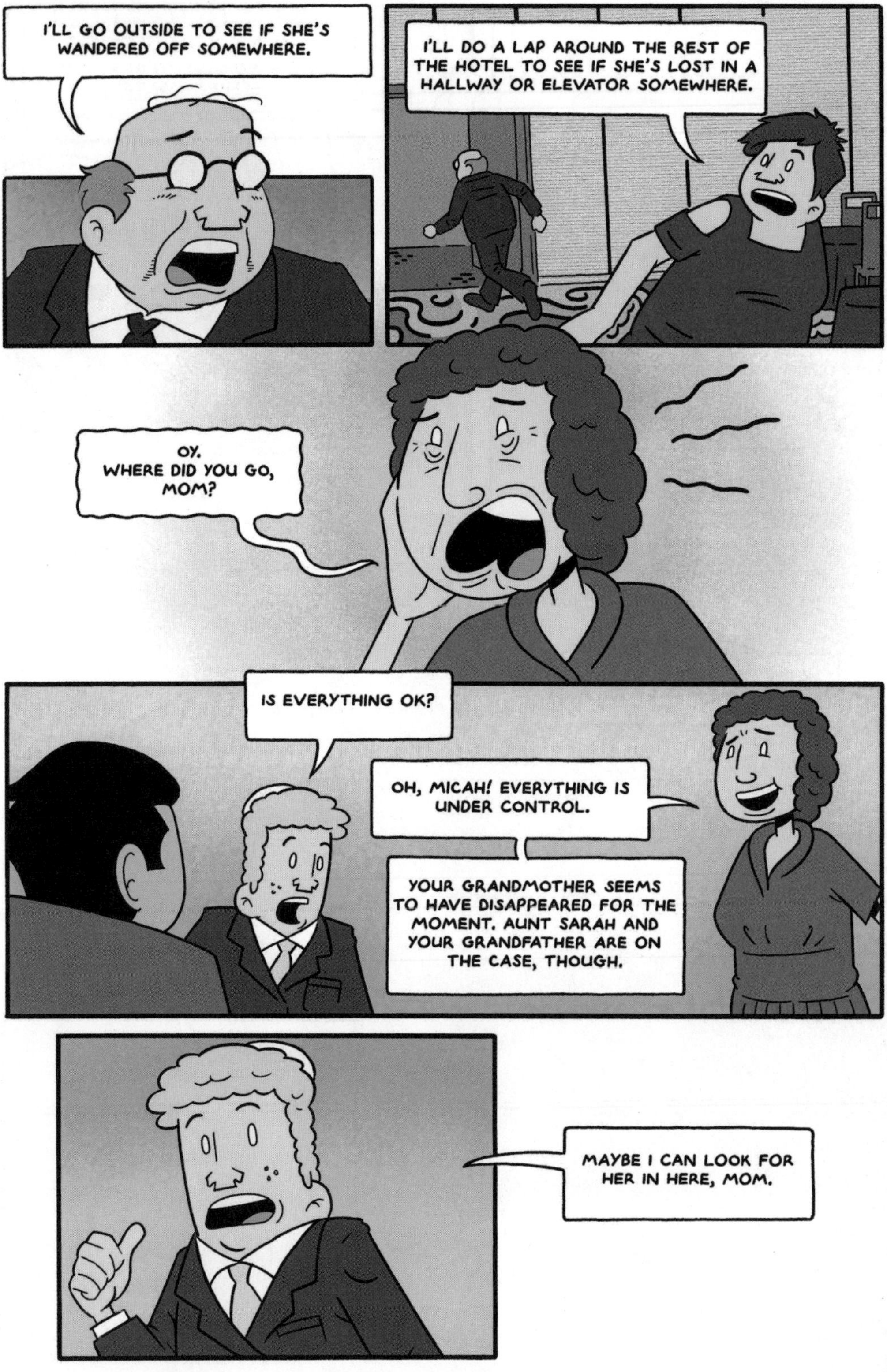
I'LL GO OUTSIDE TO SEE IF SHE'S WANDERED OFF SOMEWHERE.
I'LL DO A LAP AROUND THE REST OF THE HOTEL TO SEE IF SHE'S LOST IN A HALLWAY OR ELEVATOR SOMEWHERE.
OY. WHERE DID YOU GO, MOM?
IS EVERYTHING OK?
OH, MICAH! EVERYTHING IS UNDER CONTROL.
YOUR GRANDMOTHER SEEMS TO HAVE DISAPPEARED FOR THE MOMENT. AUNT SARAH AND YOUR GRANDFATHER ARE ON THE CASE, THOUGH.
MAYBE I CAN LOOK FOR HER IN HERE, MOM.

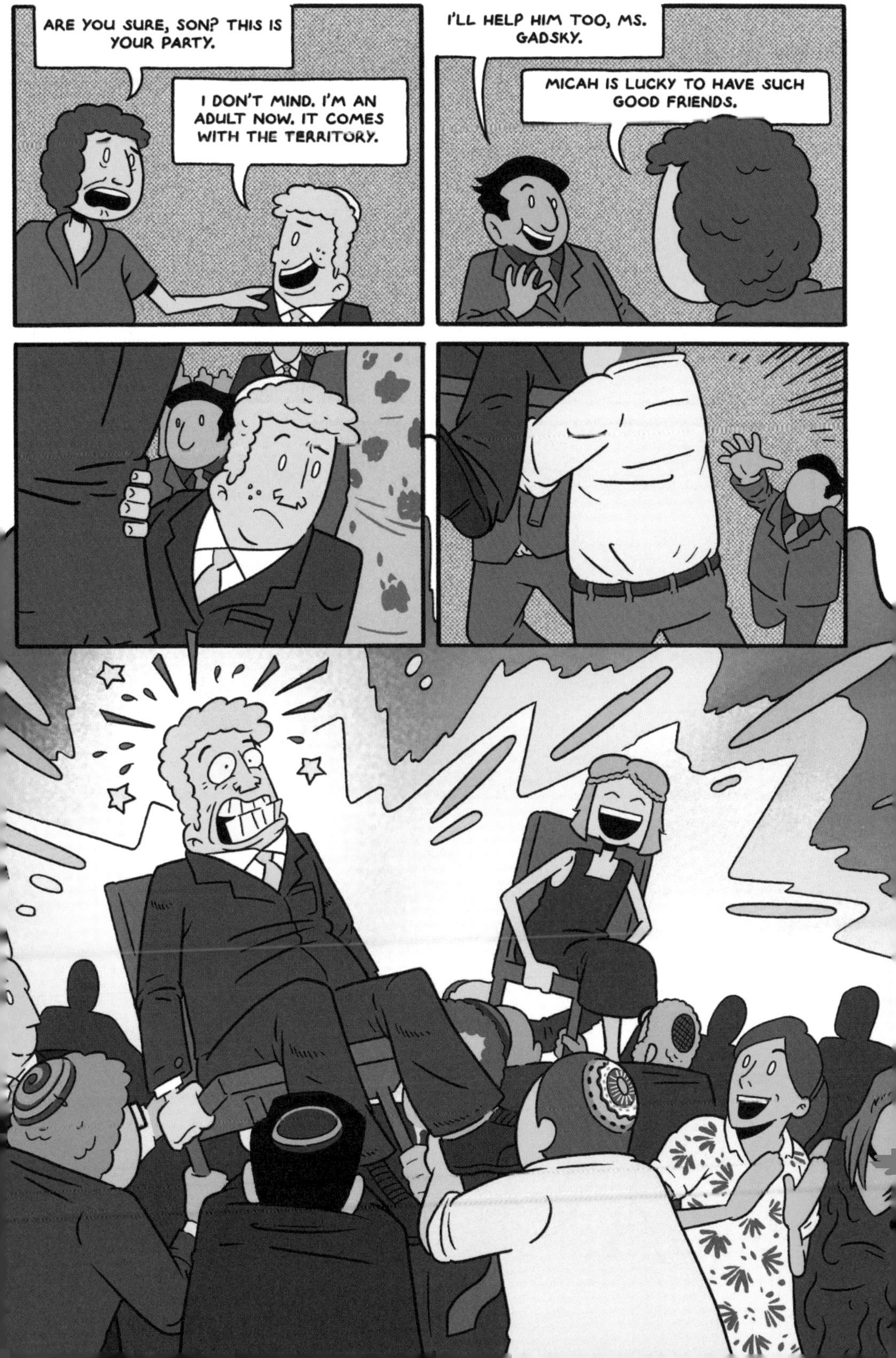
ARE YOU SURE, SON? THIS IS YOUR PARTY.
I DON'T MIND. I'M AN ADULT NOW. IT COMES WITH THE TERRITORY.
I'LL HELP HIM TOO, MS. GADSKY.
MICAH IS LUCKY TO HAVE SUCH GOOD FRIENDS.

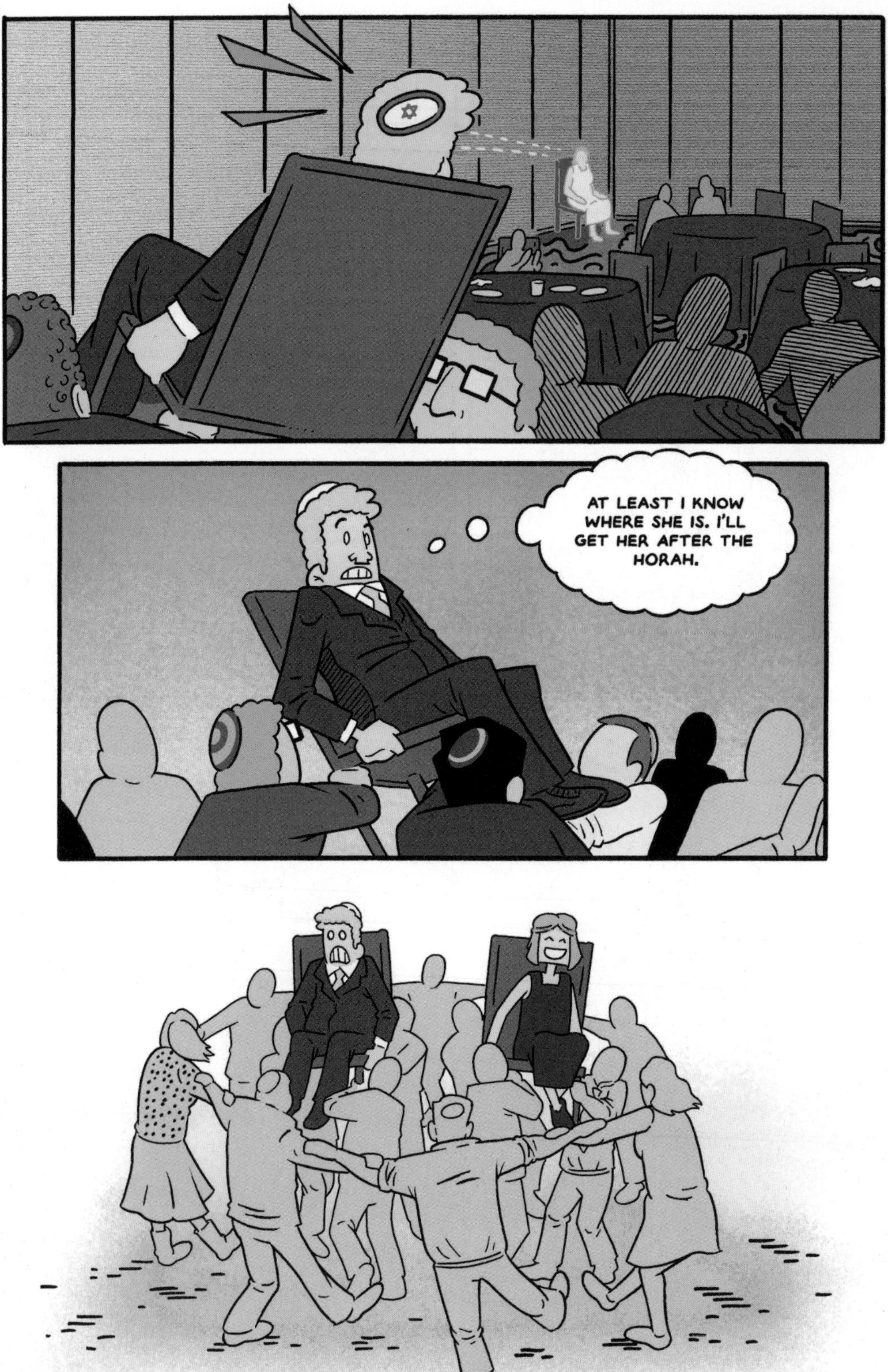
AT LEAST I KNOW WHERE SHE IS. I'LL GET HER AFTER THE HORAH.

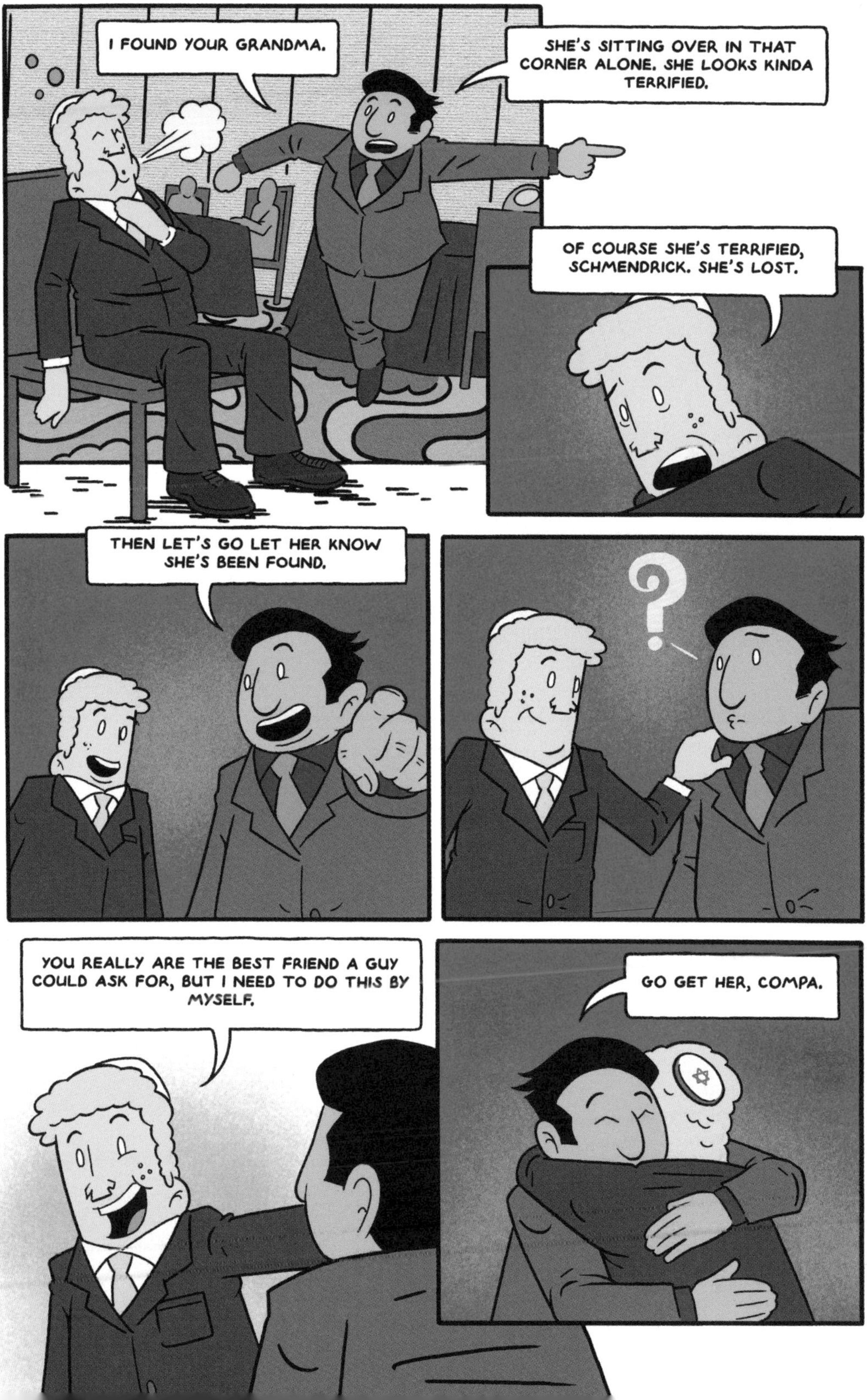
I FOUND YOUR GRANDMA.
SHE'S SITTING OVER IN THAT CORNER ALONE. SHE LOOKS KINDA TERRIFIED.
OF COURSE SHE'S TERRIFIED, SCHMENDRICK. SHE'S LOST.
THEN LET'S GO LET HER KNOW SHE'S BEEN FOUND.
?
YOU REALLY ARE THE BEST FRIEND A GUY COULD ASK FOR, BUT I NEED TO DO THIS BY MYSELF.
GO GET HER, COMPA.

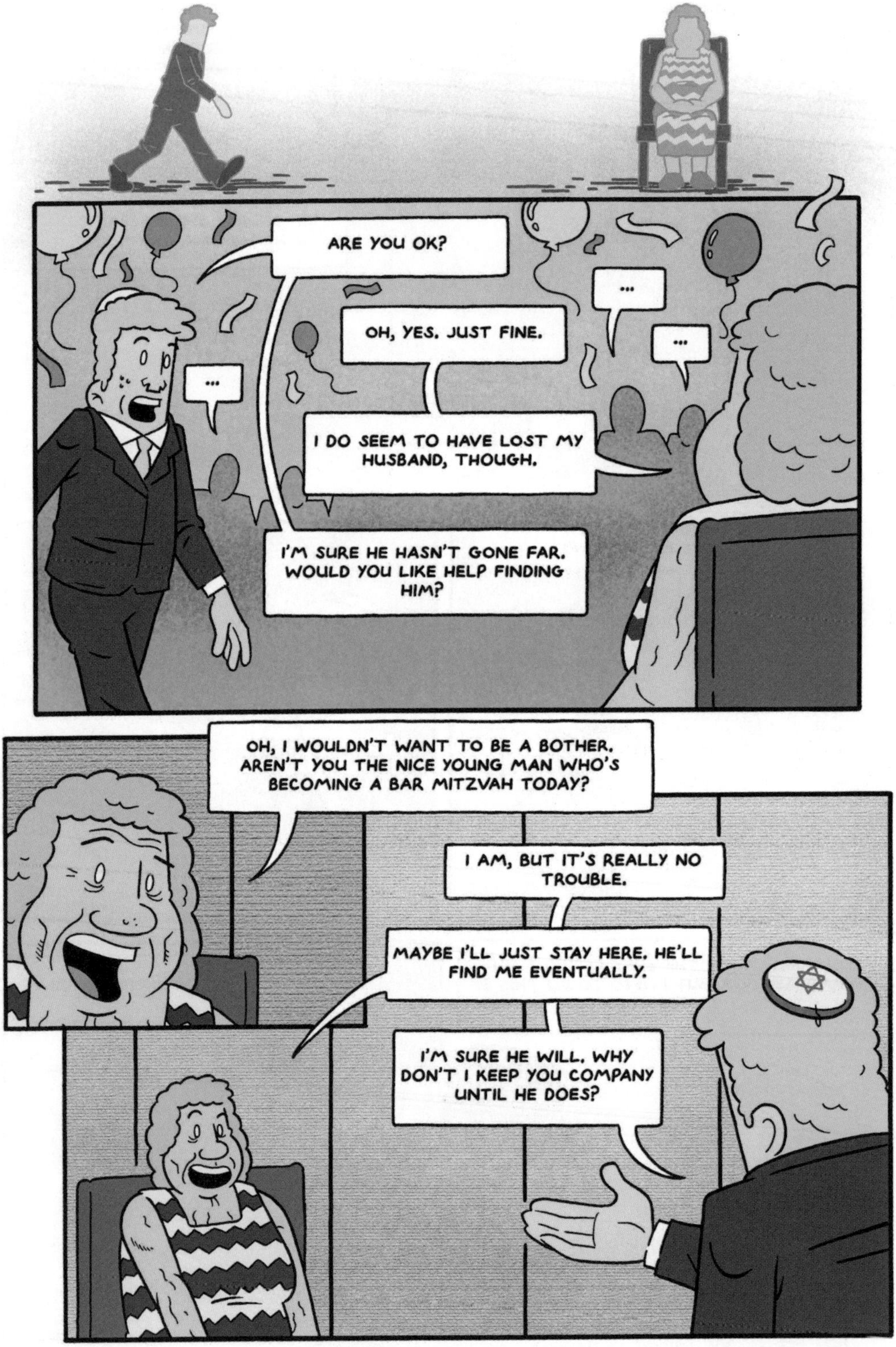
ARE YOU OK?
...
OH, YES. JUST FINE.
...
...
I DO SEEM TO HAVE LOST MY HUSBAND, THOUGH.
I'M SURE HE HASN'T GONE FAR. WOULD YOU LIKE HELP FINDING HIM?
OH, I WOULDN'T WANT TO BE A BOTHER. AREN'T YOU THE NICE YOUNG MAN WHO'S BECOMING A BAR MITZVAH TODAY?
I AM, BUT IT'S REALLY NO TROUBLE.
MAYBE I'LL JUST STAY HERE. HE'LL FIND ME EVENTUALLY.
I'M SURE HE WILL. WHY DON'T I KEEP YOU COMPANY UNTIL HE DOES?

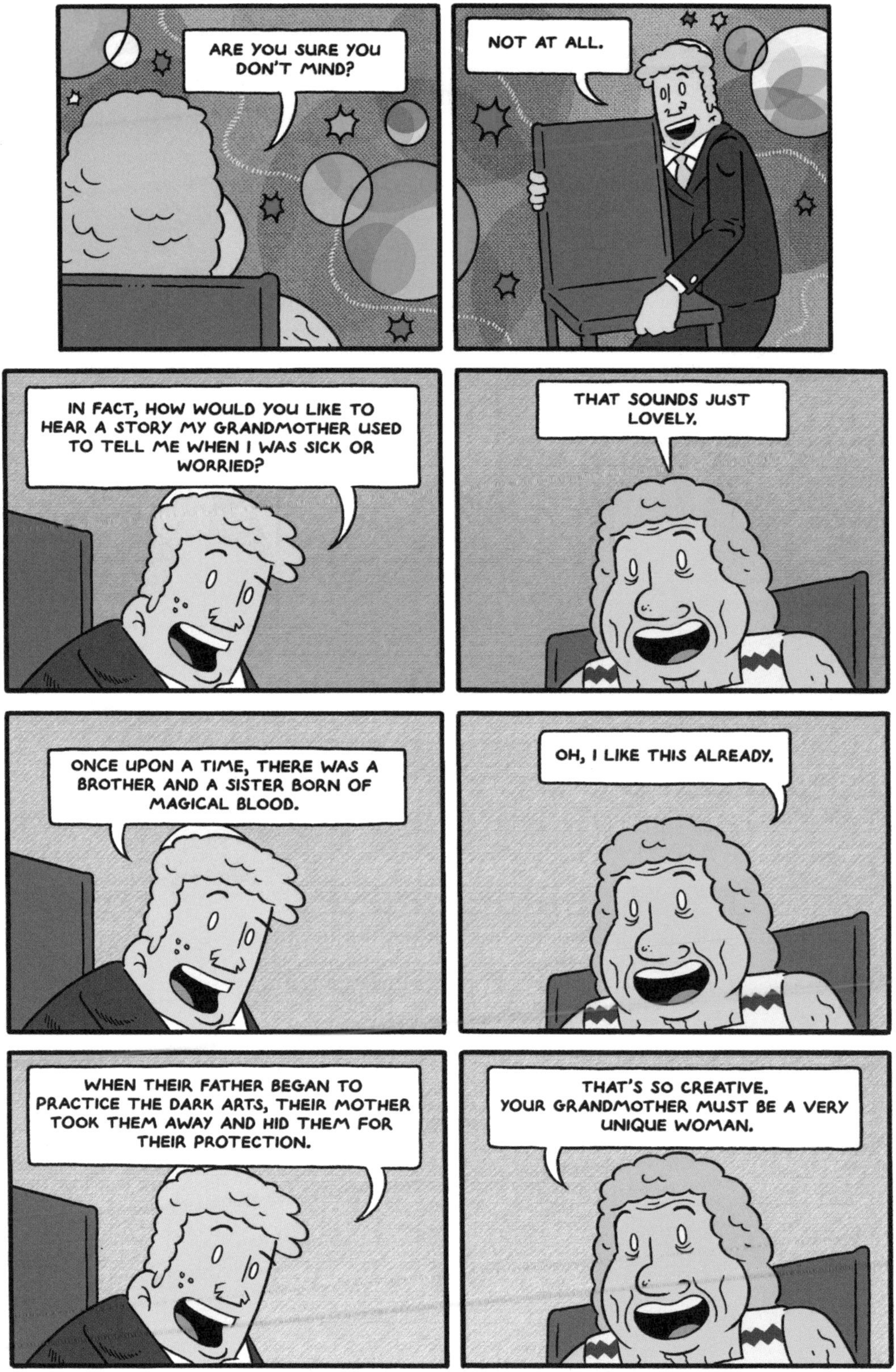
ARE YOU SURE YOU DON'T MIND?
NOT AT ALL.
IN FACT, HOW WOULD YOU LIKE TO HEAR A STORY MY GRANDMOTHER USED TO TELL ME WHEN I WAS SICK OR WORRIED?
THAT SOUNDS JUST LOVELY.
ONCE UPON A TIME, THERE WAS A BROTHER AND A SISTER BORN OF MAGICAL BLOOD.
OH, I LIKE THIS ALREADY.
WHEN THEIR FATHER BEGAN TO PRACTICE THE DARK ARTS, THEIR MOTHER TOOK THEM AWAY AND HID THEM FOR THEIR PROTECTION.
THAT'S SO CREATIVE. YOUR GRANDMOTHER MUST BE A VERY UNIQUE WOMAN.

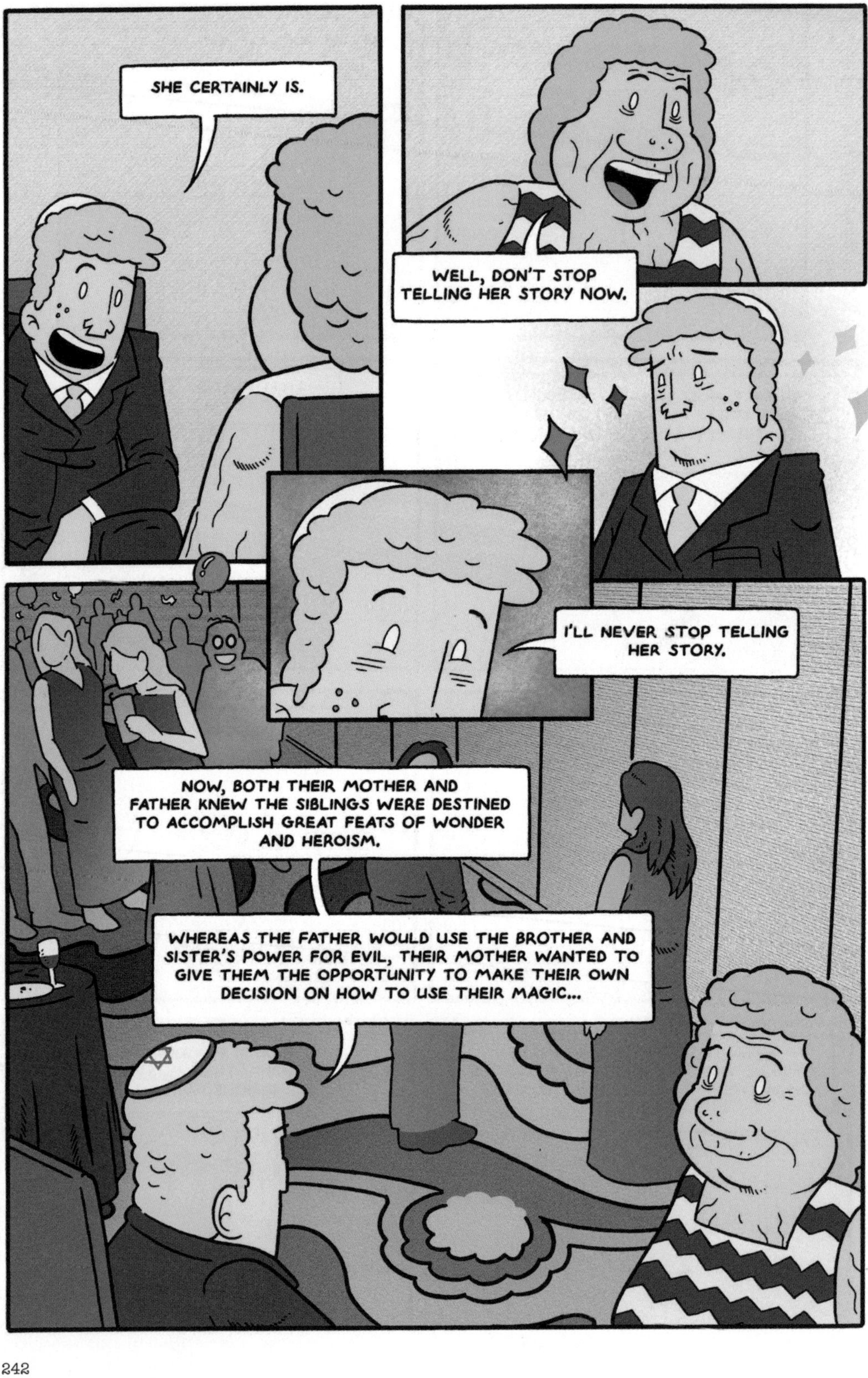
SHE CERTAINLY IS.
WELL, DON'T STOP TELLING HER STORY NOW.
I'LL NEVER STOP TELLING HER STORY.
NOW, BOTH THEIR MOTHER AND FATHER KNEW THE SIBLINGS WERE DESTINED TO ACCOMPLISH GREAT FEATS OF WONDER AND HEROISM.
WHEREAS THE FATHER WOULD USE THE BROTHER AND SISTER'S POWER FOR EVIL, THEIR MOTHER WANTED TO GIVE THEM THE OPPORTUNITY TO MAKE THEIR OWN DECISION ON HOW TO USE THEIR MAGIC...

Author's Note

Grams always called us "toots."

She called us "bubbeleh" from time to time, as Jewish grandmothers are known to do, but for some reason "toots" is the term of endearment I remember the most. I'm not even entirely sure why. Our memories can be funny that way. Since I didn't keep any sort of consistent record when I was younger, be it a diary, journal, blog (when those were a thing), etc., I had to rely mostly on memories to write. Well, memories and countless conversations with my family. It was interesting to see what came back to us.

For instance, I remember the incident when she emerged from the bedroom in only a vest. I remember the warmth of arriving at my grandparents' house for the weekly breakfast feast before Sunday school. I remember the smell of her signature Passover brisket wafting from the kitchen every spring. Though it's hazy, since it happened way back in the dark ages of 1993, I even remember how proud Grams looked during my b'nai mitzvah ceremony with my sister—who is, and always will be, ten months older.

But I can't recall exactly when I learned that Grams had Alzheimer's. I suppose in some ways it doesn't matter. The disease is not what defined her in the slightest. I don't remember her as the woman who couldn't tell you what she ordered at a restaurant the moment after the waiter left; I remember her as the person that could, with one silly expression or ridiculous sound, send you into a fit of giggles. My grandmother was nothing if not a goofball, so I come by that honestly.

Though it isn't specific to any one time, I also remember the aching sadness of realizing she was never going to be the same. But sometimes finding the humor in things that are sad can be healing. Talking about both the highs and lows of Alzheimer's was a way for me to honor the memory of my grandmother, and celebrating my grandparents was a huge part of the inspiration behind *The Effects of Pickled Herring*. I was lucky enough to have them as a daily part of my life since I was four years old. The lessons I learned from them, wisdom they shared with me, and love they expressed for our Jewish community can be found in every line on every page of the book you just read.

No two people would have been happier to see this published than Grams and Gramps. I hope you enjoyed getting to know them a bit.

Thanks to...

Zephyr Lister for providing Micah's handwriting.

Peter Ryan, Leah Harris, Francis Lombard, and Matt Guerrero for their invaluable insight at various stages of development.

Olivia Ngai and Jennifer Newens for their recognition, vision, and indispensable editorial input. You are both forever a part of this

Hugo Villabona, Robin Miller, Elina Diaz, and the magnificent Mango Publishing team for their enthusiasm, expertise, and commitment to this project. I would still be lost in the woods without you.

Allan Ferguson for being an absolute champ throughout the process and providing stunning color which elevates every single panel.

My agent Allison Hellegers for her guidance, compassion, and unyielding belief in my work. My gratitude and admiration for you know no bounds!

Jaime Mora for lending his services as sensitivity reader. We've been through it all together, and it was such a privilege to have you contribute.

My family for being effortlessly and endlessly nurturing, motivating, considerate of imagination, and quirky enough to perpetually supply me with material.

Caitlin for her steadfast support, limitless patience, and never allowing me to surrender to imposter syndrome. You are, without a doubt, the absolute besto. I love you.

Grams and Gramps for their eternal love and light, without whom this book In your hands would not exist. I miss them every single day.

And last, but certainly not least, to all of you for reading!

Glossary

Yiddish/Hebrew (in Order of Appearance)

Mishegas: Insanity or craziness.

Adonai/HaShem: God.

Aliyot: The calling of a member of a Jewish congregation to the bimah for a segment of reading from the Torah.

Fershnikit: Hopelessly drunk, so much so that you can barely function.

Schmendrick: A foolish, bumbling, or incompetent person.

Schluff: A nap.

Bupkis: Nothing of value, significance, or substance.

Meshuggeneh: A person who is nonsensical, silly or crazy; a jackass.

Chutzpah: Nerve, extreme arrogance, brazen presumption. In English, it often connotes courage or confidence.

Shiksa: A non-Jewish girl.

Mishpocha: Family.

Strudel: Layered pastry with a filling that is usually sweet.

Rugelach: Bite-size cookie made with cream-cheese dough rolled around a filling of nuts, poppy seed paste, chocolate, or jam.

Dybbuk: a malicious possessing spirit believed to be the dislocated soul of a dead person.

Seder: Ritual service and ceremonial dinner for the first night or first two nights of Passover.

Four Questions: The impetus for telling why this (Passover) night is different from all other nights, asked/chanted by the youngest person at the Seder.

Matzah: Thin, crisp, unleavened bread, traditionally eaten by Jews during Passover.

Charoset: A sweet, dark-colored paste made of fruits and nuts eaten at the Passover Seder.

Boychik: Term of endearment for a young boy.

Oy Vey Iz Mir: Exclamation of dismay, grief, or exasperation. Literally translated as "Oh, woe is me."

Oneg: Casual festive gathering on Friday night after the first Shabbat meal, usually involving food, singing, and dancing.

Mi Shebeirach: Public prayer or blessing of healing for an individual or group.

Goyim: Plural term for a gentile, a non-Jew.

Pisher: A diminutive for a child that combines amusement and annoyance. Literally translated as "bedwetter."

Verkakta: Lousy, messed up, or ridiculous.

Tallit: Fringed garment, traditionally worn as a prayer shawl by religious Jews.

Shpilkes: A state of impatience, agitation, anxiety, or any combination thereof.

Kiddush: Prayer and blessing over wine.

HaMotzi: Prayer and blessing over bread/grain.

Horah: Traditional circle dance for Jewish weddings and other joyous occasions in the Jewish community.

Spanish (in Order of Appearance)

Compa: Friend, short for compadre.

Simon: Yes, of course.

Novia: Love interest, crush.

¡Oye! ¿Qué te pasó?: Hey, what happened?

Oración por los Enfermos: Prayer for the sick.

Sí, güey: Yeah, dude.

About the Author

Alex Schumacher is an author/illustrator whose work has appeared in picture books, comic strips, graphic novels, and on too many paper napkins to count. From an early age, his cartoons were regularly displayed in a number of respectable kitchens by adoring relatives. Alex has also written for periodicals and websites such as Comicon.com, The Comic Book Yeti, and *Monkeys Fighting Robots Magazine*. While often lost in his imagination, he can mostly be found in San Francisco where he lives with his wonderful wife and beloved—but incredibly clingy—dog, Meldrick. Visit him online at alexschumacherart.com.

Mango Publishing, established in 2014, publishes an eclectic list of books by diverse authors—both new and established voices—on topics ranging from business, personal growth, women's empowerment, LGBTQ studies, health, and spirituality to history, popular culture, time management, decluttering, lifestyle, mental wellness, aging, and sustainable living. We were named 2019 and 2020's #1 fastest growing independent publisher by Publishers Weekly. Our success is driven by our main goal, which is to publish high-quality books that will entertain readers as well as make a positive difference in their lives.

Our readers are our most important resource; we value your input, suggestions, and ideas. We'd love to hear from you—after all, we are publishing books for you!

Please stay in touch with us and follow us at:

Facebook: Mango Publishing
Twitter: @MangoPublishing
Instagram: @MangoPublishing
LinkedIn: Mango Publishing
Pinterest: Mango Publishing
Newsletter: mangopublishinggroup.com/newsletter

Join us on Mango's journey to reinvent publishing, one book at a time.